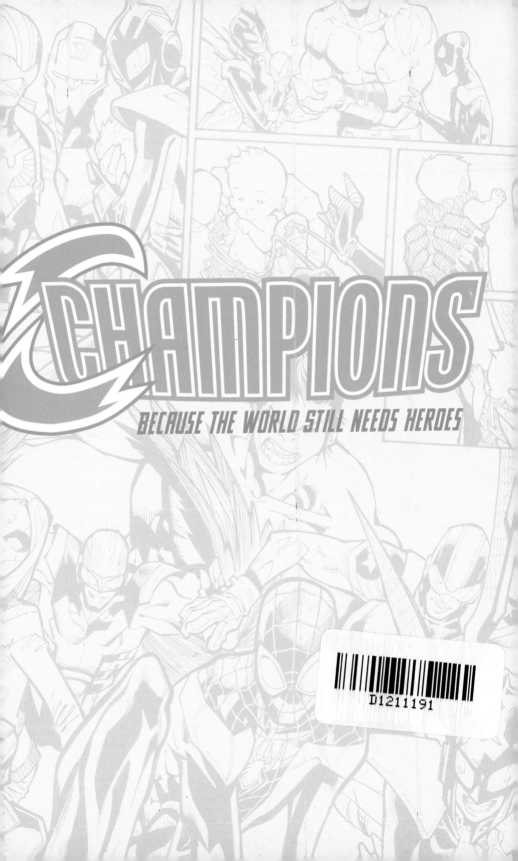

CHAMPIONS

BECAUSE THE WORLD STILL NEEDS HEROES

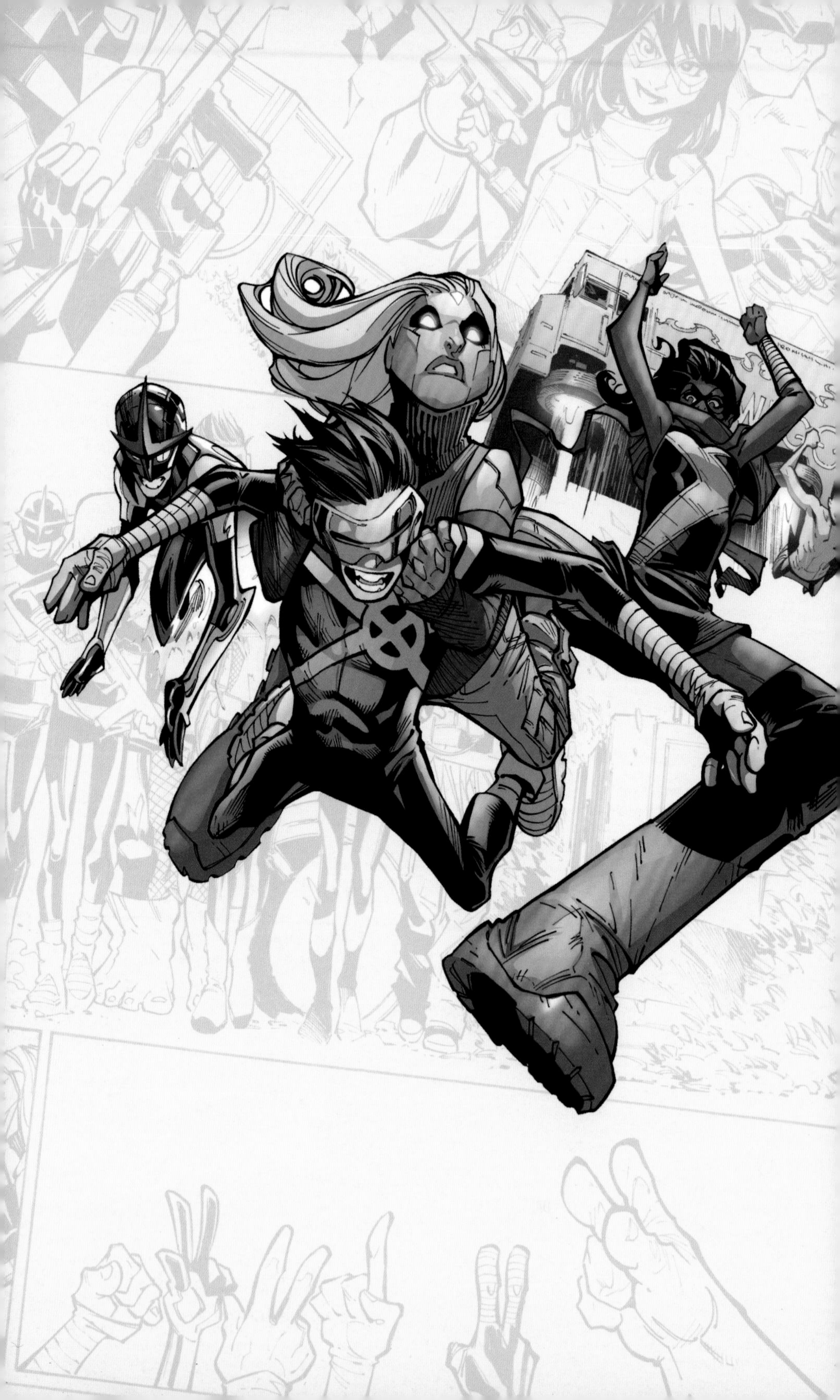

CHAMPIONS

BECAUSE THE WORLD STILL NEEDS HEROES

WRITER
MARK WAID

PENCILER
HUMBERTO RAMOS

INKER
VICTOR OLAZABA

COLORIST
EDGAR DELGADO
WITH **NOLAN WOODARD** (#6 & #8)

LETTERER
VC's CLAYTON COWLES

COVER ART
HUMBERTO RAMOS & EDGAR DELGADO

ASSOCIATE EDITOR
ALANNA SMITH

EDITOR
TOM BREVOORT

SPECIAL THANKS TO
DENNIS MALLONEE

collection editor JENNIFER GRÜNWALD
assistant editor CAITLIN O'CONNELL • associate managing editor KATERI WOODY
editor, special projects MARK D. BEAZLEY • vp production & special projects JEFF YOUNGQUIST
svp print, sales & marketing DAVID GABRIEL

editor in chief C.B. CEBULSKI • chief creative officer JOE QUESADA
president DAN BUCKLEY • executive producer ALAN FINE

MPIONS: BECAUSE THE WORLD STILL NEEDS HEROES. Contains material originally published in magazine form as CHAMPIONS #1-12. First printing 2019. ISBN 978-1-302-91794-4. shed by MARVEL WORLDWIDE, INC., a subsidiary of MARVEL ENTERTAINMENT, LLC. OFFICE OF PUBLICATION: 135 West 50th Street, New York, NY 10020. **Printed in Canada.** DAN BUCKLEY, President, Marvel Entertainment; JOHN NEE, Publisher; JOE QUESADA, Chief Creative Officer; TOM BREVOORT, SVP of Publishing; DAVID BOGART, iate Publisher & SVP of Talent Affairs; DAVID GABRIEL, SVP of Sales & Marketing, Publishing; JEFF YOUNGQUIST, VP of Production & Special Projects; DAN CARR, Executive Director of Publishing nology; ALEX MORALES, Director of Publishing Operations; DAN EDINGTON, Managing Editor; SUSAN CRESPI, Production Manager; STAN LEE, Chairman Emeritus. For information regarding tising in Marvel Comics or on Marvel.com, please contact Vit DeBellis, Custom Solutions & Integrated Advertising Manager, at vdebellis@marvel.com. For Marvel subscription inquiries, please 88-511-5480. **Manufactured between 3/15/2019 and 4/16/2019 by SOLISCO PRINTERS, SCOTT, QC, CANADA.**

87654321

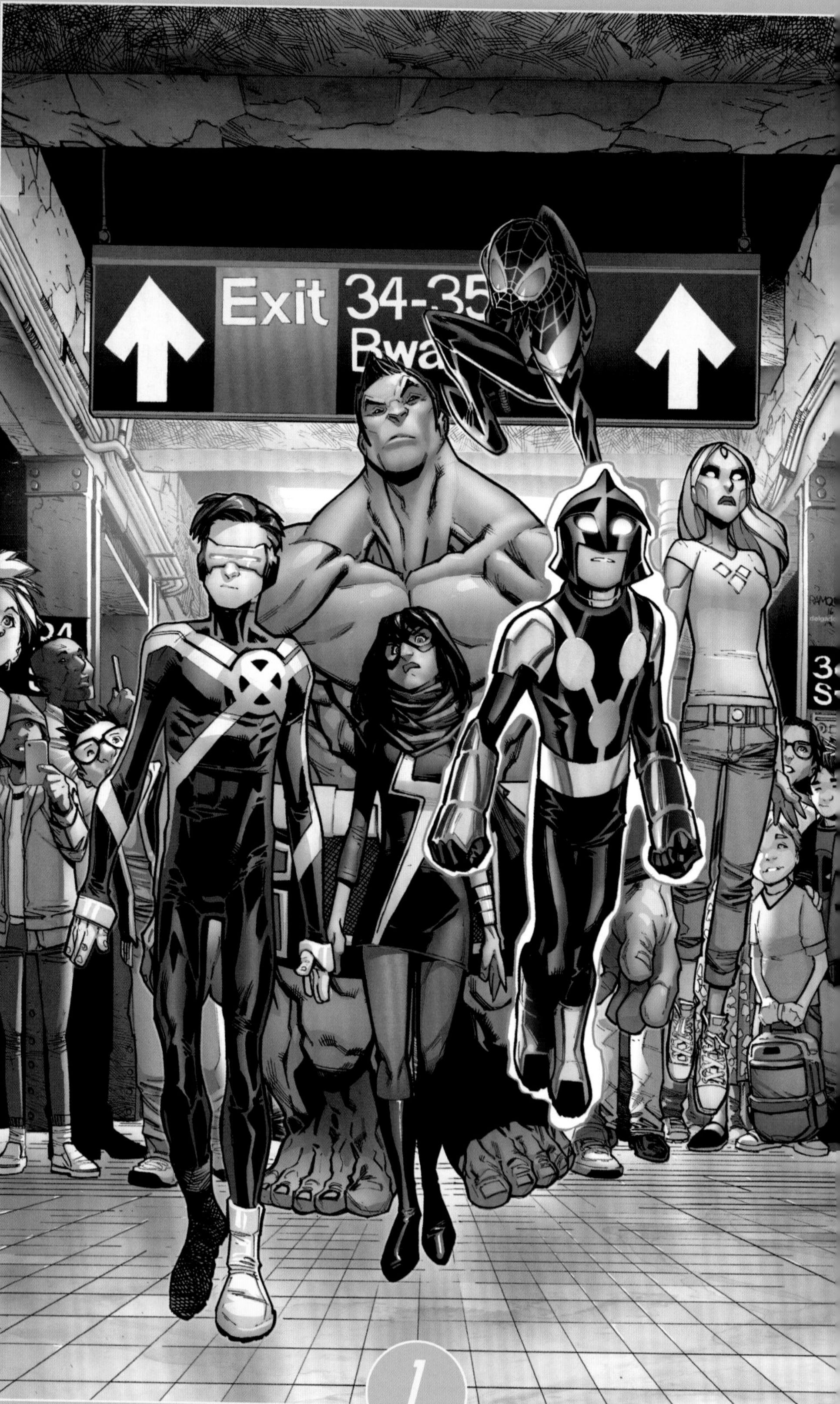
Exit
34-35

1

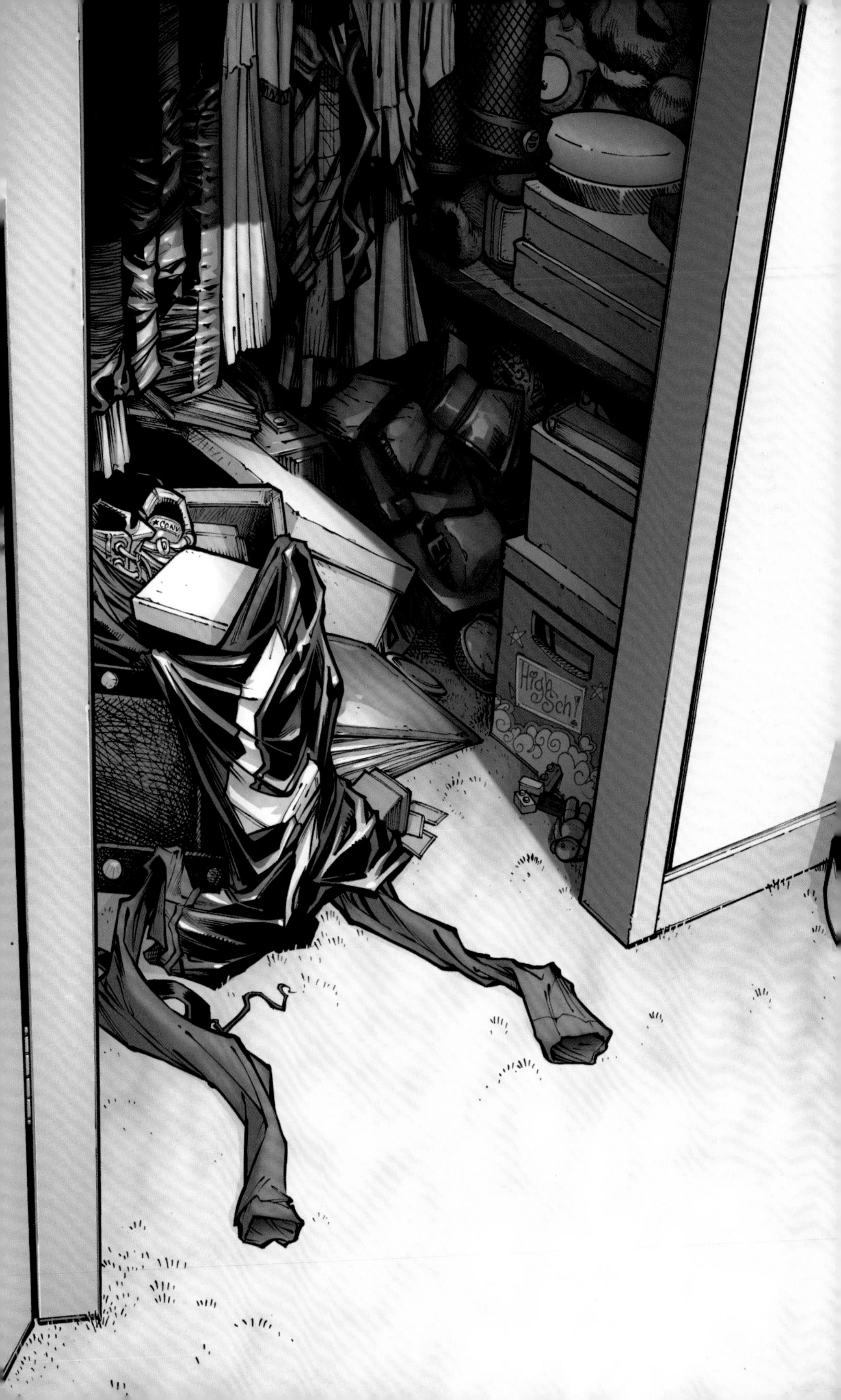
High Sch!

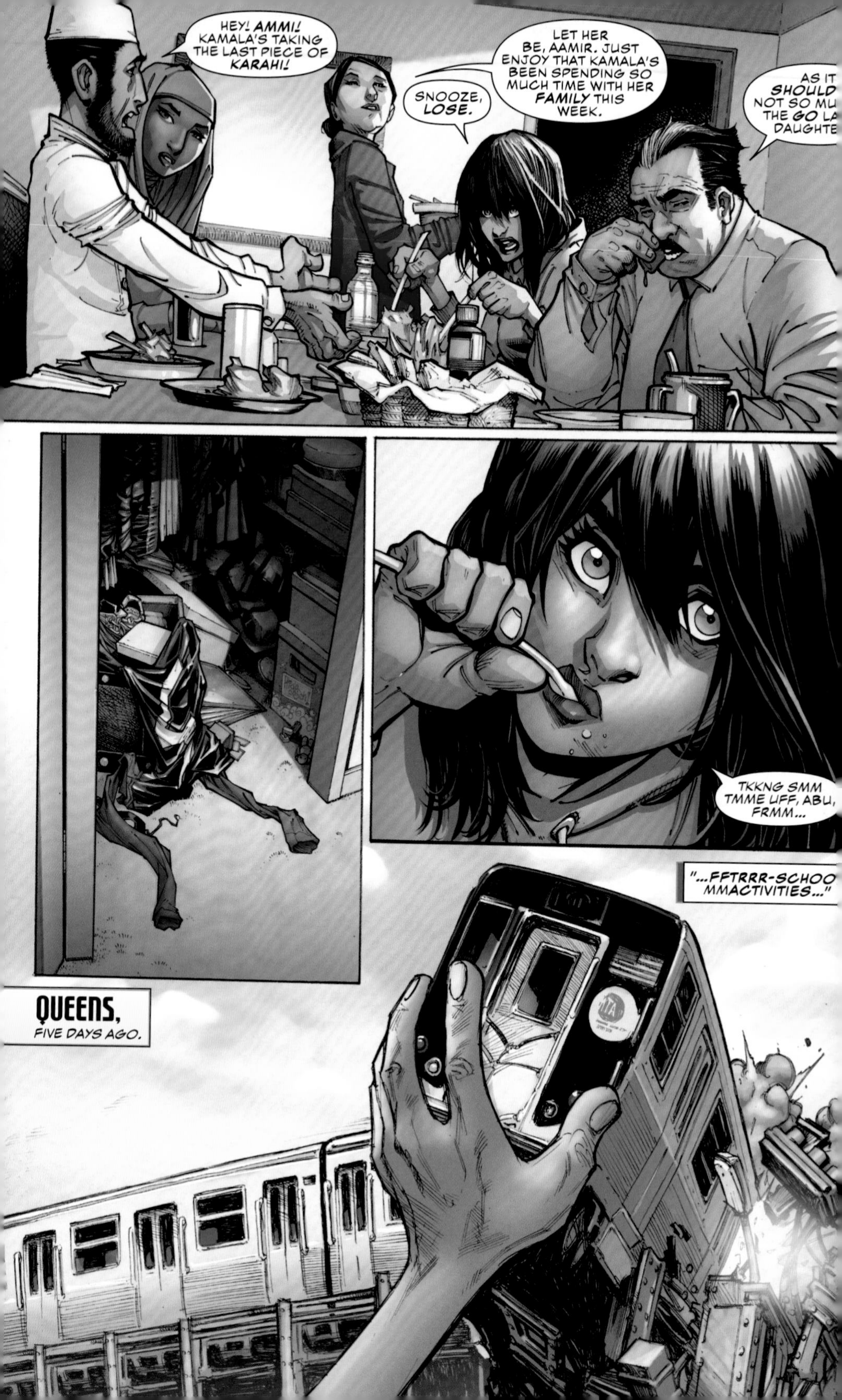
HEY! AMMI! KAMALA'S TAKING THE LAST PIECE OF KARAHI!
SNOOZE, LOSE.
LET HER BE, AAMIR. JUST ENJOY THAT KAMALA'S BEEN SPENDING SO MUCH TIME WITH HER FAMILY THIS WEEK.
AS IT SHOULD NOT SO MU THE GO LA DAUGHTE
TKKNG SMM TMME UFF, ABU, FRMM...
"...FFTRRR-SCHOO MMACTIVITIES..."
QUEENS, FIVE DAYS AGO.

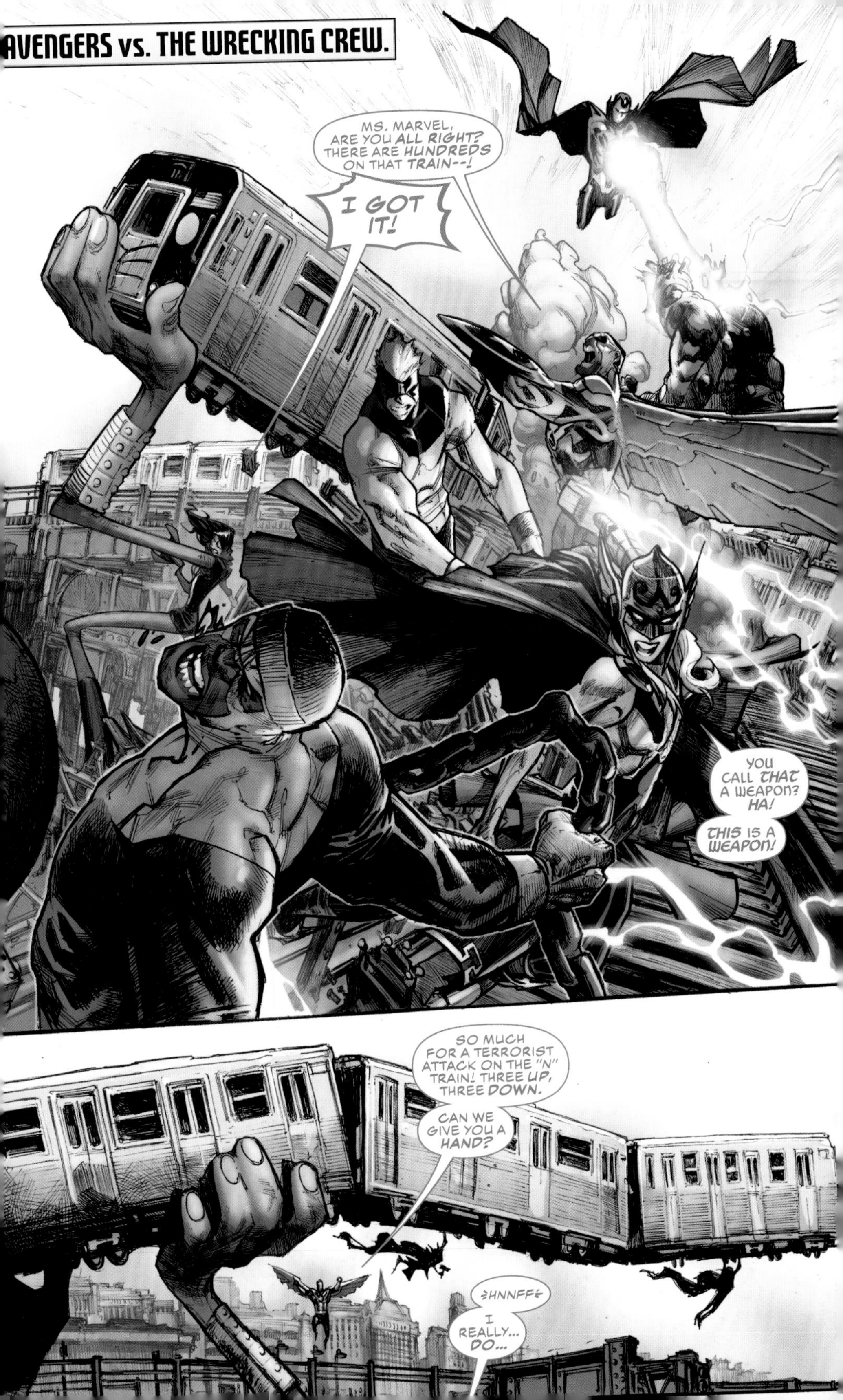
AVENGERS vs. THE WRECKING CREW.
MS. MARVEL, ARE YOU ALL RIGHT? THERE ARE HUNDREDS ON THAT TRAIN--!
I GOT IT!
YOU CALL THAT A WEAPON? HA!
THIS IS A WEAPON!
SO MUCH FOR A TERRORIST ATTACK ON THE "N" TRAIN! THREE UP, THREE DOWN.
CAN WE GIVE YOU A HAND?
HNNFF
I REALLY... DO...

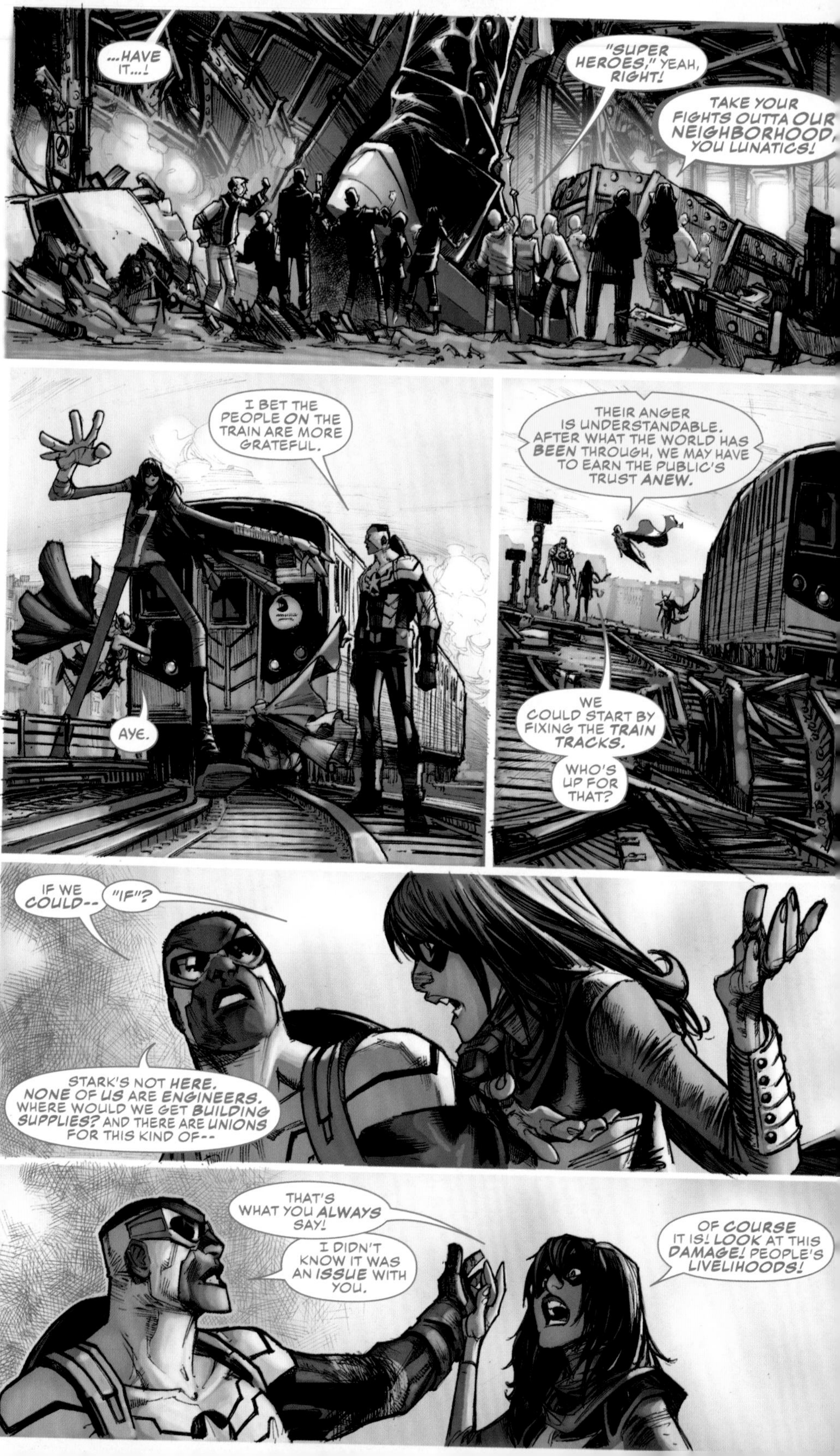
...HAVE IT...!
"SUPER HEROES," YEAH, RIGHT!
TAKE YOUR FIGHTS OUTTA OUR NEIGHBORHOOD, YOU LUNATICS!
I BET THE PEOPLE ON THE TRAIN ARE MORE GRATEFUL.
AYE.
THEIR ANGER IS UNDERSTANDABLE. AFTER WHAT THE WORLD HAS BEEN THROUGH, WE MAY HAVE TO EARN THE PUBLIC'S TRUST ANEW.
WE COULD START BY FIXING THE TRAIN TRACKS.
WHO'S UP FOR THAT?
IF WE COULD--
"IF"?
STARK'S NOT HERE. NONE OF US ARE ENGINEERS. WHERE WOULD WE GET BUILDING SUPPLIES? AND THERE ARE UNIONS FOR THIS KIND OF--
THAT'S WHAT YOU ALWAYS SAY!
I DIDN'T KNOW IT WAS AN ISSUE WITH YOU.
OF COURSE IT IS! LOOK AT THIS DAMAGE! PEOPLE'S LIVELIHOODS!

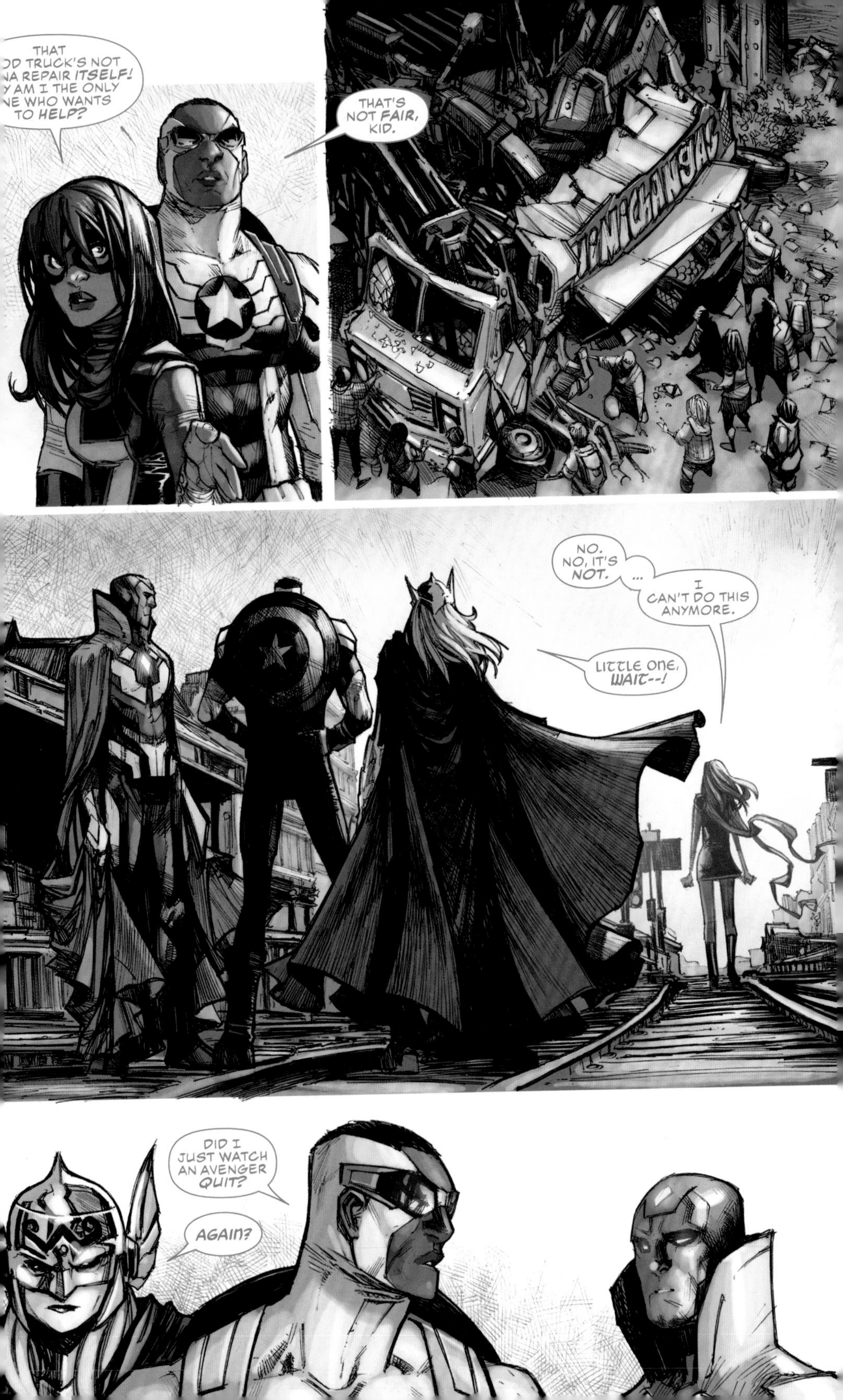

THAT
DD TRUCK'S NOT
NA REPAIR ITSELF!
Y AM I THE ONLY
NE WHO WANTS
TO HELP?
THAT'S NOT FAIR, KID.
NO. NO, IT'S NOT.
...
I CAN'T DO THIS ANYMORE.
LITTLE ONE, WAIT--!
DID I JUST WATCH AN AVENGER QUIT?
AGAIN?

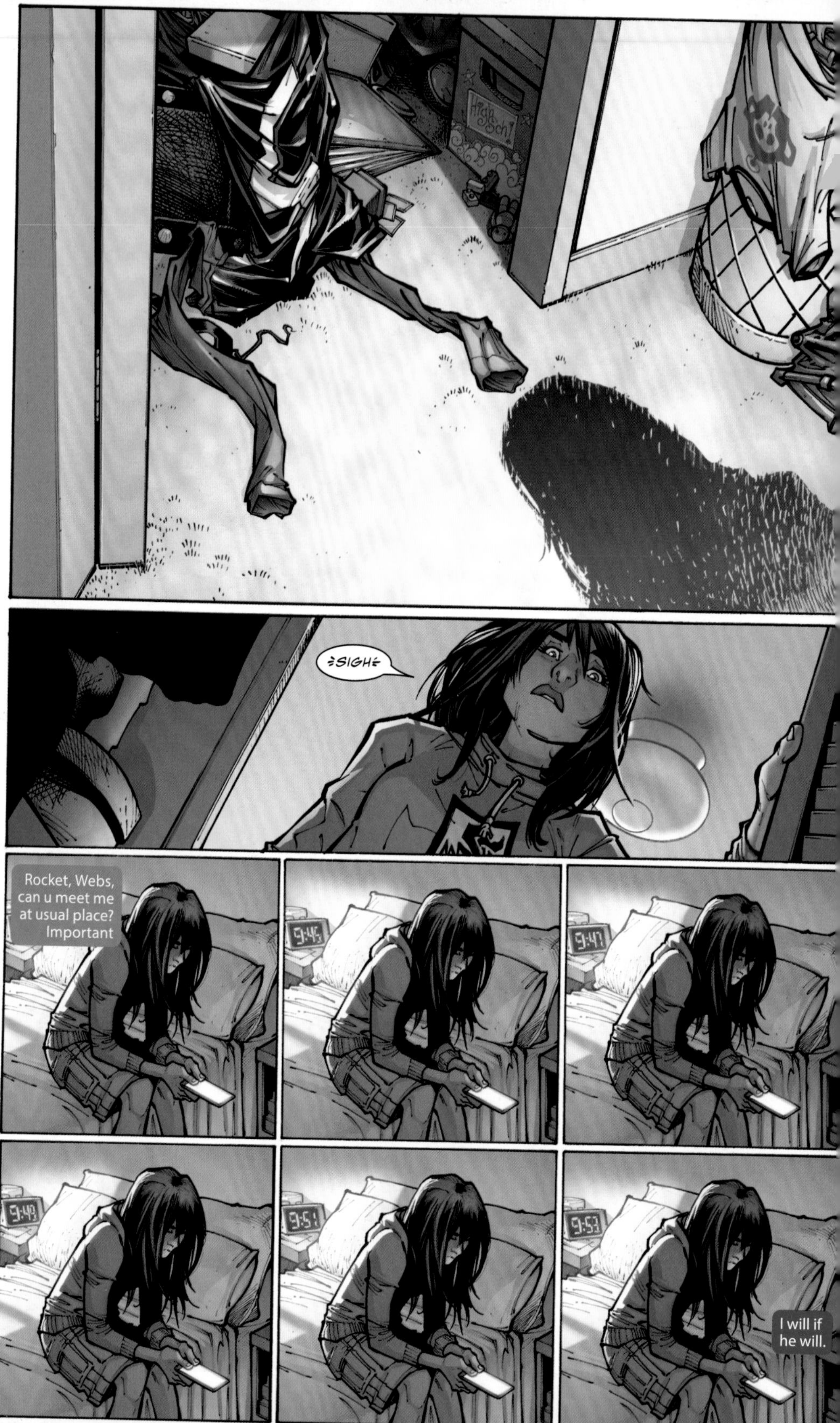

SIGH
Rocket, Webs, can u meet me at usual place? Important
I will if he will.

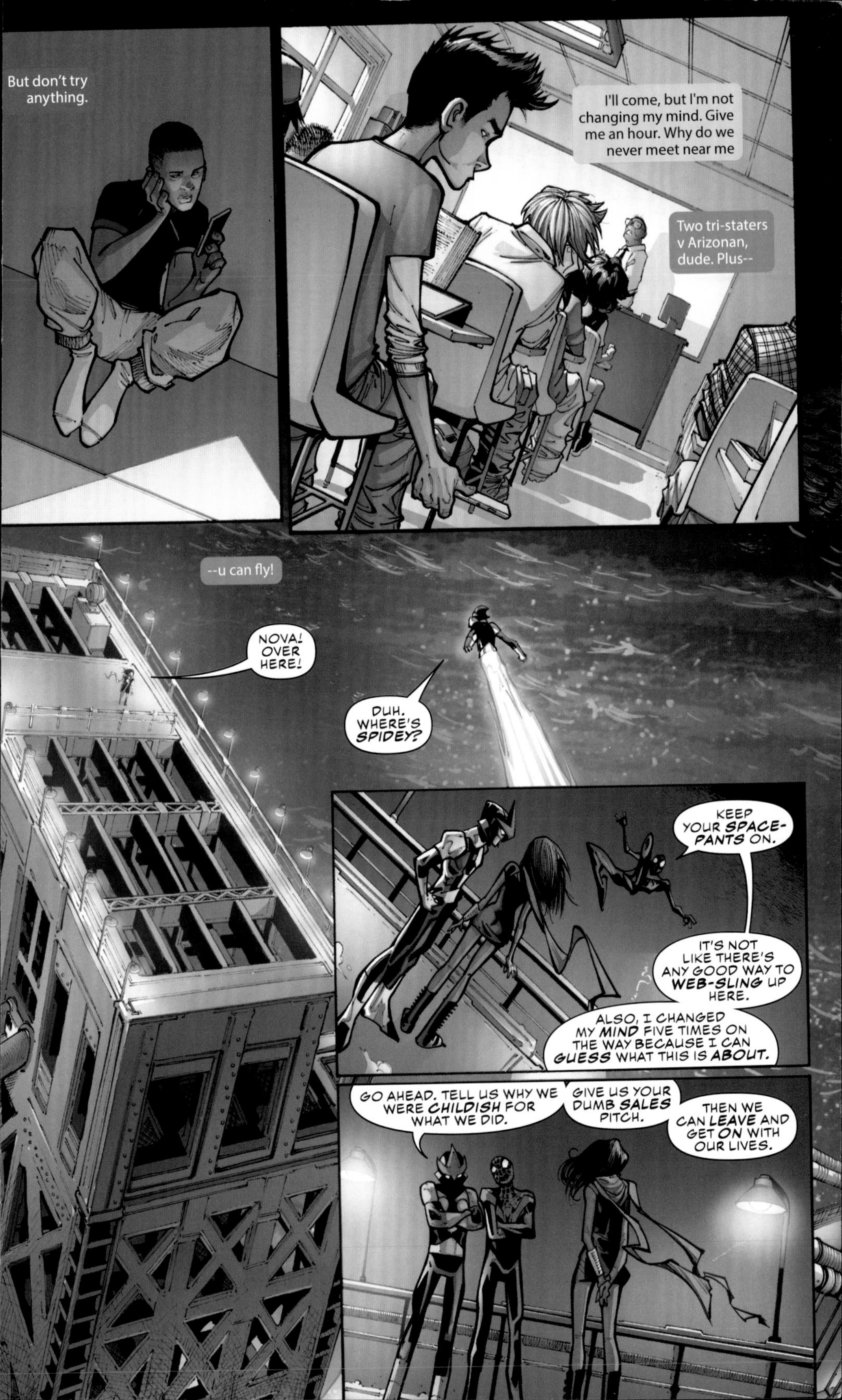

But don't try anything.
I'll come, but I'm not changing my mind. Give me an hour. Why do we never meet near me
Two tri-staters v Arizonan, dude. Plus--
--u can fly!
NOVA! OVER HERE!
DUH. WHERE'S SPIDEY?
KEEP YOUR SPACE-PANTS ON.
IT'S NOT LIKE THERE'S ANY GOOD WAY TO WEB-SLING UP HERE.
ALSO, I CHANGED MY MIND FIVE TIMES ON THE WAY BECAUSE I CAN GUESS WHAT THIS IS ABOUT.
GO AHEAD. TELL US WHY WE WERE CHILDISH FOR WHAT WE DID.
GIVE US YOUR DUMB SALES PITCH.
THEN WE CAN LEAVE AND GET ON WITH OUR LIVES.

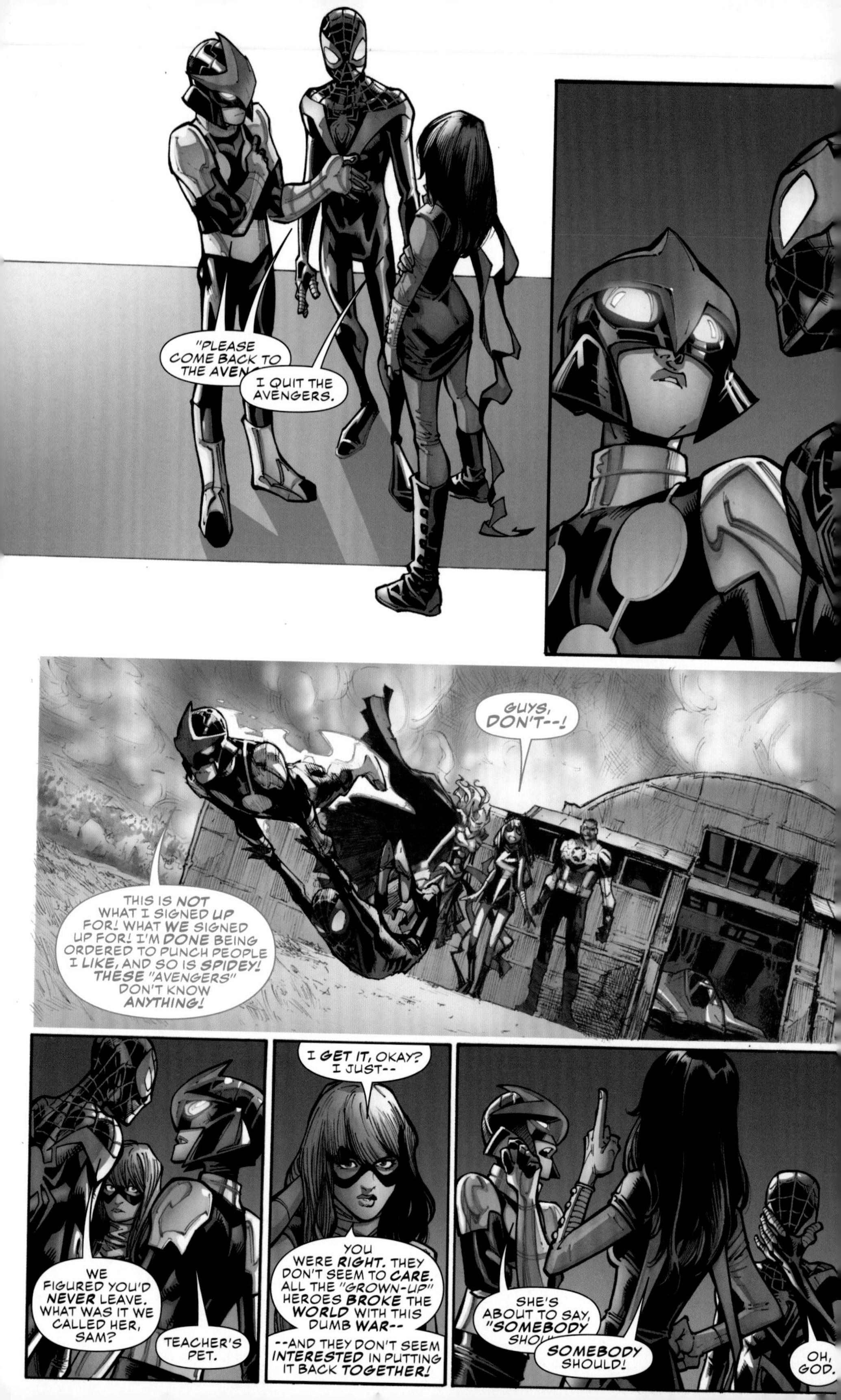
"PLEASE COME BACK TO THE AVEN
I QUIT THE AVENGERS.
GUYS, DON'T--!
THIS IS NOT WHAT I SIGNED UP FOR! WHAT WE SIGNED UP FOR! I'M DONE BEING ORDERED TO PUNCH PEOPLE I LIKE, AND SO IS SPIDEY! THESE "AVENGERS" DON'T KNOW ANYTHING!
WE FIGURED YOU'D NEVER LEAVE. WHAT WAS IT WE CALLED HER, SAM?
TEACHER'S PET.
I GET IT, OKAY? I JUST--
YOU WERE RIGHT. THEY DON'T SEEM TO CARE. ALL THE "GROWN-UP" HEROES BROKE THE WORLD WITH THIS DUMB WAR--
--AND THEY DON'T SEEM INTERESTED IN PUTTING IT BACK TOGETHER!
SHE'S ABOUT TO SAY, "SOMEBODY SHOU
SOMEBODY SHOULD!
OH, GOD.

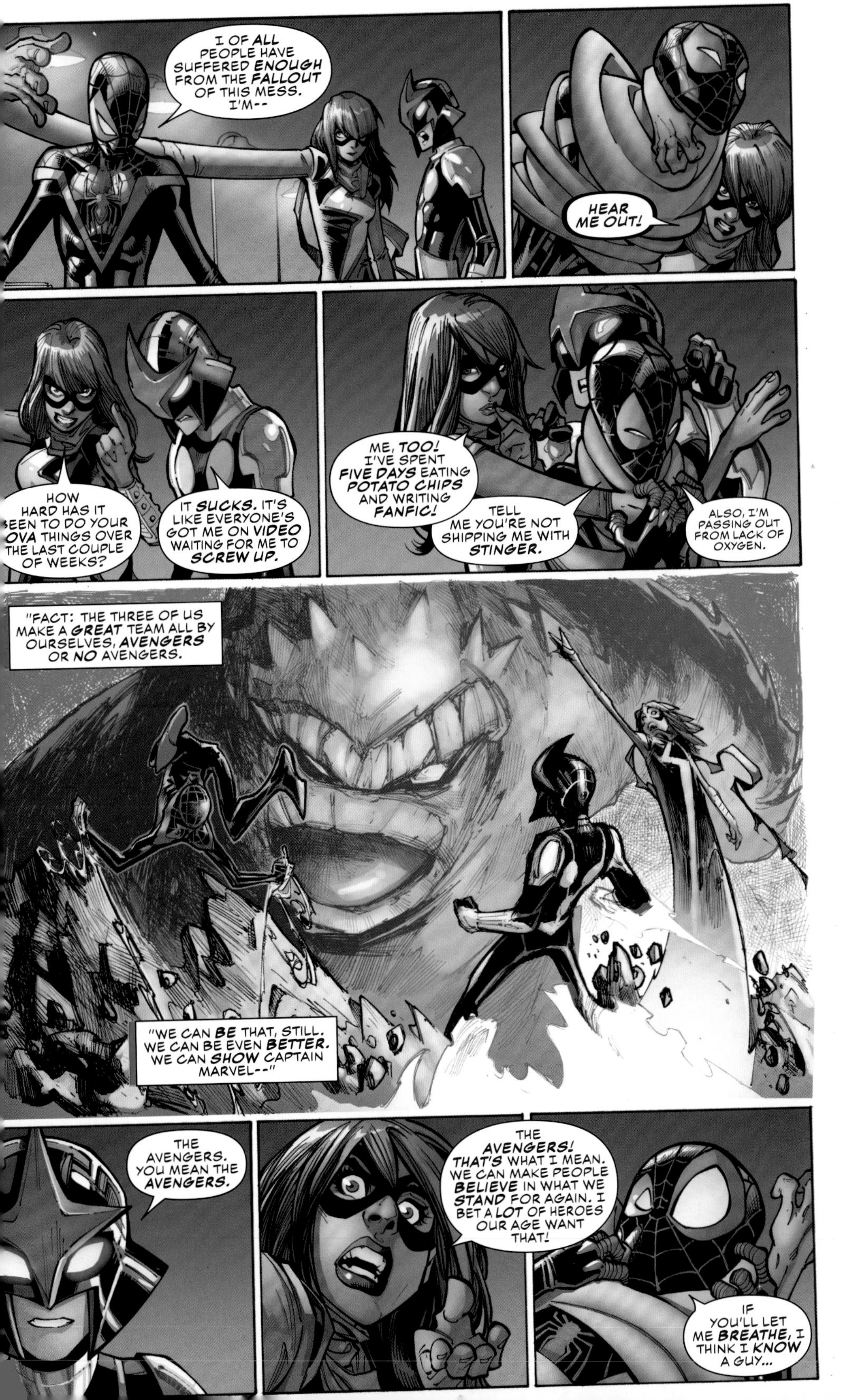

I OF ALL PEOPLE HAVE SUFFERED ENOUGH FROM THE FALLOUT OF THIS MESS. I'M--
HEAR ME OUT!
HOW HARD HAS IT BEEN TO DO YOUR NOVA THINGS OVER THE LAST COUPLE OF WEEKS?
IT SUCKS. IT'S LIKE EVERYONE'S GOT ME ON VIDEO WAITING FOR ME TO SCREW UP.
ME, TOO! I'VE SPENT FIVE DAYS EATING POTATO CHIPS AND WRITING FANFIC!
TELL ME YOU'RE NOT SHIPPING ME WITH STINGER.
ALSO, I'M PASSING OUT FROM LACK OF OXYGEN.
"FACT: THE THREE OF US MAKE A GREAT TEAM ALL BY OURSELVES, AVENGERS OR NO AVENGERS.
"WE CAN BE THAT, STILL. WE CAN BE EVEN BETTER. WE CAN SHOW CAPTAIN MARVEL--"
THE AVENGERS. YOU MEAN THE AVENGERS.
THE AVENGERS! THAT'S WHAT I MEAN. WE CAN MAKE PEOPLE BELIEVE IN WHAT WE STAND FOR AGAIN. I BET A LOT OF HEROES OUR AGE WANT THAT!
IF YOU'LL LET ME BREATHE, I THINK I KNOW A GUY...

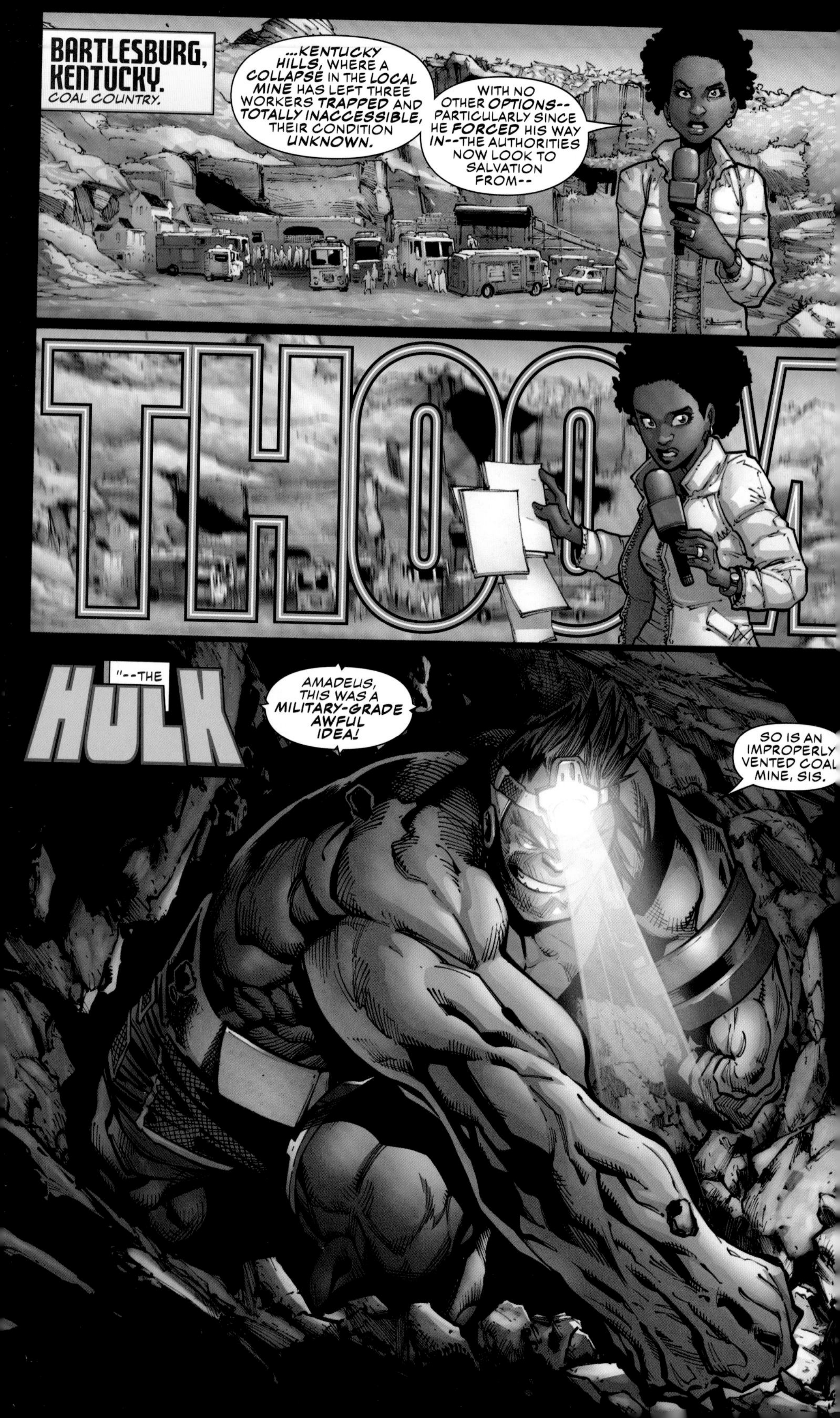

BARTLESBURG, KENTUCKY.
COAL COUNTRY.
...KENTUCKY HILLS, WHERE A COLLAPSE IN THE LOCAL MINE HAS LEFT THREE WORKERS TRAPPED AND TOTALLY INACCESSIBLE, THEIR CONDITION UNKNOWN.
WITH NO OTHER OPTIONS-- PARTICULARLY SINCE HE FORCED HIS WAY IN--THE AUTHORITIES NOW LOOK TO SALVATION FROM--
THOOOM
"--THE
HULK
AMADEUS, THIS WAS A MILITARY-GRADE AWFUL IDEA!
SO IS AN IMPROPERLY VENTED COAL MINE, SIS.

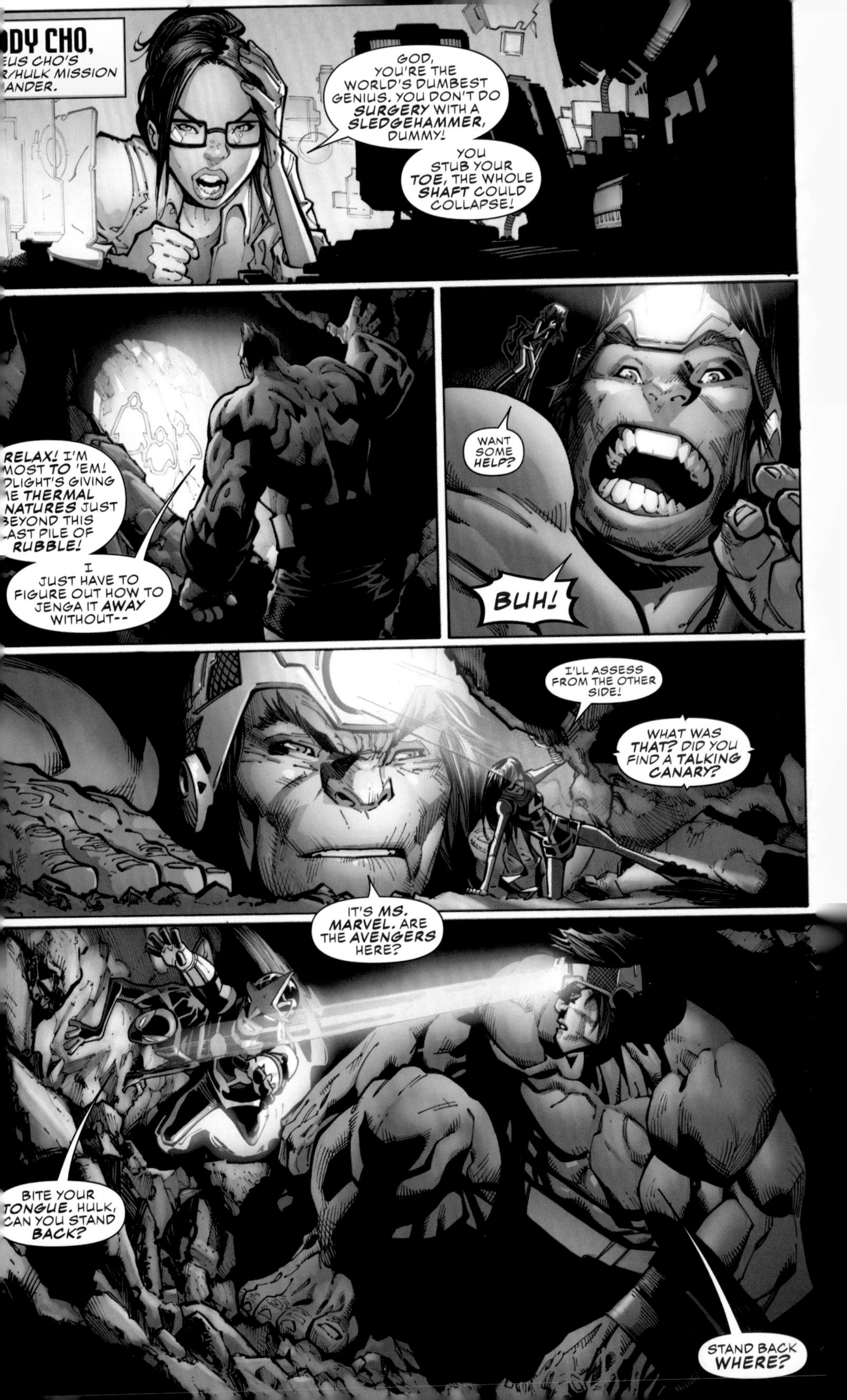
ODY CHO,
EUS CHO'S
R/HULK MISSION
MANDER.
GOD, YOU'RE THE WORLD'S DUMBEST GENIUS. YOU DON'T DO SURGERY WITH A SLEDGEHAMMER, DUMMY!
YOU STUB YOUR TOE, THE WHOLE SHAFT COULD COLLAPSE!
RELAX! I'M MOST TO 'EM! DLIGHT'S GIVING ME THERMAL NATURES JUST BEYOND THIS LAST PILE OF RUBBLE!
I JUST HAVE TO FIGURE OUT HOW TO JENGA IT AWAY WITHOUT--
WANT SOME HELP?
BUH!
I'LL ASSESS FROM THE OTHER SIDE!
WHAT WAS THAT? DID YOU FIND A TALKING CANARY?
IT'S MS. MARVEL. ARE THE AVENGERS HERE?
BITE YOUR TONGUE. HULK, CAN YOU STAND BACK?
STAND BACK WHERE?

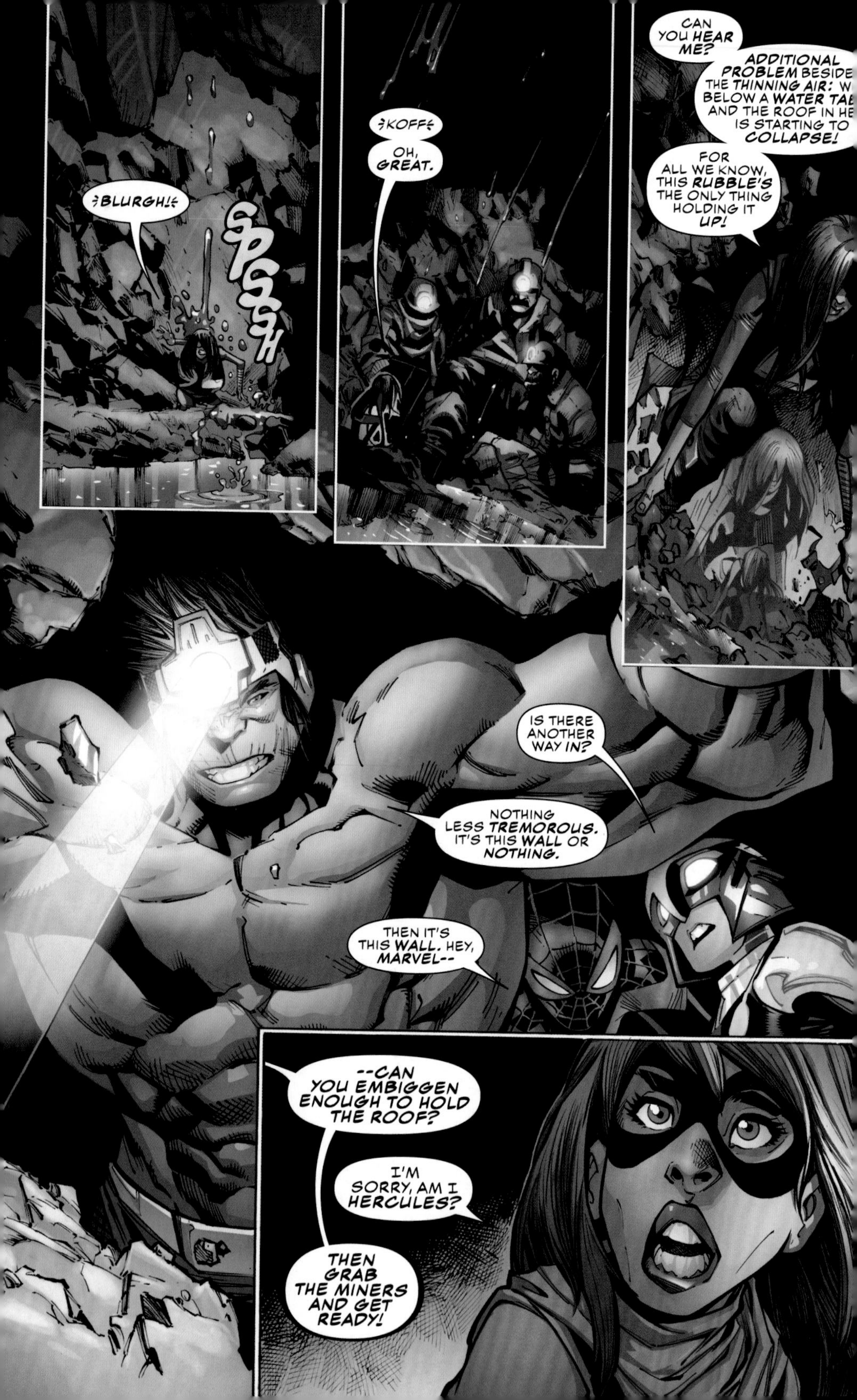

BLURGH!
SPSSH
KOFF
OH, GREAT.
CAN YOU HEAR ME?
ADDITIONAL PROBLEM BESIDE THE THINNING AIR: W BELOW A WATER TAB AND THE ROOF IN HE IS STARTING TO COLLAPSE!
FOR ALL WE KNOW, THIS RUBBLE'S THE ONLY THING HOLDING IT UP!
IS THERE ANOTHER WAY IN?
NOTHING LESS TREMOROUS. IT'S THIS WALL OR NOTHING.
THEN IT'S THIS WALL. HEY, MARVEL--
--CAN YOU EMBIGGEN ENOUGH TO HOLD THE ROOF?
I'M SORRY, AM I HERCULES?
THEN GRAB THE MINERS AND GET READY!

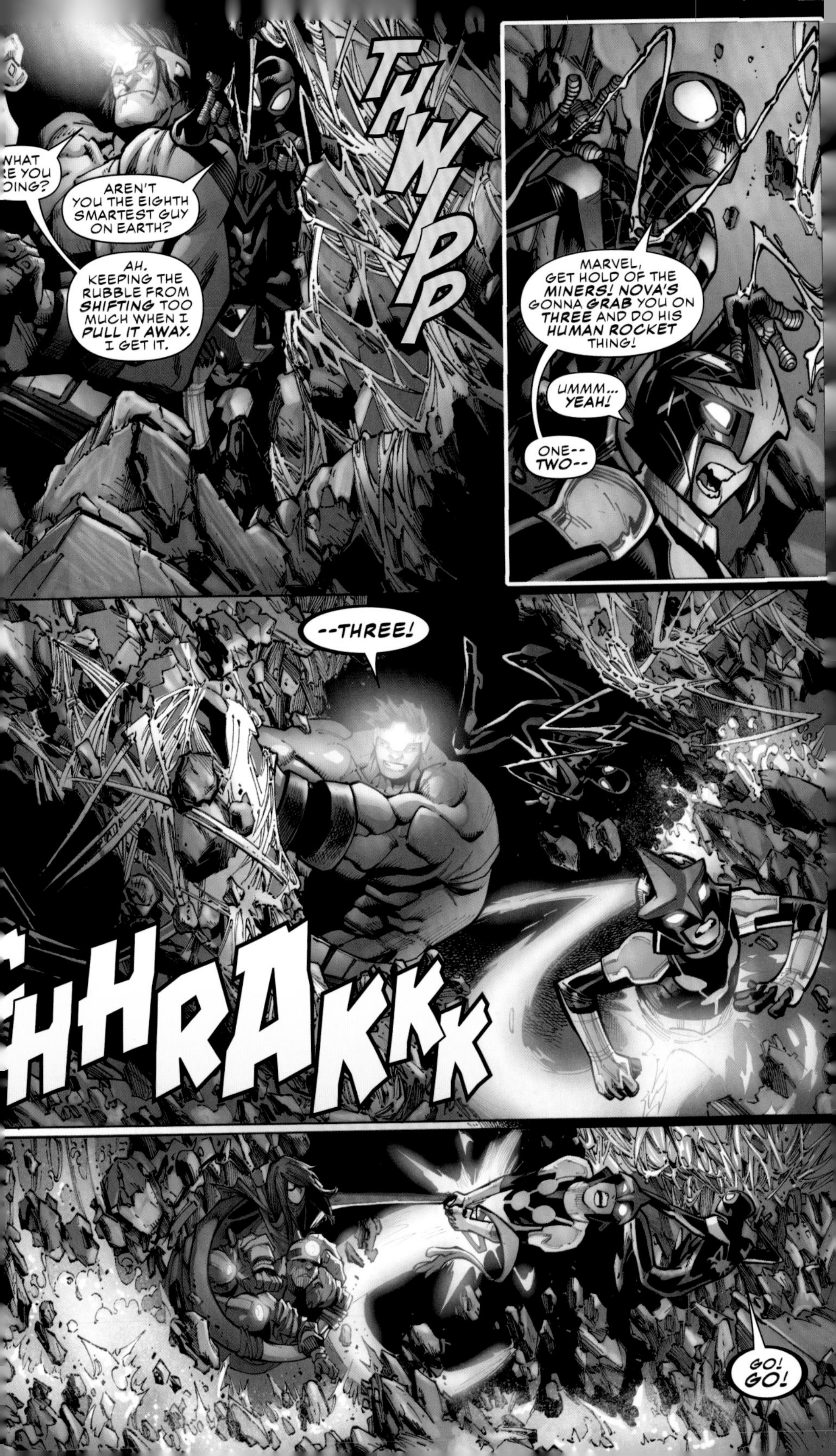
THWIPP
WHAT 'RE YOU DOING?
AREN'T YOU THE EIGHTH SMARTEST GUY ON EARTH?
AH. KEEPING THE RUBBLE FROM SHIFTING TOO MUCH WHEN I PULL IT AWAY. I GET IT.
MARVEL, GET HOLD OF THE MINERS! NOVA'S GONNA GRAB YOU ON THREE AND DO HIS HUMAN ROCKET THING!
UMMM... YEAH!
ONE-- TWO--
--THREE!
SHHRAKKK
GO! GO!

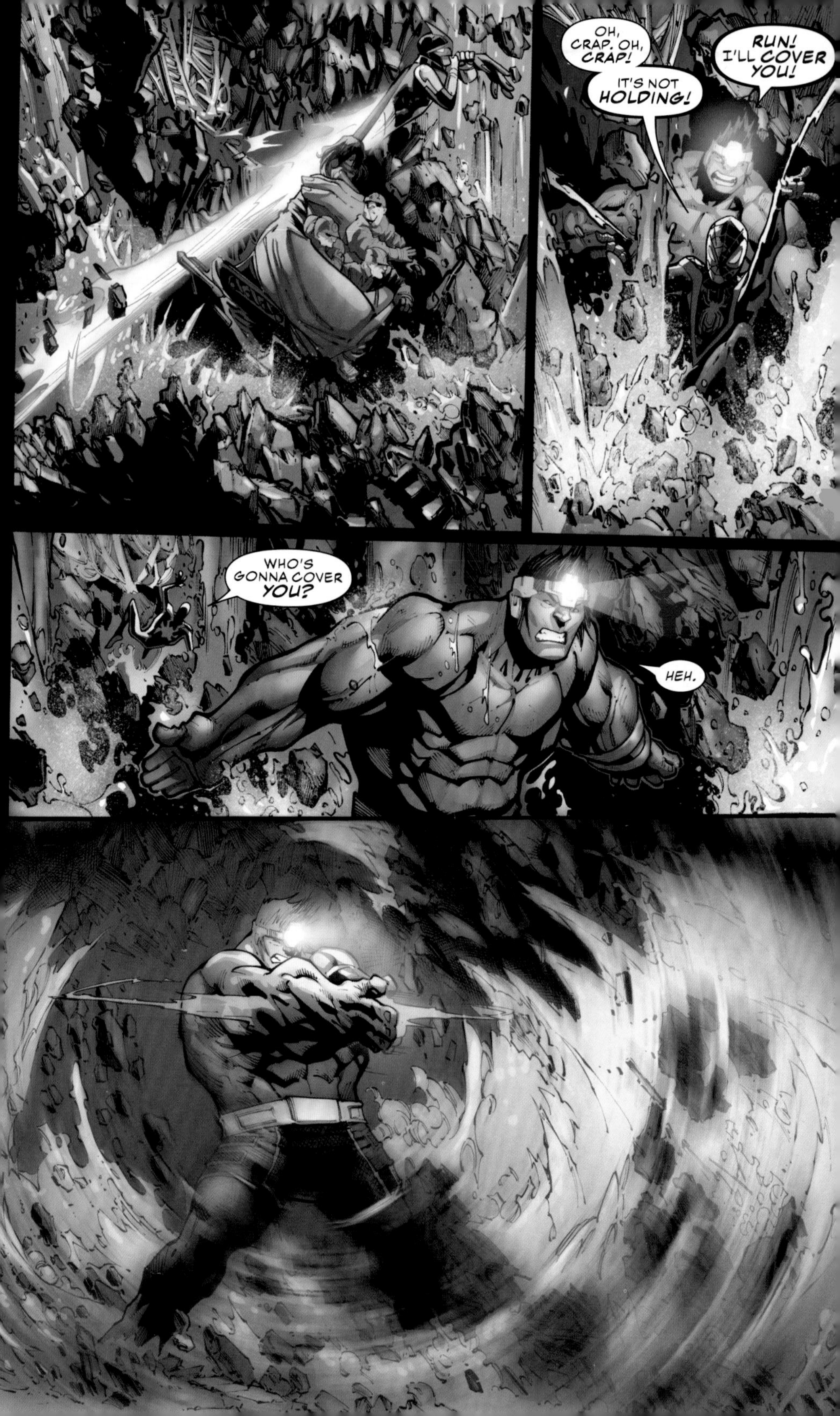
OH, CRAP. OH, CRAP!
IT'S NOT HOLDING!
RUN! I'LL COVER YOU!
WHO'S GONNA COVER YOU?
HEH.

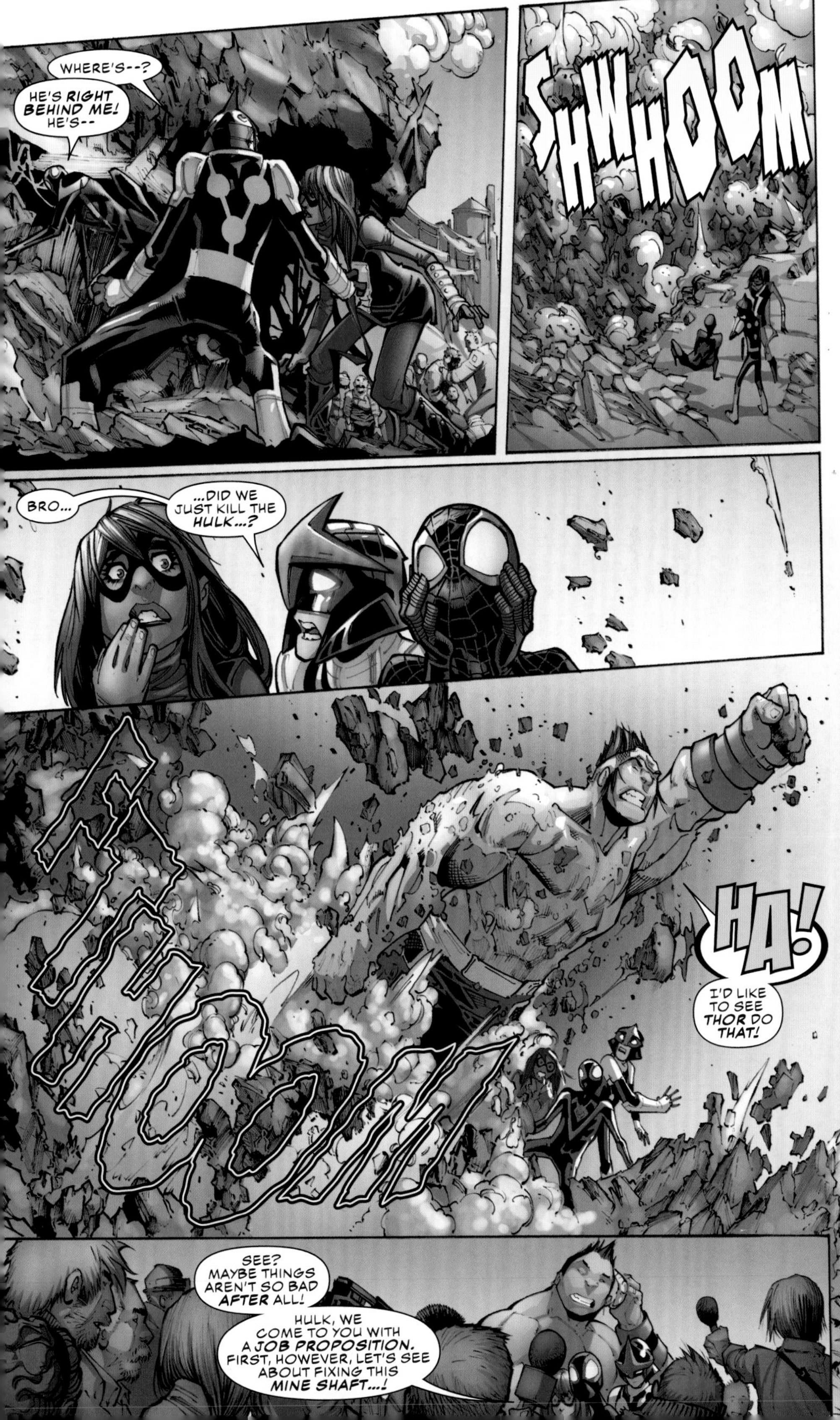
WHERE'S--?
HE'S RIGHT BEHIND ME! HE'S--
SHWHOOM
BRO...
...DID WE JUST KILL THE HULK...?
HA!
I'D LIKE TO SEE THOR DO THAT!
SEE? MAYBE THINGS AREN'T SO BAD AFTER ALL!
HULK, WE COME TO YOU WITH A JOB PROPOSITION. FIRST, HOWEVER, LET'S SEE ABOUT FIXING THIS MINE SHAFT...!

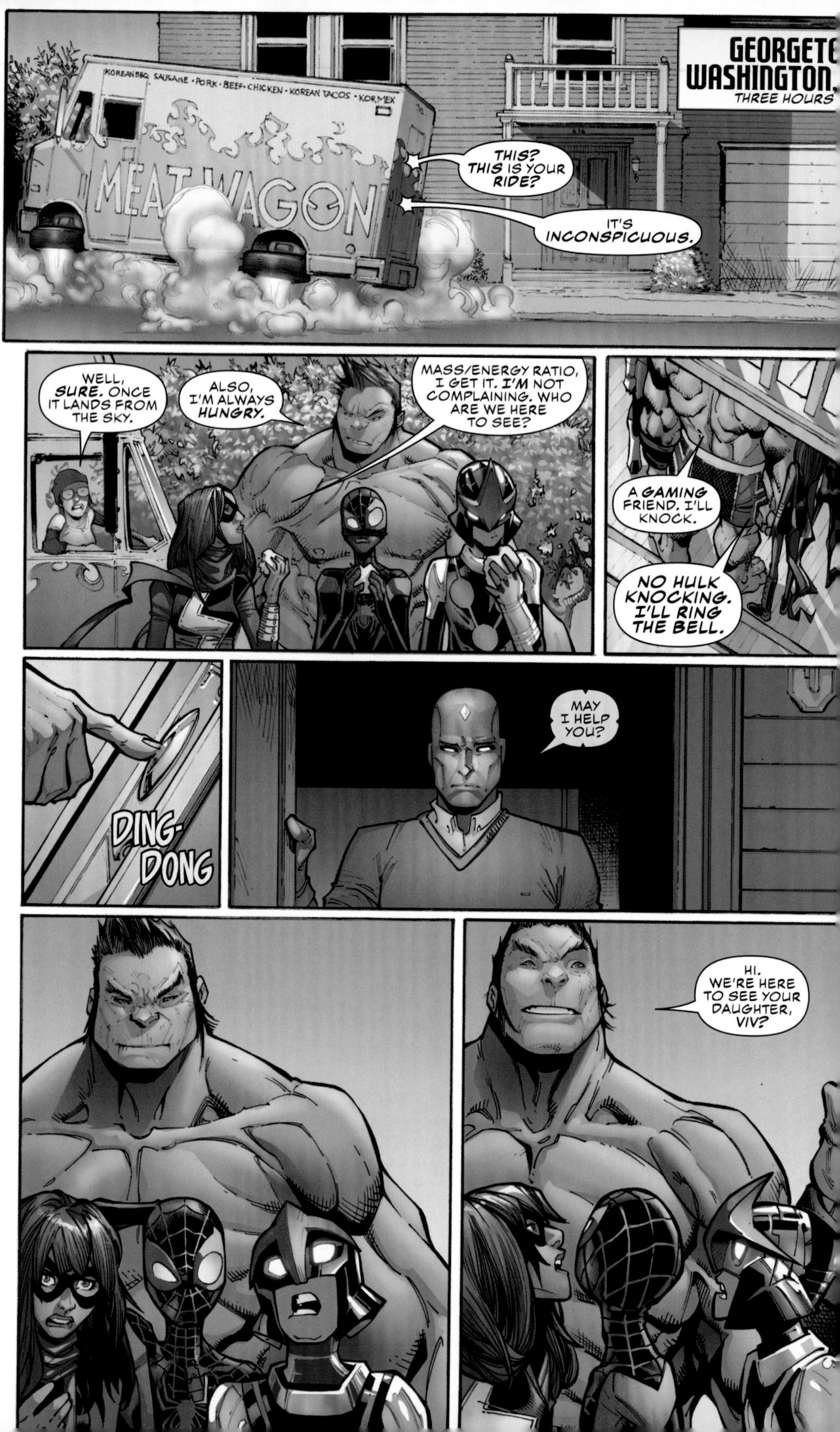
GEORGETO
WASHINGTON,
THREE HOURS
KOREAN BBQ SAUSAGE • PORK • BEEF • CHICKEN • KOREAN TACOS • KOR-MEX
MEAT WAGON
THIS? THIS IS YOUR RIDE?
IT'S INCONSPICUOUS.
WELL, SURE. ONCE IT LANDS FROM THE SKY.
ALSO, I'M ALWAYS HUNGRY.
MASS/ENERGY RATIO, I GET IT. I'M NOT COMPLAINING. WHO ARE WE HERE TO SEE?
A GAMING FRIEND. I'LL KNOCK.
NO HULK KNOCKING. I'LL RING THE BELL.
DING-DONG
MAY I HELP YOU?
HI. WE'RE HERE TO SEE YOUR DAUGHTER, VIV?

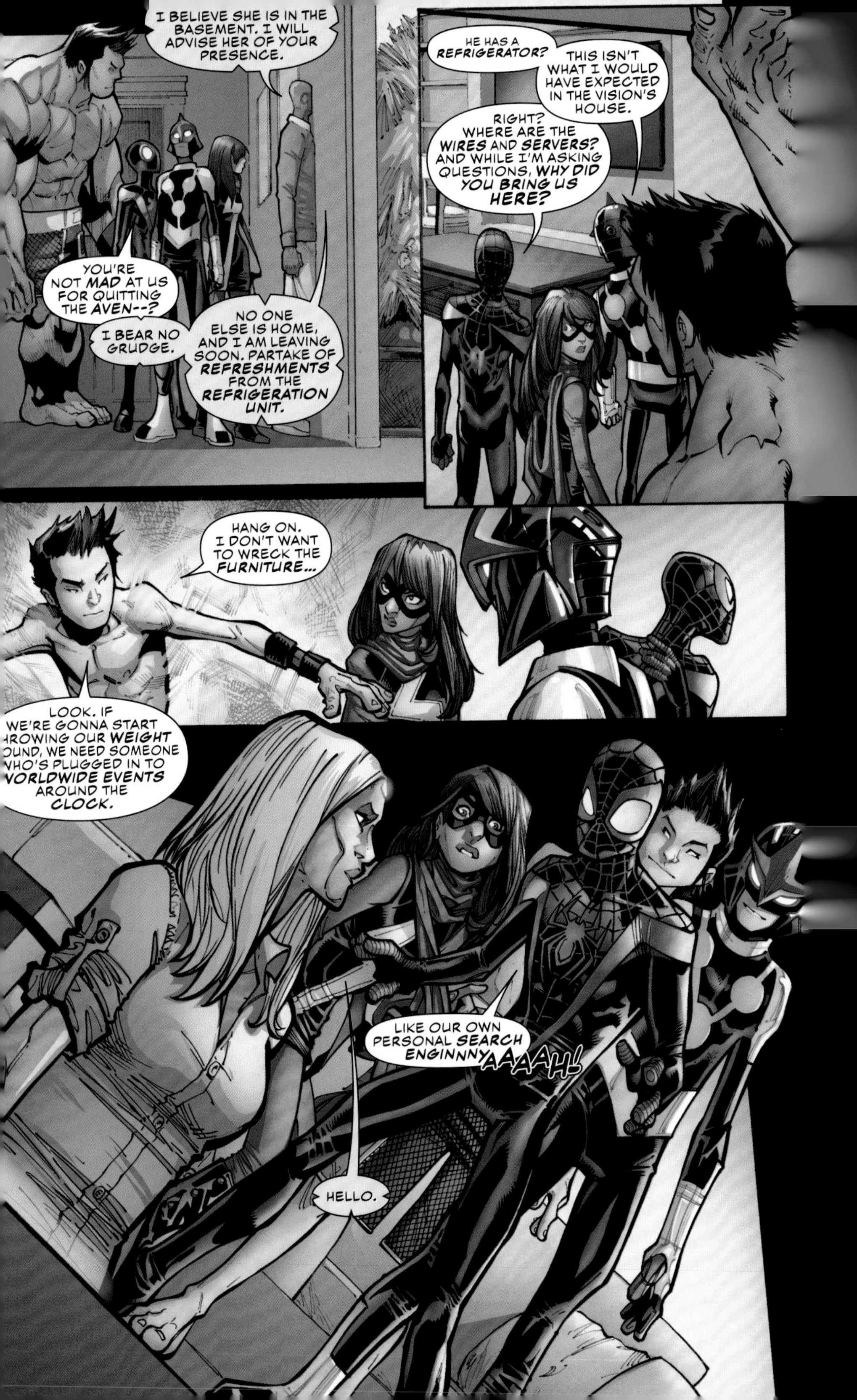
I BELIEVE SHE IS IN THE BASEMENT. I WILL ADVISE HER OF YOUR PRESENCE.
YOU'RE NOT MAD AT US FOR QUITTING THE AVEN--?
I BEAR NO GRUDGE.
NO ONE ELSE IS HOME, AND I AM LEAVING SOON. PARTAKE OF REFRESHMENTS FROM THE REFRIGERATION UNIT.
HE HAS A REFRIGERATOR?
THIS ISN'T WHAT I WOULD HAVE EXPECTED IN THE VISION'S HOUSE.
RIGHT? WHERE ARE THE WIRES AND SERVERS? AND WHILE I'M ASKING QUESTIONS, WHY DID YOU BRING US HERE?
HANG ON. I DON'T WANT TO WRECK THE FURNITURE...
LOOK. IF WE'RE GONNA START HROWING OUR WEIGHT OUND, WE NEED SOMEONE VHO'S PLUGGED IN TO VORLDWIDE EVENTS AROUND THE CLOCK.
LIKE OUR OWN PERSONAL SEARCH ENGINNNYAAAAH!
HELLO.

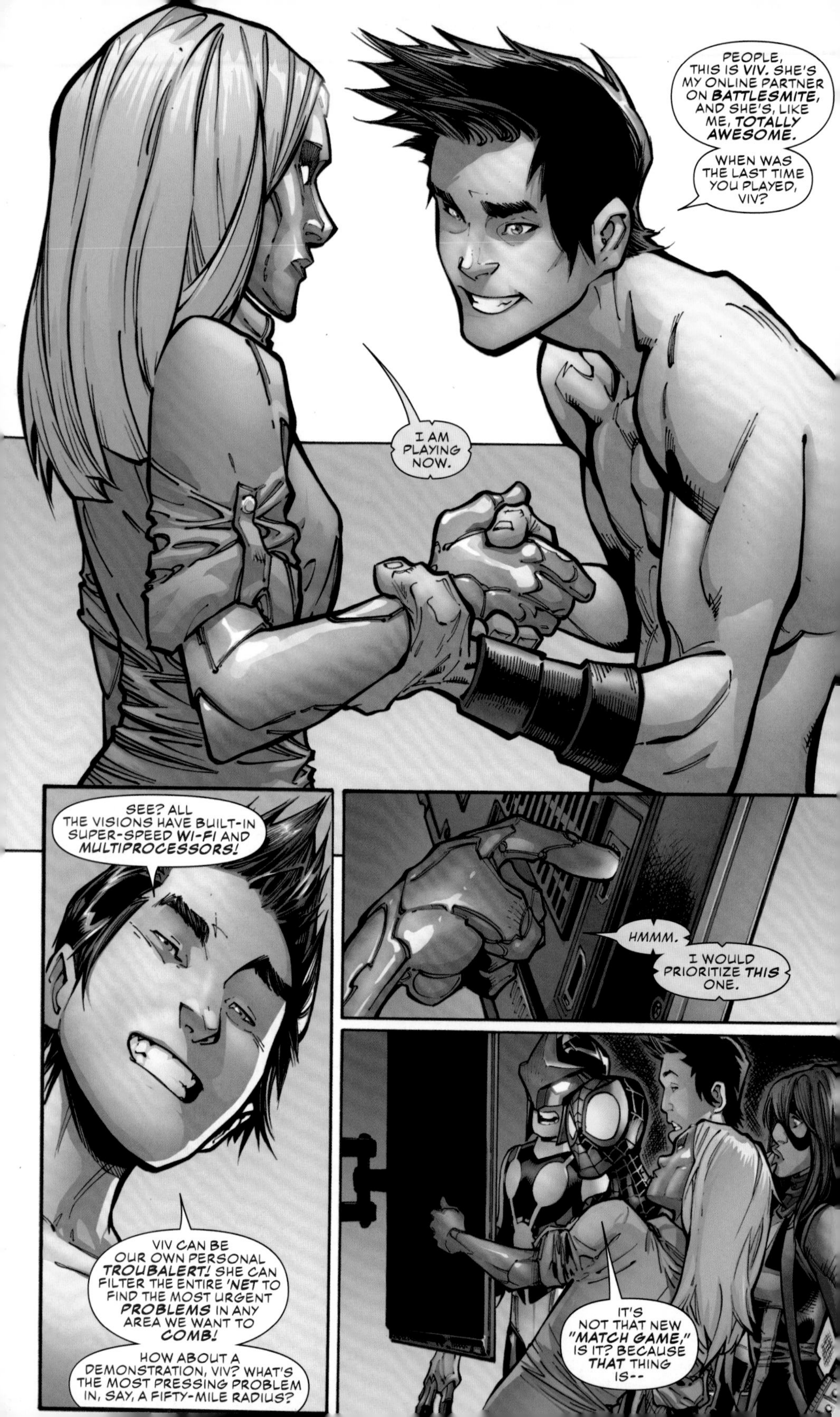
PEOPLE, THIS IS VIV. SHE'S MY ONLINE PARTNER ON BATTLESMITE, AND SHE'S, LIKE ME, TOTALLY AWESOME.
WHEN WAS THE LAST TIME YOU PLAYED, VIV?
I AM PLAYING NOW.
SEE? ALL THE VISIONS HAVE BUILT-IN SUPER-SPEED WI-FI AND MULTIPROCESSORS!
VIV CAN BE OUR OWN PERSONAL TROUBALERT! SHE CAN FILTER THE ENTIRE 'NET TO FIND THE MOST URGENT PROBLEMS IN ANY AREA WE WANT TO COMB!
HOW ABOUT A DEMONSTRATION, VIV? WHAT'S THE MOST PRESSING PROBLEM IN, SAY, A FIFTY-MILE RADIUS?
HMMM.
I WOULD PRIORITIZE THIS ONE.
IT'S NOT THAT NEW "MATCH GAME," IS IT? BECAUSE THAT THING IS--

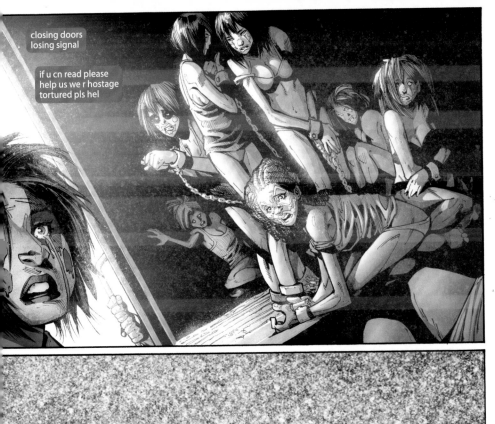

closing doors
losing signal

if u cn read please
help us we r hostage
tortured pls hel

... VIV, FIND
THEM.

FIND
THEM!

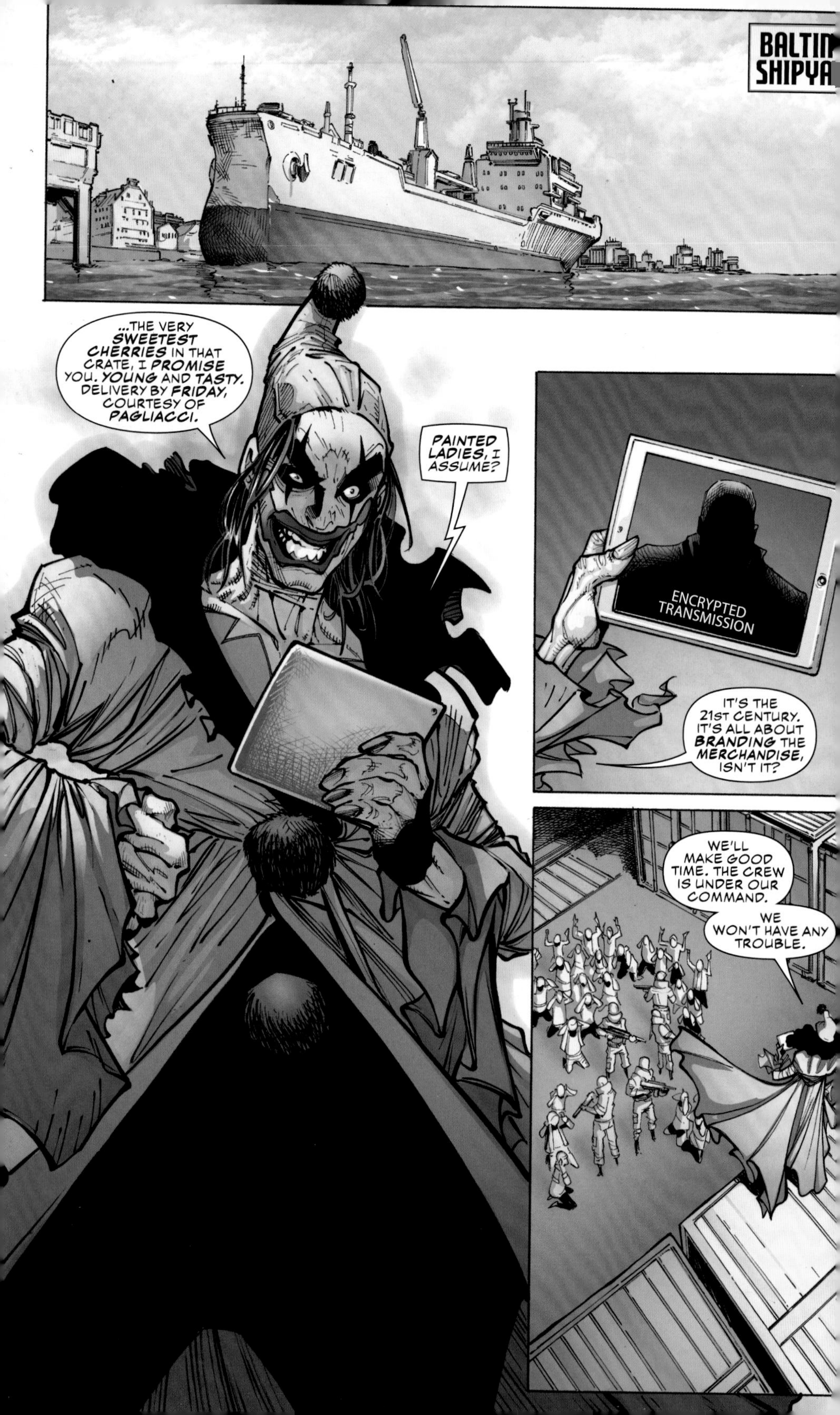
BALTIM
SHIPYA
...THE VERY SWEETEST CHERRIES IN THAT CRATE, I PROMISE YOU. YOUNG AND TASTY. DELIVERY BY FRIDAY, COURTESY OF PAGLIACCI.
PAINTED LADIES, I ASSUME?
ENCRYPTED TRANSMISSION
IT'S THE 21ST CENTURY. IT'S ALL ABOUT BRANDING THE MERCHANDISE, ISN'T IT?
WE'LL MAKE GOOD TIME. THE CREW IS UNDER OUR COMMAND.
WE WON'T HAVE ANY TROUBLE.

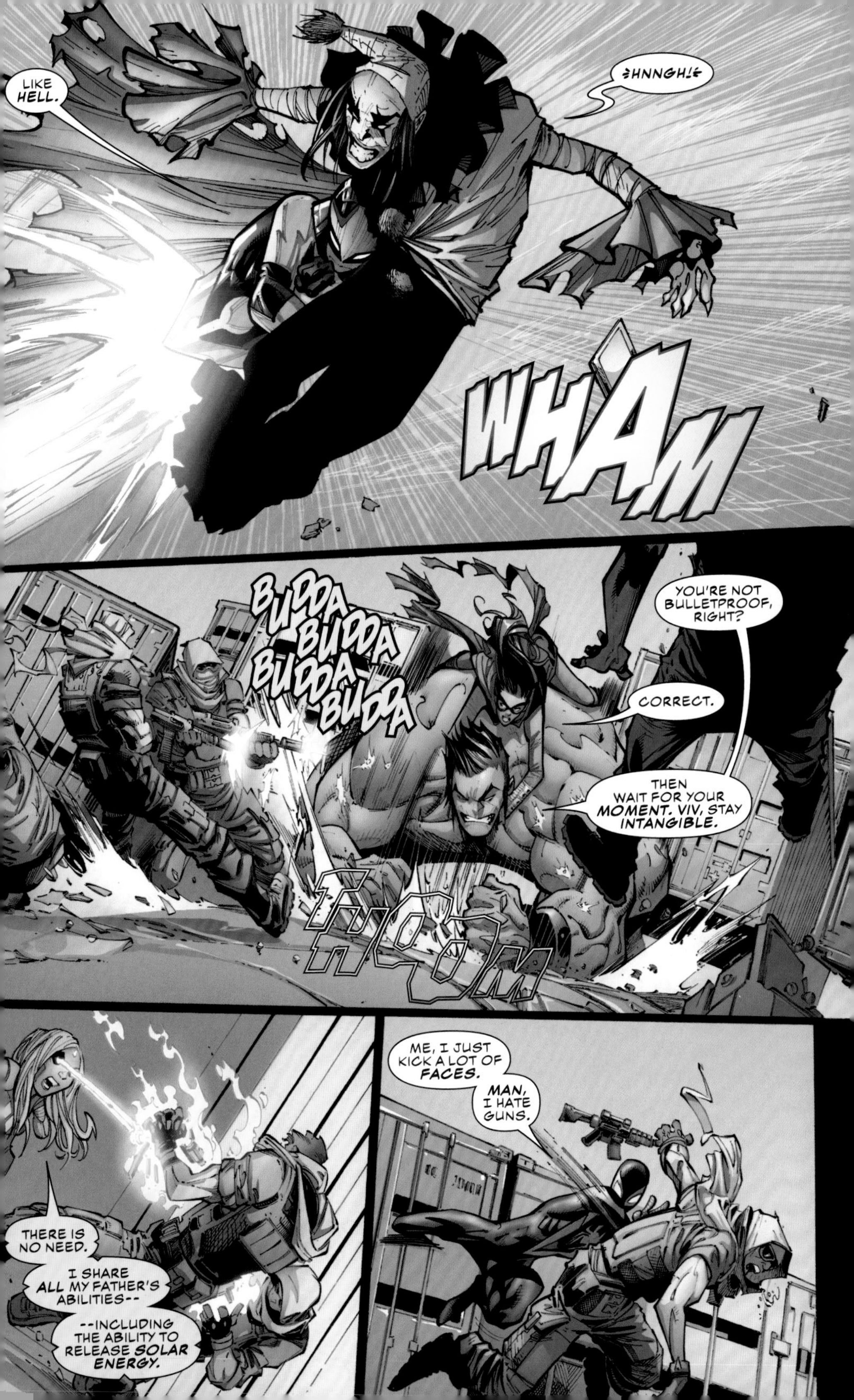
LIKE HELL.
HNNGH!
WHAM
BUDDA BUDDA BUDDA BUDDA
YOU'RE NOT BULLETPROOF, RIGHT?
CORRECT.
THEN WAIT FOR YOUR MOMENT. VIV, STAY INTANGIBLE.
FWOOM
THERE IS NO NEED.
I SHARE ALL MY FATHER'S ABILITIES--
--INCLUDING THE ABILITY TO RELEASE SOLAR ENERGY.
ME, I JUST KICK A LOT OF FACES.
MAN, I HATE GUNS.

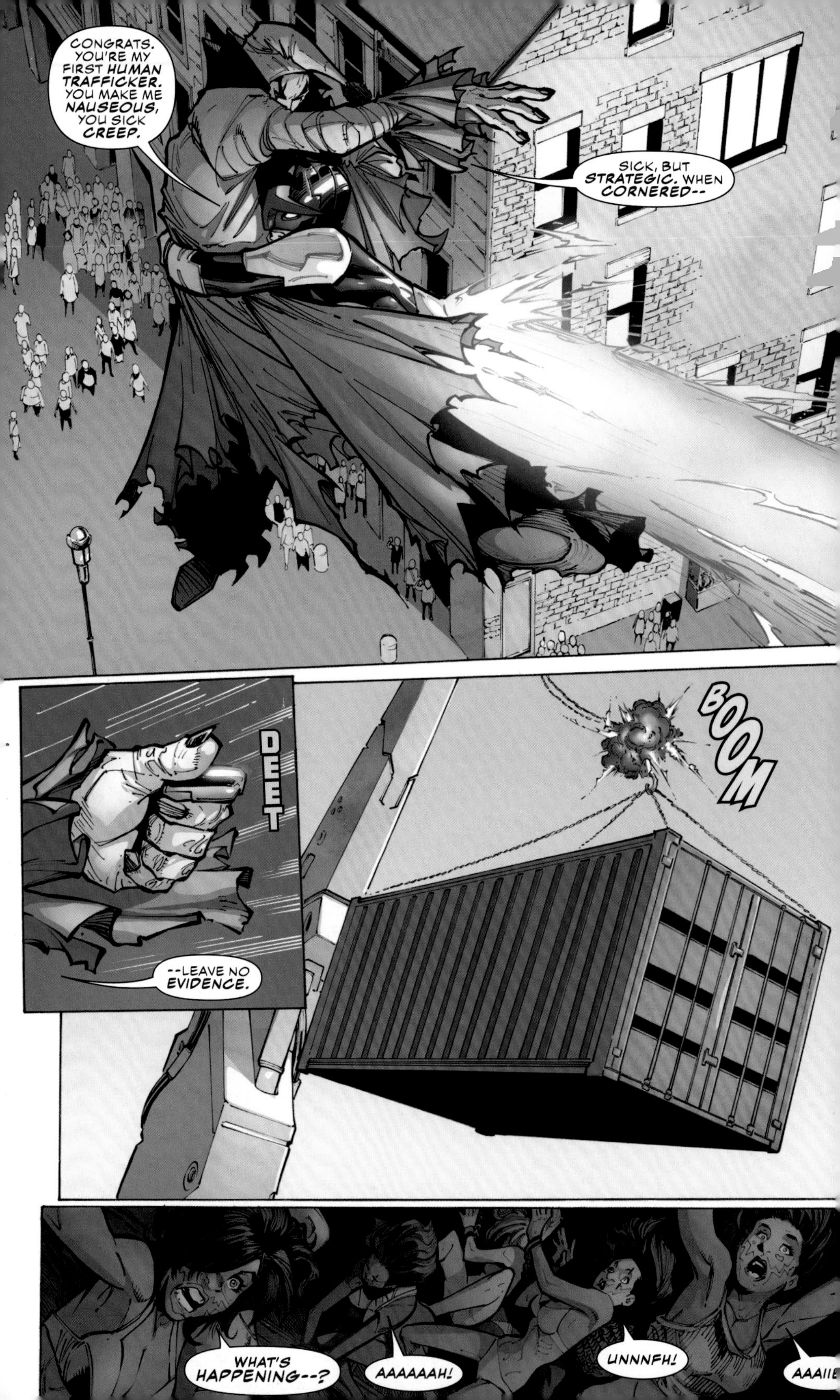
CONGRATS. YOU'RE MY FIRST HUMAN TRAFFICKER. YOU MAKE ME NAUSEOUS, YOU SICK CREEP.
SICK, BUT STRATEGIC. WHEN CORNERED--
DEET
--LEAVE NO EVIDENCE.
BOOM
WHAT'S HAPPENING--?
AAAAAAH!
UNNNFH!

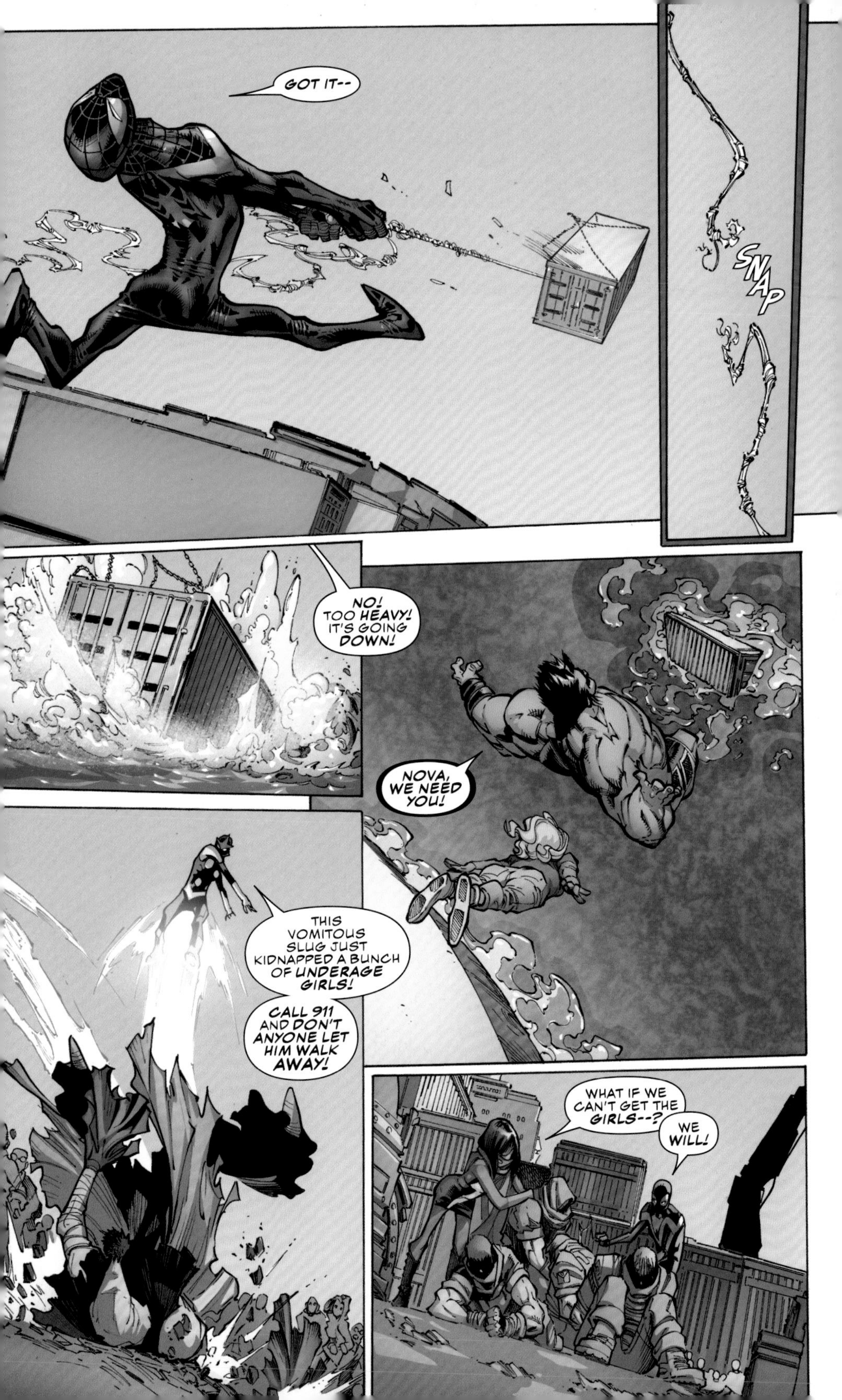
GOT IT--
SNAP
NO! TOO HEAVY! IT'S GOING DOWN!
NOVA, WE NEED YOU!
THIS VOMITOUS SLUG JUST KIDNAPPED A BUNCH OF UNDERAGE GIRLS!
CALL 911 AND DON'T ANYONE LET HIM WALK AWAY!
WHAT IF WE CAN'T GET THE GIRLS--?
WE WILL!

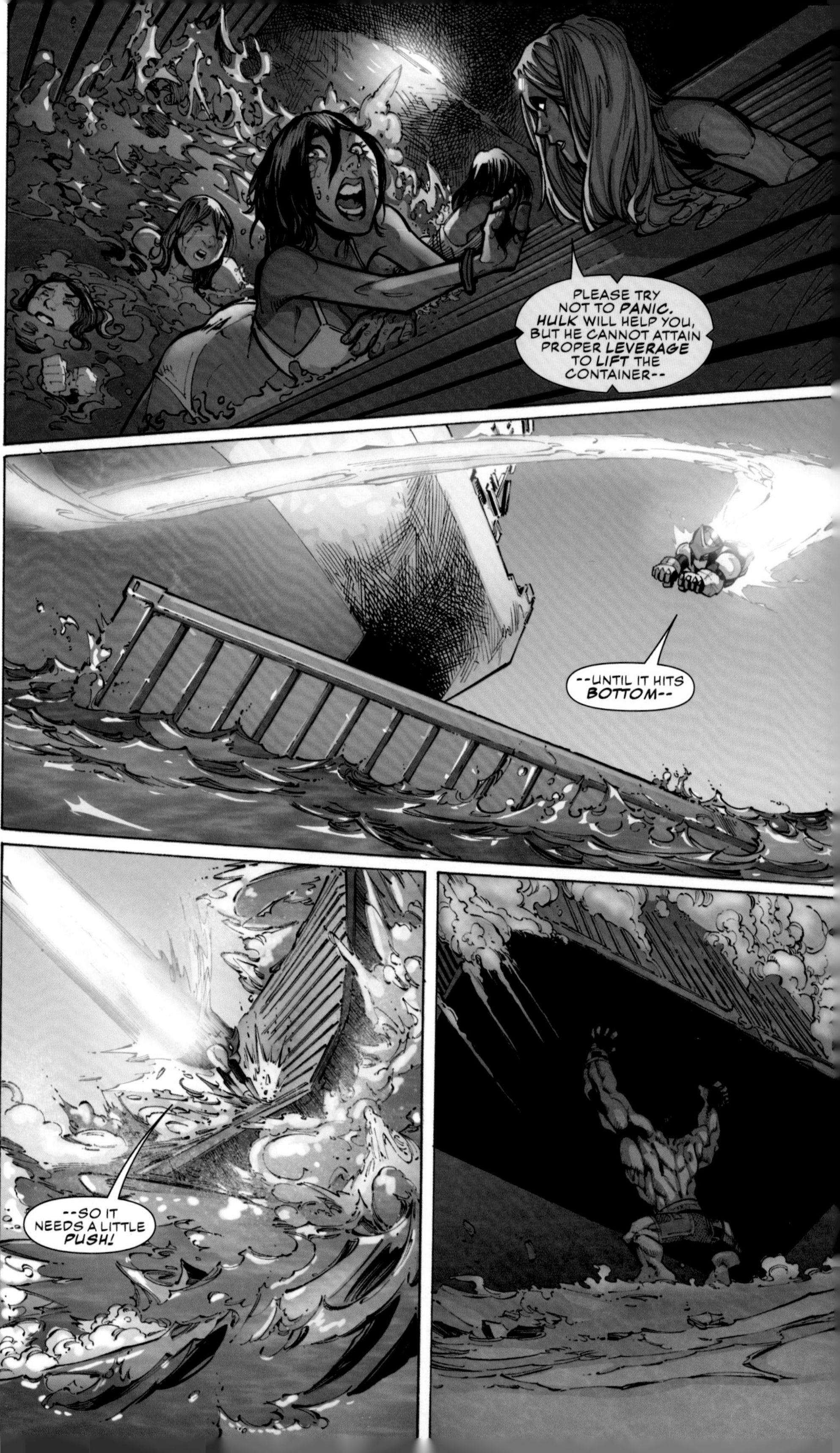
PLEASE TRY NOT TO PANIC. HULK WILL HELP YOU, BUT HE CANNOT ATTAIN PROPER LEVERAGE TO LIFT THE CONTAINER--
--UNTIL IT HITS BOTTOM--
--SO IT NEEDS A LITTLE PUSH!

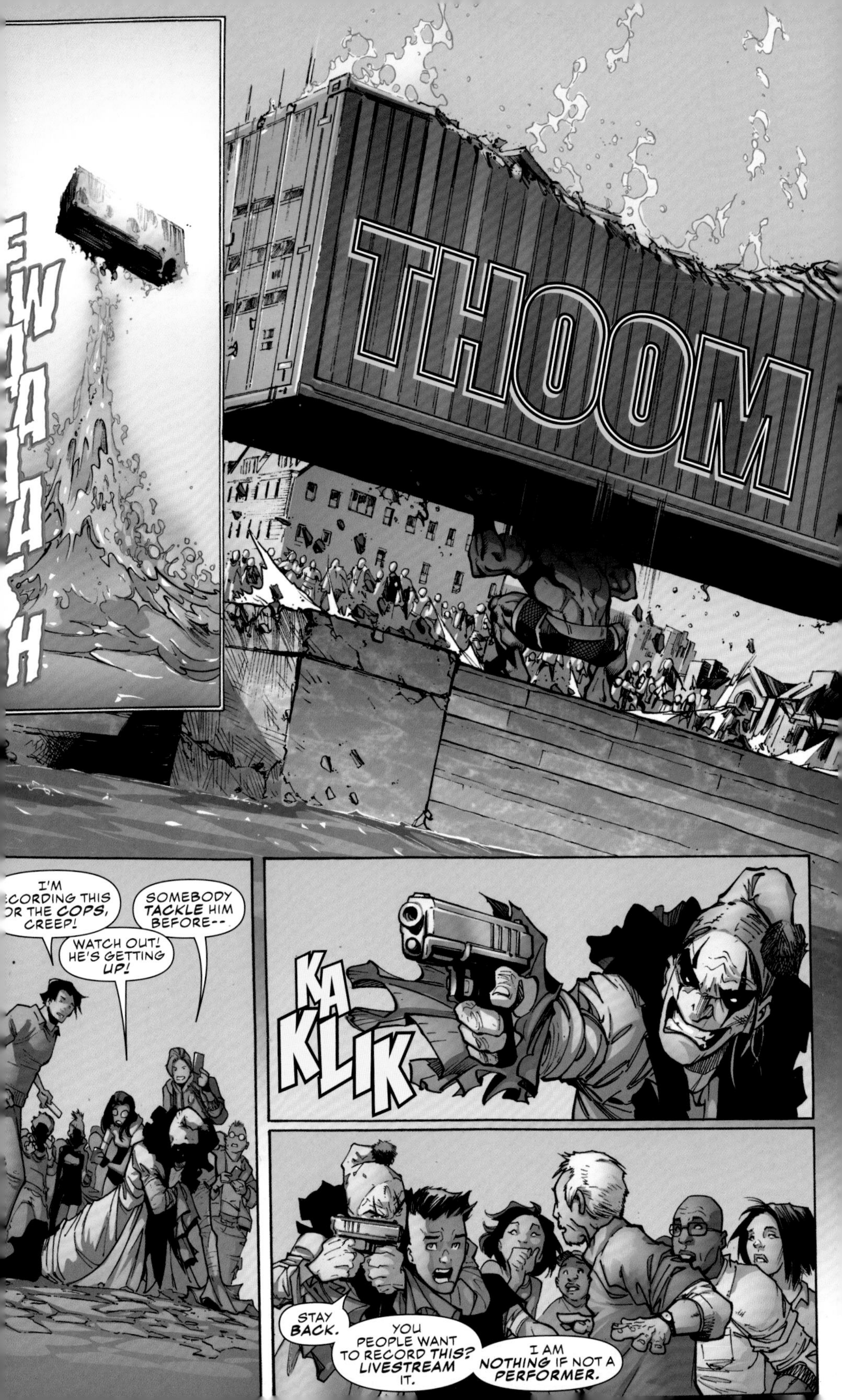
THOOM
SPLAAASH
I'M RECORDING THIS FOR THE COPS, CREEP!
SOMEBODY TACKLE HIM BEFORE--
WATCH OUT! HE'S GETTING UP!
KA KLIK
STAY BACK.
YOU PEOPLE WANT TO RECORD THIS? LIVESTREAM IT.
I AM NOTHING IF NOT A PERFORMER.

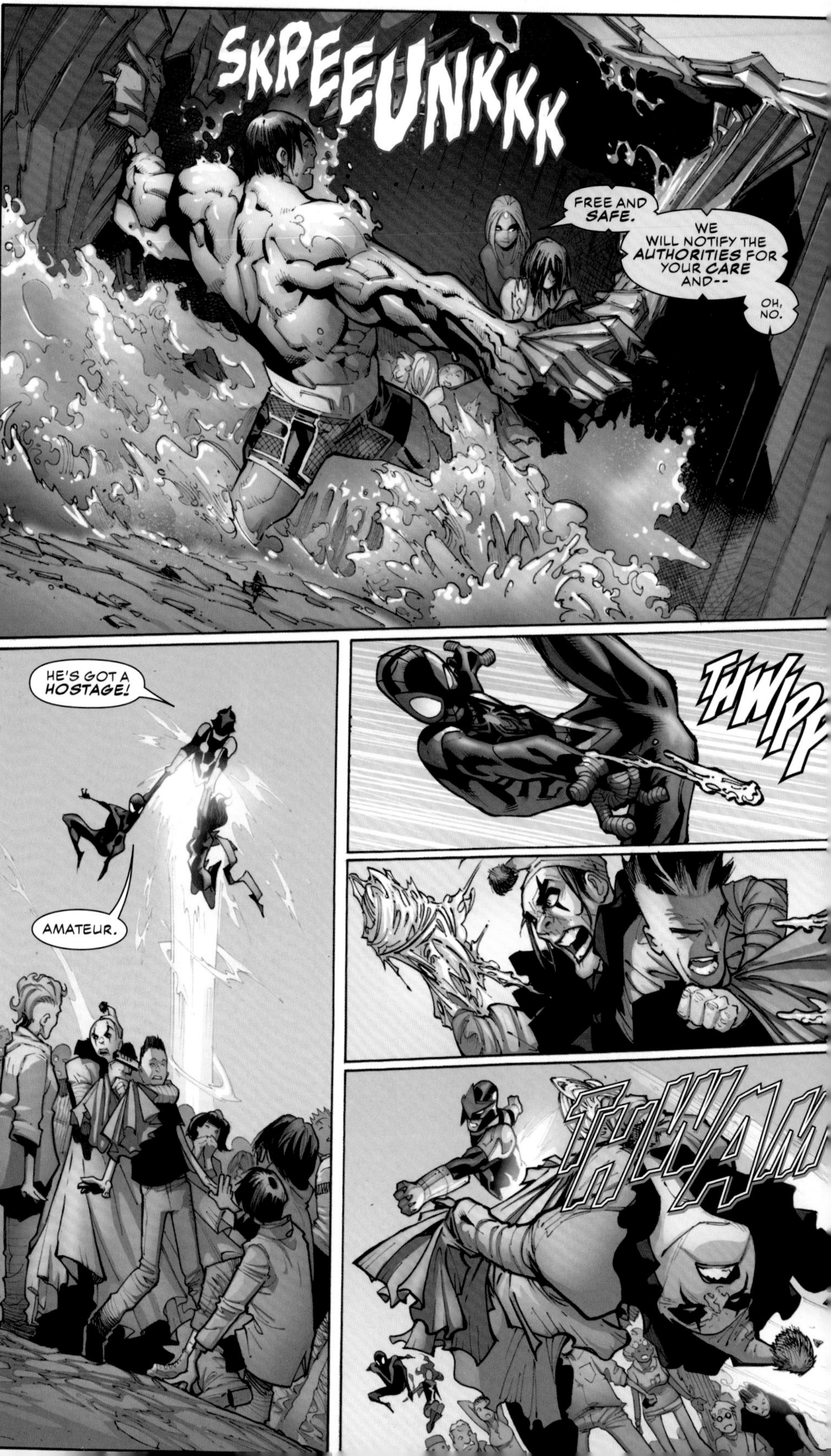

SKREEUNKKK
FREE AND SAFE.
WE WILL NOTIFY THE AUTHORITIES FOR YOUR CARE AND--
OH, NO.
HE'S GOT A HOSTAGE!
AMATEUR.
THWIPP
THWAM

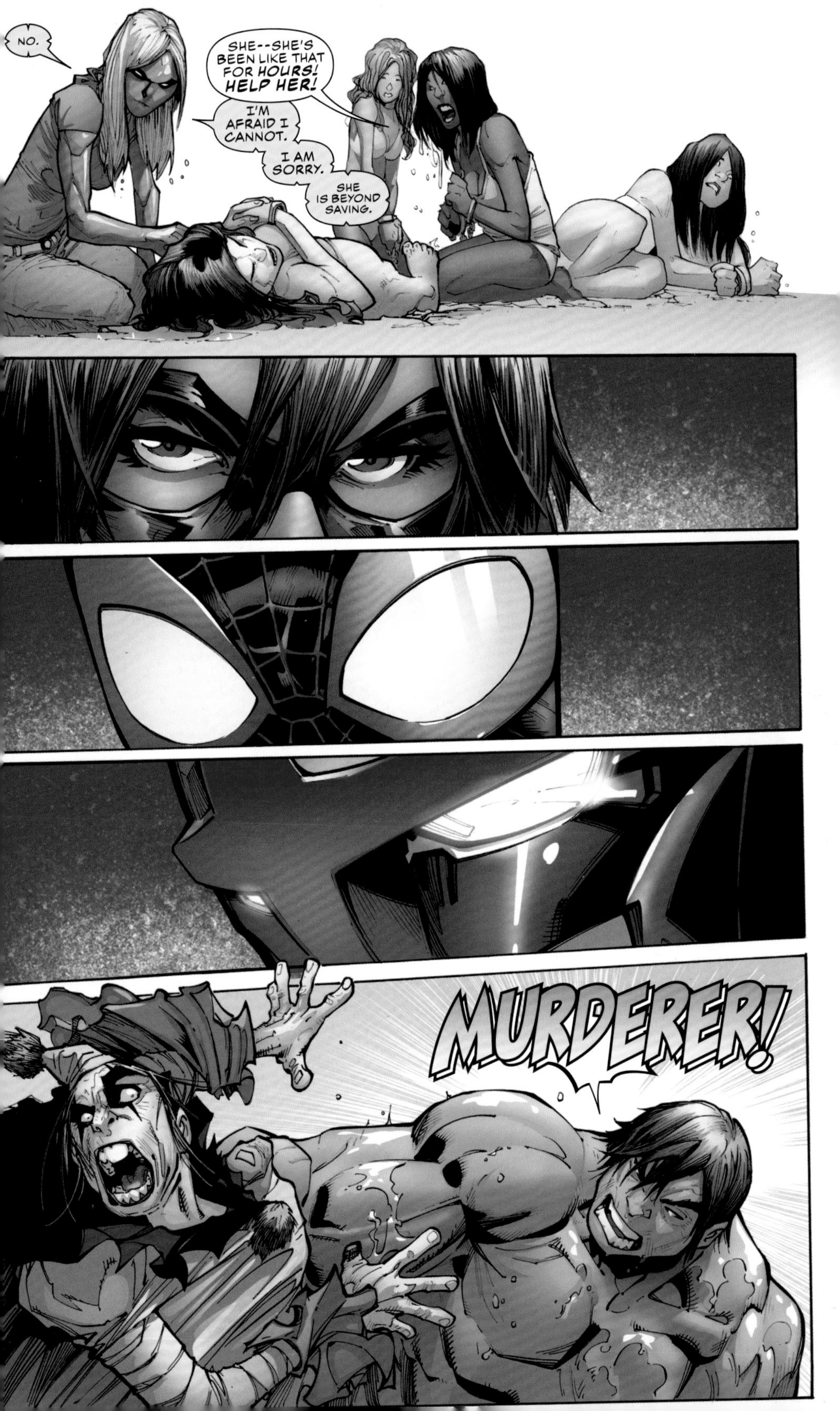
NO.
SHE--SHE'S BEEN LIKE THAT FOR HOURS! HELP HER!
I'M AFRAID I CANNOT.
I AM SORRY.
SHE IS BEYOND SAVING.
MURDERER!

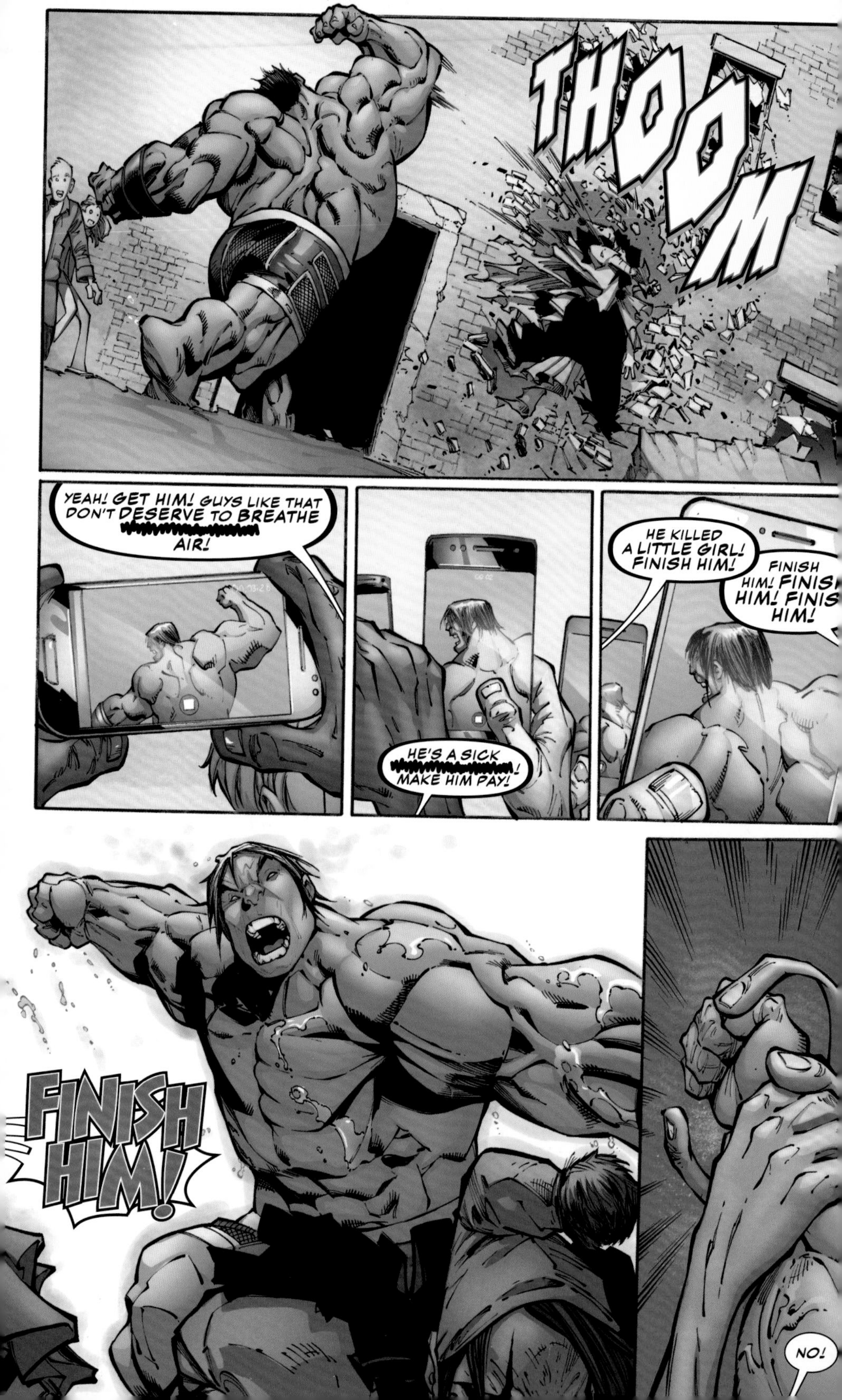
THOOM
YEAH! GET HIM! GUYS LIKE THAT DON'T DESERVE TO BREATHE AIR!
HE'S A SICK ! MAKE HIM PAY!
HE KILLED A LITTLE GIRL! FINISH HIM!
FINISH HIM! FINIS HIM! FINIS HIM!
FINISH HIM!
NO!

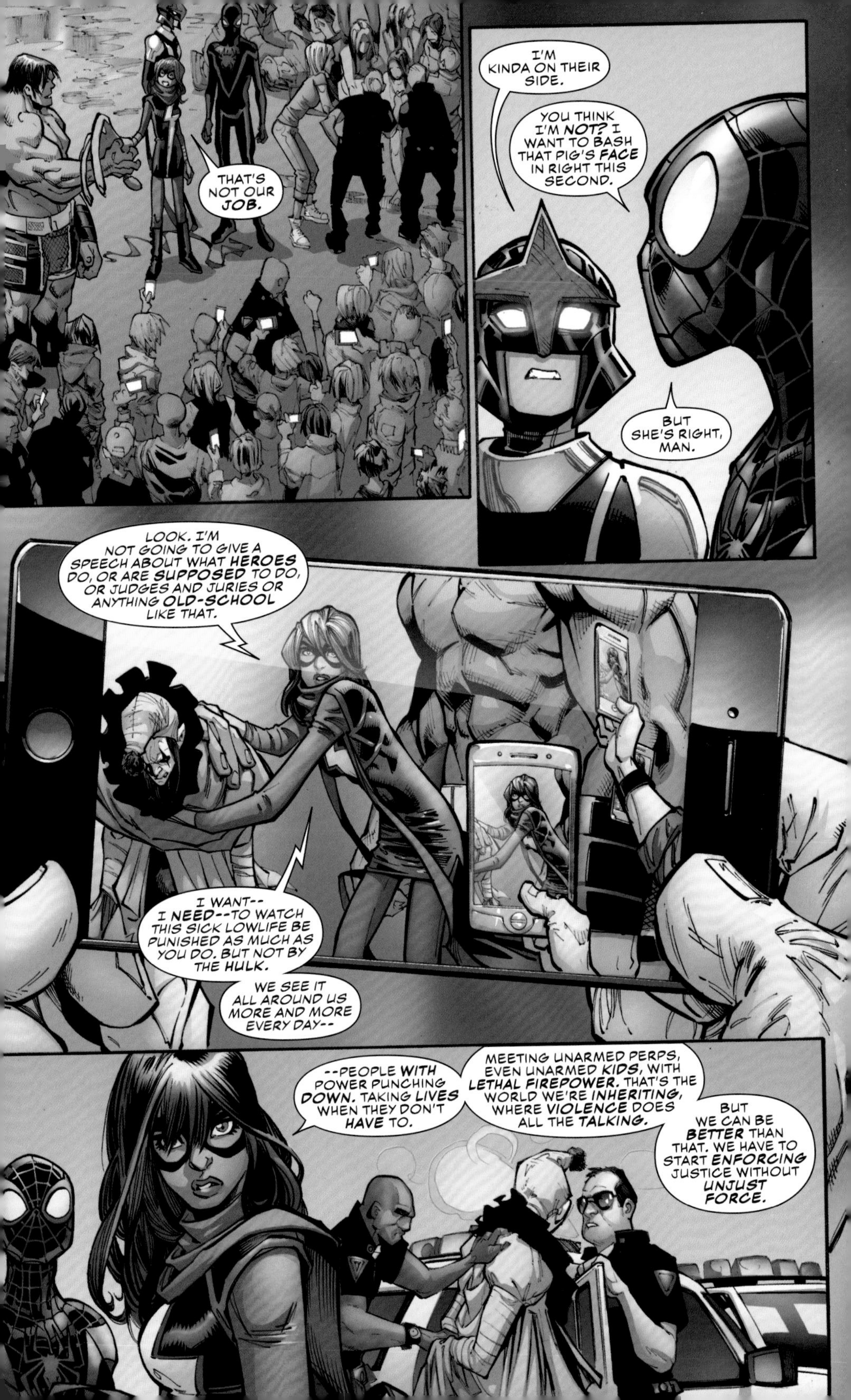
THAT'S NOT OUR JOB.
I'M KINDA ON THEIR SIDE.
YOU THINK I'M NOT? I WANT TO BASH THAT PIG'S FACE IN RIGHT THIS SECOND.
BUT SHE'S RIGHT, MAN.
LOOK. I'M NOT GOING TO GIVE A SPEECH ABOUT WHAT HEROES DO, OR ARE SUPPOSED TO DO, OR JUDGES AND JURIES OR ANYTHING OLD-SCHOOL LIKE THAT.
I WANT-- I NEED--TO WATCH THIS SICK LOWLIFE BE PUNISHED AS MUCH AS YOU DO. BUT NOT BY THE HULK.
WE SEE IT ALL AROUND US MORE AND MORE EVERY DAY--
--PEOPLE WITH POWER PUNCHING DOWN. TAKING LIVES WHEN THEY DON'T HAVE TO.
MEETING UNARMED PERPS, EVEN UNARMED KIDS, WITH LETHAL FIREPOWER. THAT'S THE WORLD WE'RE INHERITING, WHERE VIOLENCE DOES ALL THE TALKING.
BUT WE CAN BE BETTER THAN THAT. WE HAVE TO START ENFORCING JUSTICE WITHOUT UNJUST FORCE.

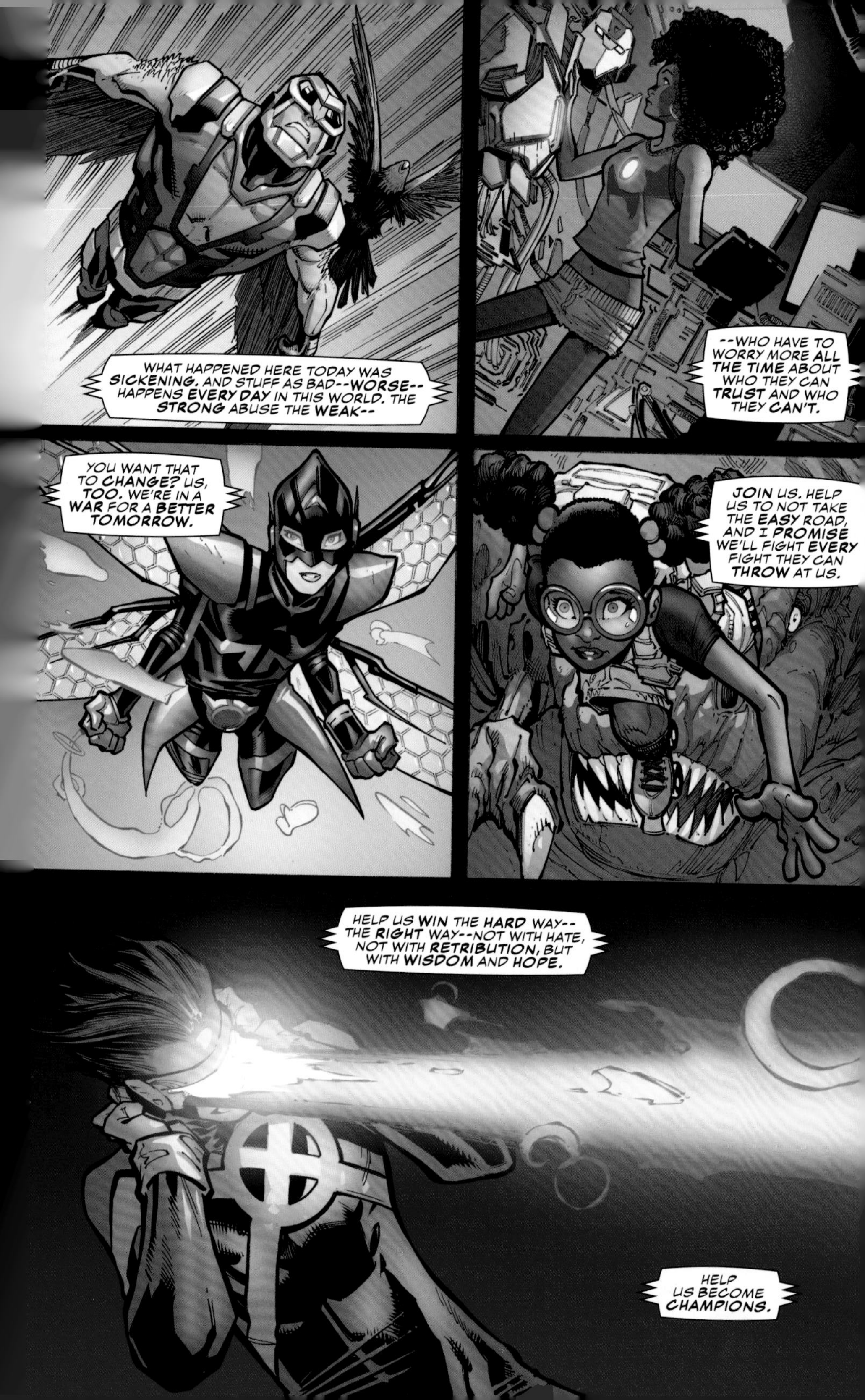

WHAT HAPPENED HERE TODAY WAS SICKENING. AND STUFF AS BAD--WORSE--HAPPENS EVERY DAY IN THIS WORLD. THE STRONG ABUSE THE WEAK--
--WHO HAVE TO WORRY MORE ALL THE TIME ABOUT WHO THEY CAN TRUST AND WHO THEY CAN'T.
YOU WANT THAT TO CHANGE? US, TOO. WE'RE IN A WAR FOR A BETTER TOMORROW.
JOIN US. HELP US TO NOT TAKE THE EASY ROAD, AND I PROMISE WE'LL FIGHT EVERY FIGHT THEY CAN THROW AT US.
HELP US WIN THE HARD WAY--THE RIGHT WAY--NOT WITH HATE, NOT WITH RETRIBUTION, BUT WITH WISDOM AND HOPE.
HELP US BECOME CHAMPIONS.

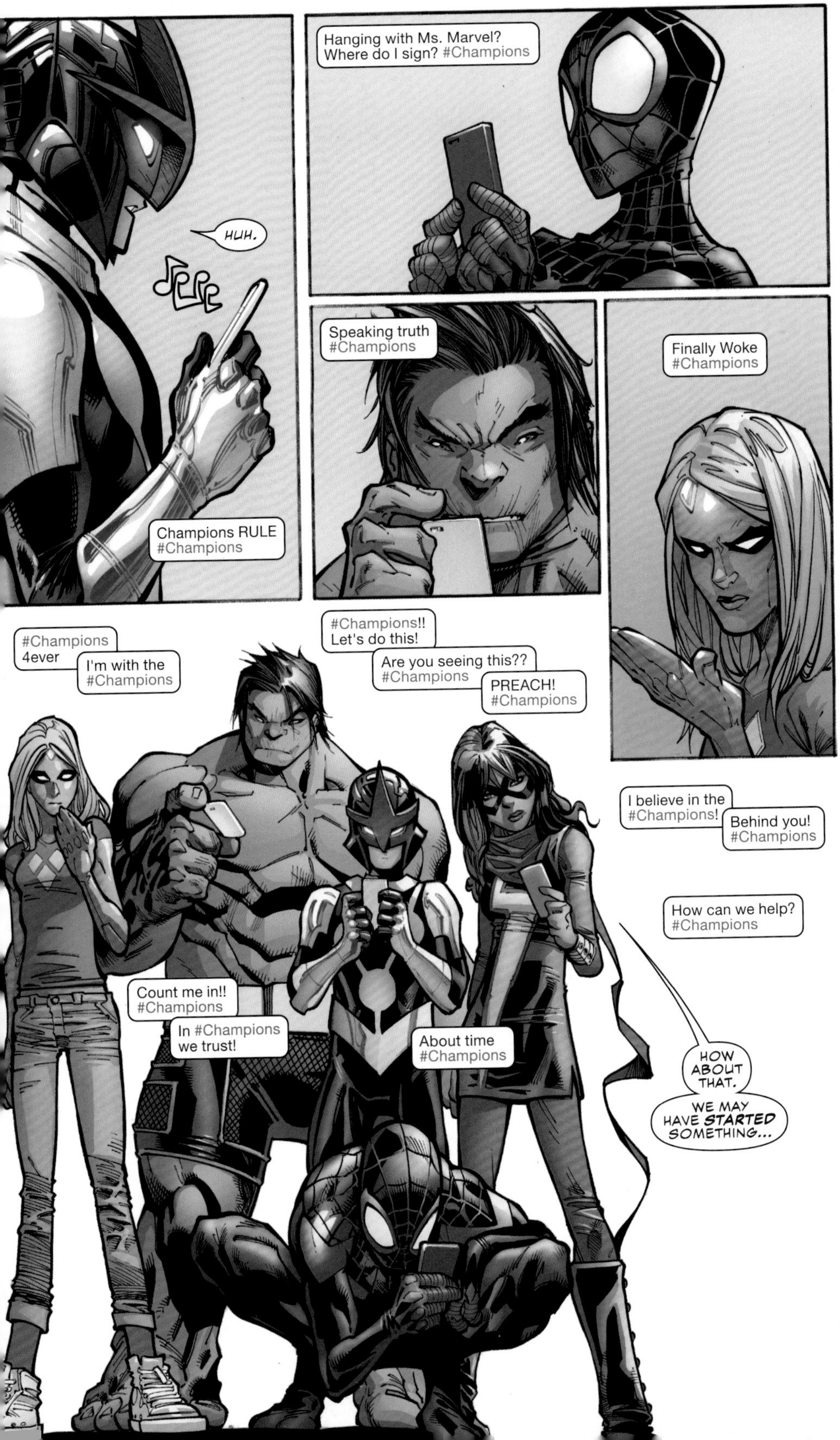
HUH.
SPLE
Champions RULE #Champions
Hanging with Ms. Marvel? Where do I sign? #Champions
Speaking truth #Champions
Finally Woke #Champions
#Champions 4ever
I'm with the #Champions
#Champions!! Let's do this!
Are you seeing this?? #Champions
PREACH! #Champions
I believe in the #Champions!
Behind you! #Champions
How can we help? #Champions
Count me in!! #Champions
In #Champions we trust!
About time #Champions
HOW ABOUT THAT.
WE MAY HAVE STARTED SOMETHING...

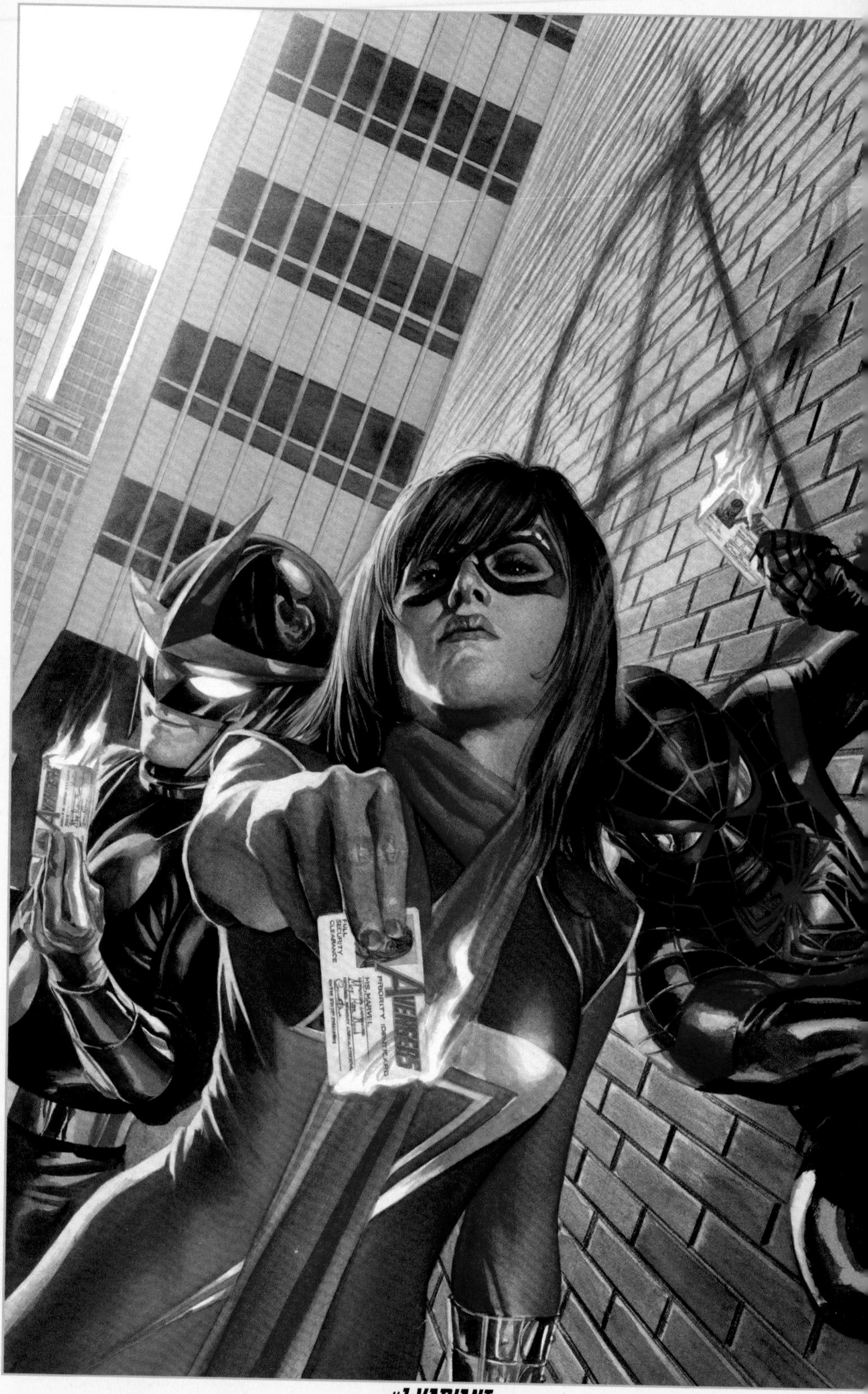
AVENGERS
PRIORITY IDENTICARD
MS.MARVEL
FULL SECURITY CLEARANCE

#1 VARIANT
BY ALEX ROSS

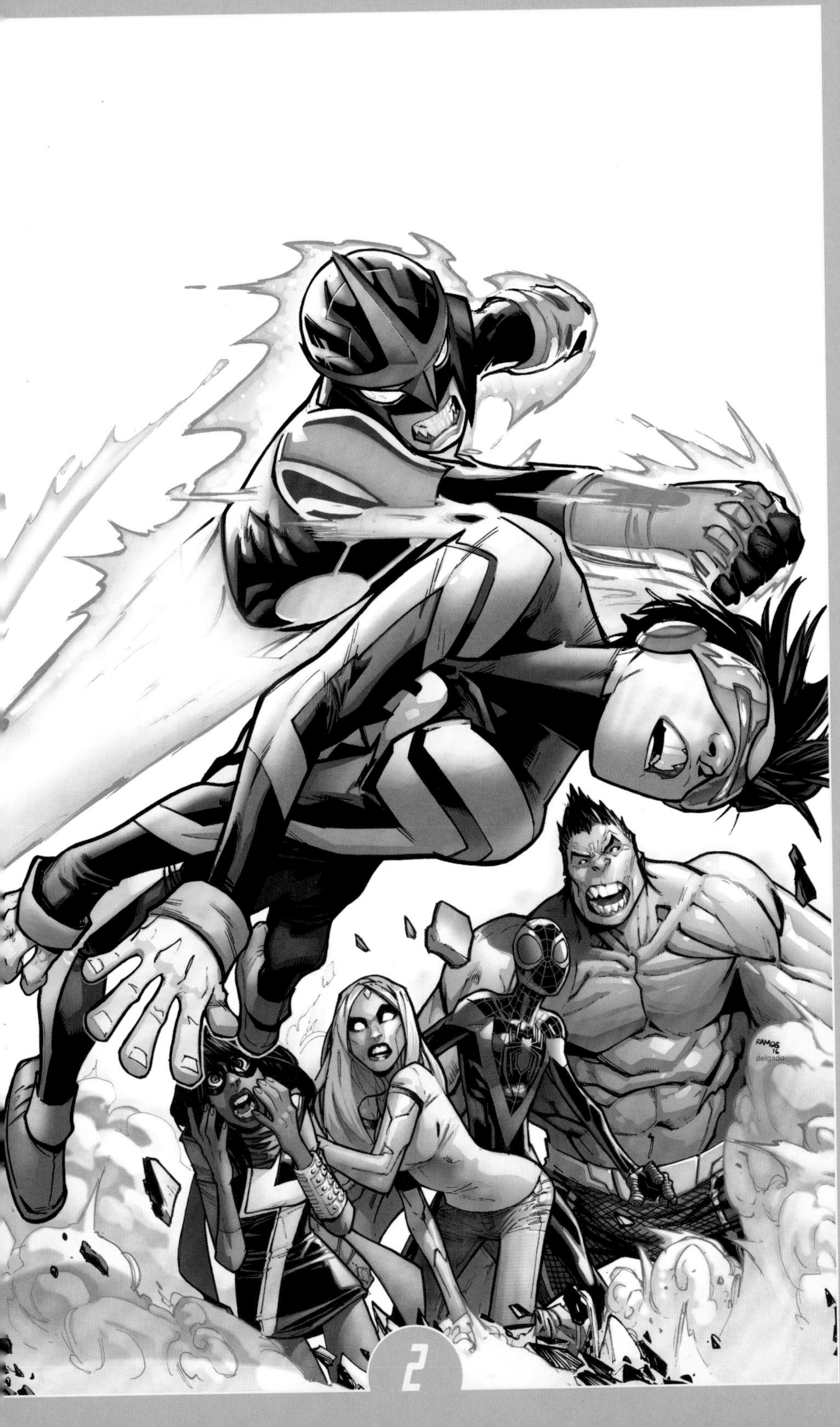
RAMOS 16
delgado
2

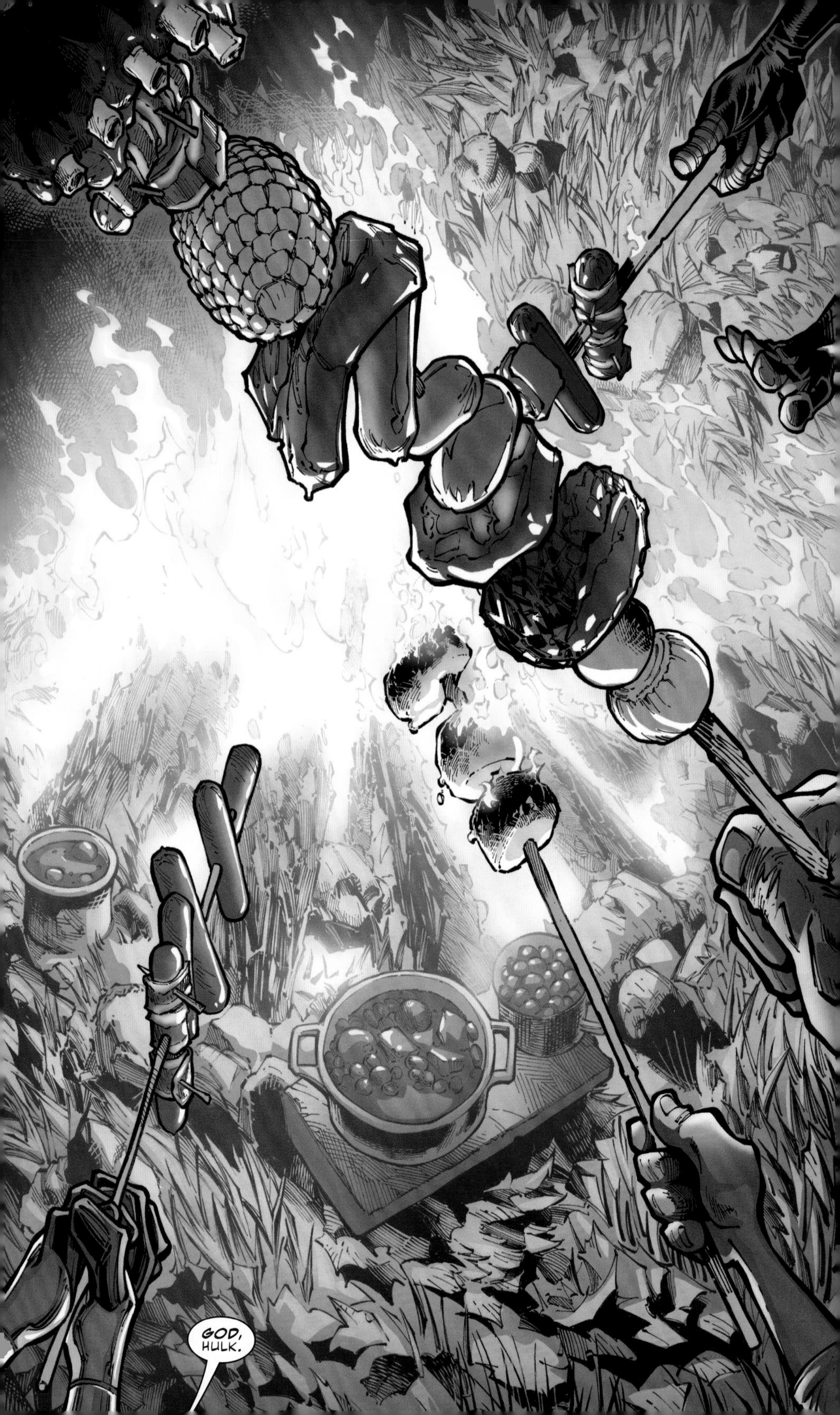
GOD, HULK.

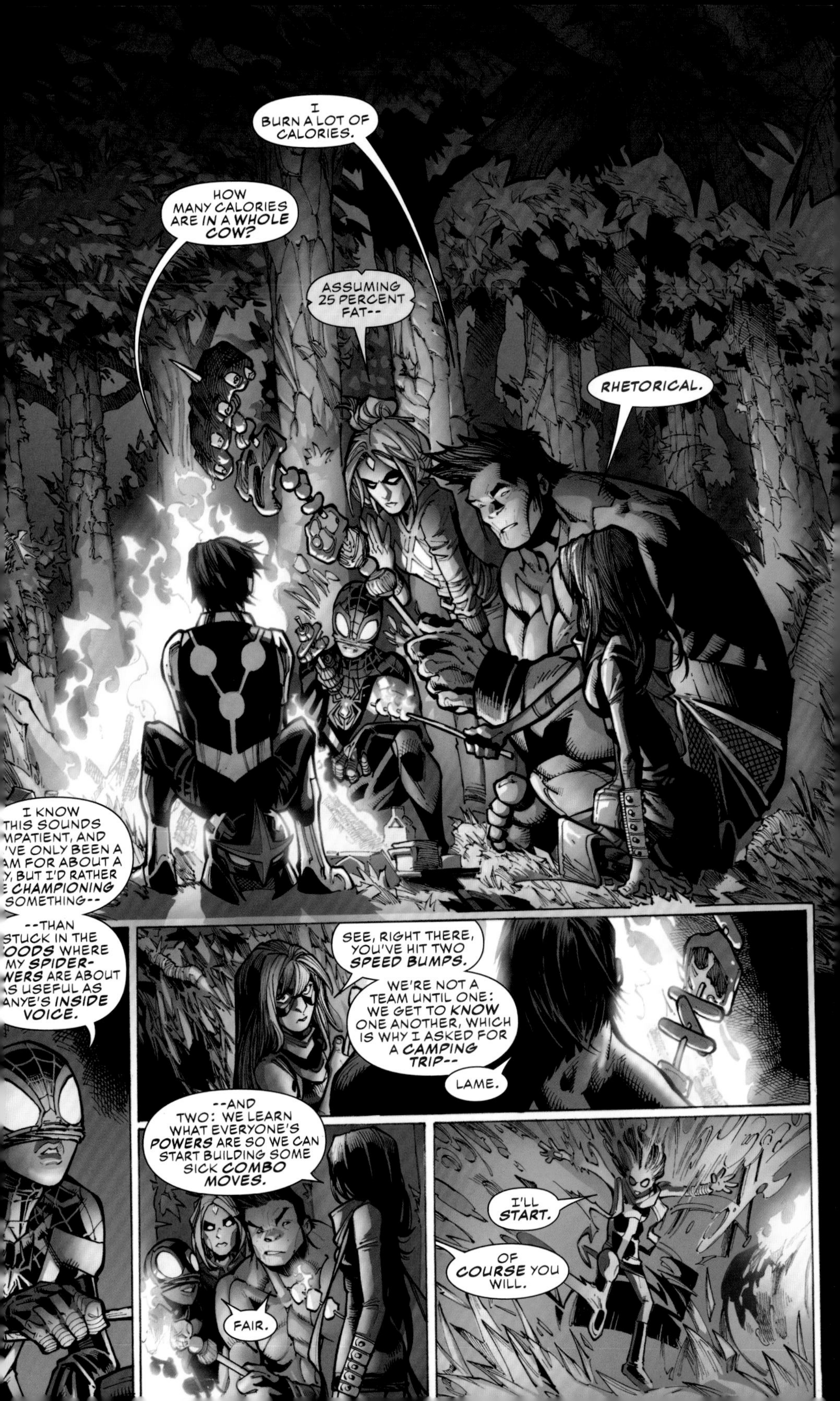
HOW MANY CALORIES ARE IN A WHOLE COW?
I BURN A LOT OF CALORIES.
ASSUMING 25 PERCENT FAT--
RHETORICAL.
I KNOW THIS SOUNDS MPATIENT, AND 'VE ONLY BEEN A AM FOR ABOUT A Y, BUT I'D RATHER E CHAMPIONING SOMETHING--
--THAN STUCK IN THE OODS WHERE MY SPIDER-WERS ARE ABOUT S USEFUL AS ANYE'S INSIDE VOICE.
SEE, RIGHT THERE, YOU'VE HIT TWO SPEED BUMPS.
WE'RE NOT A TEAM UNTIL ONE: WE GET TO KNOW ONE ANOTHER, WHICH IS WHY I ASKED FOR A CAMPING TRIP--
LAME.
--AND TWO: WE LEARN WHAT EVERYONE'S POWERS ARE SO WE CAN START BUILDING SOME SICK COMBO MOVES.
FAIR.
I'LL START.
OF COURSE YOU WILL.

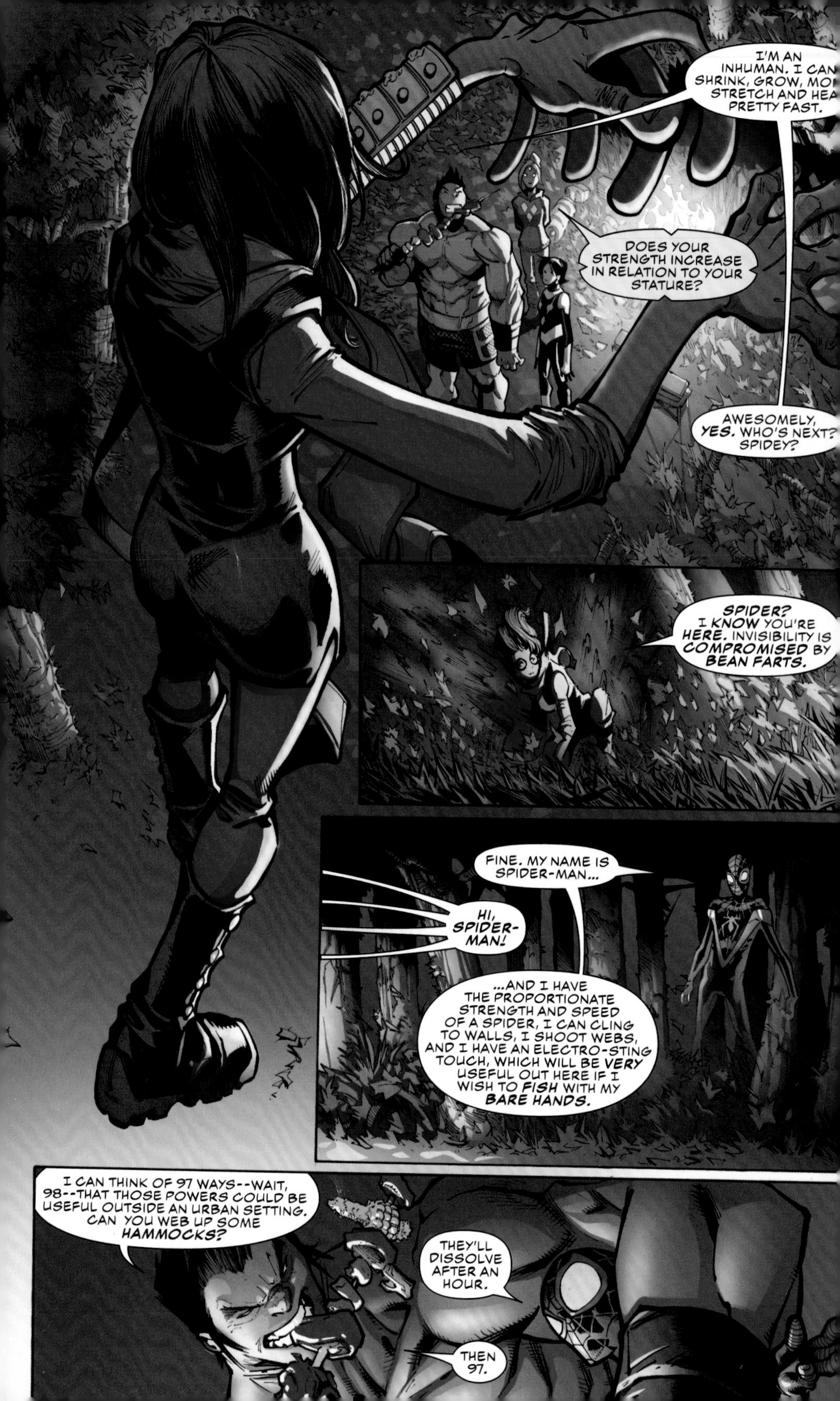
I'M AN INHUMAN. I CAN SHRINK, GROW, MO STRETCH AND HEA PRETTY FAST.
DOES YOUR STRENGTH INCREASE IN RELATION TO YOUR STATURE?
AWESOMELY, YES. WHO'S NEXT? SPIDEY?
SPIDER? I KNOW YOU'RE HERE. INVISIBILITY IS COMPROMISED BY BEAN FARTS.
FINE. MY NAME IS SPIDER-MAN...
HI, SPIDER-MAN!
...AND I HAVE THE PROPORTIONATE STRENGTH AND SPEED OF A SPIDER, I CAN CLING TO WALLS, I SHOOT WEBS, AND I HAVE AN ELECTRO-STING TOUCH, WHICH WILL BE VERY USEFUL OUT HERE IF I WISH TO FISH WITH MY BARE HANDS.
I CAN THINK OF 97 WAYS--WAIT, 98--THAT THOSE POWERS COULD BE USEFUL OUTSIDE AN URBAN SETTING. CAN YOU WEB UP SOME HAMMOCKS?
THEY'LL DISSOLVE AFTER AN HOUR.
THEN 97.

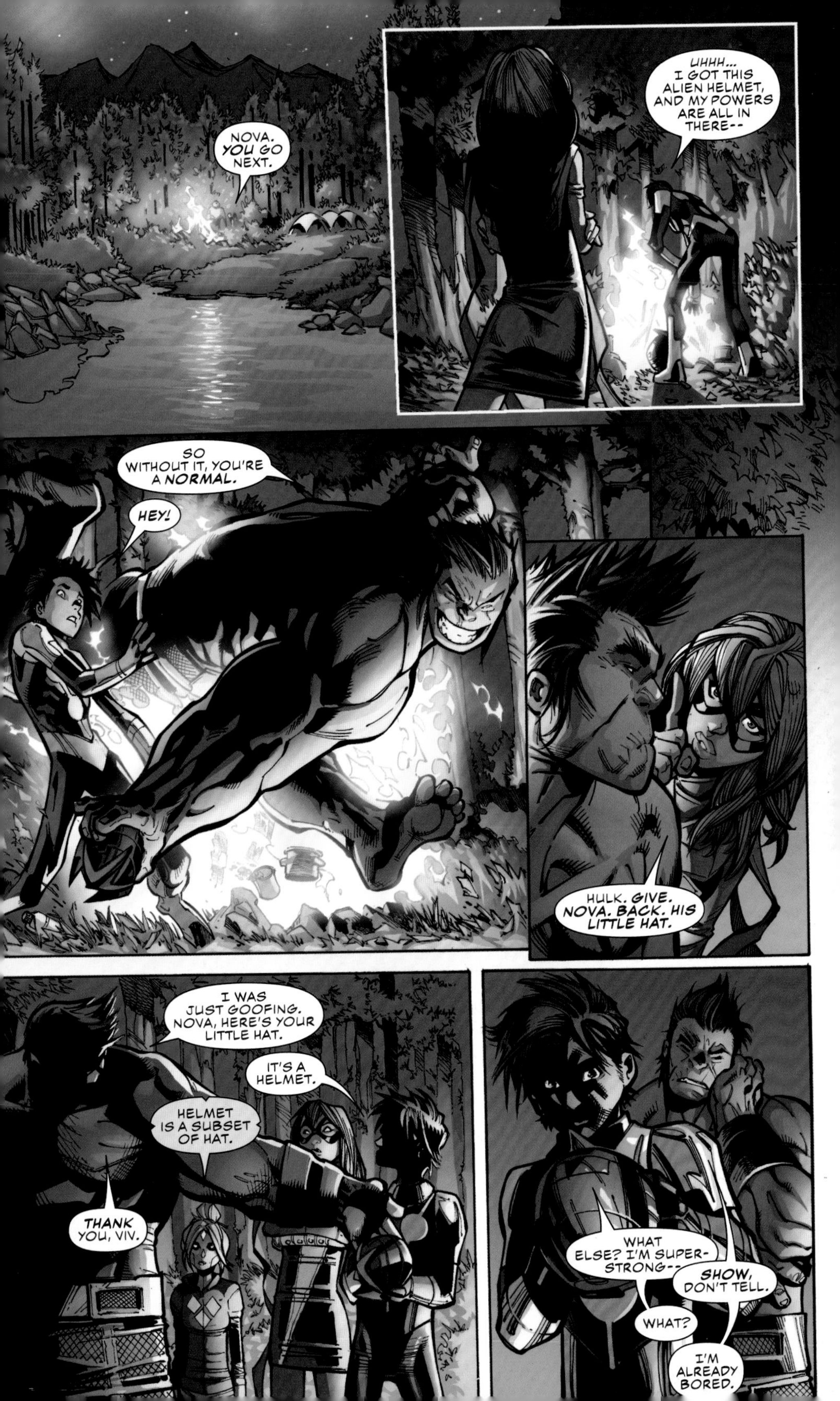
NOVA. YOU GO NEXT.
UHHH... I GOT THIS ALIEN HELMET, AND MY POWERS ARE ALL IN THERE--
SO WITHOUT IT, YOU'RE A NORMAL.
HEY!
HULK. GIVE. NOVA. BACK. HIS LITTLE HAT.
I WAS JUST GOOFING. NOVA, HERE'S YOUR LITTLE HAT.
IT'S A HELMET.
HELMET IS A SUBSET OF HAT.
THANK YOU, VIV.
WHAT ELSE? I'M SUPER-STRONG--
SHOW, DON'T TELL.
WHAT?
I'M ALREADY BORED.

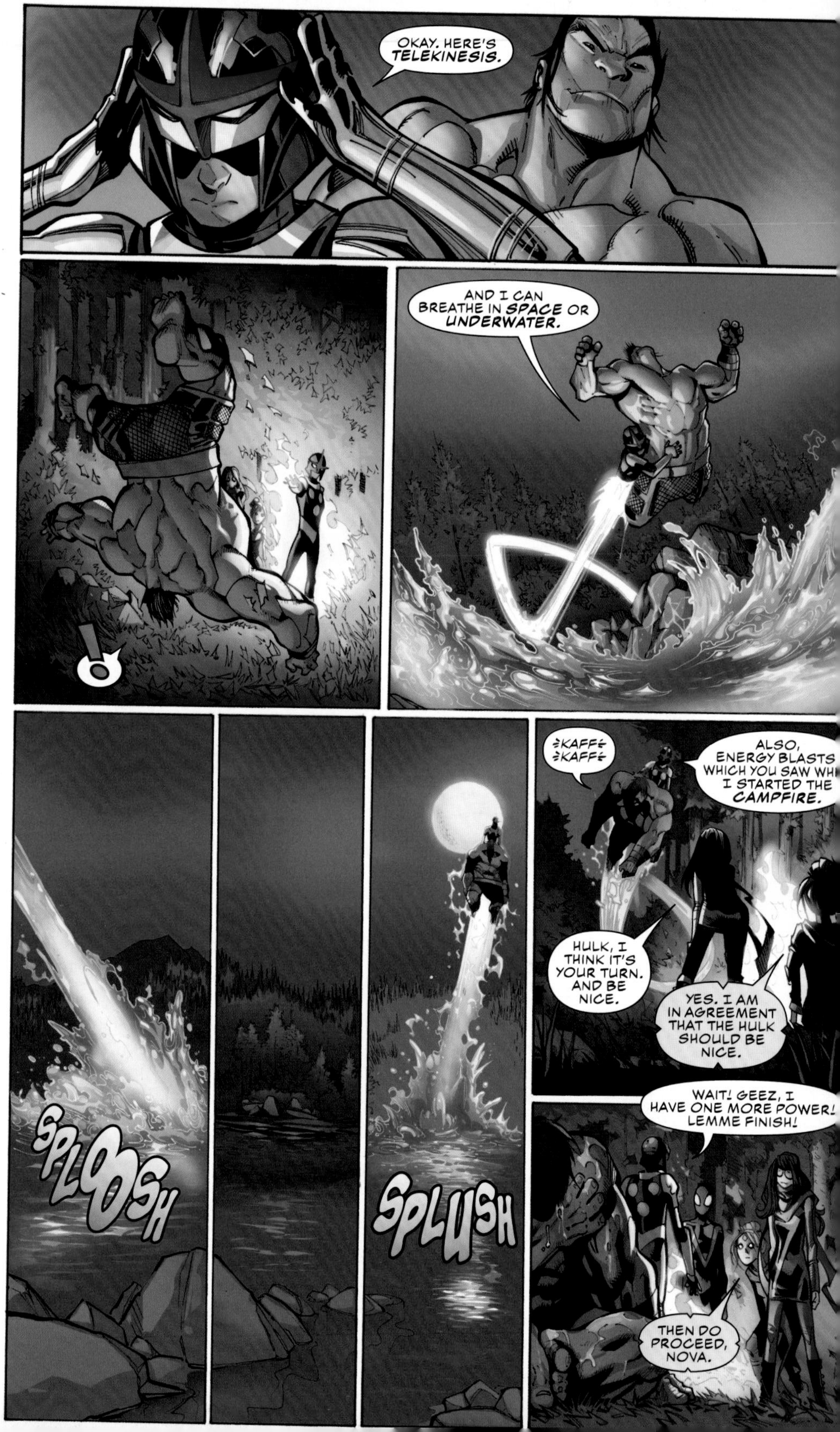

OKAY. HERE'S TELEKINESIS.
!
AND I CAN BREATHE IN SPACE OR UNDERWATER.
SPLOOSH
SPLUSH
=KAFF= =KAFF=
ALSO, ENERGY BLASTS WHICH YOU SAW WH I STARTED THE CAMPFIRE.
HULK, I THINK IT'S YOUR TURN. AND BE NICE.
YES. I AM IN AGREEMENT THAT THE HULK SHOULD BE NICE.
WAIT! GEEZ, I HAVE ONE MORE POWER! LEMME FINISH!
THEN DO PROCEED, NOVA.

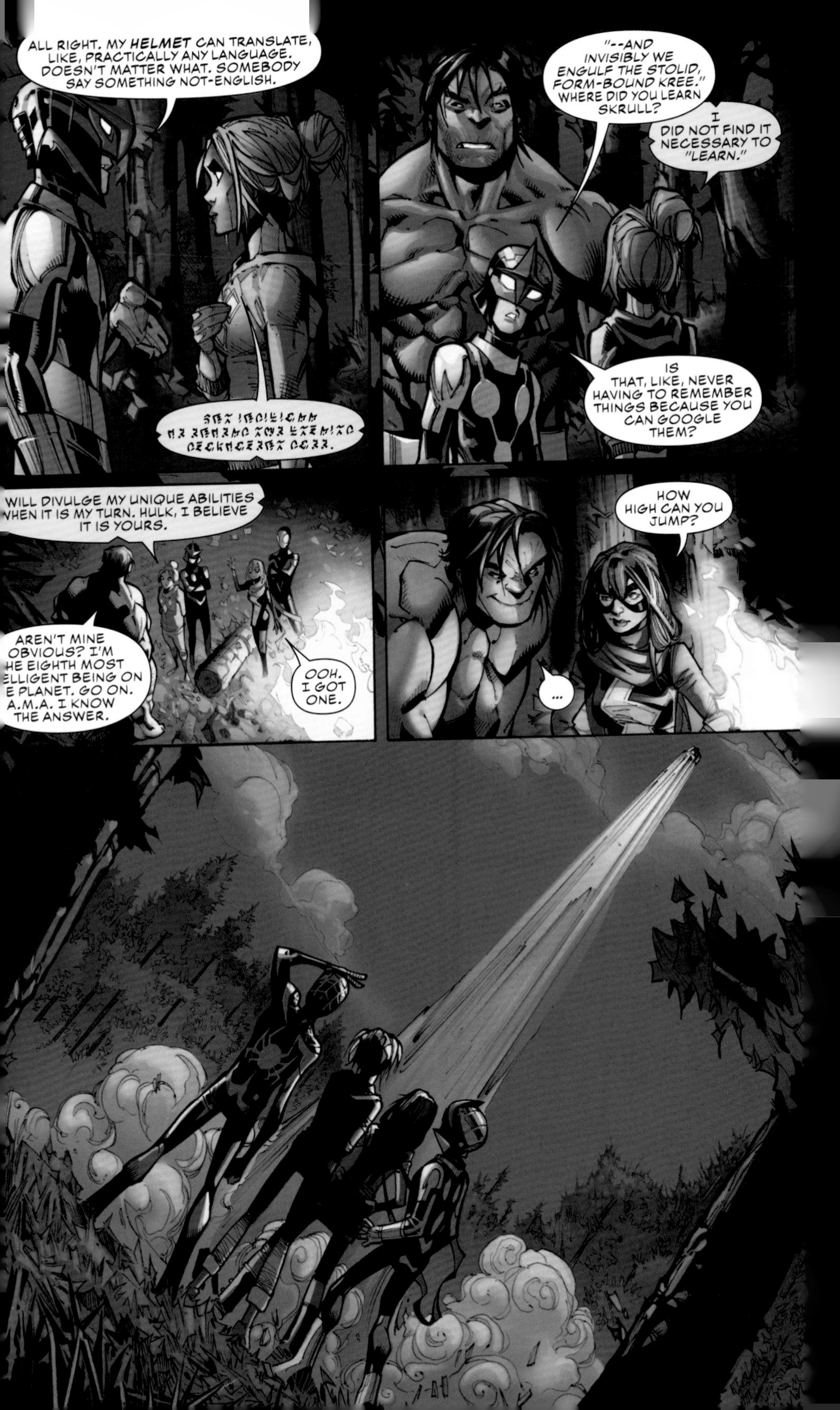

ALL RIGHT. MY HELMET CAN TRANSLATE, LIKE, PRACTICALLY ANY LANGUAGE. DOESN'T MATTER WHAT. SOMEBODY SAY SOMETHING NOT-ENGLISH.
"--AND INVISIBLY WE ENGULF THE STOLID, FORM-BOUND KREE." WHERE DID YOU LEARN SKRULL?
I DID NOT FIND IT NECESSARY TO "LEARN."
IS THAT, LIKE, NEVER HAVING TO REMEMBER THINGS BECAUSE YOU CAN GOOGLE THEM?
WILL DIVULGE MY UNIQUE ABILITIES WHEN IT IS MY TURN. HULK, I BELIEVE IT IS YOURS.
AREN'T MINE OBVIOUS? I'M HE EIGHTH MOST ELLIGENT BEING ON E PLANET. GO ON. A.M.A. I KNOW THE ANSWER.
OOH. I GOT ONE.
HOW HIGH CAN YOU JUMP?
...

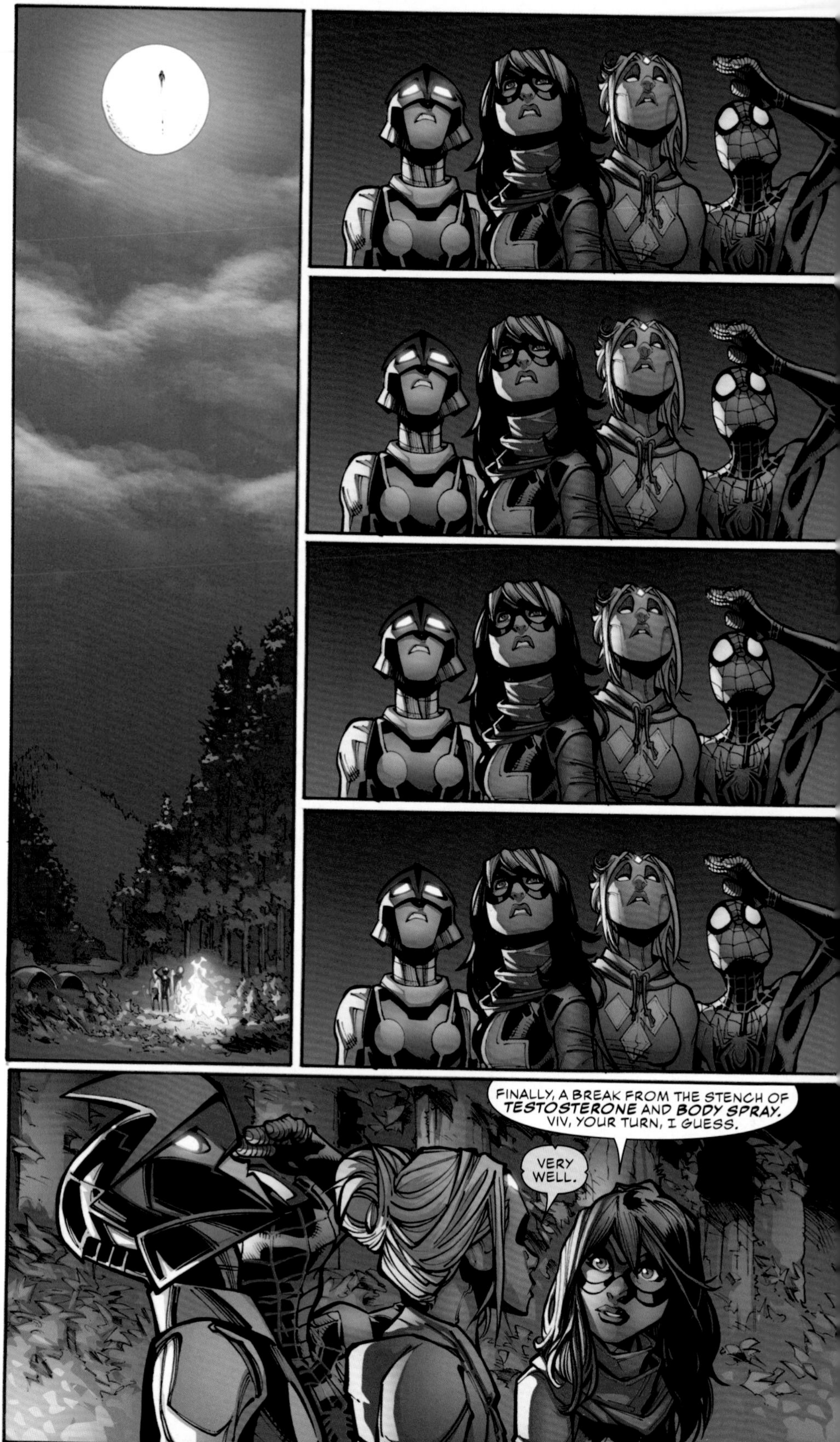
FINALLY, A BREAK FROM THE STENCH OF *TESTOSTERONE* AND *BODY SPRAY.* VIV, YOUR TURN, I GUESS.
VERY WELL.

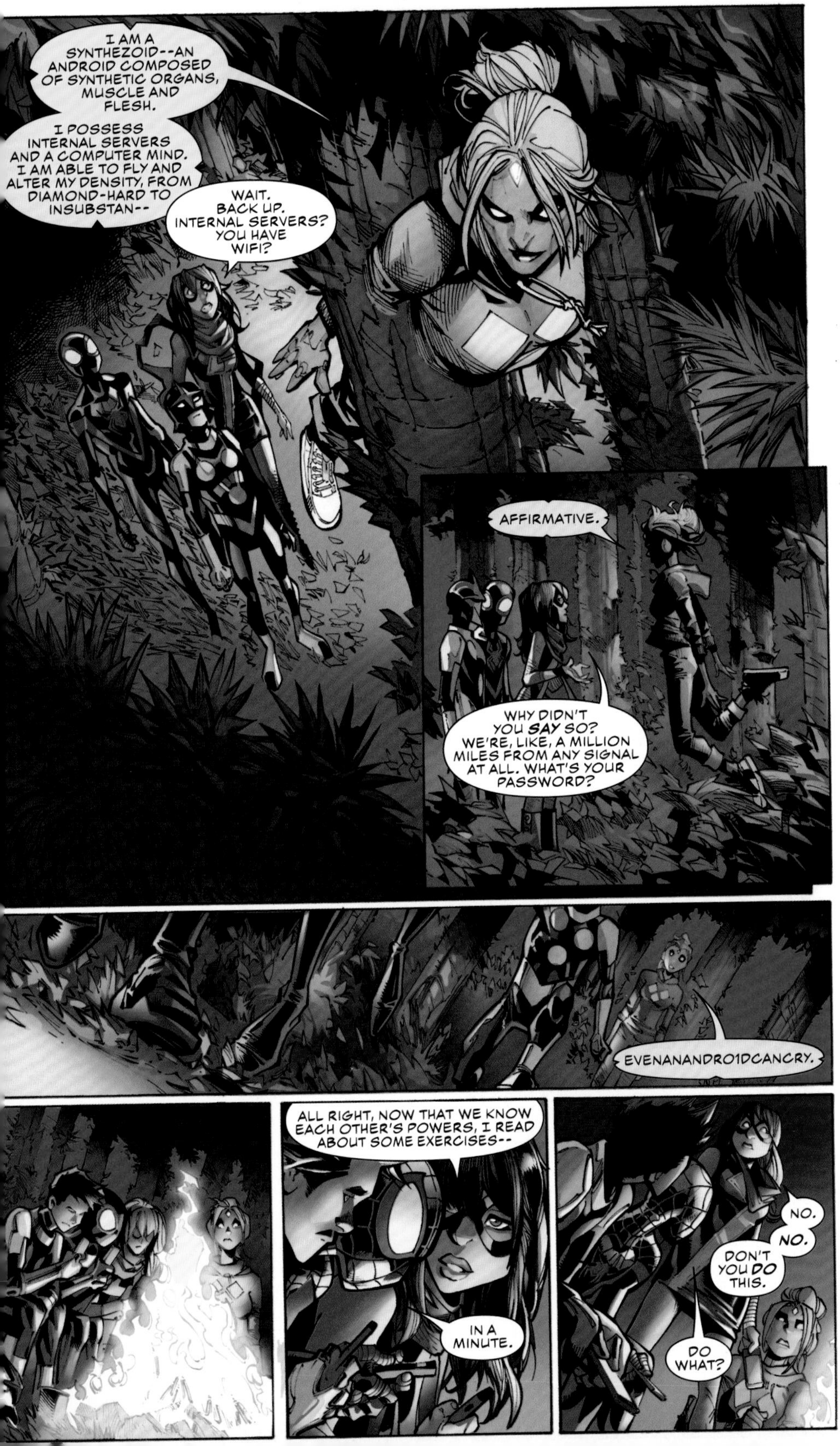
I AM A SYNTHEZOID--AN ANDROID COMPOSED OF SYNTHETIC ORGANS, MUSCLE AND FLESH.
I POSSESS INTERNAL SERVERS AND A COMPUTER MIND. I AM ABLE TO FLY AND ALTER MY DENSITY, FROM DIAMOND-HARD TO INSUBSTAN--
WAIT. BACK UP. INTERNAL SERVERS? YOU HAVE WIFI?
AFFIRMATIVE.
WHY DIDN'T YOU SAY SO? WE'RE, LIKE, A MILLION MILES FROM ANY SIGNAL AT ALL. WHAT'S YOUR PASSWORD?
EVENANANDRO1DCANCRY.
ALL RIGHT, NOW THAT WE KNOW EACH OTHER'S POWERS, I READ ABOUT SOME EXERCISES--
IN A MINUTE.
NO.
NO.
DON'T YOU DO THIS.
DO WHAT?

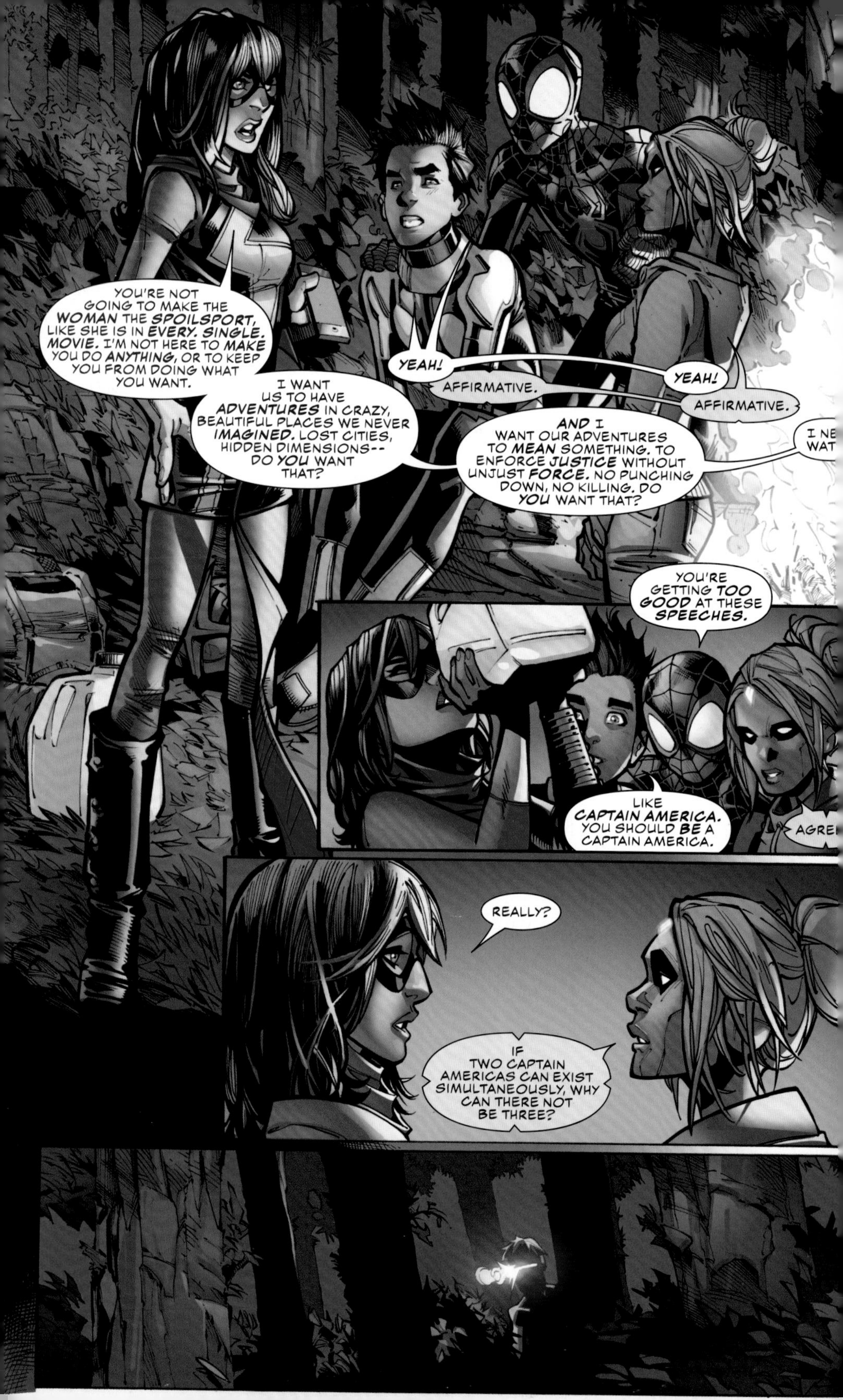

YOU'RE NOT GOING TO MAKE THE WOMAN THE SPOILSPORT, LIKE SHE IS IN EVERY. SINGLE. MOVIE. I'M NOT HERE TO MAKE YOU DO ANYTHING, OR TO KEEP YOU FROM DOING WHAT YOU WANT.
I WANT US TO HAVE ADVENTURES IN CRAZY, BEAUTIFUL PLACES WE NEVER IMAGINED. LOST CITIES, HIDDEN DIMENSIONS-- DO YOU WANT THAT?
YEAH!
AFFIRMATIVE.
AND I WANT OUR ADVENTURES TO MEAN SOMETHING. TO ENFORCE JUSTICE WITHOUT UNJUST FORCE. NO PUNCHING DOWN, NO KILLING. DO YOU WANT THAT?
YEAH!
AFFIRMATIVE.
YOU'RE GETTING TOO GOOD AT THESE SPEECHES.
LIKE CAPTAIN AMERICA. YOU SHOULD BE A CAPTAIN AMERICA.
REALLY?
IF TWO CAPTAIN AMERICAS CAN EXIST SIMULTANEOUSLY, WHY CAN THERE NOT BE THREE?

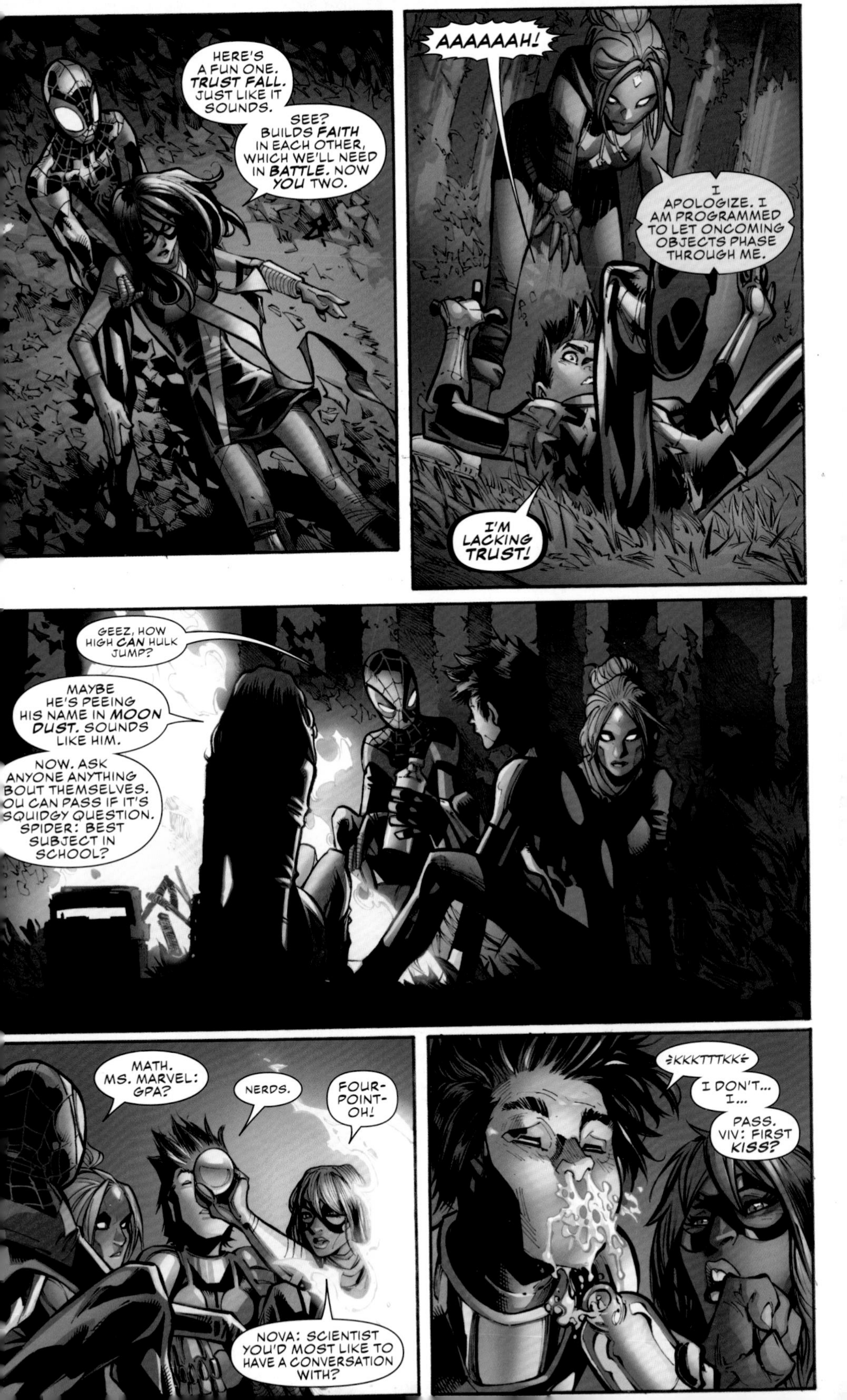

HERE'S A FUN ONE. TRUST FALL. JUST LIKE IT SOUNDS.
SEE? BUILDS FAITH IN EACH OTHER, WHICH WE'LL NEED IN BATTLE. NOW YOU TWO.
AAAAAAH!
I APOLOGIZE. I AM PROGRAMMED TO LET ONCOMING OBJECTS PHASE THROUGH ME.
I'M LACKING TRUST!
GEEZ, HOW HIGH CAN HULK JUMP?
MAYBE HE'S PEEING HIS NAME IN MOON DUST. SOUNDS LIKE HIM.
NOW. ASK ANYONE ANYTHING BOUT THEMSELVES. OU CAN PASS IF IT'S SQUIDGY QUESTION. SPIDER: BEST SUBJECT IN SCHOOL?
MATH. MS. MARVEL: GPA?
NERDS.
FOUR-POINT-OH!
NOVA: SCIENTIST YOU'D MOST LIKE TO HAVE A CONVERSATION WITH?
KKKTTTKK
I DON'T... I...
PASS. VIV: FIRST KISS?

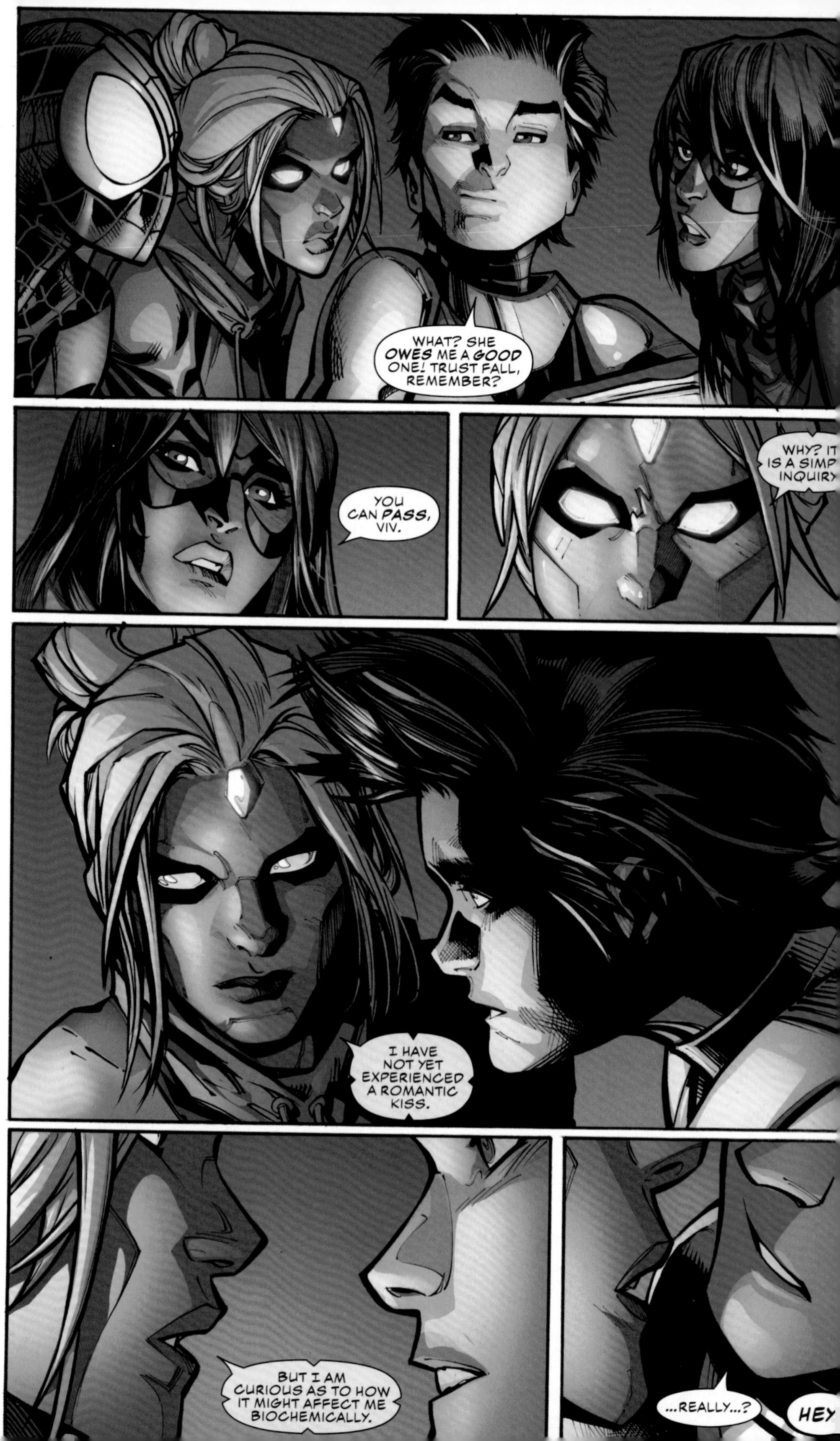
WHAT? SHE OWES ME A GOOD ONE! TRUST FALL, REMEMBER?
YOU CAN PASS, VIV.
WHY? IT IS A SIMP INQUIRY
I HAVE NOT YET EXPERIENCED A ROMANTIC KISS.
BUT I AM CURIOUS AS TO HOW IT MIGHT AFFECT ME BIOCHEMICALLY.
...REALLY...?
HEY

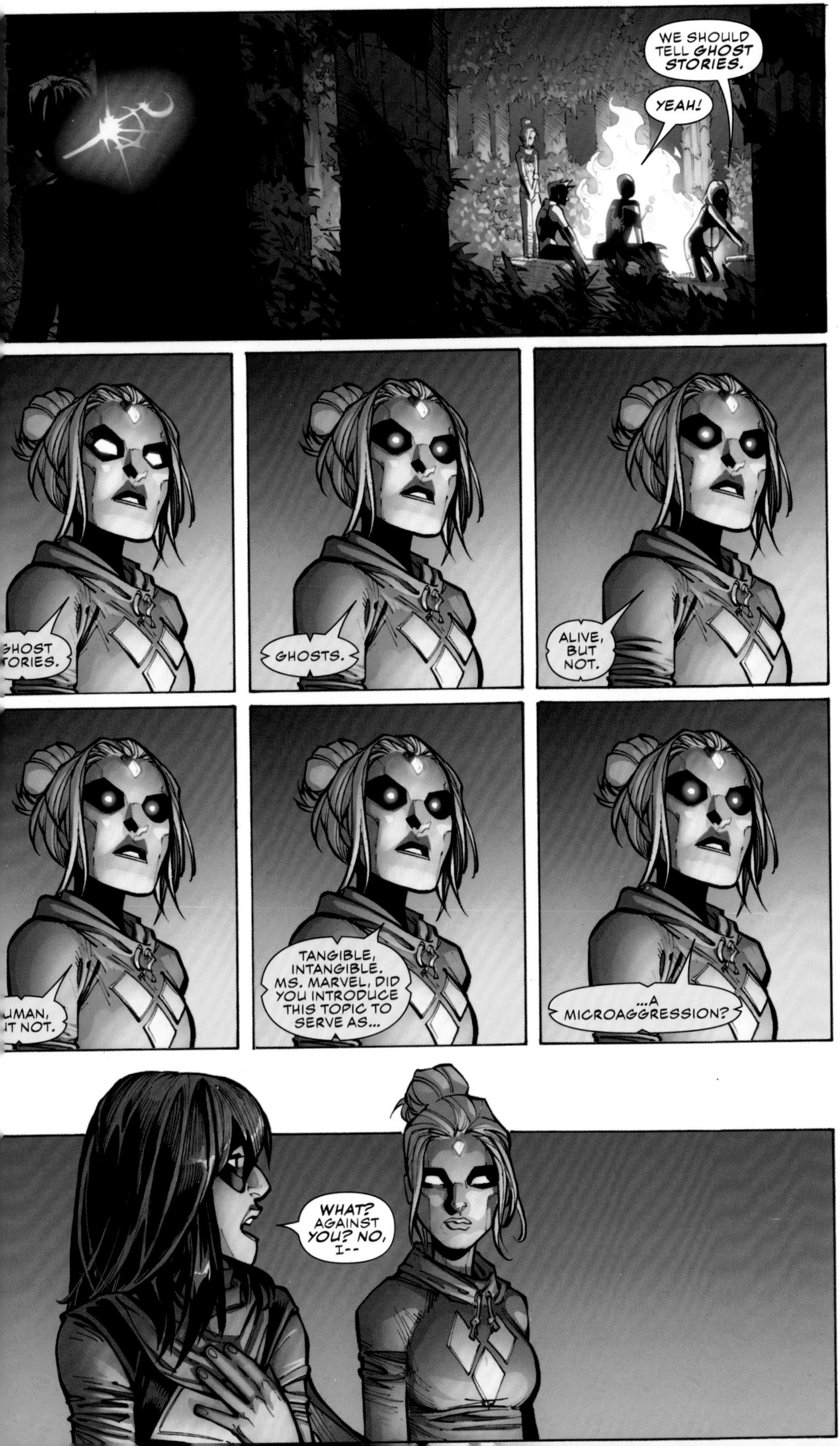
WE SHOULD TELL GHOST STORIES.
YEAH!
GHOST TORIES.
GHOSTS.
ALIVE, BUT NOT.
UMAN, T NOT.
TANGIBLE, INTANGIBLE. MS. MARVEL, DID YOU INTRODUCE THIS TOPIC TO SERVE AS...
...A MICROAGGRESSION?
WHAT? AGAINST YOU? NO, I--

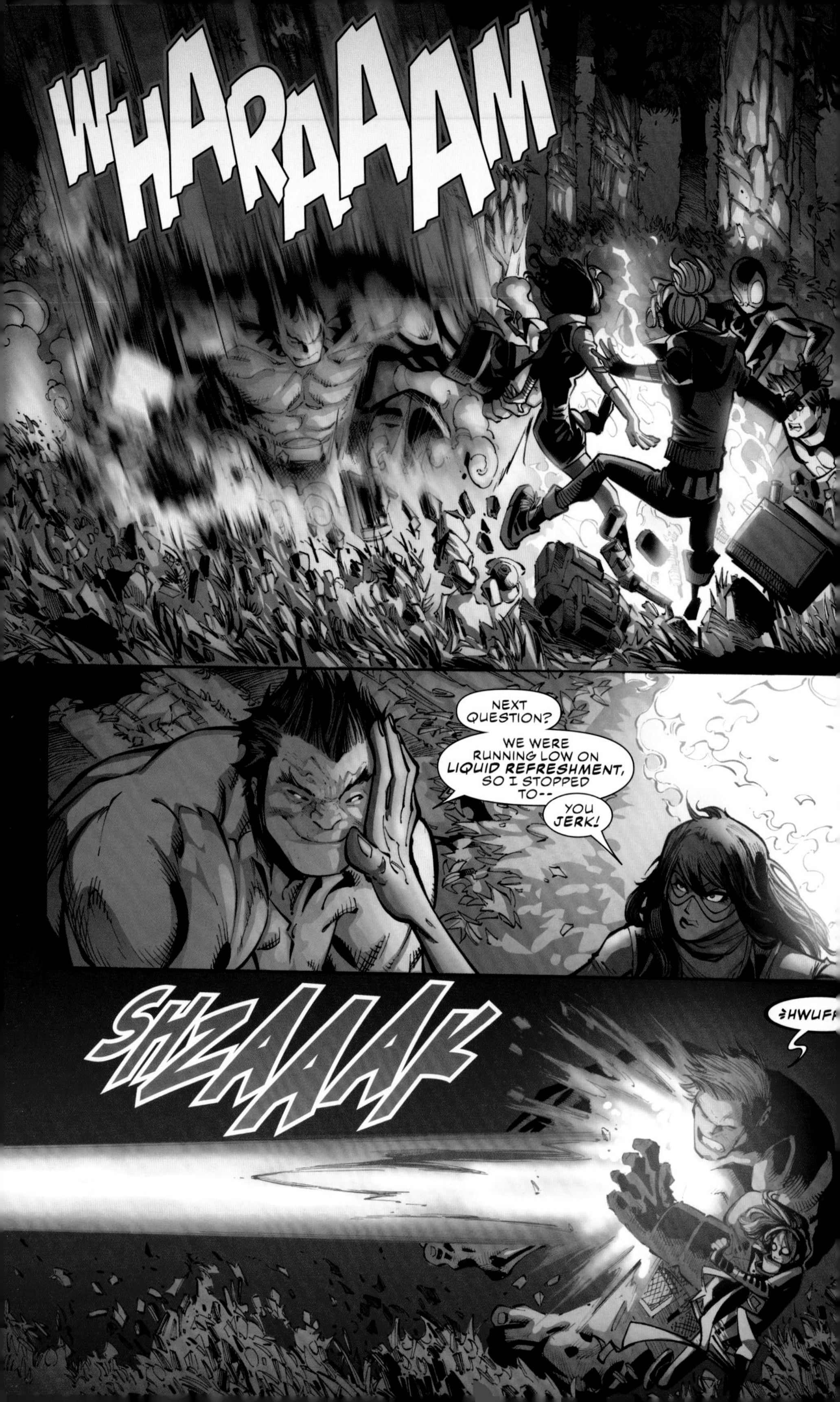
WHARAAAM
NEXT QUESTION?
WE WERE RUNNING LOW ON LIQUID REFRESHMENT, SO I STOPPED TO--
YOU JERK!
SHZAAAK
SHWUF

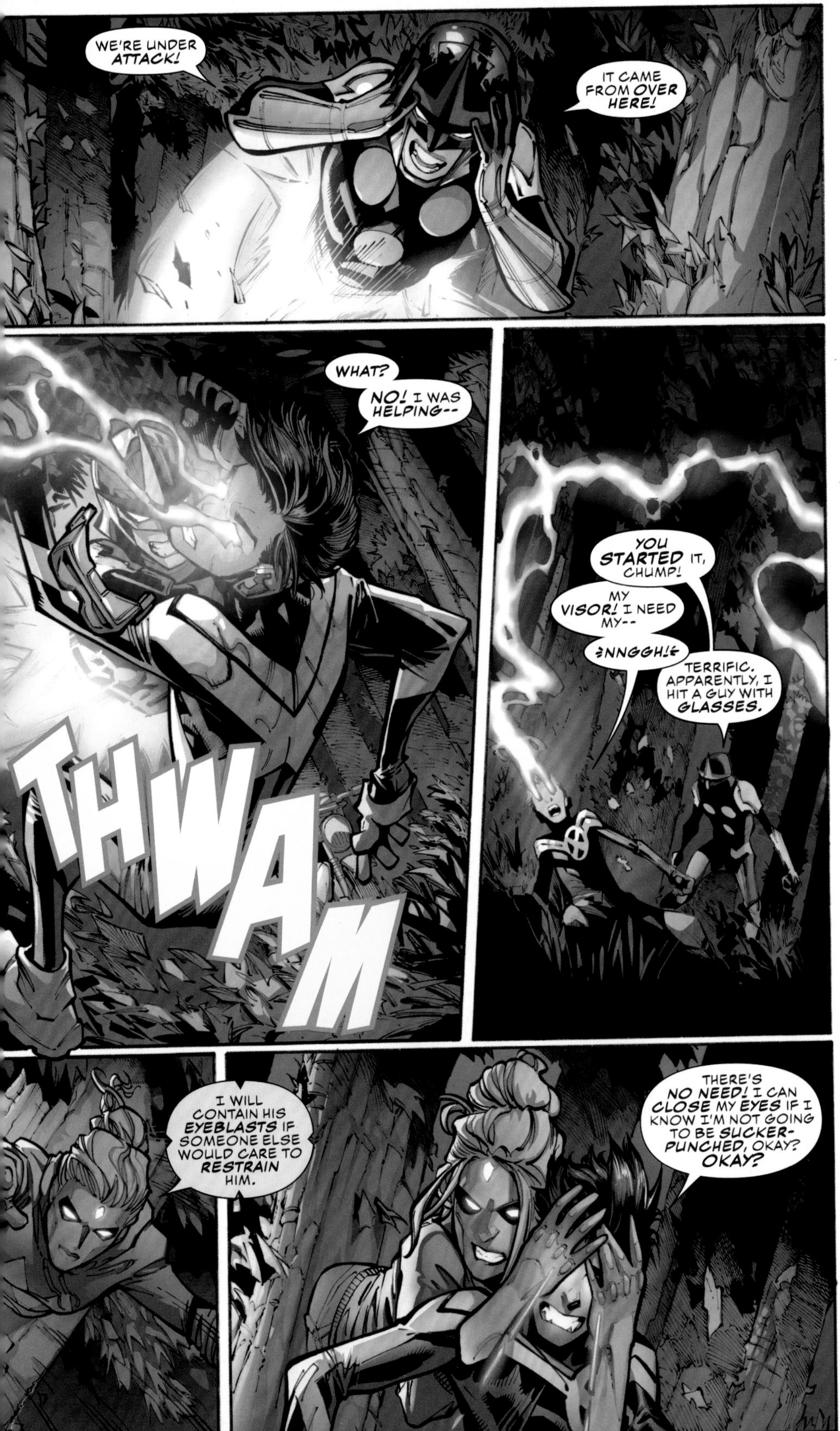
WE'RE UNDER ATTACK!
IT CAME FROM OVER HERE!
WHAT?
NO! I WAS HELPING--
THWAM
YOU STARTED IT, CHUMP!
MY VISOR! I NEED MY--
NNGGH!
TERRIFIC. APPARENTLY, I HIT A GUY WITH GLASSES.
I WILL CONTAIN HIS EYEBLASTS IF SOMEONE ELSE WOULD CARE TO RESTRAIN HIM.
THERE'S NO NEED! I CAN CLOSE MY EYES IF I KNOW I'M NOT GOING TO BE SUCKER-PUNCHED, OKAY? OKAY?

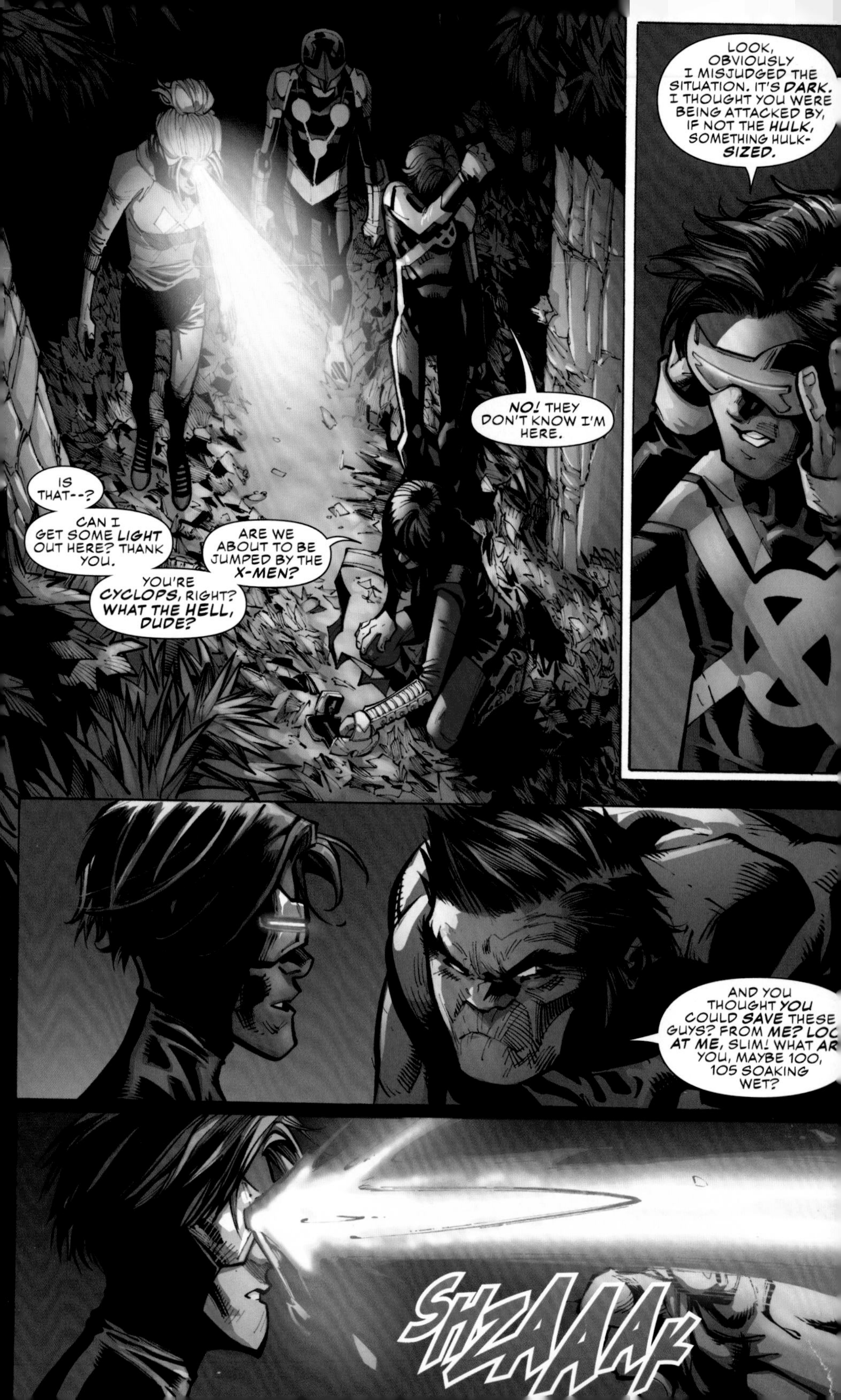
NO! THEY DON'T KNOW I'M HERE.
IS THAT--?
CAN I GET SOME LIGHT OUT HERE? THANK YOU.
ARE WE ABOUT TO BE JUMPED BY THE X-MEN?
YOU'RE CYCLOPS, RIGHT? WHAT THE HELL, DUDE?
LOOK, OBVIOUSLY I MISJUDGED THE SITUATION. IT'S DARK. I THOUGHT YOU WERE BEING ATTACKED BY, IF NOT THE HULK, SOMETHING HULK-SIZED.
AND YOU THOUGHT YOU COULD SAVE THESE GUYS? FROM ME? LOO AT ME, SLIM! WHAT AR YOU, MAYBE 100, 105 SOAKING WET?
SHZAAAK

YOU LITTLE ████████!

I ALREADY APOLOGIZED. THEN YOU GOT IN MY *FACE.* I DON'T TAKE WELL TO *BULLIES.*

HE HAS A *POINT!* HE HAS A POINT!

SO WHAT'S YOUR DEAL, THEN?

I...WANT TO TRY NEW THINGS. WALK NEW PATHS. FIND NEW PATTERNS.

I HEARD YOU DELIVER A MISSION STATEMENT ABOUT BEING A *CHAMPION* THAT REALLY *RESONATED.* I CAME TO JOIN.

...NEED TO DISCUSS THIS. THE TEAM.

THAT'S PERFECTLY UNDERSTANDABLE. I FIGURED AS MUCH.

PUT IT TO A VOTE. I'M NOT GOING TO BEG, BUT I JUST WANT TO SAY ONE THING:

I'M NOT A BAD GUY.

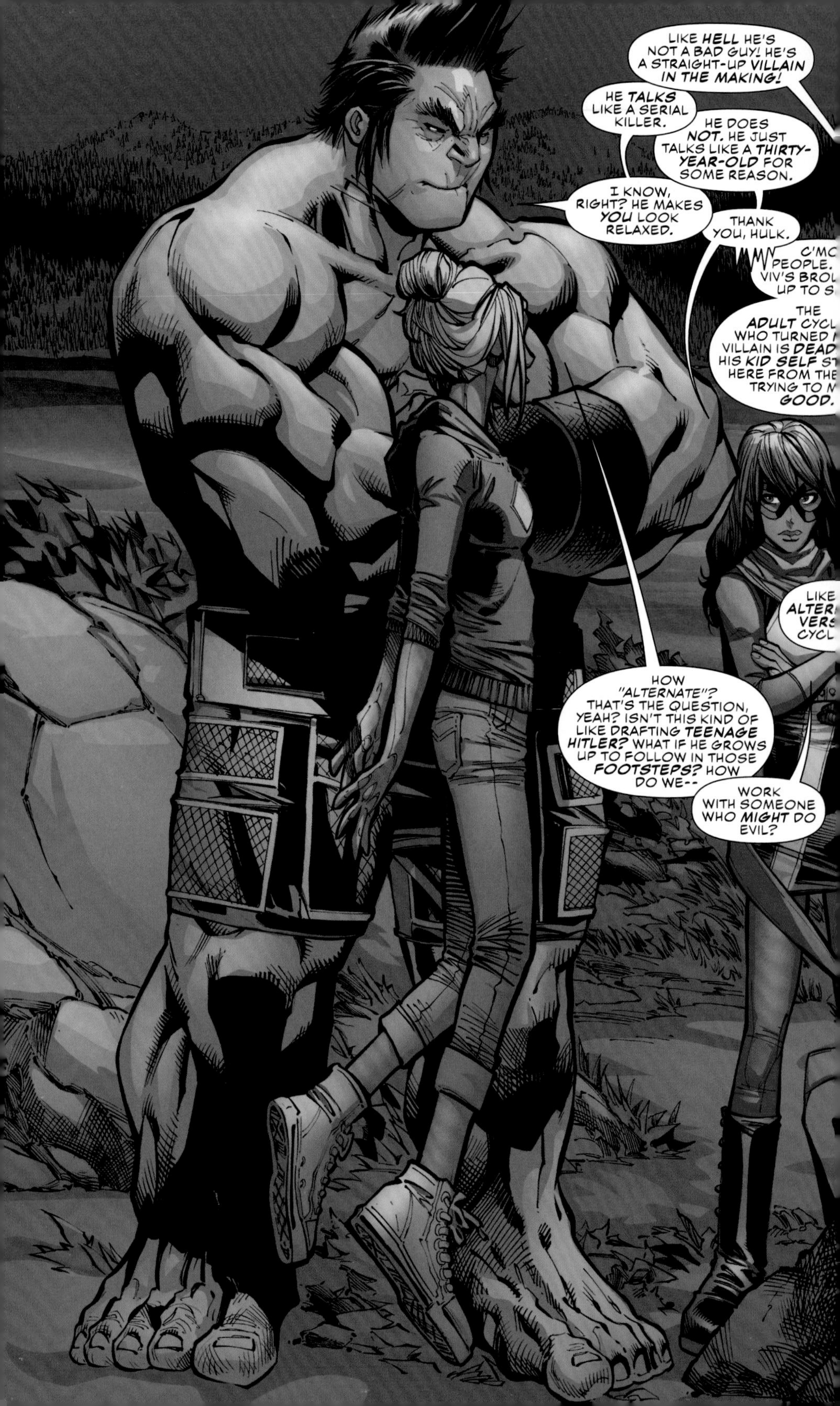
LIKE HELL HE'S NOT A BAD GUY! HE'S A STRAIGHT-UP VILLAIN IN THE MAKING!
HE TALKS LIKE A SERIAL KILLER.
HE DOES NOT. HE JUST TALKS LIKE A THIRTY-YEAR-OLD FOR SOME REASON.
I KNOW, RIGHT? HE MAKES YOU LOOK RELAXED.
THANK YOU, HULK.
C'MC PEOPLE. VIV'S BROU UP TO S
THE ADULT CYCL WHO TURNED VILLAIN IS DEAD HIS KID SELF S HERE FROM THE TRYING TO GOOD.
LIKE ALTER VERS CYCL
HOW "ALTERNATE"? THAT'S THE QUESTION, YEAH? ISN'T THIS KIND OF LIKE DRAFTING TEENAGE HITLER? WHAT IF HE GROWS UP TO FOLLOW IN THOSE FOOTSTEPS? HOW DO WE--
WORK WITH SOMEONE WHO MIGHT DO EVIL?

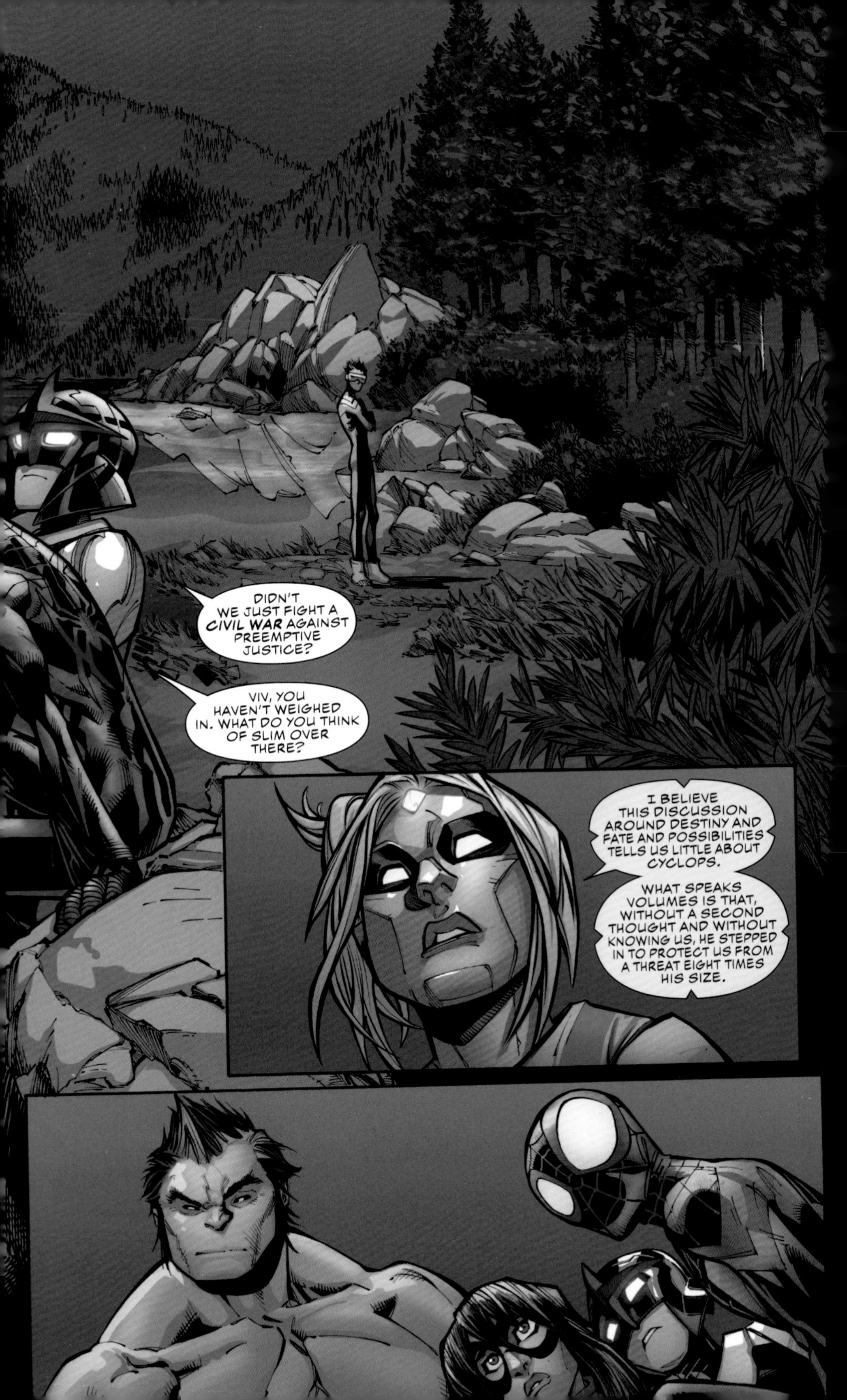
DIDN'T WE JUST FIGHT A CIVIL WAR AGAINST PREEMPTIVE JUSTICE?
VIV, YOU HAVEN'T WEIGHED IN. WHAT DO YOU THINK OF SLIM OVER THERE?
I BELIEVE THIS DISCUSSION AROUND DESTINY AND FATE AND POSSIBILITIES TELLS US LITTLE ABOUT CYCLOPS.
WHAT SPEAKS VOLUMES IS THAT, WITHOUT A SECOND THOUGHT AND WITHOUT KNOWING US, HE STEPPED IN TO PROTECT US FROM A THREAT EIGHT TIMES HIS SIZE.

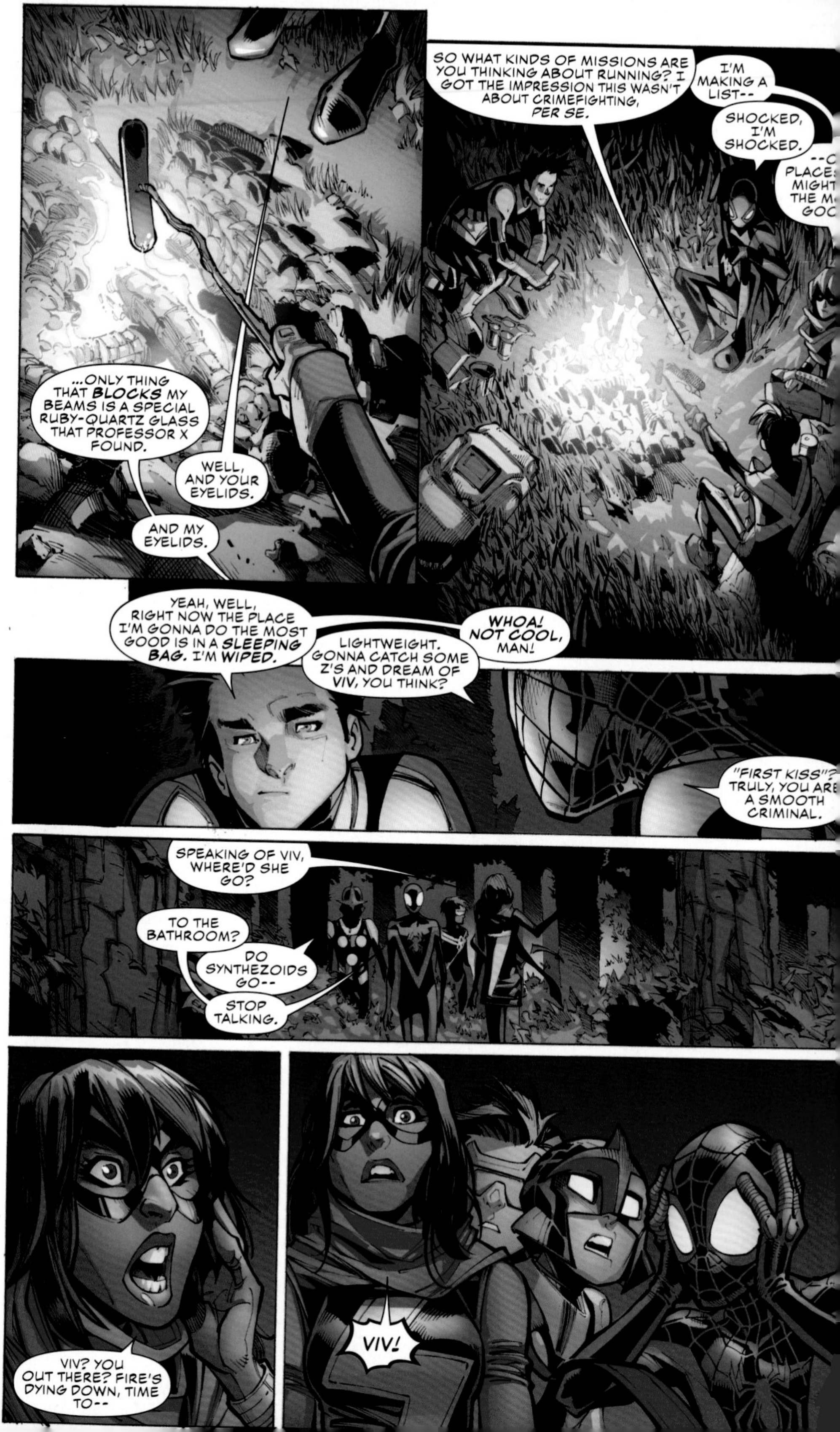
...ONLY THING THAT BLOCKS MY BEAMS IS A SPECIAL RUBY-QUARTZ GLASS THAT PROFESSOR X FOUND.
WELL, AND YOUR EYELIDS.
AND MY EYELIDS.
SO WHAT KINDS OF MISSIONS ARE YOU THINKING ABOUT RUNNING? I GOT THE IMPRESSION THIS WASN'T ABOUT CRIMEFIGHTING, PER SE.
I'M MAKING A LIST--
SHOCKED, I'M SHOCKED.
YEAH, WELL, RIGHT NOW THE PLACE I'M GONNA DO THE MOST GOOD IS IN A SLEEPING BAG. I'M WIPED.
WHOA! NOT COOL, MAN!
LIGHTWEIGHT. GONNA CATCH SOME Z'S AND DREAM OF VIV, YOU THINK?
"FIRST KISS"? TRULY, YOU ARE A SMOOTH CRIMINAL.
SPEAKING OF VIV, WHERE'D SHE GO?
TO THE BATHROOM?
DO SYNTHEZOIDS GO--
STOP TALKING.
VIV? YOU OUT THERE? FIRE'S DYING DOWN, TIME TO--
VIV!

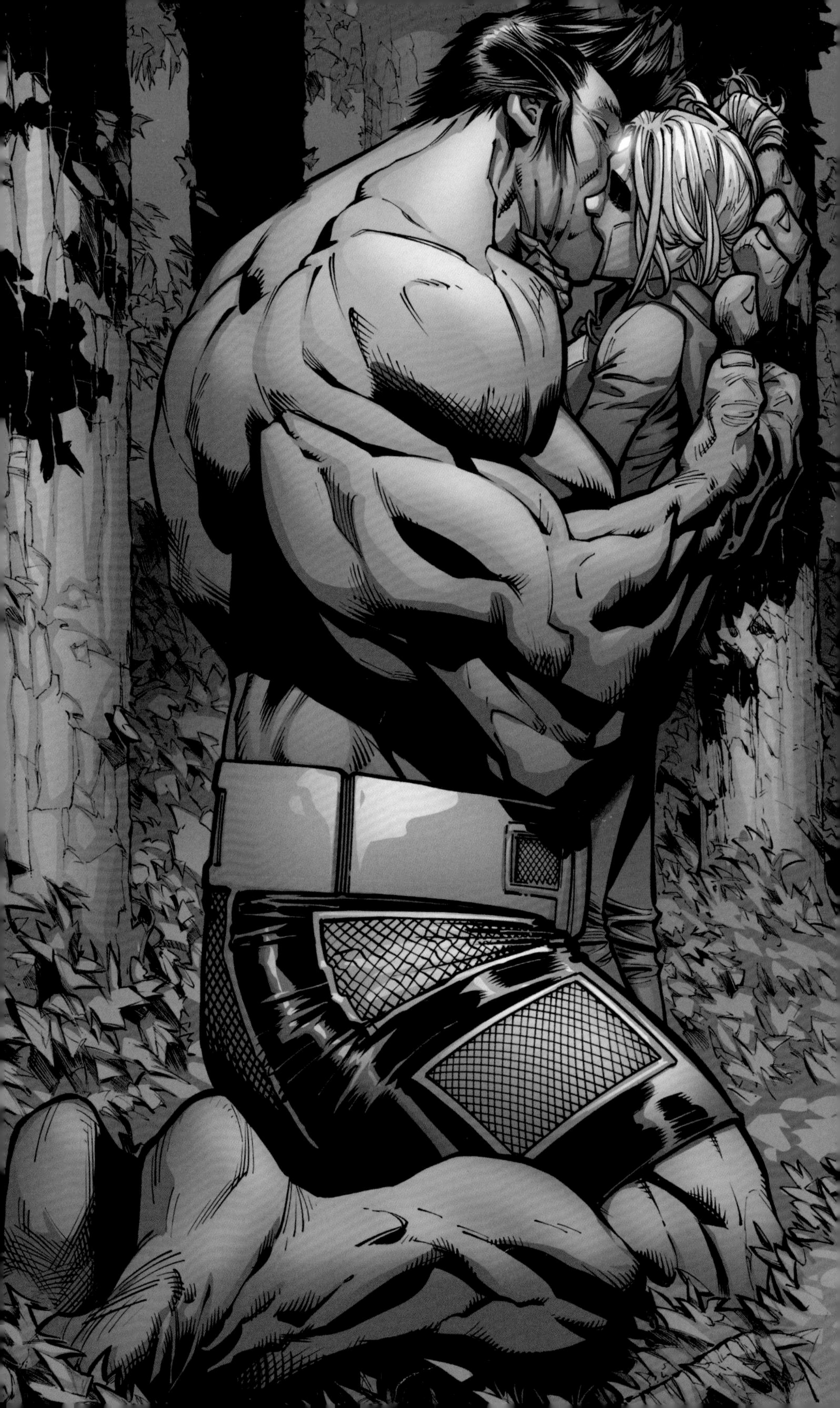

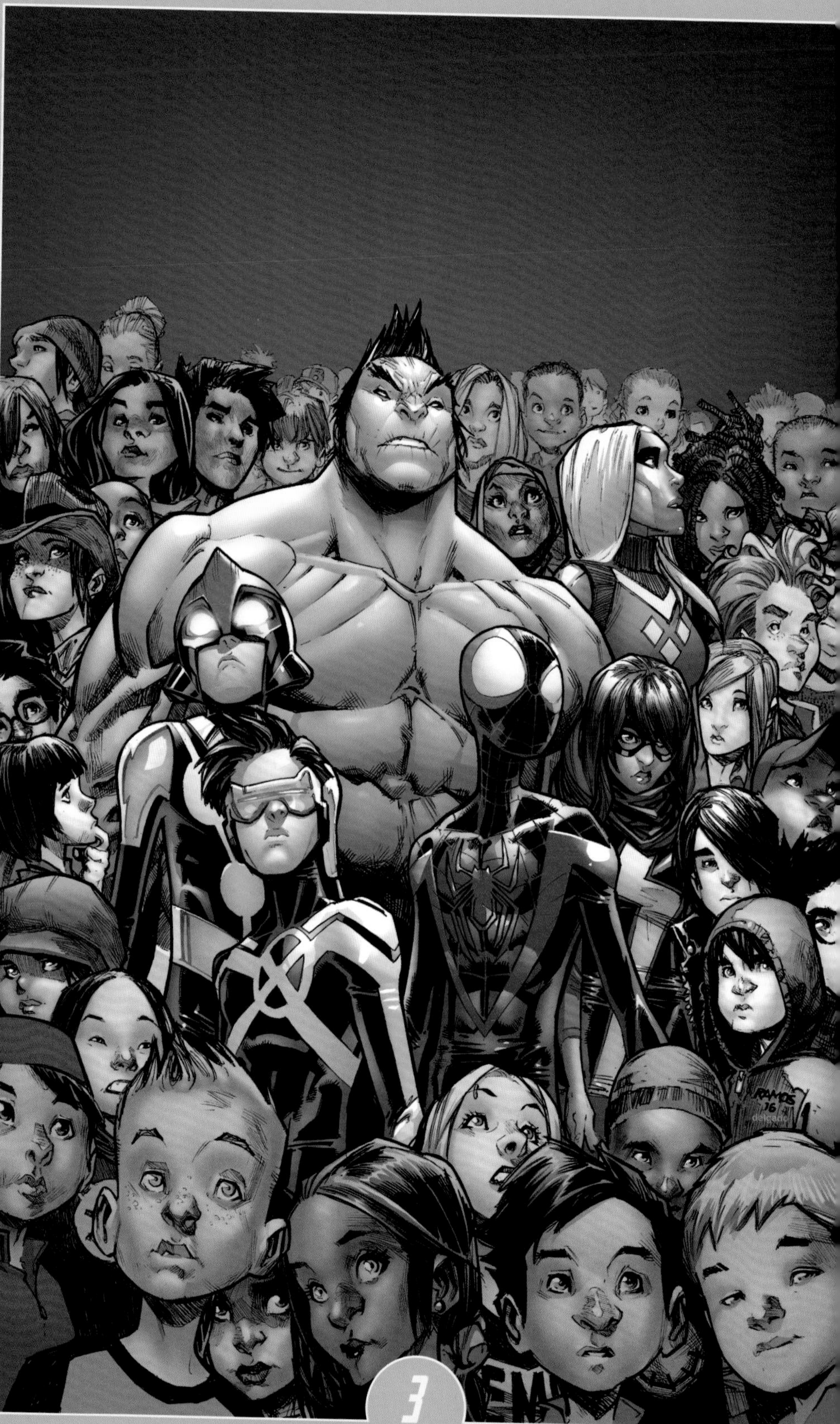
RAMOS 16
delgado

3

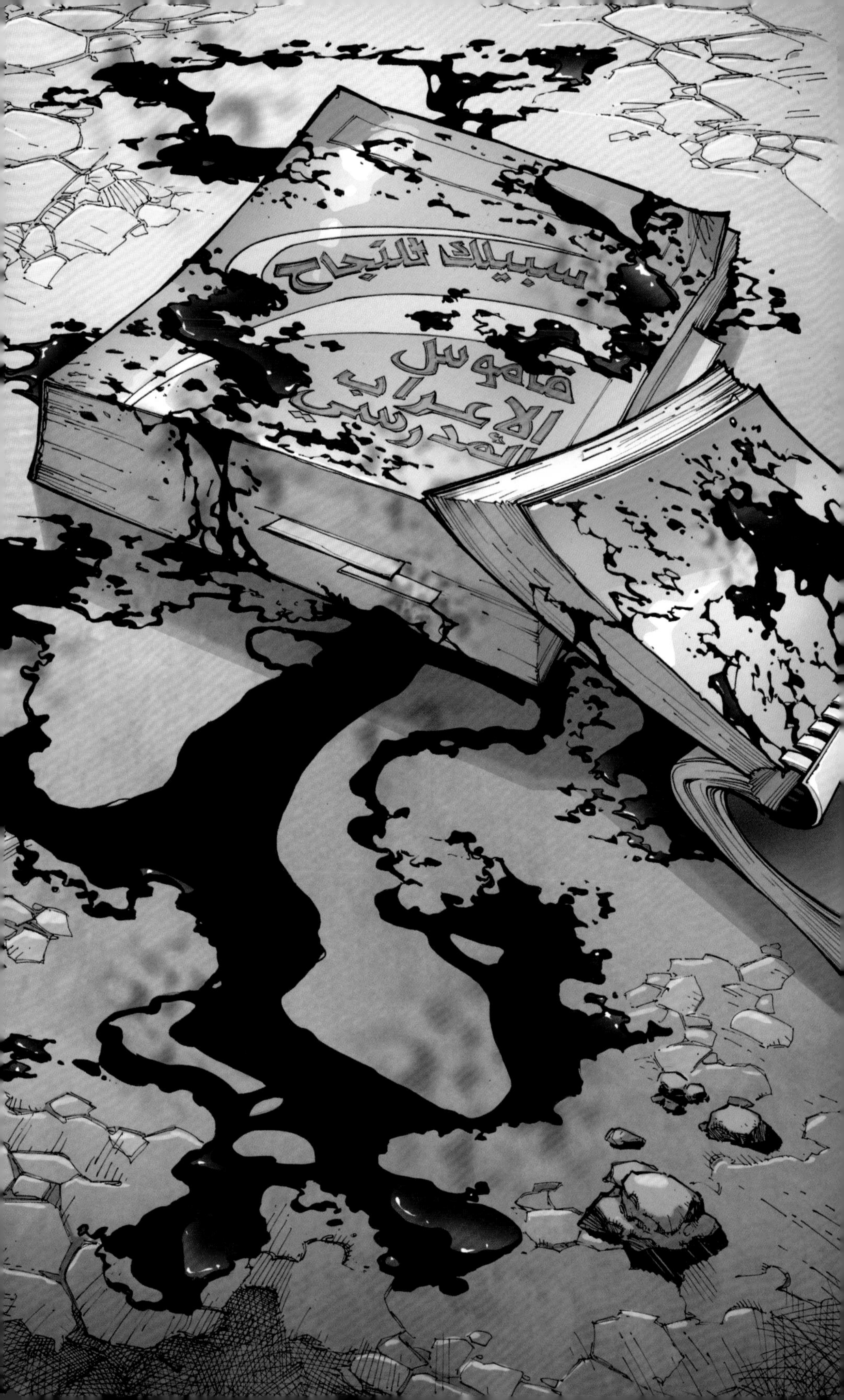
سبيلك للنجاح
قاموس
الإعراب
المدرسي

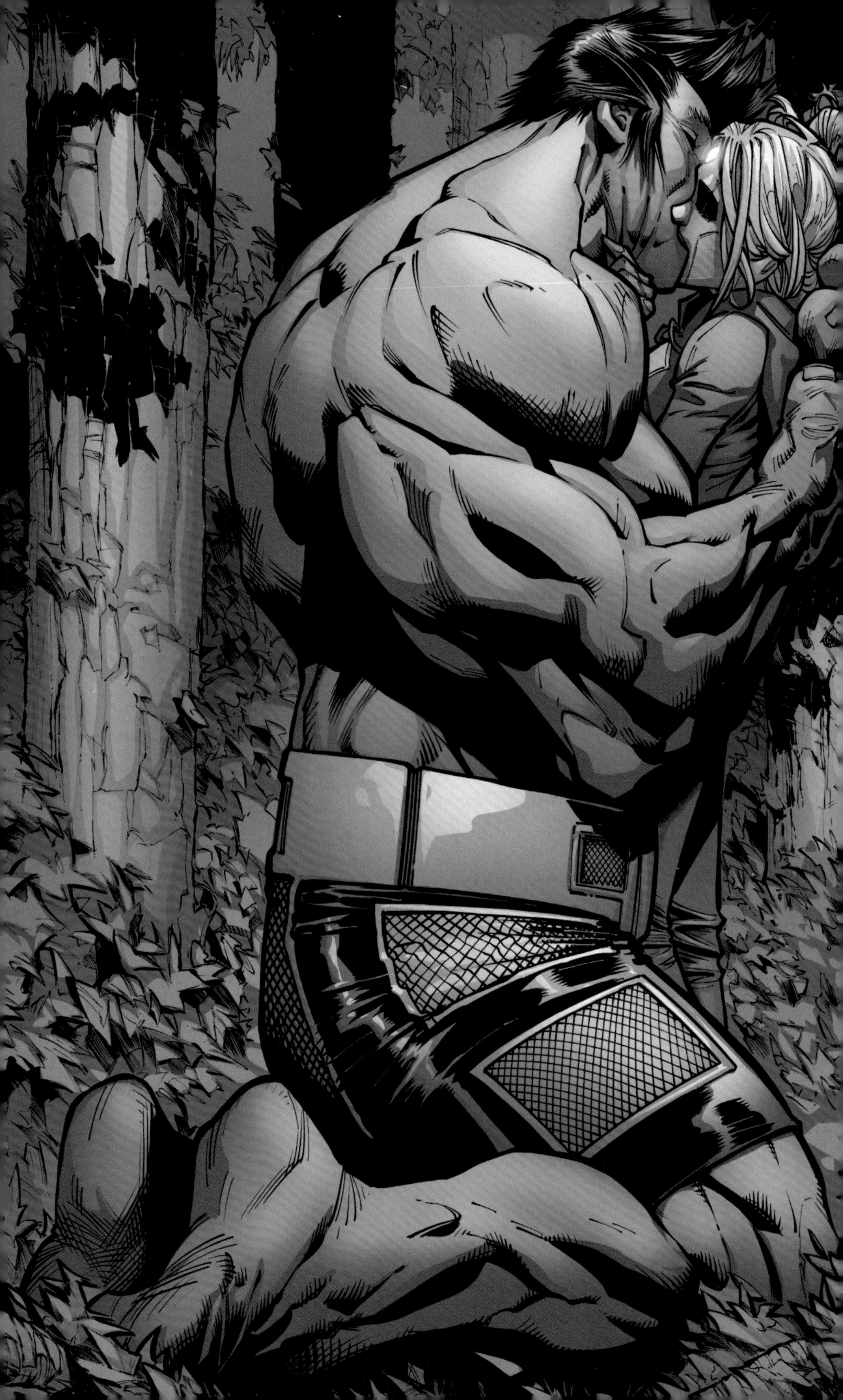

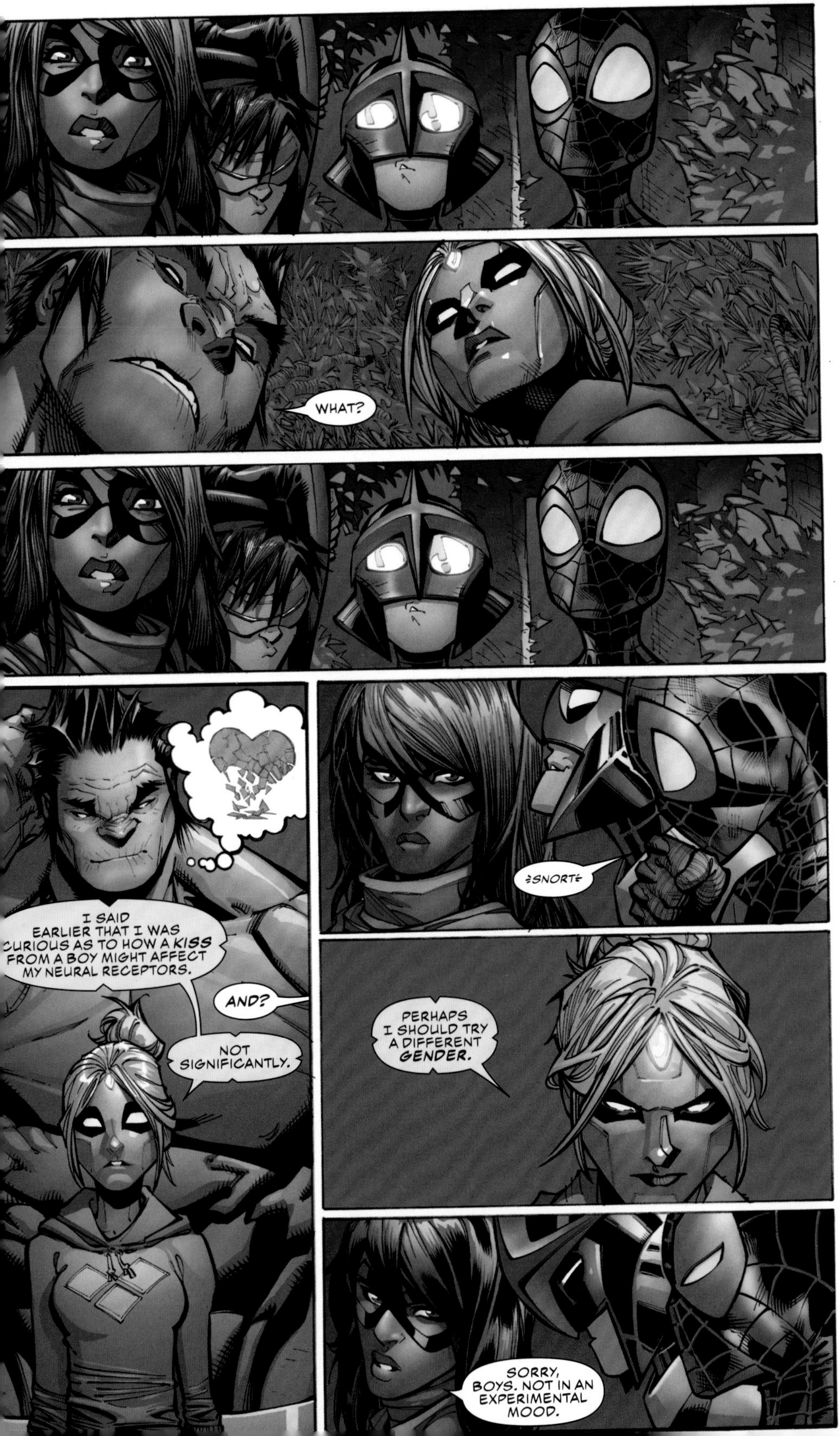
WHAT?
I SAID EARLIER THAT I WAS CURIOUS AS TO HOW A KISS FROM A BOY MIGHT AFFECT MY NEURAL RECEPTORS.
AND?
NOT SIGNIFICANTLY.
SNORT
PERHAPS I SHOULD TRY A DIFFERENT GENDER.
SORRY, BOYS. NOT IN AN EXPERIMENTAL MOOD.

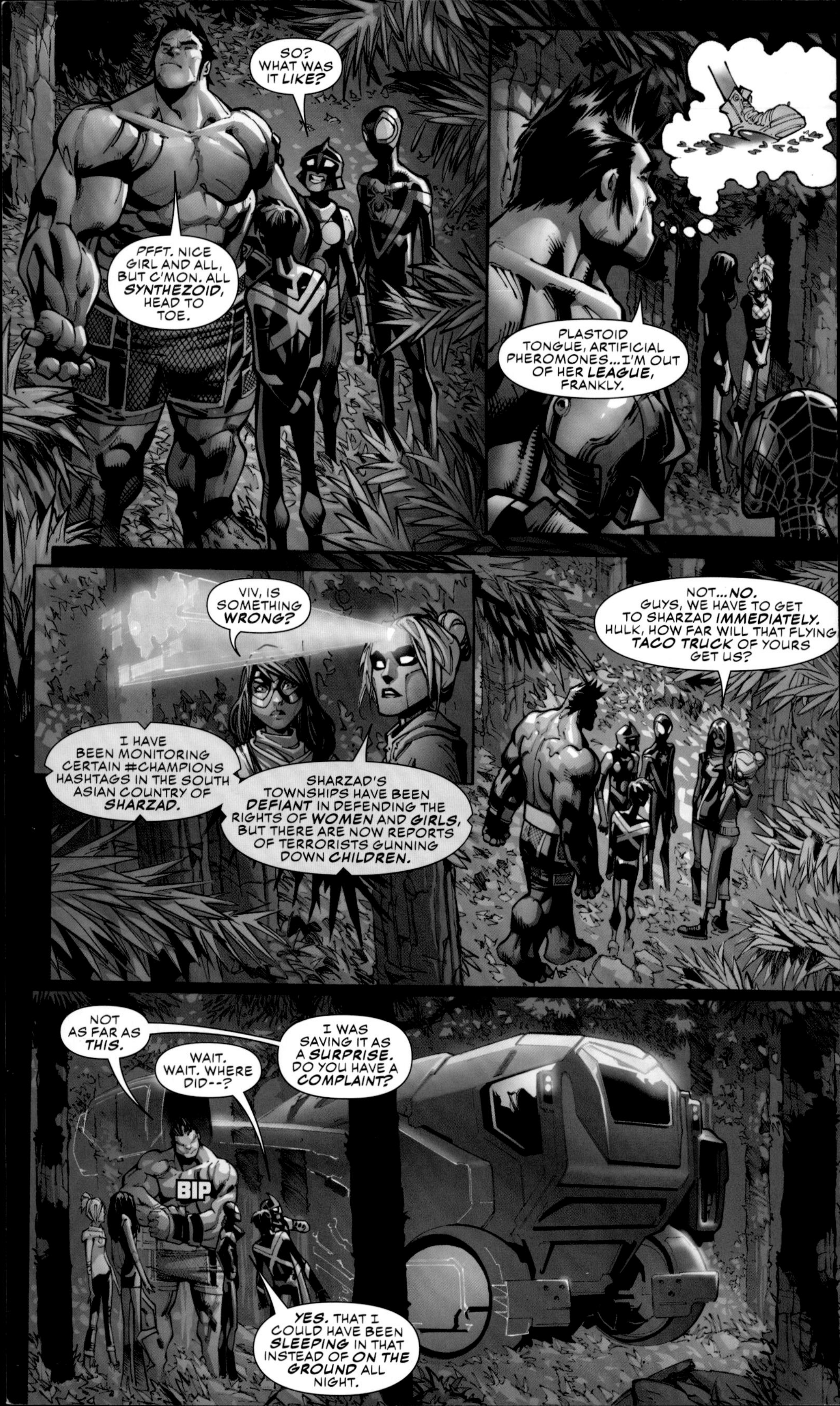
SO? WHAT WAS IT LIKE?
PFFT. NICE GIRL AND ALL, BUT C'MON. ALL SYNTHEZOID, HEAD TO TOE.
PLASTOID TONGUE, ARTIFICIAL PHEROMONES...I'M OUT OF HER LEAGUE, FRANKLY.
VIV, IS SOMETHING WRONG?
I HAVE BEEN MONITORING CERTAIN #CHAMPIONS HASHTAGS IN THE SOUTH ASIAN COUNTRY OF SHARZAD.
SHARZAD'S TOWNSHIPS HAVE BEEN DEFIANT IN DEFENDING THE RIGHTS OF WOMEN AND GIRLS, BUT THERE ARE NOW REPORTS OF TERRORISTS GUNNING DOWN CHILDREN.
NOT...NO. GUYS, WE HAVE TO GET TO SHARZAD IMMEDIATELY. HULK, HOW FAR WILL THAT FLYING TACO TRUCK OF YOURS GET US?
NOT AS FAR AS THIS.
BIP
WAIT. WAIT. WHERE DID--?
I WAS SAVING IT AS A SURPRISE. DO YOU HAVE A COMPLAINT?
YES. THAT I COULD HAVE BEEN SLEEPING IN THAT INSTEAD OF ON THE GROUND ALL NIGHT.

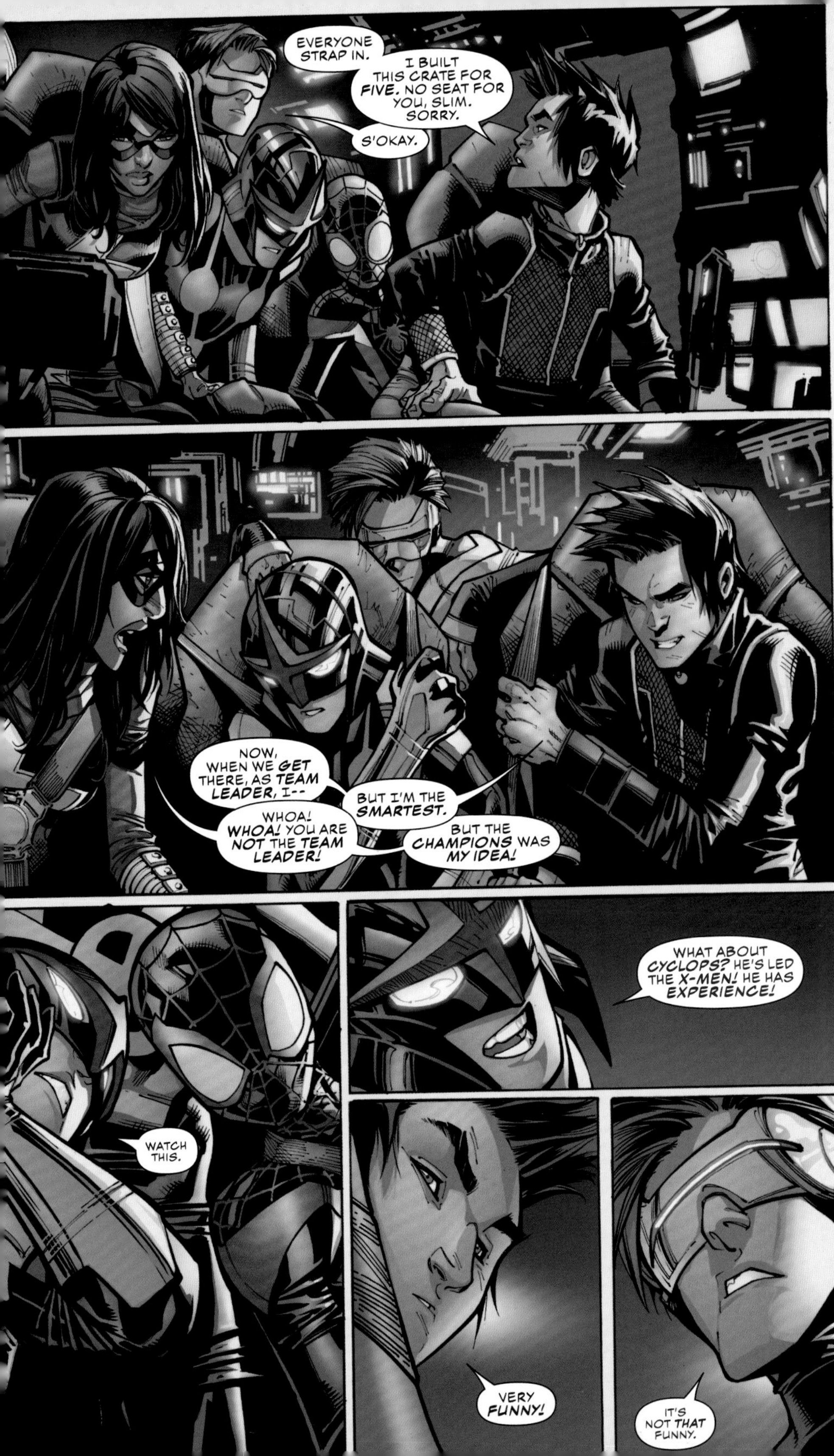
EVERYONE STRAP IN.
I BUILT THIS CRATE FOR FIVE. NO SEAT FOR YOU, SLIM. SORRY.
S'OKAY.
NOW, WHEN WE GET THERE, AS TEAM LEADER, I--
BUT I'M THE SMARTEST.
WHOA! WHOA! YOU ARE NOT THE TEAM LEADER!
BUT THE CHAMPIONS WAS MY IDEA!
WATCH THIS.
WHAT ABOUT CYCLOPS? HE'S LED THE X-MEN! HE HAS EXPERIENCE!
VERY FUNNY!
IT'S NOT THAT FUNNY.

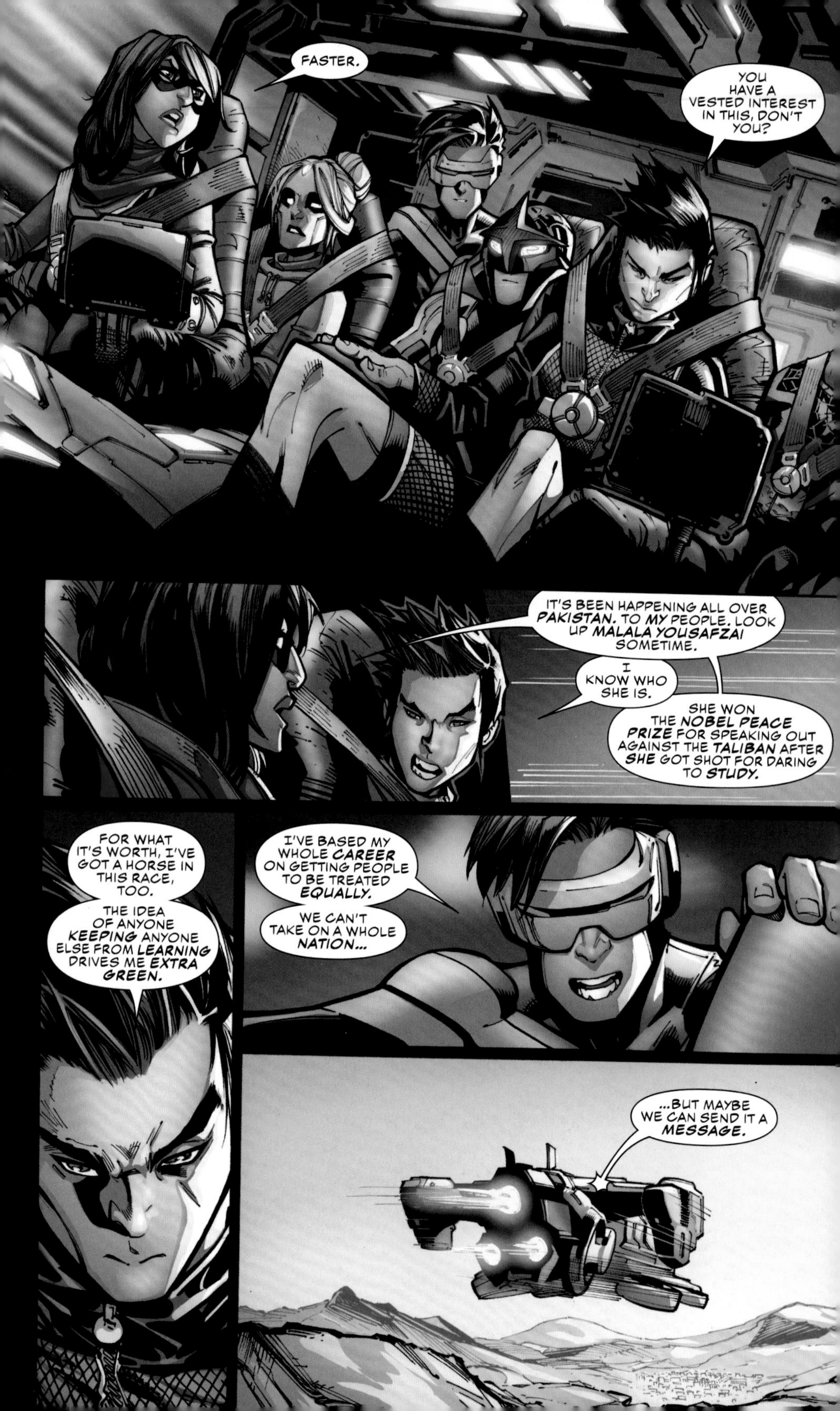
FASTER.
YOU HAVE A VESTED INTEREST IN THIS, DON'T YOU?
IT'S BEEN HAPPENING ALL OVER PAKISTAN. TO MY PEOPLE. LOOK UP MALALA YOUSAFZAI SOMETIME.
I KNOW WHO SHE IS.
SHE WON THE NOBEL PEACE PRIZE FOR SPEAKING OUT AGAINST THE TALIBAN AFTER SHE GOT SHOT FOR DARING TO STUDY.
FOR WHAT IT'S WORTH, I'VE GOT A HORSE IN THIS RACE, TOO.
THE IDEA OF ANYONE KEEPING ANYONE ELSE FROM LEARNING DRIVES ME EXTRA GREEN.
I'VE BASED MY WHOLE CAREER ON GETTING PEOPLE TO BE TREATED EQUALLY.
WE CAN'T TAKE ON A WHOLE NATION...
...BUT MAYBE WE CAN SEND IT A MESSAGE.

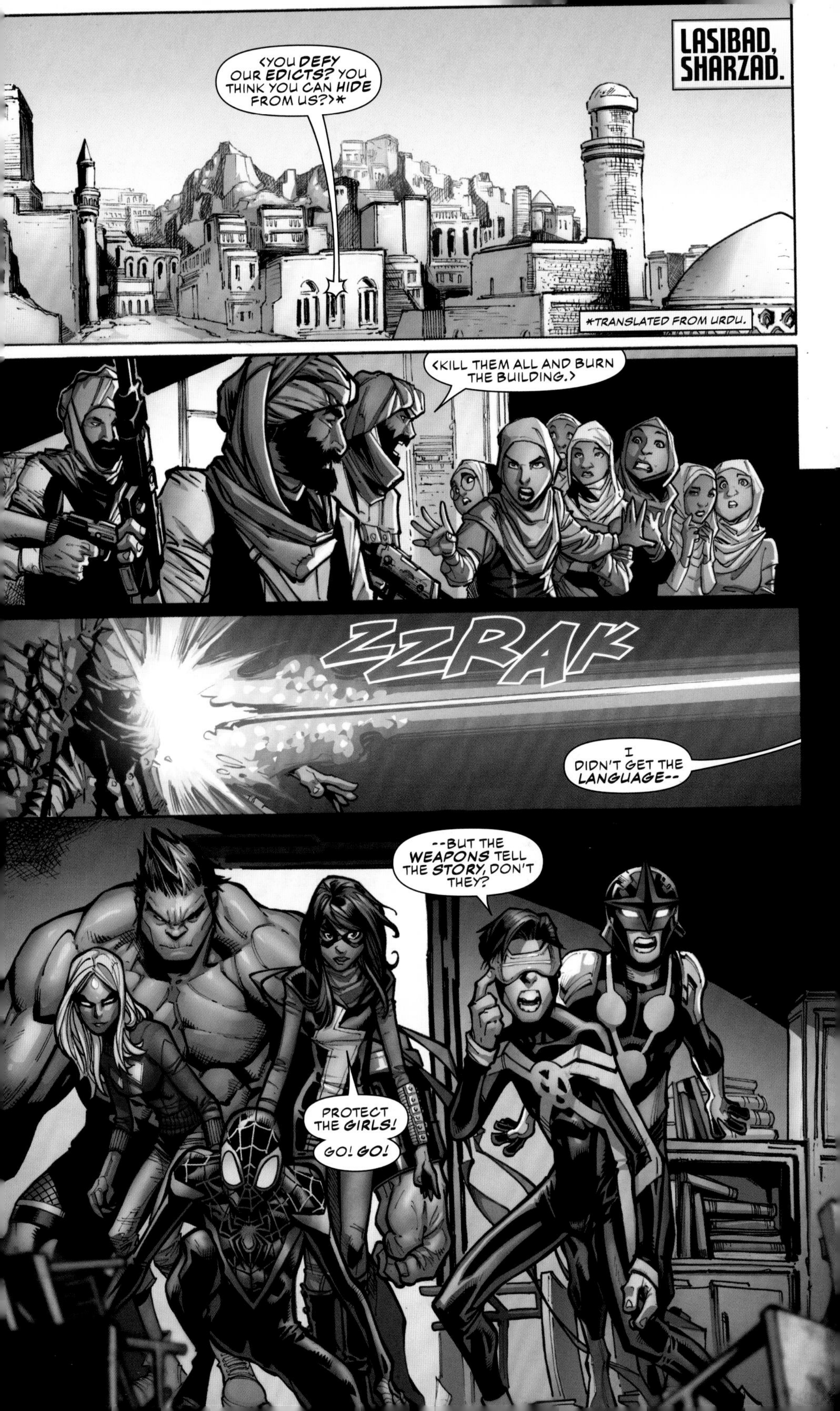
LASIBAD, SHARZAD.
<YOU DEFY OUR EDICTS? YOU THINK YOU CAN HIDE FROM US?>*
*TRANSLATED FROM URDU.
<KILL THEM ALL AND BURN THE BUILDING.>
ZZRAK
I DIDN'T GET THE LANGUAGE--
--BUT THE WEAPONS TELL THE STORY, DON'T THEY?
PROTECT THE GIRLS!
GO! GO!

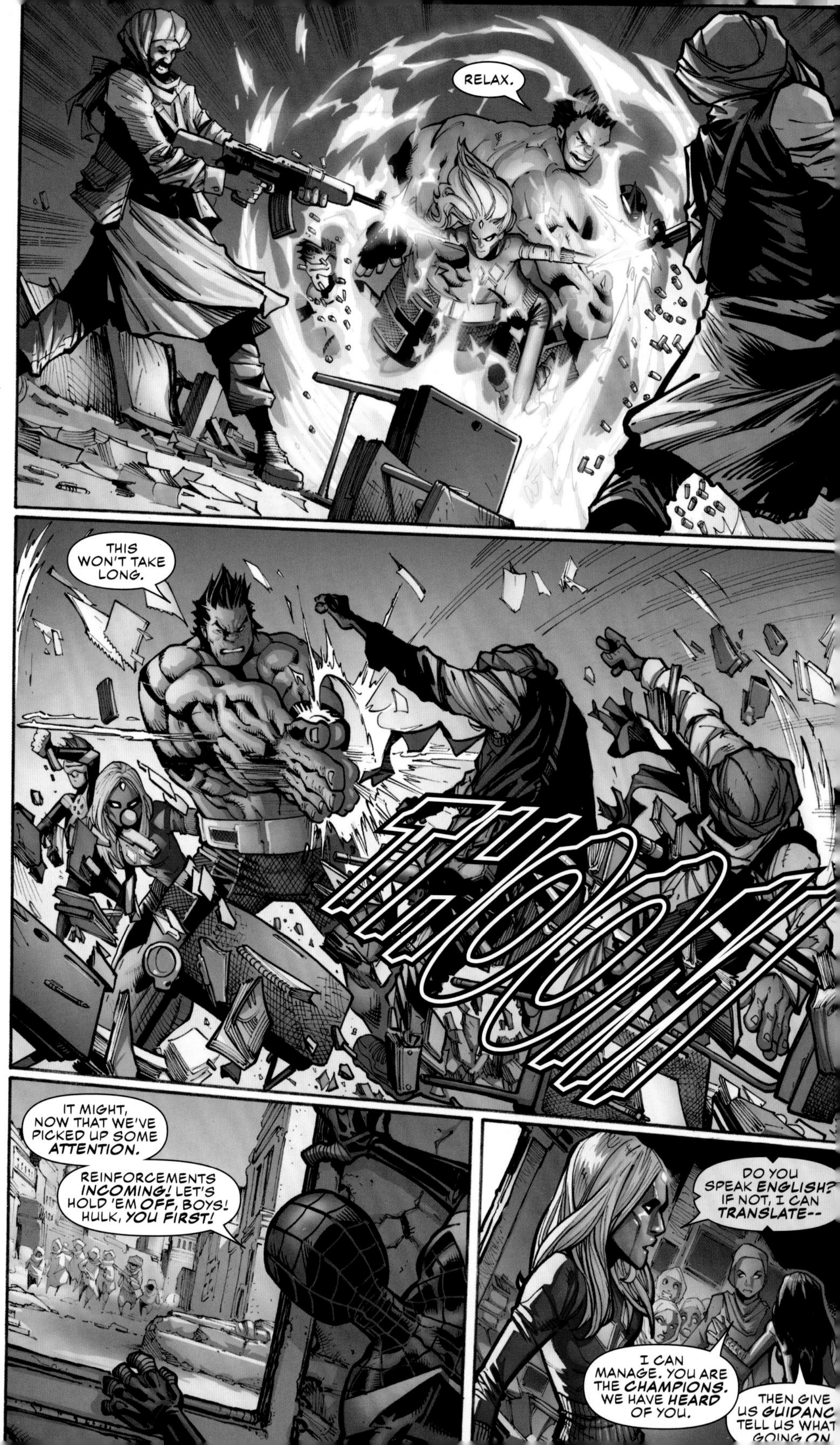
RELAX.
THIS WON'T TAKE LONG.
THOOM
IT MIGHT, NOW THAT WE'VE PICKED UP SOME ATTENTION.
REINFORCEMENTS INCOMING! LET'S HOLD 'EM OFF, BOYS! HULK, YOU FIRST!
DO YOU SPEAK ENGLISH? IF NOT, I CAN TRANSLATE--
I CAN MANAGE. YOU ARE THE CHAMPIONS. WE HAVE HEARD OF YOU.
THEN GIVE US GUIDANC TELL US WHAT

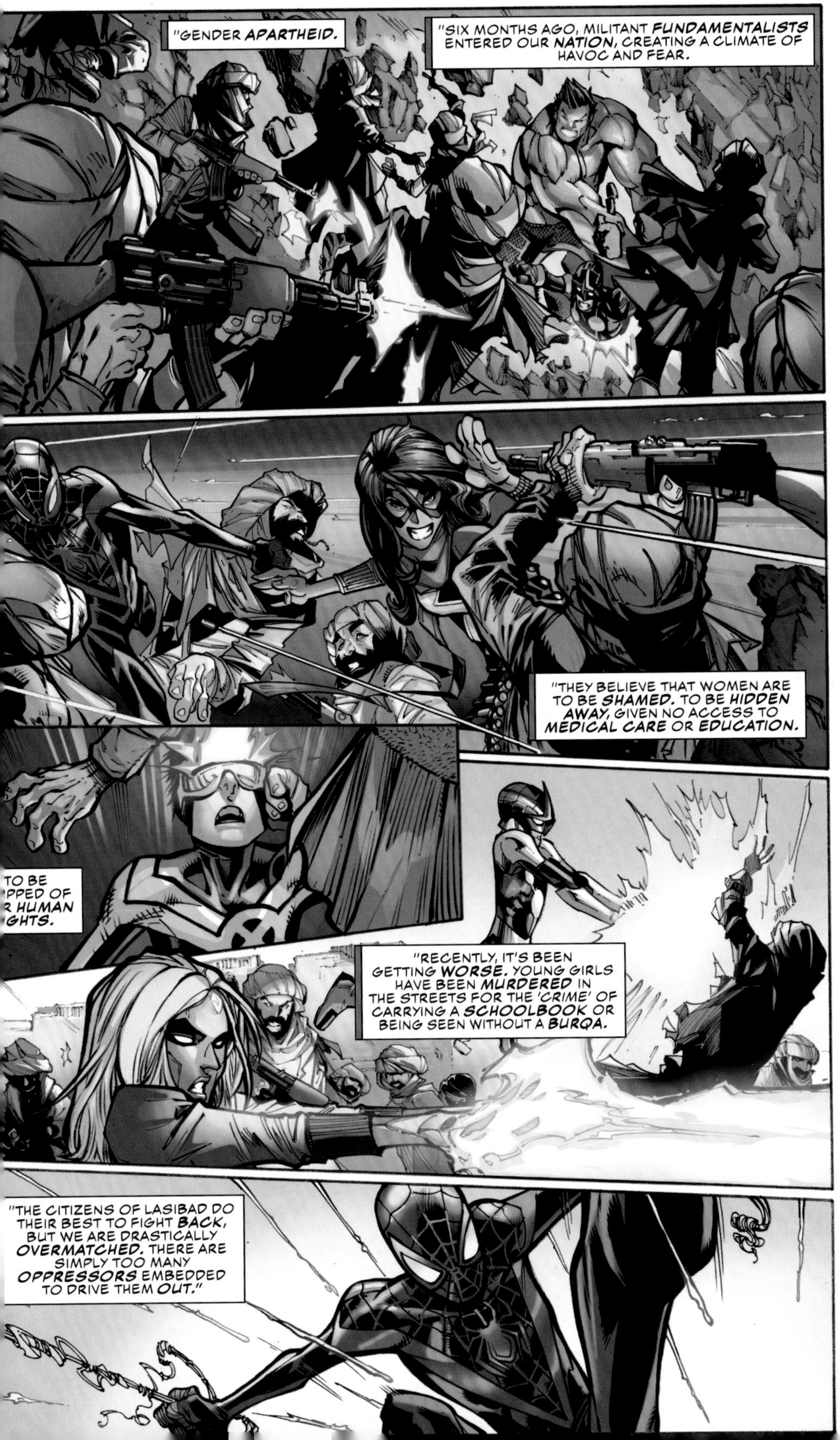

"GENDER APARTHEID.
"SIX MONTHS AGO, MILITANT FUNDAMENTALISTS ENTERED OUR NATION, CREATING A CLIMATE OF HAVOC AND FEAR.
"THEY BELIEVE THAT WOMEN ARE TO BE SHAMED. TO BE HIDDEN AWAY, GIVEN NO ACCESS TO MEDICAL CARE OR EDUCATION.
TO BE PPED OF R HUMAN GHTS.
"RECENTLY, IT'S BEEN GETTING WORSE. YOUNG GIRLS HAVE BEEN MURDERED IN THE STREETS FOR THE 'CRIME' OF CARRYING A SCHOOLBOOK OR BEING SEEN WITHOUT A BURQA.
"THE CITIZENS OF LASIBAD DO THEIR BEST TO FIGHT BACK, BUT WE ARE DRASTICALLY OVERMATCHED. THERE ARE SIMPLY TOO MANY OPPRESSORS EMBEDDED TO DRIVE THEM OUT."

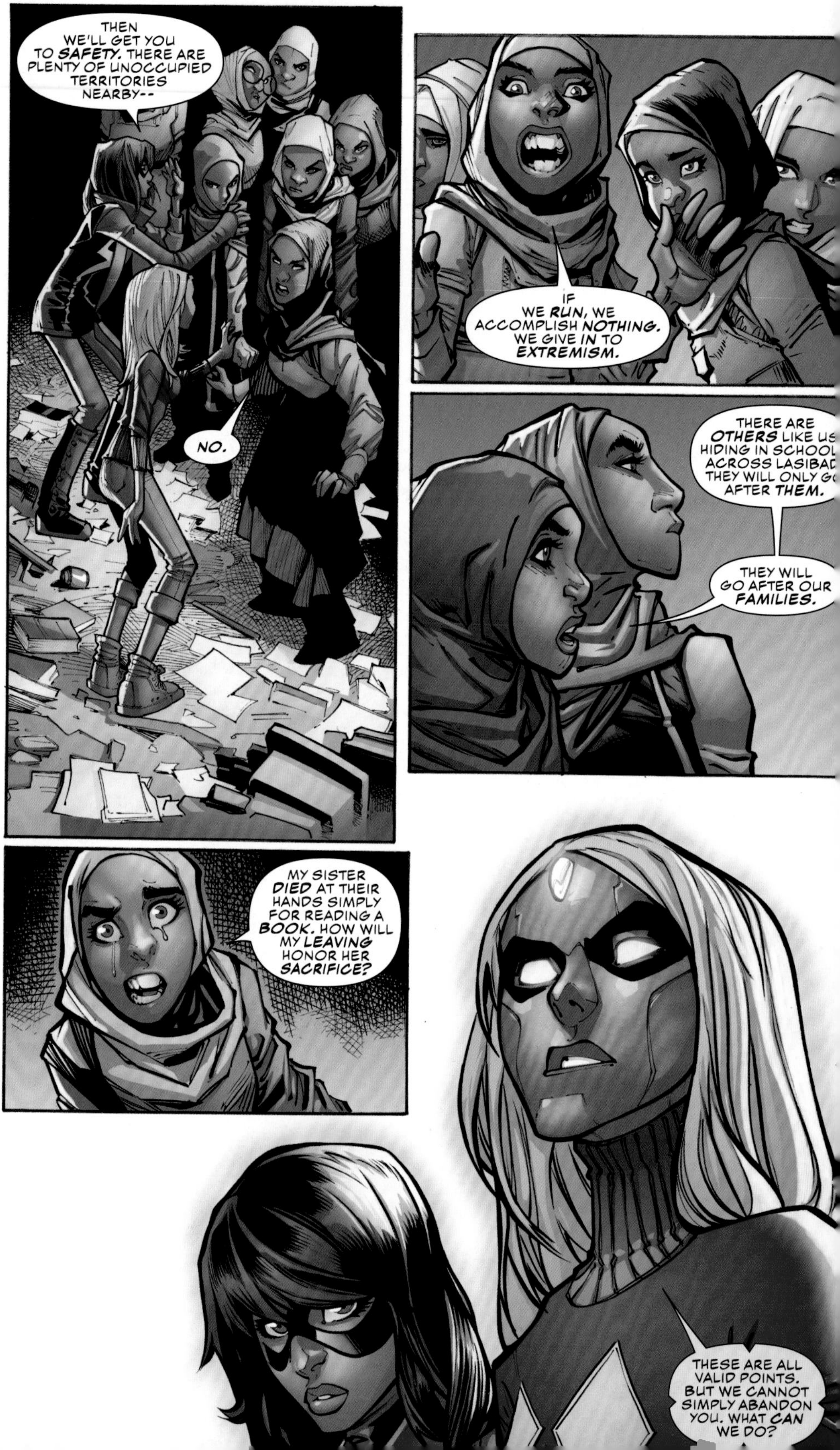

THEN WE'LL GET YOU TO SAFETY. THERE ARE PLENTY OF UNOCCUPIED TERRITORIES NEARBY--
NO.
IF WE RUN, WE ACCOMPLISH NOTHING. WE GIVE IN TO EXTREMISM.
THERE ARE OTHERS LIKE US HIDING IN SCHOOL ACROSS LASIBAD THEY WILL ONLY GO AFTER THEM.
THEY WILL GO AFTER OUR FAMILIES.
MY SISTER DIED AT THEIR HANDS SIMPLY FOR READING A BOOK. HOW WILL MY LEAVING HONOR HER SACRIFICE?
THESE ARE ALL VALID POINTS. BUT WE CANNOT SIMPLY ABANDON YOU. WHAT CAN WE DO?

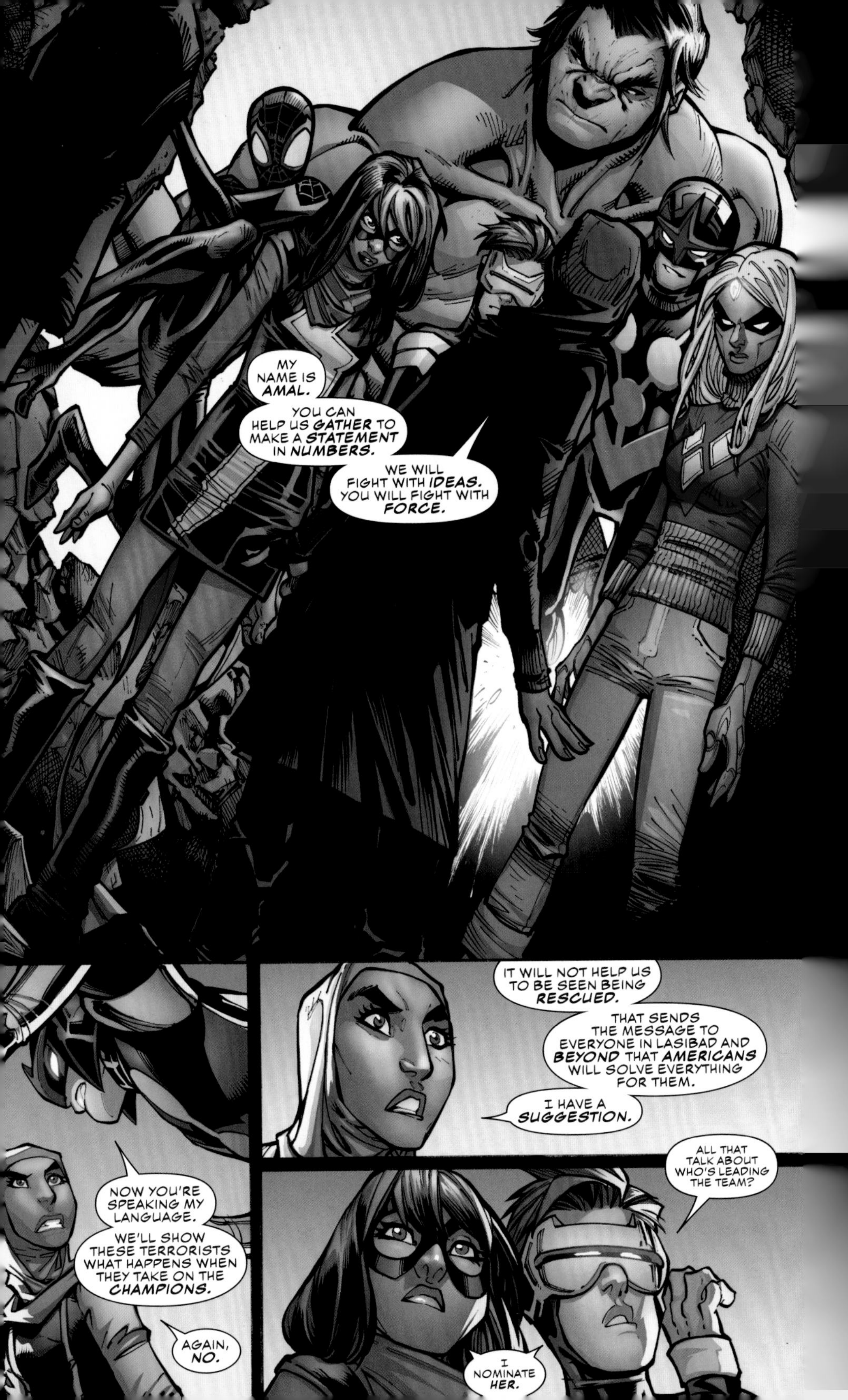
MY NAME IS AMAL.
YOU CAN HELP US GATHER TO MAKE A STATEMENT IN NUMBERS.
WE WILL FIGHT WITH IDEAS. YOU WILL FIGHT WITH FORCE.
IT WILL NOT HELP US TO BE SEEN BEING RESCUED.
THAT SENDS THE MESSAGE TO EVERYONE IN LASIBAD AND BEYOND THAT AMERICANS WILL SOLVE EVERYTHING FOR THEM.
I HAVE A SUGGESTION.
NOW YOU'RE SPEAKING MY LANGUAGE.
WE'LL SHOW THESE TERRORISTS WHAT HAPPENS WHEN THEY TAKE ON THE CHAMPIONS.
AGAIN, NO.
ALL THAT TALK ABOUT WHO'S LEADING THE TEAM?
I NOMINATE HER.

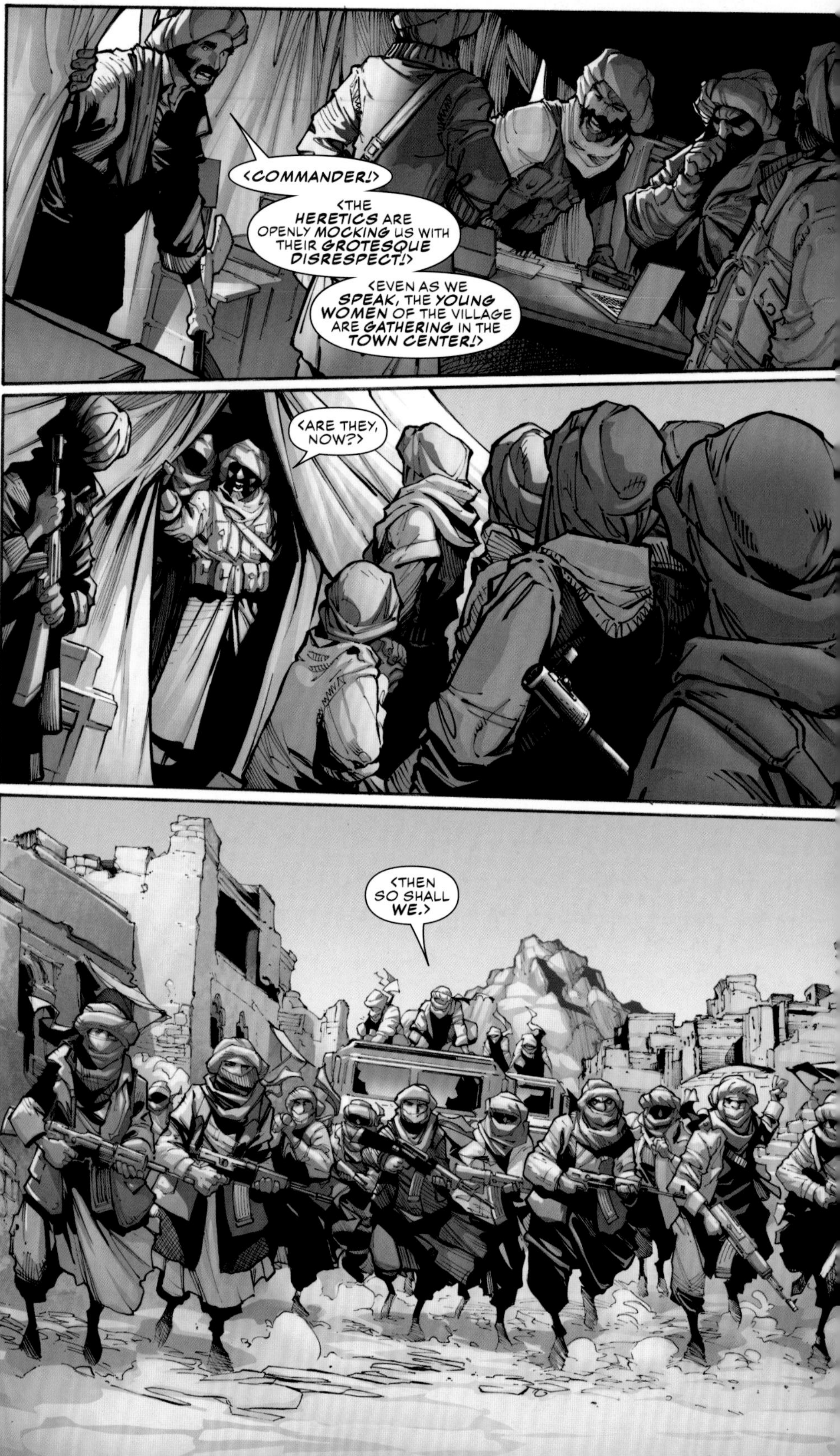
<COMMANDER!>
<THE HERETICS ARE OPENLY MOCKING US WITH THEIR GROTESQUE DISRESPECT!>
<EVEN AS WE SPEAK, THE YOUNG WOMEN OF THE VILLAGE ARE GATHERING IN THE TOWN CENTER!>
<ARE THEY, NOW?>
<THEN SO SHALL WE.>

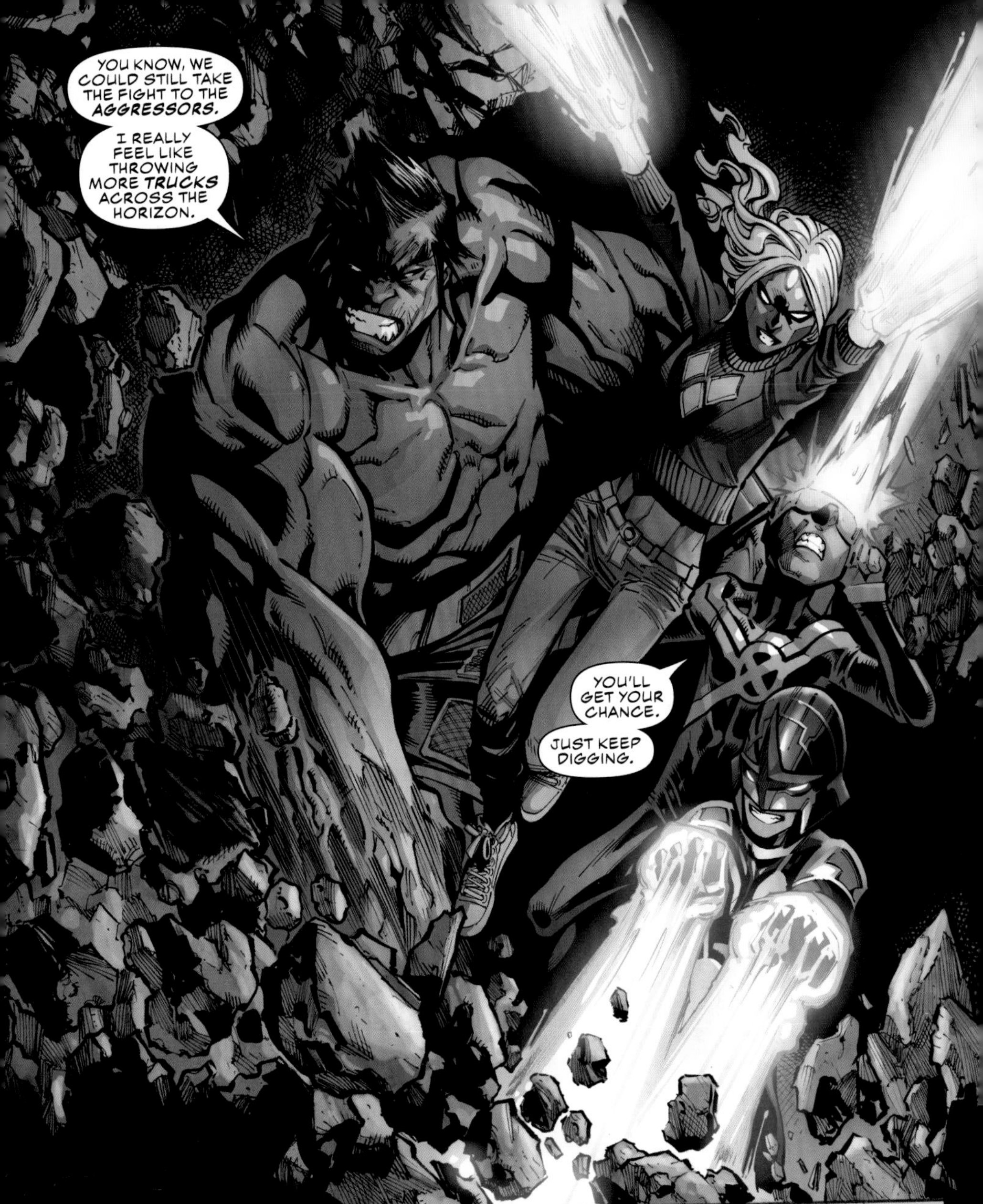
YOU KNOW, WE COULD STILL TAKE THE FIGHT TO THE AGGRESSORS.
I REALLY FEEL LIKE THROWING MORE TRUCKS ACROSS THE HORIZON.
YOU'LL GET YOUR CHANCE.
JUST KEEP DIGGING.

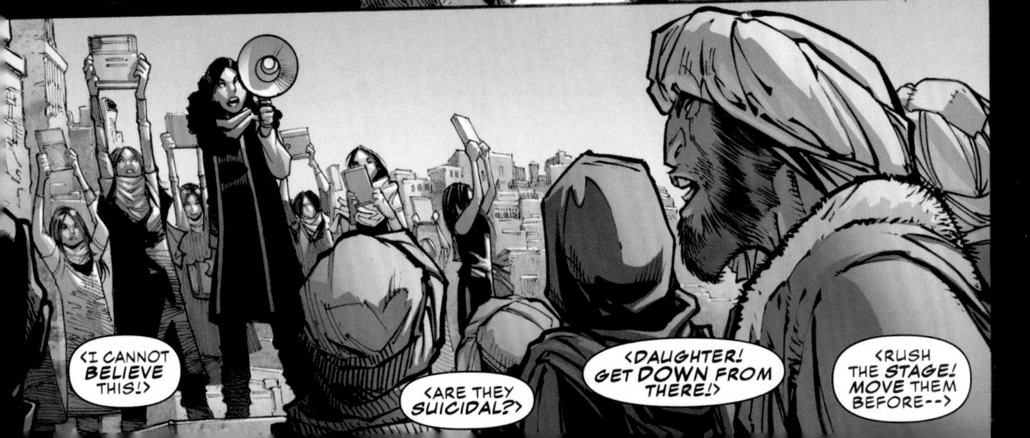
<I CANNOT BELIEVE THIS!>
<ARE THEY SUICIDAL?>
<DAUGHTER! GET DOWN FROM THERE!>
<RUSH THE STAGE! MOVE THEM BEFORE-->

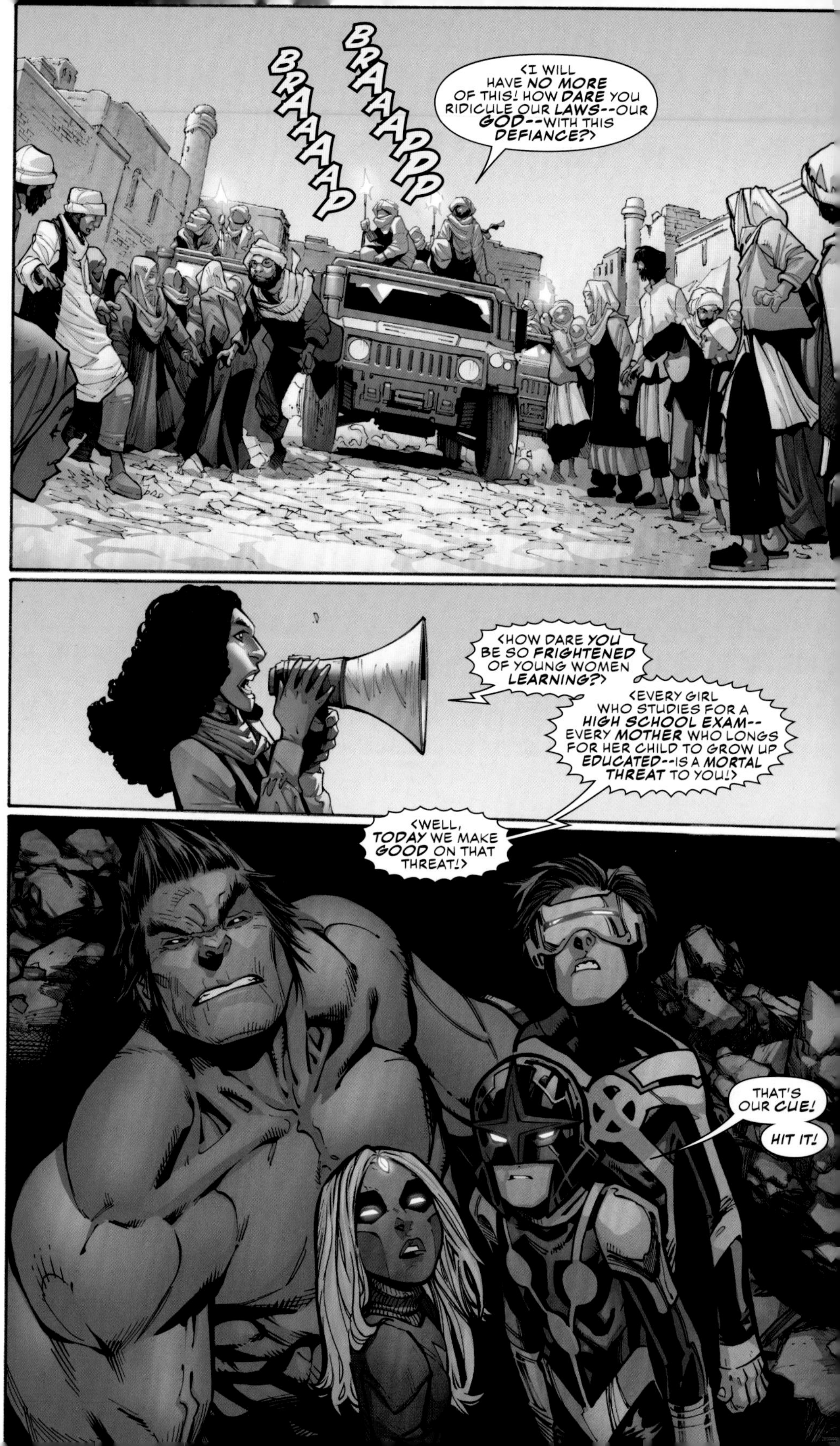
BRAAAAP
BRAAAPPP
<I WILL HAVE NO MORE OF THIS! HOW DARE YOU RIDICULE OUR LAWS--OUR GOD--WITH THIS DEFIANCE?>
<HOW DARE YOU BE SO FRIGHTENED OF YOUNG WOMEN LEARNING?>
<EVERY GIRL WHO STUDIES FOR A HIGH SCHOOL EXAM--EVERY MOTHER WHO LONGS FOR HER CHILD TO GROW UP EDUCATED--IS A MORTAL THREAT TO YOU!>
<WELL, TODAY WE MAKE GOOD ON THAT THREAT!>
THAT'S OUR CUE!
HIT IT!

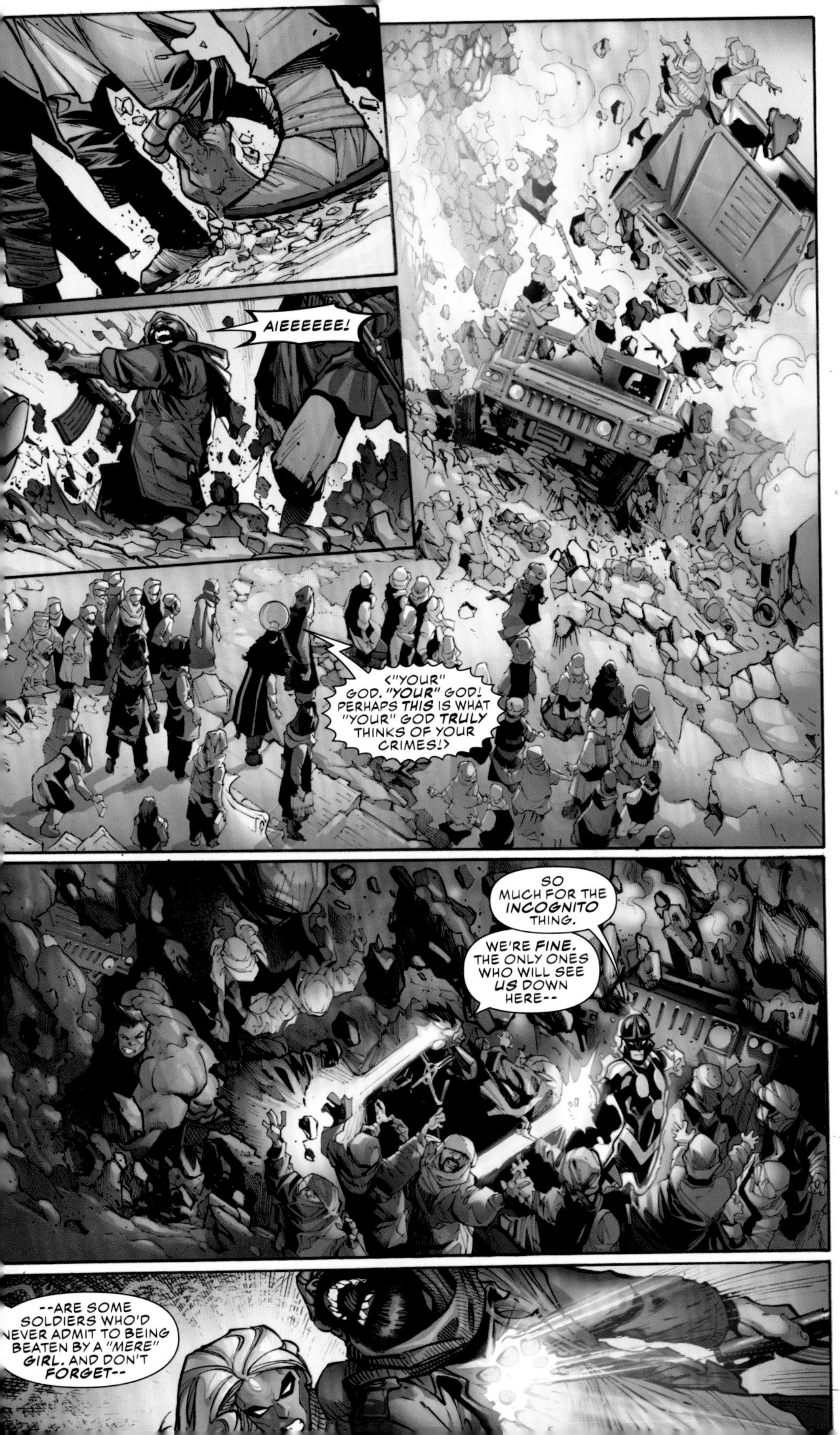
AIEEEEEE!
<"YOUR" GOD. "YOUR" GOD! PERHAPS THIS IS WHAT "YOUR" GOD TRULY THINKS OF YOUR CRIMES!>
SO MUCH FOR THE INCOGNITO THING.
WE'RE FINE. THE ONLY ONES WHO WILL SEE US DOWN HERE--
--ARE SOME SOLDIERS WHO'D NEVER ADMIT TO BEING BEATEN BY A "MERE" GIRL. AND DON'T FORGET--

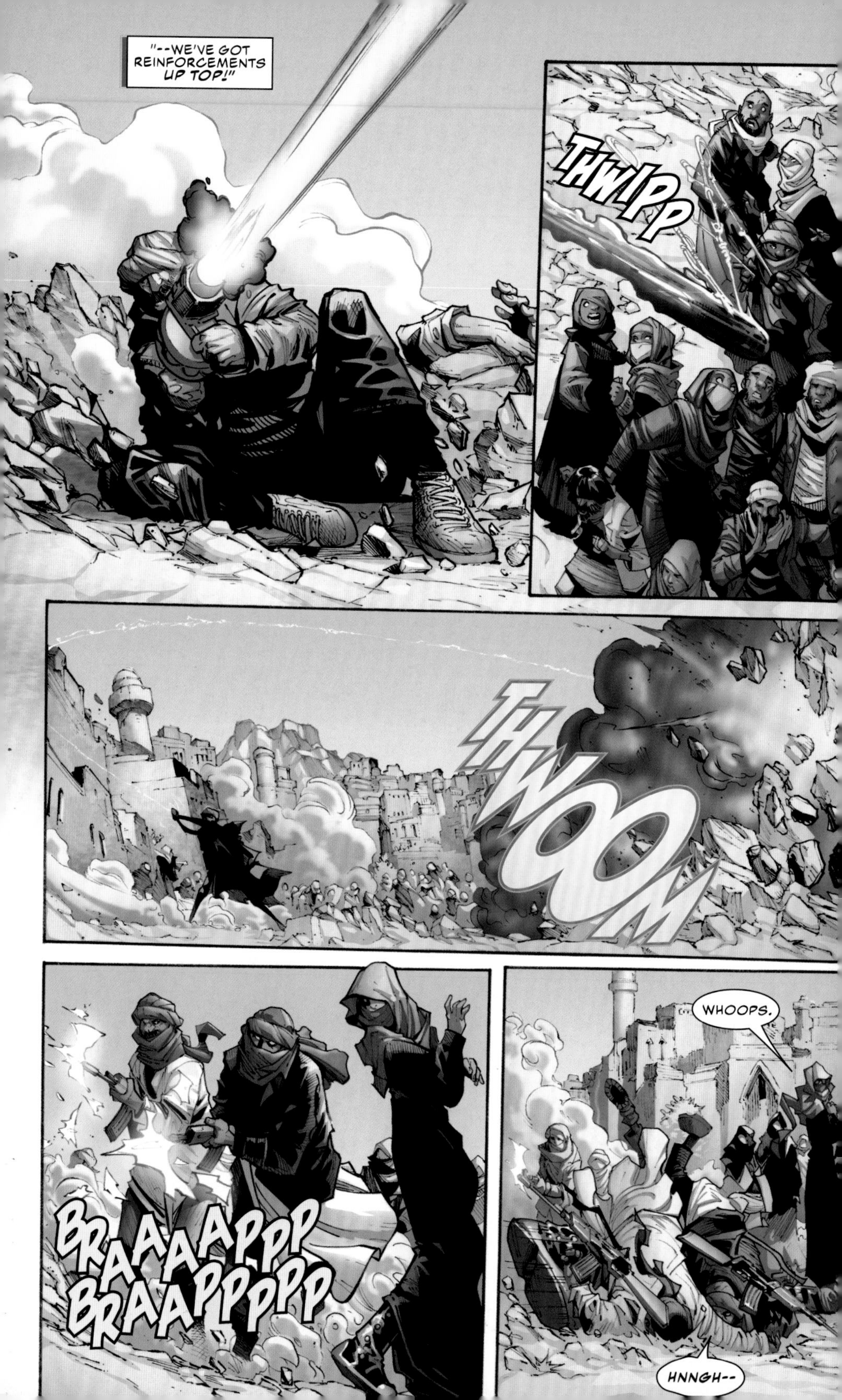
"--WE'VE GOT REINFORCEMENTS UP TOP!"
THWIPP
THWOOM
BRAAAAPPP
BRAAPPPPP
WHOOPS.
HNNGH--

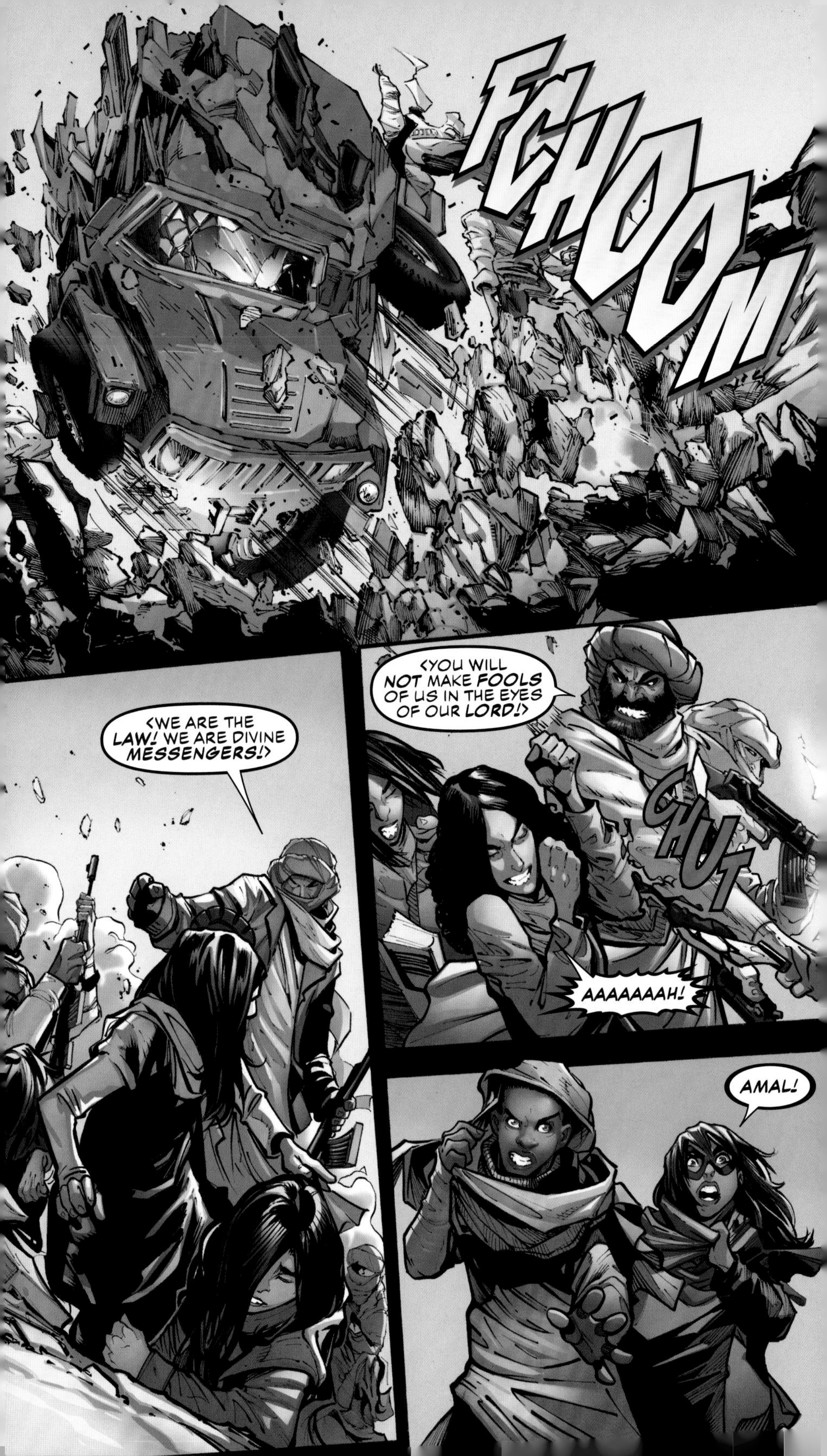

FCHOOM
<WE ARE THE LAW! WE ARE DIVINE MESSENGERS!>
<YOU WILL NOT MAKE FOOLS OF US IN THE EYES OF OUR LORD!>
CHUT
AAAAAAAH!
AMAL!

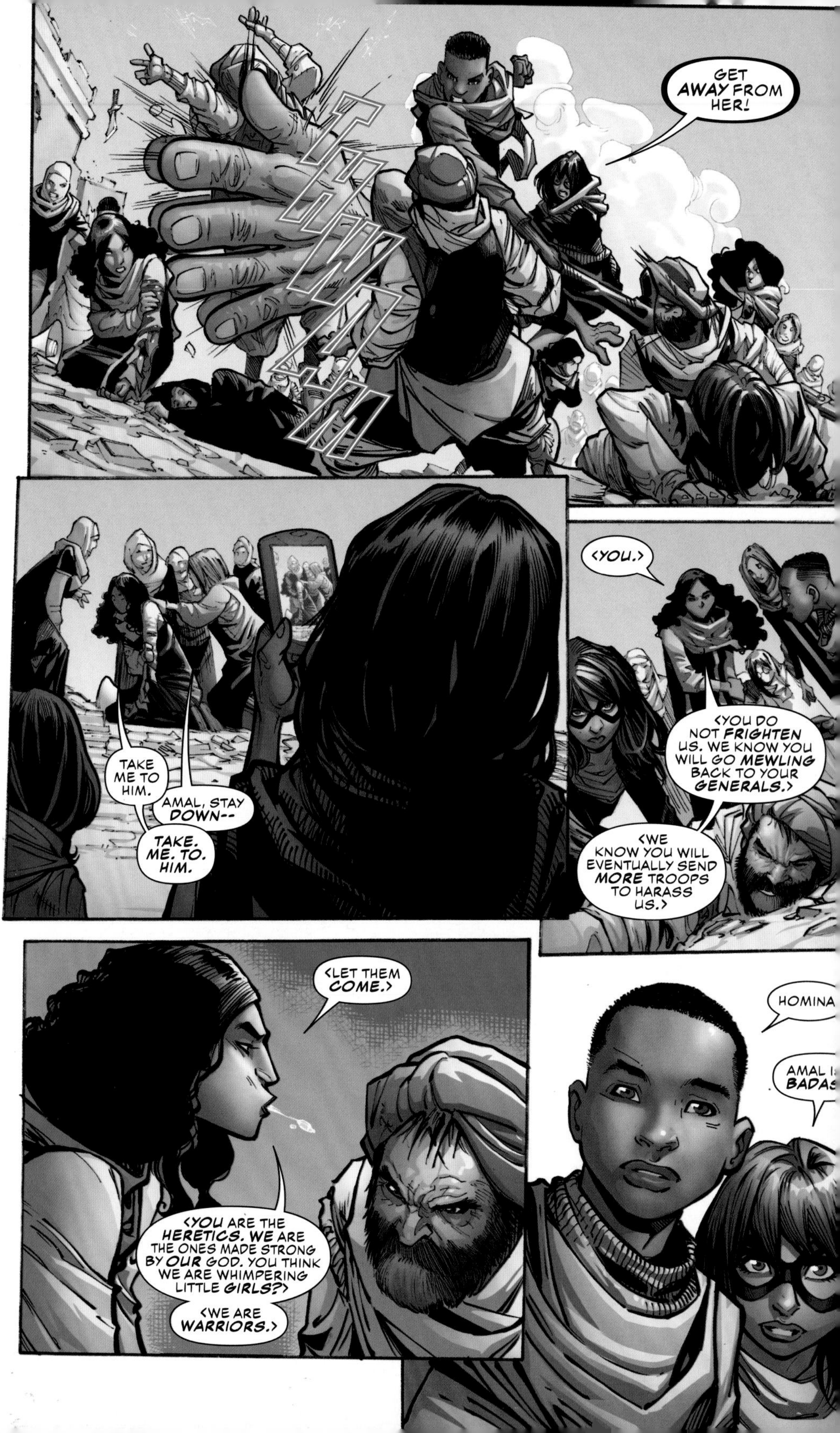
GET AWAY FROM HER!
<YOU.>
TAKE ME TO HIM.
AMAL, STAY DOWN--
TAKE. ME. TO. HIM.
<YOU DO NOT FRIGHTEN US. WE KNOW YOU WILL GO MEWLING BACK TO YOUR GENERALS.>
<WE KNOW YOU WILL EVENTUALLY SEND MORE TROOPS TO HARASS US.>
<LET THEM COME.>
<YOU ARE THE HERETICS. WE ARE THE ONES MADE STRONG BY OUR GOD. YOU THINK WE ARE WHIMPERING LITTLE GIRLS?>
<WE ARE WARRIORS.>
HOMINA
AMAL I
BADAS

--NO NEED TO ACT SO *HUMBLE.* WERE IT NOT FOR *YOU,* WE MIGHT NEVER HAVE FOUND THE COURAGE TO *ACT.*

WE'LL MAKE SURE THE *CAMERA FOOTAGE* OF YOUR VICTORY GETS BROADCAST *WORLDWIDE* TO OUR *FOLLOWERS--* AND *BEYOND.*

YOU'LL CONTACT US IF YOU NEED US AGAIN?

I PROMISE.

YOU'D *BETTER.*

WE'RE ALL PART OF THE SAME *TEAM* NOW.

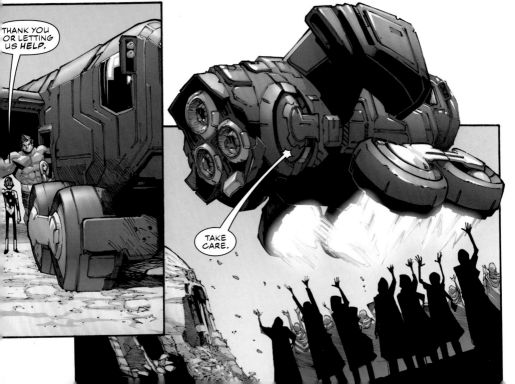

THANK YOU FOR LETTING US HELP.

TAKE CARE.

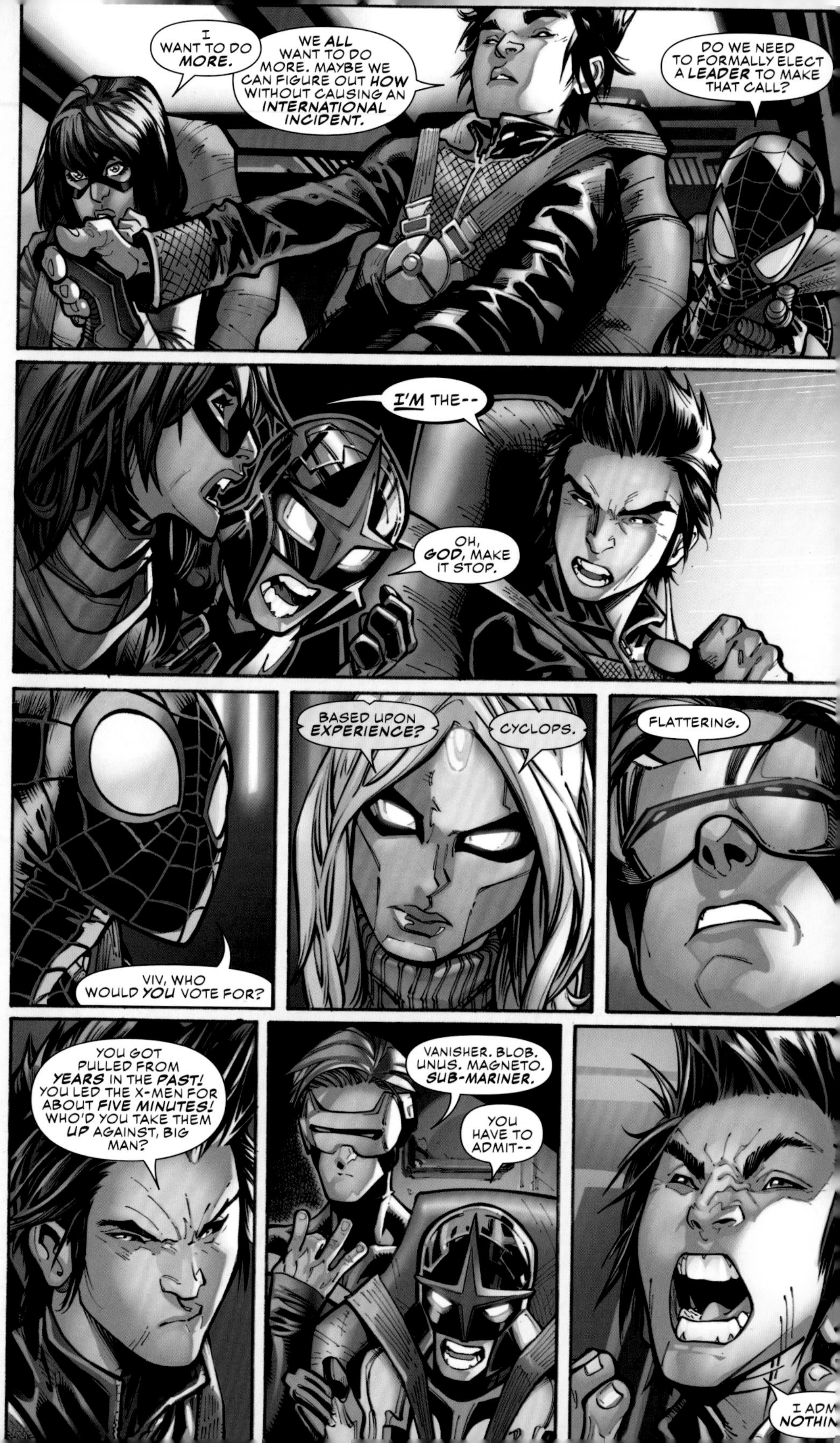

I WANT TO DO MORE.
WE ALL WANT TO DO MORE. MAYBE WE CAN FIGURE OUT HOW WITHOUT CAUSING AN INTERNATIONAL INCIDENT.
DO WE NEED TO FORMALLY ELECT A LEADER TO MAKE THAT CALL?
I'M THE--
OH, GOD, MAKE IT STOP.
VIV, WHO WOULD YOU VOTE FOR?
BASED UPON EXPERIENCE?
CYCLOPS.
FLATTERING.
YOU GOT PULLED FROM YEARS IN THE PAST! YOU LED THE X-MEN FOR ABOUT FIVE MINUTES! WHO'D YOU TAKE THEM UP AGAINST, BIG MAN?
VANISHER. BLOB. UNUS. MAGNETO. SUB-MARINER.
YOU HAVE TO ADMIT--

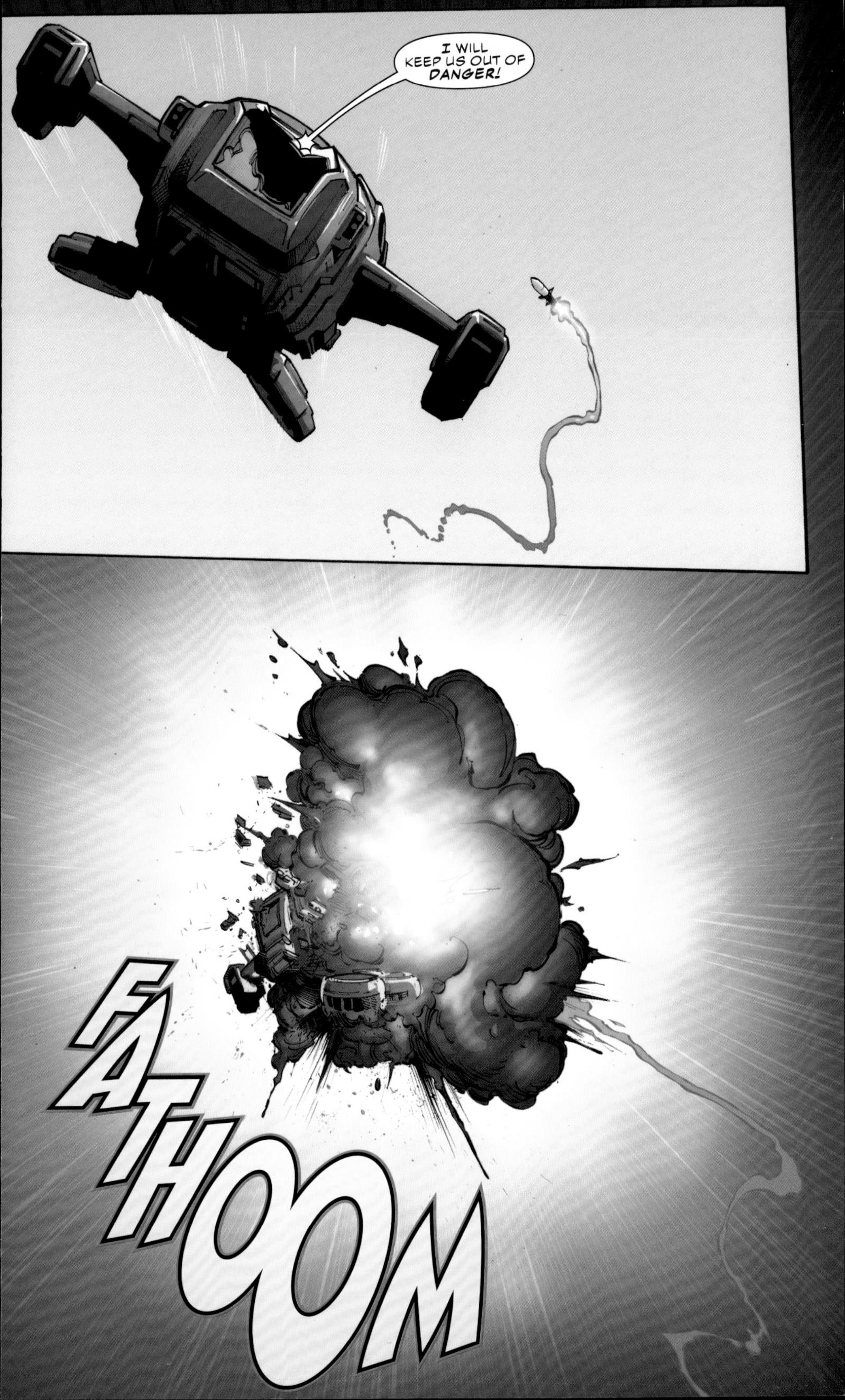
I WILL KEEP US OUT OF DANGER!
FATHOOM

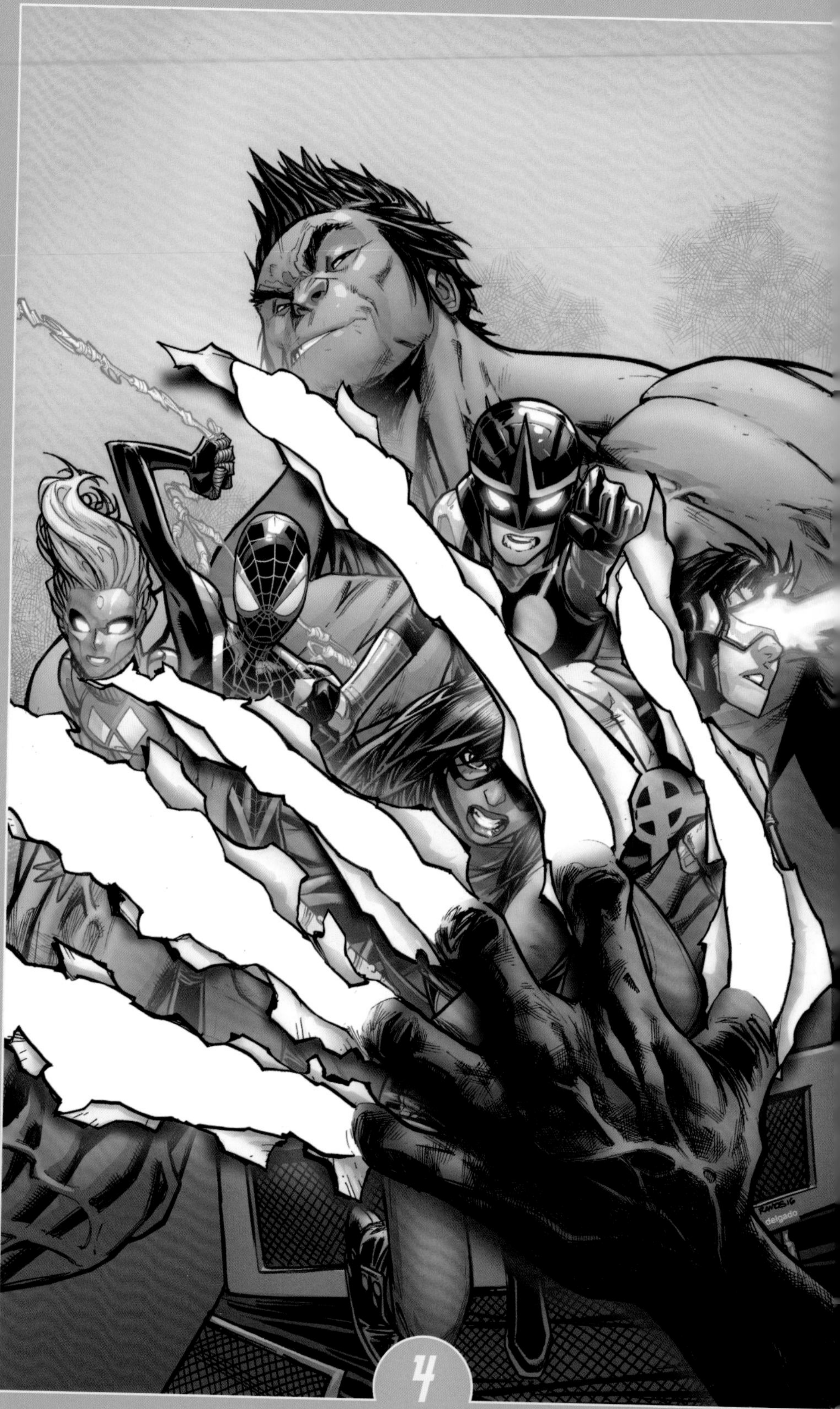

delgado

4

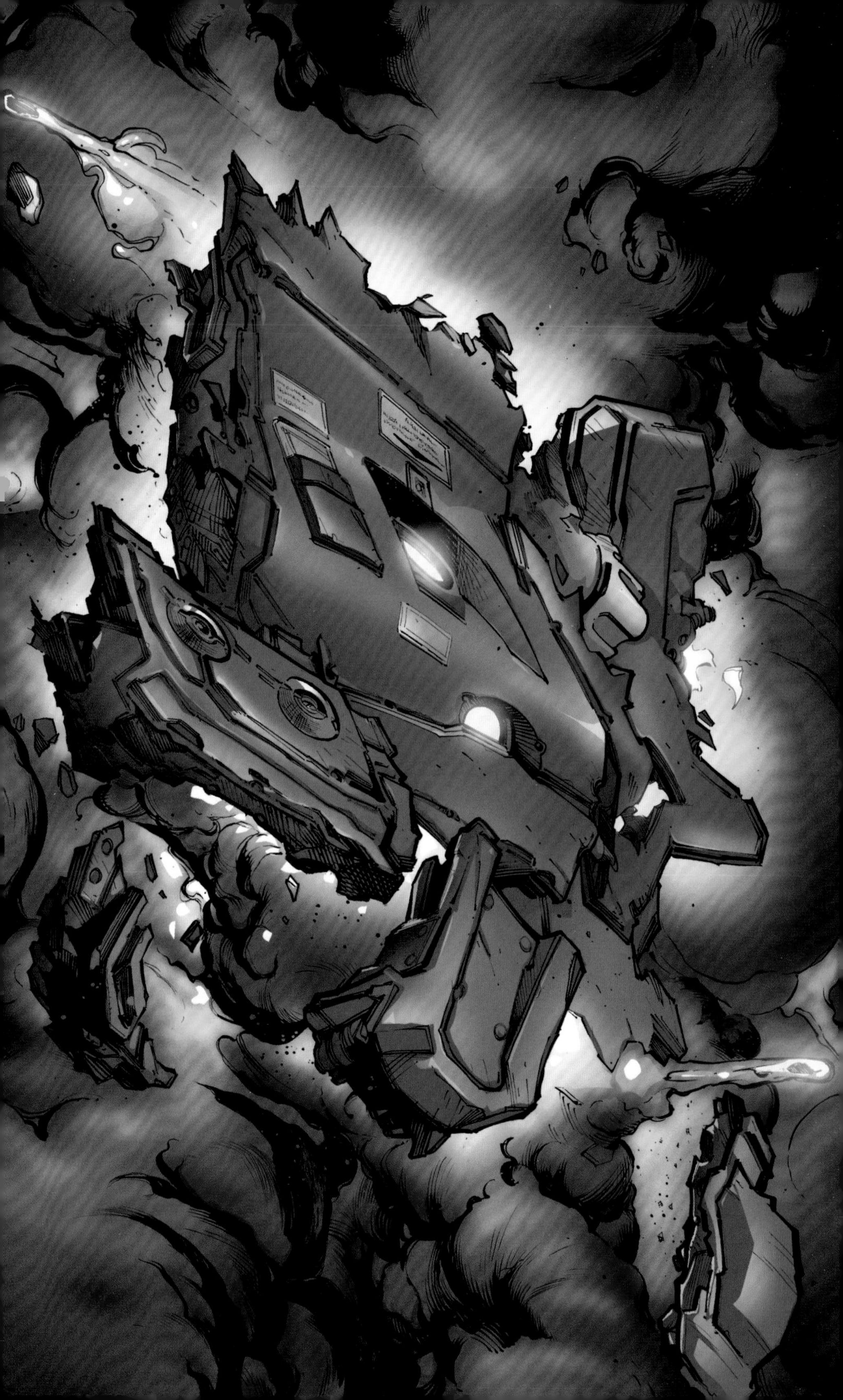

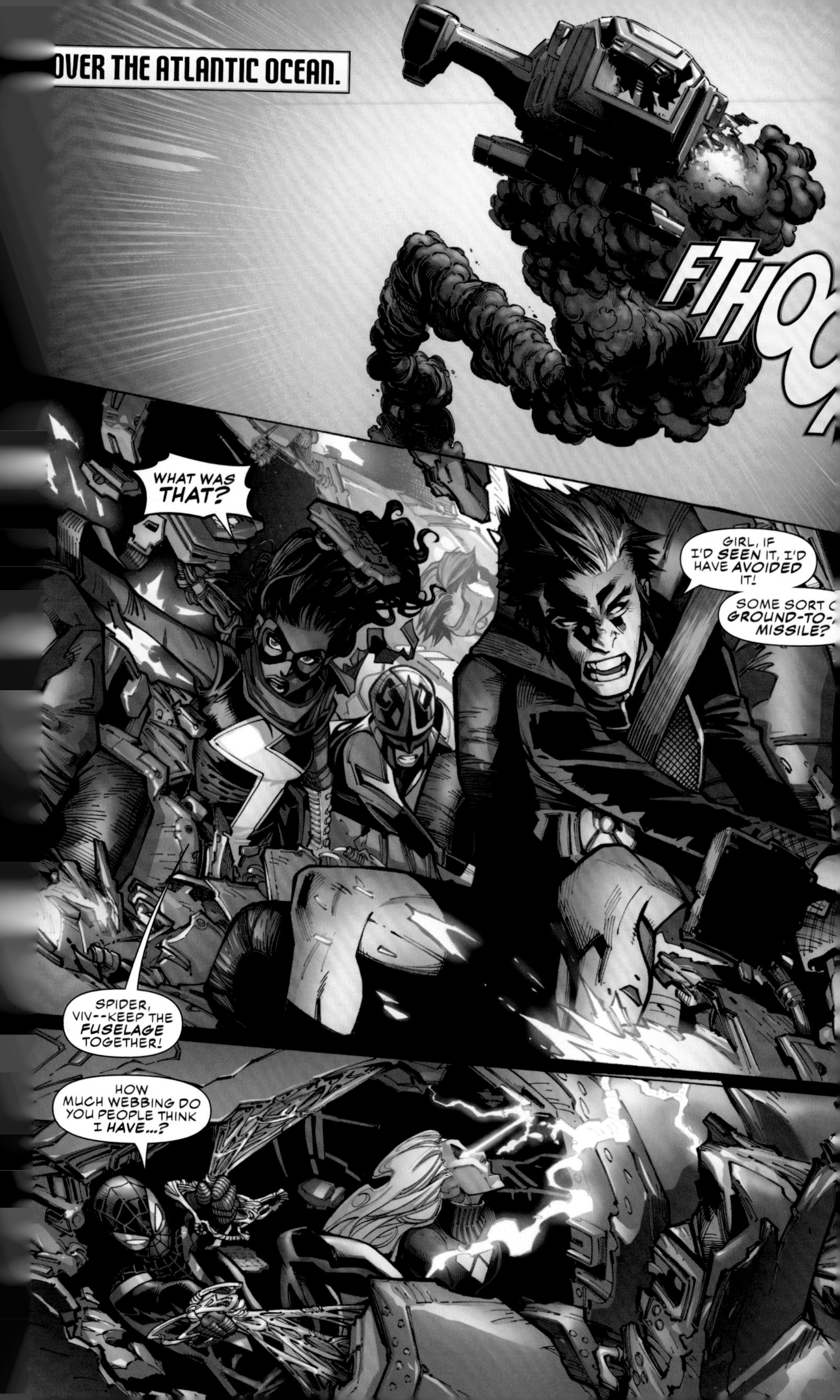
OVER THE ATLANTIC OCEAN.
FTHOO
WHAT WAS THAT?
GIRL, IF I'D SEEN IT, I'D HAVE AVOIDED IT!
SOME SORT O GROUND-TO- MISSILE?
SPIDER, VIV--KEEP THE FUSELAGE TOGETHER!
HOW MUCH WEBBING DO YOU PEOPLE THINK I HAVE...?

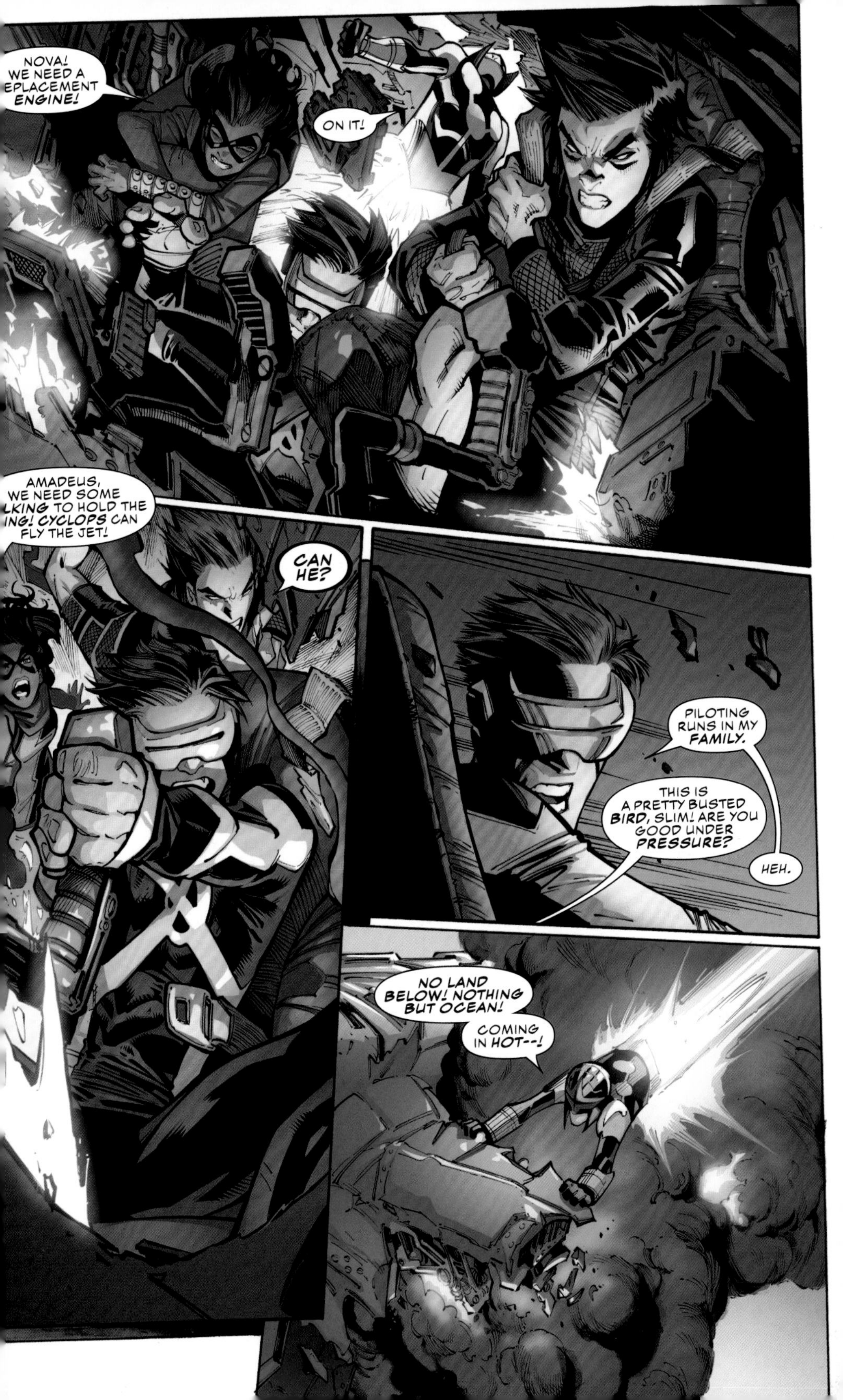
NOVA! WE NEED A EPLACEMENT ENGINE!
ON IT!
AMADEUS, WE NEED SOME LKING TO HOLD THE ING! CYCLOPS CAN FLY THE JET!
CAN HE?
PILOTING RUNS IN MY FAMILY.
THIS IS A PRETTY BUSTED BIRD, SLIM! ARE YOU GOOD UNDER PRESSURE?
HEH.
NO LAND BELOW! NOTHING BUT OCEAN!
COMING IN HOT--!

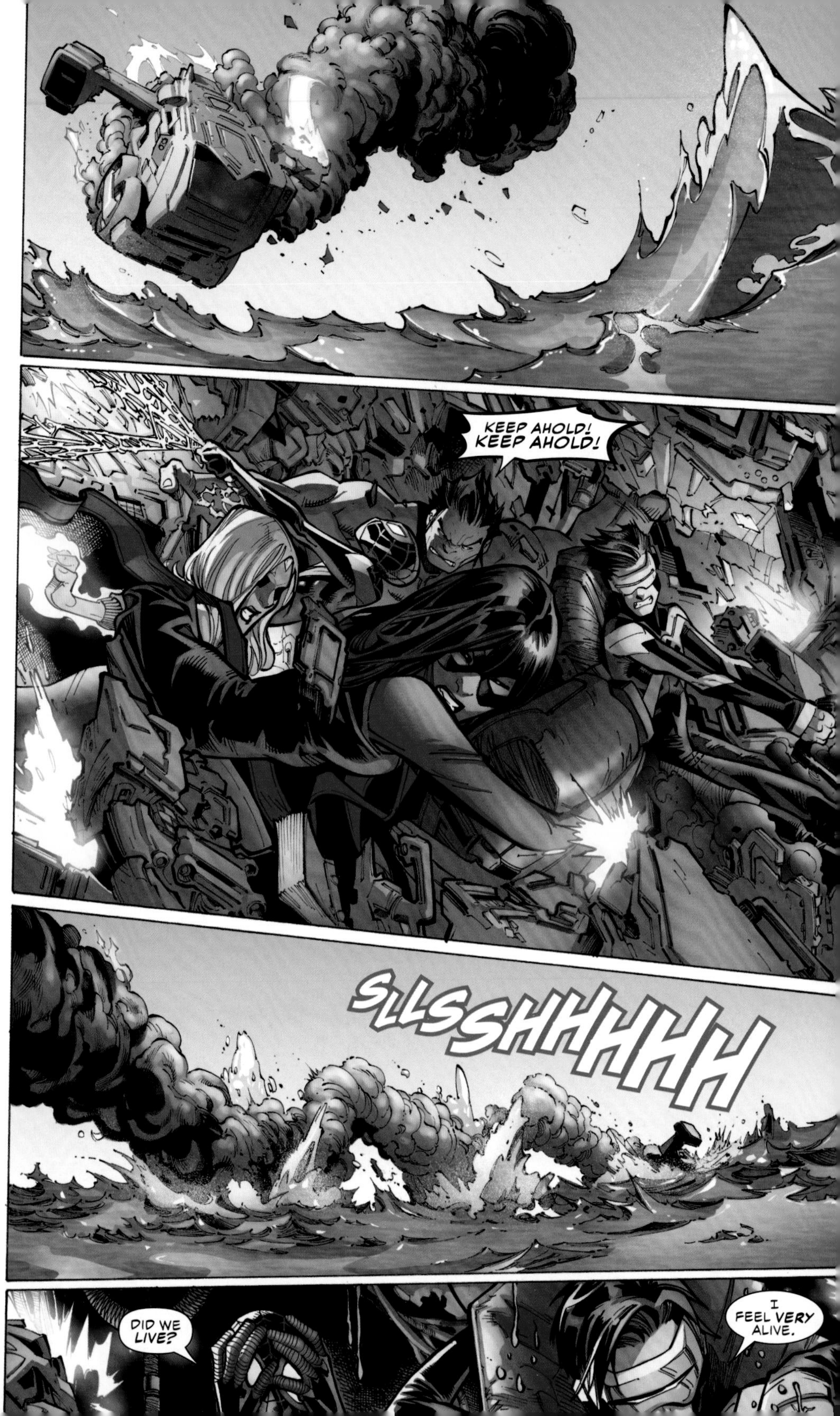
KEEP AHOLD!
KEEP AHOLD!
SLLSSHHHHHH
DID WE LIVE?
I FEEL VERY ALIVE.

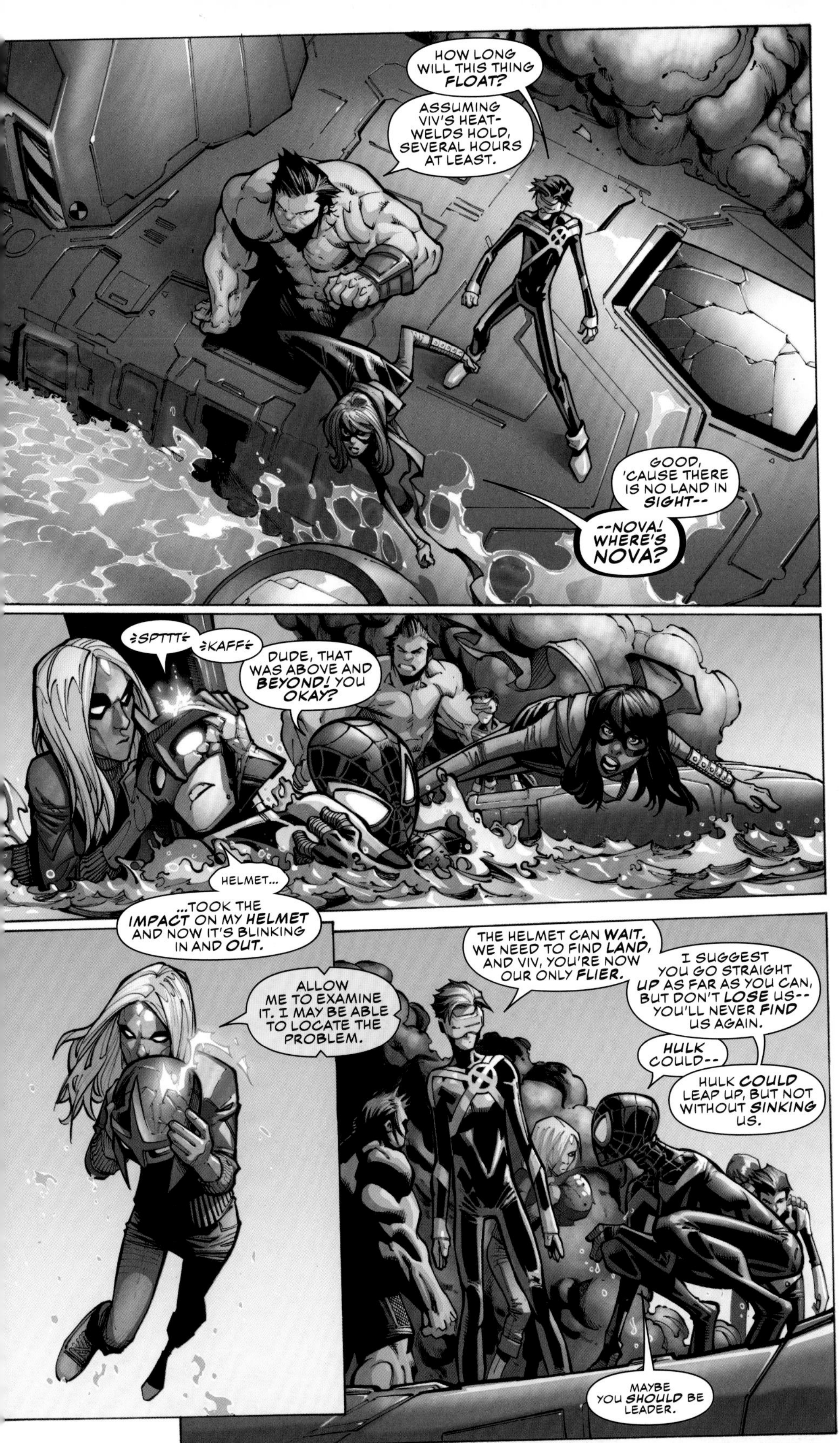
HOW LONG WILL THIS THING FLOAT?
ASSUMING VIV'S HEAT-WELDS HOLD, SEVERAL HOURS AT LEAST.
GOOD, 'CAUSE THERE IS NO LAND IN SIGHT--
--NOVA! WHERE'S NOVA?
SPTTT
KAFF
DUDE, THAT WAS ABOVE AND BEYOND! YOU OKAY?
HELMET...
...TOOK THE IMPACT ON MY HELMET AND NOW IT'S BLINKING IN AND OUT.
ALLOW ME TO EXAMINE IT. I MAY BE ABLE TO LOCATE THE PROBLEM.
THE HELMET CAN WAIT. WE NEED TO FIND LAND, AND VIV, YOU'RE NOW OUR ONLY FLIER.
I SUGGEST YOU GO STRAIGHT UP AS FAR AS YOU CAN, BUT DON'T LOSE US--YOU'LL NEVER FIND US AGAIN.
HULK COULD--
HULK COULD LEAP UP, BUT NOT WITHOUT SINKING US.
MAYBE YOU SHOULD BE LEADER.

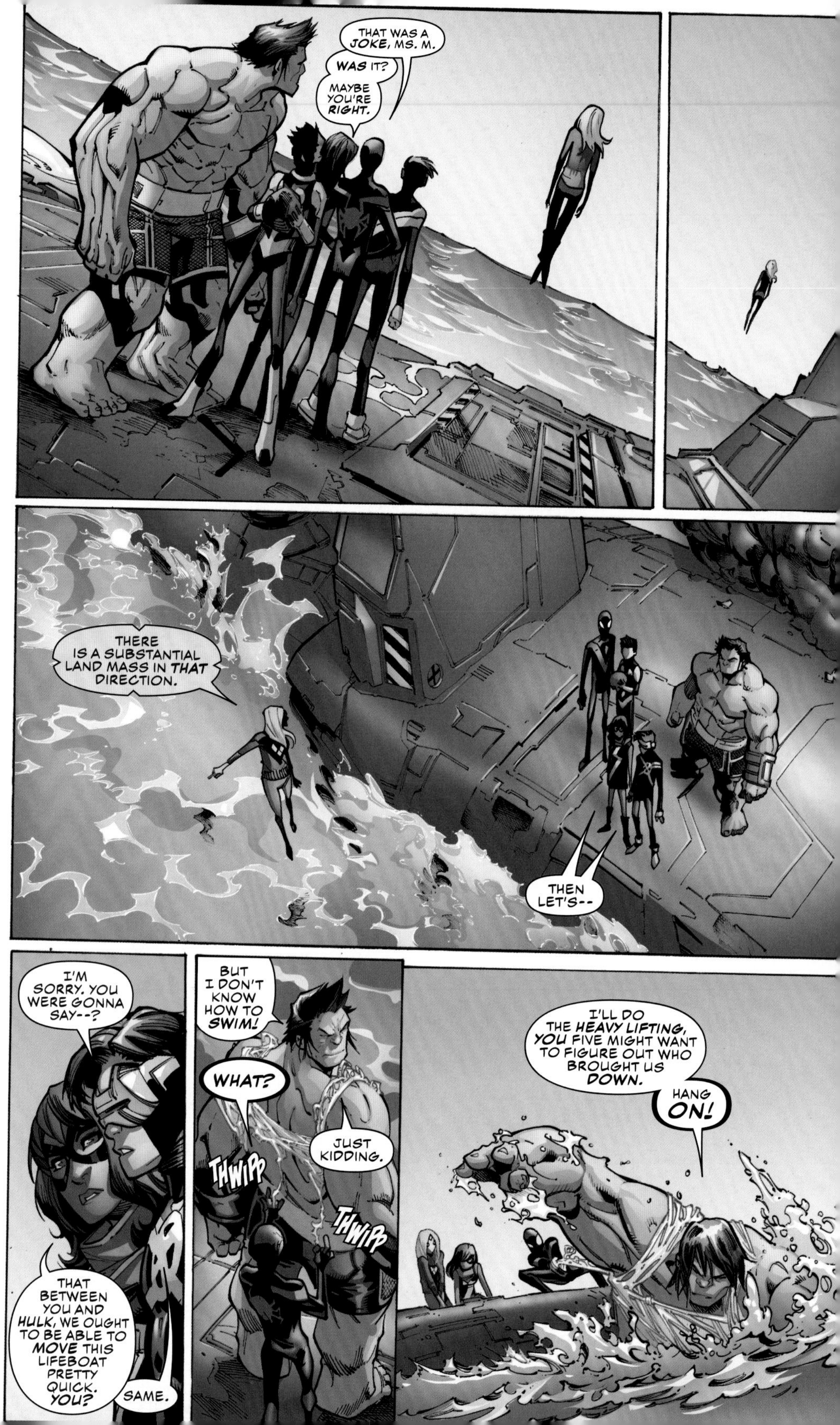

THAT WAS A JOKE, MS. M.
WAS IT?
MAYBE YOU'RE RIGHT.
THERE IS A SUBSTANTIAL LAND MASS IN THAT DIRECTION.
THEN LET'S--
I'M SORRY. YOU WERE GONNA SAY--?
THAT BETWEEN YOU AND HULK, WE OUGHT TO BE ABLE TO MOVE THIS LIFEBOAT PRETTY QUICK. YOU?
SAME.
BUT I DON'T KNOW HOW TO SWIM!
WHAT?
JUST KIDDING.
THWIPP
THWIPP
I'LL DO THE HEAVY LIFTING, YOU FIVE MIGHT WANT TO FIGURE OUT WHO BROUGHT US DOWN.
HANG ON!

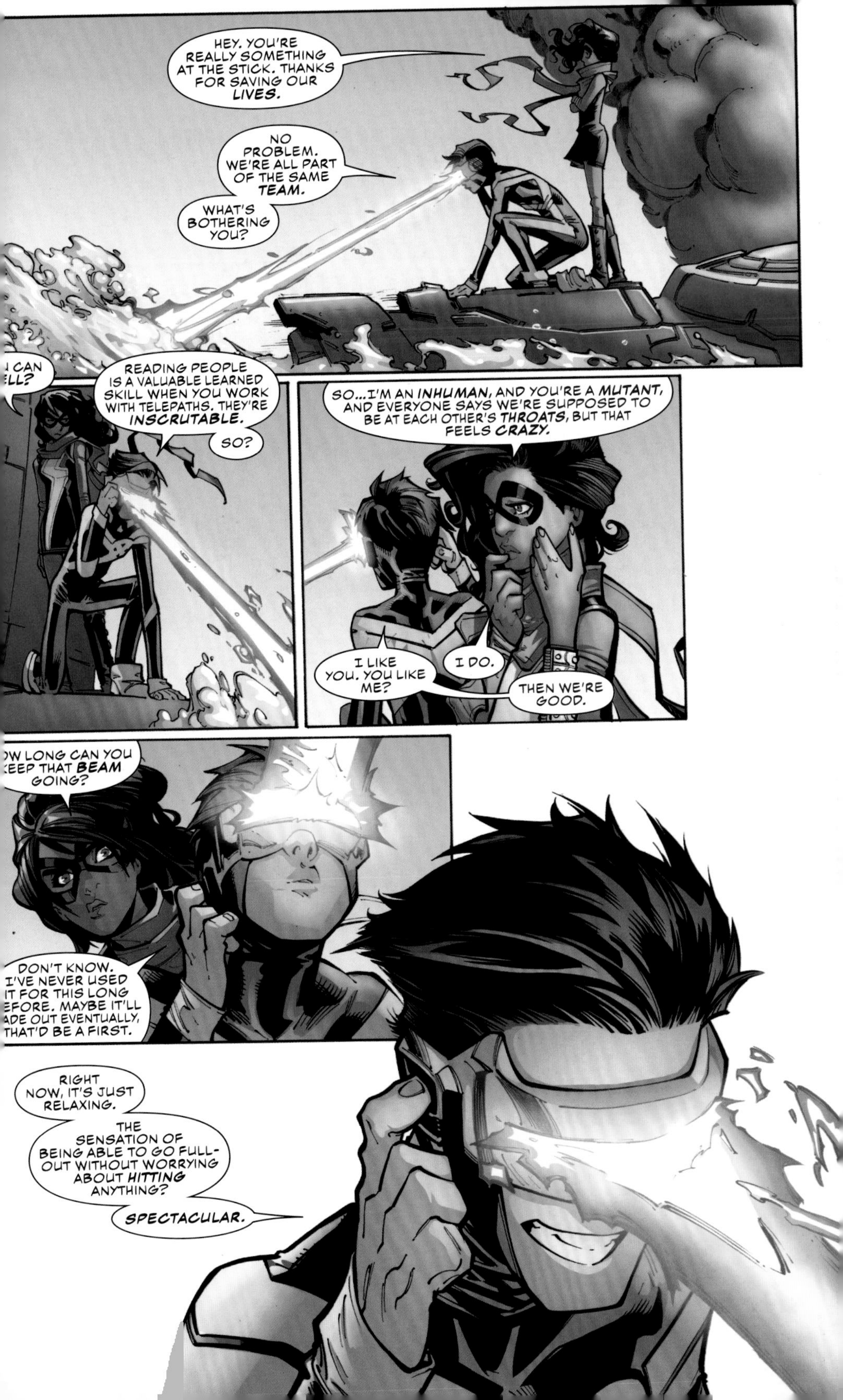
HEY. YOU'RE REALLY SOMETHING AT THE STICK. THANKS FOR SAVING OUR LIVES.
NO PROBLEM. WE'RE ALL PART OF THE SAME TEAM.
WHAT'S BOTHERING YOU?
READING PEOPLE IS A VALUABLE LEARNED SKILL WHEN YOU WORK WITH TELEPATHS. THEY'RE INSCRUTABLE.
SO?
SO...I'M AN INHUMAN, AND YOU'RE A MUTANT, AND EVERYONE SAYS WE'RE SUPPOSED TO BE AT EACH OTHER'S THROATS, BUT THAT FEELS CRAZY.
I LIKE YOU. YOU LIKE ME?
I DO.
THEN WE'RE GOOD.
KEEP THAT BEAM GOING?
DON'T KNOW. I'VE NEVER USED IT FOR THIS LONG
RIGHT NOW, IT'S JUST RELAXING.
THE SENSATION OF BEING ABLE TO GO FULL-OUT WITHOUT WORRYING ABOUT HITTING ANYTHING?
SPECTACULAR.

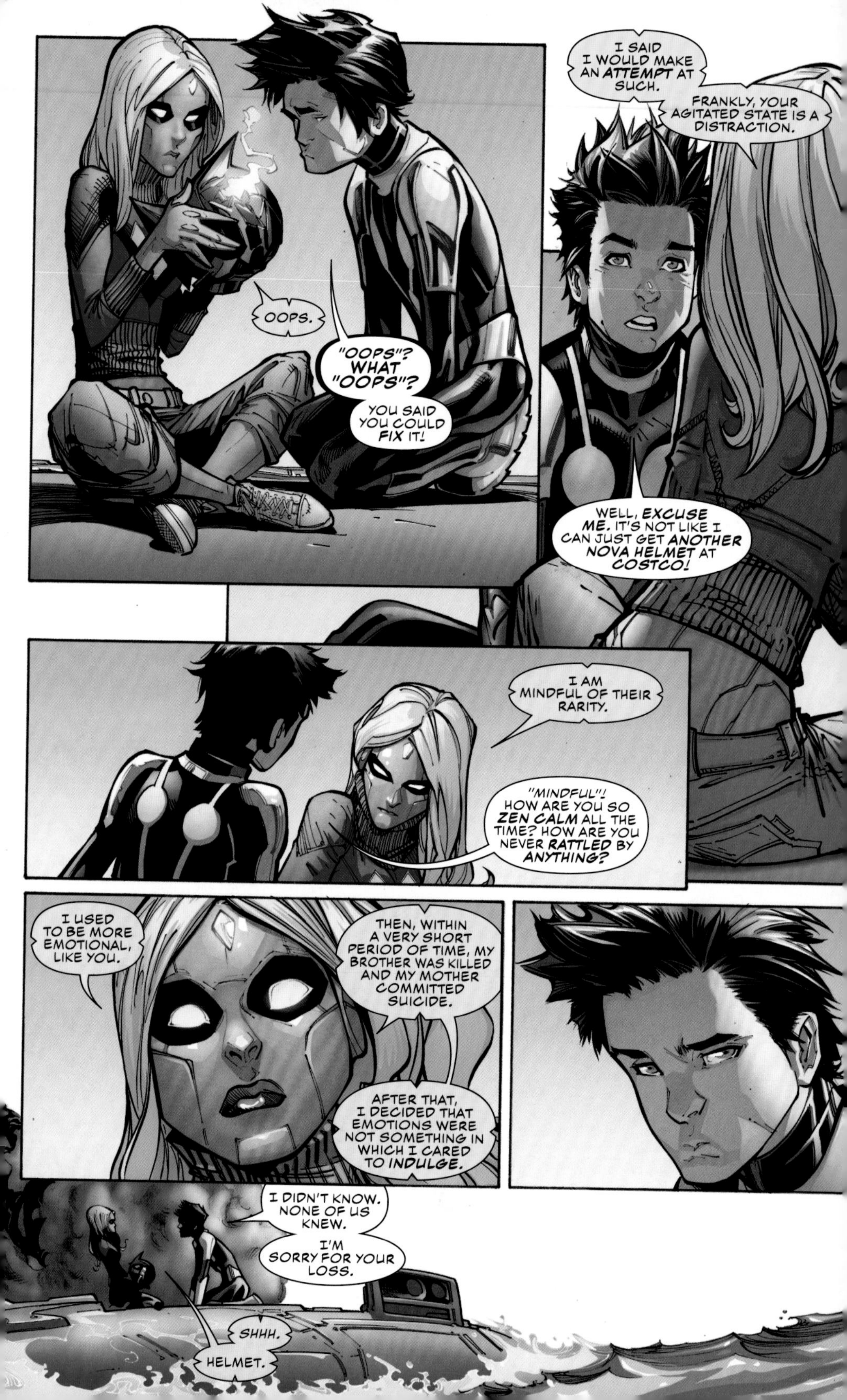
OOPS.
"OOPS"? WHAT "OOPS"?
YOU SAID YOU COULD FIX IT!
I SAID I WOULD MAKE AN ATTEMPT AT SUCH.
FRANKLY, YOUR AGITATED STATE IS A DISTRACTION.
WELL, EXCUSE ME. IT'S NOT LIKE I CAN JUST GET ANOTHER NOVA HELMET AT COSTCO!
I AM MINDFUL OF THEIR RARITY.
"MINDFUL"! HOW ARE YOU SO ZEN CALM ALL THE TIME? HOW ARE YOU NEVER RATTLED BY ANYTHING?
I USED TO BE MORE EMOTIONAL, LIKE YOU.
THEN, WITHIN A VERY SHORT PERIOD OF TIME, MY BROTHER WAS KILLED AND MY MOTHER COMMITTED SUICIDE.
AFTER THAT, I DECIDED THAT EMOTIONS WERE NOT SOMETHING IN WHICH I CARED TO INDULGE.
I DIDN'T KNOW. NONE OF US KNEW.
I'M SORRY FOR YOUR LOSS.
SHHH.
HELMET.

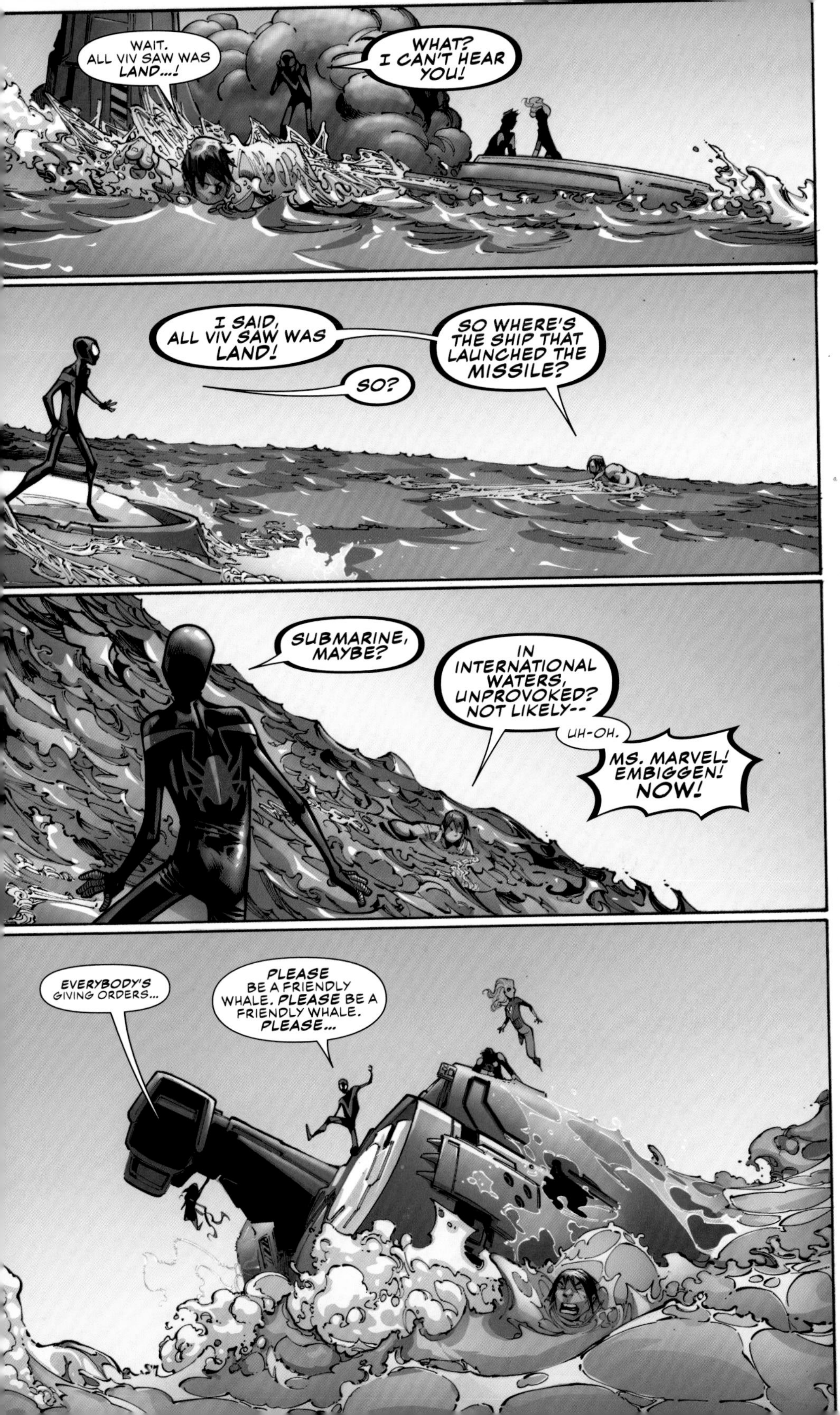

WAIT. ALL VIV SAW WAS LAND...!
WHAT? I CAN'T HEAR YOU!
I SAID, ALL VIV SAW WAS LAND!
SO?
SO WHERE'S THE SHIP THAT LAUNCHED THE MISSILE?
SUBMARINE, MAYBE?
IN INTERNATIONAL WATERS, UNPROVOKED? NOT LIKELY--
UH-OH.
MS. MARVEL! EMBIGGEN! NOW!
EVERYBODY'S GIVING ORDERS...
PLEASE BE A FRIENDLY WHALE. PLEASE BE A FRIENDLY WHALE. PLEASE...

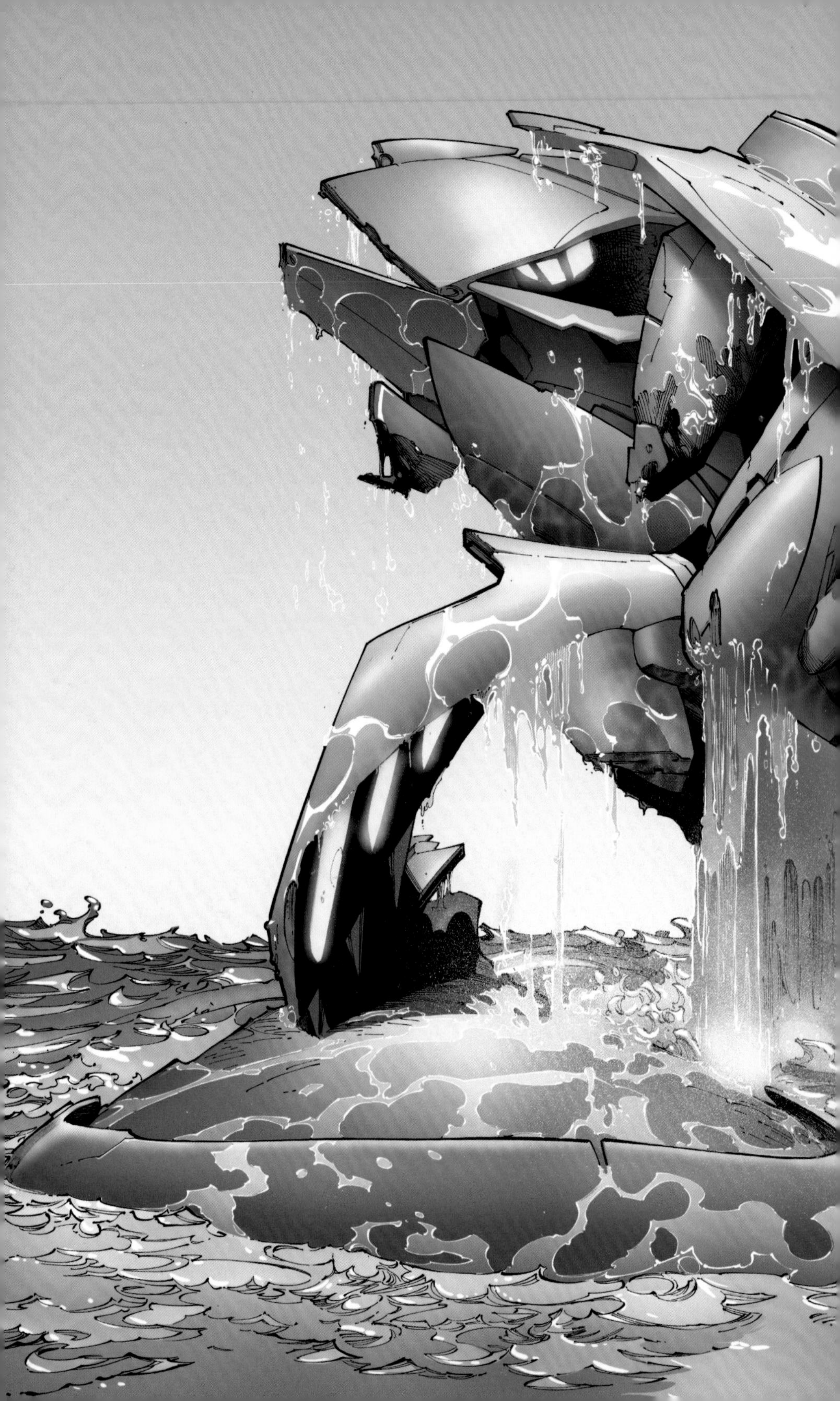

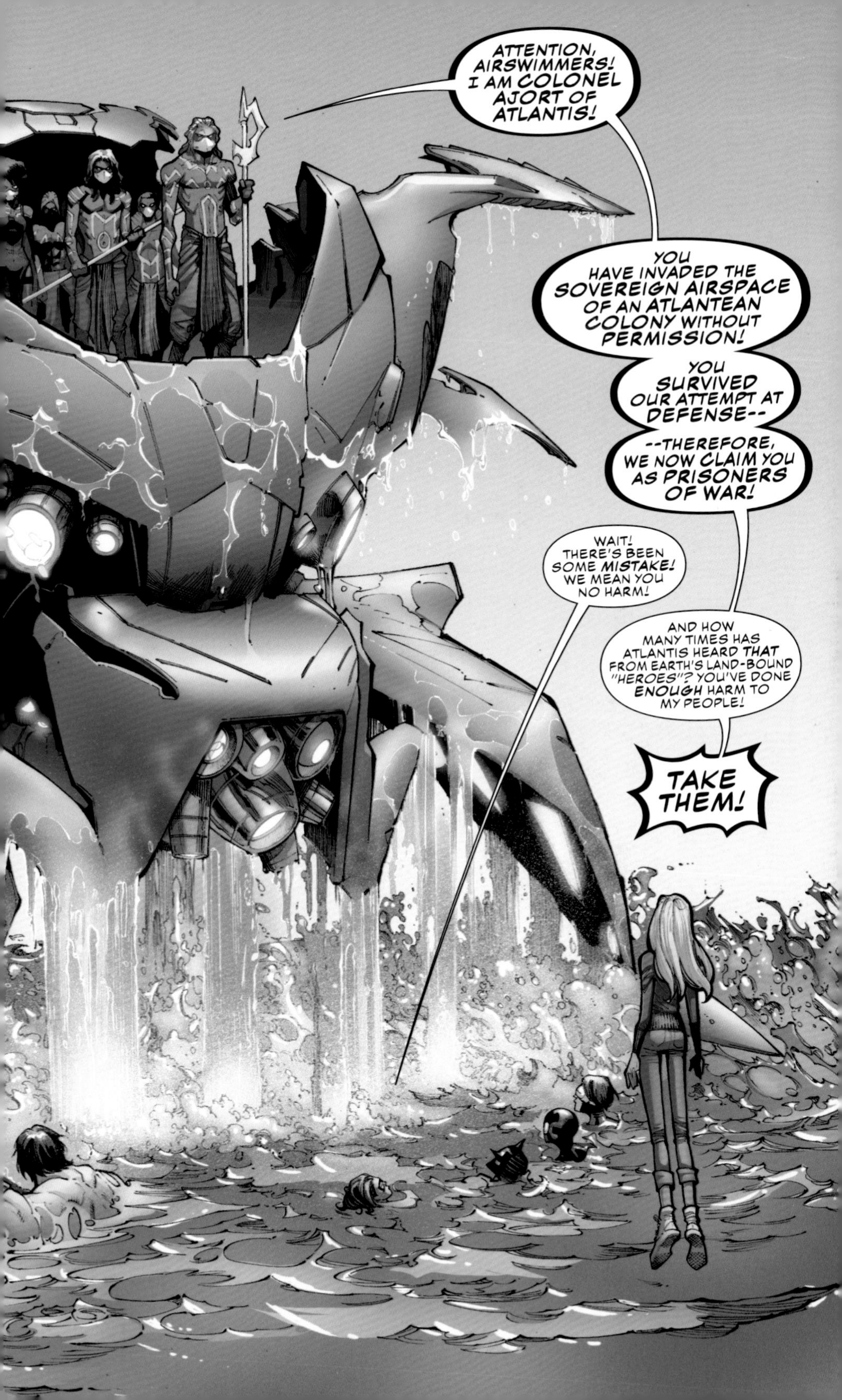
ATTENTION, AIRSWIMMERS! I AM COLONEL AJORT OF ATLANTIS!
YOU HAVE INVADED THE SOVEREIGN AIRSPACE OF AN ATLANTEAN COLONY WITHOUT PERMISSION!
YOU SURVIVED OUR ATTEMPT AT DEFENSE--
--THEREFORE, WE NOW CLAIM YOU AS PRISONERS OF WAR!
WAIT! THERE'S BEEN SOME MISTAKE! WE MEAN YOU NO HARM!
AND HOW MANY TIMES HAS ATLANTIS HEARD THAT FROM EARTH'S LAND-BOUND "HEROES"? YOU'VE DONE ENOUGH HARM TO MY PEOPLE!
TAKE THEM!

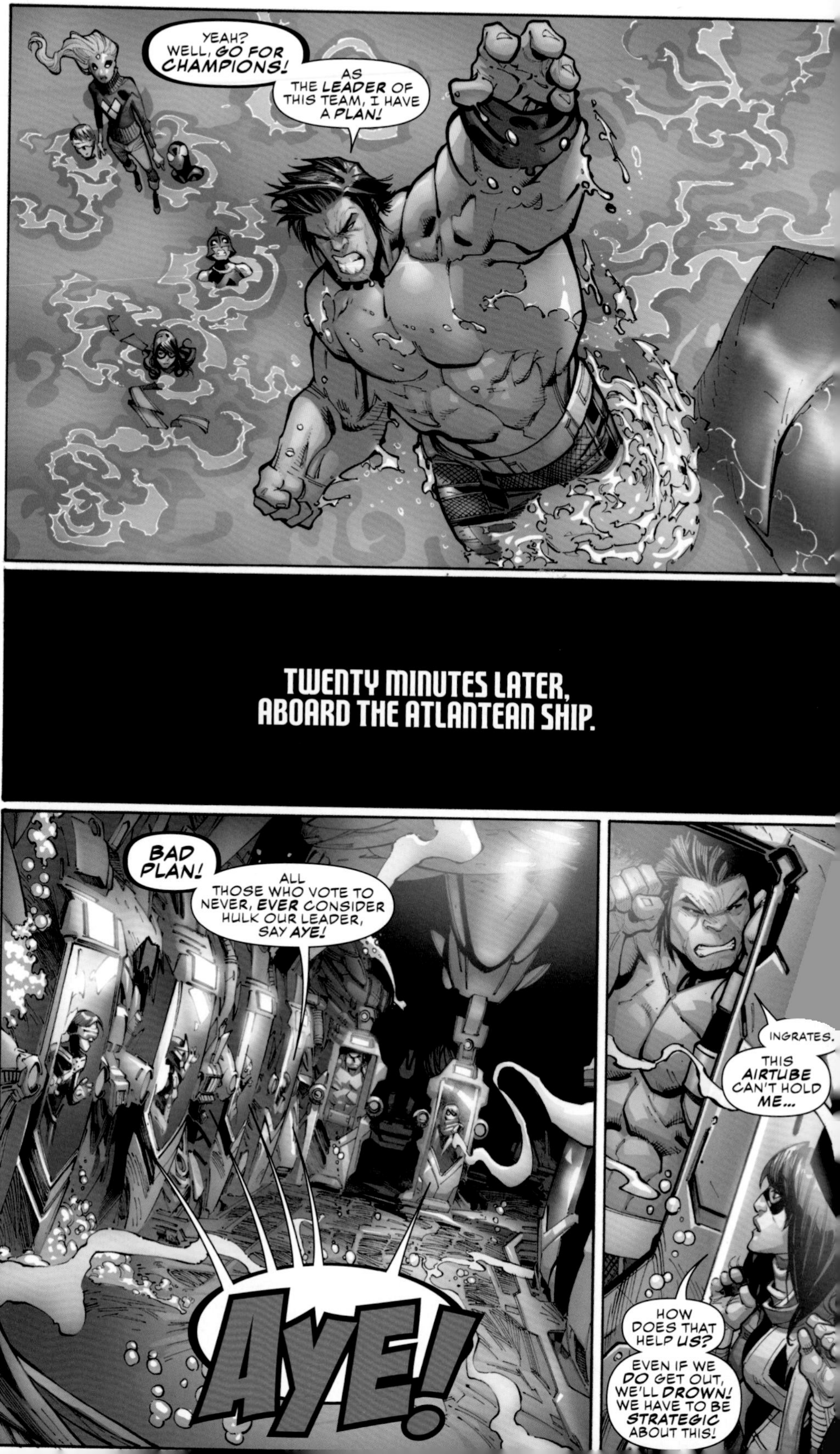
YEAH? WELL, GO FOR CHAMPIONS!
AS THE LEADER OF THIS TEAM, I HAVE A PLAN!
TWENTY MINUTES LATER, ABOARD THE ATLANTEAN SHIP.
BAD PLAN!
ALL THOSE WHO VOTE TO NEVER, EVER CONSIDER HULK OUR LEADER, SAY AYE!
AYE!
INGRATES.
THIS AIRTUBE CAN'T HOLD ME...
HOW DOES THAT HELP US?
EVEN IF WE DO GET OUT, WE'LL DROWN! WE HAVE TO BE STRATEGIC ABOUT THIS!

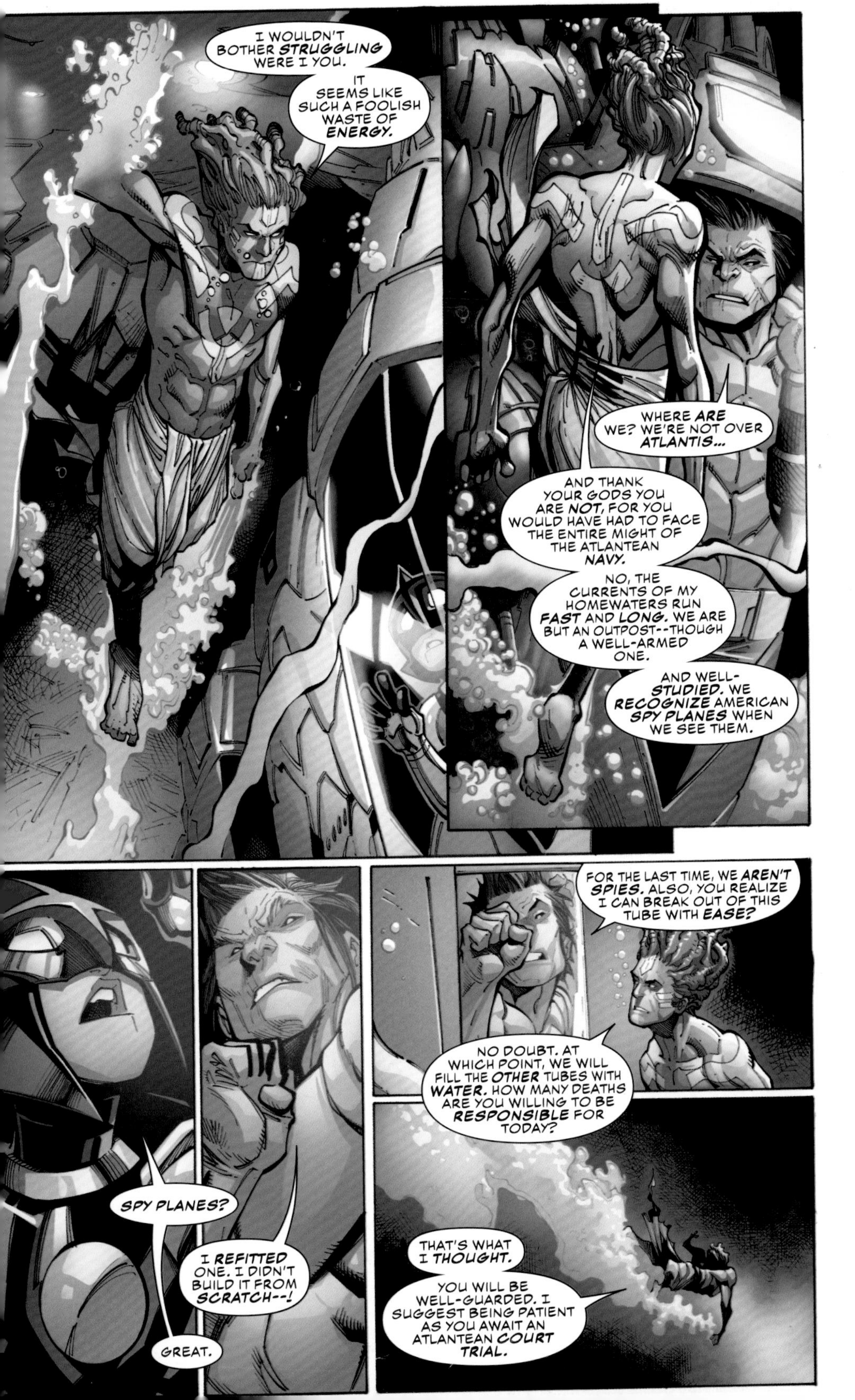
I WOULDN'T BOTHER STRUGGLING WERE I YOU.
IT SEEMS LIKE SUCH A FOOLISH WASTE OF ENERGY.
WHERE ARE WE? WE'RE NOT OVER ATLANTIS...
AND THANK YOUR GODS YOU ARE NOT, FOR YOU WOULD HAVE HAD TO FACE THE ENTIRE MIGHT OF THE ATLANTEAN NAVY.
NO, THE CURRENTS OF MY HOMEWATERS RUN FAST AND LONG. WE ARE BUT AN OUTPOST--THOUGH A WELL-ARMED ONE.
AND WELL-STUDIED. WE RECOGNIZE AMERICAN SPY PLANES WHEN WE SEE THEM.
SPY PLANES?
I REFITTED ONE. I DIDN'T BUILD IT FROM SCRATCH--!
GREAT.
FOR THE LAST TIME, WE AREN'T SPIES. ALSO, YOU REALIZE I CAN BREAK OUT OF THIS TUBE WITH EASE?
NO DOUBT. AT WHICH POINT, WE WILL FILL THE OTHER TUBES WITH WATER. HOW MANY DEATHS ARE YOU WILLING TO BE RESPONSIBLE FOR TODAY?
THAT'S WHAT I THOUGHT.
YOU WILL BE WELL-GUARDED. I SUGGEST BEING PATIENT AS YOU AWAIT AN ATLANTEAN COURT TRIAL.

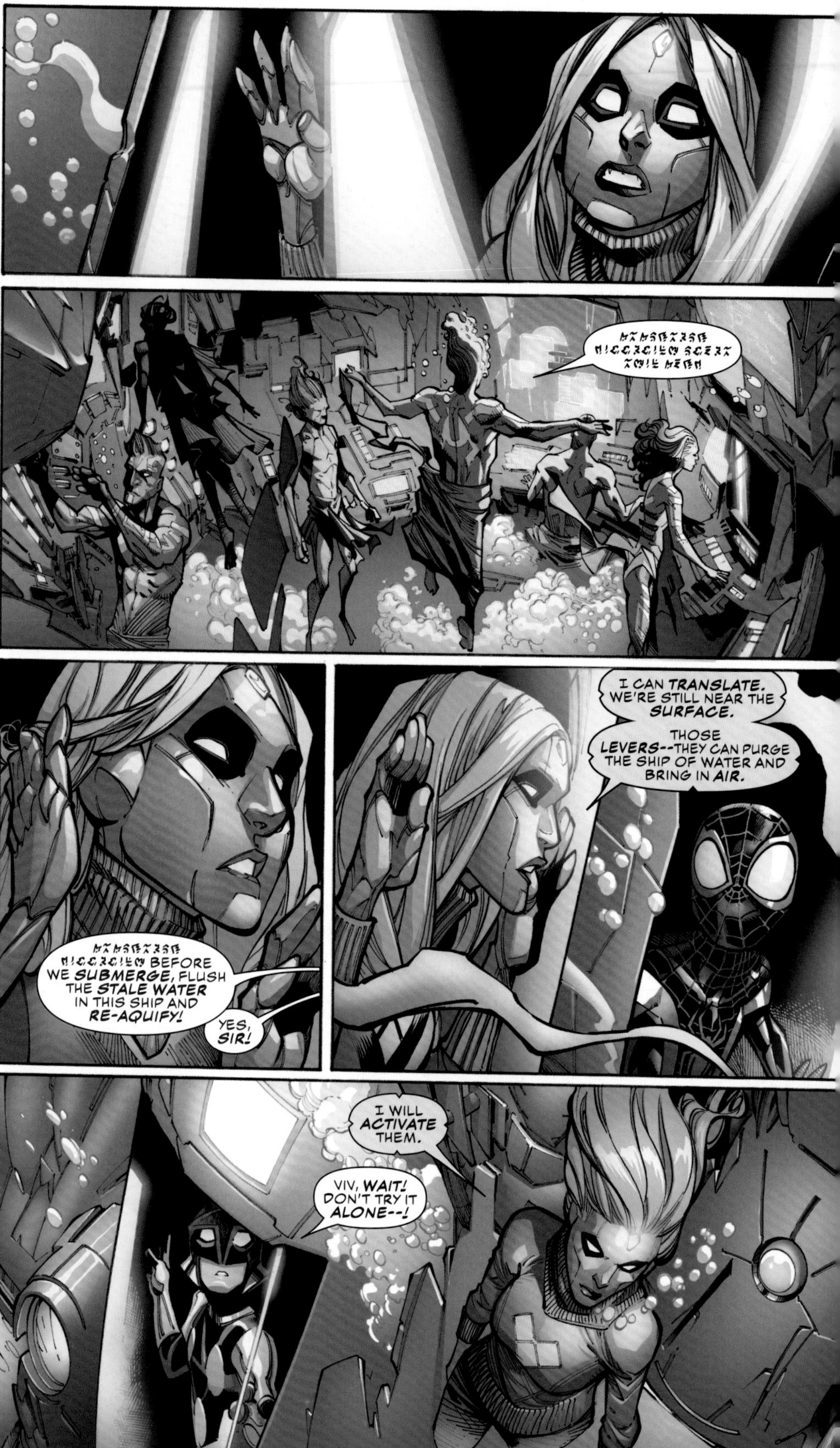
I CAN TRANSLATE. WE'RE STILL NEAR THE SURFACE.
THOSE LEVERS--THEY CAN PURGE THE SHIP OF WATER AND BRING IN AIR.
BEFORE WE SUBMERGE, FLUSH THE STALE WATER IN THIS SHIP AND RE-AQUIFY!
YES, SIR!
I WILL ACTIVATE THEM.
VIV, WAIT! DON'T TRY IT ALONE--!

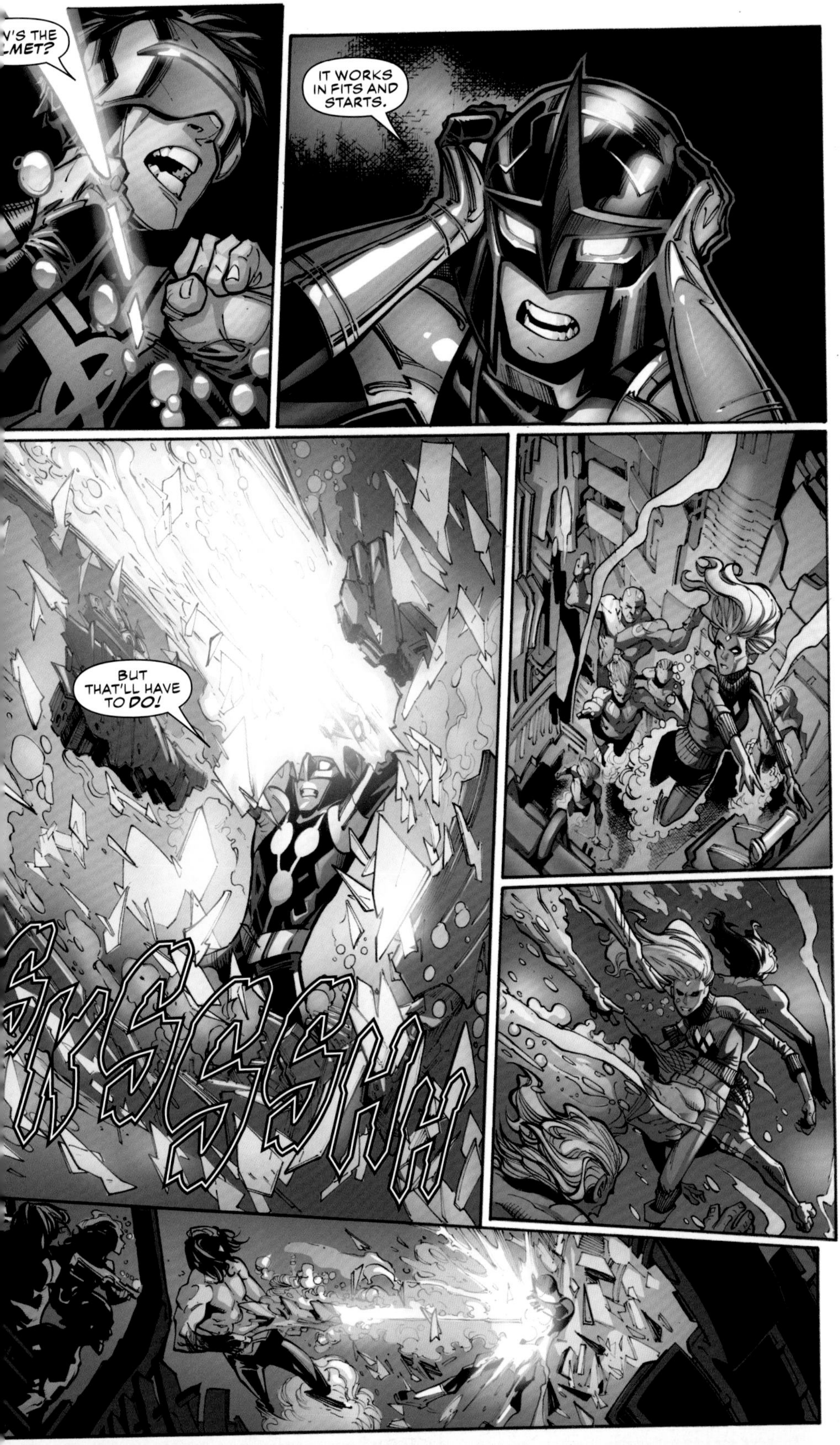

'S THE
MET?
IT WORKS IN FITS AND STARTS.
BUT THAT'LL HAVE TO DO!
SHSSSHH

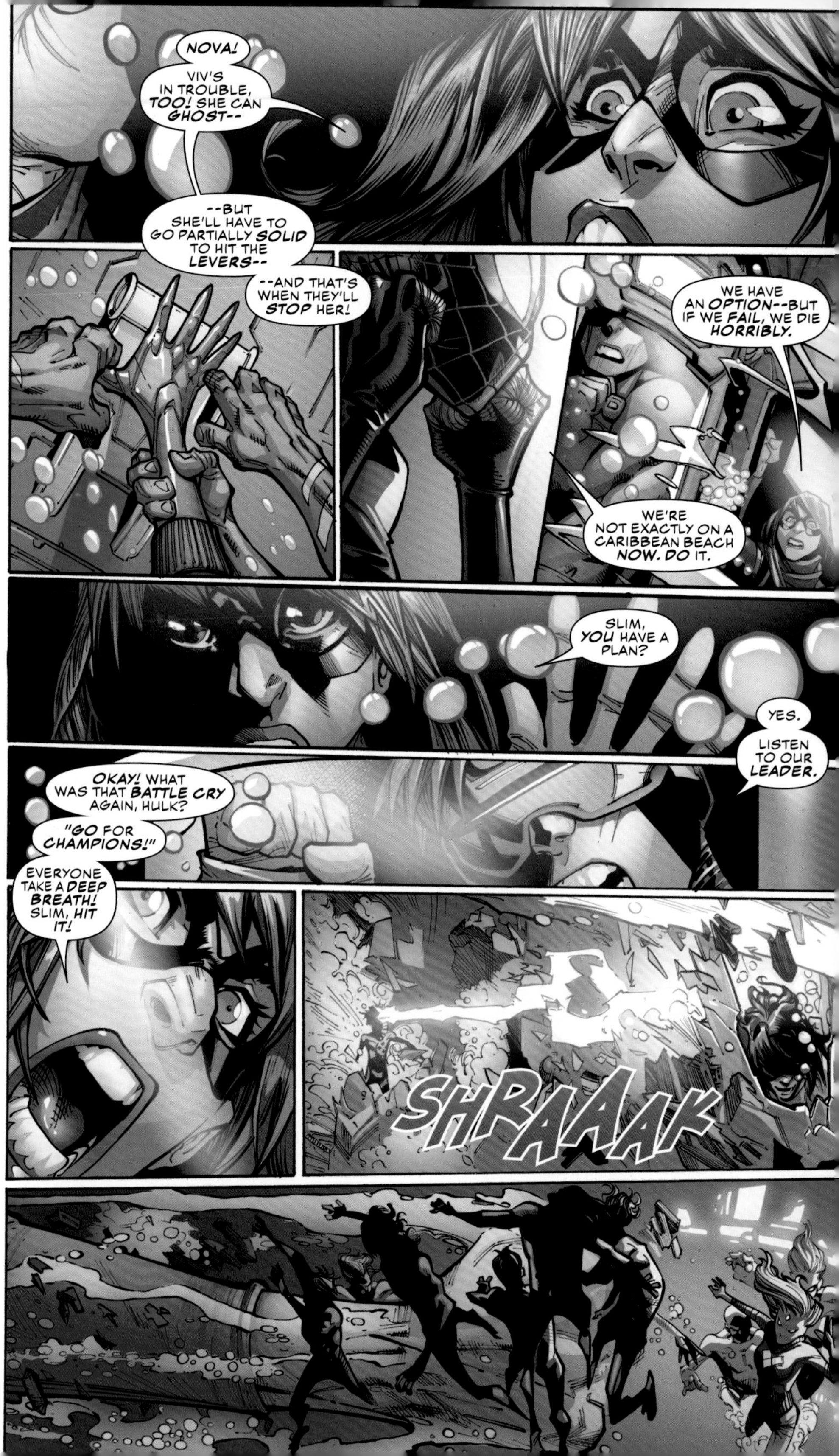
NOVA!
VIV'S IN TROUBLE, TOO! SHE CAN GHOST--
--BUT SHE'LL HAVE TO GO PARTIALLY SOLID TO HIT THE LEVERS--
--AND THAT'S WHEN THEY'LL STOP HER!
WE HAVE AN OPTION--BUT IF WE FAIL, WE DIE HORRIBLY.
WE'RE NOT EXACTLY ON A CARIBBEAN BEACH NOW. DO IT.
SLIM, YOU HAVE A PLAN?
YES.
LISTEN TO OUR LEADER.
OKAY! WHAT WAS THAT BATTLE CRY AGAIN, HULK?
"GO FOR CHAMPIONS!"
EVERYONE TAKE A DEEP BREATH! SLIM, HIT IT!
SHRAAAK

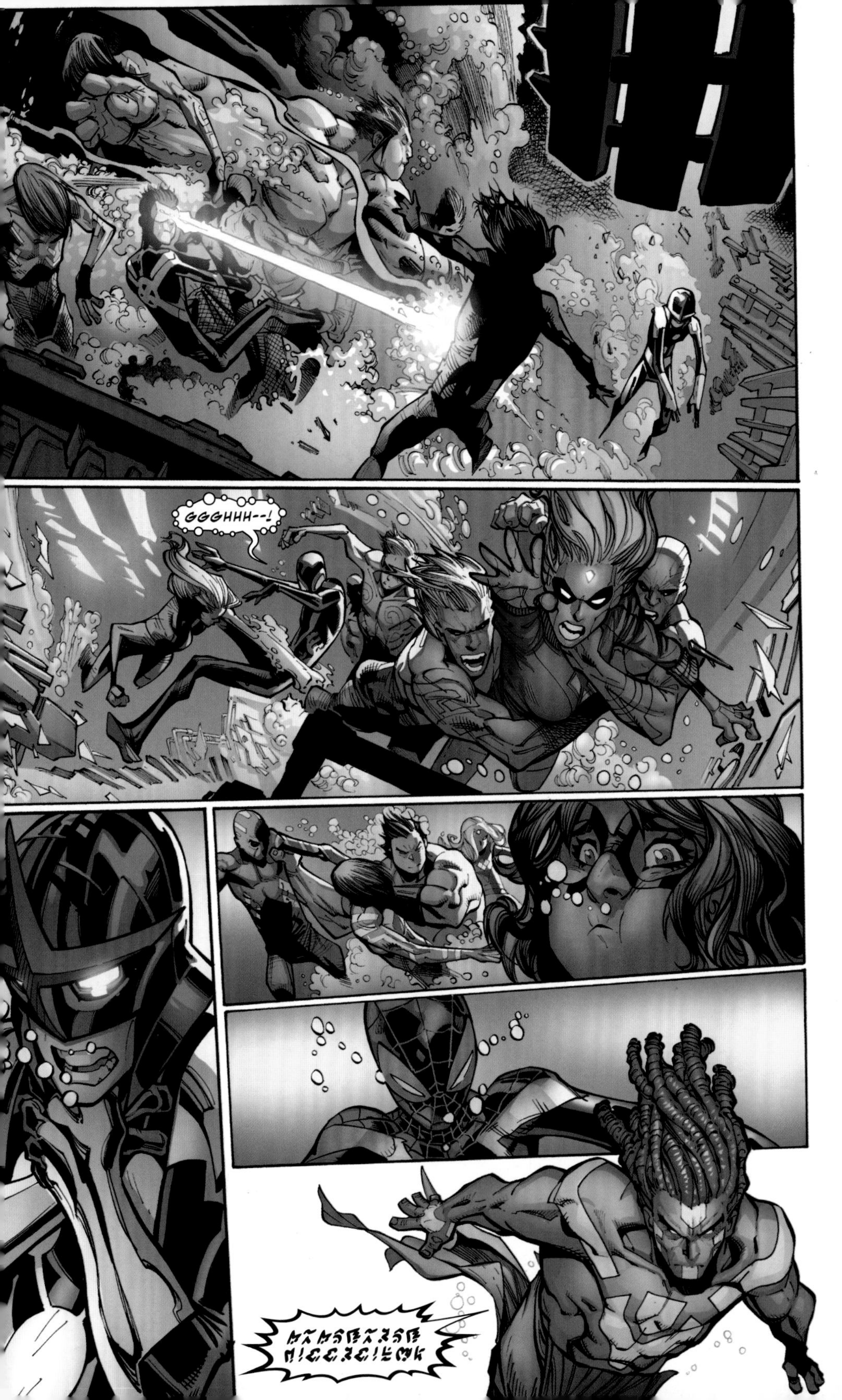
GGGHHH--!

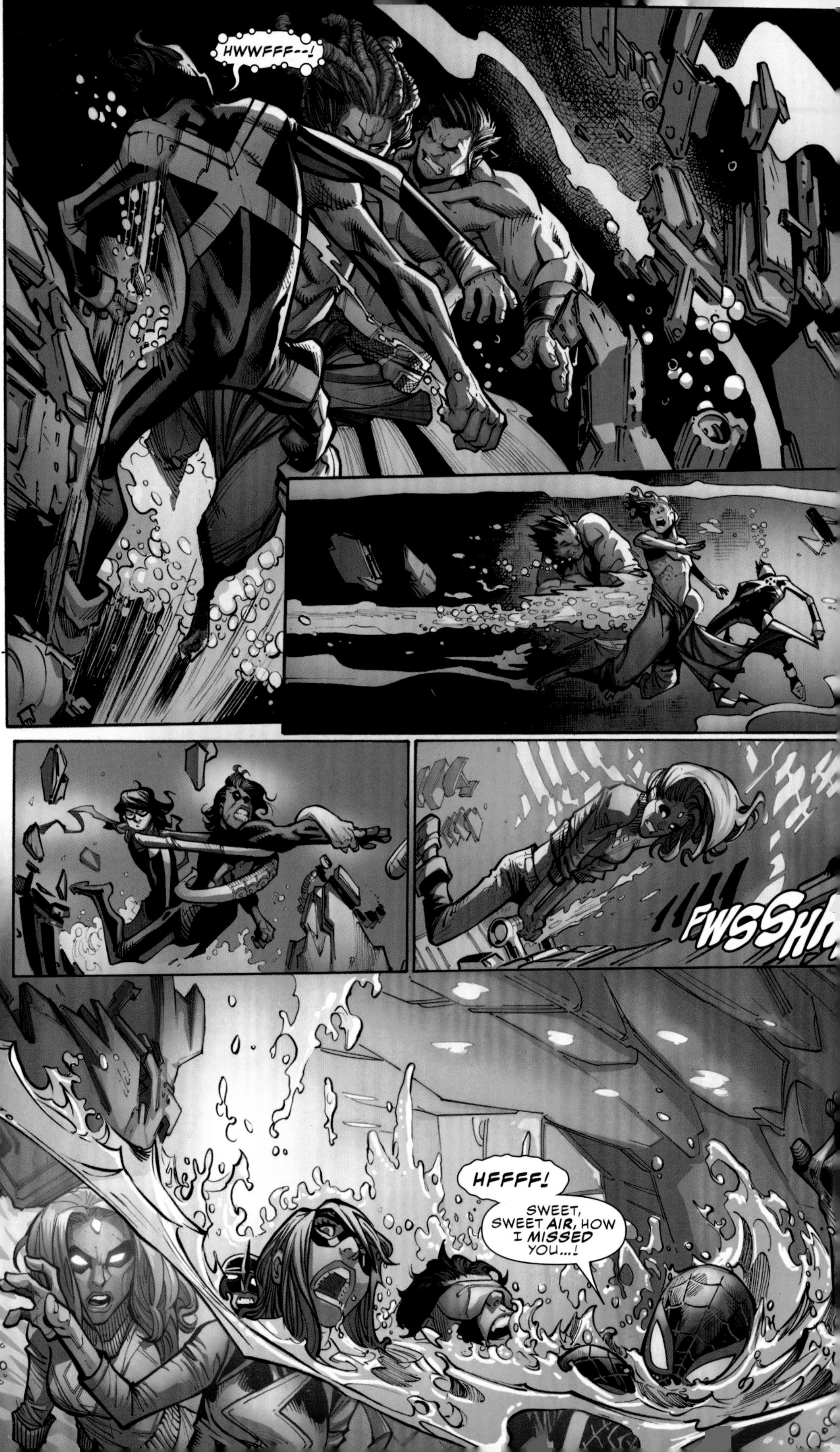
HWWFFF--!
FWSSHH
HFFFF!
SWEET, SWEET AIR, HOW I MISSED YOU...!

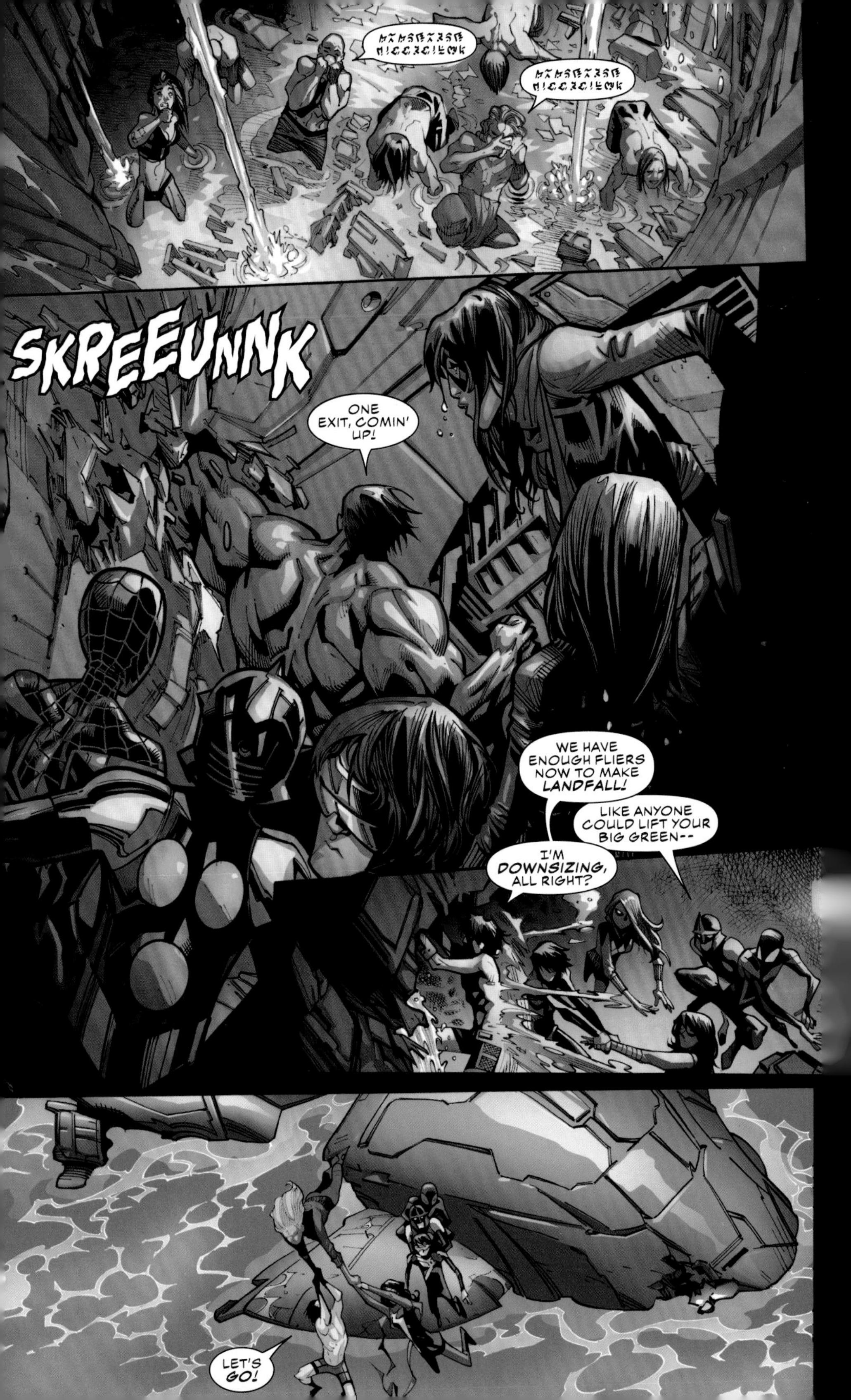
SKREEUNNK
ONE EXIT, COMIN' UP!
WE HAVE ENOUGH FLIERS NOW TO MAKE LANDFALL!
LIKE ANYONE COULD LIFT YOUR BIG GREEN--
I'M DOWNSIZING, ALL RIGHT?
LET'S GO!

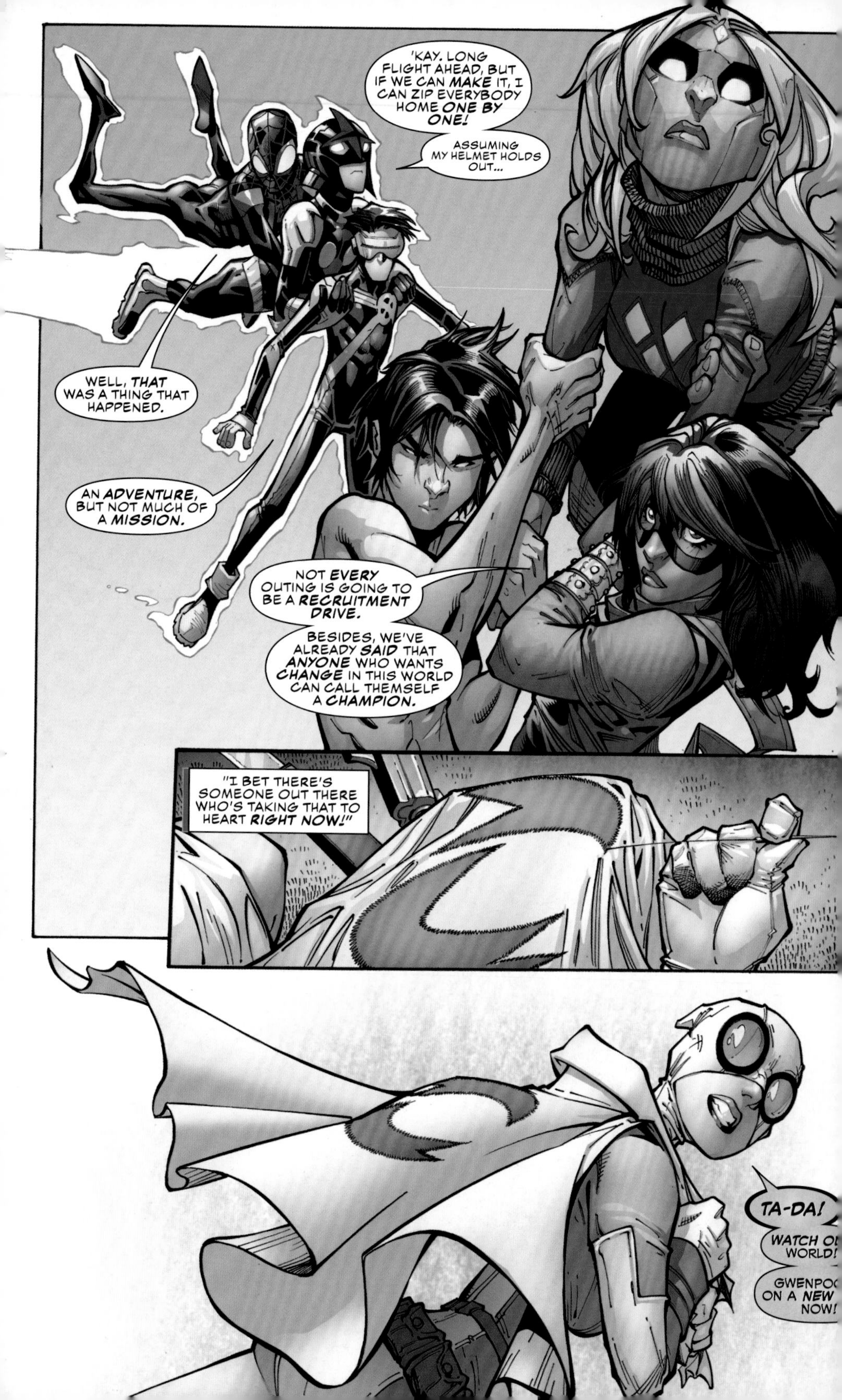
'KAY. LONG FLIGHT AHEAD, BUT IF WE CAN MAKE IT, I CAN ZIP EVERYBODY HOME ONE BY ONE!
ASSUMING MY HELMET HOLDS OUT...
WELL, THAT WAS A THING THAT HAPPENED.
AN ADVENTURE, BUT NOT MUCH OF A MISSION.
NOT EVERY OUTING IS GOING TO BE A RECRUITMENT DRIVE.
BESIDES, WE'VE ALREADY SAID THAT ANYONE WHO WANTS CHANGE IN THIS WORLD CAN CALL THEMSELF A CHAMPION.
"I BET THERE'S SOMEONE OUT THERE WHO'S TAKING THAT TO HEART RIGHT NOW!"
TA-DA!

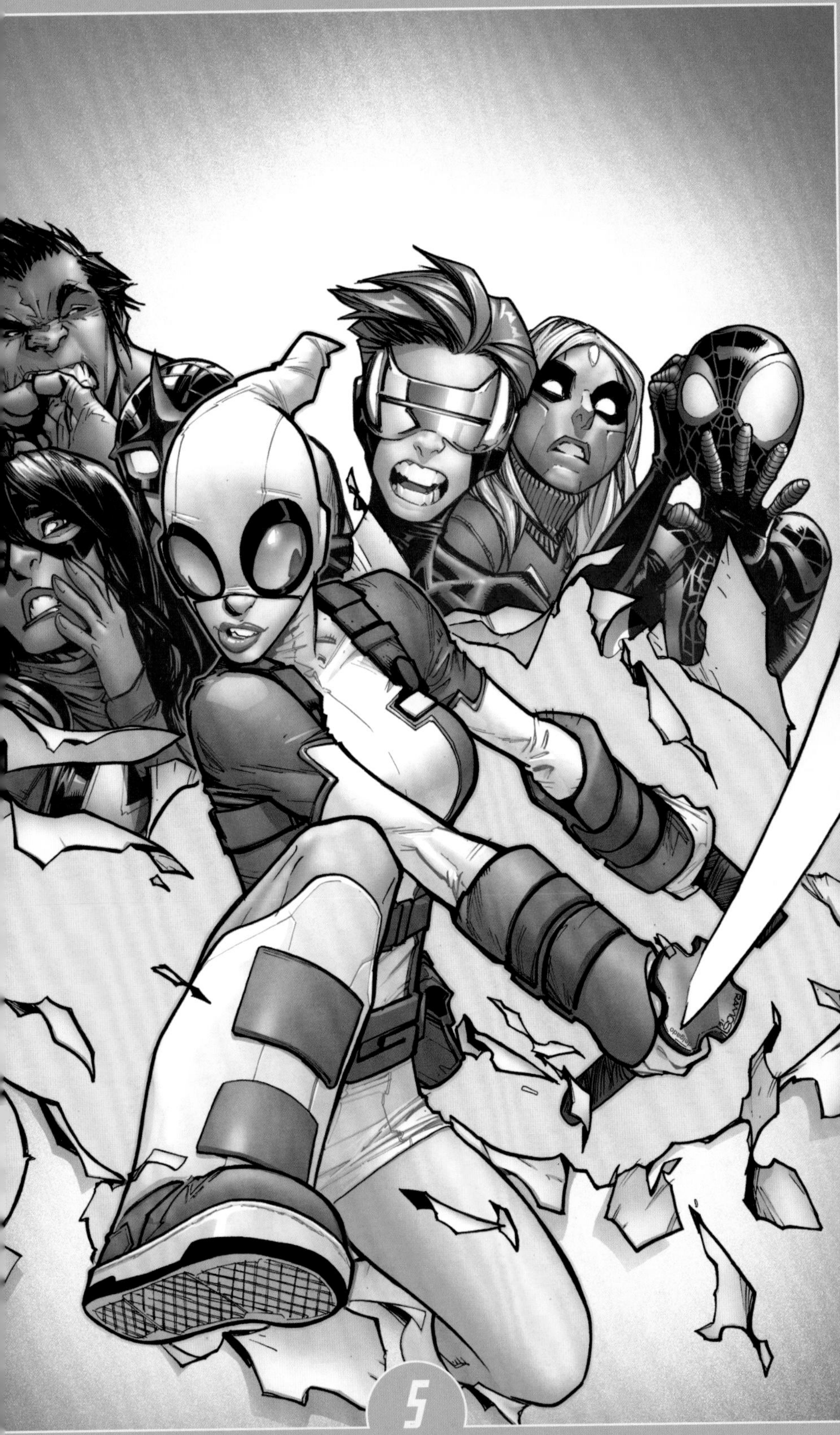

5

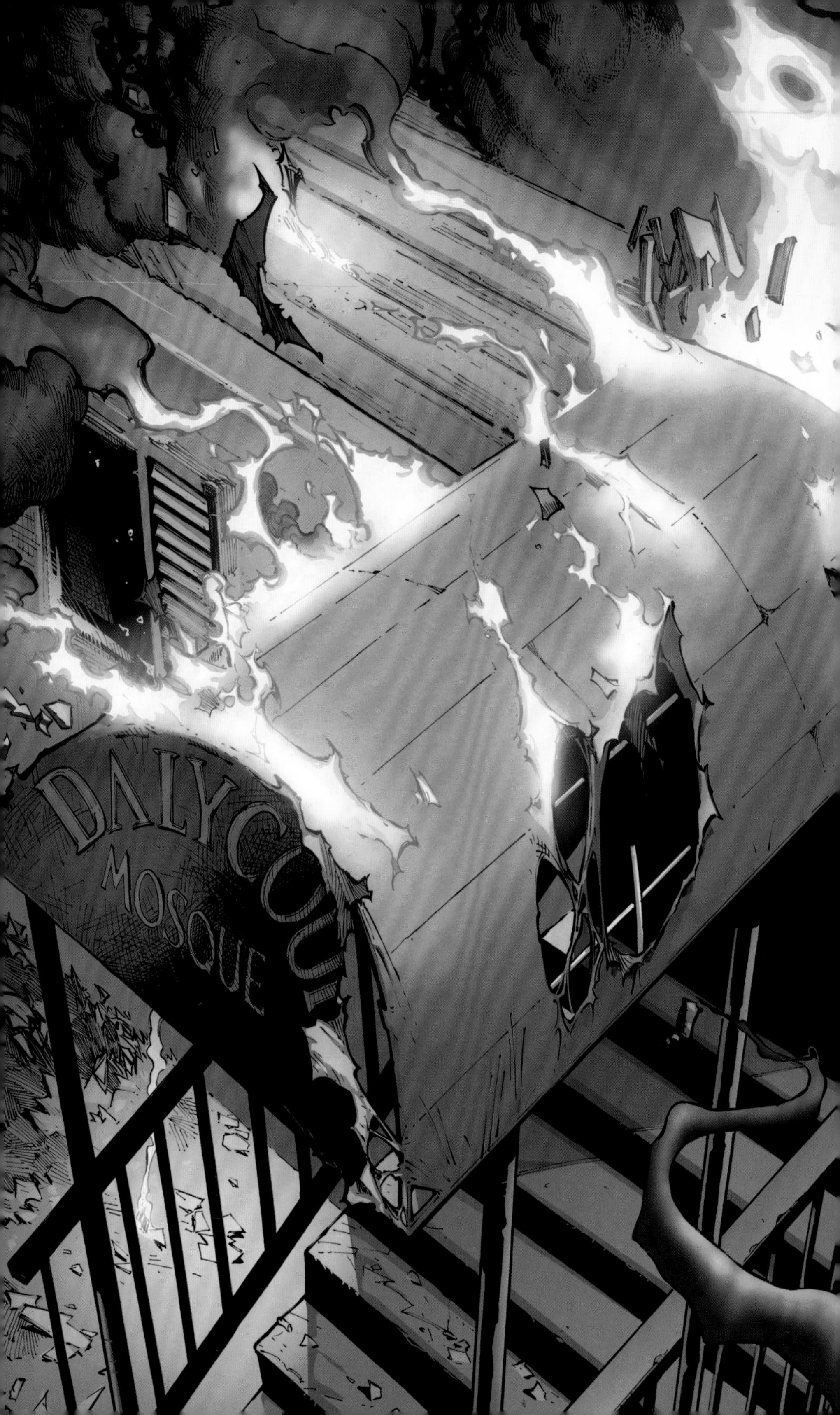
MOSQUE

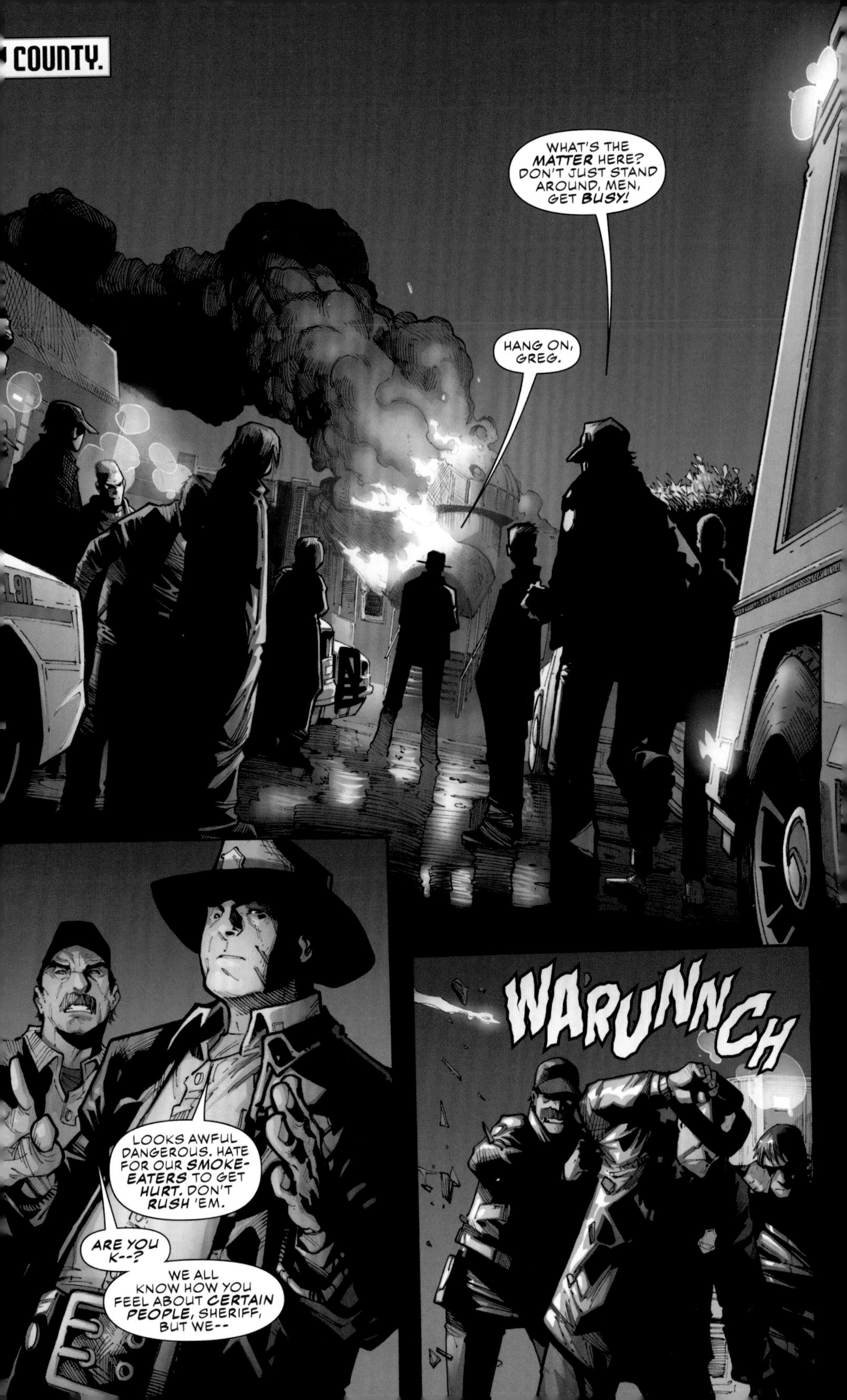
COUNTY.
WHAT'S THE MATTER HERE? DON'T JUST STAND AROUND, MEN, GET BUSY!
HANG ON, GREG.
LOOKS AWFUL DANGEROUS. HATE FOR OUR SMOKE-EATERS TO GET HURT. DON'T RUSH 'EM.
ARE YOU K--?
WE ALL KNOW HOW YOU FEEL ABOUT CERTAIN PEOPLE, SHERIFF, BUT WE--
WARUNNCH

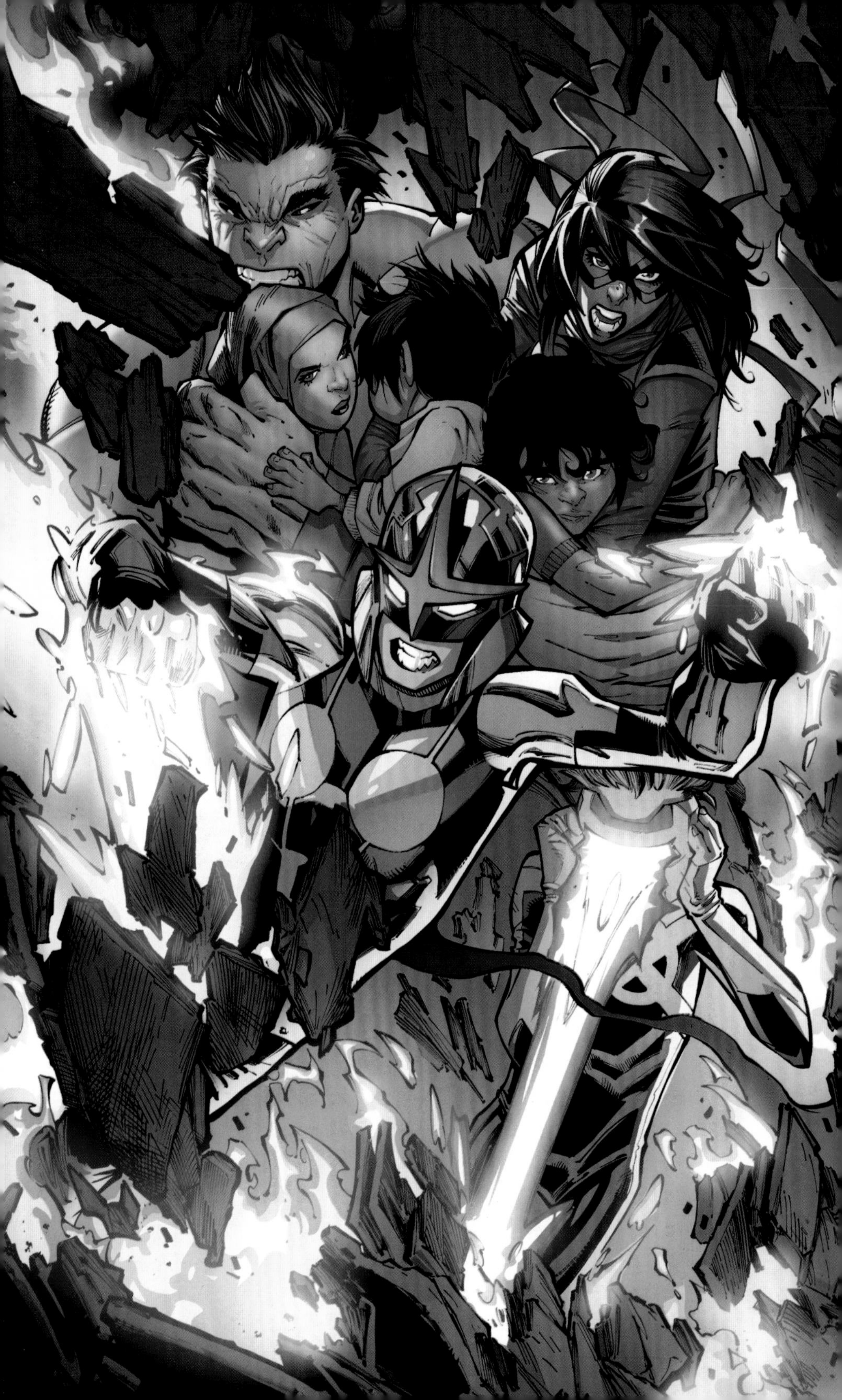

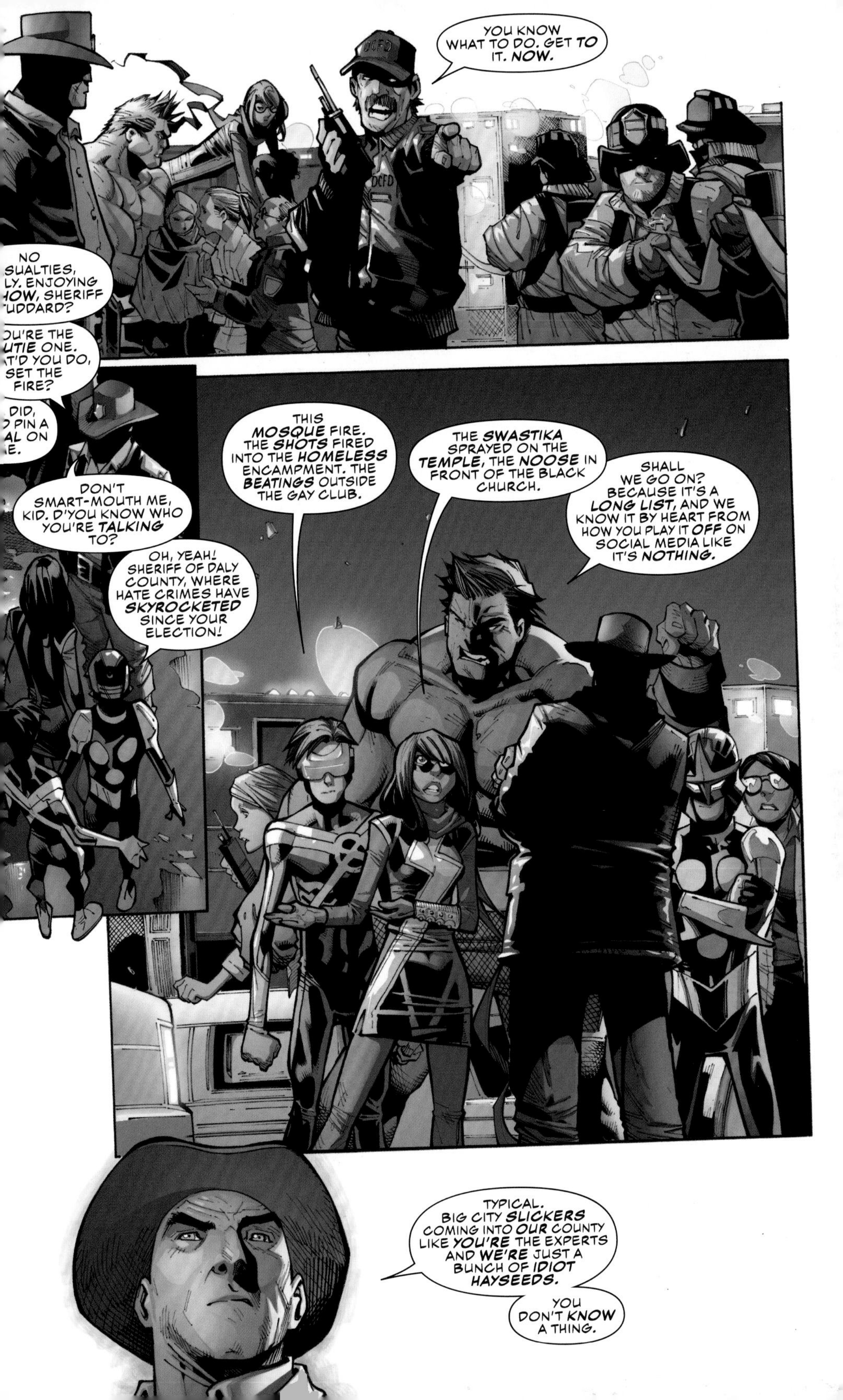

YOU KNOW WHAT TO DO. GET TO IT. NOW.
NO SUALTIES, LY. ENJOYING HOW, SHERIFF TUDDARD?
OU'RE THE UTIE ONE. T'D YOU DO, SET THE FIRE?
DID, PIN A AL ON E.
DON'T SMART-MOUTH ME, KID. D'YOU KNOW WHO YOU'RE TALKING TO?
OH, YEAH! SHERIFF OF DALY COUNTY, WHERE HATE CRIMES HAVE SKYROCKETED SINCE YOUR ELECTION!
THIS MOSQUE FIRE. THE SHOTS FIRED INTO THE HOMELESS ENCAMPMENT. THE BEATINGS OUTSIDE THE GAY CLUB.
THE SWASTIKA SPRAYED ON THE TEMPLE, THE NOOSE IN FRONT OF THE BLACK CHURCH.
SHALL WE GO ON? BECAUSE IT'S A LONG LIST, AND WE KNOW IT BY HEART FROM HOW YOU PLAY IT OFF ON SOCIAL MEDIA LIKE IT'S NOTHING.
TYPICAL. BIG CITY SLICKERS COMING INTO OUR COUNTY LIKE YOU'RE THE EXPERTS AND WE'RE JUST A BUNCH OF IDIOT HAYSEEDS.
YOU DON'T KNOW A THING.

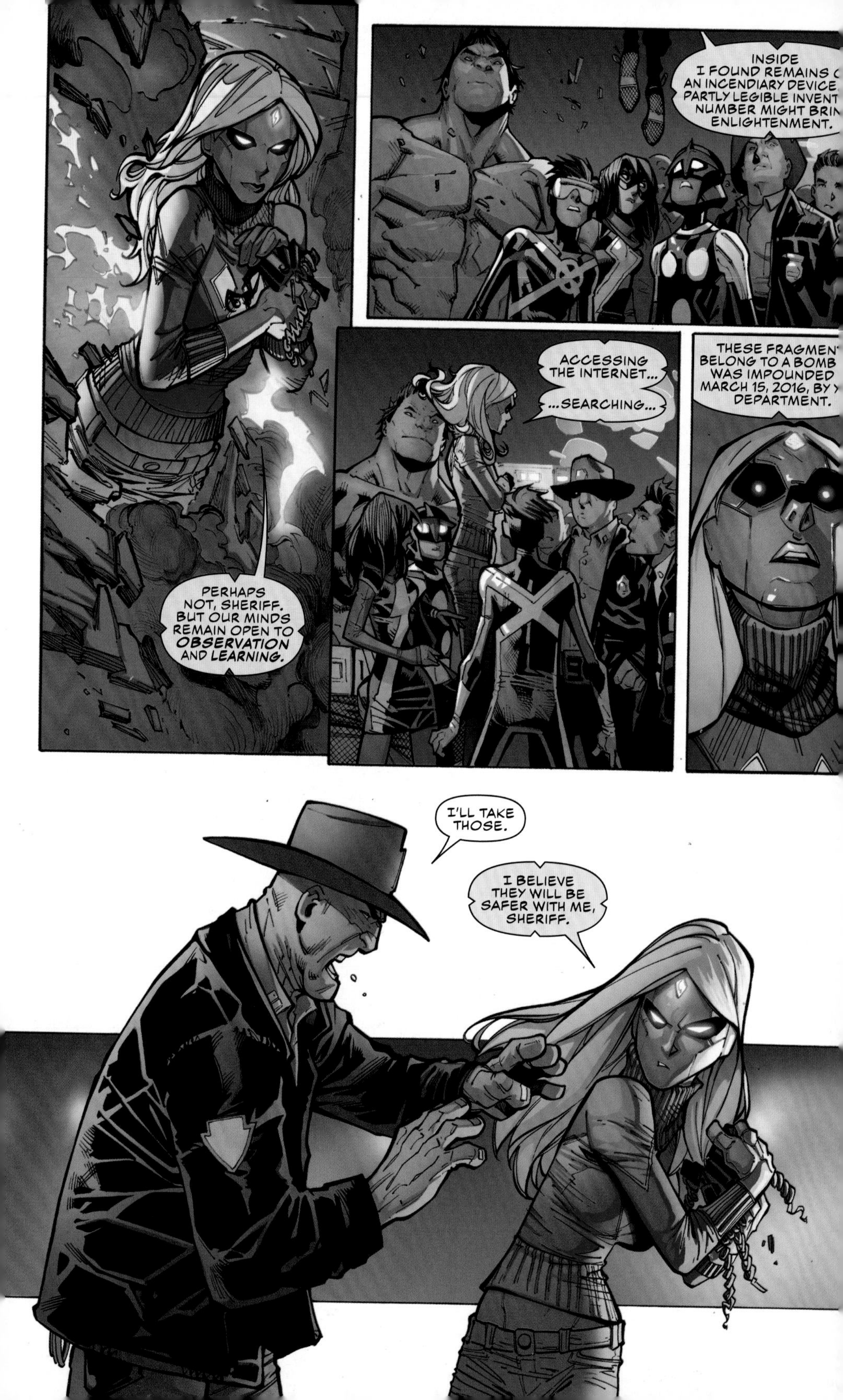
PERHAPS NOT, SHERIFF. BUT OUR MINDS REMAIN OPEN TO OBSERVATION AND LEARNING.
INSIDE I FOUND REMAINS O AN INCENDIARY DEVICE PARTLY LEGIBLE INVENT NUMBER MIGHT BRIN ENLIGHTENMENT.
ACCESSING THE INTERNET...
...SEARCHING...
THESE FRAGMENT BELONG TO A BOMB WAS IMPOUNDED MARCH 15, 2016, BY Y DEPARTMENT.
I'LL TAKE THOSE.
I BELIEVE THEY WILL BE SAFER WITH ME, SHERIFF.

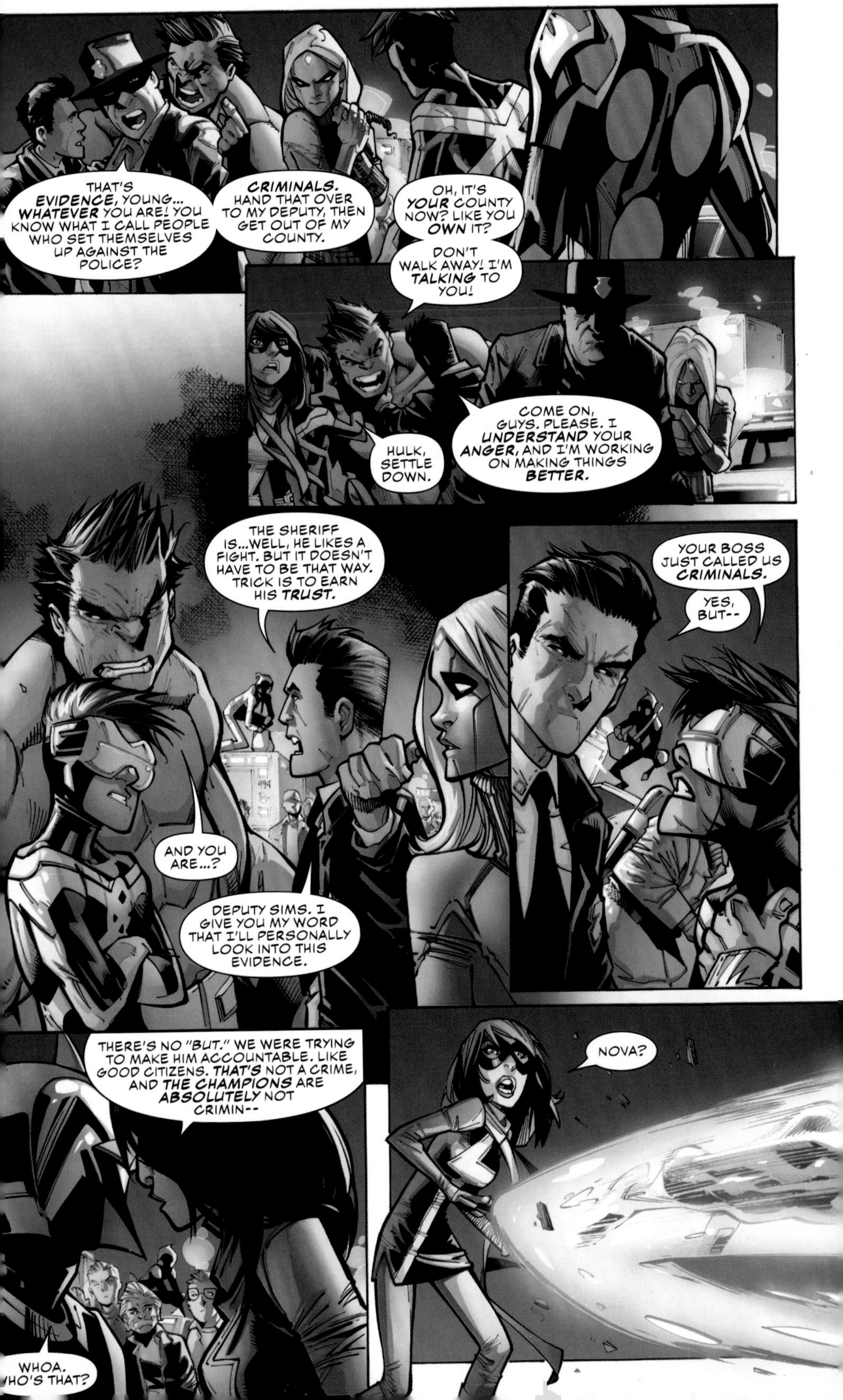

THAT'S EVIDENCE, YOUNG... WHATEVER YOU ARE! YOU KNOW WHAT I CALL PEOPLE WHO SET THEMSELVES UP AGAINST THE POLICE?
CRIMINALS. HAND THAT OVER TO MY DEPUTY, THEN GET OUT OF MY COUNTY.
OH, IT'S YOUR COUNTY NOW? LIKE YOU OWN IT?
DON'T WALK AWAY! I'M TALKING TO YOU!
HULK, SETTLE DOWN.
COME ON, GUYS. PLEASE. I UNDERSTAND YOUR ANGER, AND I'M WORKING ON MAKING THINGS BETTER.
THE SHERIFF IS...WELL, HE LIKES A FIGHT. BUT IT DOESN'T HAVE TO BE THAT WAY. TRICK IS TO EARN HIS TRUST.
AND YOU ARE...?
DEPUTY SIMS. I GIVE YOU MY WORD THAT I'LL PERSONALLY LOOK INTO THIS EVIDENCE.
YOUR BOSS JUST CALLED US CRIMINALS.
YES, BUT--
THERE'S NO "BUT." WE WERE TRYING TO MAKE HIM ACCOUNTABLE. LIKE GOOD CITIZENS. THAT'S NOT A CRIME, AND THE CHAMPIONS ARE ABSOLUTELY NOT CRIMIN--
WHOA. WHO'S THAT?
NOVA?

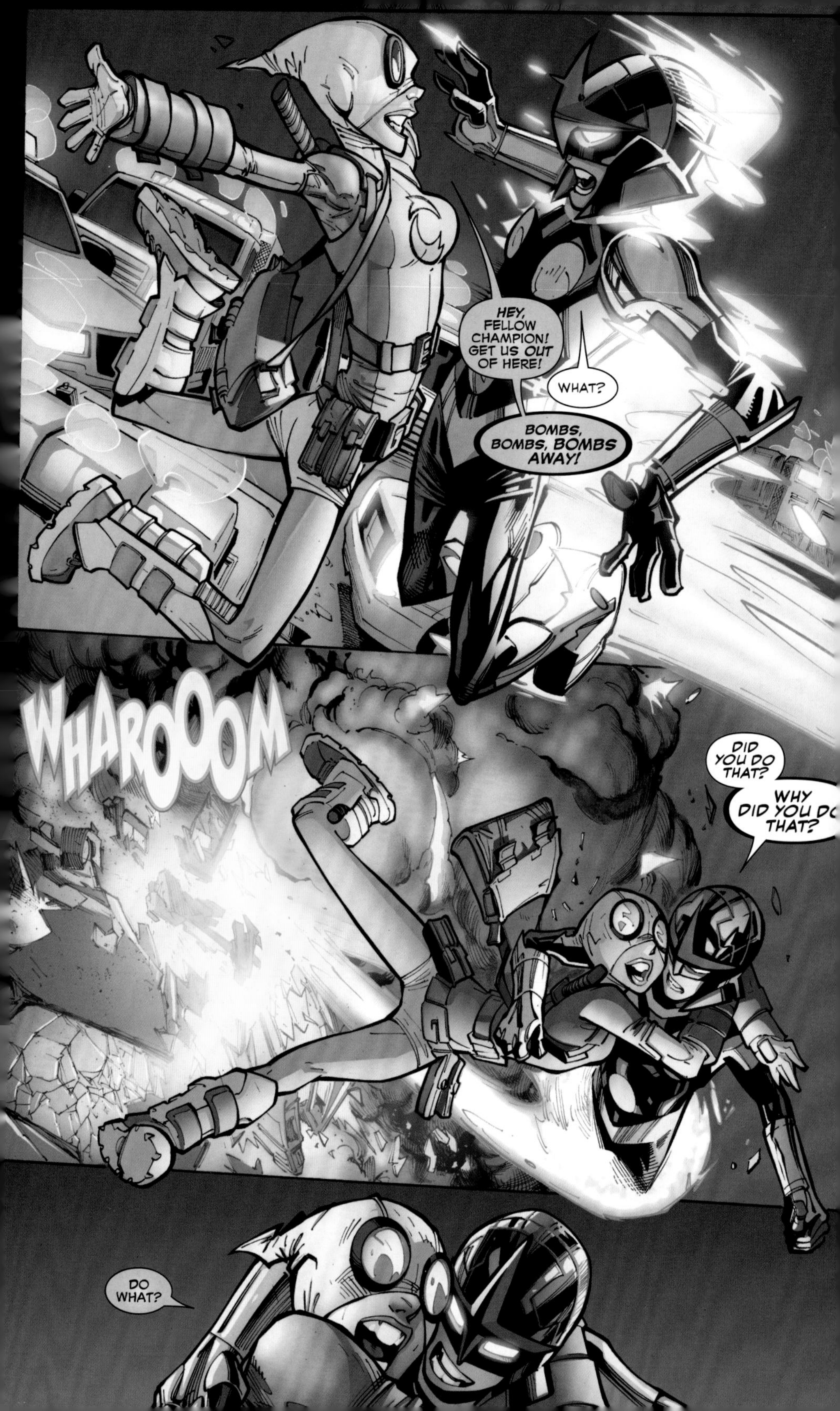

HEY, FELLOW CHAMPION! GET US OUT OF HERE!
WHAT?
BOMBS, BOMBS, BOMBS AWAY!
WHAROOOM
DID YOU DO THAT?
WHY DID YOU DO THAT?
DO WHAT?

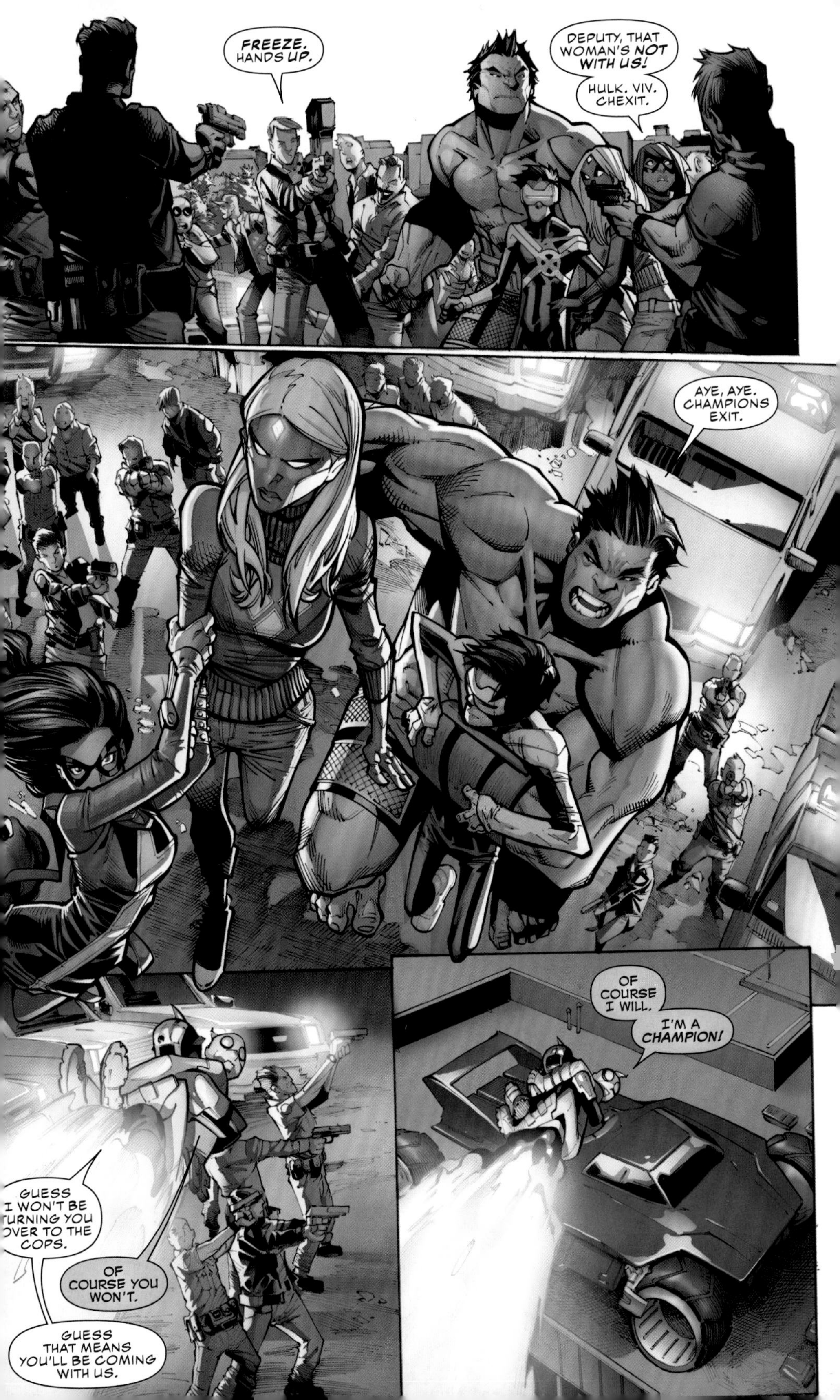
FREEZE. HANDS UP.
DEPUTY, THAT WOMAN'S NOT WITH US!
HULK. VIV. CHEXIT.
AYE, AYE. CHAMPIONS EXIT.
GUESS I WON'T BE TURNING YOU OVER TO THE COPS.
OF COURSE YOU WON'T.
GUESS THAT MEANS YOU'LL BE COMING WITH US.
OF COURSE I WILL.
I'M A CHAMPION!

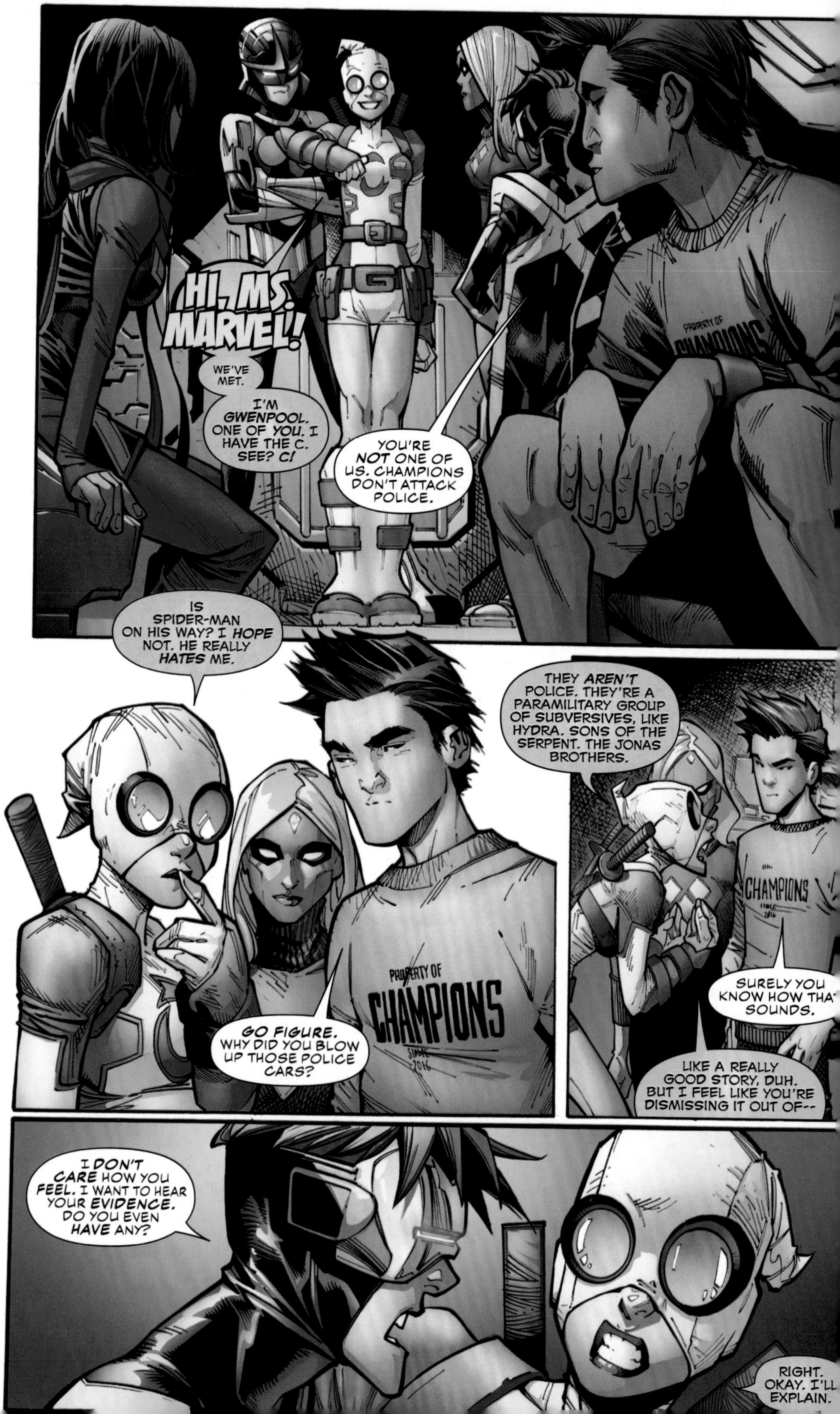
HI, MS. MARVEL!
WE'VE MET.
I'M GWENPOOL. ONE OF YOU. I HAVE THE C. SEE? C!
YOU'RE NOT ONE OF US. CHAMPIONS DON'T ATTACK POLICE.
PROPERTY OF CHAMPIONS
IS SPIDER-MAN ON HIS WAY? I HOPE NOT. HE REALLY HATES ME.
GO FIGURE. WHY DID YOU BLOW UP THOSE POLICE CARS?
PROPERTY OF CHAMPIONS
THEY AREN'T POLICE. THEY'RE A PARAMILITARY GROUP OF SUBVERSIVES, LIKE HYDRA. SONS OF THE SERPENT. THE JONAS BROTHERS.
CHAMPIONS
SURELY YOU KNOW HOW THA SOUNDS.
LIKE A REALLY GOOD STORY, DUH. BUT I FEEL LIKE YOU'RE DISMISSING IT OUT OF--
I DON'T CARE HOW YOU FEEL. I WANT TO HEAR YOUR EVIDENCE. DO YOU EVEN HAVE ANY?
RIGHT. OKAY. I'LL EXPLAIN.

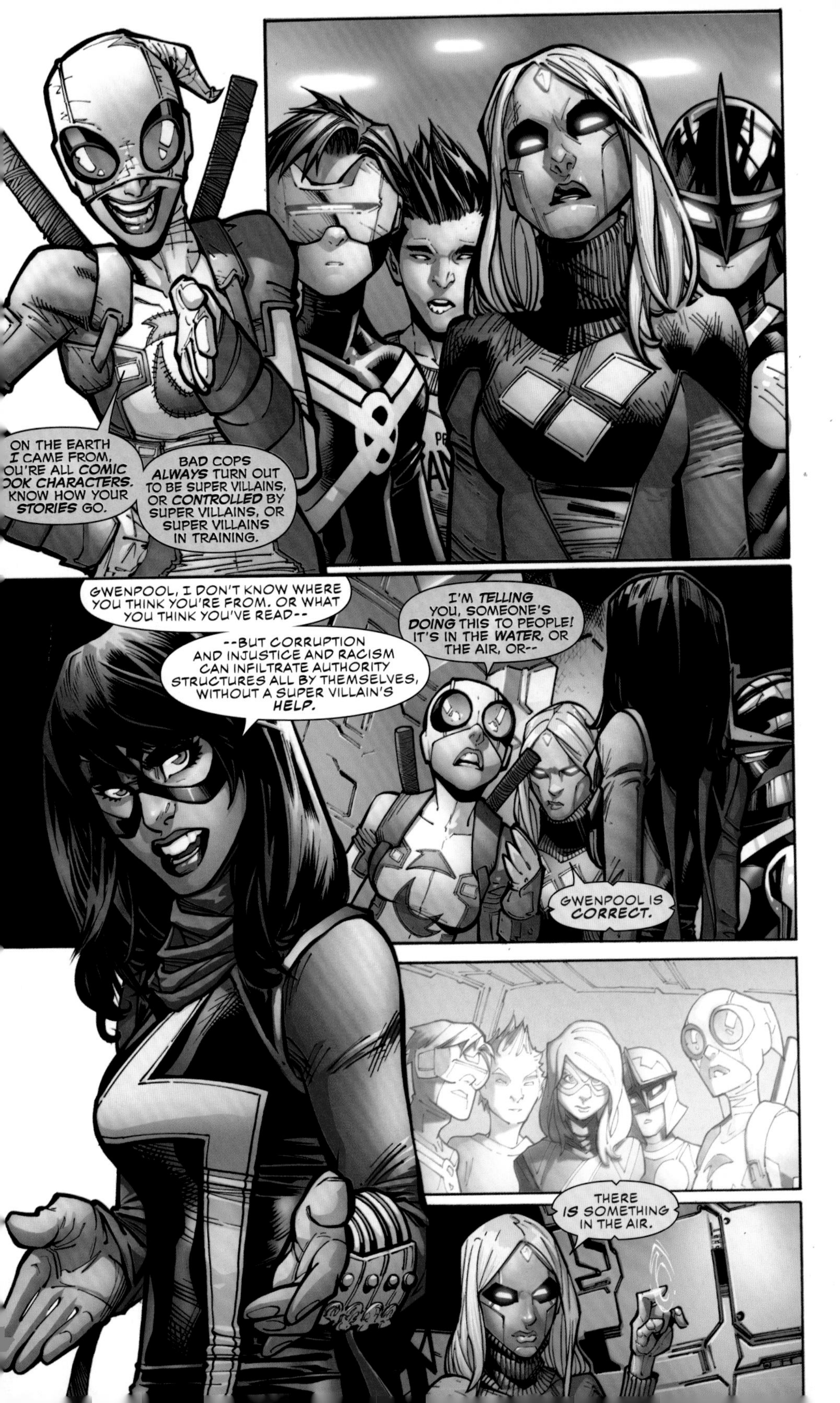

ON THE EARTH I CAME FROM, OU'RE ALL COMIC OOK CHARACTERS. KNOW HOW YOUR STORIES GO.
BAD COPS ALWAYS TURN OUT TO BE SUPER VILLAINS, OR CONTROLLED BY SUPER VILLAINS, OR SUPER VILLAINS IN TRAINING.
GWENPOOL, I DON'T KNOW WHERE YOU THINK YOU'RE FROM. OR WHAT YOU THINK YOU'VE READ--
--BUT CORRUPTION AND INJUSTICE AND RACISM CAN INFILTRATE AUTHORITY STRUCTURES ALL BY THEMSELVES, WITHOUT A SUPER VILLAIN'S HELP.
I'M TELLING YOU, SOMEONE'S DOING THIS TO PEOPLE! IT'S IN THE WATER, OR THE AIR, OR--
GWENPOOL IS CORRECT.
THERE IS SOMETHING IN THE AIR.

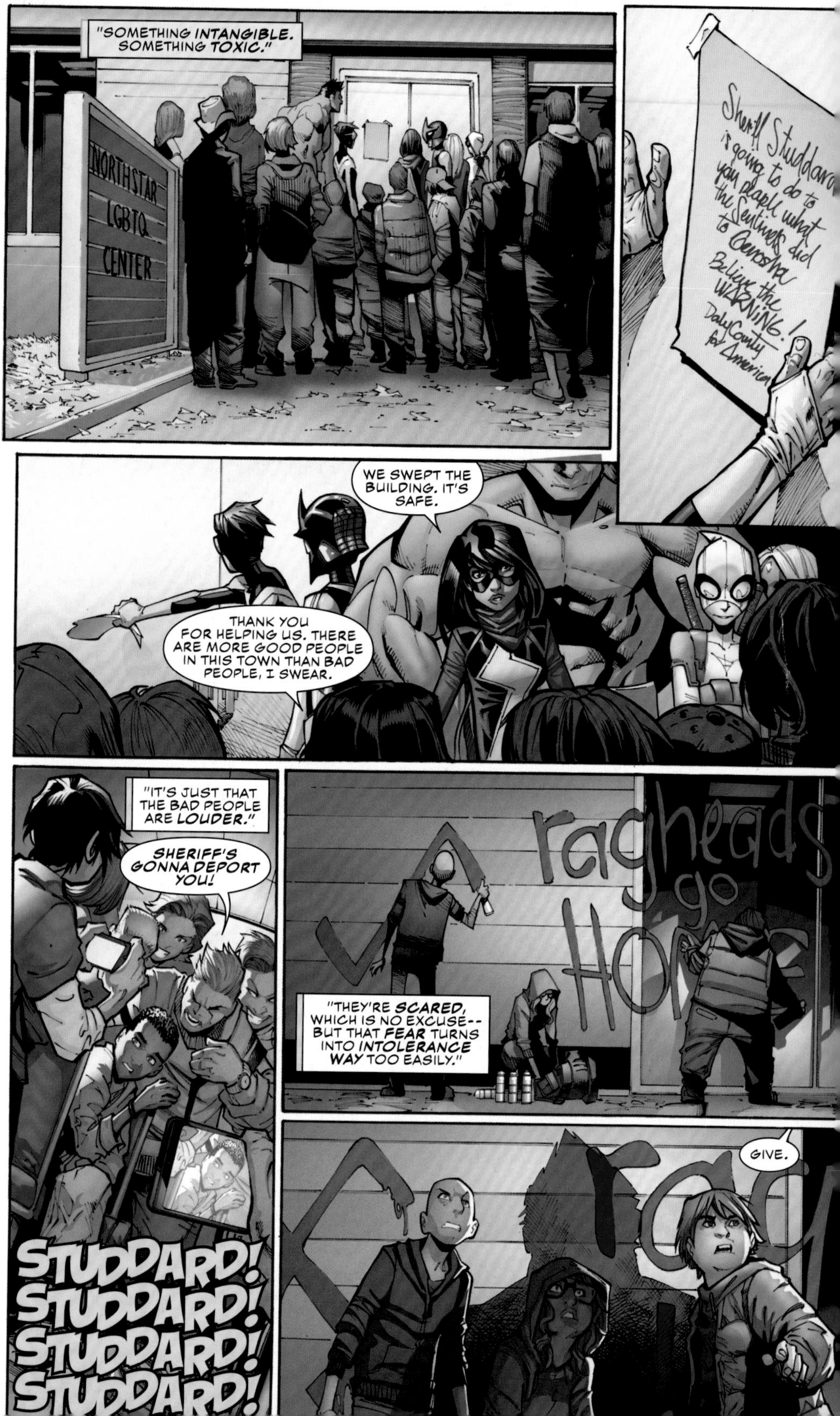
"SOMETHING INTANGIBLE. SOMETHING TOXIC."
NORTHSTAR LGBTQ CENTER
Sheriff Studdard is going to do to you people what the Sentinels did to Genosha
Believe the WARNING!
Daly County for America
WE SWEPT THE BUILDING. IT'S SAFE.
THANK YOU FOR HELPING US. THERE ARE MORE GOOD PEOPLE IN THIS TOWN THAN BAD PEOPLE, I SWEAR.
"IT'S JUST THAT THE BAD PEOPLE ARE LOUDER."
SHERIFF'S GONNA DEPORT YOU!
STUDDARD! STUDDARD! STUDDARD! STUDDARD!
ragheads go Ho
"THEY'RE SCARED, WHICH IS NO EXCUSE-- BUT THAT FEAR TURNS INTO INTOLERANCE WAY TOO EASILY."
GIVE.

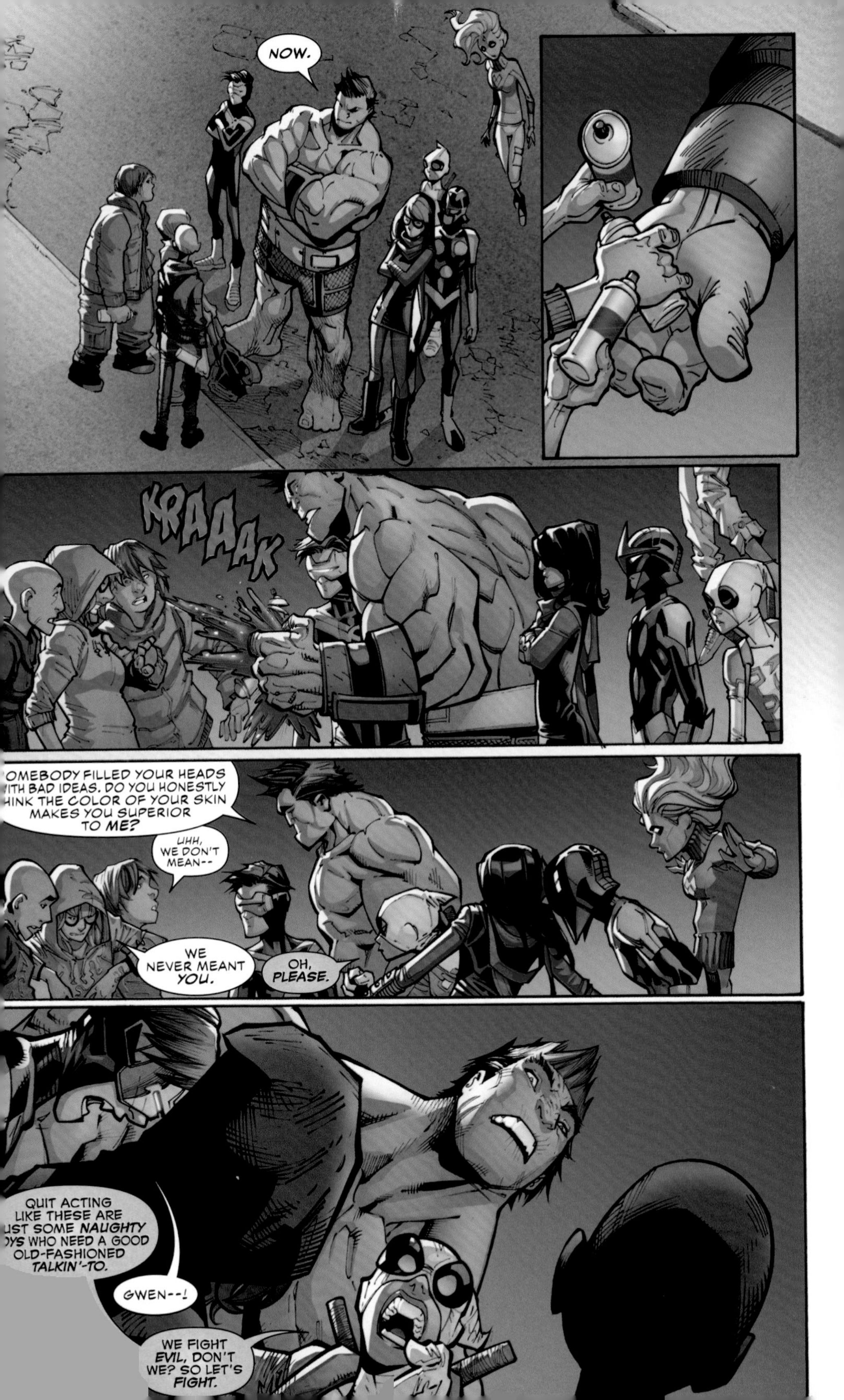
NOW.
KRAAAK
OMEBODY FILLED YOUR HEADS
ITH BAD IDEAS. DO YOU HONESTLY
HINK THE COLOR OF YOUR SKIN
MAKES YOU SUPERIOR
TO ME?
UHH, WE DON'T MEAN--
WE NEVER MEANT YOU.
OH, PLEASE.
QUIT ACTING LIKE THESE ARE UST SOME NAUGHTY OYS WHO NEED A GOOD OLD-FASHIONED TALKIN'-TO.
GWEN--!
WE FIGHT EVIL, DON'T WE? SO LET'S FIGHT.

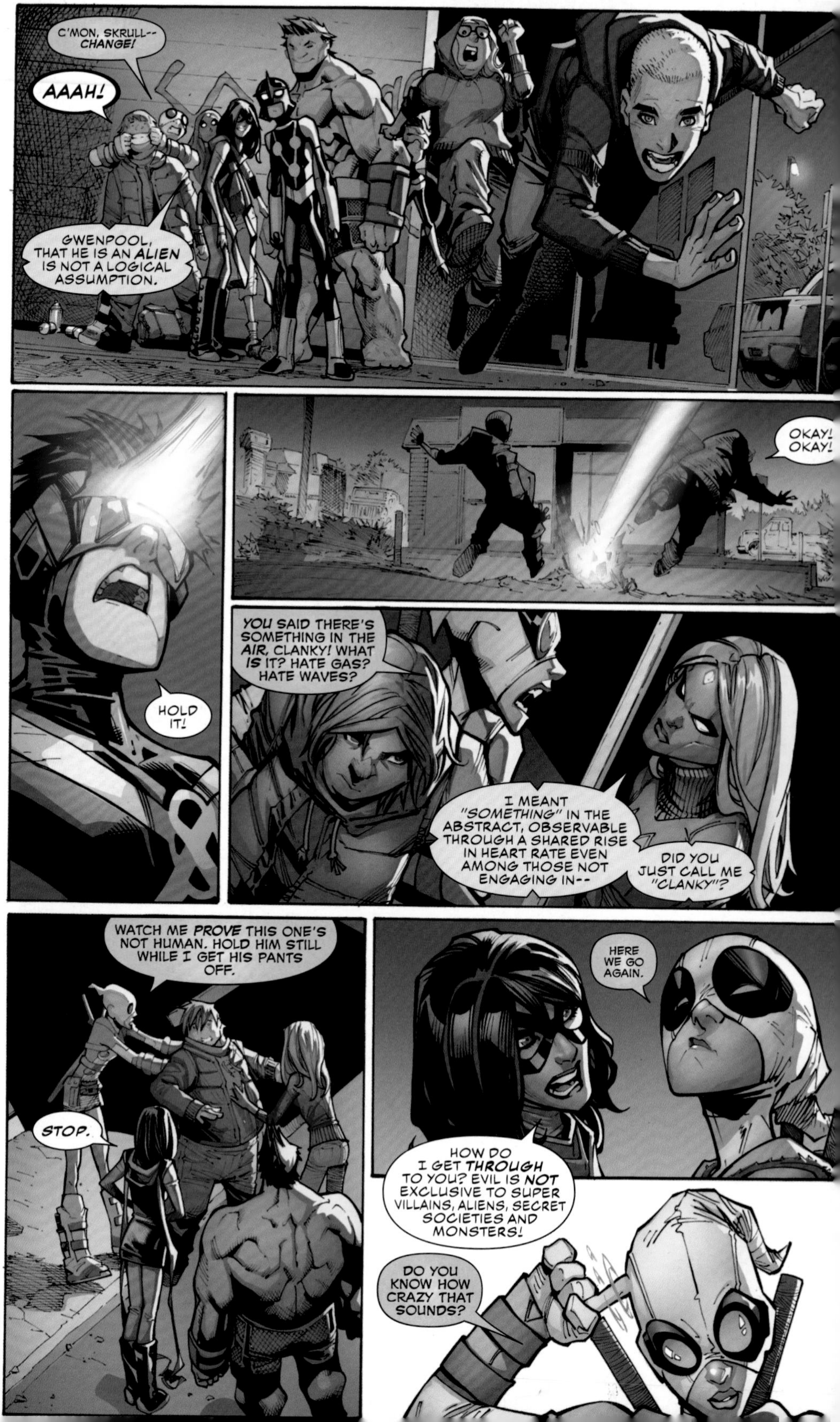

C'MON, SKRULL-- CHANGE!
AAAH!
GWENPOOL, THAT HE IS AN ALIEN IS NOT A LOGICAL ASSUMPTION.
HOLD IT!
OKAY! OKAY!
YOU SAID THERE'S SOMETHING IN THE AIR, CLANKY! WHAT IS IT? HATE GAS? HATE WAVES?
I MEANT "SOMETHING" IN THE ABSTRACT, OBSERVABLE THROUGH A SHARED RISE IN HEART RATE EVEN AMONG THOSE NOT ENGAGING IN--
DID YOU JUST CALL ME "CLANKY"?
WATCH ME PROVE THIS ONE'S NOT HUMAN. HOLD HIM STILL WHILE I GET HIS PANTS OFF.
STOP.
HERE WE GO AGAIN.
HOW DO I GET THROUGH TO YOU? EVIL IS NOT EXCLUSIVE TO SUPER VILLAINS, ALIENS, SECRET SOCIETIES AND MONSTERS!
DO YOU KNOW HOW CRAZY THAT SOUNDS?

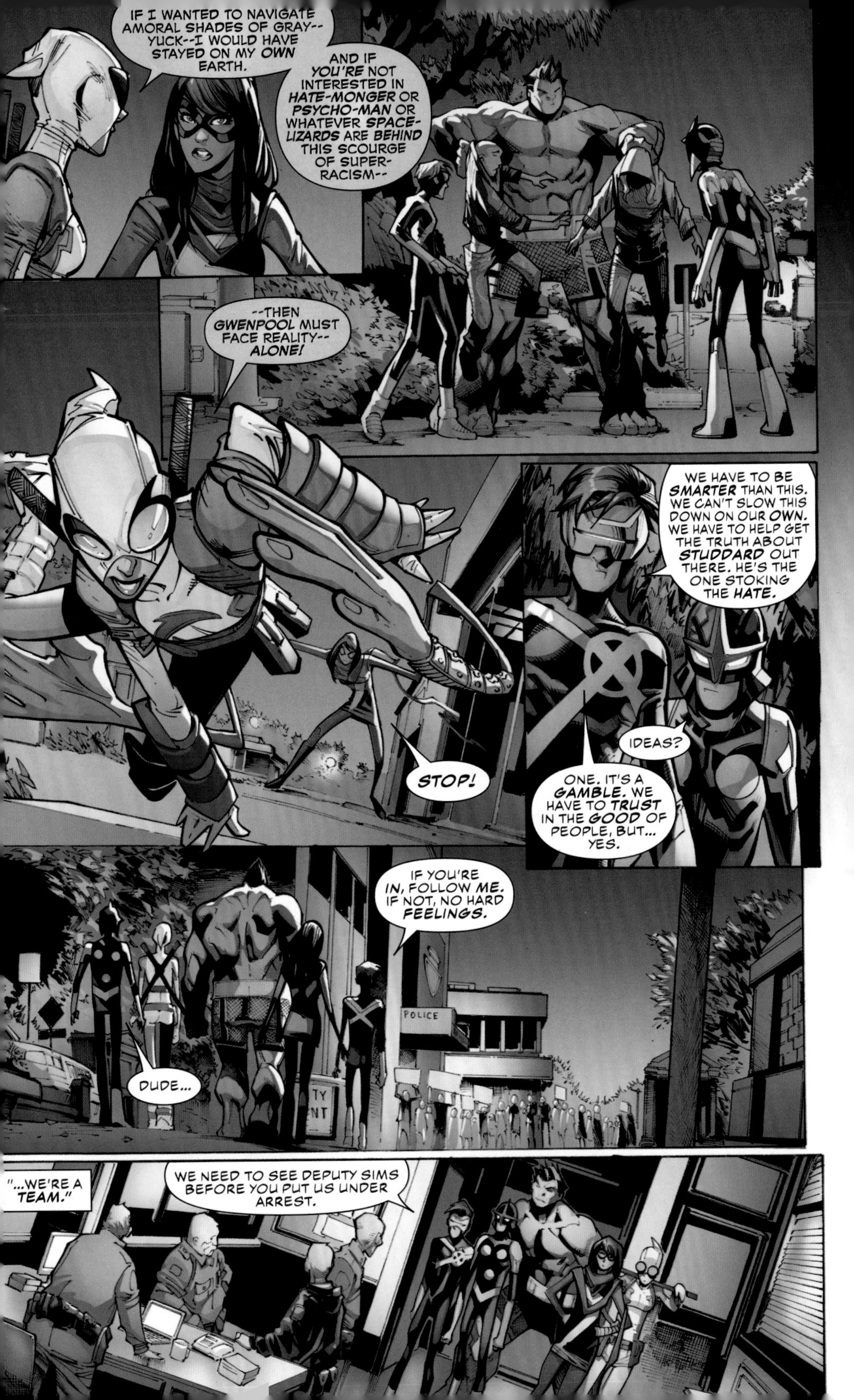

IF I WANTED TO NAVIGATE AMORAL SHADES OF GRAY-- YUCK--I WOULD HAVE STAYED ON MY OWN EARTH.
AND IF YOU'RE NOT INTERESTED IN HATE-MONGER OR PSYCHO-MAN OR WHATEVER SPACE-LIZARDS ARE BEHIND THIS SCOURGE OF SUPER-RACISM--
--THEN GWENPOOL MUST FACE REALITY-- ALONE!
STOP!
WE HAVE TO BE SMARTER THAN THIS. WE CAN'T SLOW THIS DOWN ON OUR OWN. WE HAVE TO HELP GET THE TRUTH ABOUT STUDDARD OUT THERE. HE'S THE ONE STOKING THE HATE.
IDEAS?
ONE. IT'S A GAMBLE. WE HAVE TO TRUST IN THE GOOD OF PEOPLE, BUT... YES.
IF YOU'RE IN, FOLLOW ME. IF NOT, NO HARD FEELINGS.
POLICE
DUDE...
"...WE'RE A TEAM."
WE NEED TO SEE DEPUTY SIMS BEFORE YOU PUT US UNDER ARREST.

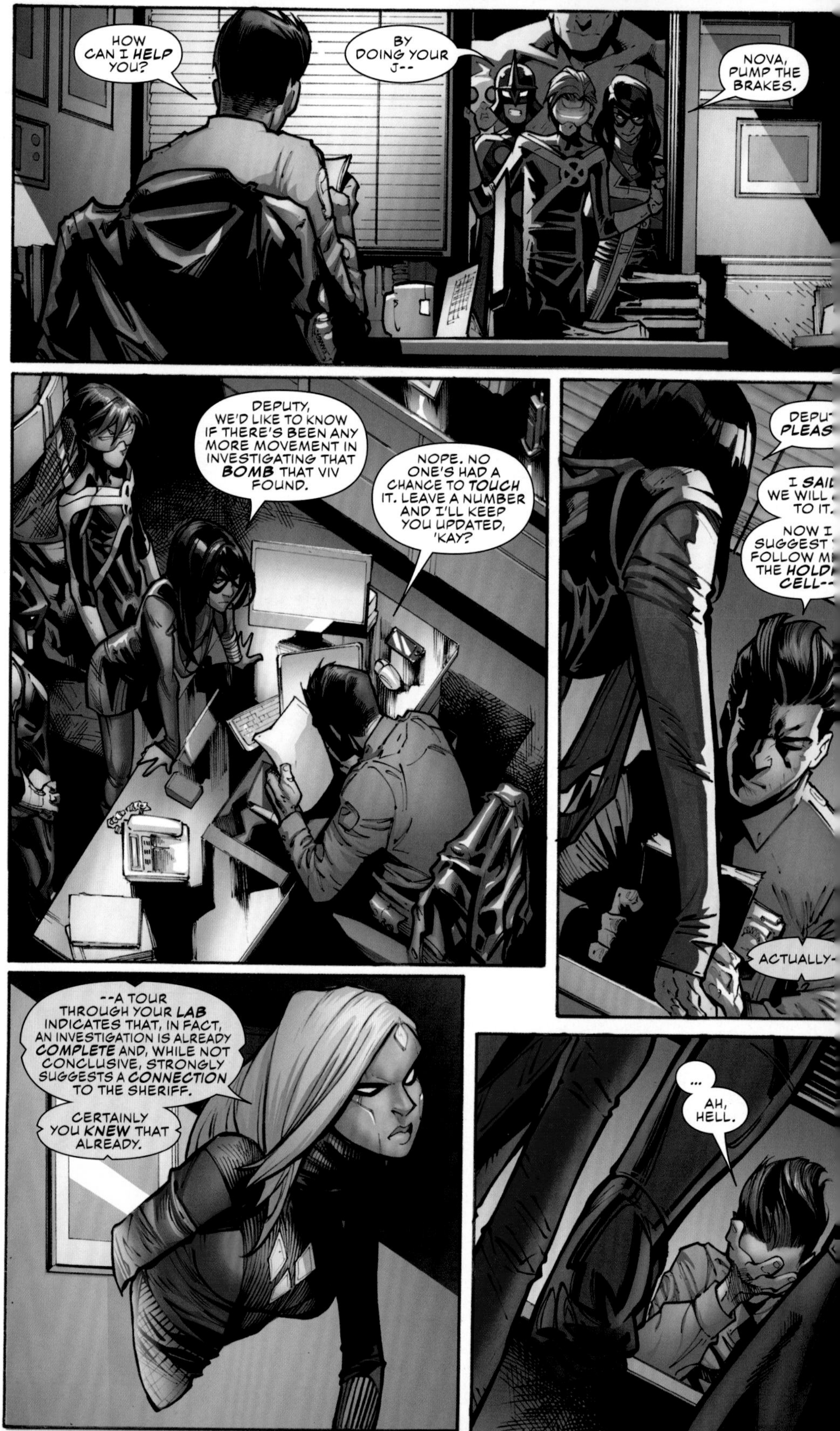

HOW CAN I HELP YOU?
BY DOING YOUR J--
NOVA, PUMP THE BRAKES.
DEPUTY, WE'D LIKE TO KNOW IF THERE'S BEEN ANY MORE MOVEMENT IN INVESTIGATING THAT BOMB THAT VIV FOUND.
NOPE. NO ONE'S HAD A CHANCE TO TOUCH IT. LEAVE A NUMBER AND I'LL KEEP YOU UPDATED, 'KAY?
DEPU PLEAS
I SAI WE WILL TO IT.
NOW I SUGGEST FOLLOW M THE HOLD CELL--
ACTUALLY-
--A TOUR THROUGH YOUR LAB INDICATES THAT, IN FACT, AN INVESTIGATION IS ALREADY COMPLETE AND, WHILE NOT CONCLUSIVE, STRONGLY SUGGESTS A CONNECTION TO THE SHERIFF.
CERTAINLY YOU KNEW THAT ALREADY.
... AH, HELL.

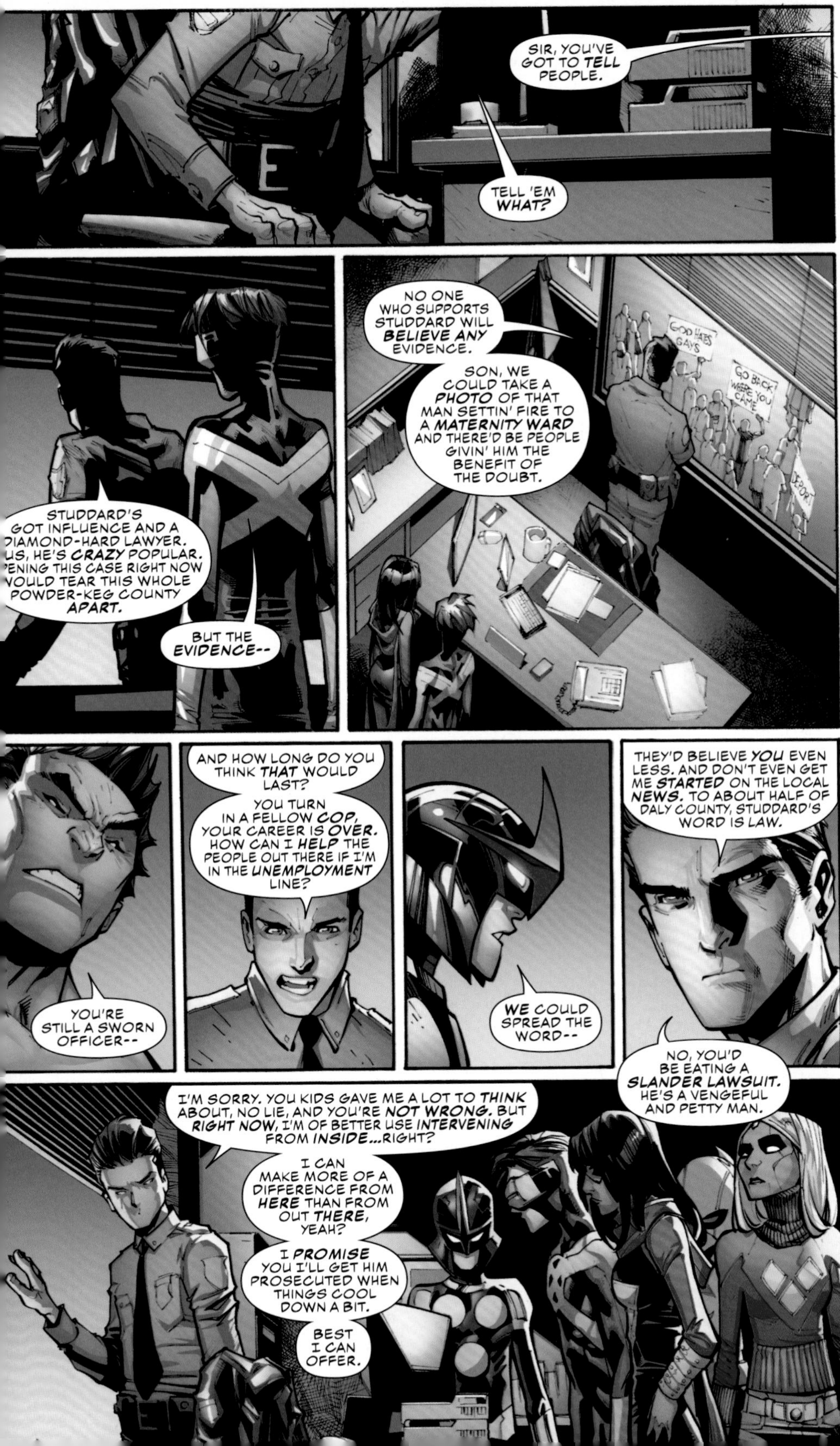

SIR, YOU'VE GOT TO TELL PEOPLE.
TELL 'EM WHAT?
STUDDARD'S GOT INFLUENCE AND A IAMOND-HARD LAWYER. US, HE'S CRAZY POPULAR. PENING THIS CASE RIGHT NOW VOULD TEAR THIS WHOLE POWDER-KEG COUNTY APART.
BUT THE EVIDENCE--
NO ONE WHO SUPPORTS STUDDARD WILL BELIEVE ANY EVIDENCE.
SON, WE COULD TAKE A PHOTO OF THAT MAN SETTIN' FIRE TO A MATERNITY WARD AND THERE'D BE PEOPLE GIVIN' HIM THE BENEFIT OF THE DOUBT.
GOD HATES GAYS
GO BACK WHERE YOU CAME
DEPORT
YOU'RE STILL A SWORN OFFICER--
AND HOW LONG DO YOU THINK THAT WOULD LAST?
YOU TURN IN A FELLOW COP, YOUR CAREER IS OVER. HOW CAN I HELP THE PEOPLE OUT THERE IF I'M IN THE UNEMPLOYMENT LINE?
WE COULD SPREAD THE WORD--
THEY'D BELIEVE YOU EVEN LESS. AND DON'T EVEN GET ME STARTED ON THE LOCAL NEWS. TO ABOUT HALF OF DALY COUNTY, STUDDARD'S WORD IS LAW.
NO, YOU'D BE EATING A SLANDER LAWSUIT. HE'S A VENGEFUL AND PETTY MAN.
I'M SORRY. YOU KIDS GAVE ME A LOT TO THINK ABOUT, NO LIE, AND YOU'RE NOT WRONG. BUT RIGHT NOW, I'M OF BETTER USE INTERVENING FROM INSIDE...RIGHT?
I CAN MAKE MORE OF A DIFFERENCE FROM HERE THAN FROM OUT THERE, YEAH?
I PROMISE YOU I'LL GET HIM PROSECUTED WHEN THINGS COOL DOWN A BIT.
BEST I CAN OFFER.

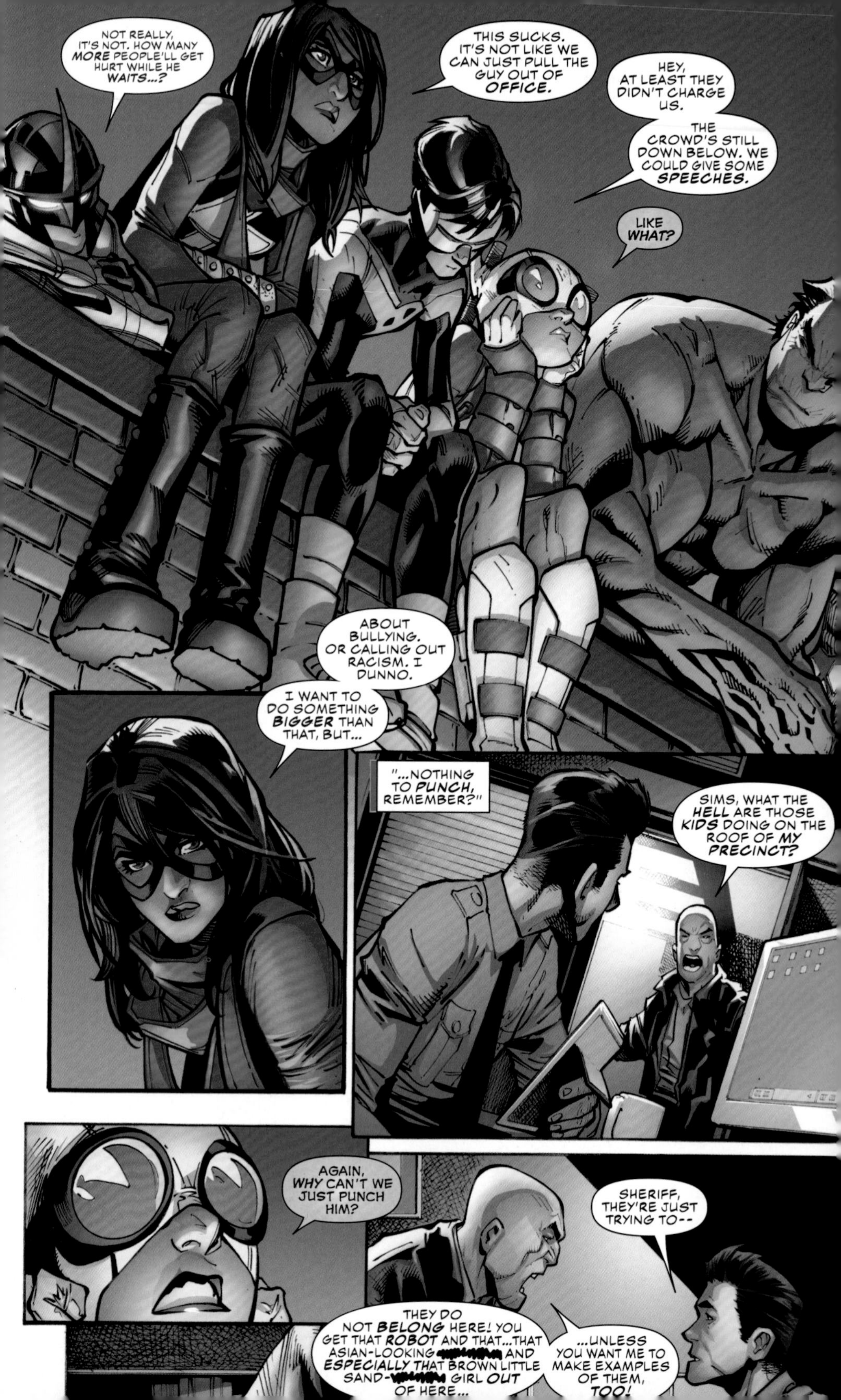

NOT REALLY, IT'S NOT. HOW MANY MORE PEOPLE'LL GET HURT WHILE HE WAITS...?
THIS SUCKS. IT'S NOT LIKE WE CAN JUST PULL THE GUY OUT OF OFFICE.
HEY, AT LEAST THEY DIDN'T CHARGE US.
THE CROWD'S STILL DOWN BELOW. WE COULD GIVE SOME SPEECHES.
LIKE WHAT?
ABOUT BULLYING. OR CALLING OUT RACISM. I DUNNO.
I WANT TO DO SOMETHING BIGGER THAN THAT, BUT...
"...NOTHING TO PUNCH, REMEMBER?"
SIMS, WHAT THE HELL ARE THOSE KIDS DOING ON THE ROOF OF MY PRECINCT?
AGAIN, WHY CAN'T WE JUST PUNCH HIM?
SHERIFF, THEY'RE JUST TRYING TO--
THEY DO NOT BELONG HERE! YOU GET THAT ROBOT AND THAT...THAT ASIAN-LOOKING [redacted] AND ESPECIALLY THAT BROWN LITTLE SAND-[redacted] GIRL OUT OF HERE...
...UNLESS YOU WANT ME TO MAKE EXAMPLES OF THEM, TOO!

...
"TOO"?

SLAM

JUST DITCH 'EM.

WELL, LET'S DO SOMETHING...

HOLD UP! CHECK IT OUT!

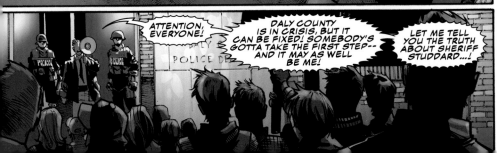

ATTENTION, EVERYONE!

DALY COUNTY IS IN CRISIS, BUT IT CAN BE FIXED! SOMEBODY'S GOTTA TAKE THE FIRST STEP-- AND IT MAY AS WELL BE ME!

LET ME TELL YOU THE TRUTH ABOUT SHERIFF STUDDARD...!

POLICE DE

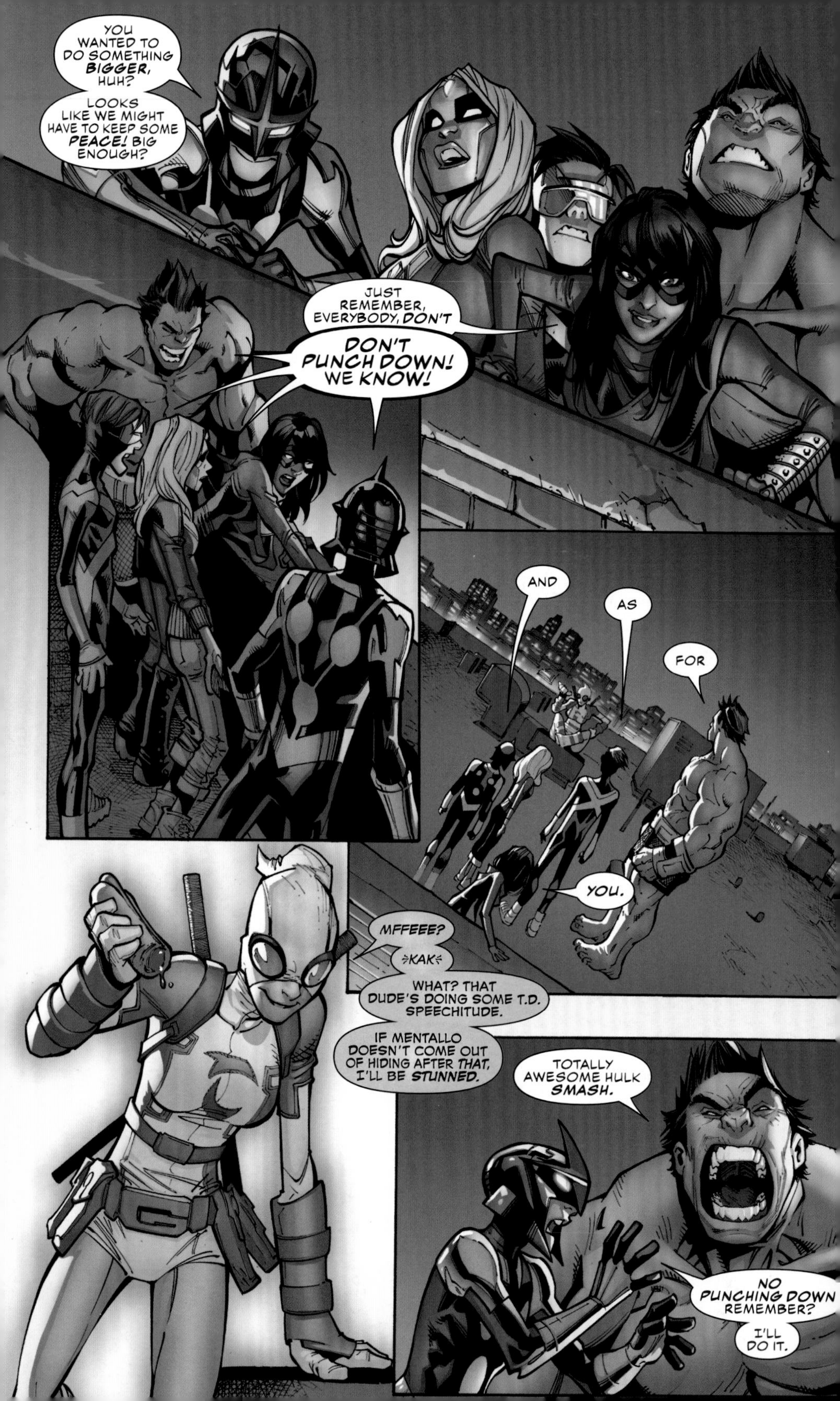
YOU WANTED TO DO SOMETHING BIGGER, HUH?
LOOKS LIKE WE MIGHT HAVE TO KEEP SOME PEACE! BIG ENOUGH?
JUST REMEMBER, EVERYBODY, DON'T
DON'T PUNCH DOWN! WE KNOW!
AND
AS
FOR
YOU.
MFFEEE?
KAK
WHAT? THAT DUDE'S DOING SOME T.D. SPEECHITUDE.
IF MENTALLO DOESN'T COME OUT OF HIDING AFTER THAT, I'LL BE STUNNED.
TOTALLY AWESOME HULK SMASH.
NO PUNCHING DOWN REMEMBER?
I'LL DO IT.

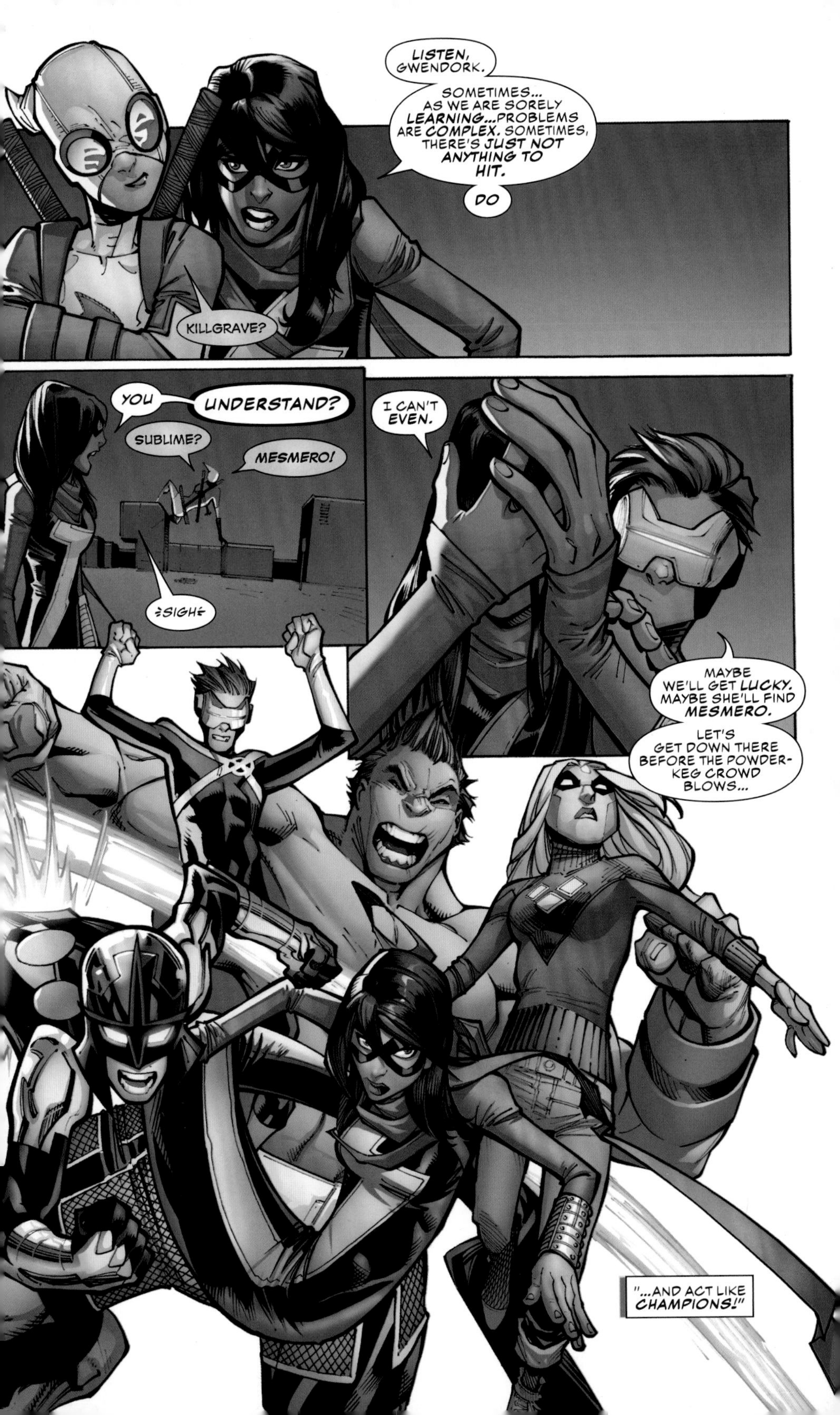
LISTEN, GWENDORK.
SOMETIMES... AS WE ARE SORELY LEARNING...PROBLEMS ARE COMPLEX. SOMETIMES, THERE'S JUST NOT ANYTHING TO HIT.
DO
KILLGRAVE?
YOU
UNDERSTAND?
SUBLIME?
MESMERO!
SIGH
I CAN'T EVEN.
MAYBE WE'LL GET LUCKY. MAYBE SHE'LL FIND MESMERO.
LET'S GET DOWN THERE BEFORE THE POWDER-KEG CROWD BLOWS...
"...AND ACT LIKE CHAMPIONS!"

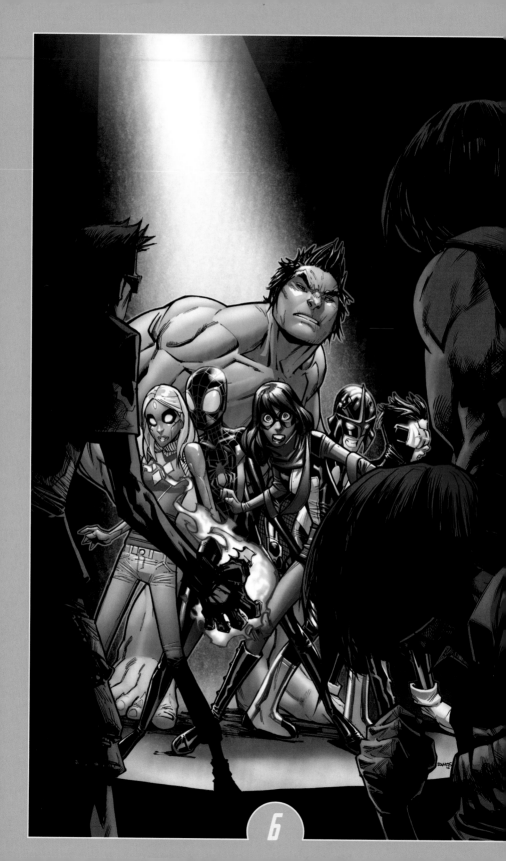

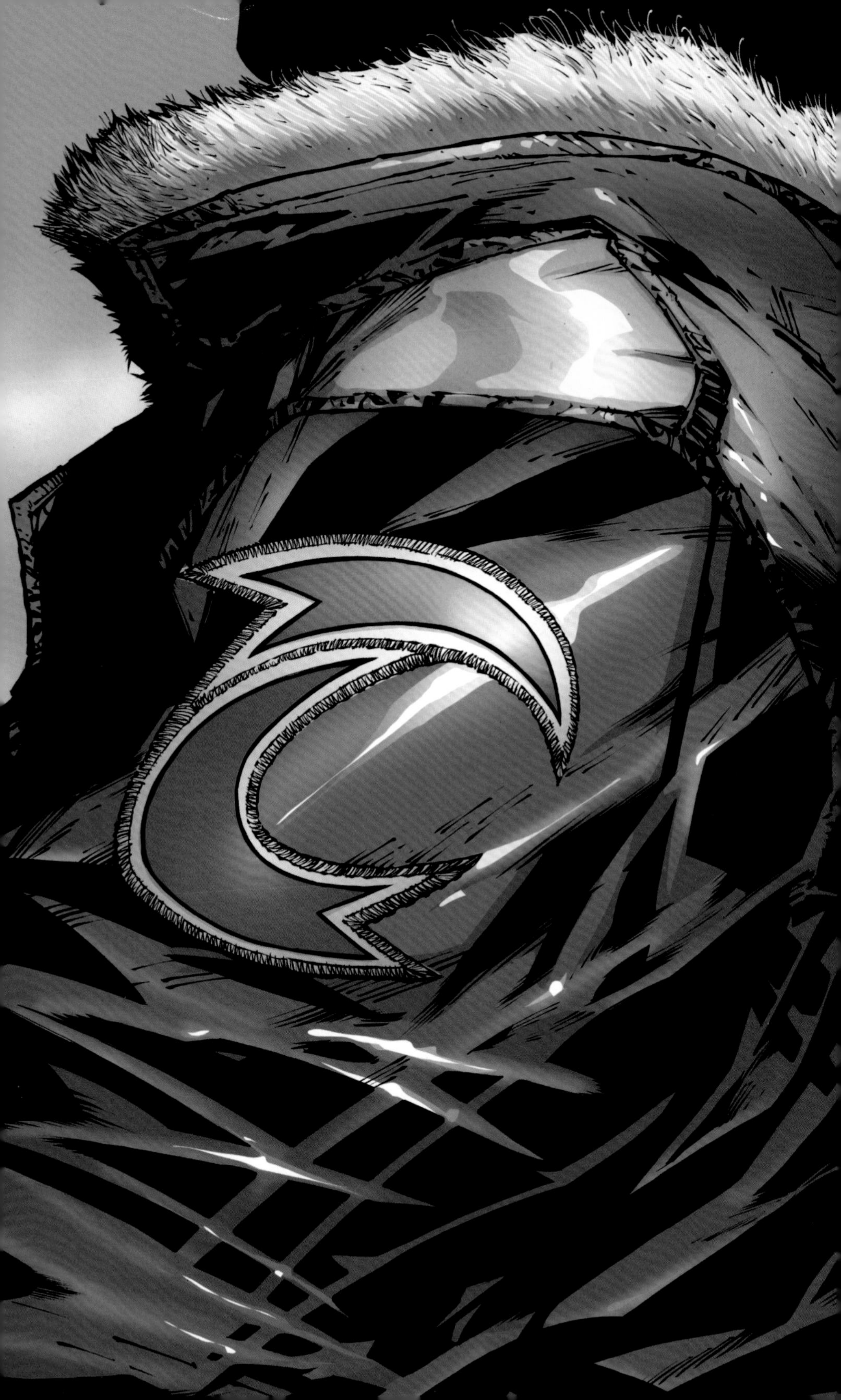

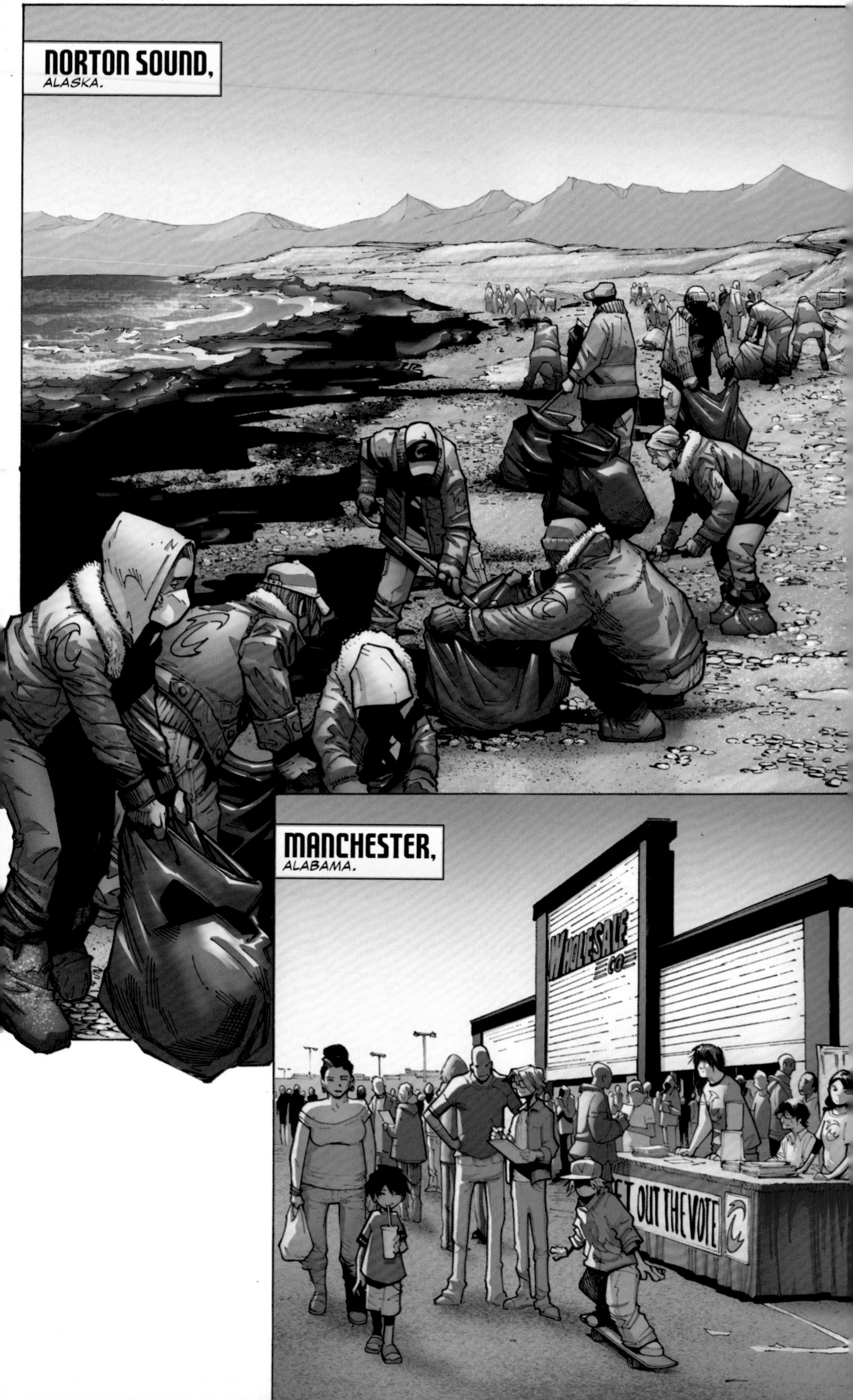

NORTON SOUND,
ALASKA.
MANCHESTER,
ALABAMA.
WHOLESALE CO
OUT THE VOTE

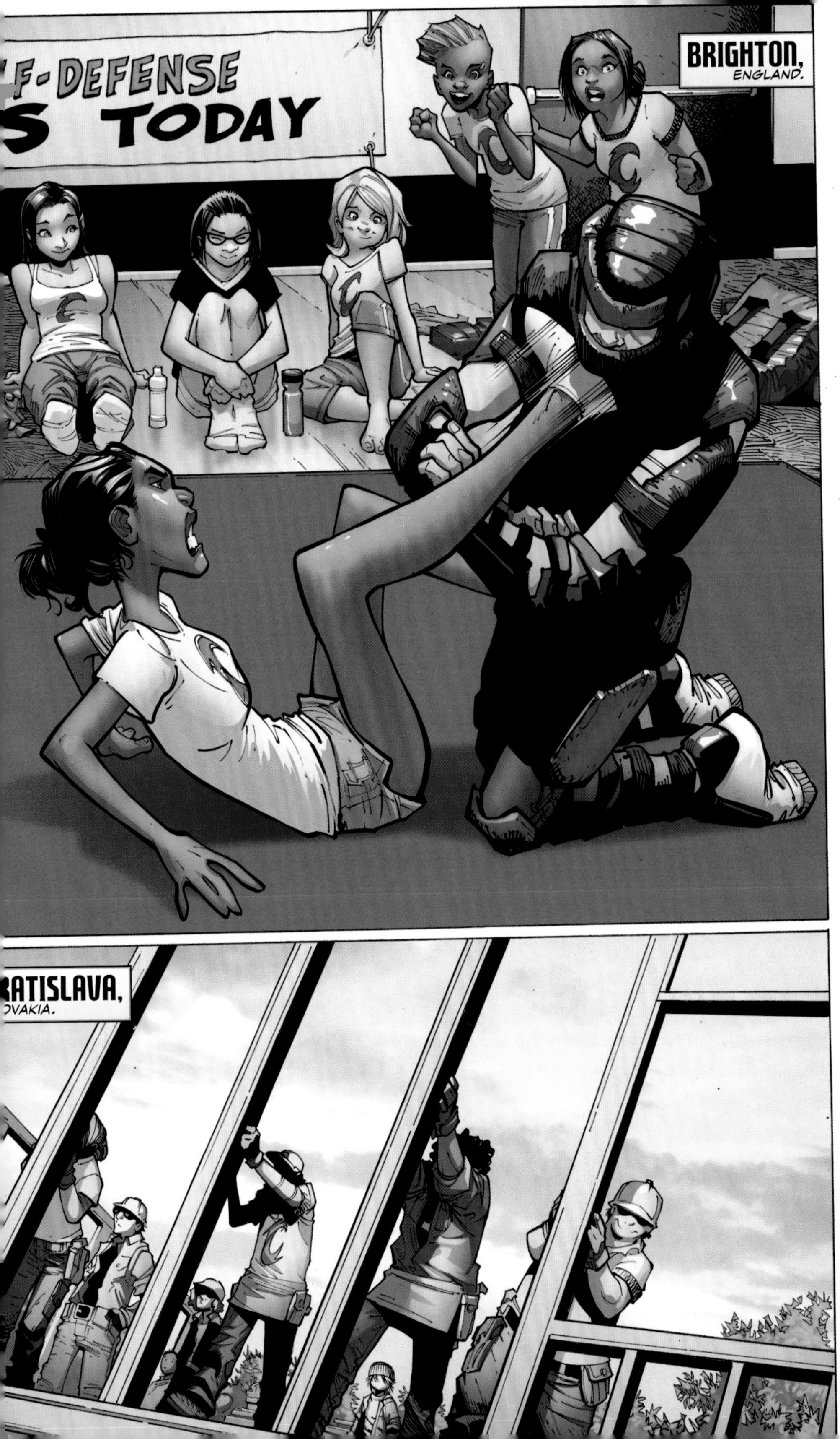

F-DEFENSE
S TODAY
BRIGHTON,
ENGLAND.
RATISLAVA,
OVAKIA.

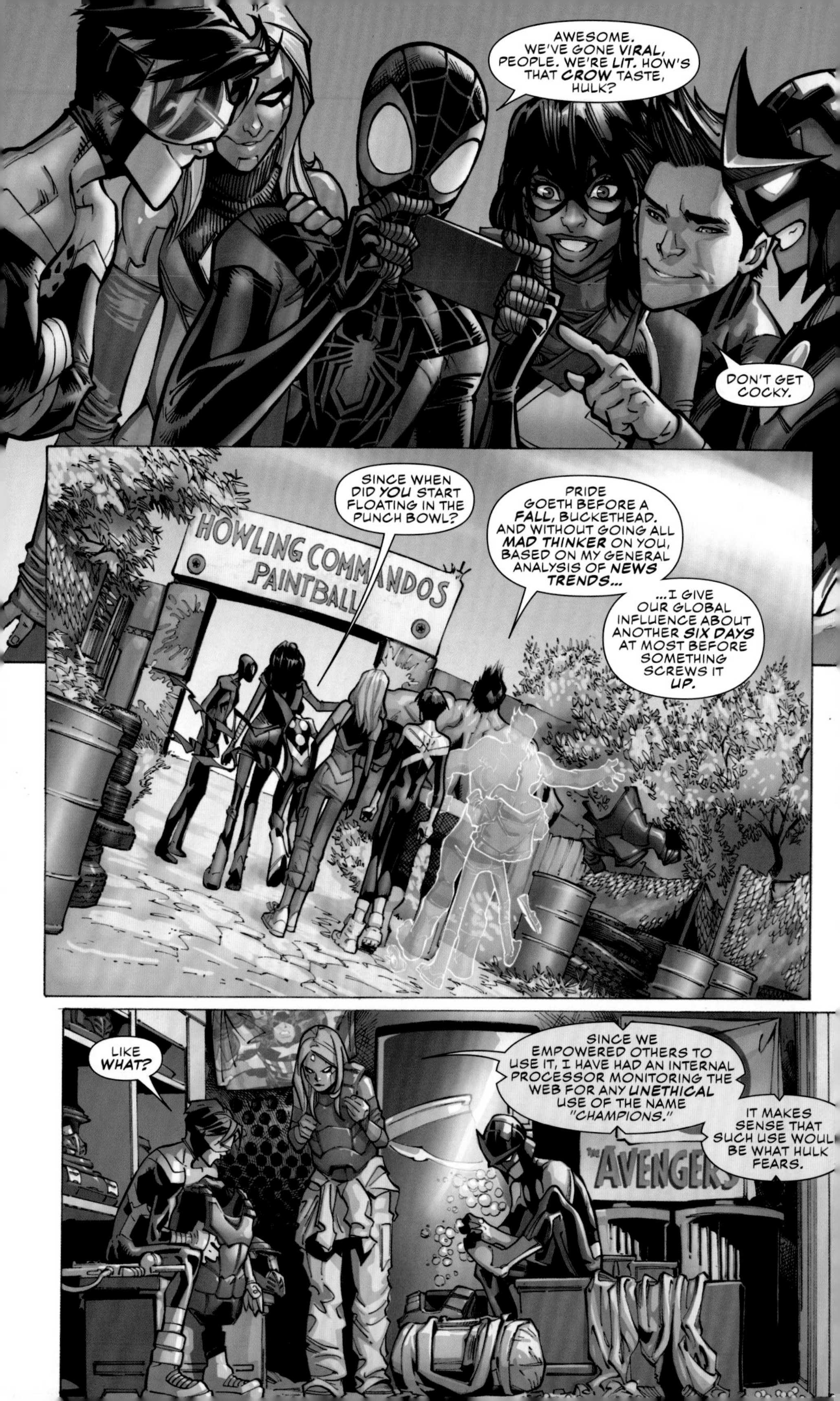
AWESOME. WE'VE GONE VIRAL, PEOPLE. WE'RE LIT. HOW'S THAT CROW TASTE, HULK?
DON'T GET COCKY.
SINCE WHEN DID YOU START FLOATING IN THE PUNCH BOWL?
HOWLING COMMANDOS PAINTBALL
PRIDE GOETH BEFORE A FALL, BUCKETHEAD. AND WITHOUT GOING ALL MAD THINKER ON YOU, BASED ON MY GENERAL ANALYSIS OF NEWS TRENDS...
...I GIVE OUR GLOBAL INFLUENCE ABOUT ANOTHER SIX DAYS AT MOST BEFORE SOMETHING SCREWS IT UP.
LIKE WHAT?
SINCE WE EMPOWERED OTHERS TO USE IT, I HAVE HAD AN INTERNAL PROCESSOR MONITORING THE WEB FOR ANY UNETHICAL USE OF THE NAME "CHAMPIONS."
IT MAKES SENSE THAT SUCH USE WOUL BE WHAT HULK FEARS.
AVENGERS

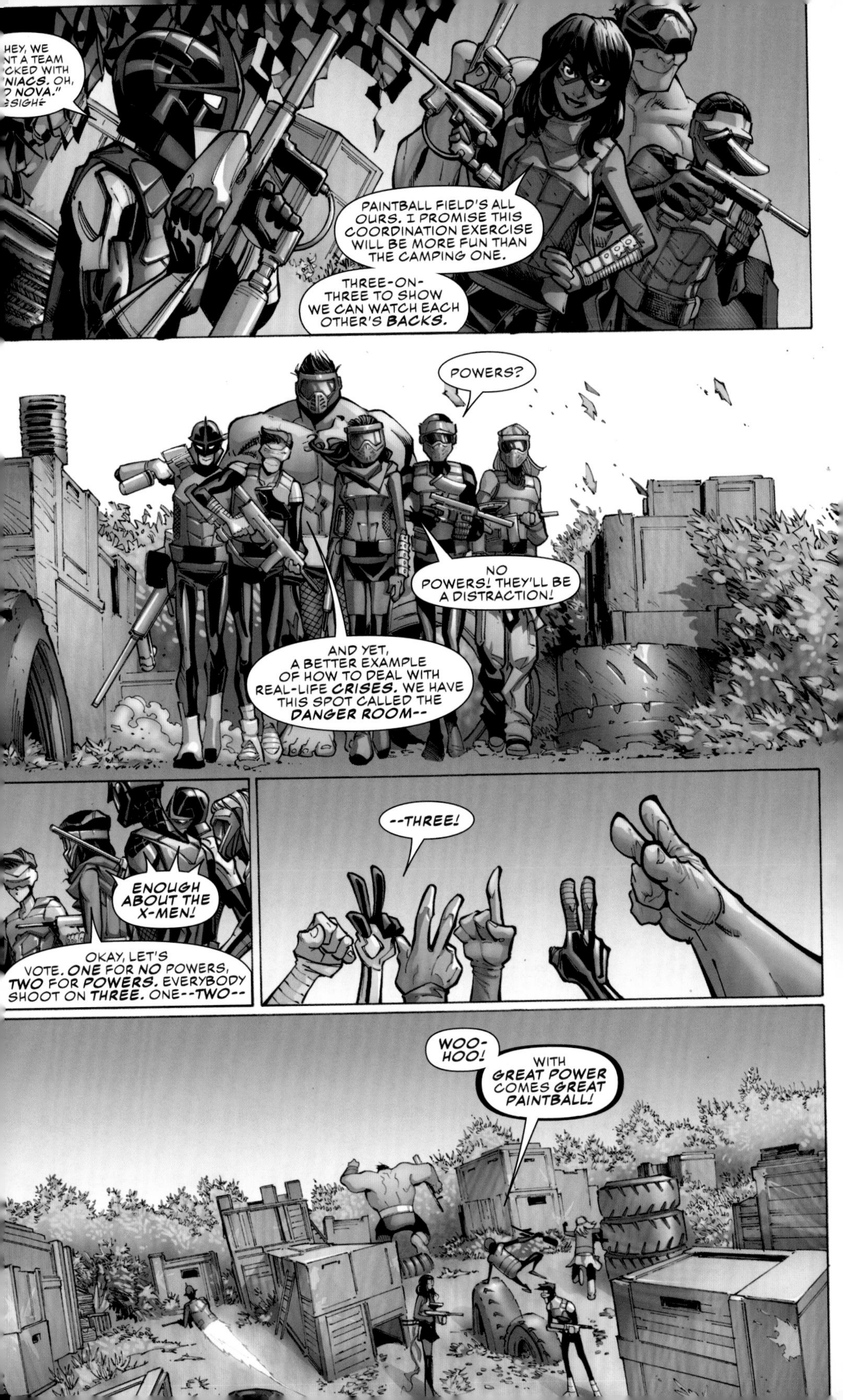
HEY, WE NT A TEAM CKED WITH NIACS. OH, D NOVA." SIGH
PAINTBALL FIELD'S ALL OURS. I PROMISE THIS COORDINATION EXERCISE WILL BE MORE FUN THAN THE CAMPING ONE.
THREE-ON-THREE TO SHOW WE CAN WATCH EACH OTHER'S BACKS.
POWERS?
NO POWERS! THEY'LL BE A DISTRACTION!
AND YET, A BETTER EXAMPLE OF HOW TO DEAL WITH REAL-LIFE CRISES. WE HAVE THIS SPOT CALLED THE DANGER ROOM--
ENOUGH ABOUT THE X-MEN!
OKAY, LET'S VOTE. ONE FOR NO POWERS, TWO FOR POWERS. EVERYBODY SHOOT ON THREE. ONE--TWO--
--THREE!
WOO-HOO!
WITH GREAT POWER COMES GREAT PAINTBALL!

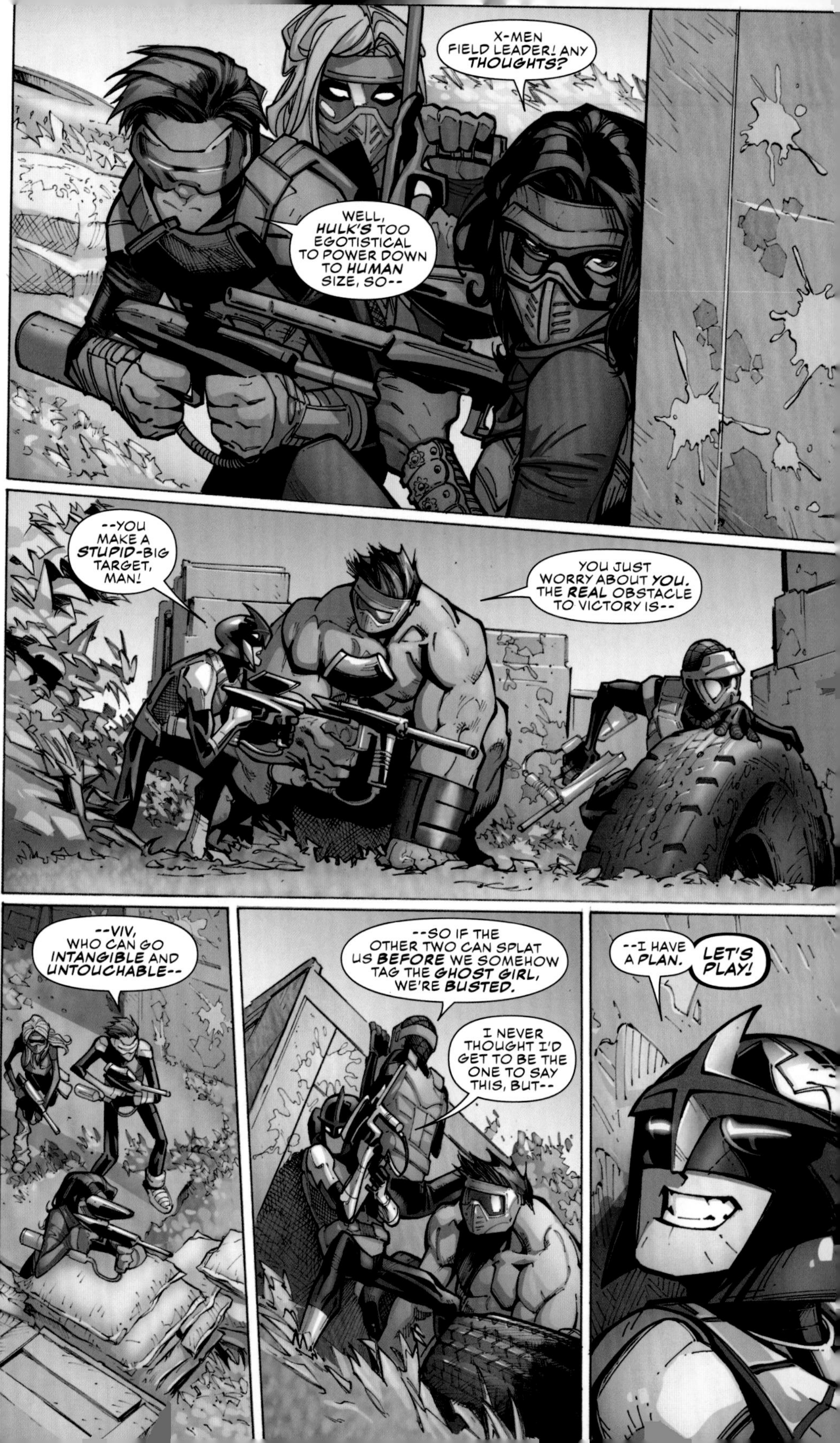
X-MEN FIELD LEADER! ANY THOUGHTS?
WELL, HULK'S TOO EGOTISTICAL TO POWER DOWN TO HUMAN SIZE, SO--
--YOU MAKE A STUPID-BIG TARGET, MAN!
YOU JUST WORRY ABOUT YOU. THE REAL OBSTACLE TO VICTORY IS--
--VIV, WHO CAN GO INTANGIBLE AND UNTOUCHABLE--
--SO IF THE OTHER TWO CAN SPLAT US BEFORE WE SOMEHOW TAG THE GHOST GIRL, WE'RE BUSTED.
I NEVER THOUGHT I'D GET TO BE THE ONE TO SAY THIS, BUT--
--I HAVE A PLAN.
LET'S PLAY!

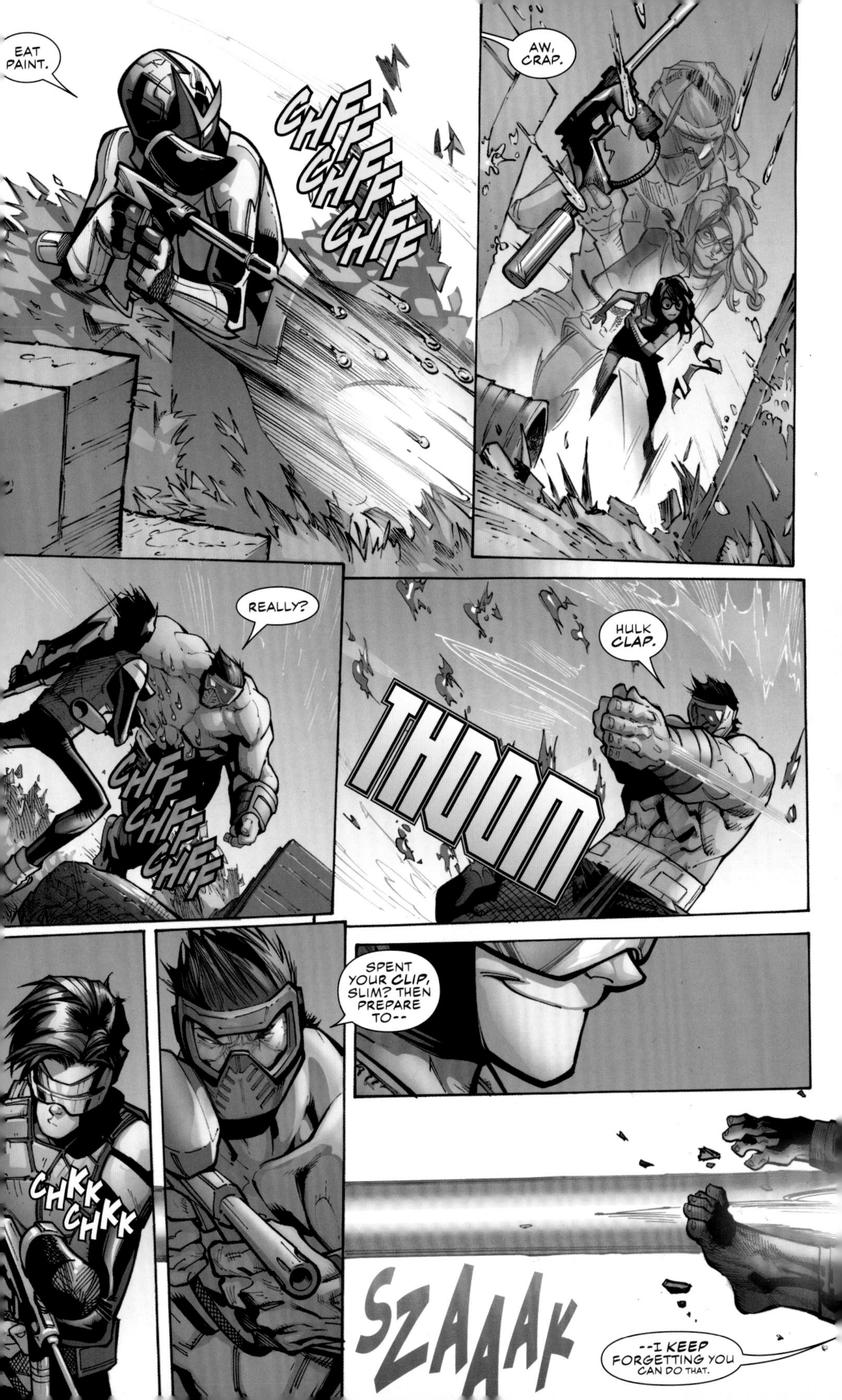

EAT PAINT.
CHFF CHFF CHFF
AW, CRAP.
REALLY?
CHFF CHFF CHFF
HULK CLAP.
THOOM
CHKK CHKK
SPENT YOUR CLIP, SLIM? THEN PREPARE TO--
SZAAAK
--I KEEP FORGETTING YOU CAN DO THAT.

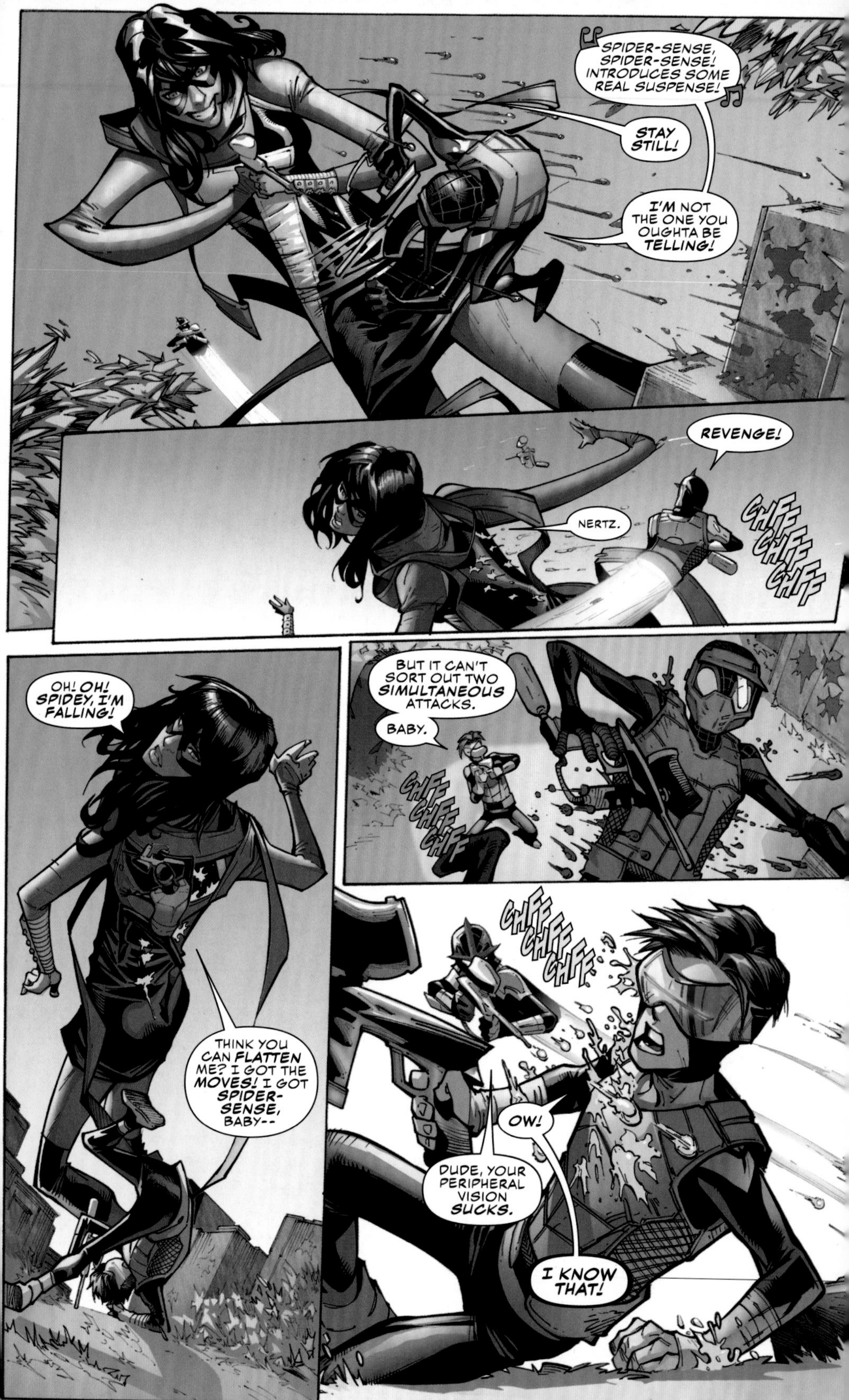

SPIDER-SENSE, SPIDER-SENSE! INTRODUCES SOME REAL SUSPENSE!
STAY STILL!
I'M NOT THE ONE YOU OUGHTA BE TELLING!
REVENGE!
NERTZ.
CHFF CHFF CHFF
OH! OH! SPIDEY, I'M FALLING!
BUT IT CAN'T SORT OUT TWO SIMULTANEOUS ATTACKS.
BABY.
CHFF CHFF CHFF
THINK YOU CAN FLATTEN ME? I GOT THE MOVES! I GOT SPIDER-SENSE, BABY--
CHFF CHFF CHFF
OW!
DUDE, YOUR PERIPHERAL VISION SUCKS.
I KNOW THAT!

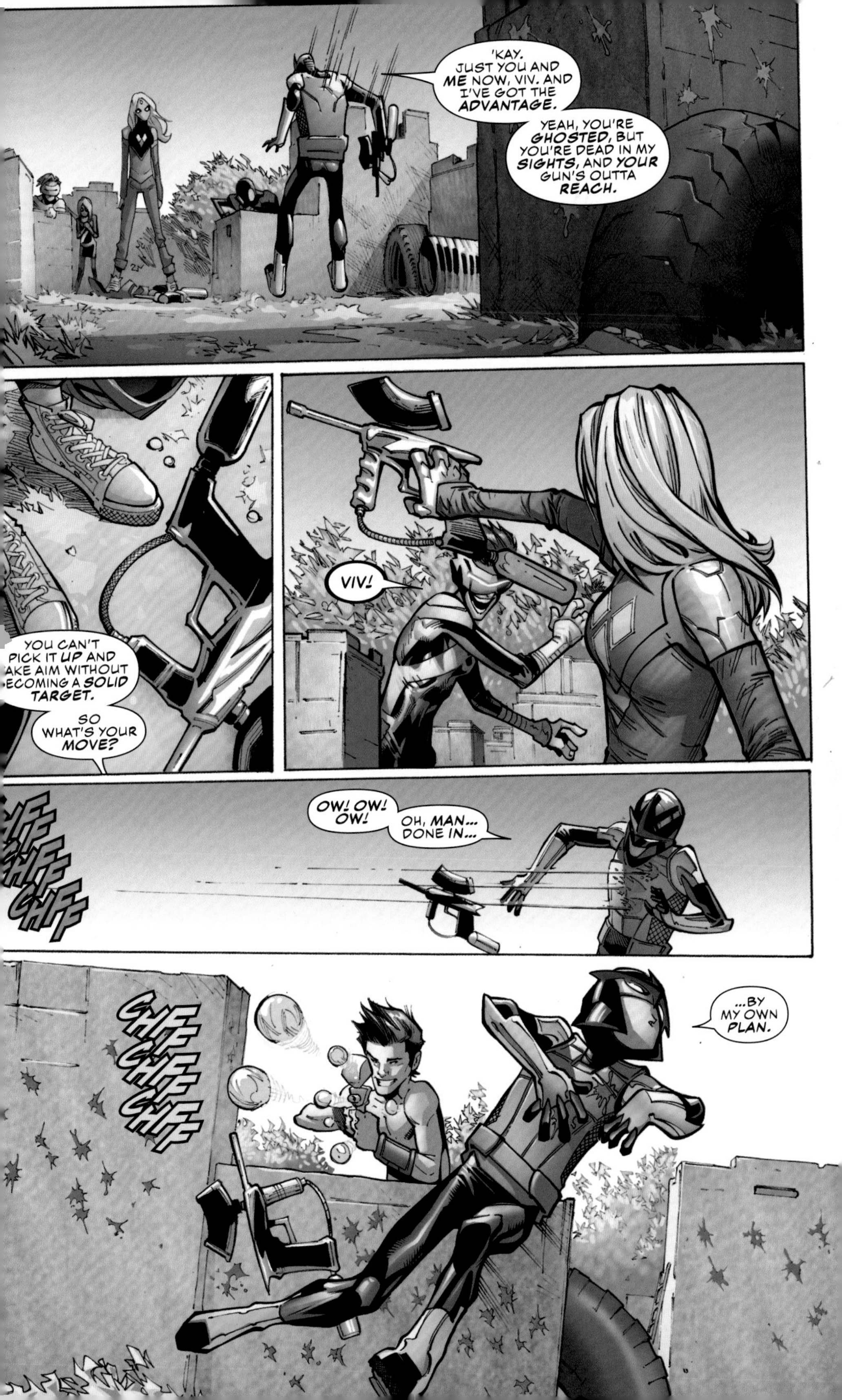

'KAY. JUST YOU AND ME NOW, VIV. AND I'VE GOT THE ADVANTAGE.
YEAH, YOU'RE GHOSTED, BUT YOU'RE DEAD IN MY SIGHTS, AND YOUR GUN'S OUTTA REACH.
YOU CAN'T PICK IT UP AND AKE AIM WITHOUT ECOMING A SOLID TARGET.
SO WHAT'S YOUR MOVE?
VIV!
CHFF
OW! OW! OW!
OH, MAN... DONE IN...
CHFF CHFF CHFF
...BY MY OWN PLAN.

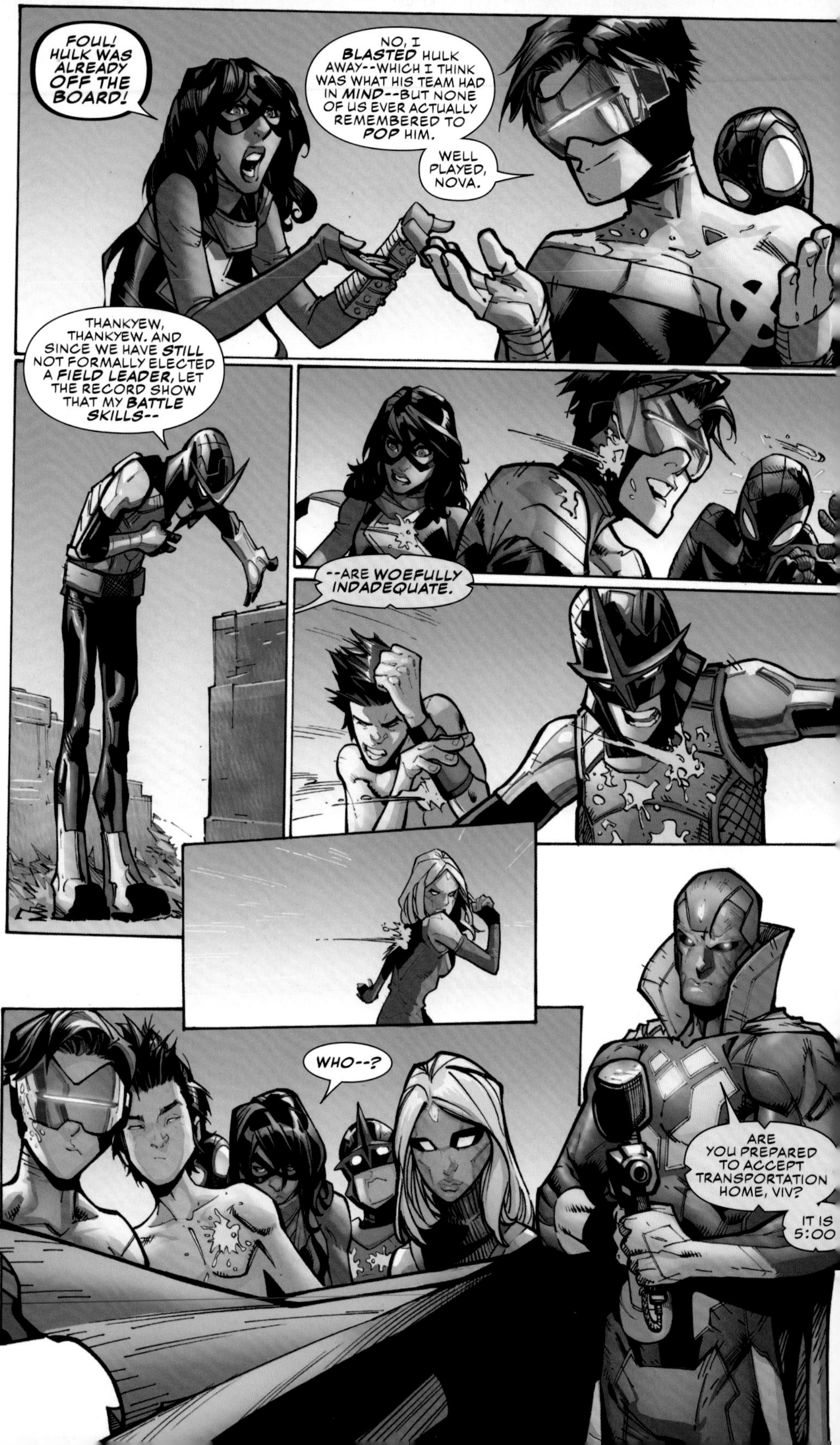
FOUL! HULK WAS ALREADY OFF THE BOARD!
NO, I BLASTED HULK AWAY--WHICH I THINK WAS WHAT HIS TEAM HAD IN MIND--BUT NONE OF US EVER ACTUALLY REMEMBERED TO POP HIM.
WELL PLAYED, NOVA.
THANKYEW, THANKYEW. AND SINCE WE HAVE STILL NOT FORMALLY ELECTED A FIELD LEADER, LET THE RECORD SHOW THAT MY BATTLE SKILLS--
--ARE WOEFULLY INDADEQUATE.
WHO--?
ARE YOU PREPARED TO ACCEPT TRANSPORTATION HOME, VIV?
IT IS 5:00

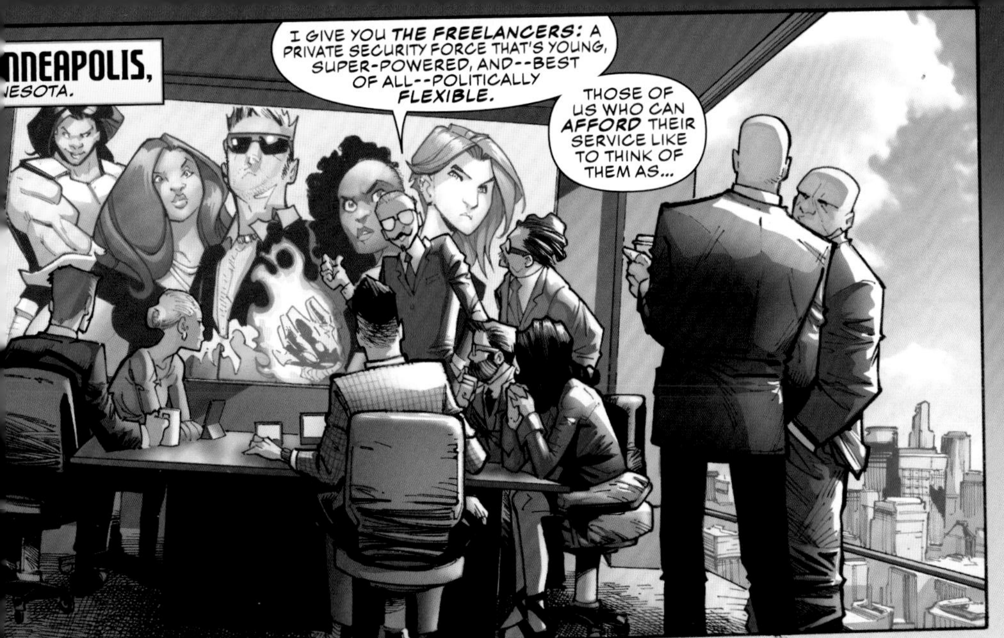

NNEAPOLIS,
NESOTA.
I GIVE YOU THE FREELANCERS: A PRIVATE SECURITY FORCE THAT'S YOUNG, SUPER-POWERED, AND--BEST OF ALL--POLITICALLY FLEXIBLE.
THOSE OF US WHO CAN AFFORD THEIR SERVICE LIKE TO THINK OF THEM AS...

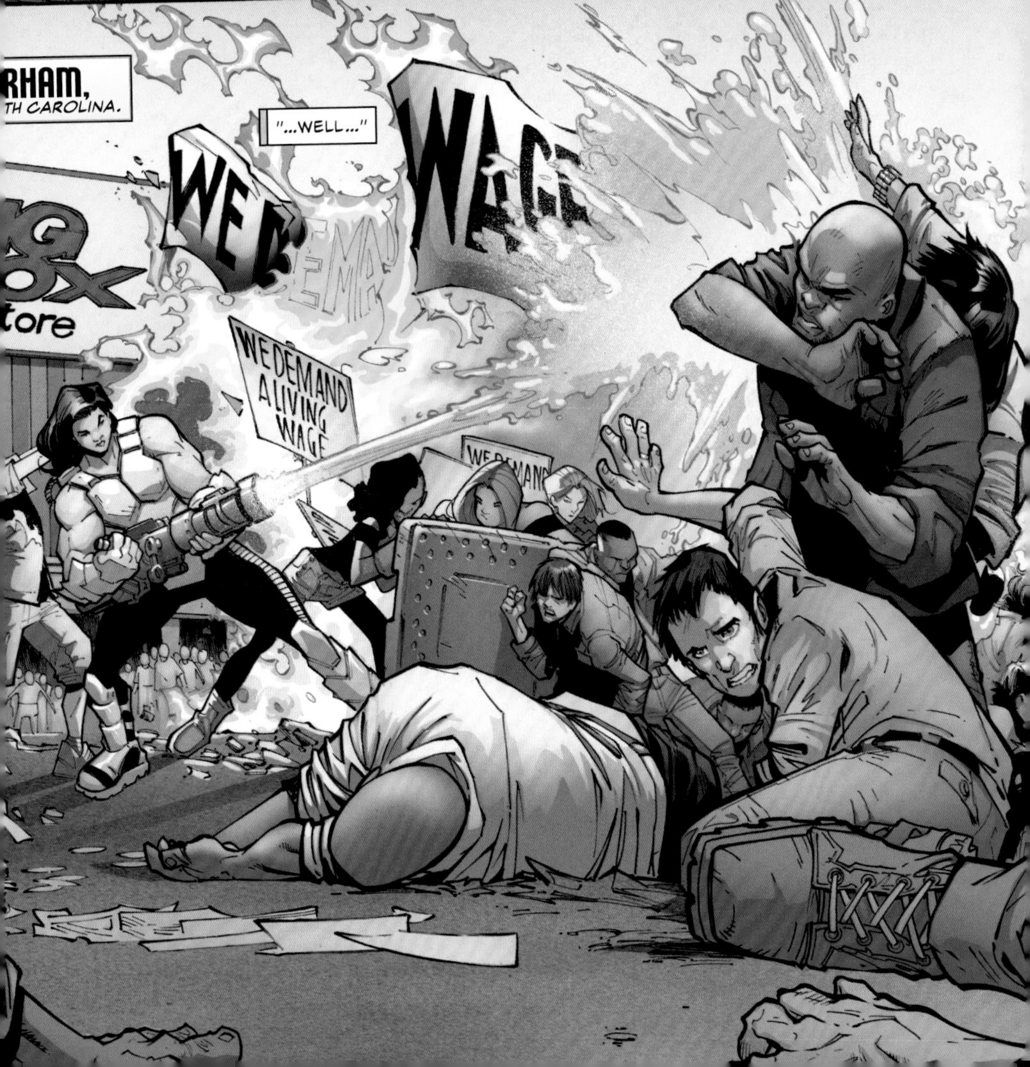

RHAM,
TH CAROLINA.
"...WELL..."
WAGE
WE DEMAND A LIVING WAGE
tore

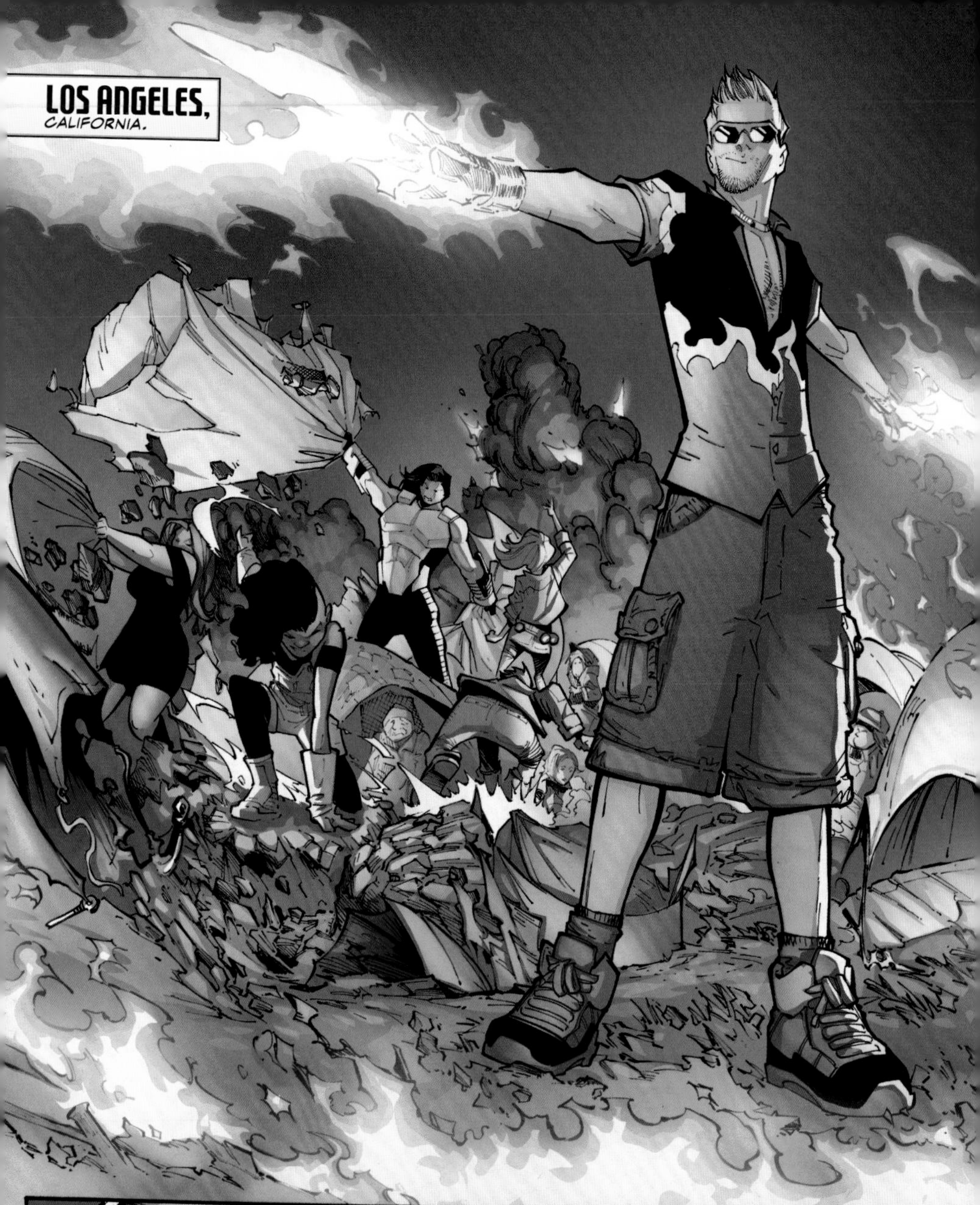
LOS ANGELES,
CALIFORNIA.

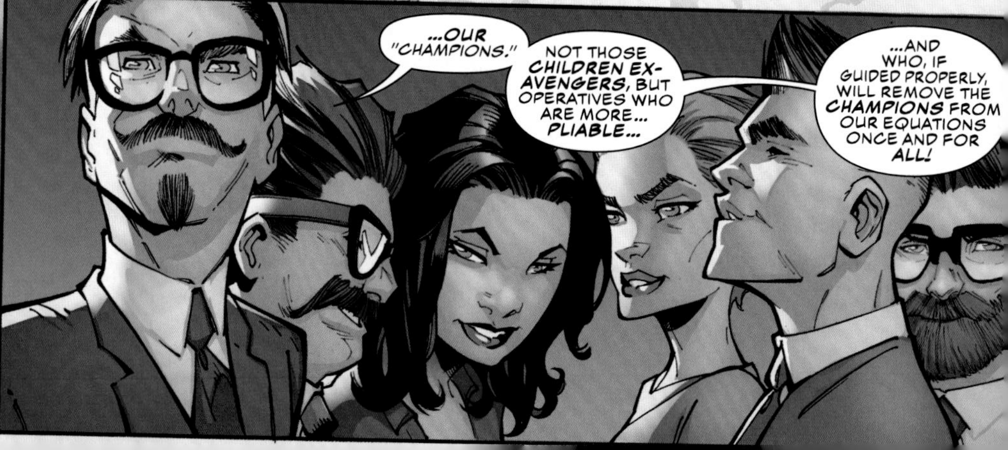
...OUR "CHAMPIONS."
NOT THOSE CHILDREN EX-AVENGERS, BUT OPERATIVES WHO ARE MORE... PLIABLE...
...AND WHO, IF GUIDED PROPERLY, WILL REMOVE THE CHAMPIONS FROM OUR EQUATIONS ONCE AND FOR ALL!

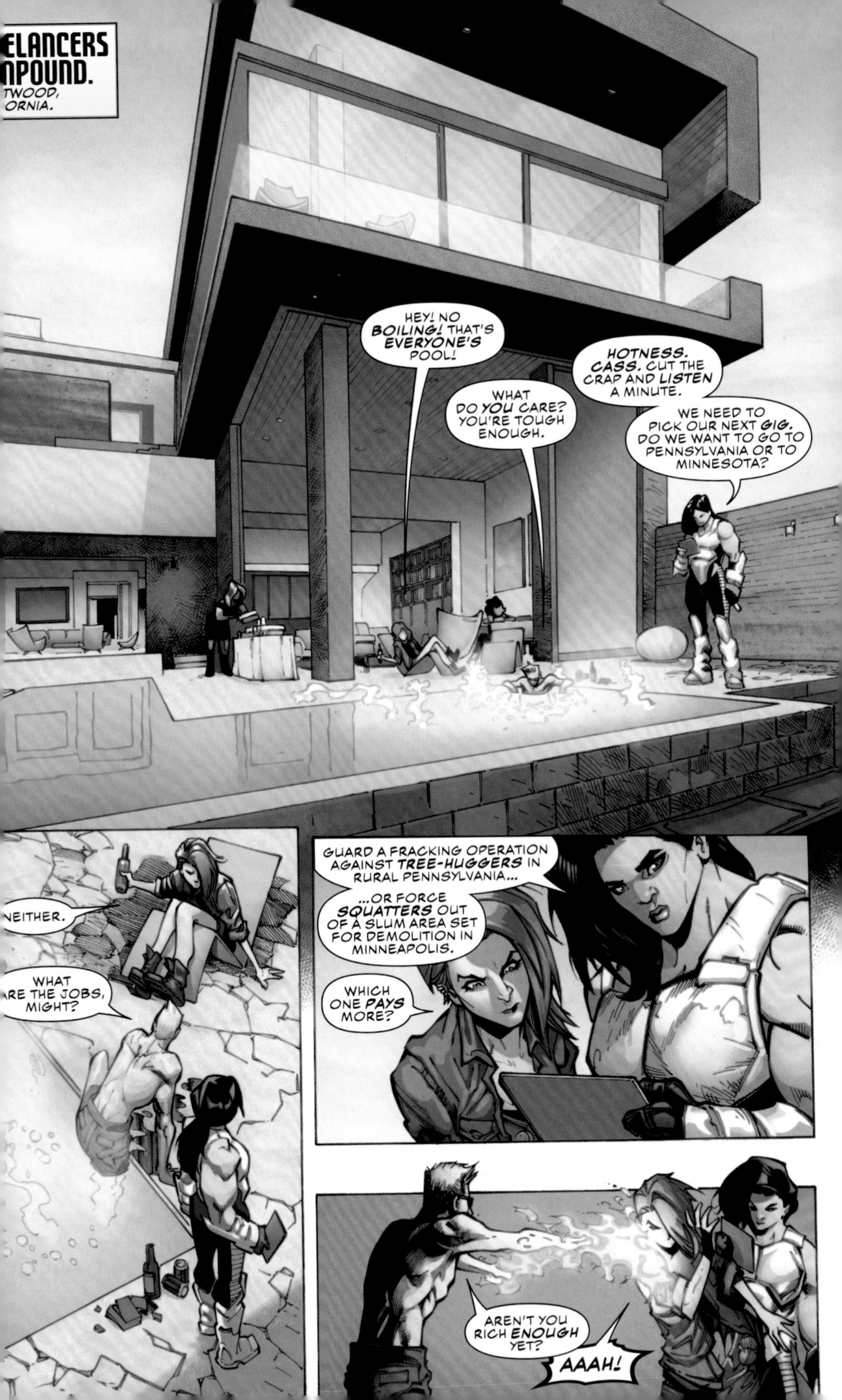

ELANCERS
NPOUND.
TWOOD,
ORNIA.
HEY! NO BOILING! THAT'S EVERYONE'S POOL!
WHAT DO YOU CARE? YOU'RE TOUGH ENOUGH.
HOTNESS. CASS. CUT THE CRAP AND LISTEN A MINUTE.
WE NEED TO PICK OUR NEXT GIG. DO WE WANT TO GO TO PENNSYLVANIA OR TO MINNESOTA?
NEITHER.
WHAT ARE THE JOBS, MIGHT?
GUARD A FRACKING OPERATION AGAINST TREE-HUGGERS IN RURAL PENNSYLVANIA...
...OR FORCE SQUATTERS OUT OF A SLUM AREA SET FOR DEMOLITION IN MINNEAPOLIS.
WHICH ONE PAYS MORE?
AREN'T YOU RICH ENOUGH YET?
AAAH!

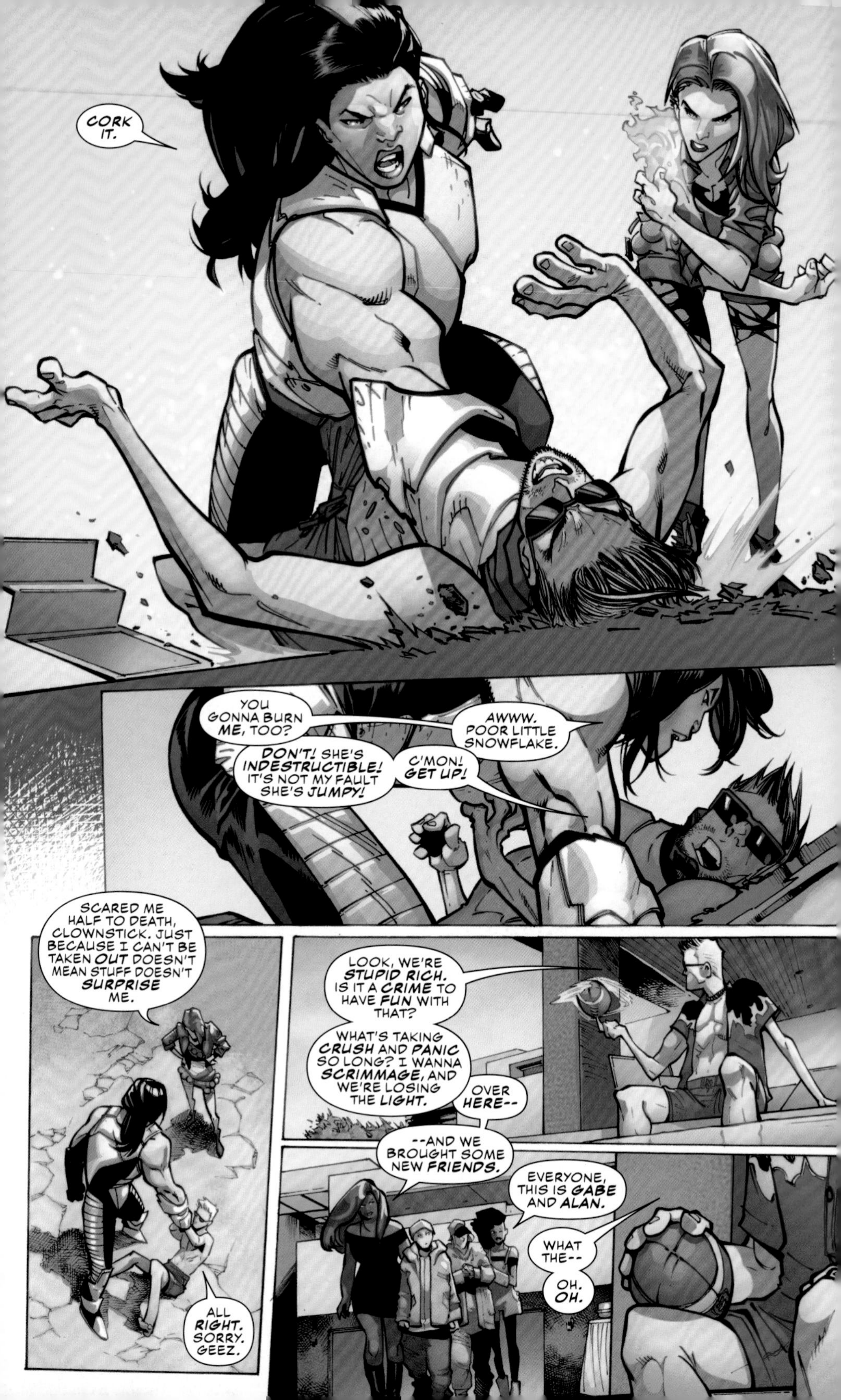
CORK IT.
YOU GONNA BURN ME, TOO?
AWWW. POOR LITTLE SNOWFLAKE.
DON'T! SHE'S INDESTRUCTIBLE! IT'S NOT MY FAULT SHE'S JUMPY!
C'MON! GET UP!
SCARED ME HALF TO DEATH, CLOWNSTICK. JUST BECAUSE I CAN'T BE TAKEN OUT DOESN'T MEAN STUFF DOESN'T SURPRISE ME.
ALL RIGHT. SORRY. GEEZ.
LOOK, WE'RE STUPID RICH. IS IT A CRIME TO HAVE FUN WITH THAT?
WHAT'S TAKING CRUSH AND PANIC SO LONG? I WANNA SCRIMMAGE, AND WE'RE LOSING THE LIGHT.
OVER HERE--
--AND WE BROUGHT SOME NEW FRIENDS.
EVERYONE, THIS IS GABE AND ALAN.
WHAT THE--
OH. OH.

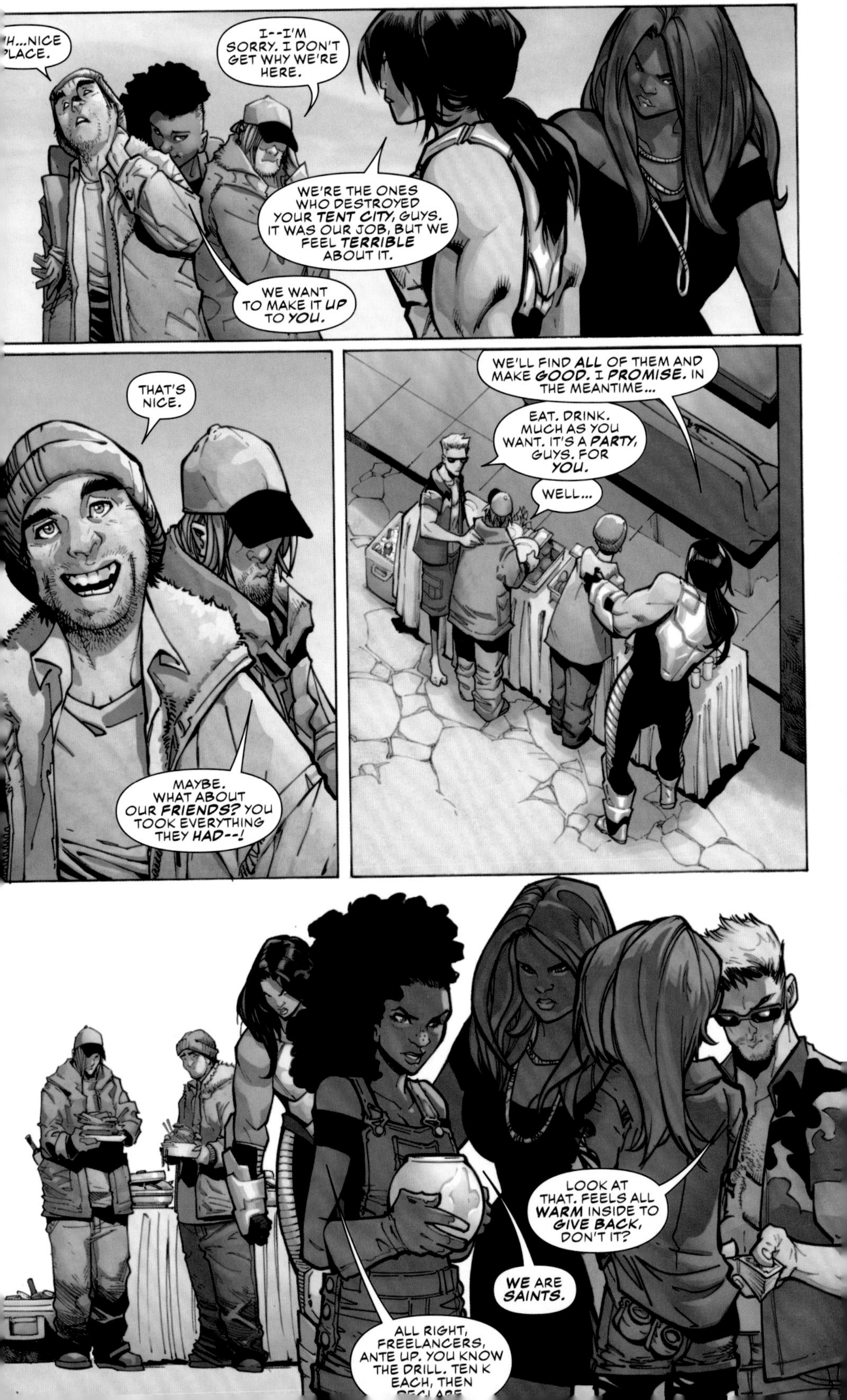

...H...NICE PLACE.
I--I'M SORRY. I DON'T GET WHY WE'RE HERE.
WE'RE THE ONES WHO DESTROYED YOUR TENT CITY, GUYS. IT WAS OUR JOB, BUT WE FEEL TERRIBLE ABOUT IT.
WE WANT TO MAKE IT UP TO YOU.
THAT'S NICE.
MAYBE. WHAT ABOUT OUR FRIENDS? YOU TOOK EVERYTHING THEY HAD--!
WE'LL FIND ALL OF THEM AND MAKE GOOD. I PROMISE. IN THE MEANTIME...
EAT. DRINK. MUCH AS YOU WANT. IT'S A PARTY, GUYS. FOR YOU.
WELL...
LOOK AT THAT. FEELS ALL WARM INSIDE TO GIVE BACK, DON'T IT?
WE ARE SAINTS.
ALL RIGHT, FREELANCERS, ANTE UP. YOU KNOW THE DRILL. TEN K EACH, THEN

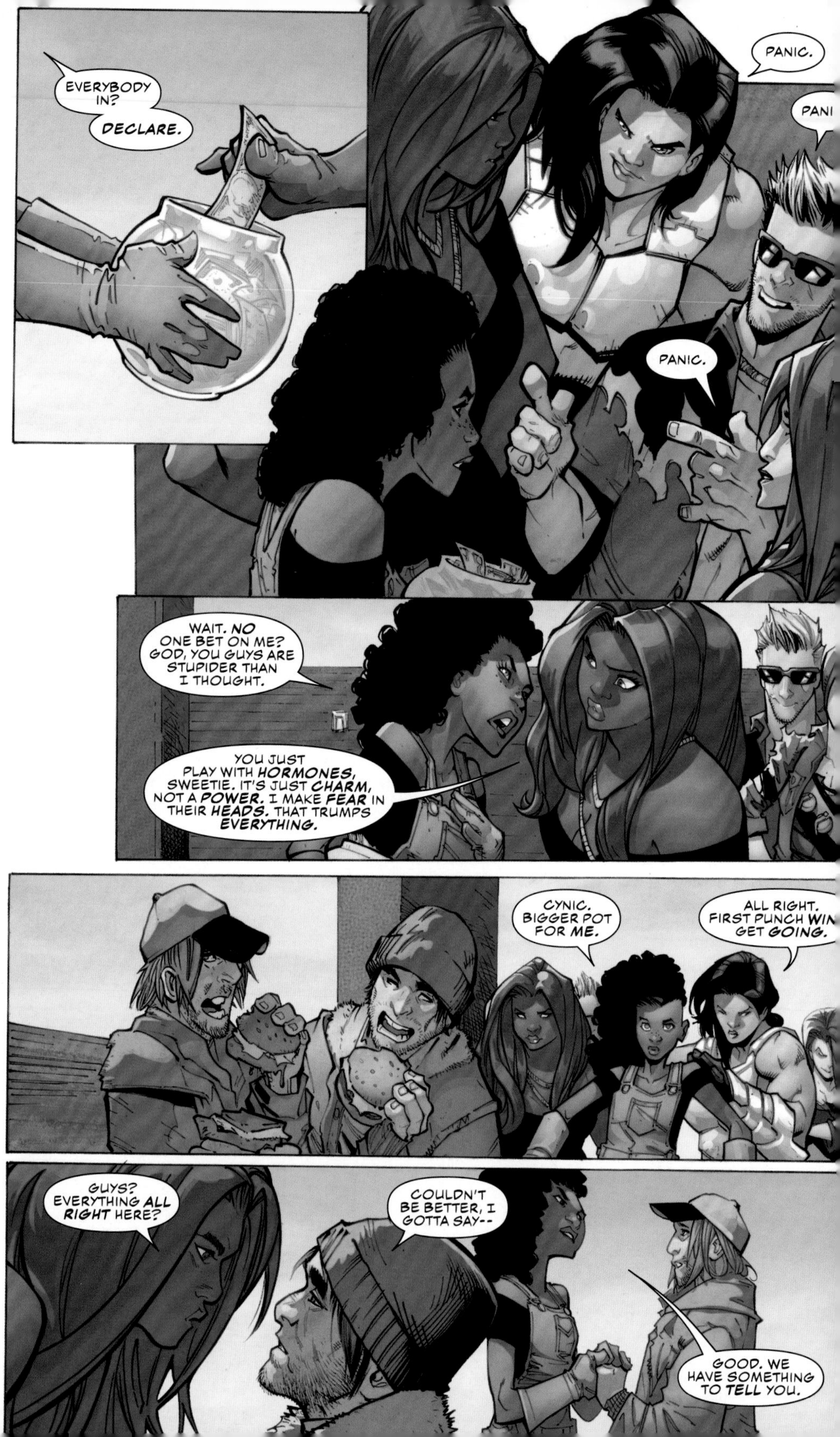
EVERYBODY IN?
DECLARE.
PANIC.
PANI
PANIC.
WAIT. NO ONE BET ON ME? GOD, YOU GUYS ARE STUPIDER THAN I THOUGHT.
YOU JUST PLAY WITH HORMONES, SWEETIE. IT'S JUST CHARM, NOT A POWER. I MAKE FEAR IN THEIR HEADS. THAT TRUMPS EVERYTHING.
CYNIC. BIGGER POT FOR ME.
ALL RIGHT. FIRST PUNCH WIN GET GOING.
GUYS? EVERYTHING ALL RIGHT HERE?
COULDN'T BE BETTER, I GOTTA SAY--
GOOD. WE HAVE SOMETHING TO TELL YOU.

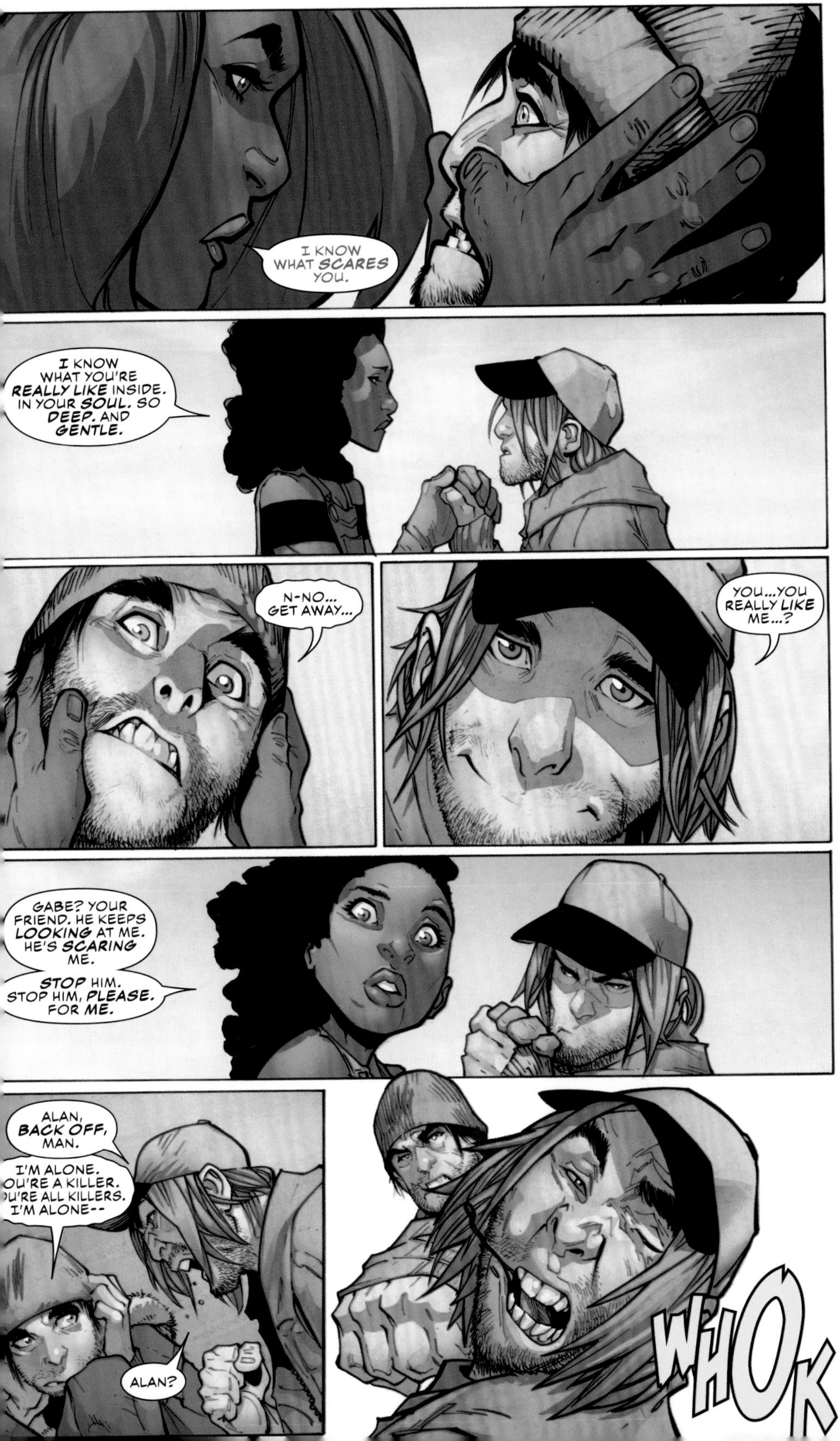
I KNOW WHAT SCARES YOU.
I KNOW WHAT YOU'RE REALLY LIKE INSIDE. IN YOUR SOUL. SO DEEP. AND GENTLE.
N-NO... GET AWAY...
YOU...YOU REALLY LIKE ME...?
GABE? YOUR FRIEND. HE KEEPS LOOKING AT ME. HE'S SCARING ME.
STOP HIM. STOP HIM, PLEASE. FOR ME.
ALAN, BACK OFF, MAN.
I'M ALONE. OU'RE A KILLER. U'RE ALL KILLERS. I'M ALONE--
ALAN?
WHOK

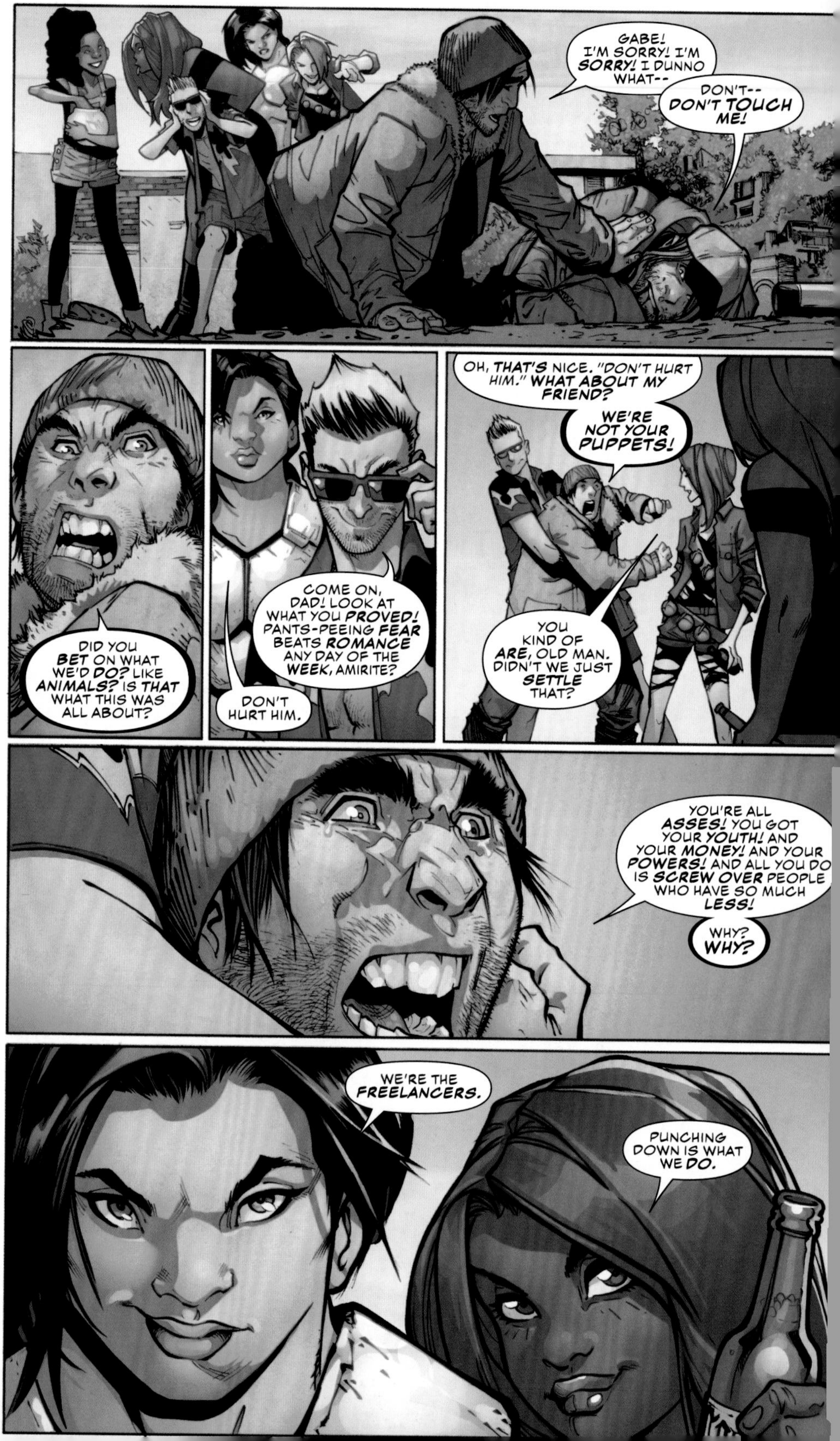
GABE! I'M SORRY! I'M SORRY! I DUNNO WHAT--
DON'T-- DON'T TOUCH ME!
DID YOU BET ON WHAT WE'D DO? LIKE ANIMALS? IS THAT WHAT THIS WAS ALL ABOUT?
DON'T HURT HIM.
COME ON, DAD! LOOK AT WHAT YOU PROVED! PANTS-PEEING FEAR BEATS ROMANCE ANY DAY OF THE WEEK, AMIRITE?
OH, THAT'S NICE. "DON'T HURT HIM." WHAT ABOUT MY FRIEND?
WE'RE NOT YOUR PUPPETS!
YOU KIND OF ARE, OLD MAN. DIDN'T WE JUST SETTLE THAT?
YOU'RE ALL ASSES! YOU GOT YOUR YOUTH! AND YOUR MONEY! AND YOUR POWERS! AND ALL YOU DO IS SCREW OVER PEOPLE WHO HAVE SO MUCH LESS!
WHY? WHY?
WE'RE THE FREELANCERS.
PUNCHING DOWN IS WHAT WE DO.

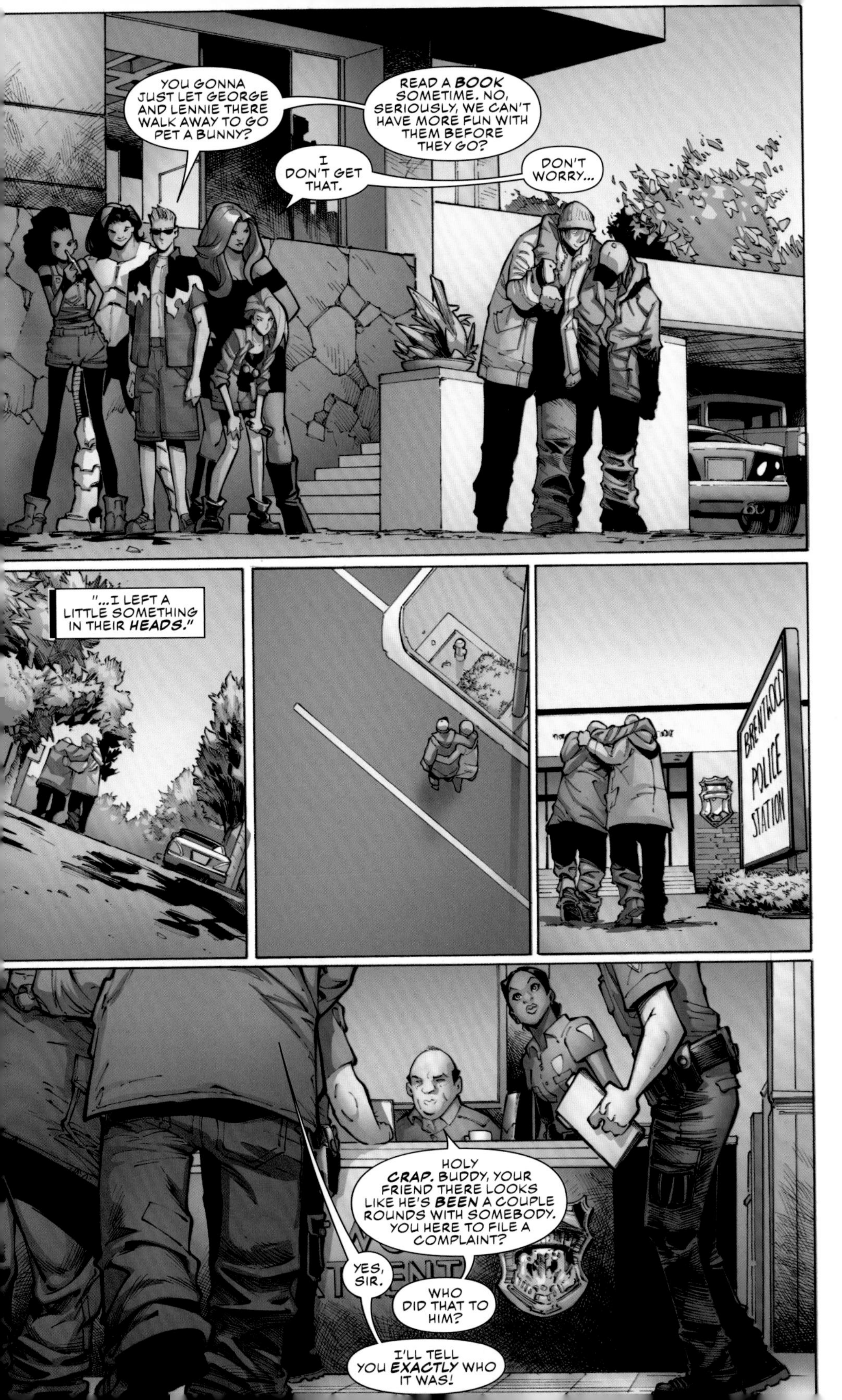
YOU GONNA JUST LET GEORGE AND LENNIE THERE WALK AWAY TO GO PET A BUNNY?
READ A BOOK SOMETIME. NO, SERIOUSLY, WE CAN'T HAVE MORE FUN WITH THEM BEFORE THEY GO?
I DON'T GET THAT.
DON'T WORRY...
"...I LEFT A LITTLE SOMETHING IN THEIR HEADS."
BRENTWOOD POLICE STATION
HOLY CRAP. BUDDY, YOUR FRIEND THERE LOOKS LIKE HE'S BEEN A COUPLE ROUNDS WITH SOMEBODY. YOU HERE TO FILE A COMPLAINT?
YES, SIR.
WHO DID THAT TO HIM?
I'LL TELL YOU EXACTLY WHO IT WAS!

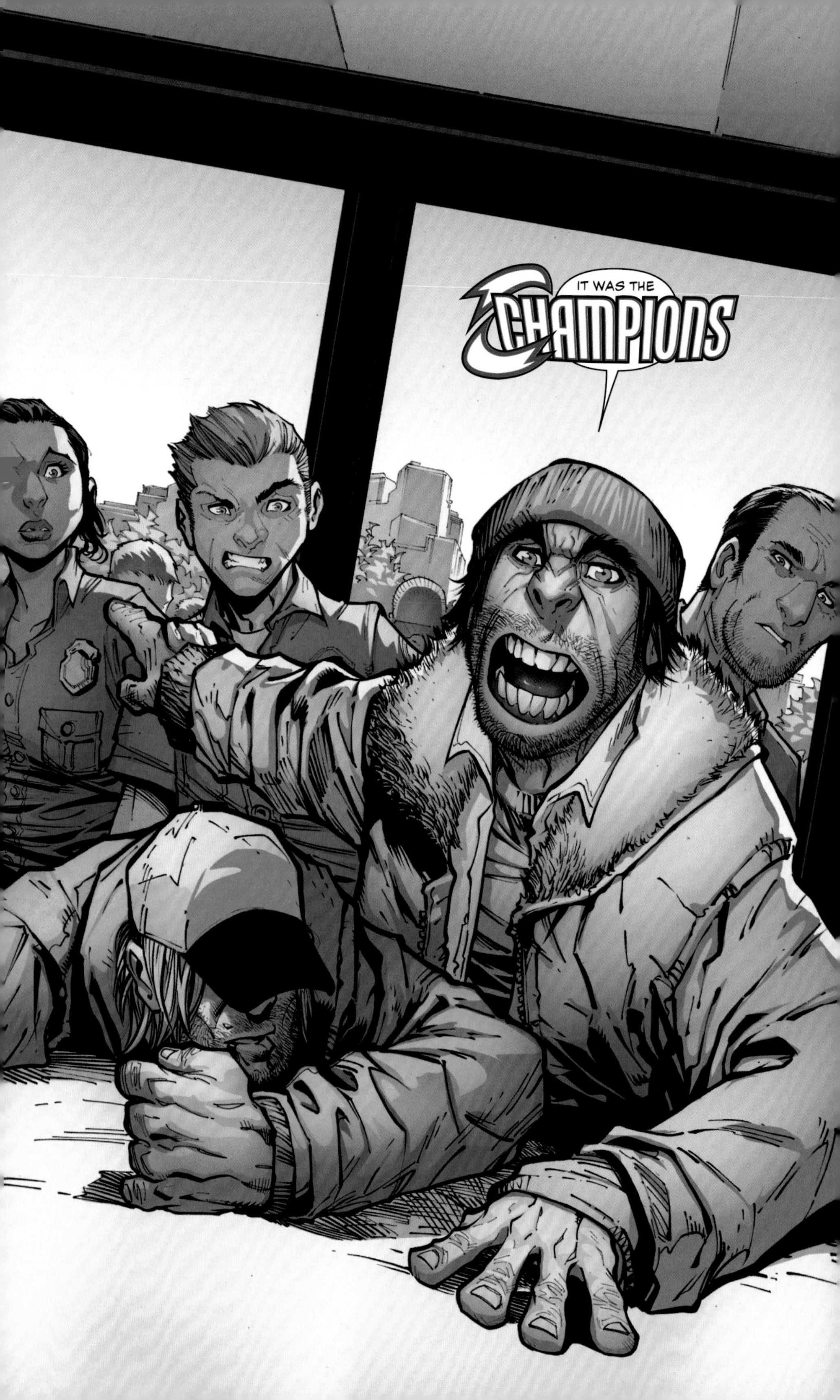
IT WAS THE CHAMPIONS

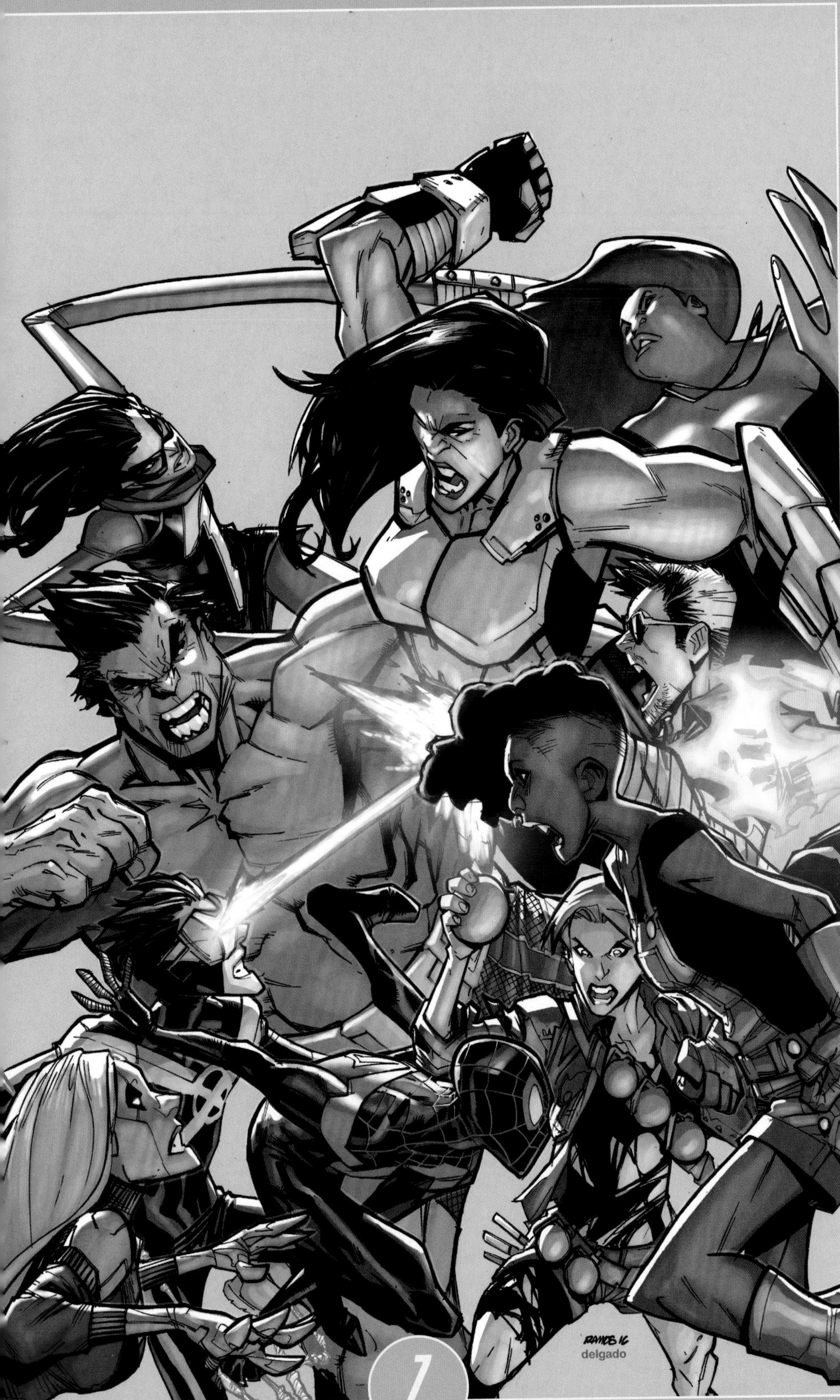
RAMOS 16
delgado

7

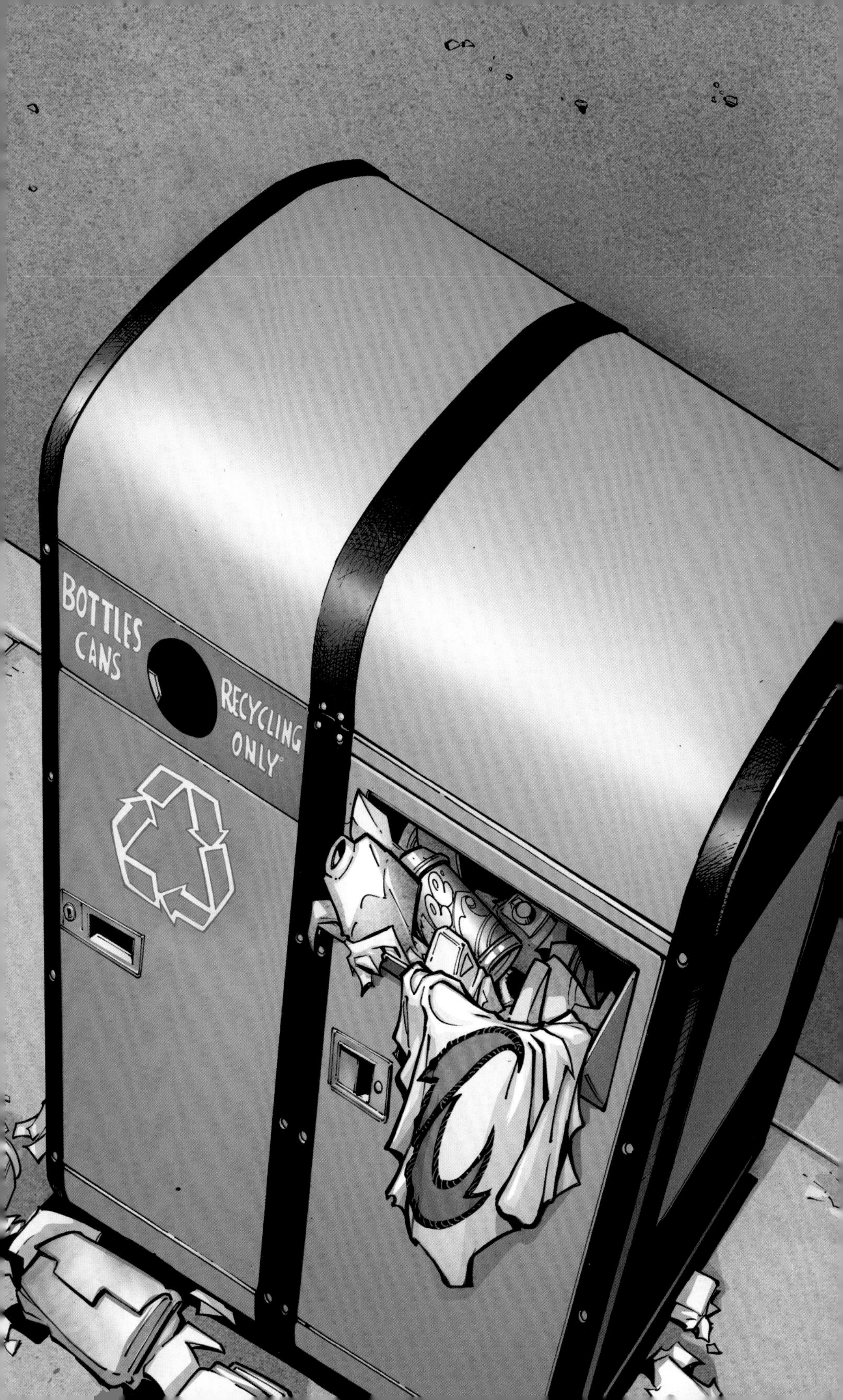
BOTTLES
CANS
RECYCLING
ONLY

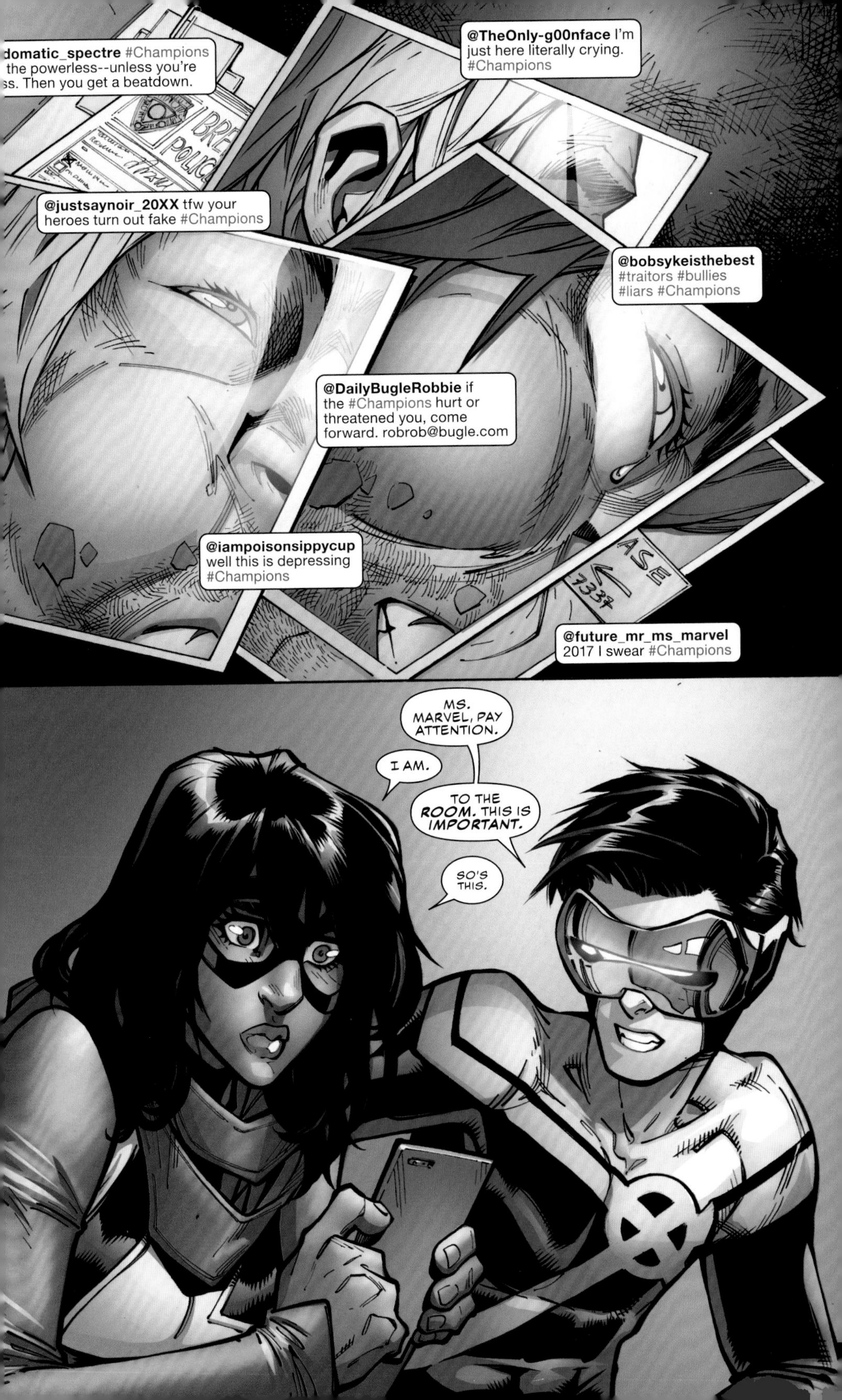

domatic_spectre #Champions the powerless--unless you're ss. Then you get a beatdown.
@TheOnly-g00nface I'm just here literally crying. #Champions
@justsaynoir_20XX tfw your heroes turn out fake #Champions
@bobsykeisthebest #traitors #bullies #liars #Champions
@DailyBugleRobbie if the #Champions hurt or threatened you, come forward. robrob@bugle.com
@iampoisonsippycup well this is depressing #Champions
@future_mr_ms_marvel 2017 I swear #Champions
MS. MARVEL, PAY ATTENTION.
I AM.
TO THE ROOM. THIS IS IMPORTANT.
SO'S THIS.

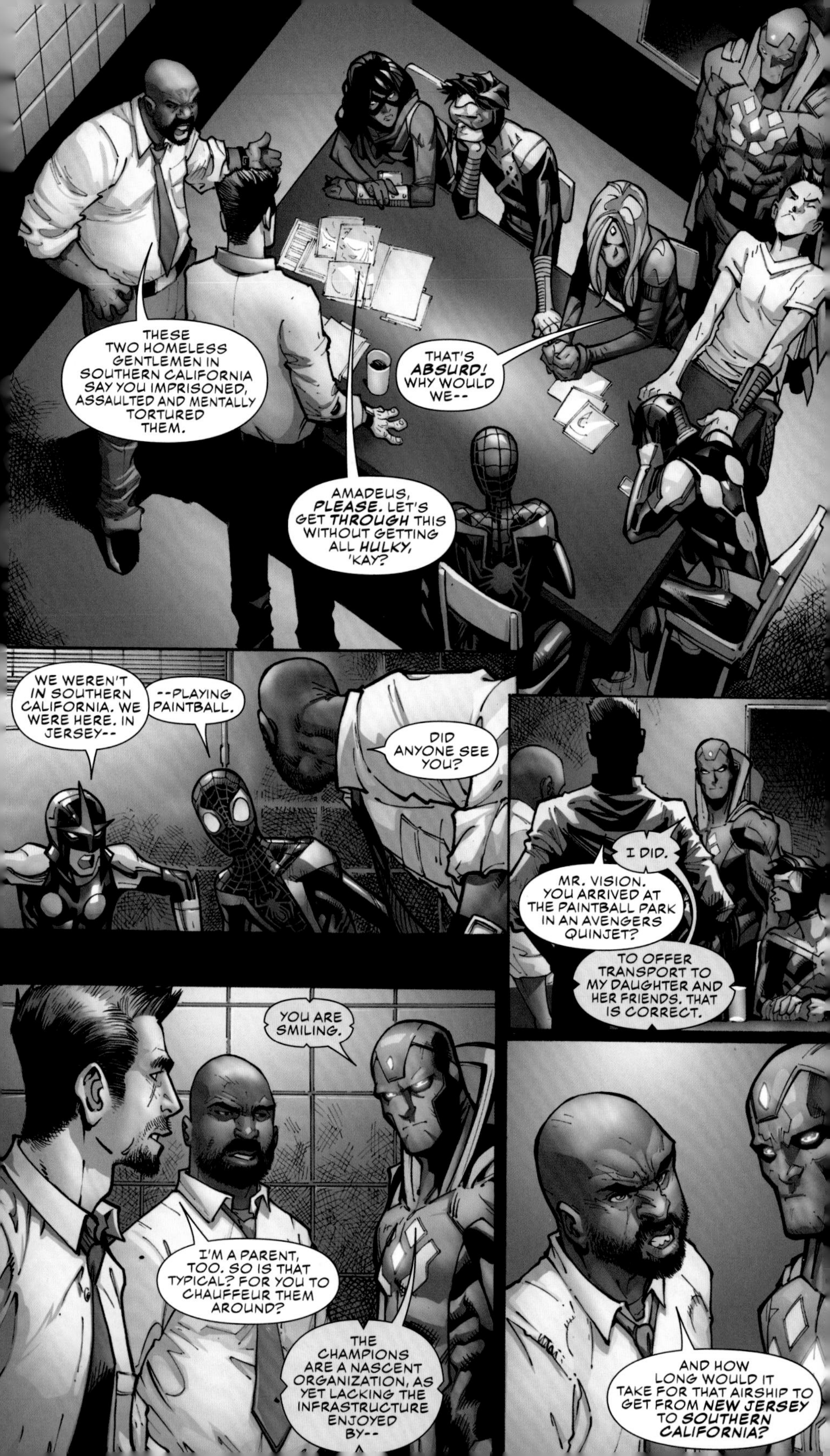

THESE TWO HOMELESS GENTLEMEN IN SOUTHERN CALIFORNIA SAY YOU IMPRISONED, ASSAULTED AND MENTALLY TORTURED THEM.
THAT'S ABSURD! WHY WOULD WE--
AMADEUS, PLEASE. LET'S GET THROUGH THIS WITHOUT GETTING ALL HULKY, 'KAY?
WE WEREN'T IN SOUTHERN CALIFORNIA. WE WERE HERE. IN JERSEY--
--PLAYING PAINTBALL.
DID ANYONE SEE YOU?
I DID.
MR. VISION. YOU ARRIVED AT THE PAINTBALL PARK IN AN AVENGERS QUINJET?
TO OFFER TRANSPORT TO MY DAUGHTER AND HER FRIENDS. THAT IS CORRECT.
YOU ARE SMILING.
I'M A PARENT, TOO. SO IS THAT TYPICAL? FOR YOU TO CHAUFFEUR THEM AROUND?
THE CHAMPIONS ARE A NASCENT ORGANIZATION, AS YET LACKING THE INFRASTRUCTURE ENJOYED BY--
AND HOW LONG WOULD IT TAKE FOR THAT AIRSHIP TO GET FROM NEW JERSEY TO SOUTHERN CALIFORNIA?

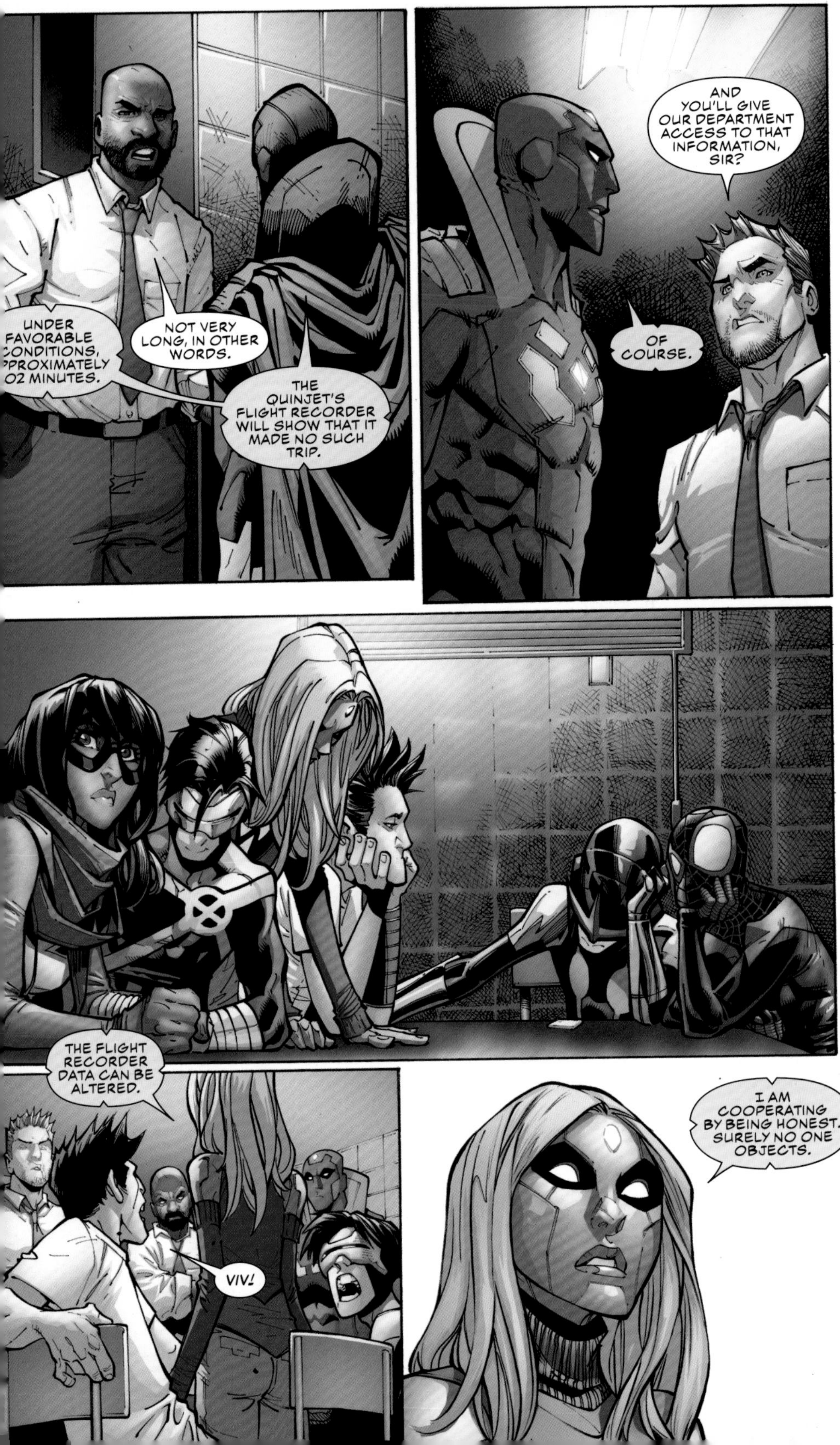
UNDER FAVORABLE CONDITIONS, APPROXIMATELY 102 MINUTES.
NOT VERY LONG, IN OTHER WORDS.
THE QUINJET'S FLIGHT RECORDER WILL SHOW THAT IT MADE NO SUCH TRIP.
AND YOU'LL GIVE OUR DEPARTMENT ACCESS TO THAT INFORMATION, SIR?
OF COURSE.
THE FLIGHT RECORDER DATA CAN BE ALTERED.
VIV!
I AM COOPERATING BY BEING HONEST. SURELY NO ONE OBJECTS.

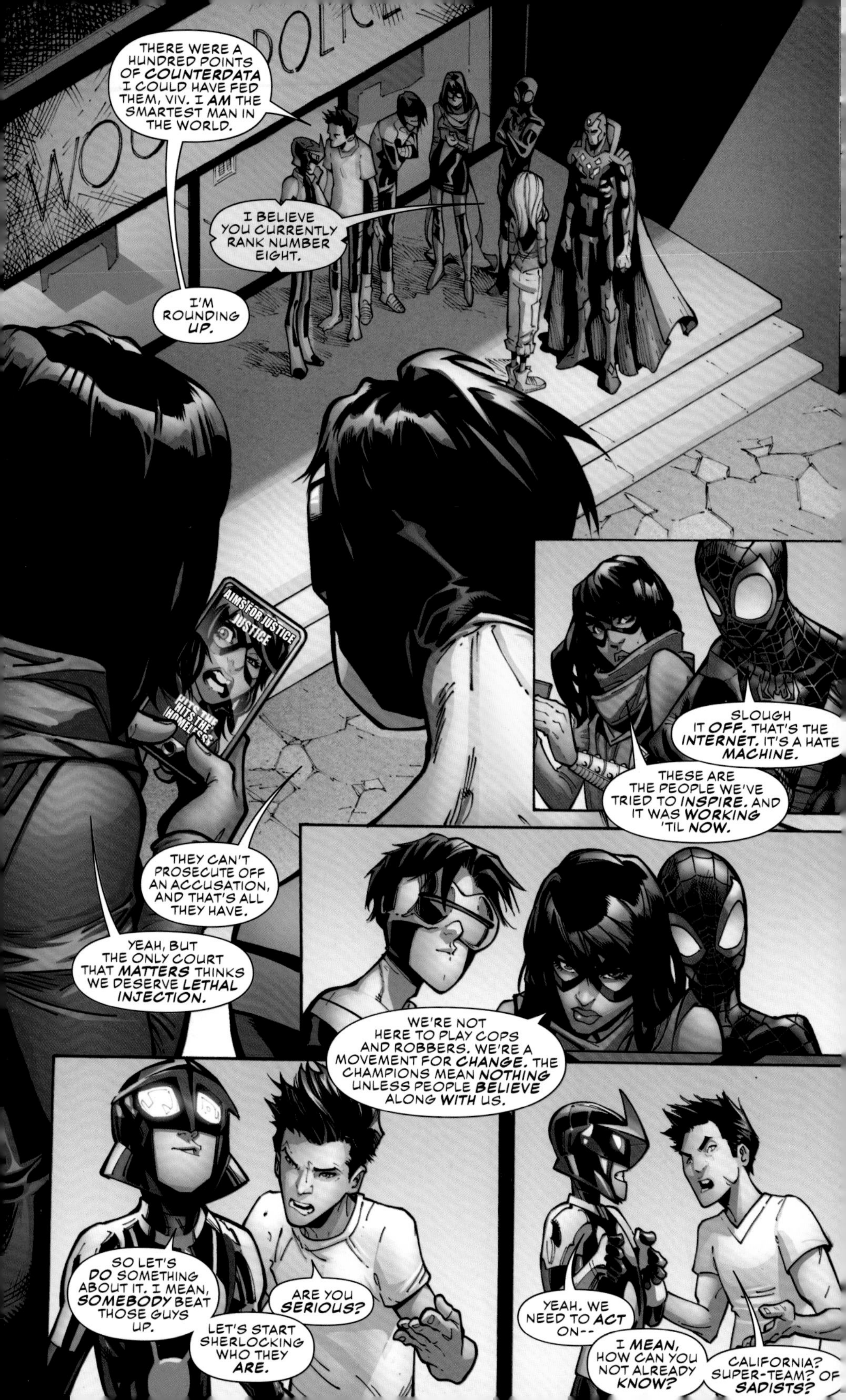

THERE WERE A HUNDRED POINTS OF COUNTERDATA I COULD HAVE FED THEM, VIV. I AM THE SMARTEST MAN IN THE WORLD.
I BELIEVE YOU CURRENTLY RANK NUMBER EIGHT.
I'M ROUNDING UP.
AIMS FOR JUSTICE
JUSTICE
SLOUGH IT OFF. THAT'S THE INTERNET. IT'S A HATE MACHINE.
THESE ARE THE PEOPLE WE'VE TRIED TO INSPIRE. AND IT WAS WORKING 'TIL NOW.
THEY CAN'T PROSECUTE OFF AN ACCUSATION, AND THAT'S ALL THEY HAVE.
YEAH, BUT THE ONLY COURT THAT MATTERS THINKS WE DESERVE LETHAL INJECTION.
WE'RE NOT HERE TO PLAY COPS AND ROBBERS. WE'RE A MOVEMENT FOR CHANGE. THE CHAMPIONS MEAN NOTHING UNLESS PEOPLE BELIEVE ALONG WITH US.
SO LET'S DO SOMETHING ABOUT IT. I MEAN, SOMEBODY BEAT THOSE GUYS UP.
LET'S START SHERLOCKING WHO THEY ARE.
ARE YOU SERIOUS?
YEAH. WE NEED TO ACT ON--
I MEAN, HOW CAN YOU NOT ALREADY KNOW?
CALIFORNIA? SUPER-TEAM? OF SADISTS?

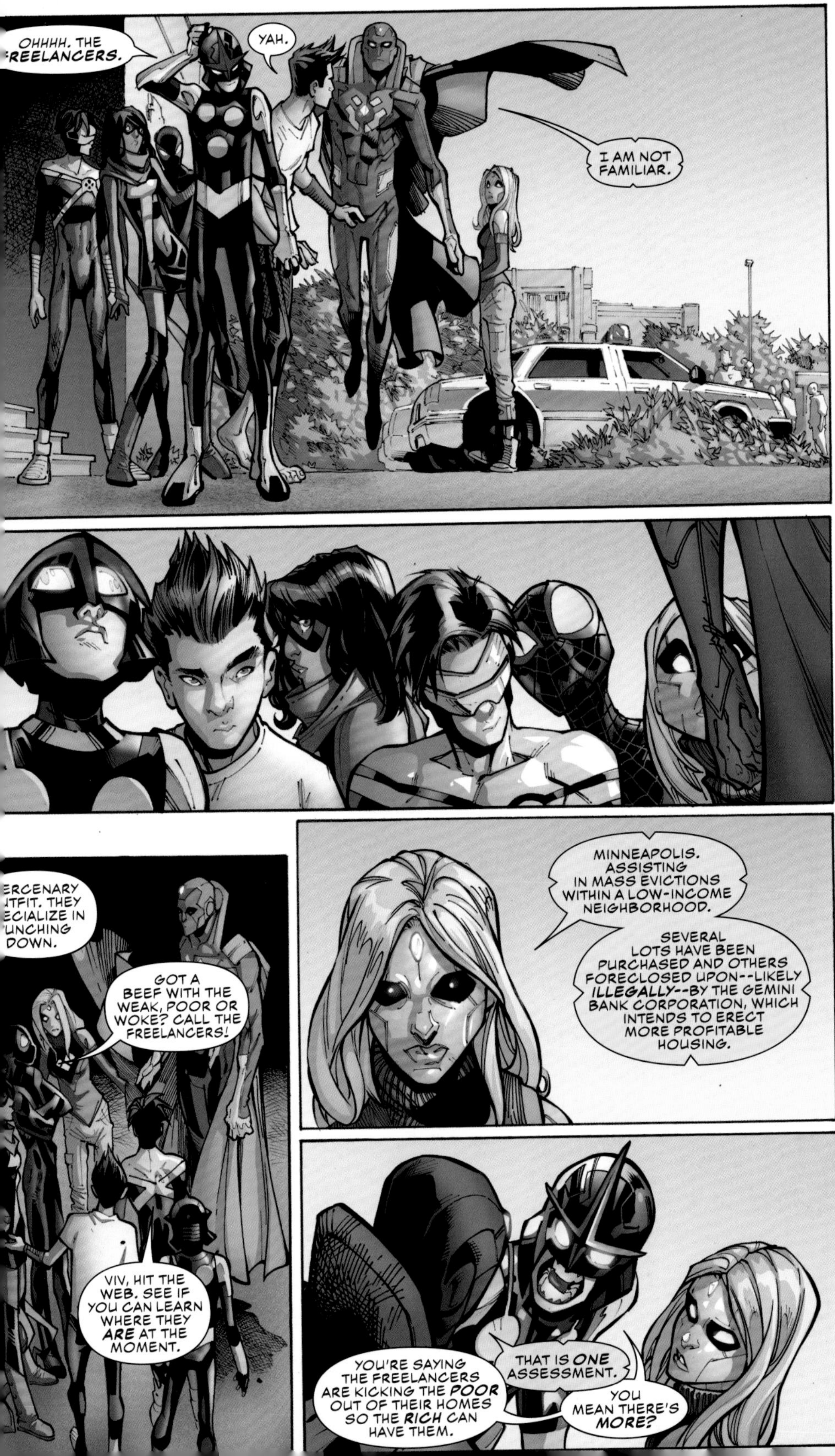
OHHHH. THE FREELANCERS.
YAH.
I AM NOT FAMILIAR.
ERCENARY UTFIT. THEY ECIALIZE IN UNCHING DOWN.
GOT A BEEF WITH THE WEAK, POOR OR WOKE? CALL THE FREELANCERS!
VIV, HIT THE WEB. SEE IF YOU CAN LEARN WHERE THEY ARE AT THE MOMENT.
MINNEAPOLIS. ASSISTING IN MASS EVICTIONS WITHIN A LOW-INCOME NEIGHBORHOOD.
SEVERAL LOTS HAVE BEEN PURCHASED AND OTHERS FORECLOSED UPON--LIKELY ILLEGALLY--BY THE GEMINI BANK CORPORATION, WHICH INTENDS TO ERECT MORE PROFITABLE HOUSING.
YOU'RE SAYING THE FREELANCERS ARE KICKING THE POOR OUT OF THEIR HOMES SO THE RICH CAN HAVE THEM.
THAT IS ONE ASSESSMENT.
YOU MEAN THERE'S MORE?

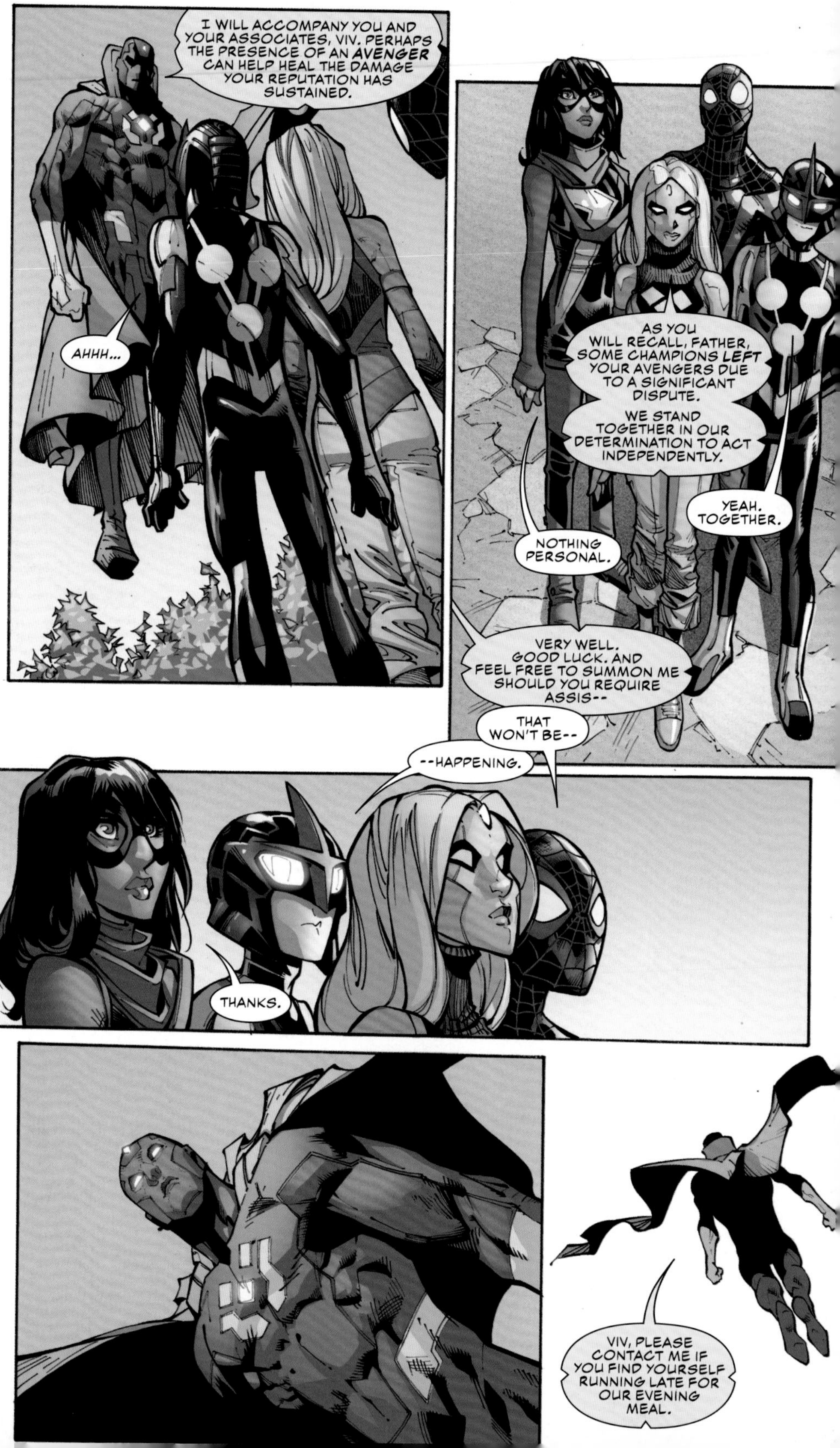
I WILL ACCOMPANY YOU AND YOUR ASSOCIATES, VIV. PERHAPS THE PRESENCE OF AN AVENGER CAN HELP HEAL THE DAMAGE YOUR REPUTATION HAS SUSTAINED.
AHHH...
AS YOU WILL RECALL, FATHER, SOME CHAMPIONS LEFT YOUR AVENGERS DUE TO A SIGNIFICANT DISPUTE.
WE STAND TOGETHER IN OUR DETERMINATION TO ACT INDEPENDENTLY.
YEAH. TOGETHER.
NOTHING PERSONAL.
VERY WELL. GOOD LUCK. AND FEEL FREE TO SUMMON ME SHOULD YOU REQUIRE ASSIS--
THAT WON'T BE--
--HAPPENING.
THANKS.
VIV, PLEASE CONTACT ME IF YOU FIND YOURSELF RUNNING LATE FOR OUR EVENING MEAL.

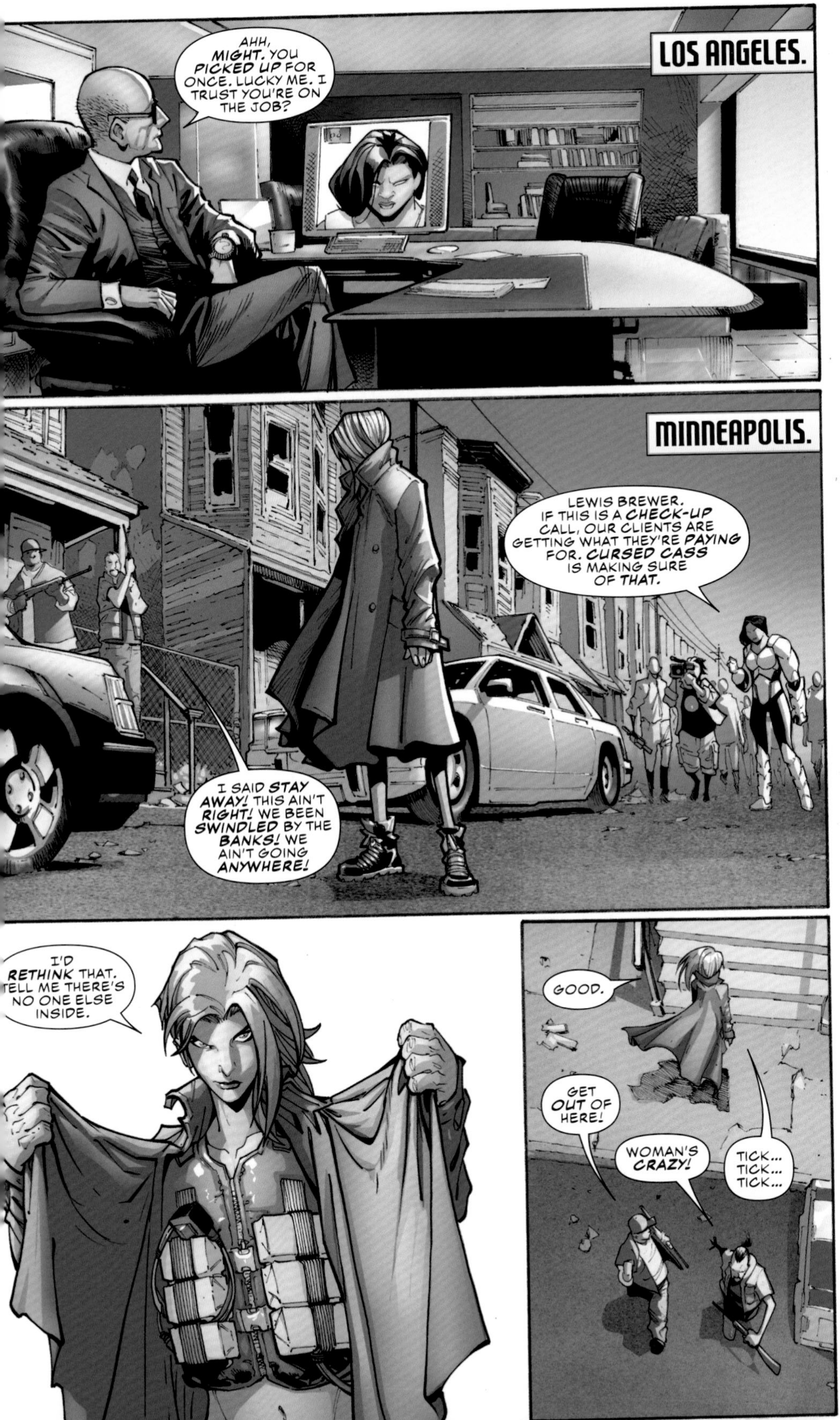
LOS ANGELES.
AHH, MIGHT. YOU PICKED UP FOR ONCE. LUCKY ME. I TRUST YOU'RE ON THE JOB?
MINNEAPOLIS.
LEWIS BREWER. IF THIS IS A CHECK-UP CALL, OUR CLIENTS ARE GETTING WHAT THEY'RE PAYING FOR. CURSED CASS IS MAKING SURE OF THAT.
I SAID STAY AWAY! THIS AIN'T RIGHT! WE BEEN SWINDLED BY THE BANKS! WE AIN'T GOING ANYWHERE!
I'D RETHINK THAT. TELL ME THERE'S NO ONE ELSE INSIDE.
GOOD.
GET OUT OF HERE!
WOMAN'S CRAZY!
TICK... TICK... TICK...

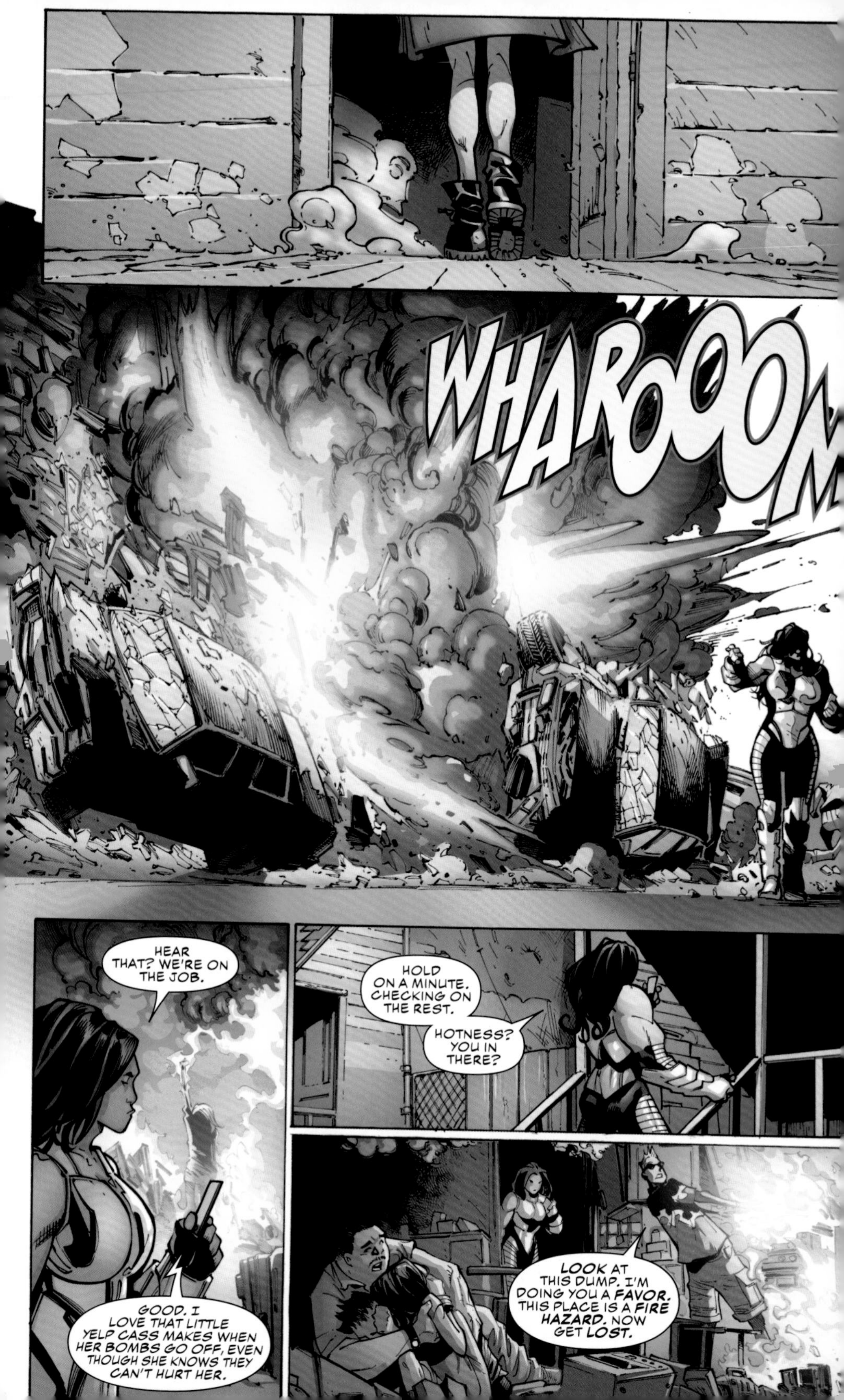
WHAROOOM
HEAR THAT? WE'RE ON THE JOB.
GOOD. I LOVE THAT LITTLE YELP CASS MAKES WHEN HER BOMBS GO OFF, EVEN THOUGH SHE KNOWS THEY CAN'T HURT HER.
HOLD ON A MINUTE. CHECKING ON THE REST.
HOTNESS? YOU IN THERE?
LOOK AT THIS DUMP. I'M DOING YOU A FAVOR. THIS PLACE IS A FIRE HAZARD. NOW GET LOST.

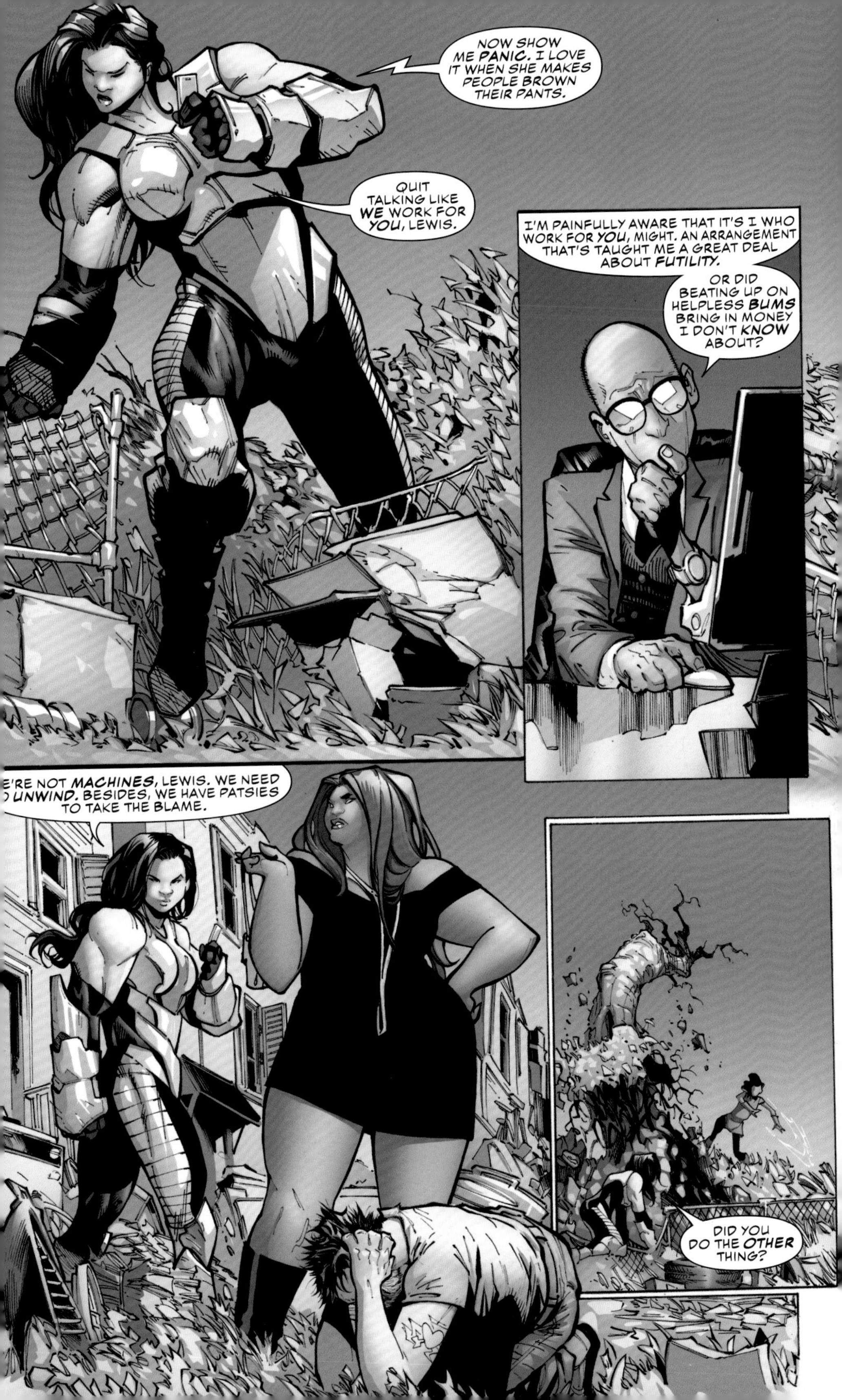

NOW SHOW ME PANIC. I LOVE IT WHEN SHE MAKES PEOPLE BROWN THEIR PANTS.
QUIT TALKING LIKE WE WORK FOR YOU, LEWIS.
I'M PAINFULLY AWARE THAT IT'S I WHO WORK FOR YOU, MIGHT. AN ARRANGEMENT THAT'S TAUGHT ME A GREAT DEAL ABOUT FUTILITY.
OR DID BEATING UP ON HELPLESS BUMS BRING IN MONEY I DON'T KNOW ABOUT?
'RE NOT MACHINES, LEWIS. WE NEED UNWIND. BESIDES, WE HAVE PATSIES TO TAKE THE BLAME.
DID YOU DO THE OTHER THING?

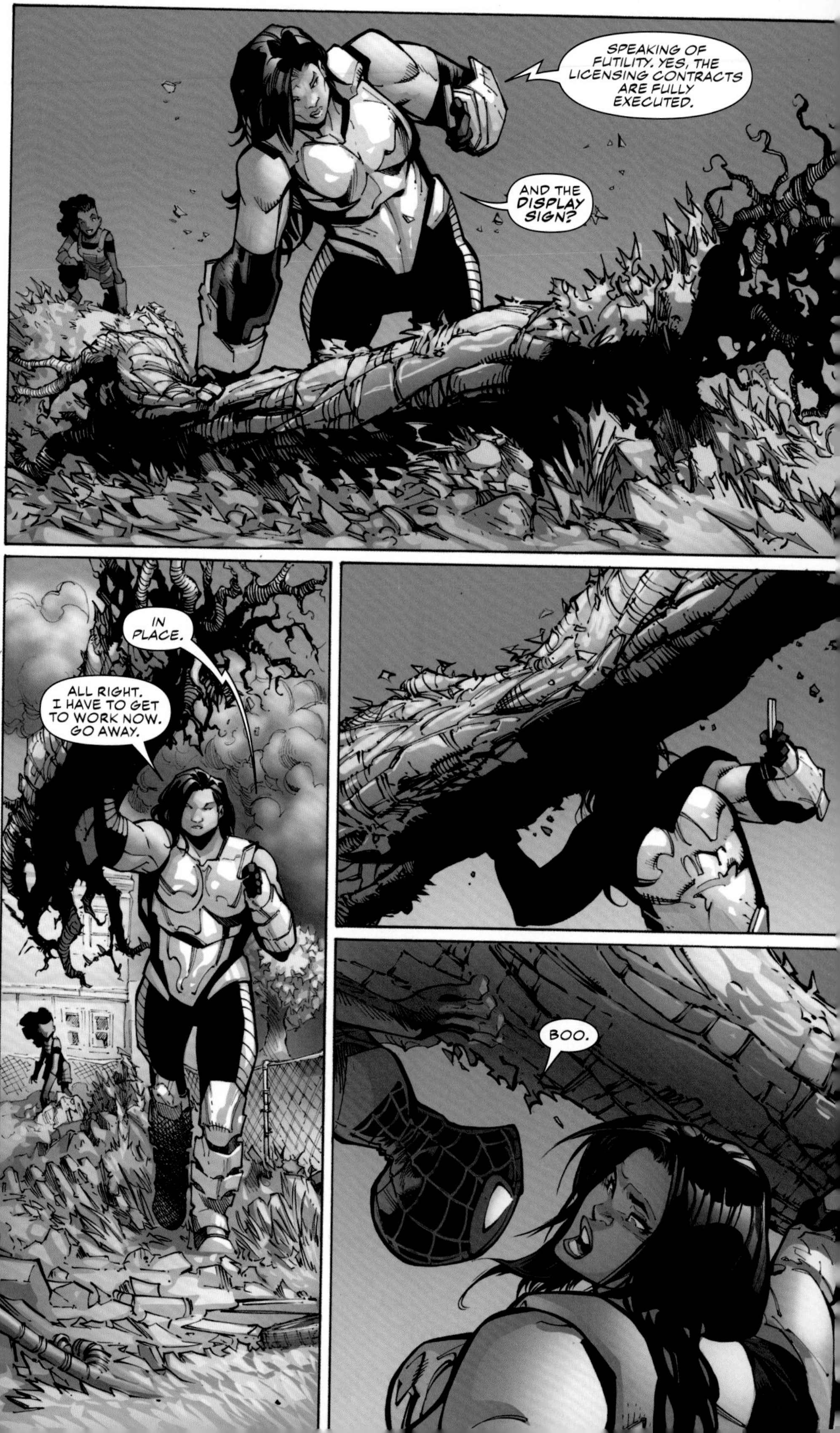
SPEAKING OF FUTILITY. YES, THE LICENSING CONTRACTS ARE FULLY EXECUTED.
AND THE DISPLAY SIGN?
IN PLACE.
ALL RIGHT. I HAVE TO GET TO WORK NOW. GO AWAY.
BOO.

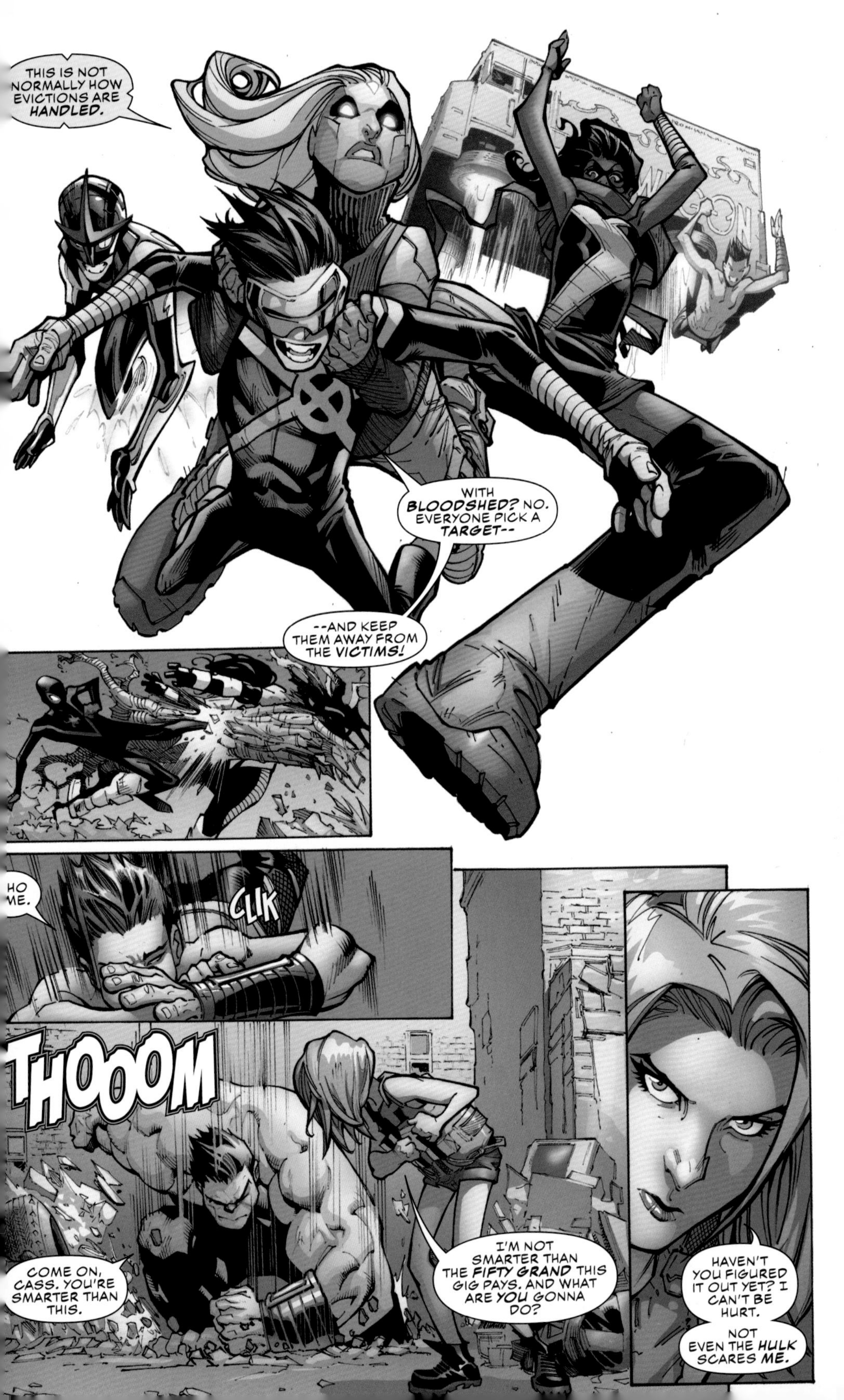
THIS IS NOT NORMALLY HOW EVICTIONS ARE HANDLED.
WITH BLOODSHED? NO. EVERYONE PICK A TARGET--
--AND KEEP THEM AWAY FROM THE VICTIMS!
HO ME.
CLIK
THOOOM
COME ON, CASS. YOU'RE SMARTER THAN THIS.
I'M NOT SMARTER THAN THE FIFTY GRAND THIS GIG PAYS. AND WHAT ARE YOU GONNA DO?
HAVEN'T YOU FIGURED IT OUT YET? I CAN'T BE HURT.
NOT EVEN THE HULK SCARES ME.

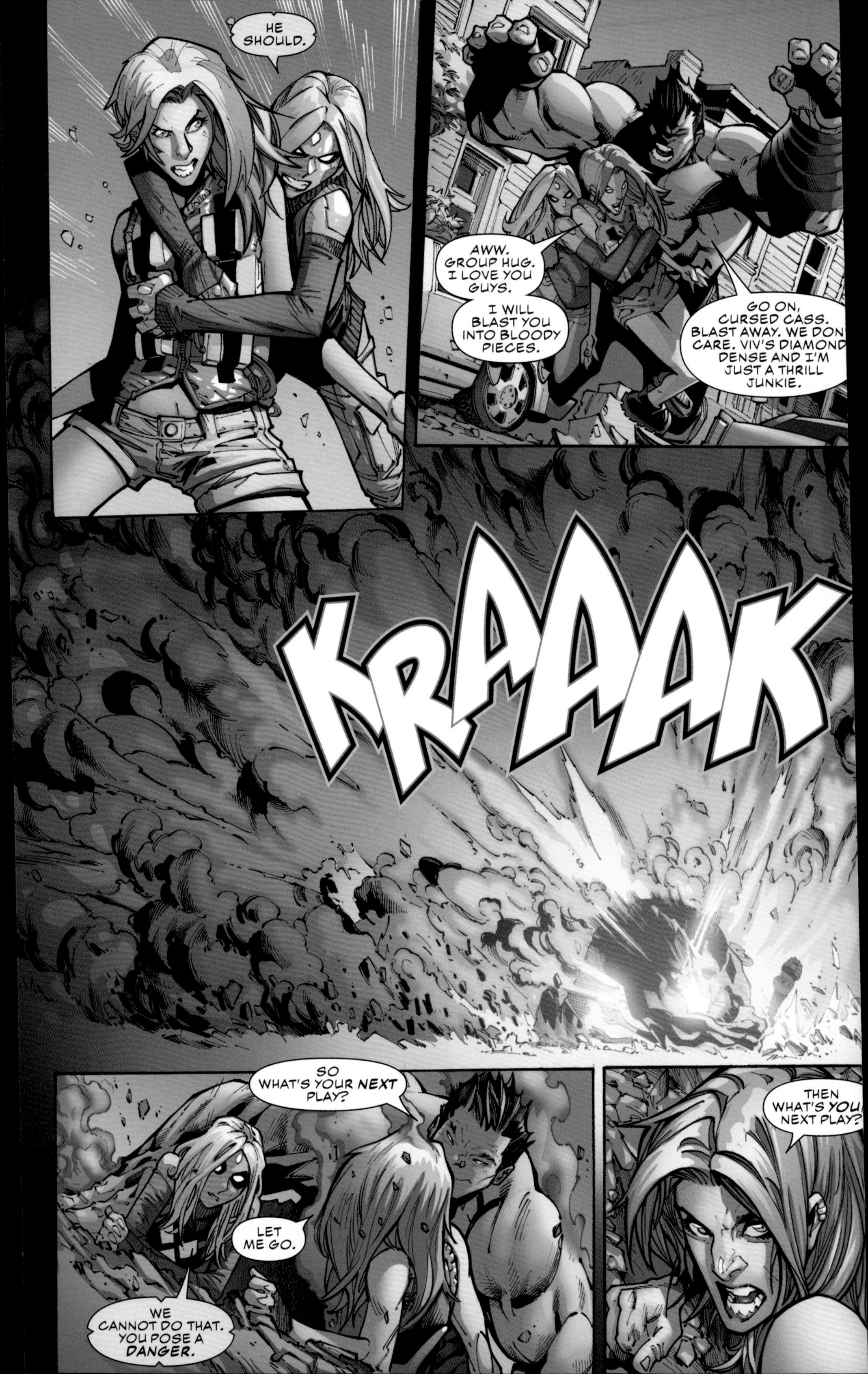
HE SHOULD.
AWW. GROUP HUG. I LOVE YOU GUYS.
I WILL BLAST YOU INTO BLOODY PIECES.
GO ON, CURSED CASS. BLAST AWAY. WE DON CARE. VIV'S DIAMOND DENSE AND I'M JUST A THRILL JUNKIE.
KRAAAK
SO WHAT'S YOUR **NEXT** PLAY?
LET ME GO.
WE CANNOT DO THAT. YOU POSE A **DANGER.**
THEN WHAT'S **YOU** NEXT PLAY?

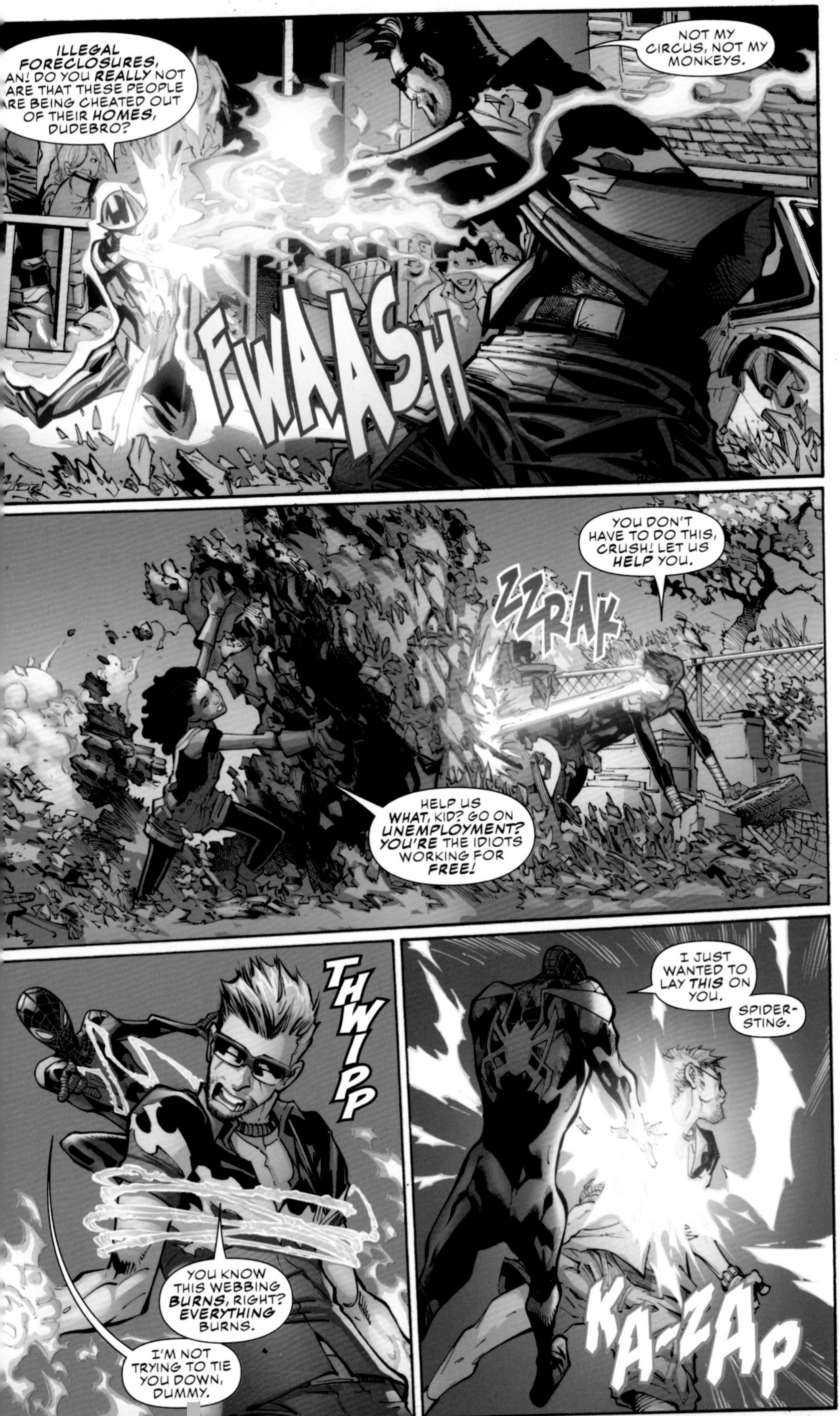
ILLEGAL FORECLOSURES, AN! DO YOU REALLY NOT ARE THAT THESE PEOPLE ARE BEING CHEATED OUT OF THEIR HOMES, DUDEBRO?
NOT MY CIRCUS, NOT MY MONKEYS.
FWAASH
YOU DON'T HAVE TO DO THIS, CRUSH! LET US HELP YOU.
ZZRAK
HELP US WHAT, KID? GO ON UNEMPLOYMENT? YOU'RE THE IDIOTS WORKING FOR FREE!
THWIPP
YOU KNOW THIS WEBBING BURNS, RIGHT? EVERYTHING BURNS.
I'M NOT TRYING TO TIE YOU DOWN, DUMMY.
I JUST WANTED TO LAY THIS ON YOU.
SPIDER-STING.
KA-ZAP

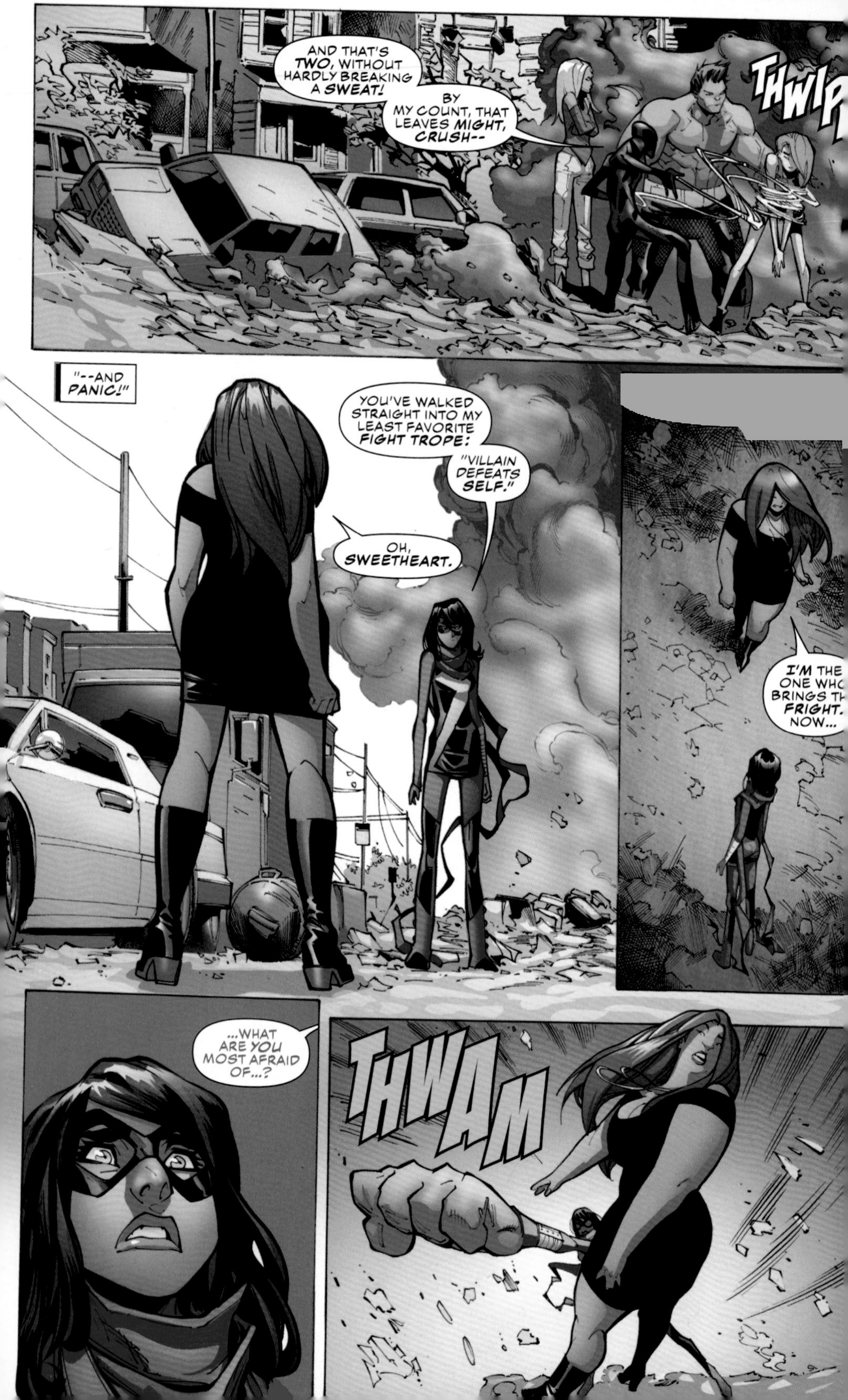
AND THAT'S TWO, WITHOUT HARDLY BREAKING A SWEAT!
BY MY COUNT, THAT LEAVES MIGHT, CRUSH--
THWIP
"--AND PANIC!"
YOU'VE WALKED STRAIGHT INTO MY LEAST FAVORITE FIGHT TROPE:
"VILLAIN DEFEATS SELF."
OH, SWEETHEART.
I'M THE ONE WHO BRINGS TH FRIGHT. NOW...
...WHAT ARE YOU MOST AFRAID OF...?
THWAM

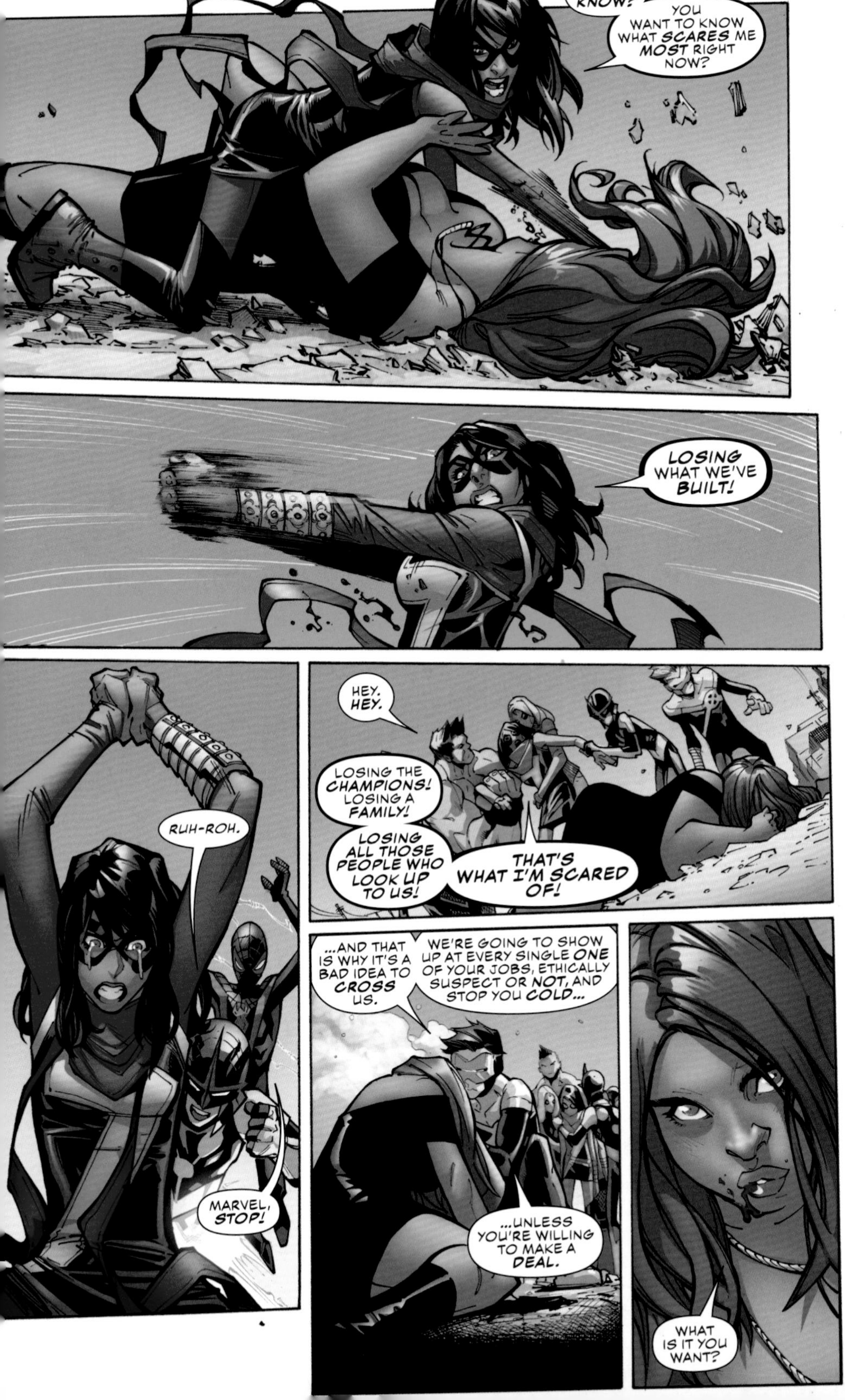

YOU WANT TO KNOW?
YOU WANT TO KNOW WHAT SCARES ME MOST RIGHT NOW?
LOSING WHAT WE'VE BUILT!
RUH-ROH.
MARVEL, STOP!
HEY. HEY.
LOSING THE CHAMPIONS! LOSING A FAMILY!
LOSING ALL THOSE PEOPLE WHO LOOK UP TO US!
THAT'S WHAT I'M SCARED OF!
...AND THAT IS WHY IT'S A BAD IDEA TO CROSS US.
WE'RE GOING TO SHOW UP AT EVERY SINGLE ONE OF YOUR JOBS, ETHICALLY SUSPECT OR NOT, AND STOP YOU COLD...
...UNLESS YOU'RE WILLING TO MAKE A DEAL.
WHAT IS IT YOU WANT?

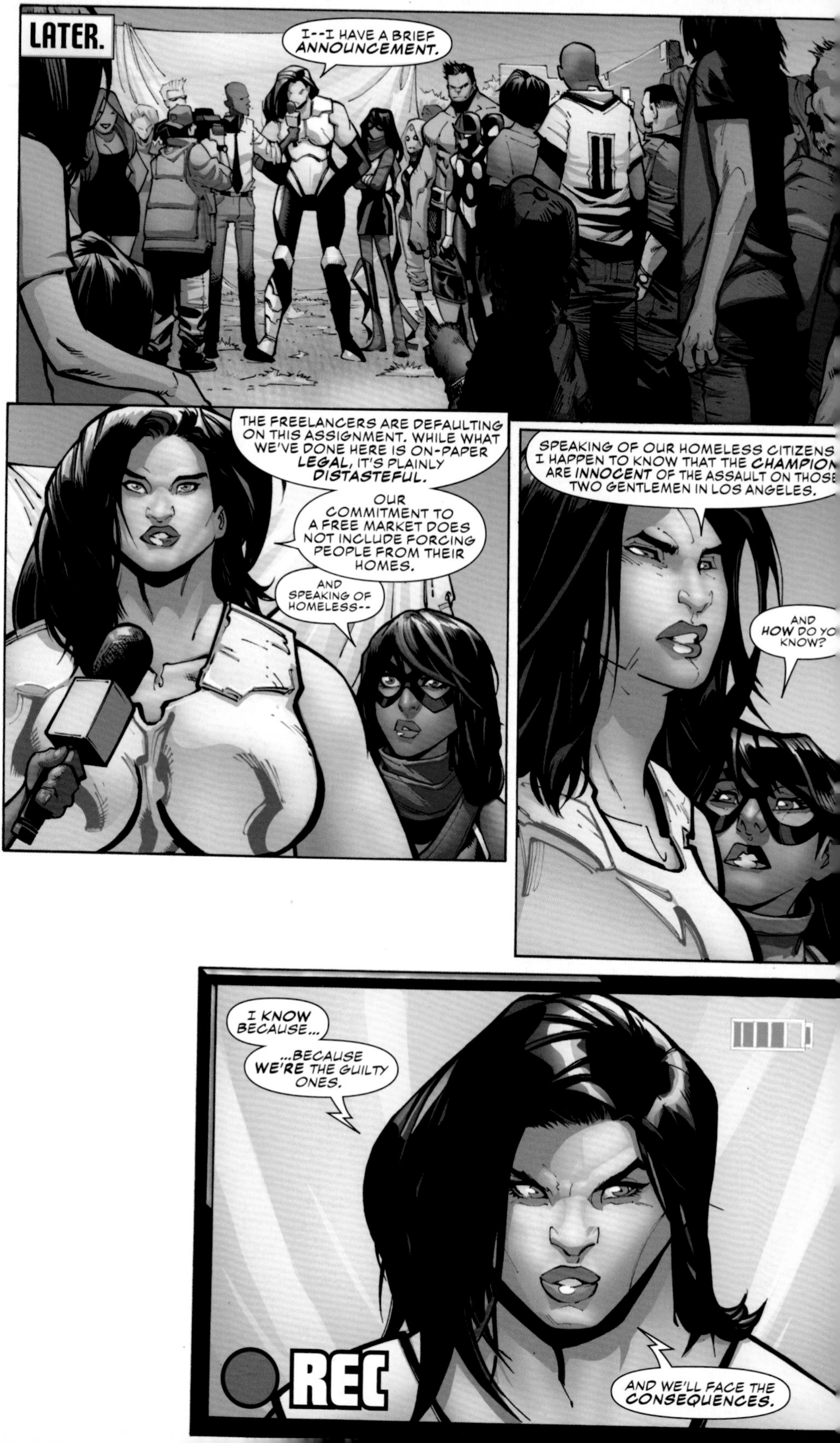

LATER.
I--I HAVE A BRIEF ANNOUNCEMENT.
THE FREELANCERS ARE DEFAULTING ON THIS ASSIGNMENT. WHILE WHAT WE'VE DONE HERE IS ON-PAPER LEGAL, IT'S PLAINLY DISTASTEFUL.
OUR COMMITMENT TO A FREE MARKET DOES NOT INCLUDE FORCING PEOPLE FROM THEIR HOMES.
AND SPEAKING OF HOMELESS--
SPEAKING OF OUR HOMELESS CITIZENS I HAPPEN TO KNOW THAT THE CHAMPION ARE INNOCENT OF THE ASSAULT ON THOSE TWO GENTLEMEN IN LOS ANGELES.
AND HOW DO YO KNOW?
I KNOW BECAUSE...
...BECAUSE WE'RE THE GUILTY ONES.
REC
AND WE'LL FACE THE CONSEQUENCES.

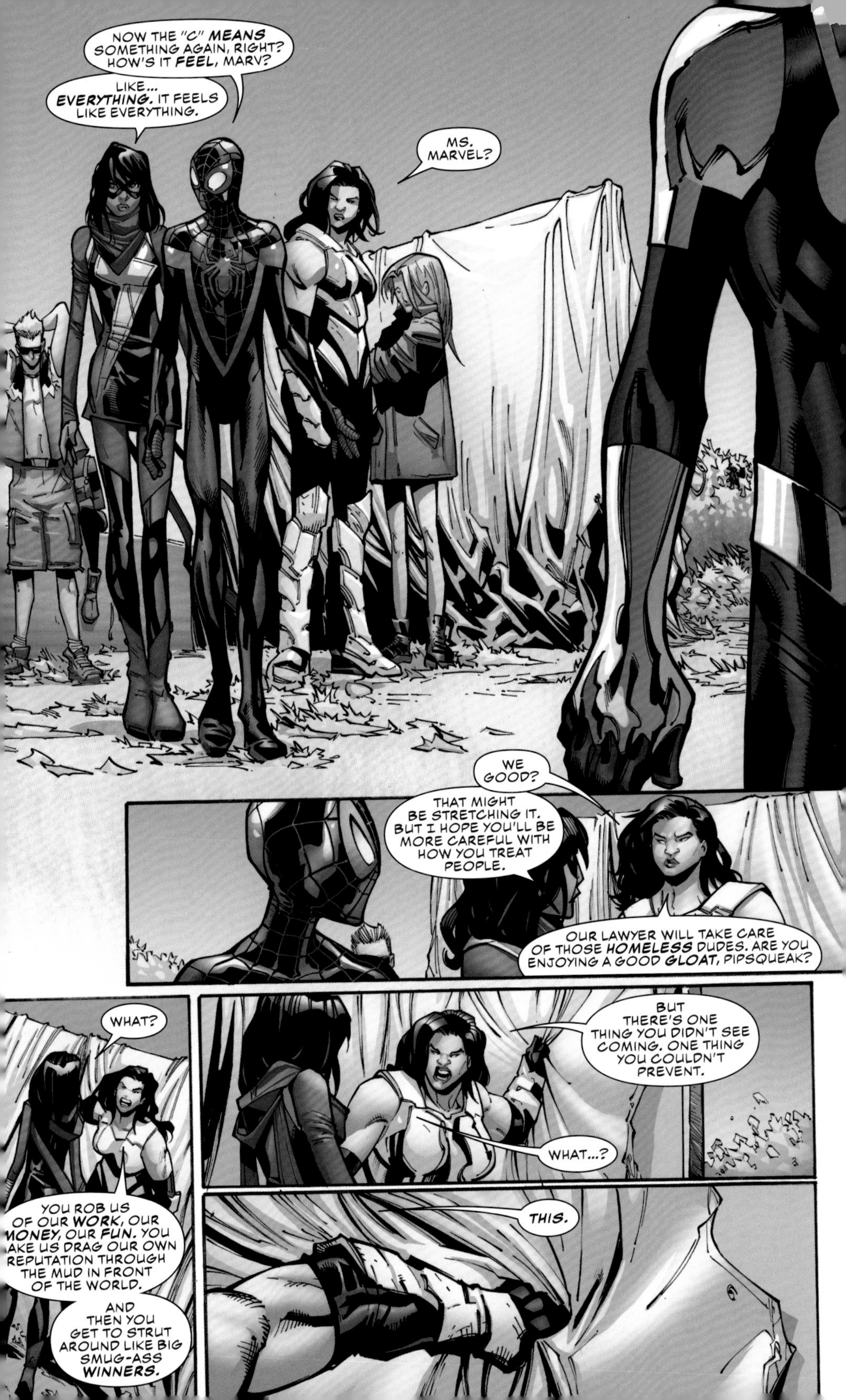

NOW THE "C" MEANS SOMETHING AGAIN, RIGHT? HOW'S IT FEEL, MARV?
LIKE... EVERYTHING. IT FEELS LIKE EVERYTHING.
MS. MARVEL?
WE GOOD?
THAT MIGHT BE STRETCHING IT. BUT I HOPE YOU'LL BE MORE CAREFUL WITH HOW YOU TREAT PEOPLE.
OUR LAWYER WILL TAKE CARE OF THOSE HOMELESS DUDES. ARE YOU ENJOYING A GOOD GLOAT, PIPSQUEAK?
WHAT?
YOU ROB US OF OUR WORK, OUR MONEY, OUR FUN. YOU MAKE US DRAG OUR OWN REPUTATION THROUGH THE MUD IN FRONT OF THE WORLD.
AND THEN YOU GET TO STRUT AROUND LIKE BIG SMUG-ASS WINNERS.
BUT THERE'S ONE THING YOU DIDN'T SEE COMING. ONE THING YOU COULDN'T PREVENT.
WHAT...?
THIS.

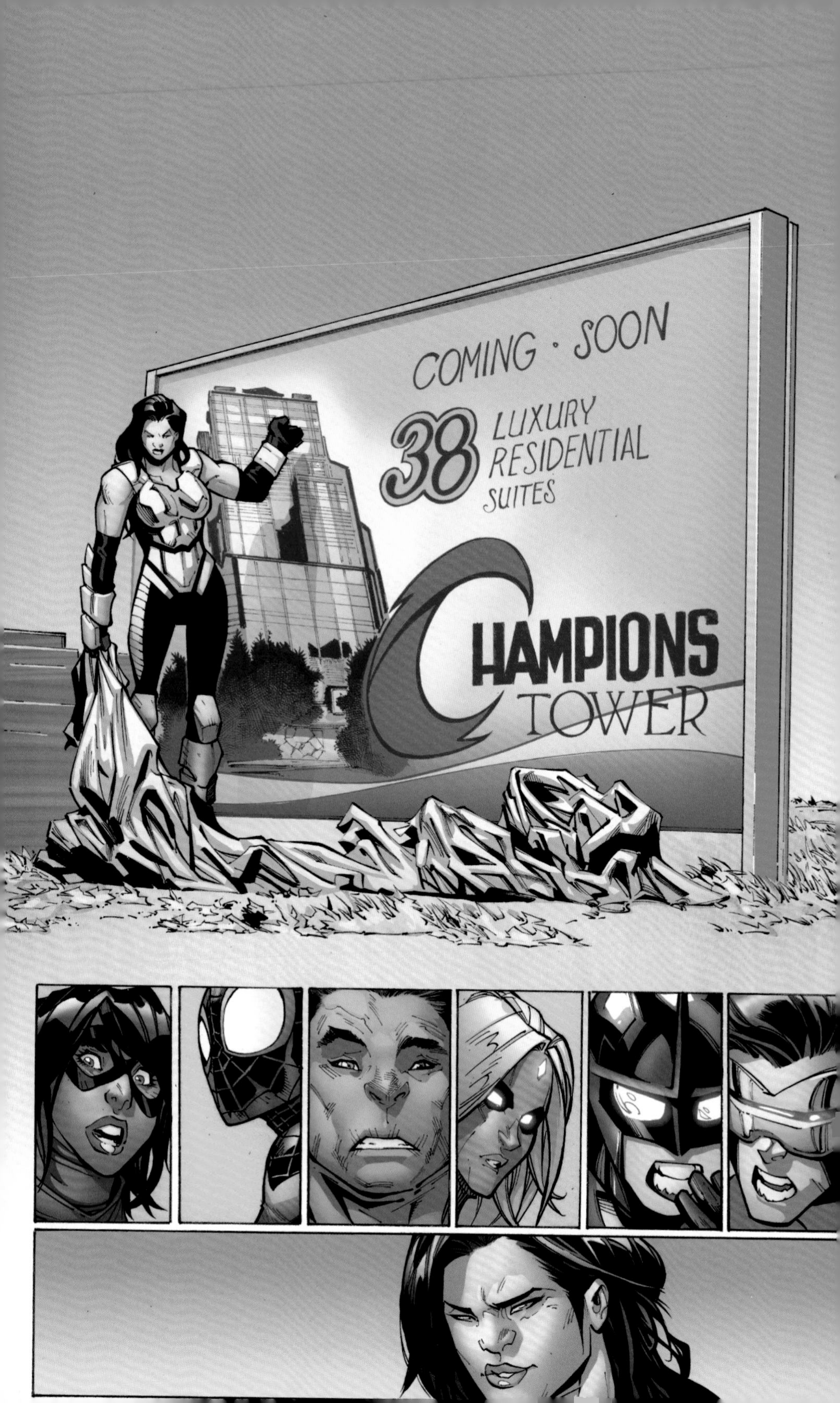

COMING · SOON
38 LUXURY RESIDENTIAL SUITES
CHAMPIONS TOWER

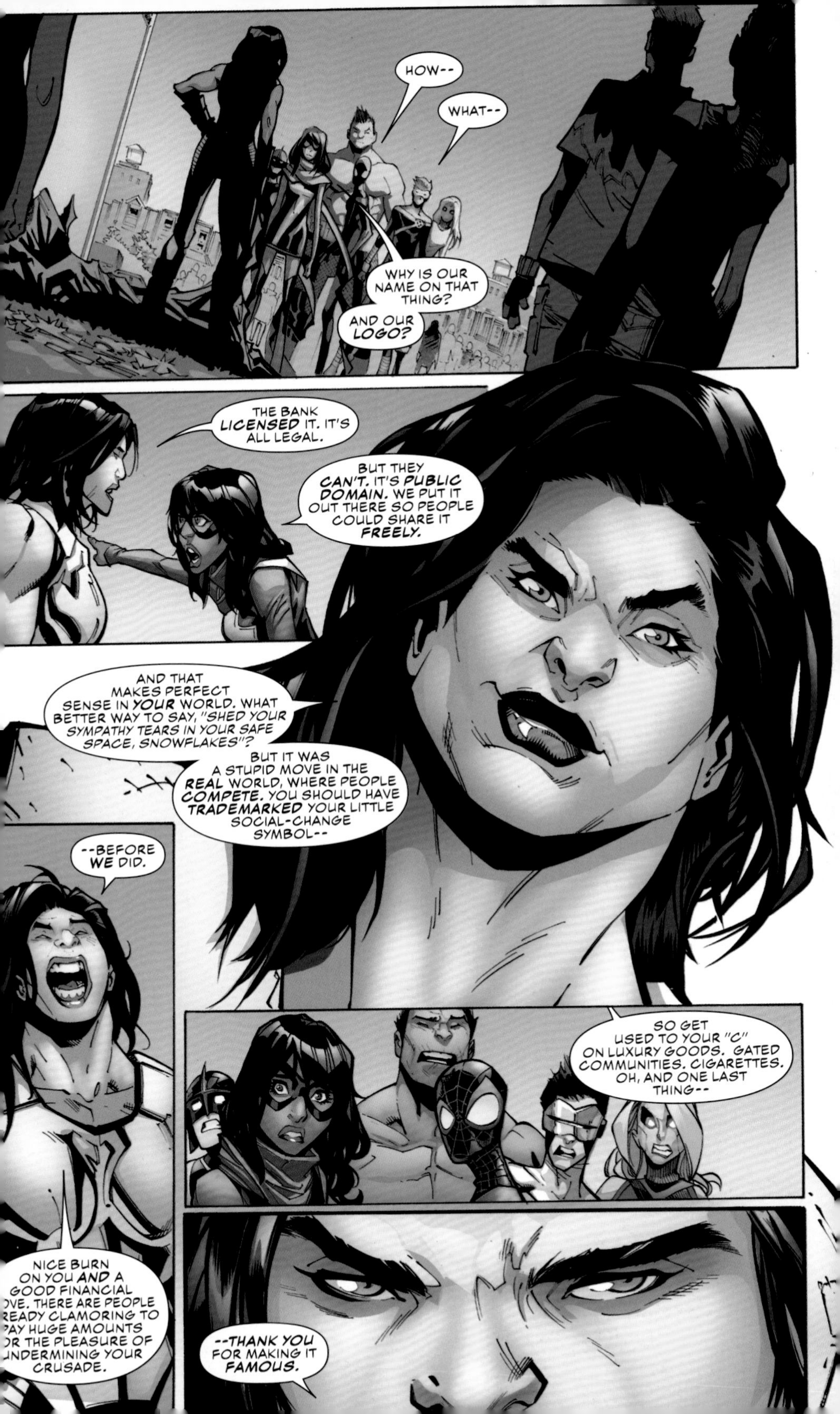
HOW--
WHAT--
WHY IS OUR NAME ON THAT THING?
AND OUR LOGO?
THE BANK LICENSED IT. IT'S ALL LEGAL.
BUT THEY CAN'T. IT'S PUBLIC DOMAIN. WE PUT IT OUT THERE SO PEOPLE COULD SHARE IT FREELY.
AND THAT MAKES PERFECT SENSE IN YOUR WORLD. WHAT BETTER WAY TO SAY, "SHED YOUR SYMPATHY TEARS IN YOUR SAFE SPACE, SNOWFLAKES"?
BUT IT WAS A STUPID MOVE IN THE REAL WORLD, WHERE PEOPLE COMPETE. YOU SHOULD HAVE TRADEMARKED YOUR LITTLE SOCIAL-CHANGE SYMBOL--
--BEFORE WE DID.
SO GET USED TO YOUR "C" ON LUXURY GOODS. GATED COMMUNITIES. CIGARETTES. OH, AND ONE LAST THING--
NICE BURN ON YOU AND A GOOD FINANCIAL OVE. THERE ARE PEOPLE READY CLAMORING TO PAY HUGE AMOUNTS OR THE PLEASURE OF UNDERMINING YOUR CRUSADE.
--THANK YOU FOR MAKING IT FAMOUS.

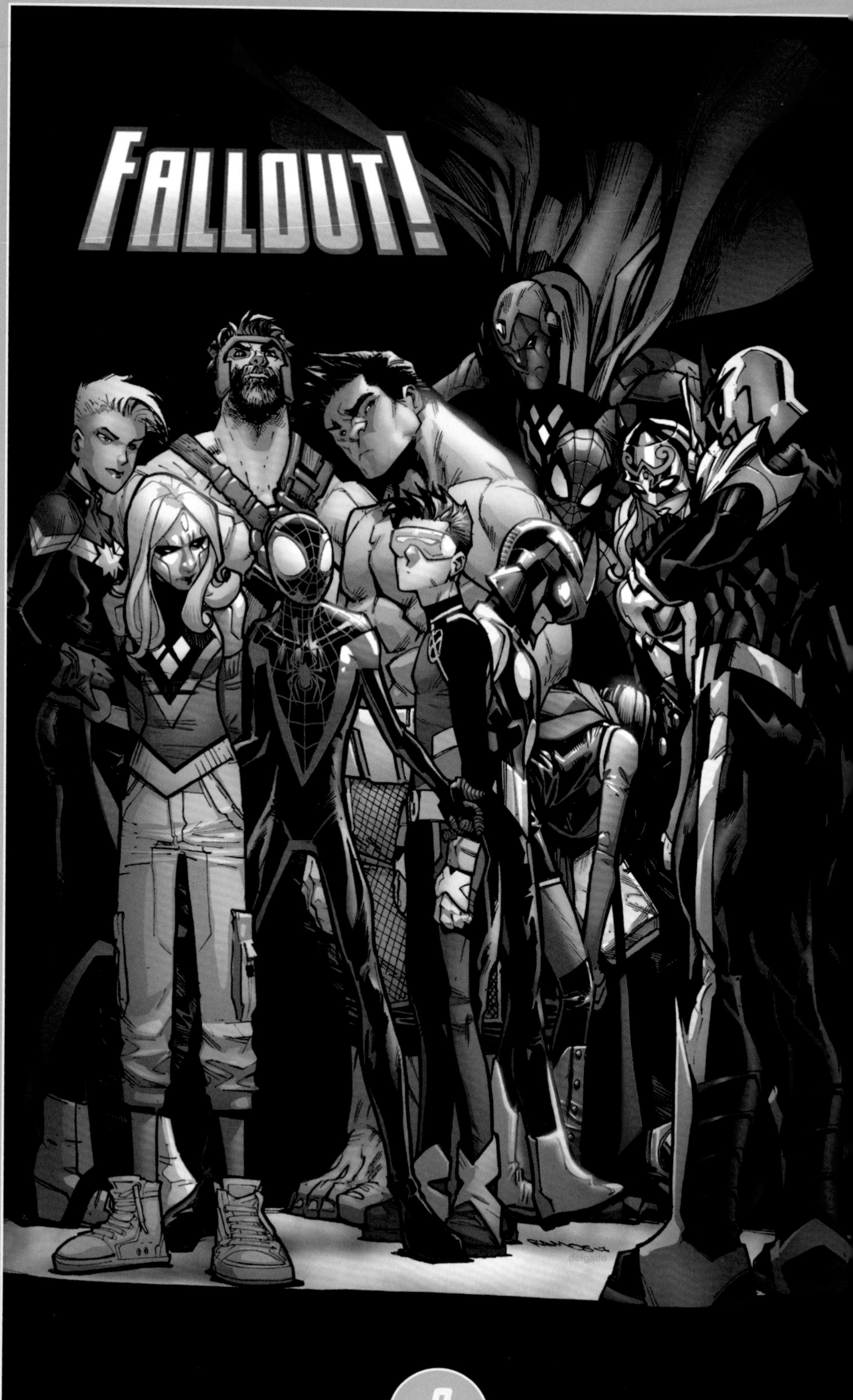
FALLOUT!

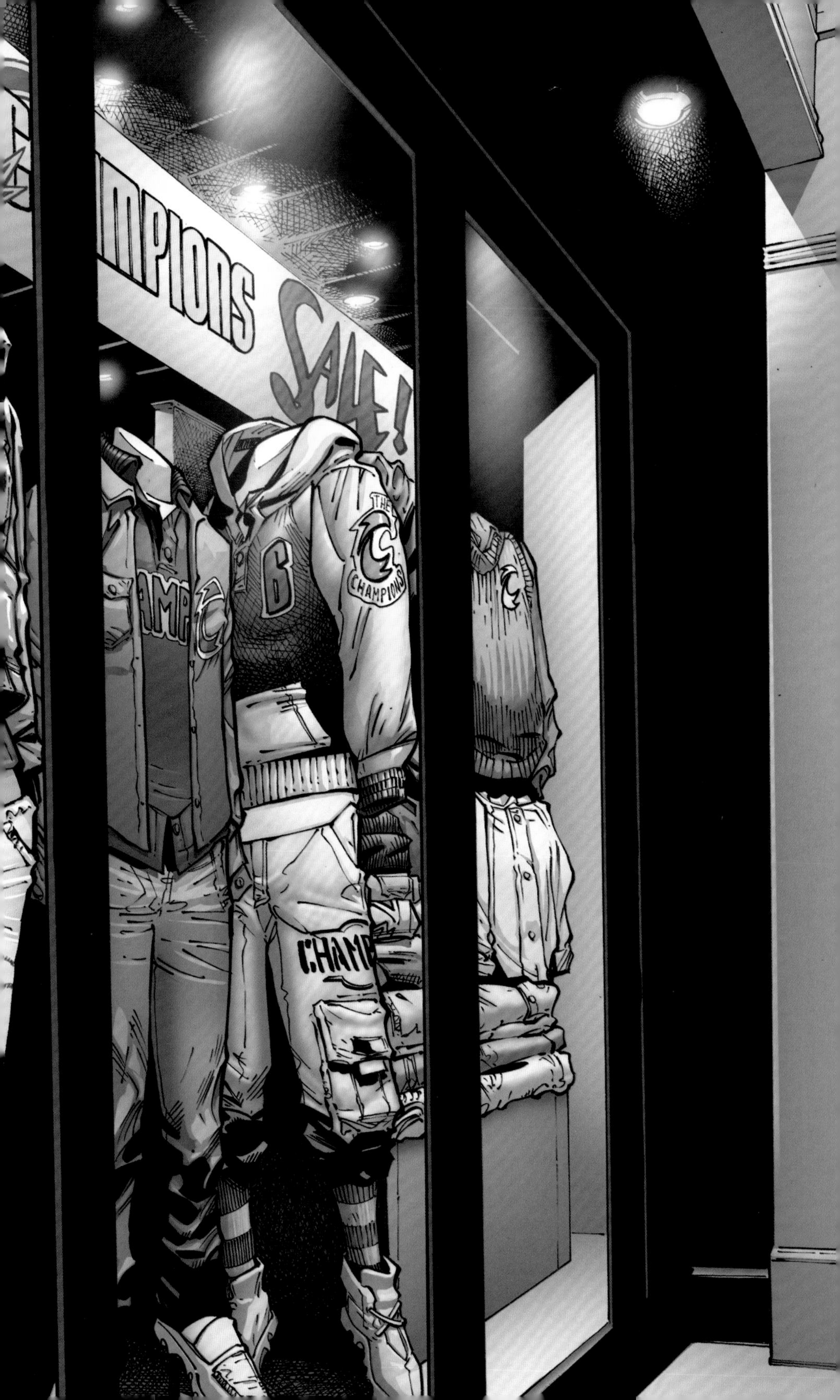
SALE!
THE
CHAMPIONS
6
CHAMP
CHAMP

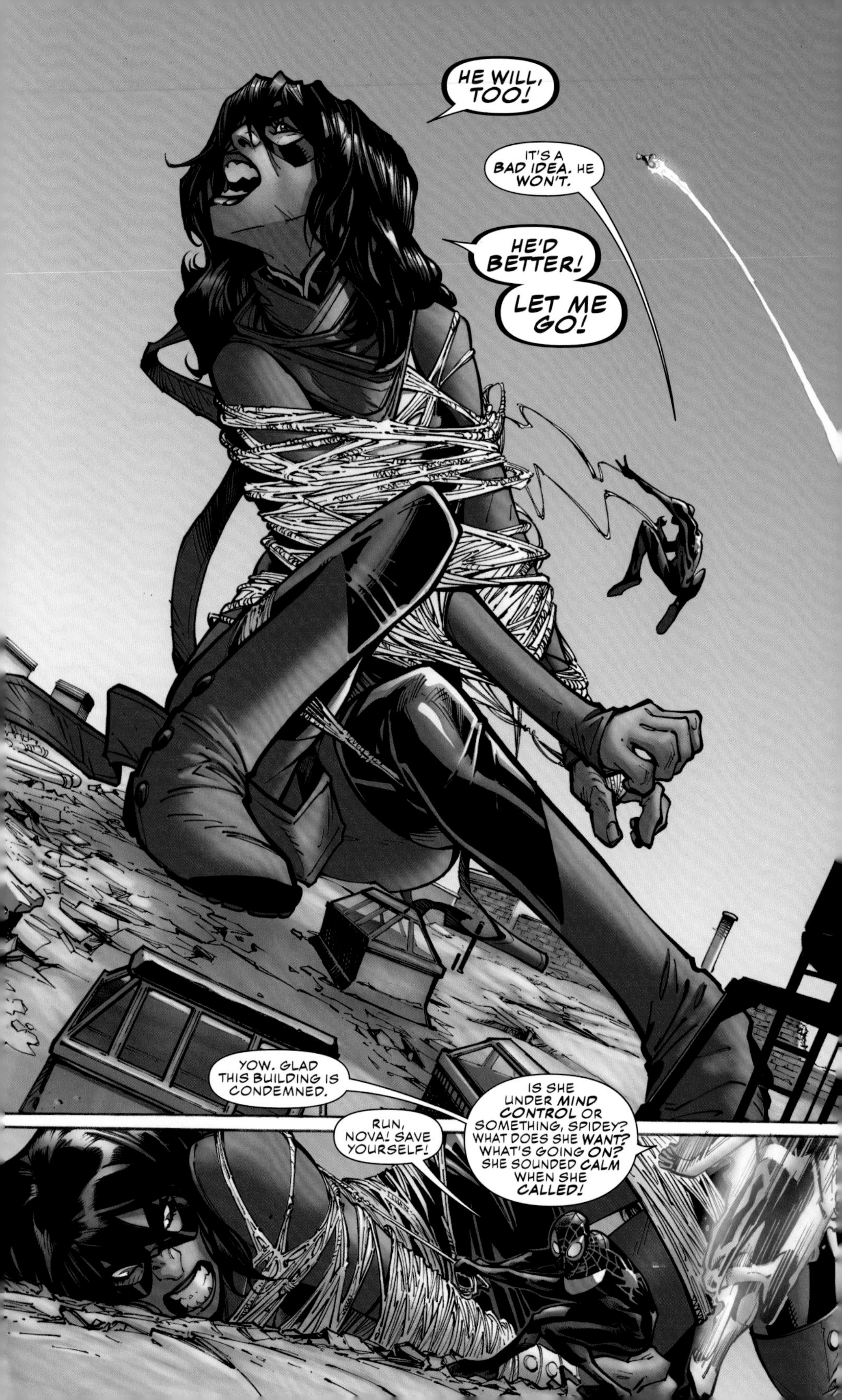
HE WILL, TOO!
IT'S A BAD IDEA. HE WON'T.
HE'D BETTER!
LET ME GO!
YOW. GLAD THIS BUILDING IS CONDEMNED.
RUN, NOVA! SAVE YOURSELF!
IS SHE UNDER MIND CONTROL OR SOMETHING, SPIDEY? WHAT DOES SHE WANT? WHAT'S GOING ON? SHE SOUNDED CALM WHEN SHE CALLED!

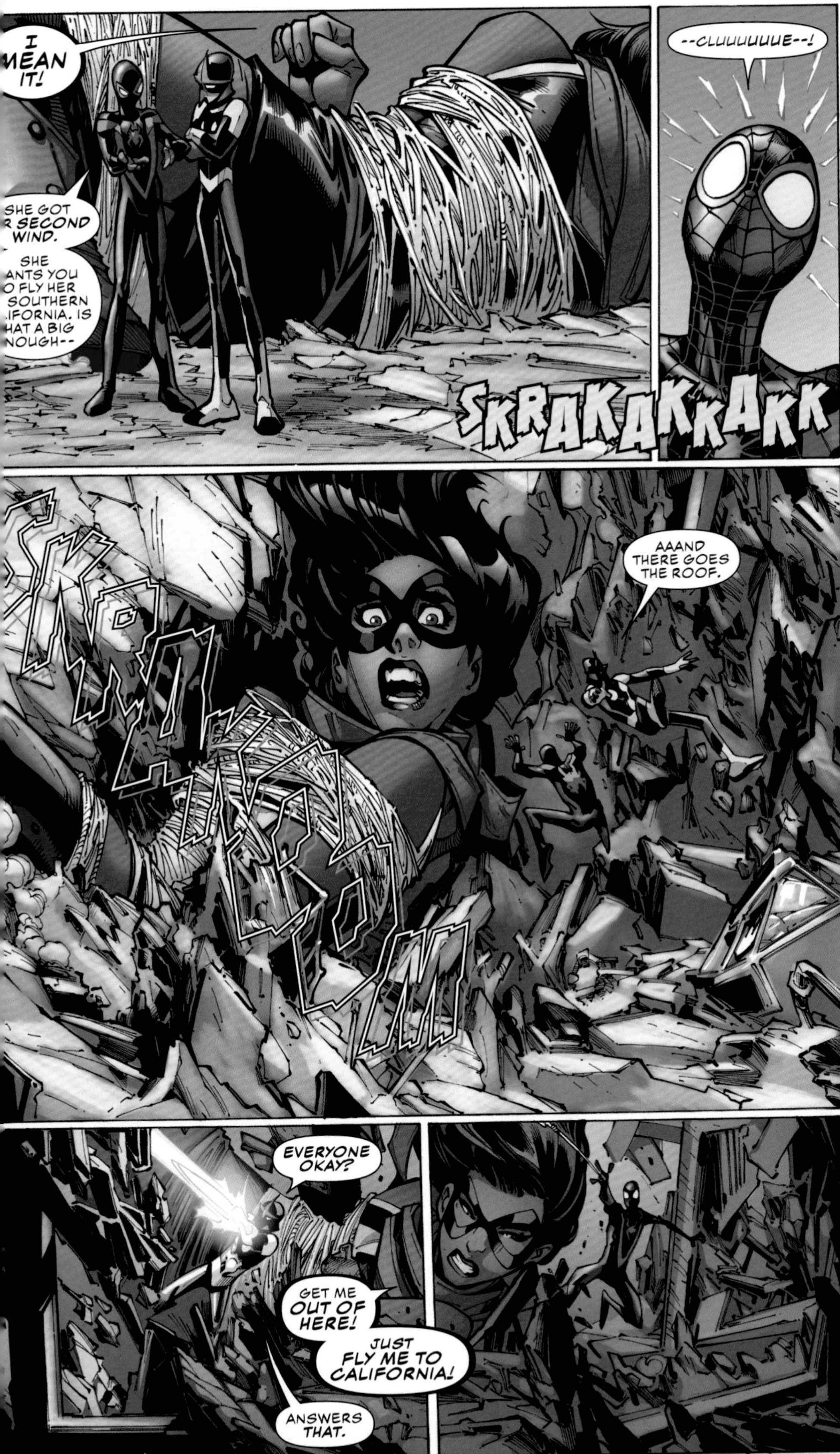
I MEAN IT!
SHE GOT R SECOND WIND.
SHE ANTS YOU O FLY HER SOUTHERN IFORNIA. IS HAT A BIG NOUGH--
--CLUUUUUUE--!
SKRAKAKKKAKK
AAAND THERE GOES THE ROOF.
EVERYONE OKAY?
GET ME OUT OF HERE!
JUST FLY ME TO CALIFORNIA!
ANSWERS THAT.

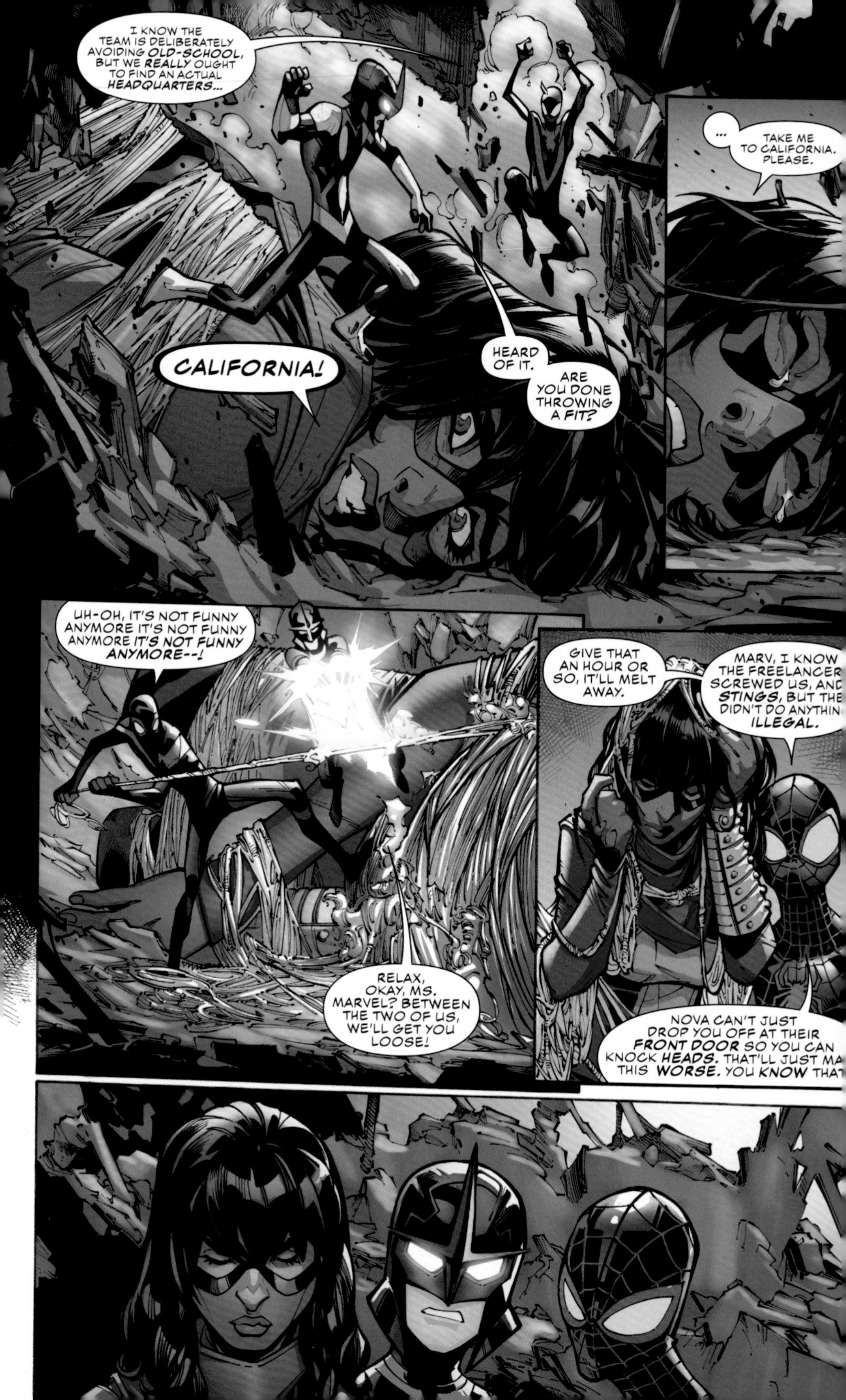
I KNOW THE TEAM IS DELIBERATELY AVOIDING OLD-SCHOOL, BUT WE REALLY OUGHT TO FIND AN ACTUAL HEADQUARTERS...
CALIFORNIA!
HEARD OF IT.
ARE YOU DONE THROWING A FIT?
...
TAKE ME TO CALIFORNIA. PLEASE.
UH-OH, IT'S NOT FUNNY ANYMORE IT'S NOT FUNNY ANYMORE IT'S NOT FUNNY ANYMORE--!
RELAX, OKAY, MS. MARVEL? BETWEEN THE TWO OF US, WE'LL GET YOU LOOSE!
GIVE THAT AN HOUR OR SO, IT'LL MELT AWAY.
MARV, I KNOW THE FREELANCER SCREWED US, AND STINGS, BUT THE DIDN'T DO ANYTHIN ILLEGAL.
NOVA CAN'T JUST DROP YOU OFF AT THEIR FRONT DOOR SO YOU CAN KNOCK HEADS. THAT'LL JUST MA THIS WORSE. YOU KNOW THAT

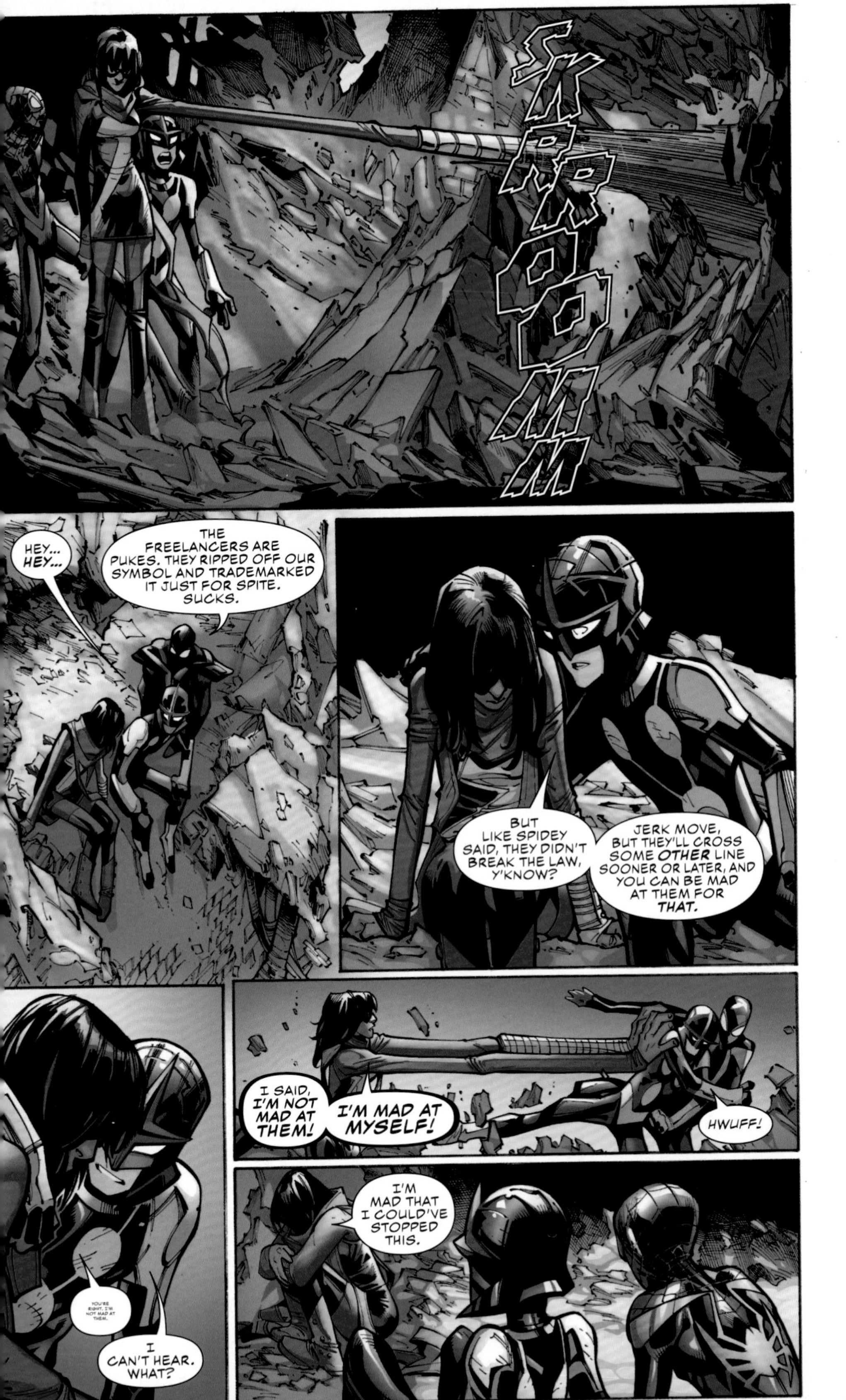
SKRROOMM
HEY... HEY...
THE FREELANCERS ARE PUKES. THEY RIPPED OFF OUR SYMBOL AND TRADEMARKED IT JUST FOR SPITE. SUCKS.
BUT LIKE SPIDEY SAID, THEY DIDN'T BREAK THE LAW, Y'KNOW?
JERK MOVE, BUT THEY'LL CROSS SOME OTHER LINE SOONER OR LATER, AND YOU CAN BE MAD AT THEM FOR THAT.
YOU'RE RIGHT. I'M NOT MAD AT THEM.
I CAN'T HEAR. WHAT?
I SAID, I'M NOT MAD AT THEM!
I'M MAD AT MYSELF!
HWUFF!
I'M MAD THAT I COULD'VE STOPPED THIS.

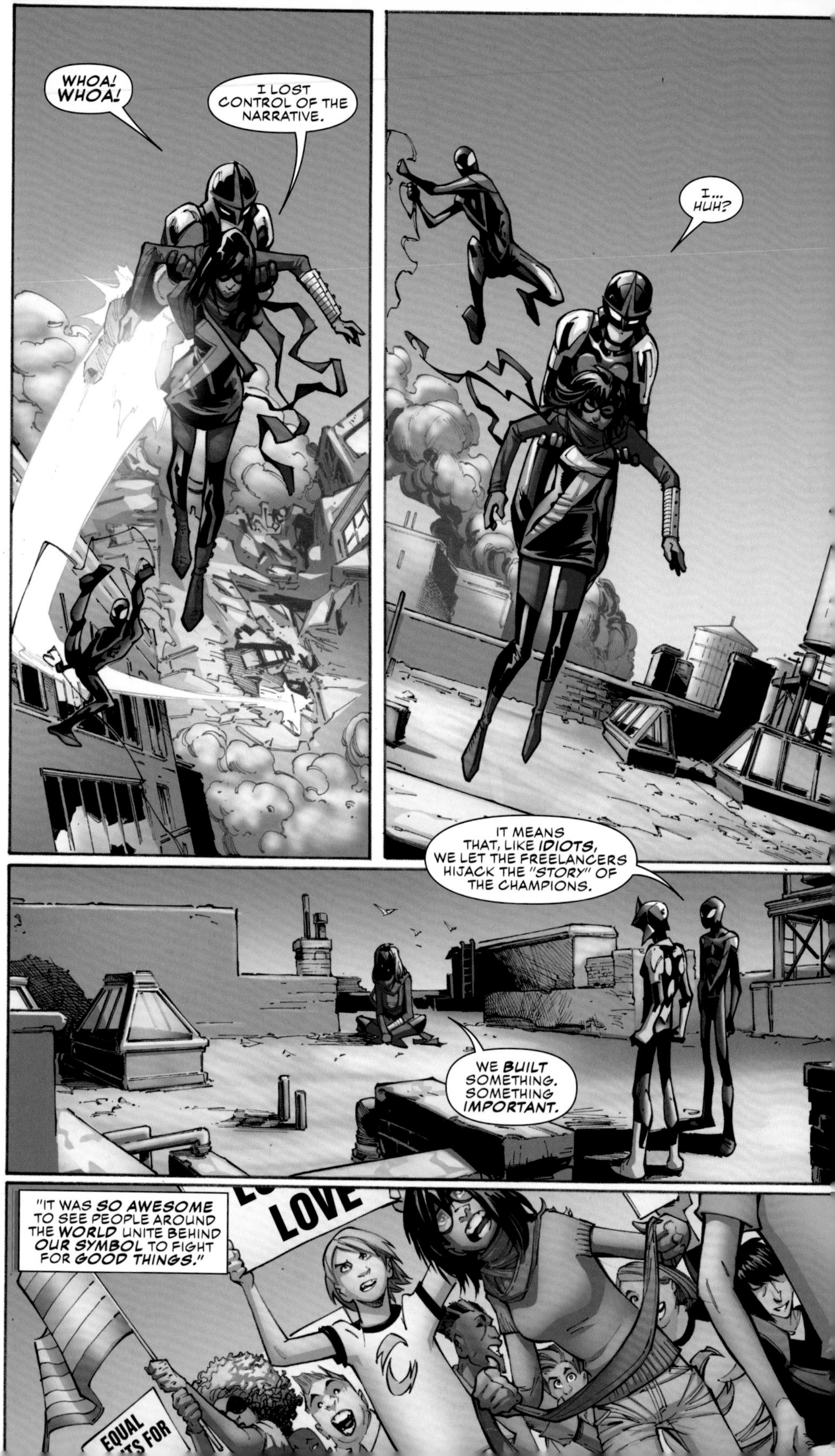

WHOA! WHOA!
I LOST CONTROL OF THE NARRATIVE.
I... HUH?
IT MEANS THAT, LIKE IDIOTS, WE LET THE FREELANCERS HIJACK THE "STORY" OF THE CHAMPIONS.
WE BUILT SOMETHING. SOMETHING IMPORTANT.
"IT WAS SO AWESOME TO SEE PEOPLE AROUND THE WORLD UNITE BEHIND OUR SYMBOL TO FIGHT FOR GOOD THINGS."
LOVE
EQUAL

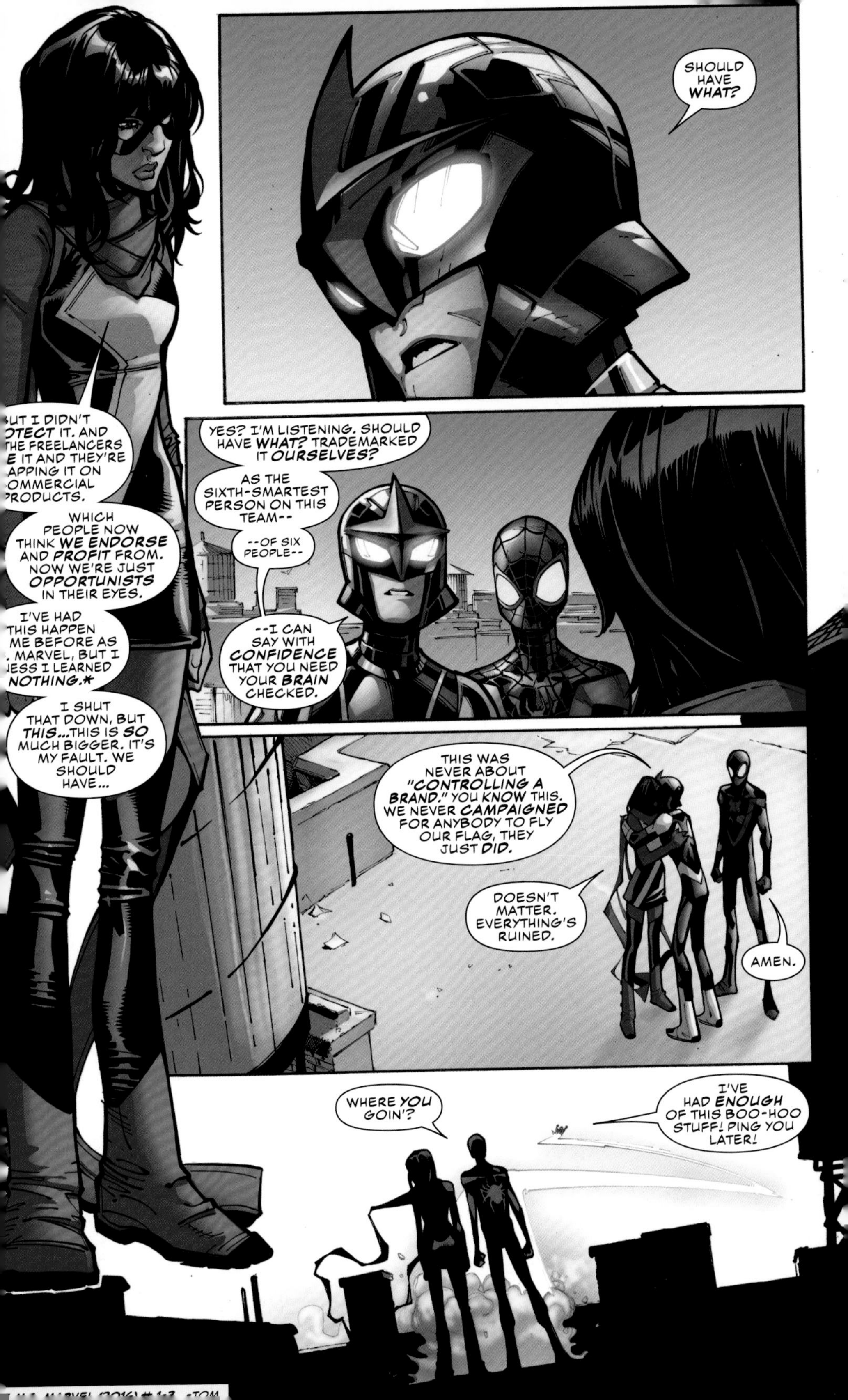

UT I DIDN'T OTECT IT. AND THE FREELANCERS E IT AND THEY'RE APPING IT ON OMMERCIAL PRODUCTS.
WHICH PEOPLE NOW THINK WE ENDORSE AND PROFIT FROM. NOW WE'RE JUST OPPORTUNISTS IN THEIR EYES.
I'VE HAD THIS HAPPEN ME BEFORE AS . MARVEL, BUT I JESS I LEARNED NOTHING.*
I SHUT THAT DOWN, BUT THIS...THIS IS SO MUCH BIGGER. IT'S MY FAULT. WE SHOULD HAVE...
SHOULD HAVE WHAT?
YES? I'M LISTENING. SHOULD HAVE WHAT? TRADEMARKED IT OURSELVES?
AS THE SIXTH-SMARTEST PERSON ON THIS TEAM--
--OF SIX PEOPLE--
--I CAN SAY WITH CONFIDENCE THAT YOU NEED YOUR BRAIN CHECKED.
THIS WAS NEVER ABOUT "CONTROLLING A BRAND." YOU KNOW THIS. WE NEVER CAMPAIGNED FOR ANYBODY TO FLY OUR FLAG, THEY JUST DID.
DOESN'T MATTER. EVERYTHING'S RUINED.
AMEN.
WHERE YOU GOIN'?
I'VE HAD ENOUGH OF THIS BOO-HOO STUFF! PING YOU LATER!

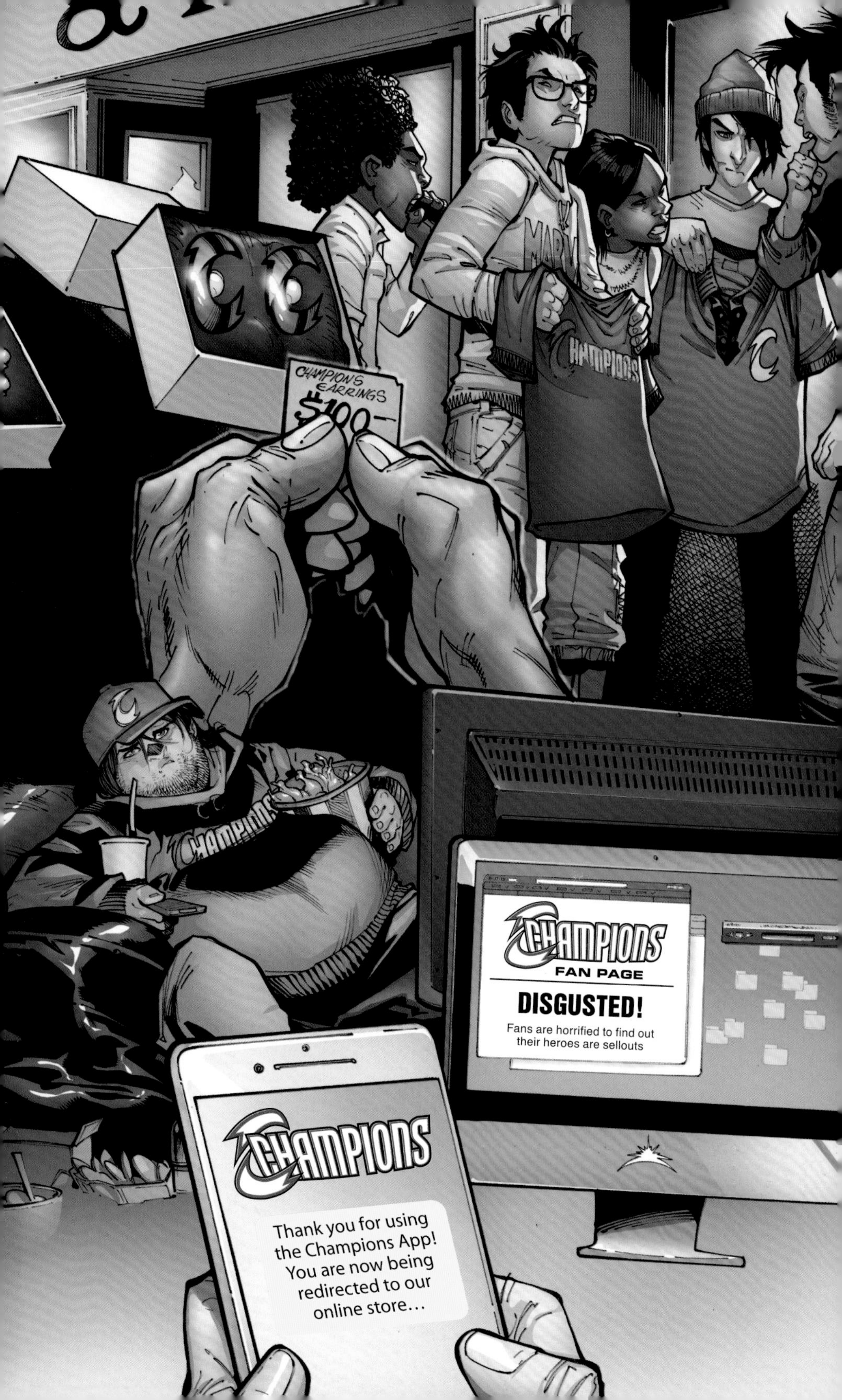
CHAMPIONS EARRINGS
$100
CHAMPIONS
CHAMPIONS
CHAMPIONS
CHAMPIONS
FAN PAGE
DISGUSTED!
Fans are horrified to find out their heroes are sellouts
CHAMPIONS
Thank you for using the Champions App! You are now being redirected to our online store...

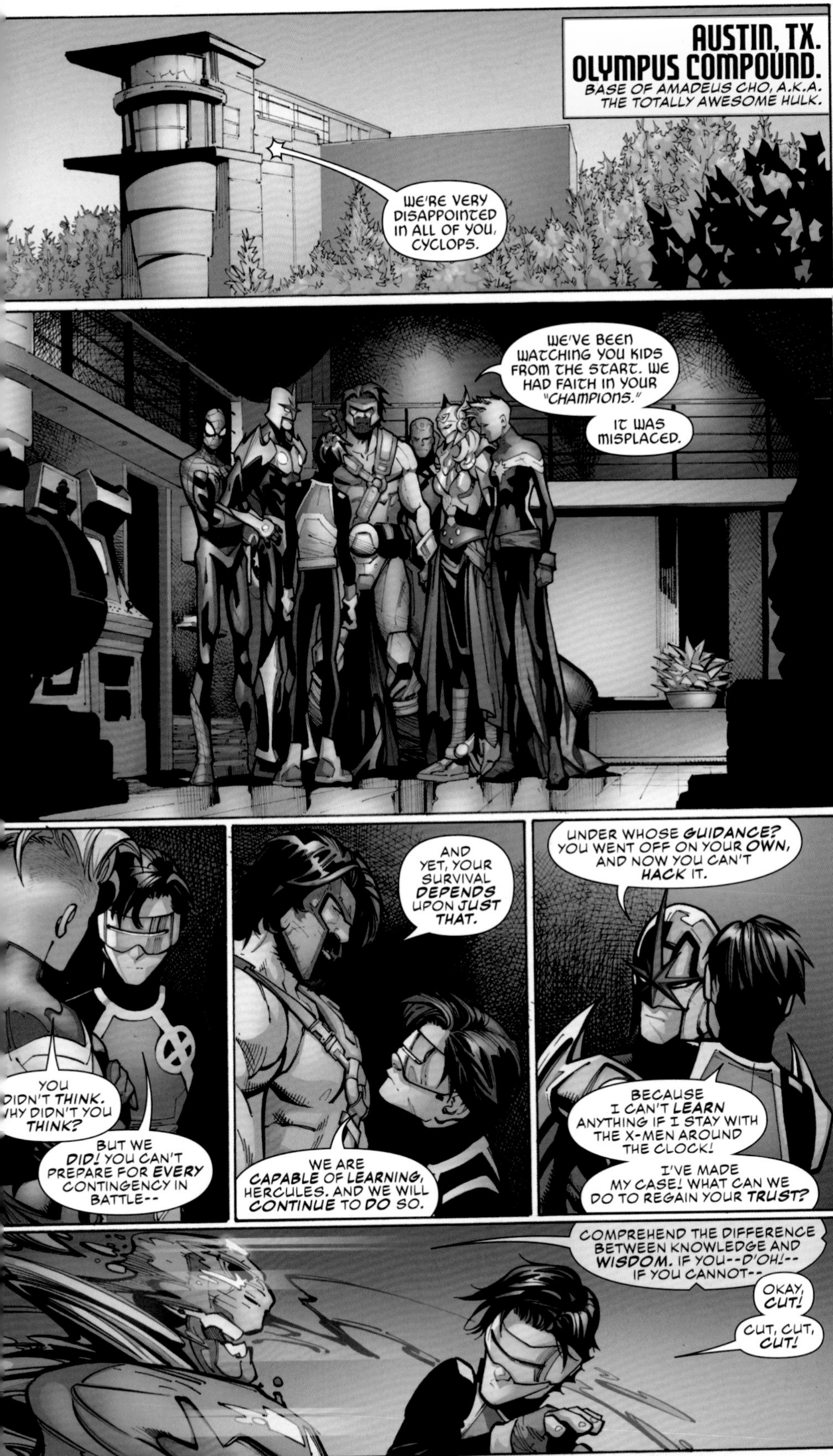
AUSTIN, TX.
OLYMPUS COMPOUND.
BASE OF AMADEUS CHO, A.K.A. THE TOTALLY AWESOME HULK.
WE'RE VERY DISAPPOINTED IN ALL OF YOU, CYCLOPS.
WE'VE BEEN WATCHING YOU KIDS FROM THE START. WE HAD FAITH IN YOUR "CHAMPIONS."
IT WAS MISPLACED.
YOU DIDN'T THINK. WHY DIDN'T YOU THINK?
BUT WE DID! YOU CAN'T PREPARE FOR EVERY CONTINGENCY IN BATTLE--
AND YET, YOUR SURVIVAL DEPENDS UPON JUST THAT.
WE ARE CAPABLE OF LEARNING, HERCULES. AND WE WILL CONTINUE TO DO SO.
UNDER WHOSE GUIDANCE? YOU WENT OFF ON YOUR OWN, AND NOW YOU CAN'T HACK IT.
BECAUSE I CAN'T LEARN ANYTHING IF I STAY WITH THE X-MEN AROUND THE CLOCK!
I'VE MADE MY CASE! WHAT CAN WE DO TO REGAIN YOUR TRUST?
COMPREHEND THE DIFFERENCE BETWEEN KNOWLEDGE AND WISDOM. IF YOU--D'OH!-- IF YOU CANNOT--
OKAY, CUT!
CUT, CUT, CUT!

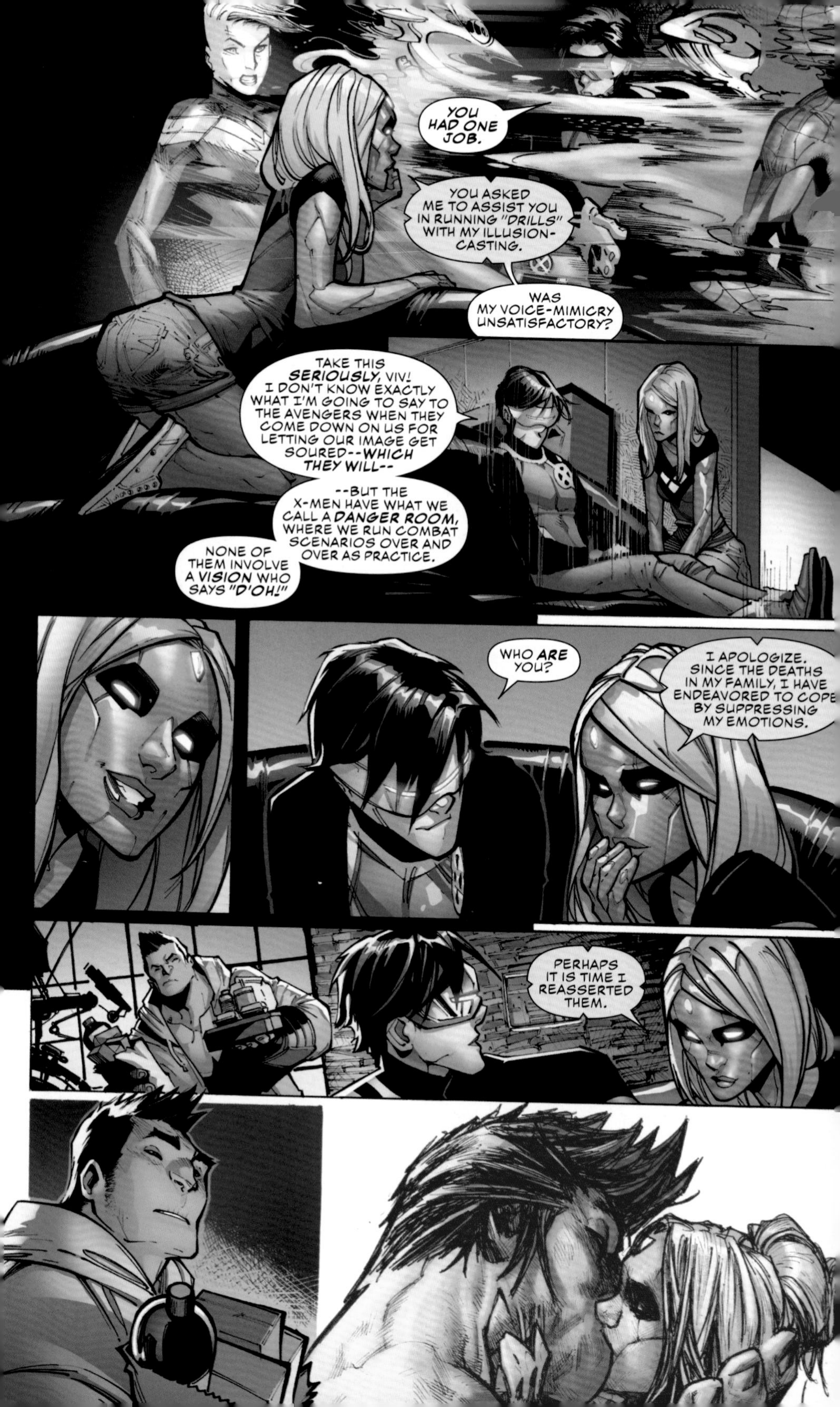

YOU HAD ONE JOB.
YOU ASKED ME TO ASSIST YOU IN RUNNING "DRILLS" WITH MY ILLUSION-CASTING.
WAS MY VOICE-MIMICRY UNSATISFACTORY?
TAKE THIS SERIOUSLY, VIV! I DON'T KNOW EXACTLY WHAT I'M GOING TO SAY TO THE AVENGERS WHEN THEY COME DOWN ON US FOR LETTING OUR IMAGE GET SOURED--WHICH THEY WILL--
--BUT THE X-MEN HAVE WHAT WE CALL A DANGER ROOM, WHERE WE RUN COMBAT SCENARIOS OVER AND OVER AS PRACTICE.
NONE OF THEM INVOLVE A VISION WHO SAYS "D'OH!"
WHO ARE YOU?
I APOLOGIZE. SINCE THE DEATHS IN MY FAMILY, I HAVE ENDEAVORED TO COPE BY SUPPRESSING MY EMOTIONS.
PERHAPS IT IS TIME I REASSERTED THEM.

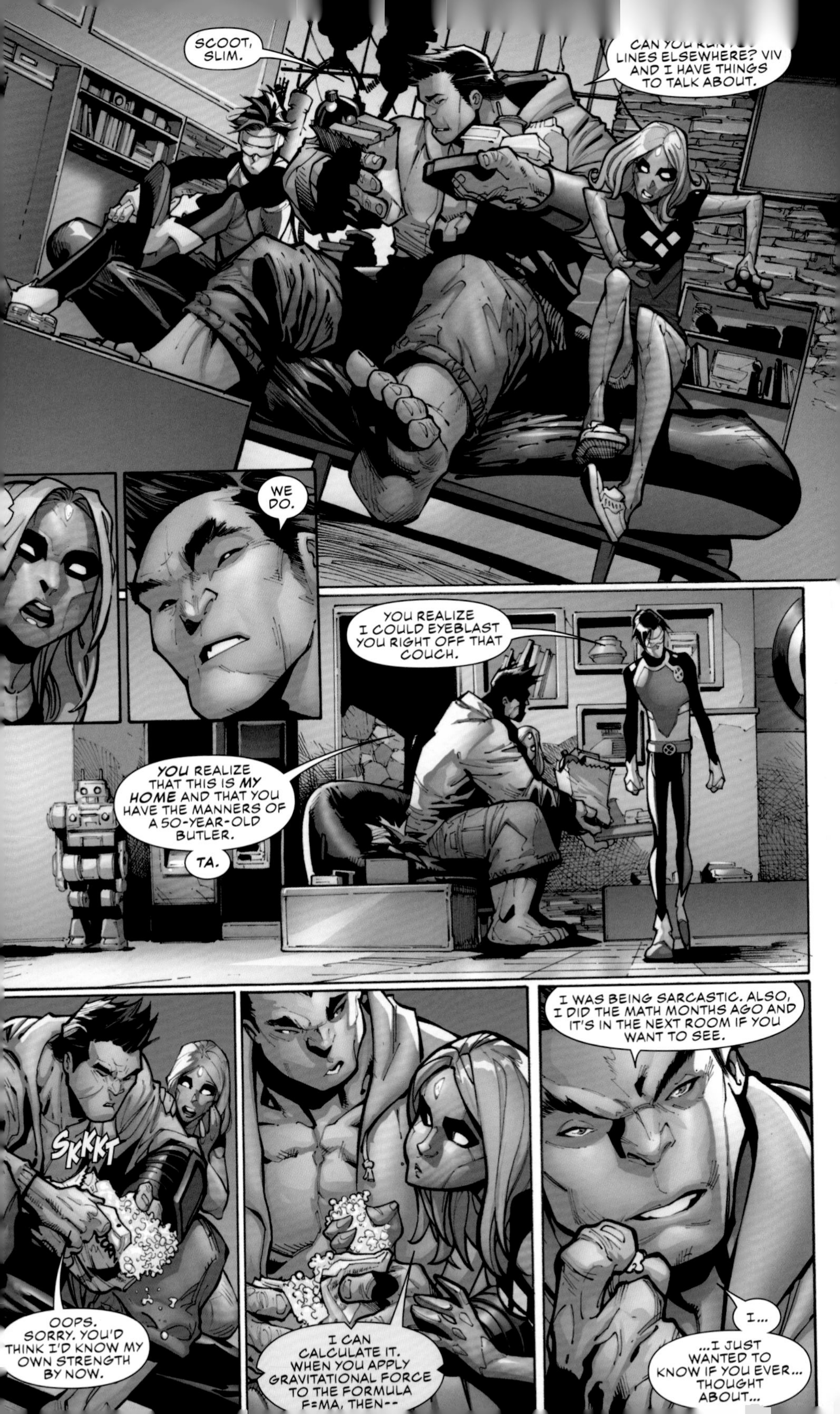
SCOOT, SLIM.
CAN YOU RUN LINES ELSEWHERE? VIV AND I HAVE THINGS TO TALK ABOUT.
WE DO.
YOU REALIZE I COULD EYEBLAST YOU RIGHT OFF THAT COUCH.
YOU REALIZE THAT THIS IS *MY HOME* AND THAT YOU HAVE THE MANNERS OF A 50-YEAR-OLD BUTLER.
TA.
SKKKT
OOPS. SORRY. YOU'D THINK I'D KNOW MY OWN STRENGTH BY NOW.
I CAN CALCULATE IT. WHEN YOU APPLY GRAVITATIONAL FORCE TO THE FORMULA F=MA, THEN--
I WAS BEING SARCASTIC. ALSO, I DID THE MATH MONTHS AGO AND IT'S IN THE NEXT ROOM IF YOU WANT TO SEE.
I...
...I JUST WANTED TO KNOW IF YOU EVER... THOUGHT ABOUT...

...ABOUT YOUR TONGUE IN MY MOUTH?

PFFF-ZZZ

ARE YOU ALL RIGHT?

...IF YOU EVER THINK NOTHING HURTS A *HULK*...

...WATCH HIM COUGH *SODA* THROUGH HIS NOSE...

YES, ABOUT...THAT. IT'S PROBABLY BETTER TO JUST CALL IT A *KISS*, MS. LITERAL.

I FIGURED IF YOU WERE KICK-STARTING YOUR EMOTIONS, MAYBE WE COULD TAKE UP WHERE WE LEFT *OFF*...?

WE COULD.

EXCEPT

EXCEPT.

AMADEUS, I HAVE BEEN ANALYZING MY FEELINGS SURROUNDING THAT MOMENT FOR SOME TIME NOW.

SIMILARLY, I HAVE BEEN PROCESSING THE EMOTIONAL EFFECTS OF VARIOUS OTHER STIMULI.

AND WHILE I HAVE YET TO THOROUGHLY ACQUAINT MYSELF WITH A FULL ENOUGH SAMPLING OF SEXUAL AND GENDER IDENTITIES TO AS YET DETERMINE MY *OWN*--

--AN ATTRACTION TO BOYS IS NOWHERE WITHIN ME.

I DO NOT WISH TO INJURE YOUR FEELINGS.

YOU DIDN'T. YOU JUST GAVE *ME* NEW ONES. C'MERE.

YOU KNOW WHAT I WANT FOR YOU TO *HAPPY*.

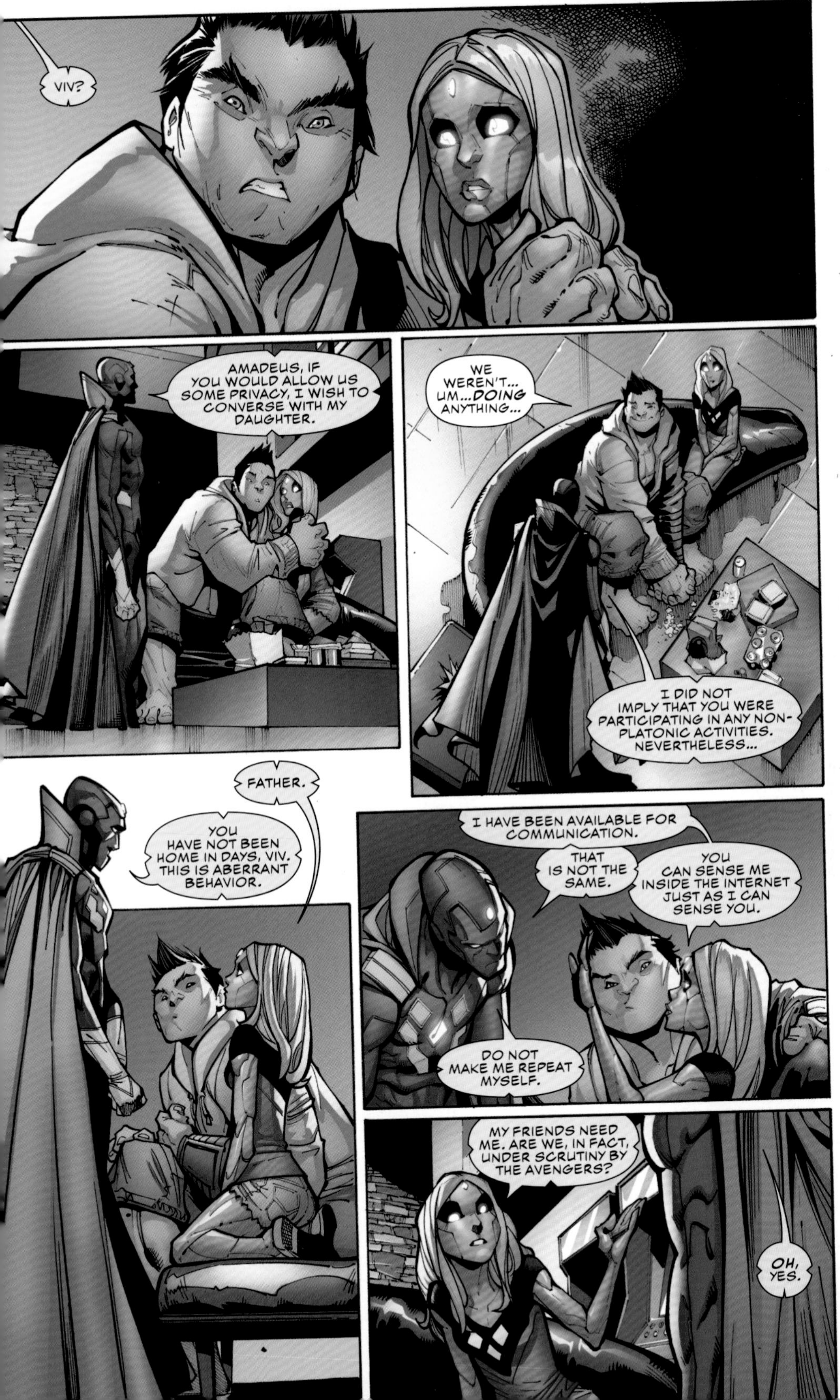
VIV?
AMADEUS, IF YOU WOULD ALLOW US SOME PRIVACY, I WISH TO CONVERSE WITH MY DAUGHTER.
WE WEREN'T... UM...DOING ANYTHING...
I DID NOT IMPLY THAT YOU WERE PARTICIPATING IN ANY NON-PLATONIC ACTIVITIES. NEVERTHELESS...
FATHER.
YOU HAVE NOT BEEN HOME IN DAYS, VIV. THIS IS ABERRANT BEHAVIOR.
I HAVE BEEN AVAILABLE FOR COMMUNICATION.
THAT IS NOT THE SAME.
YOU CAN SENSE ME INSIDE THE INTERNET JUST AS I CAN SENSE YOU.
DO NOT MAKE ME REPEAT MYSELF.
MY FRIENDS NEED ME. ARE WE, IN FACT, UNDER SCRUTINY BY THE AVENGERS?
OH, YES.

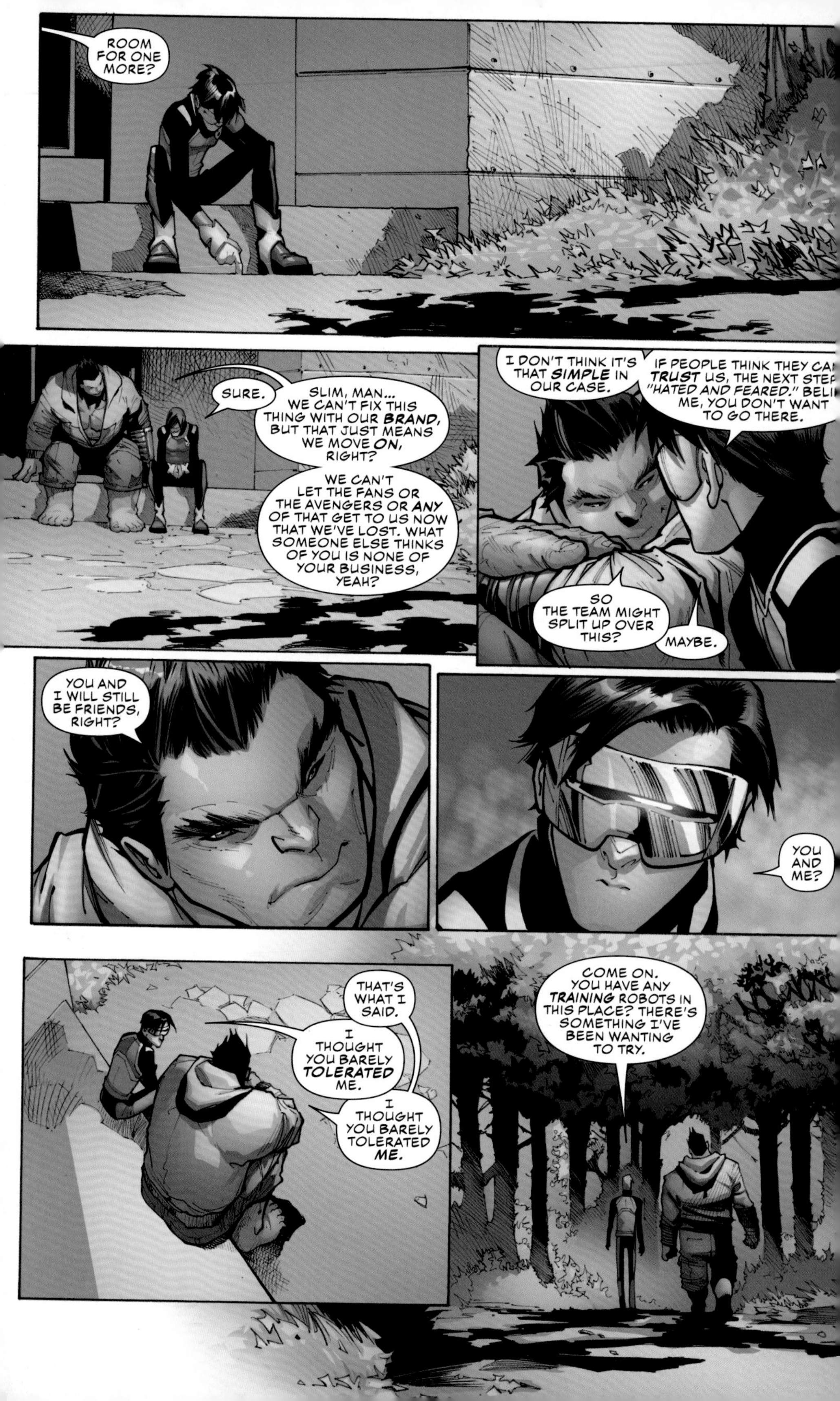
ROOM FOR ONE MORE?
SURE.
SLIM, MAN... WE CAN'T FIX THIS THING WITH OUR BRAND, BUT THAT JUST MEANS WE MOVE ON, RIGHT?
WE CAN'T LET THE FANS OR THE AVENGERS OR ANY OF THAT GET TO US NOW THAT WE'VE LOST. WHAT SOMEONE ELSE THINKS OF YOU IS NONE OF YOUR BUSINESS, YEAH?
I DON'T THINK IT'S THAT SIMPLE IN OUR CASE.
IF PEOPLE THINK THEY CA TRUST US, THE NEXT STE "HATED AND FEARED." BELI ME, YOU DON'T WANT TO GO THERE.
SO THE TEAM MIGHT SPLIT UP OVER THIS?
MAYBE.
YOU AND I WILL STILL BE FRIENDS, RIGHT?
YOU AND ME?
THAT'S WHAT I SAID.
I THOUGHT YOU BARELY TOLERATED ME.
I THOUGHT YOU BARELY TOLERATED ME.
COME ON. YOU HAVE ANY TRAINING ROBOTS IN THIS PLACE? THERE'S SOMETHING I'VE BEEN WANTING TO TRY.

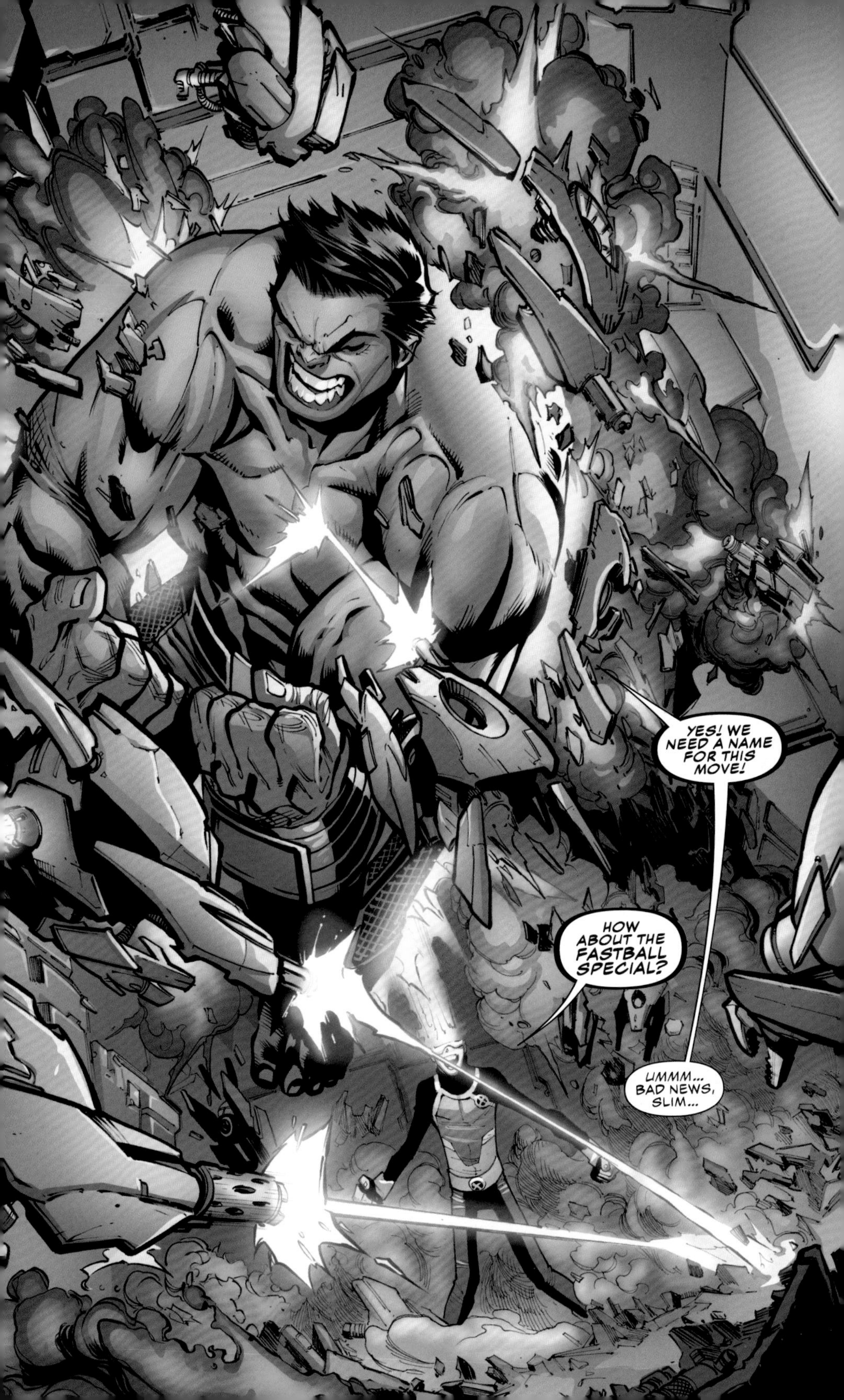
YES! WE NEED A NAME FOR THIS MOVE!
HOW ABOUT THE FASTBALL SPECIAL?
UMMM... BAD NEWS, SLIM...

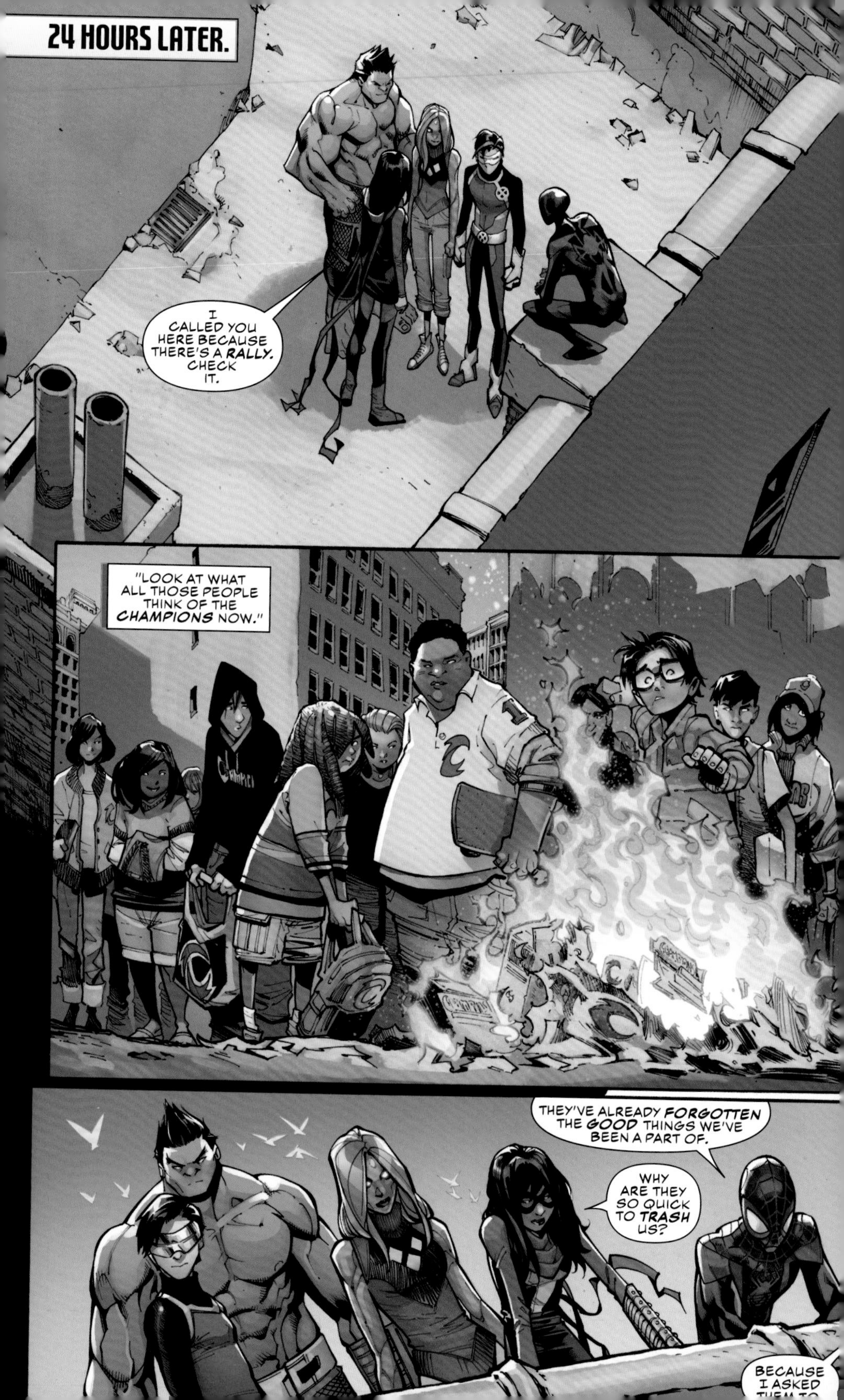
24 HOURS LATER.
I CALLED YOU HERE BECAUSE THERE'S A RALLY. CHECK IT.
"LOOK AT WHAT ALL THOSE PEOPLE THINK OF THE CHAMPIONS NOW."
THEY'VE ALREADY FORGOTTEN THE GOOD THINGS WE'VE BEEN A PART OF.
WHY ARE THEY SO QUICK TO TRASH US?
BECAUSE I ASKED

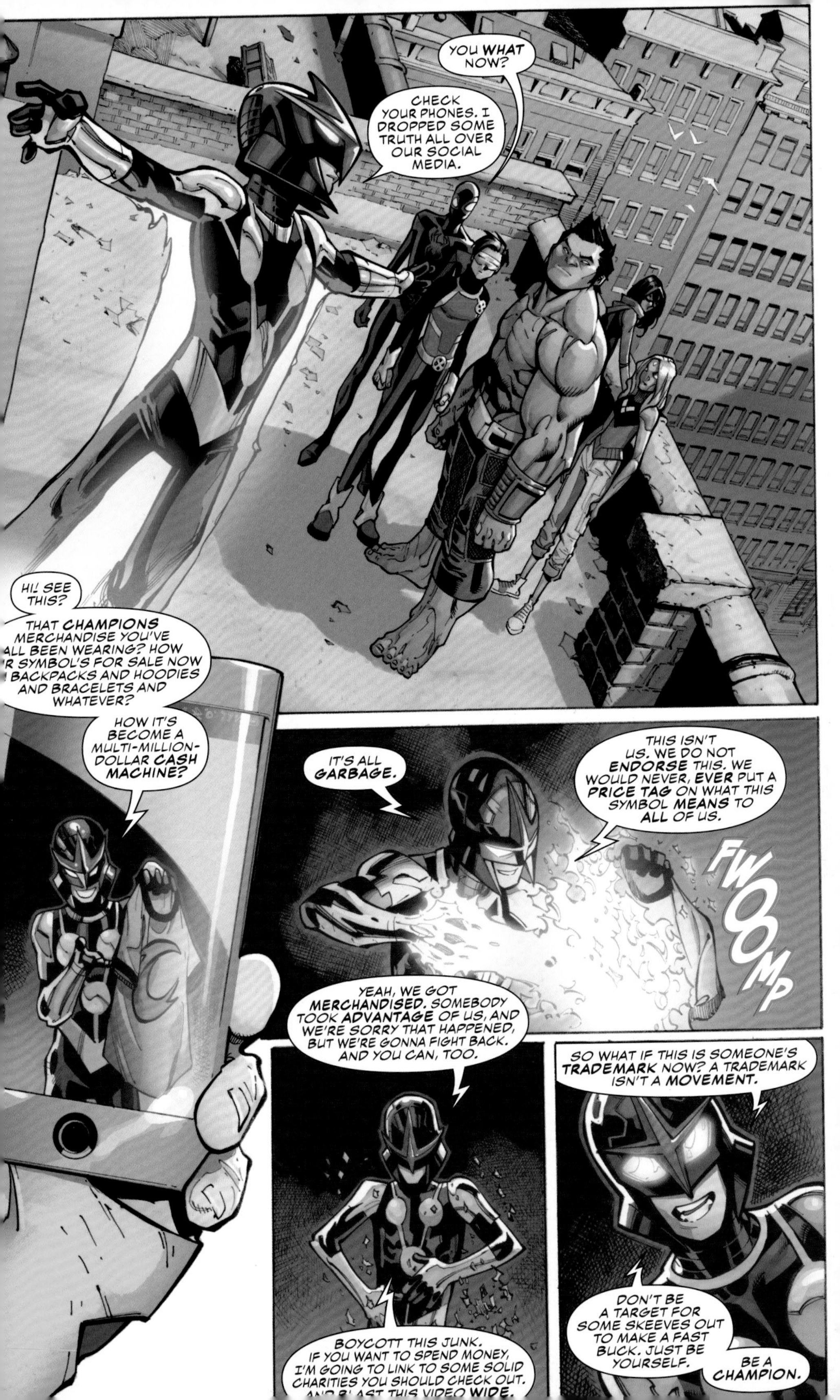
YOU WHAT NOW?
CHECK YOUR PHONES. I DROPPED SOME TRUTH ALL OVER OUR SOCIAL MEDIA.
HI! SEE THIS?
THAT CHAMPIONS MERCHANDISE YOU'VE ALL BEEN WEARING? HOW R SYMBOL'S FOR SALE NOW BACKPACKS AND HOODIES AND BRACELETS AND WHATEVER?
HOW IT'S BECOME A MULTI-MILLION-DOLLAR CASH MACHINE?
IT'S ALL GARBAGE.
THIS ISN'T US. WE DO NOT ENDORSE THIS. WE WOULD NEVER, EVER PUT A PRICE TAG ON WHAT THIS SYMBOL MEANS TO ALL OF US.
FWOOMP
YEAH, WE GOT MERCHANDISED. SOMEBODY TOOK ADVANTAGE OF US, AND WE'RE SORRY THAT HAPPENED, BUT WE'RE GONNA FIGHT BACK. AND YOU CAN, TOO.
BOYCOTT THIS JUNK. IF YOU WANT TO SPEND MONEY, I'M GOING TO LINK TO SOME SOLID CHARITIES YOU SHOULD CHECK OUT.
SO WHAT IF THIS IS SOMEONE'S TRADEMARK NOW? A TRADEMARK ISN'T A MOVEMENT.
DON'T BE A TARGET FOR SOME SKEEVES OUT TO MAKE A FAST BUCK. JUST BE YOURSELF.
BE A CHAMPION.

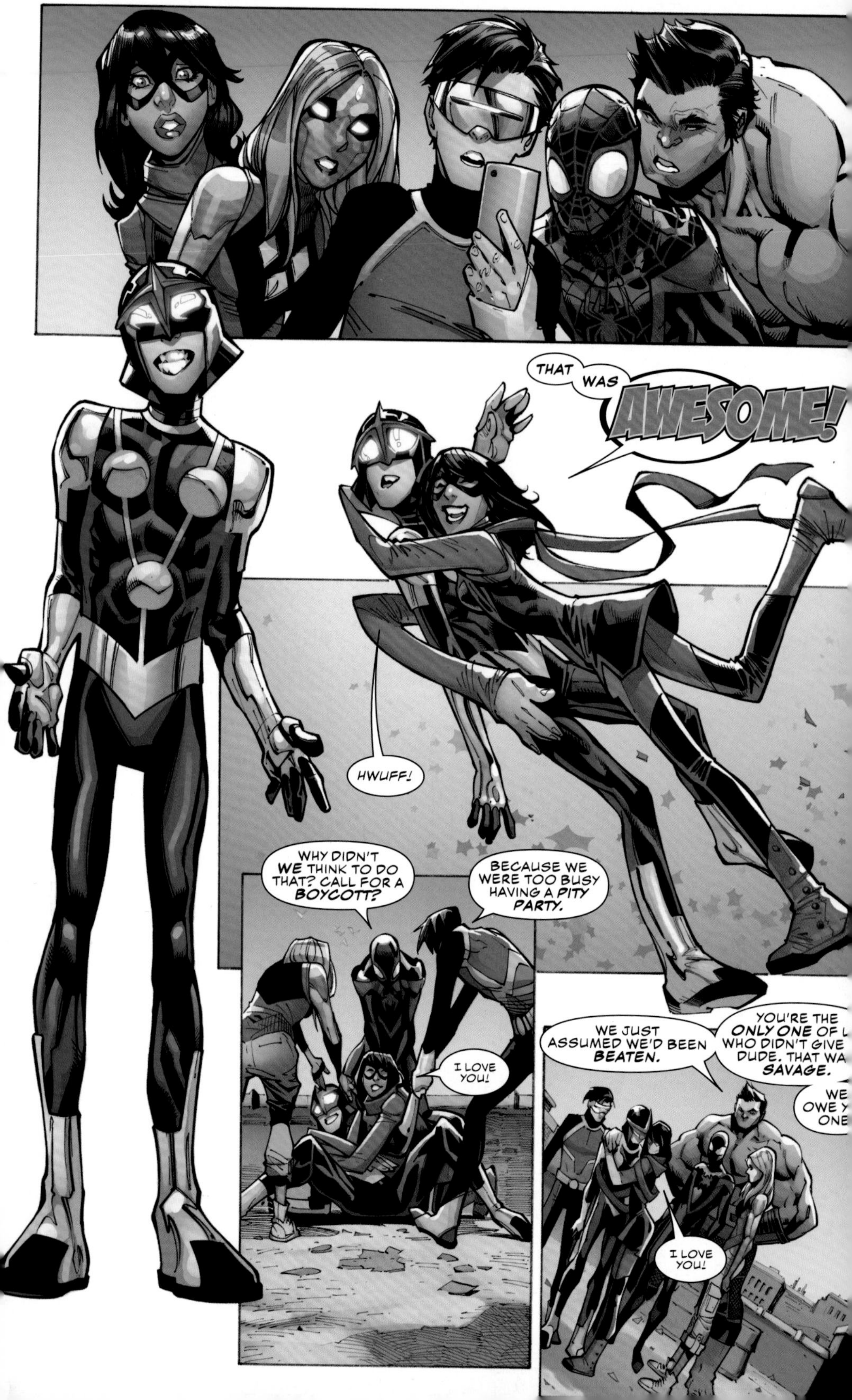

THAT WAS AWESOME!
HWUFF!
WHY DIDN'T WE THINK TO DO THAT? CALL FOR A BOYCOTT?
BECAUSE WE WERE TOO BUSY HAVING A PITY PARTY.
I LOVE YOU!
WE JUST ASSUMED WE'D BEEN BEATEN.
YOU'RE THE ONLY ONE OF WHO DIDN'T GIVE DUDE. THAT WA SAVAGE.
WE OWE Y ONE
I LOVE YOU!

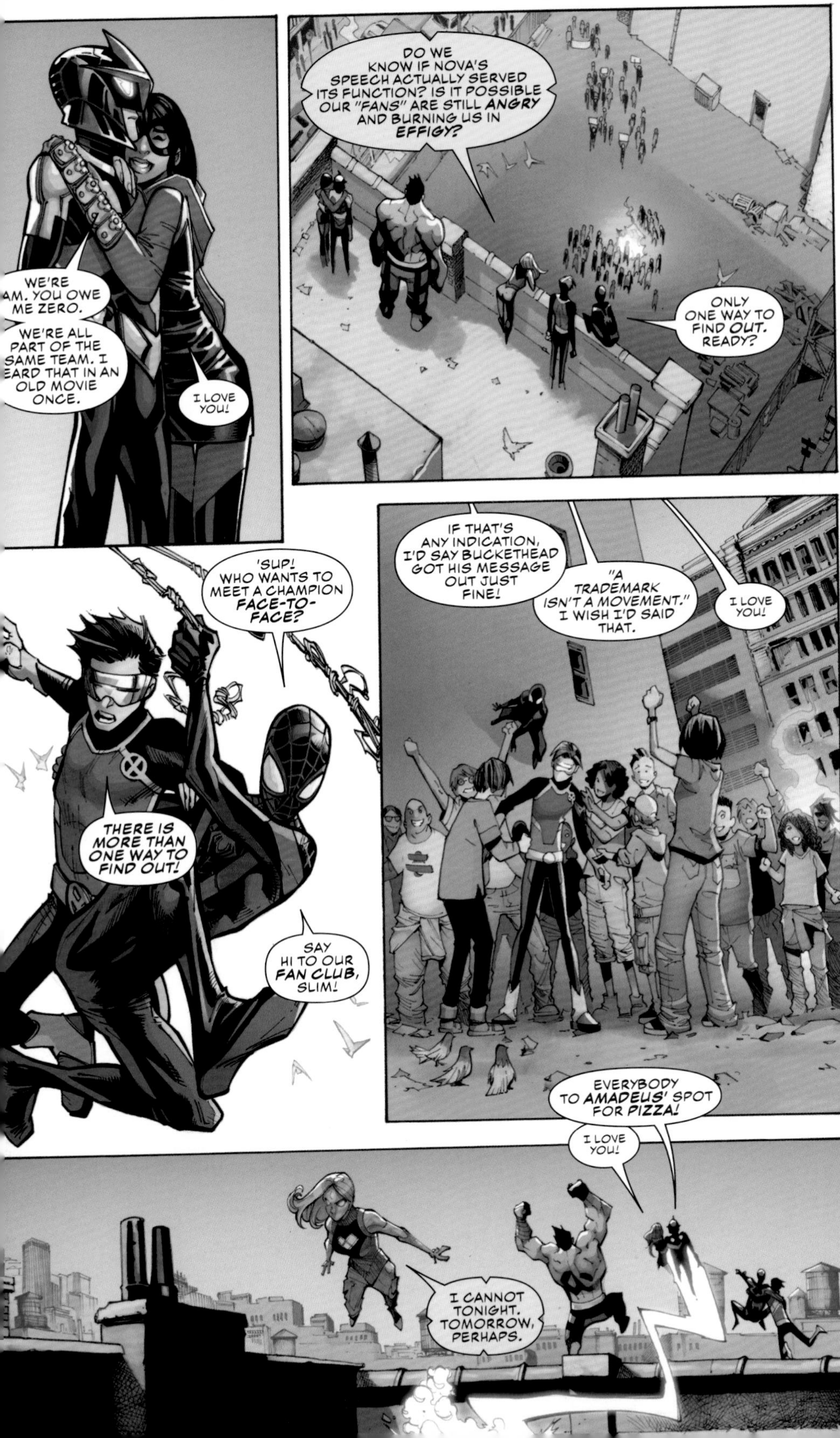
WE'RE
AM. YOU OWE
ME ZERO.
WE'RE ALL
PART OF THE
SAME TEAM. I
EARD THAT IN AN
OLD MOVIE
ONCE.
I LOVE
YOU!
DO WE KNOW IF NOVA'S SPEECH ACTUALLY SERVED ITS FUNCTION? IS IT POSSIBLE OUR "FANS" ARE STILL ANGRY AND BURNING US IN EFFIGY?
ONLY ONE WAY TO FIND OUT. READY?
'SUP! WHO WANTS TO MEET A CHAMPION FACE-TO-FACE?
THERE IS MORE THAN ONE WAY TO FIND OUT!
SAY HI TO OUR FAN CLUB, SLIM!
IF THAT'S ANY INDICATION, I'D SAY BUCKETHEAD GOT HIS MESSAGE OUT JUST FINE!
"A TRADEMARK ISN'T A MOVEMENT." I WISH I'D SAID THAT.
I LOVE YOU!
EVERYBODY TO AMADEUS' SPOT FOR PIZZA!
I LOVE YOU!
I CANNOT TONIGHT. TOMORROW, PERHAPS.

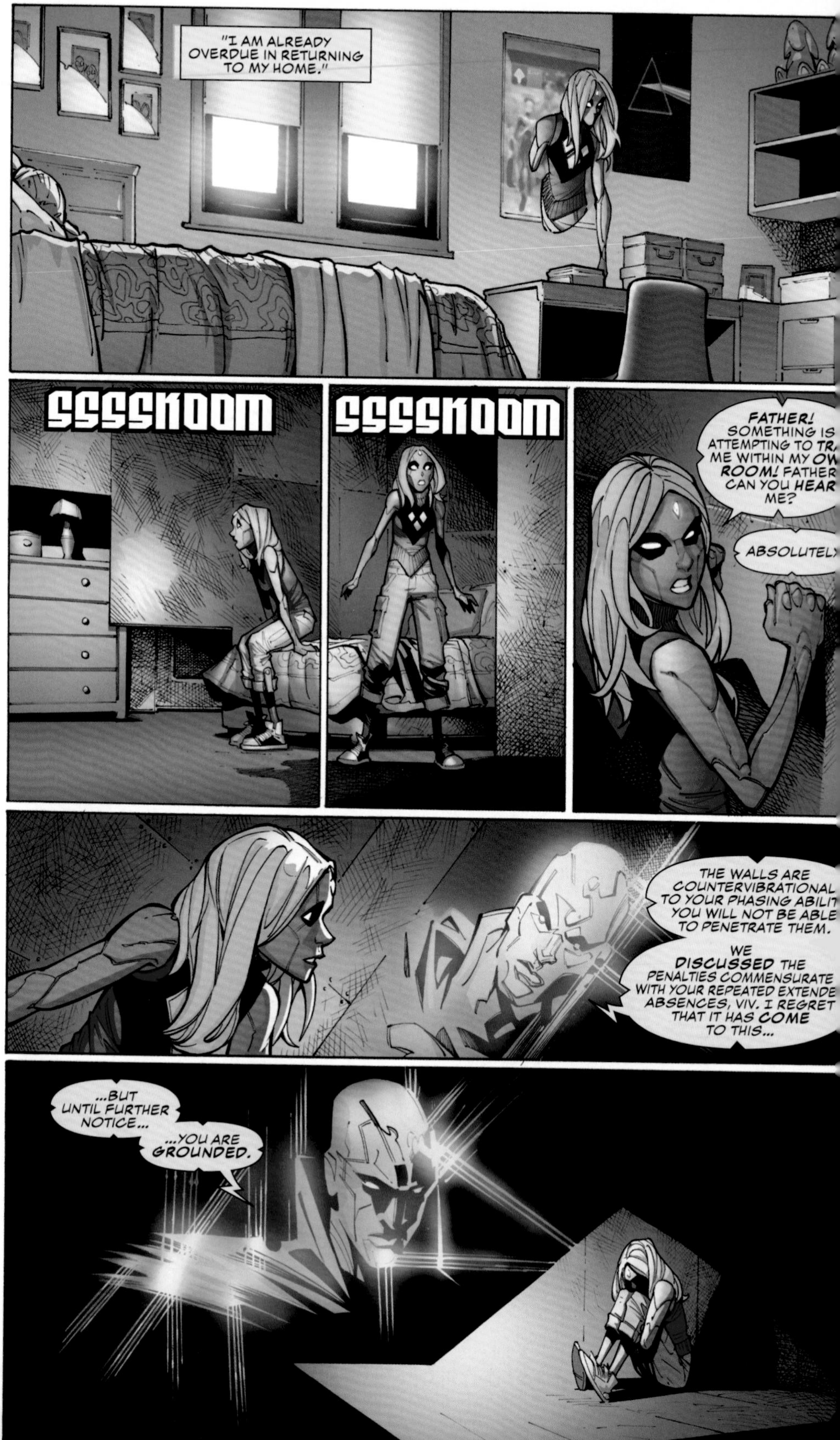
"I AM ALREADY OVERDUE IN RETURNING TO MY HOME."
SSSSKOOM
SSSSKOOM
FATHER! SOMETHING IS ATTEMPTING TO TR ME WITHIN MY OW ROOM! FATHER CAN YOU HEAR ME?
ABSOLUTEL
THE WALLS ARE COUNTERVIBRATIONAL TO YOUR PHASING ABILIT YOU WILL NOT BE ABLE TO PENETRATE THEM.
WE DISCUSSED THE PENALTIES COMMENSURATE WITH YOUR REPEATED EXTENDE ABSENCES, VIV. I REGRET THAT IT HAS COME TO THIS...
...BUT UNTIL FURTHER NOTICE...
...YOU ARE GROUNDED.

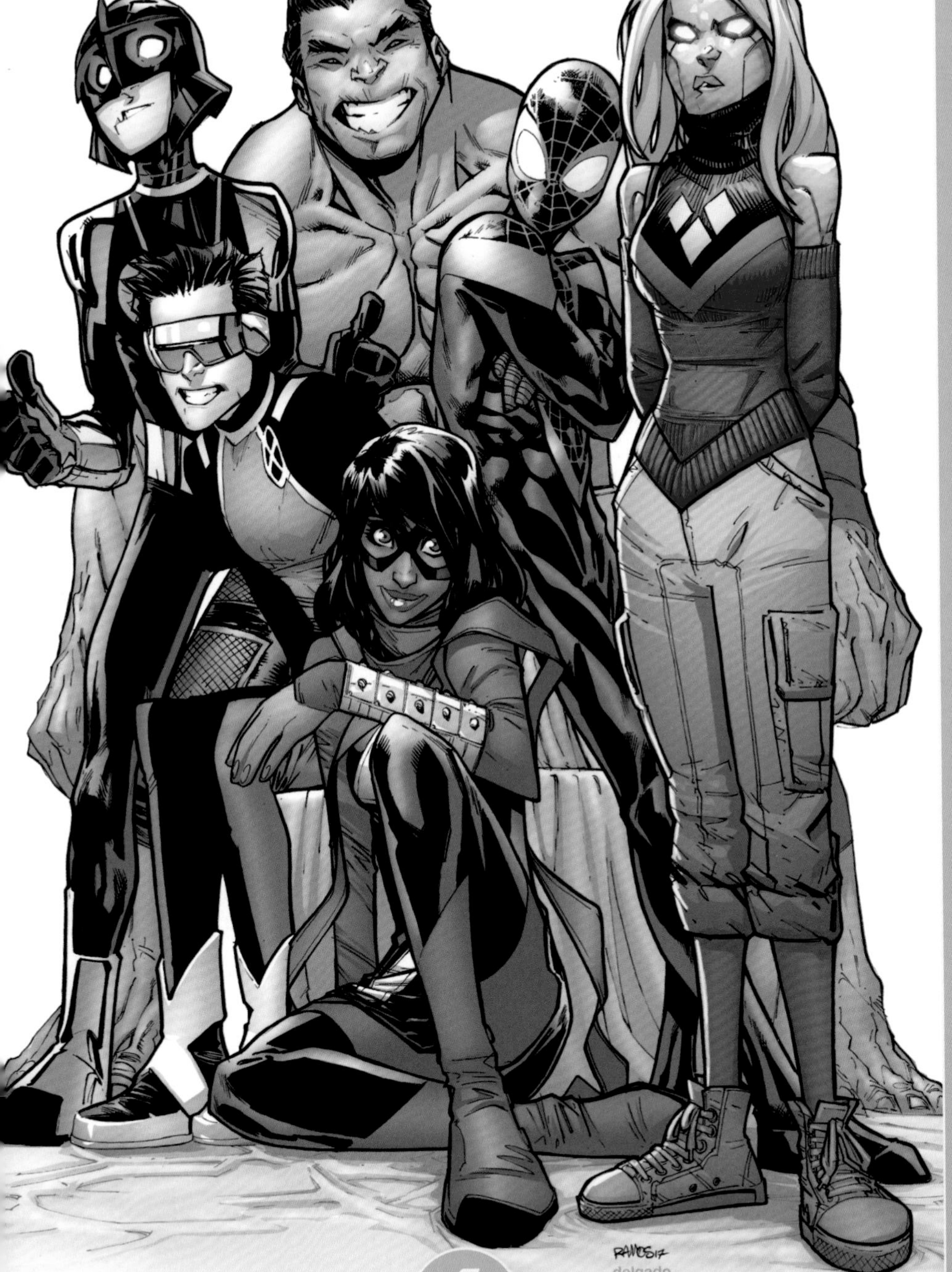
RAMOS17
delgado

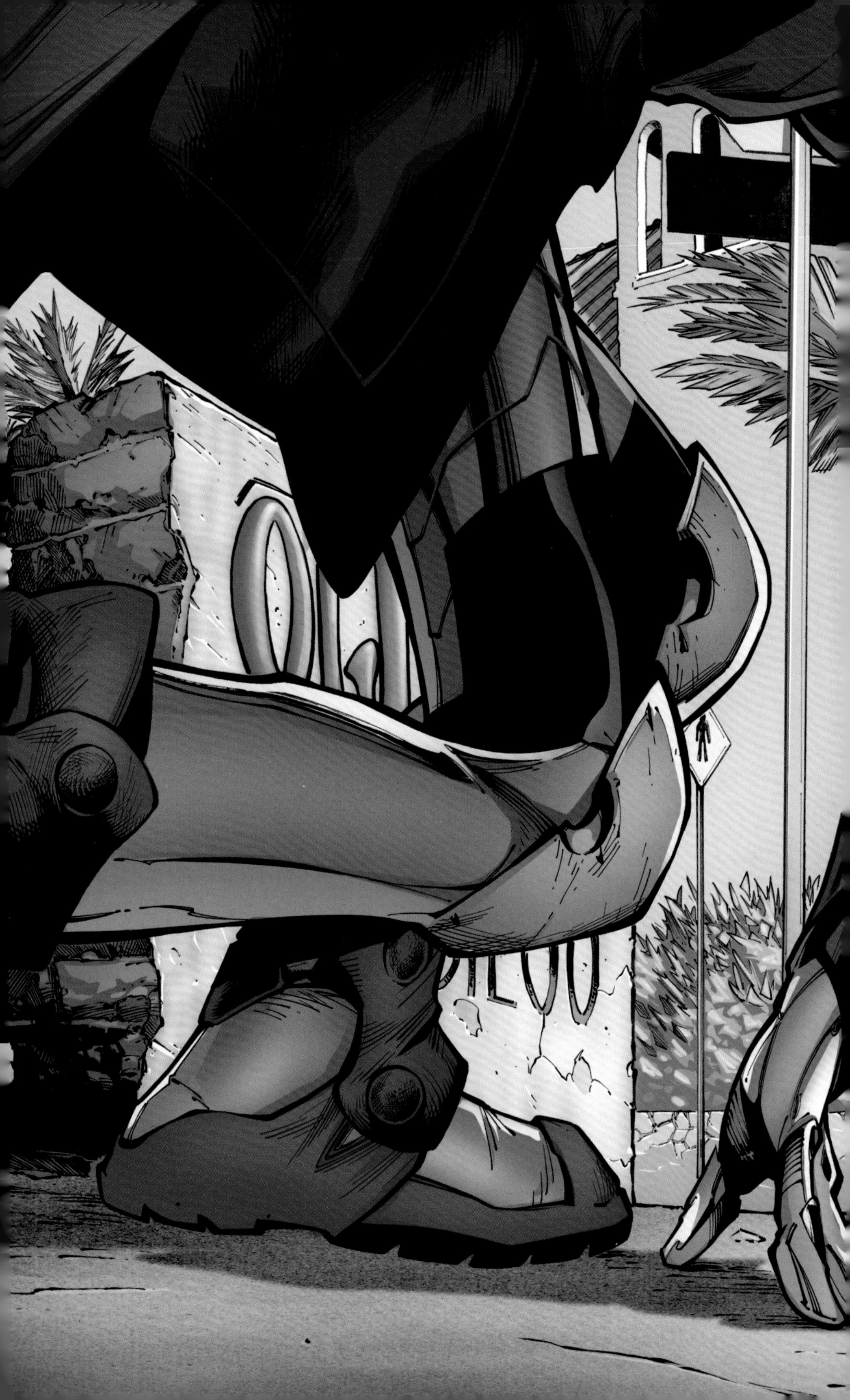

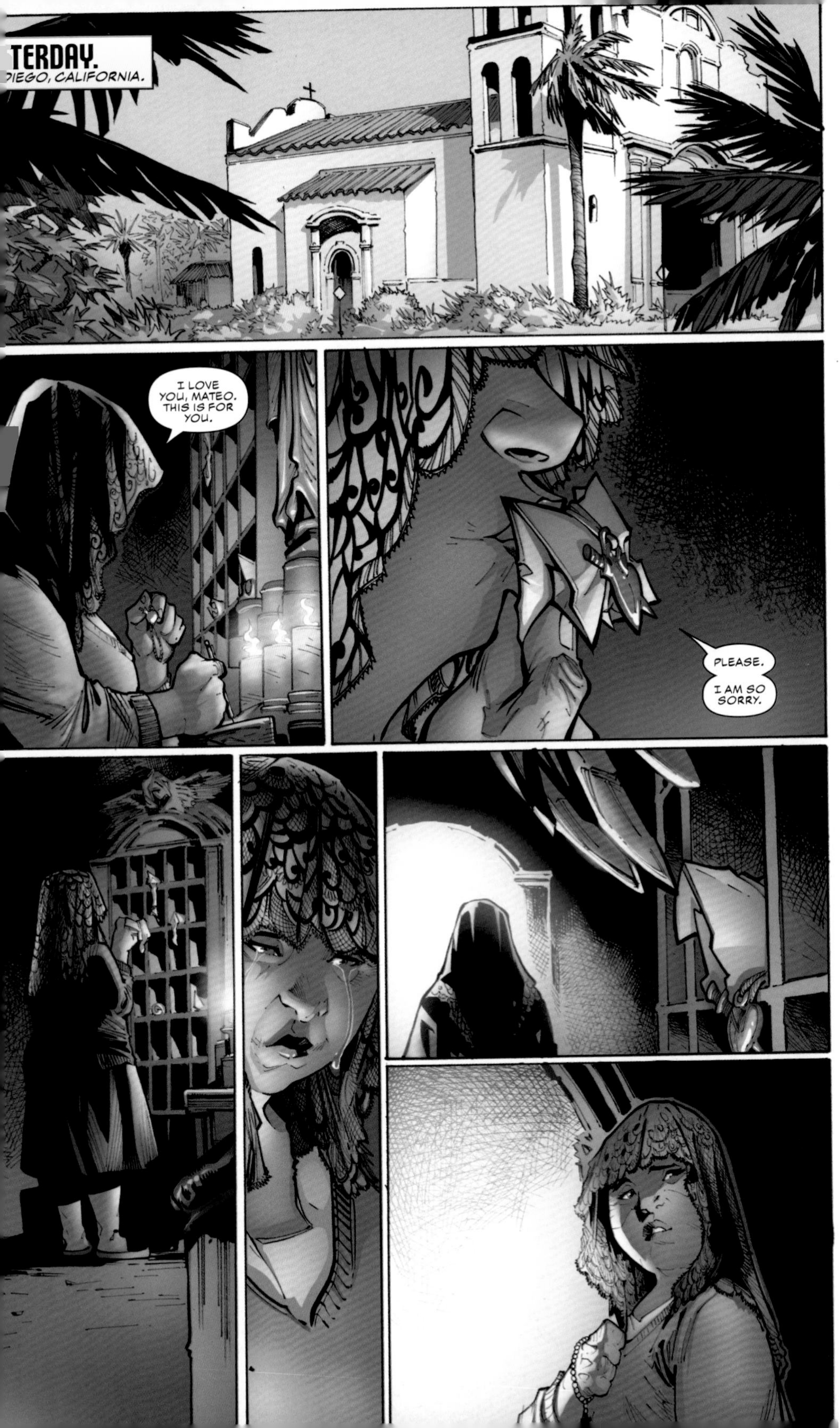
TERDAY.
DIEGO, CALIFORNIA.
I LOVE YOU, MATEO. THIS IS FOR YOU.
PLEASE.
I AM SO SORRY.

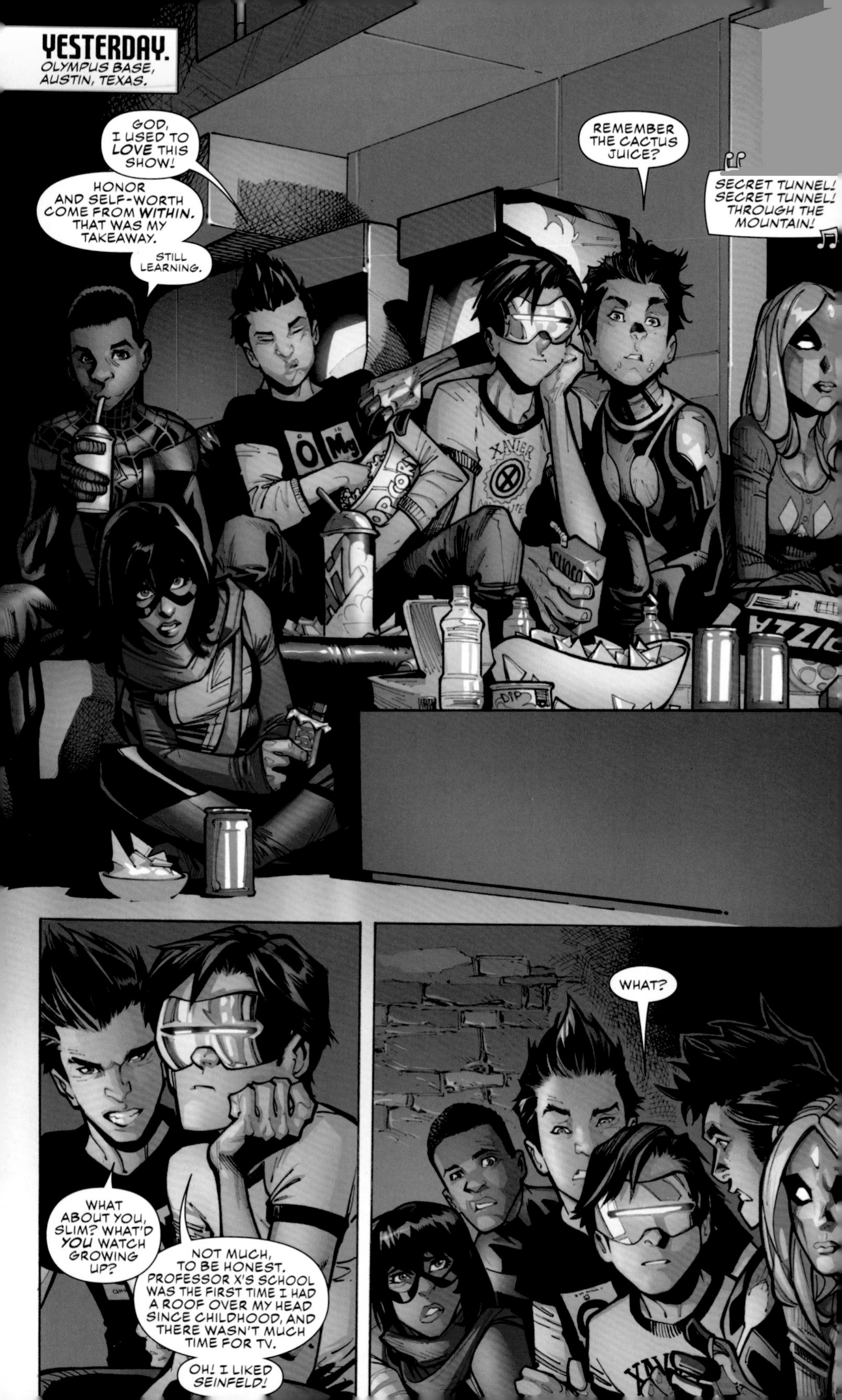

YESTERDAY.
OLYMPUS BASE, AUSTIN, TEXAS.
GOD, I USED TO LOVE THIS SHOW!
HONOR AND SELF-WORTH COME FROM WITHIN. THAT WAS MY TAKEAWAY.
STILL LEARNING.
REMEMBER THE CACTUS JUICE?
SECRET TUNNEL! SECRET TUNNEL! THROUGH THE MOUNTAIN!
WHAT ABOUT YOU, SLIM? WHAT'D YOU WATCH GROWING UP?
NOT MUCH, TO BE HONEST. PROFESSOR X'S SCHOOL WAS THE FIRST TIME I HAD A ROOF OVER MY HEAD SINCE CHILDHOOD, AND THERE WASN'T MUCH TIME FOR TV.
OH! I LIKED SEINFELD!
WHAT?

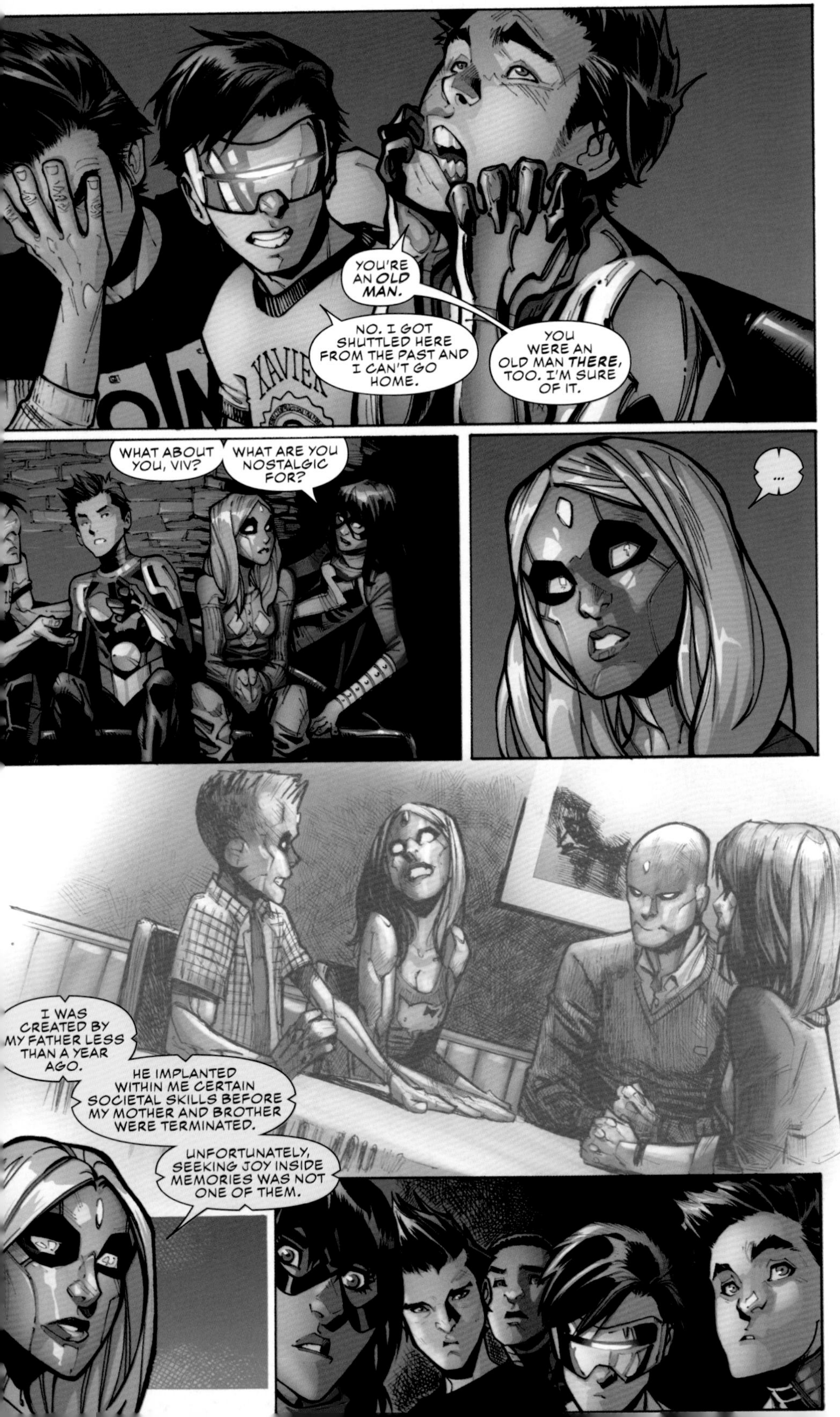
YOU'RE AN OLD MAN.
NO. I GOT SHUTTLED HERE FROM THE PAST AND I CAN'T GO HOME.
YOU WERE AN OLD MAN THERE, TOO. I'M SURE OF IT.
WHAT ABOUT YOU, VIV?
WHAT ARE YOU NOSTALGIC FOR?
...
I WAS CREATED BY MY FATHER LESS THAN A YEAR AGO.
HE IMPLANTED WITHIN ME CERTAIN SOCIETAL SKILLS BEFORE MY MOTHER AND BROTHER WERE TERMINATED.
UNFORTUNATELY, SEEKING JOY INSIDE MEMORIES WAS NOT ONE OF THEM.
XAVIER

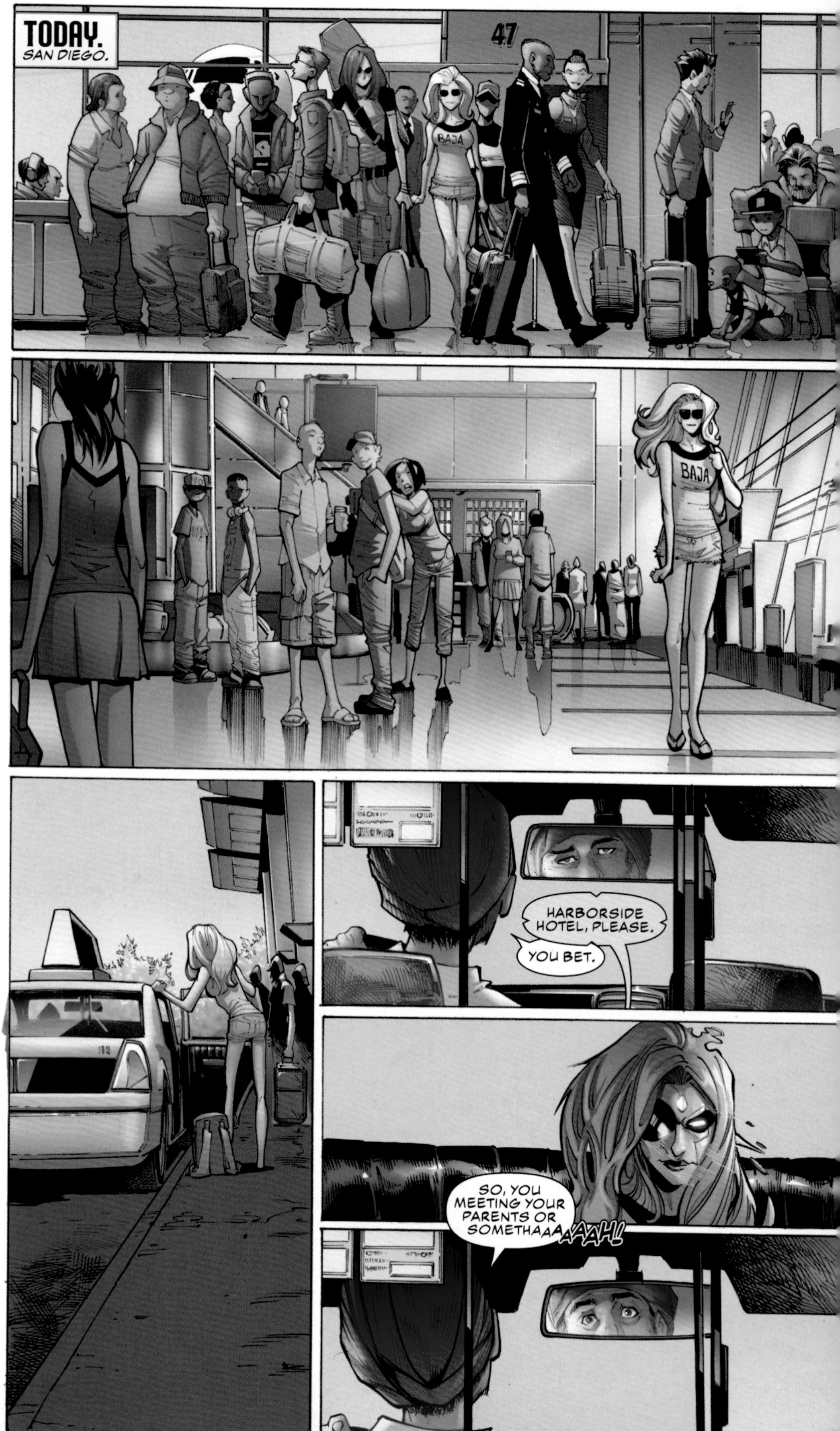
TODAY.
SAN DIEGO.
47
BAJA
BAJA
HARBORSIDE HOTEL, PLEASE.
YOU BET.
SO, YOU MEETING YOUR PARENTS OR SOMETHAAAAAAH!!

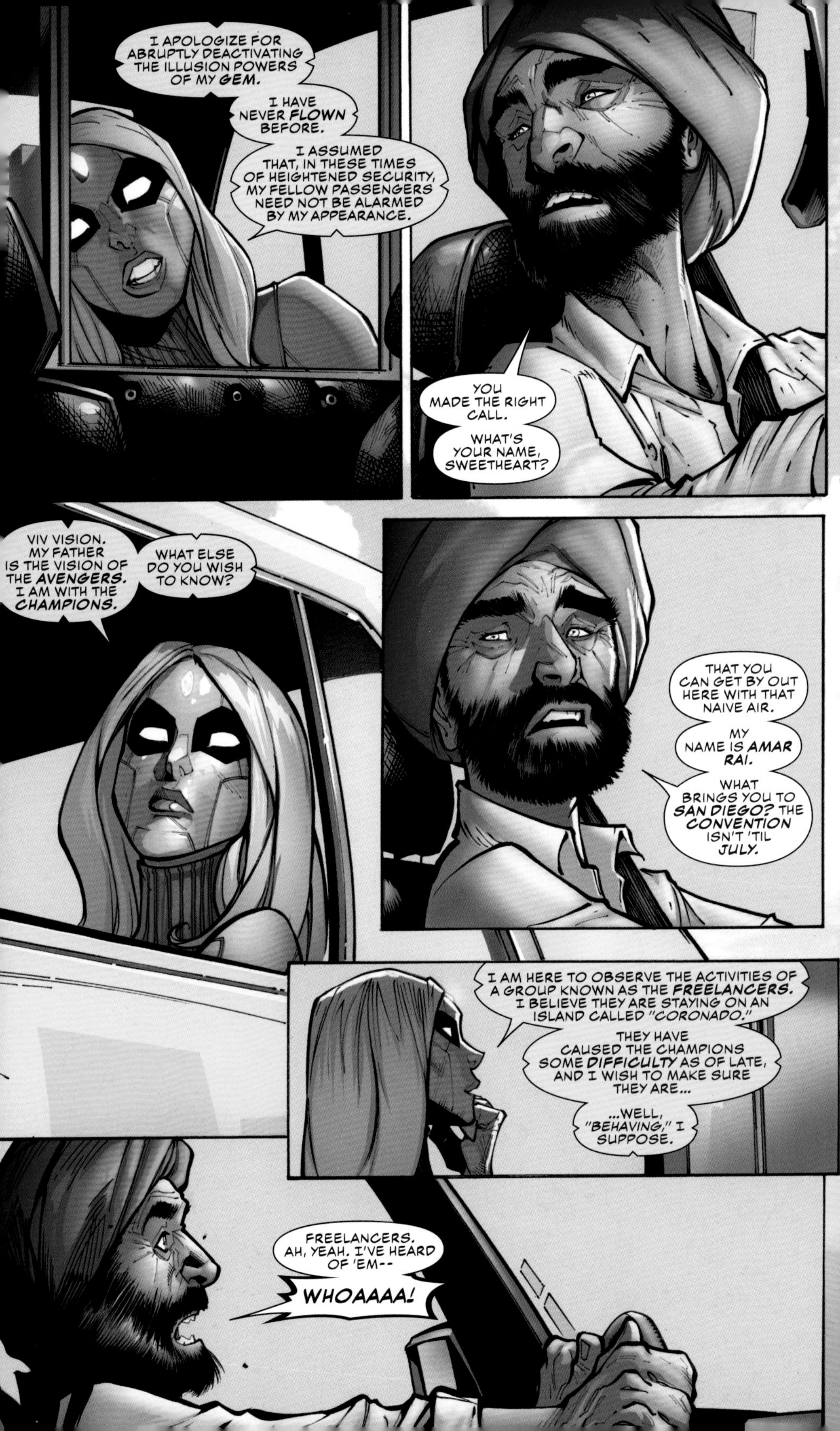
I APOLOGIZE FOR ABRUPTLY DEACTIVATING THE ILLUSION POWERS OF MY GEM.
I HAVE NEVER FLOWN BEFORE.
I ASSUMED THAT, IN THESE TIMES OF HEIGHTENED SECURITY, MY FELLOW PASSENGERS NEED NOT BE ALARMED BY MY APPEARANCE.
YOU MADE THE RIGHT CALL.
WHAT'S YOUR NAME, SWEETHEART?
VIV VISION. MY FATHER IS THE VISION OF THE AVENGERS. I AM WITH THE CHAMPIONS.
WHAT ELSE DO YOU WISH TO KNOW?
THAT YOU CAN GET BY OUT HERE WITH THAT NAIVE AIR.
MY NAME IS AMAR RAI.
WHAT BRINGS YOU TO SAN DIEGO? THE CONVENTION ISN'T 'TIL JULY.
I AM HERE TO OBSERVE THE ACTIVITIES OF A GROUP KNOWN AS THE FREELANCERS. I BELIEVE THEY ARE STAYING ON AN ISLAND CALLED "CORONADO."
THEY HAVE CAUSED THE CHAMPIONS SOME DIFFICULTY AS OF LATE, AND I WISH TO MAKE SURE THEY ARE...
...WELL, "BEHAVING," I SUPPOSE.
FREELANCERS. AH, YEAH. I'VE HEARD OF 'EM--
WHOAAAA!

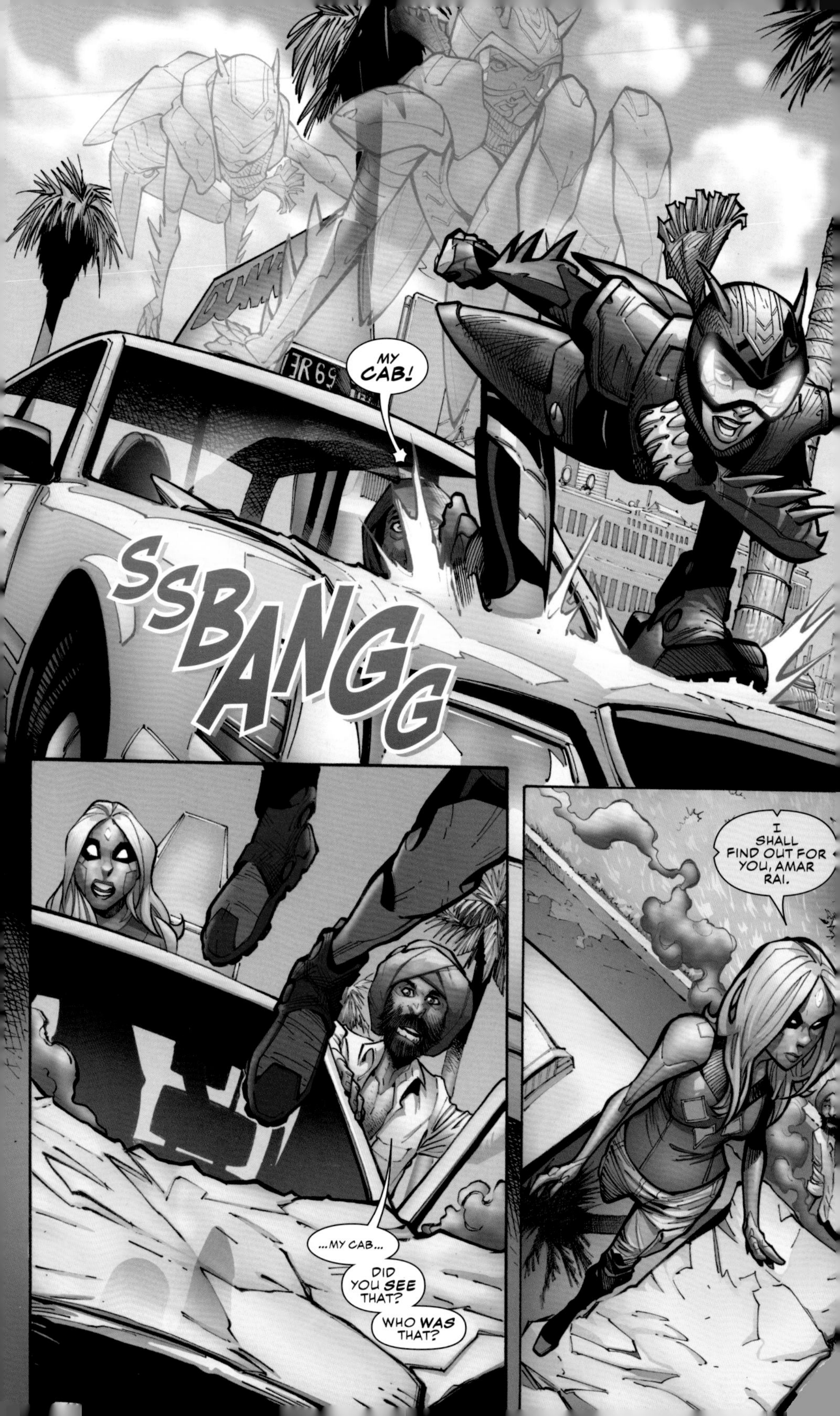
MY CAB!
SSBANGG
...MY CAB...
DID YOU SEE THAT?
WHO WAS THAT?
I SHALL FIND OUT FOR YOU, AMAR RAI.

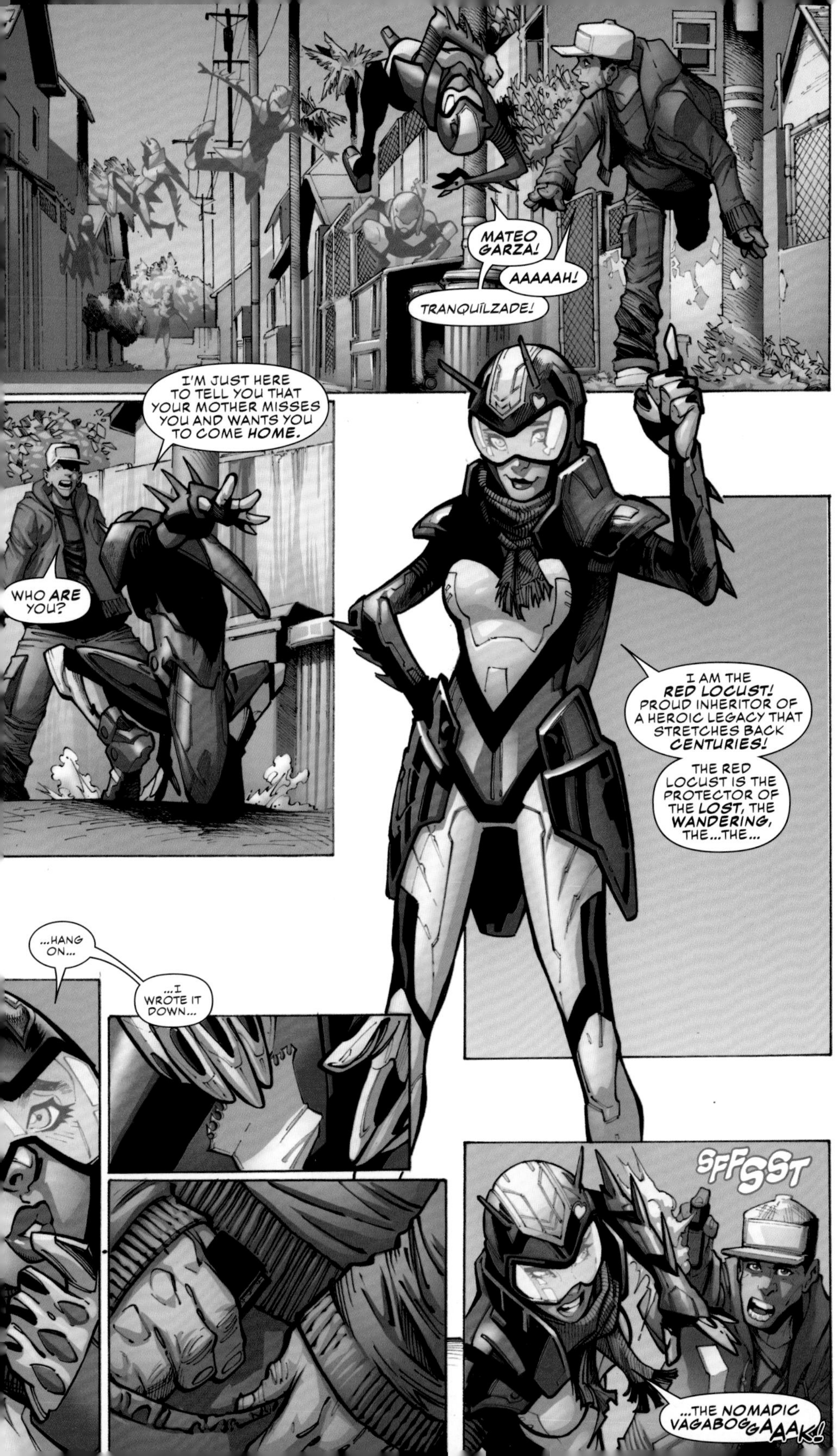
MATEO GARZA!
AAAAAH!
TRANQUILZADE!
I'M JUST HERE TO TELL YOU THAT YOUR MOTHER MISSES YOU AND WANTS YOU TO COME HOME.
WHO ARE YOU?
I AM THE RED LOCUST! PROUD INHERITOR OF A HEROIC LEGACY THAT STRETCHES BACK CENTURIES!
THE RED LOCUST IS THE PROTECTOR OF THE LOST, THE WANDERING, THE...THE...
...HANG ON...
...I WROTE IT DOWN...
SFFSST
...THE NOMADIC VAGABOGGAAAK!

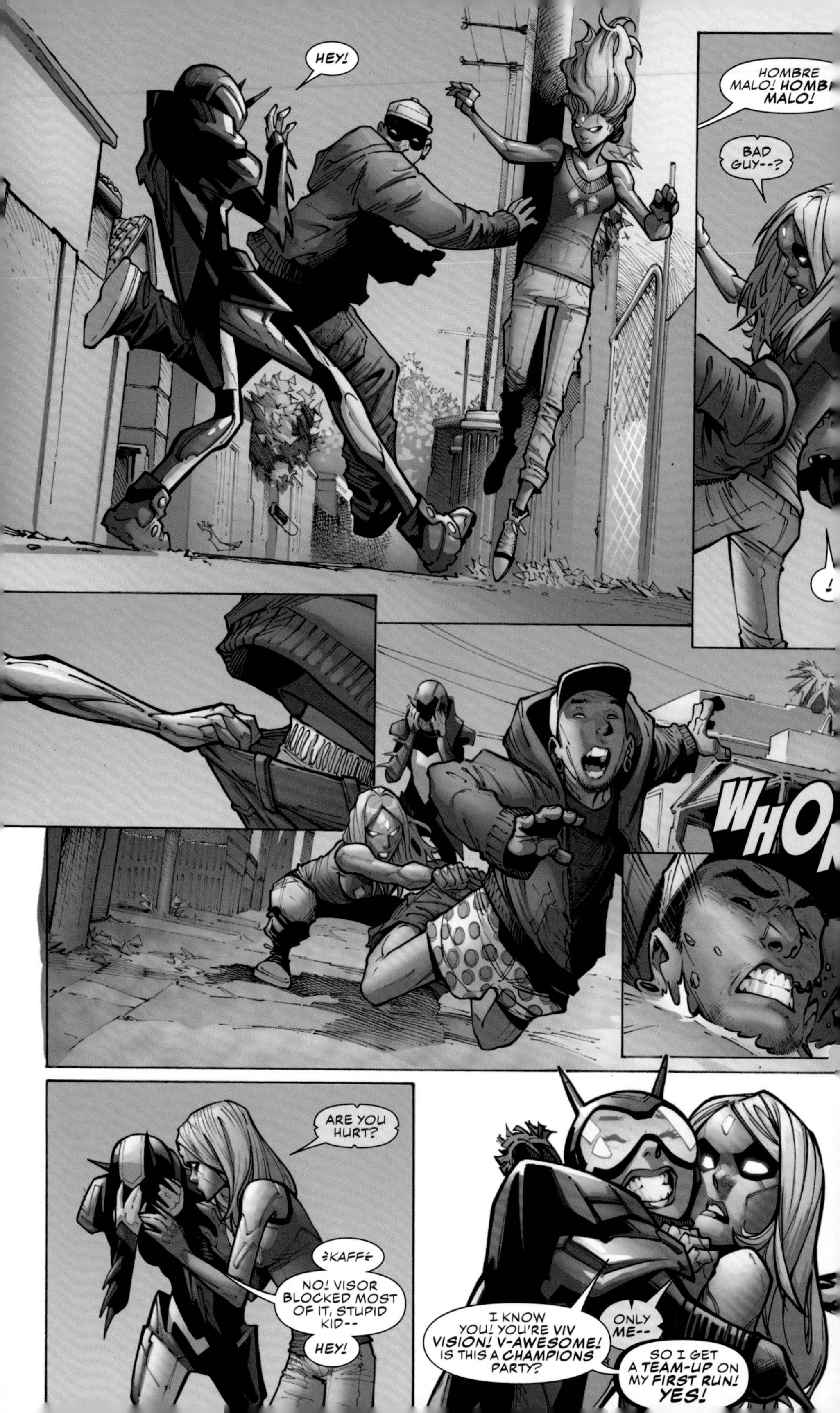
HEY!
HOMBRE MALO! HOMBI MALO!
BAD GUY--?
!
WHO
ARE YOU HURT?
≠KAFF≠
NO! VISOR BLOCKED MOST OF IT, STUPID KID--
HEY!
I KNOW YOU! YOU'RE VIV VISION! V-AWESOME! IS THIS A CHAMPIONS PARTY?
ONLY ME--
SO I GET A TEAM-UP ON MY FIRST RUN! YES!

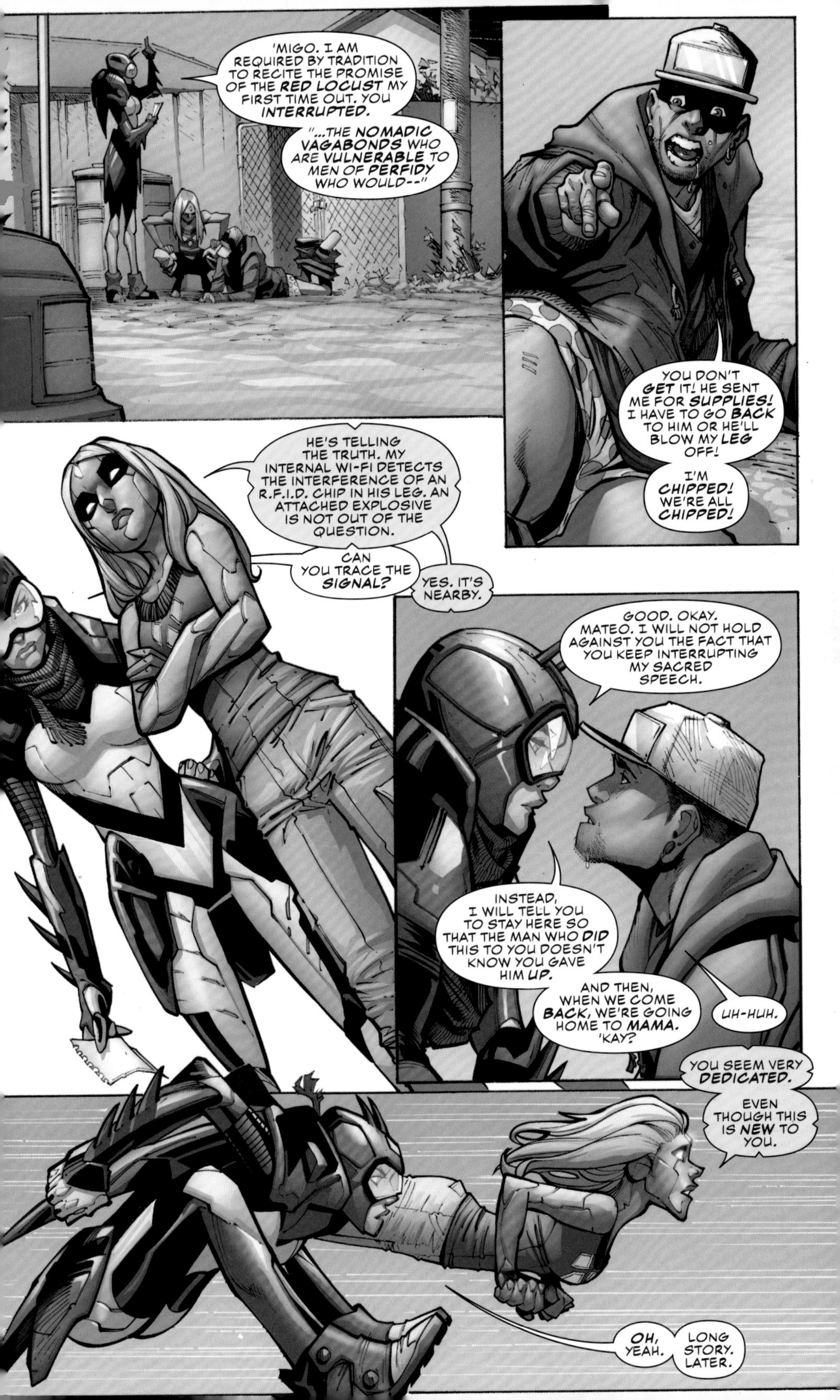

'MIGO. I AM REQUIRED BY TRADITION TO RECITE THE PROMISE OF THE RED LOCUST MY FIRST TIME OUT. YOU INTERRUPTED.
"...THE NOMADIC VAGABONDS WHO ARE VULNERABLE TO MEN OF PERFIDY WHO WOULD--"
YOU DON'T GET IT! HE SENT ME FOR SUPPLIES! I HAVE TO GO BACK TO HIM OR HE'LL BLOW MY LEG OFF!
I'M CHIPPED! WE'RE ALL CHIPPED!
HE'S TELLING THE TRUTH. MY INTERNAL WI-FI DETECTS THE INTERFERENCE OF AN R.F.I.D. CHIP IN HIS LEG. AN ATTACHED EXPLOSIVE IS NOT OUT OF THE QUESTION.
CAN YOU TRACE THE SIGNAL?
YES. IT'S NEARBY.
GOOD. OKAY. MATEO. I WILL NOT HOLD AGAINST YOU THE FACT THAT YOU KEEP INTERRUPTING MY SACRED SPEECH.
INSTEAD, I WILL TELL YOU TO STAY HERE SO THAT THE MAN WHO DID THIS TO YOU DOESN'T KNOW YOU GAVE HIM UP.
AND THEN, WHEN WE COME BACK, WE'RE GOING HOME TO MAMA. 'KAY?
UH-HUH.
YOU SEEM VERY DEDICATED.
EVEN THOUGH THIS IS NEW TO YOU.
OH, YEAH.
LONG STORY. LATER.

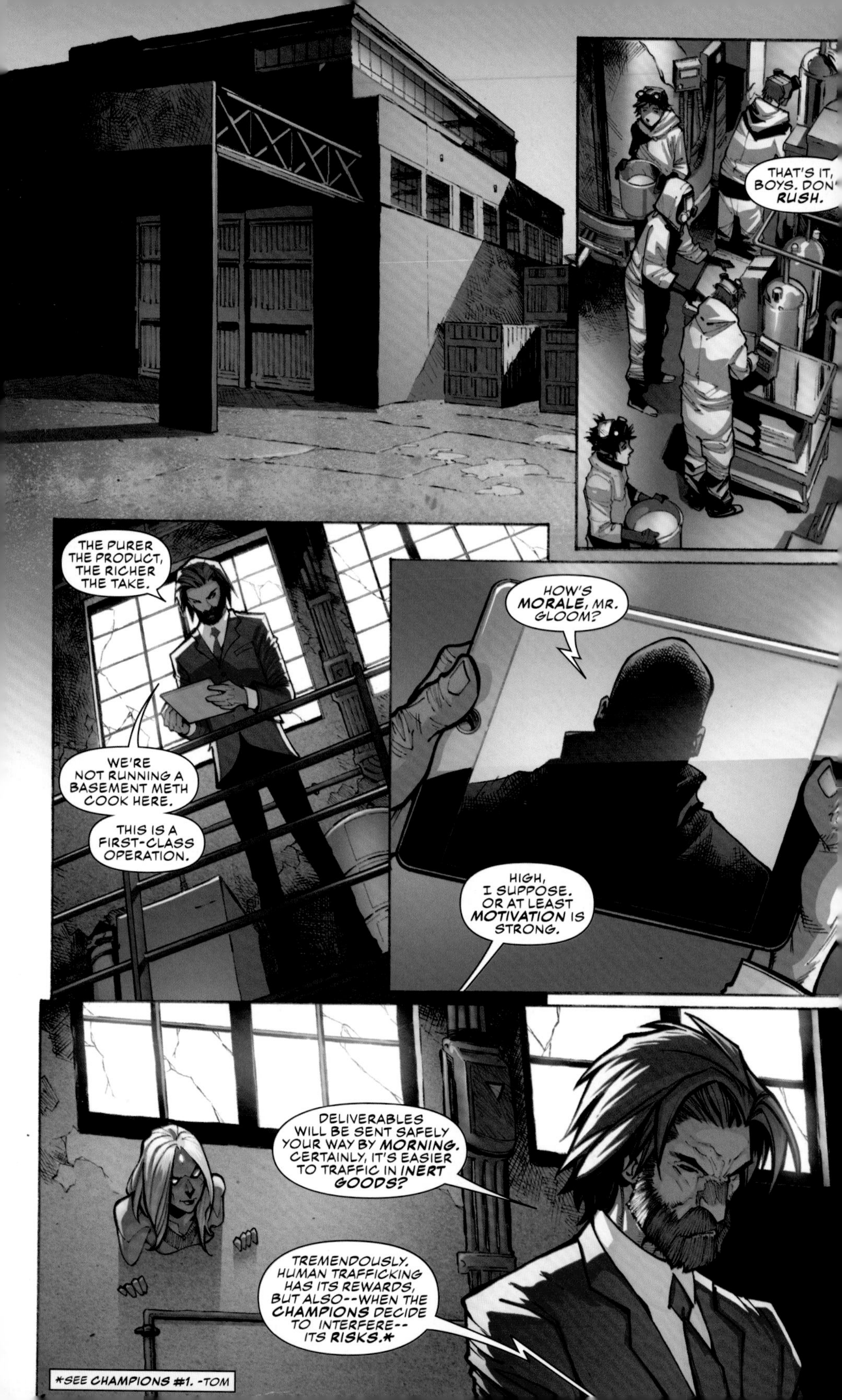

THAT'S IT, BOYS. DON' RUSH.
THE PURER THE PRODUCT, THE RICHER THE TAKE.
WE'RE NOT RUNNING A BASEMENT METH COOK HERE.
THIS IS A FIRST-CLASS OPERATION.
HOW'S MORALE, MR. GLOOM?
HIGH, I SUPPOSE. OR AT LEAST MOTIVATION IS STRONG.
DELIVERABLES WILL BE SENT SAFELY YOUR WAY BY MORNING. CERTAINLY, IT'S EASIER TO TRAFFIC IN INERT GOODS?
TREMENDOUSLY. HUMAN TRAFFICKING HAS ITS REWARDS, BUT ALSO--WHEN THE CHAMPIONS DECIDE TO INTERFERE--ITS RISKS.*
*SEE CHAMPIONS #1. -TOM

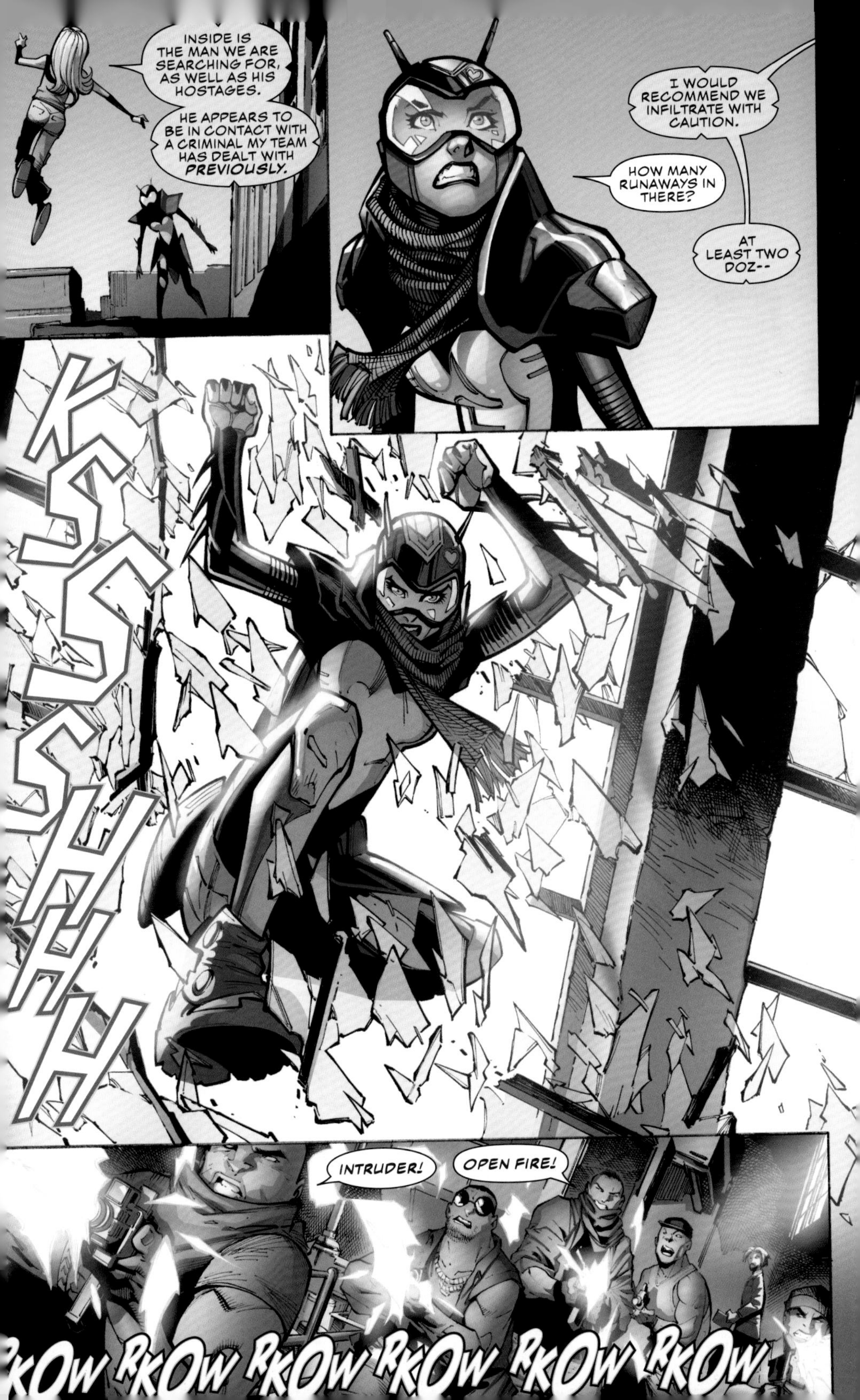
INSIDE IS THE MAN WE ARE SEARCHING FOR, AS WELL AS HIS HOSTAGES.
HE APPEARS TO BE IN CONTACT WITH A CRIMINAL MY TEAM HAS DEALT WITH PREVIOUSLY.
I WOULD RECOMMEND WE INFILTRATE WITH CAUTION.
HOW MANY RUNAWAYS IN THERE?
AT LEAST TWO DOZ--
KSSSHHHH
INTRUDER!
OPEN FIRE!
RKOW RKOW RKOW RKOW RKOW RKOW

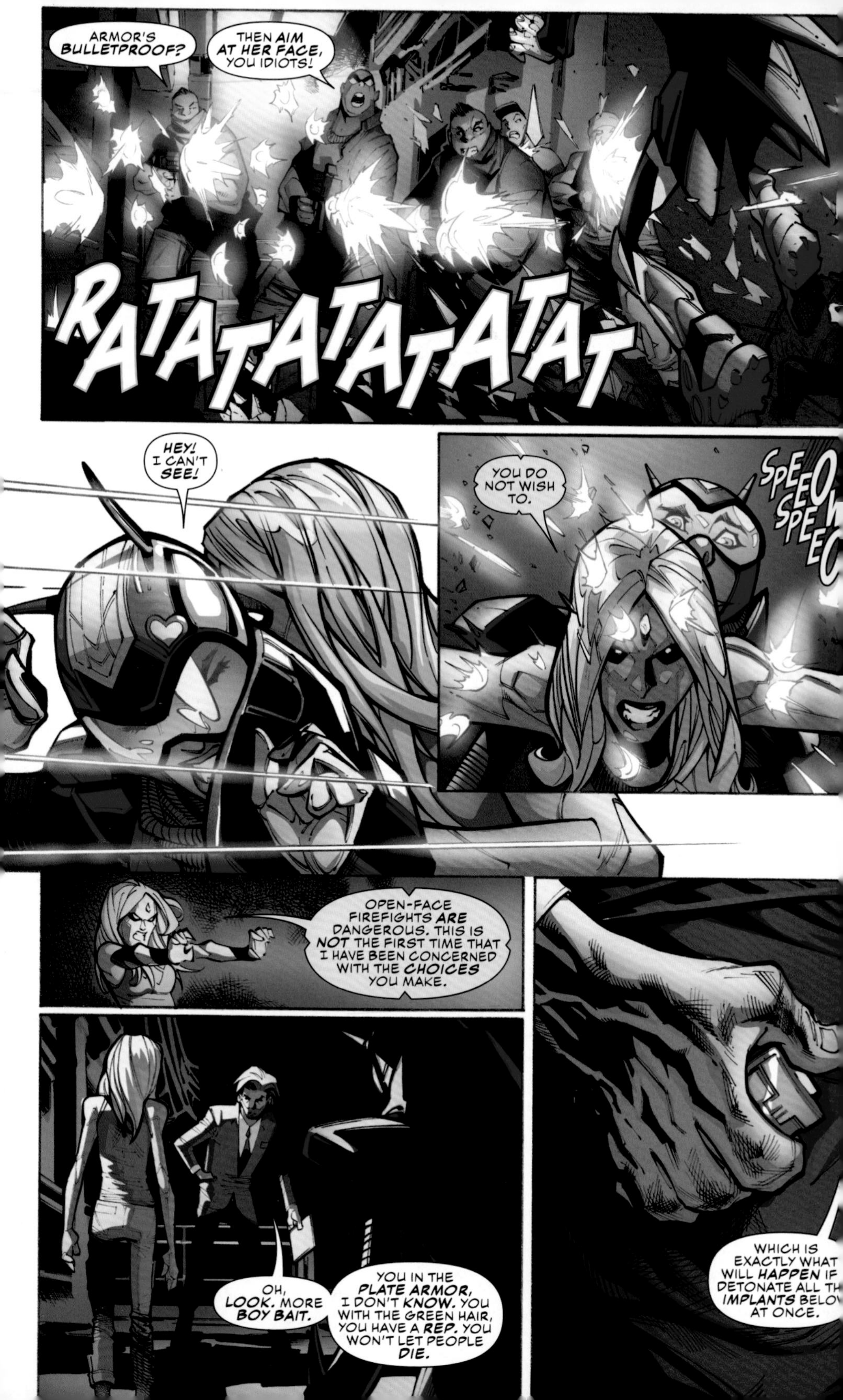

ARMOR'S BULLETPROOF?
THEN AIM AT HER FACE, YOU IDIOTS!
RATATATATATATAT
HEY! I CAN'T SEE!
YOU DO NOT WISH TO.
SPEEOW SPEEOW
OPEN-FACE FIREFIGHTS ARE DANGEROUS. THIS IS NOT THE FIRST TIME THAT I HAVE BEEN CONCERNED WITH THE CHOICES YOU MAKE.
OH, LOOK. MORE BOY BAIT.
YOU IN THE PLATE ARMOR, I DON'T KNOW. YOU WITH THE GREEN HAIR, YOU HAVE A REP. YOU WON'T LET PEOPLE DIE.
WHICH IS EXACTLY WHAT WILL HAPPEN IF DETONATE ALL TH IMPLANTS BELOW AT ONCE.

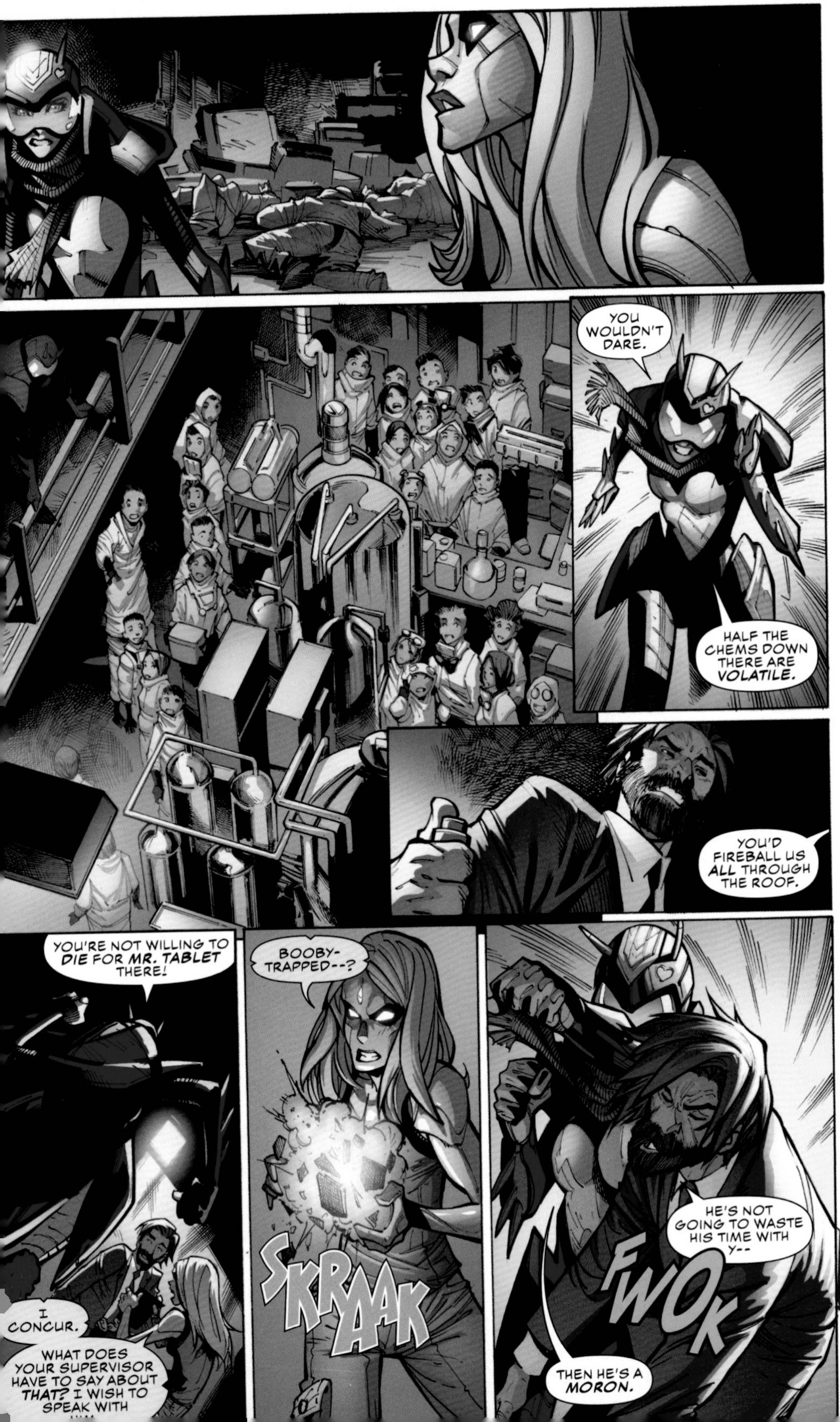

YOU WOULDN'T DARE.
HALF THE CHEMS DOWN THERE ARE VOLATILE.
YOU'D FIREBALL US ALL THROUGH THE ROOF.
YOU'RE NOT WILLING TO DIE FOR MR. TABLET THERE!
I CONCUR.
WHAT DOES YOUR SUPERVISOR HAVE TO SAY ABOUT THAT? I WISH TO SPEAK WITH
BOOBY-TRAPPED--?
SKRAAAK
HE'S NOT GOING TO WASTE HIS TIME WITH Y--
FWOK
THEN HE'S A MORON.

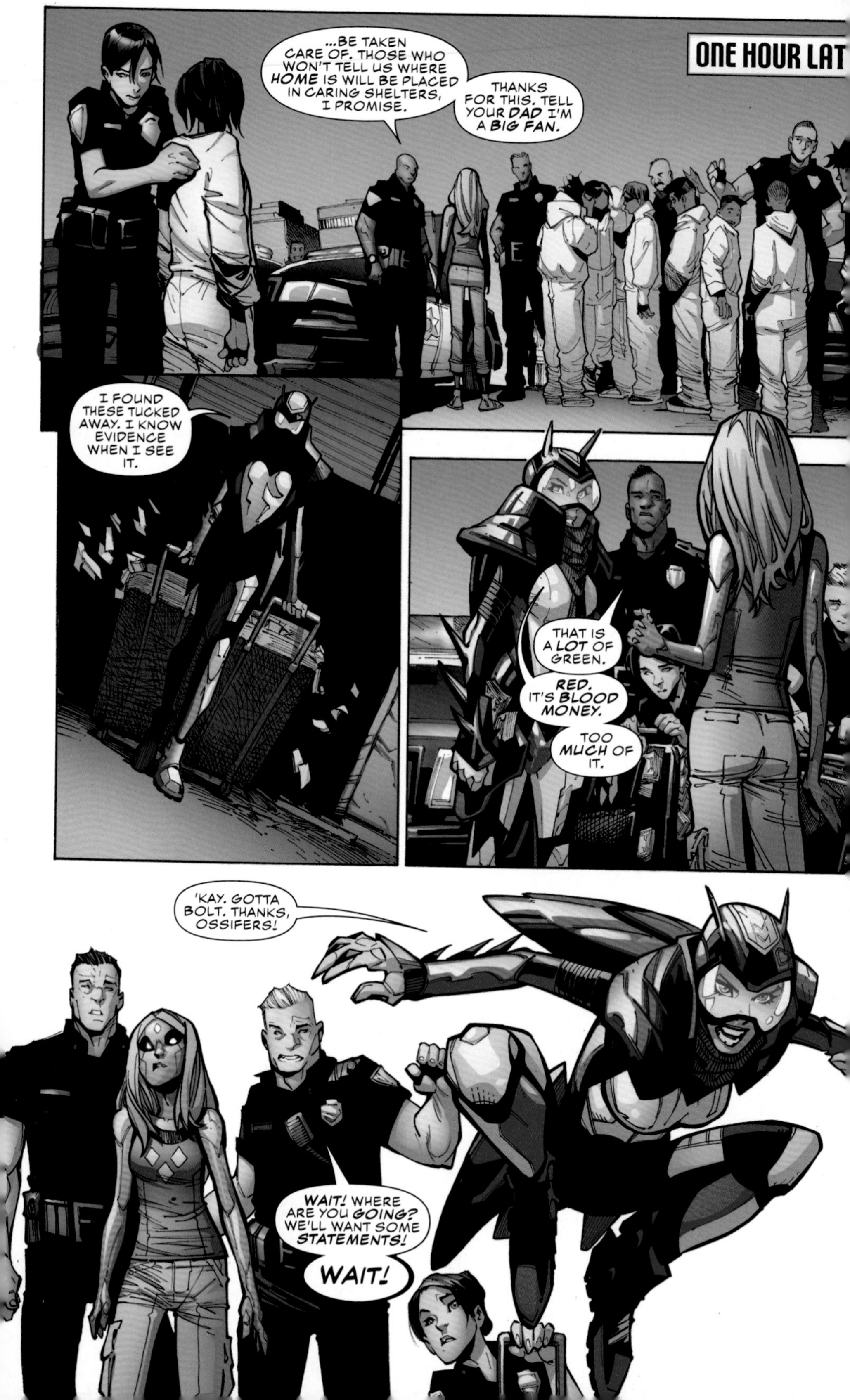
ONE HOUR LAT
...BE TAKEN CARE OF. THOSE WHO WON'T TELL US WHERE HOME IS WILL BE PLACED IN CARING SHELTERS, I PROMISE.
THANKS FOR THIS. TELL YOUR DAD I'M A BIG FAN.
I FOUND THESE TUCKED AWAY. I KNOW EVIDENCE WHEN I SEE IT.
THAT IS A LOT OF GREEN.
RED. IT'S BLOOD MONEY.
TOO MUCH OF IT.
'KAY. GOTTA BOLT. THANKS, OSSIFERS!
WAIT! WHERE ARE YOU GOING? WE'LL WANT SOME STATEMENTS!
WAIT!

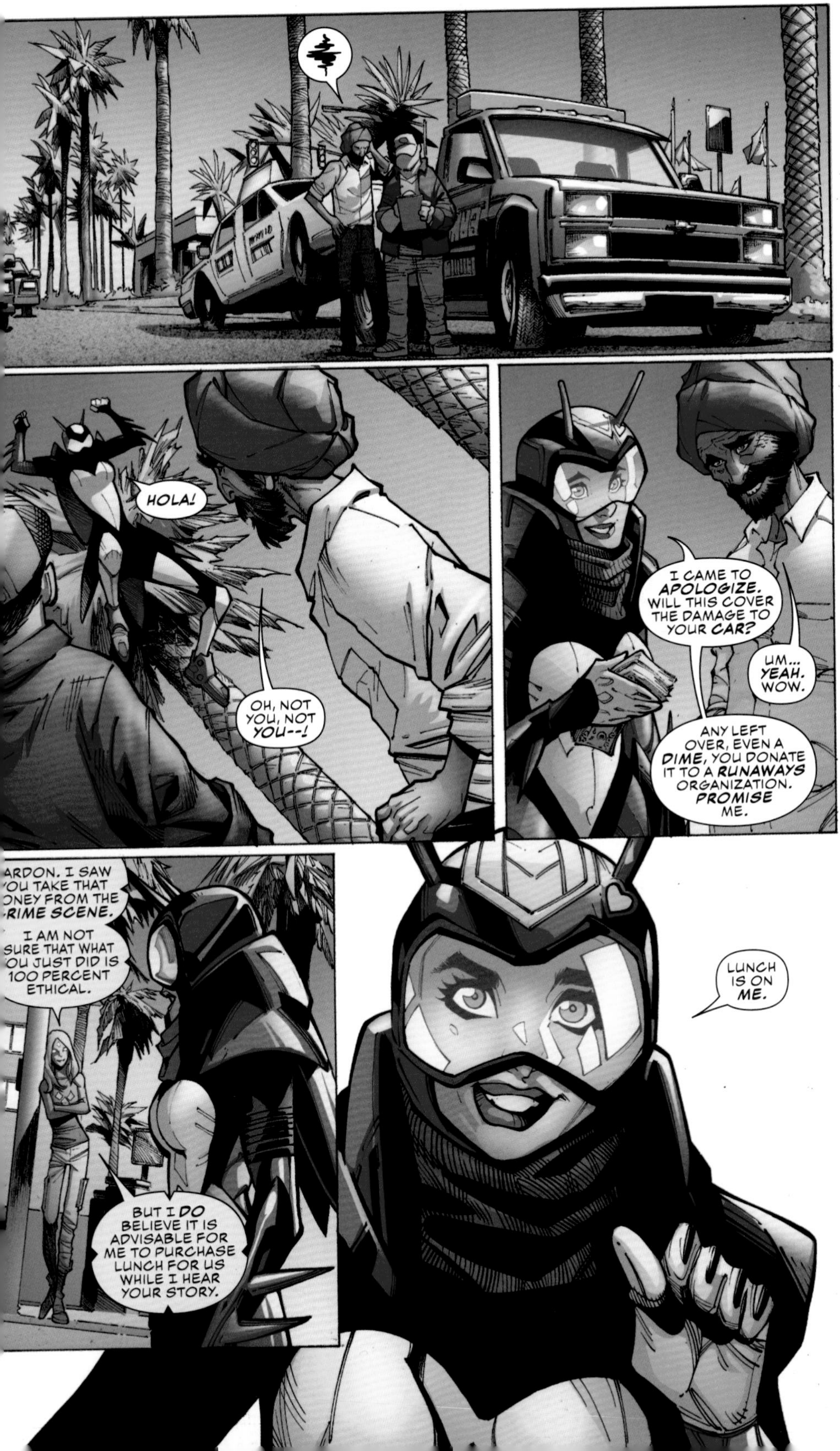
HOLA!
OH, NOT YOU, NOT YOU--!
I CAME TO APOLOGIZE. WILL THIS COVER THE DAMAGE TO YOUR CAR?
UM... YEAH. WOW.
ANY LEFT OVER, EVEN A DIME, YOU DONATE IT TO A RUNAWAYS ORGANIZATION. PROMISE ME.
ARDON. I SAW OU TAKE THAT ONEY FROM THE RIME SCENE.
I AM NOT URE THAT WHAT OU JUST DID IS 100 PERCENT ETHICAL.
BUT I DO BELIEVE IT IS ADVISABLE FOR ME TO PURCHASE LUNCH FOR US WHILE I HEAR YOUR STORY.
LUNCH IS ON ME.

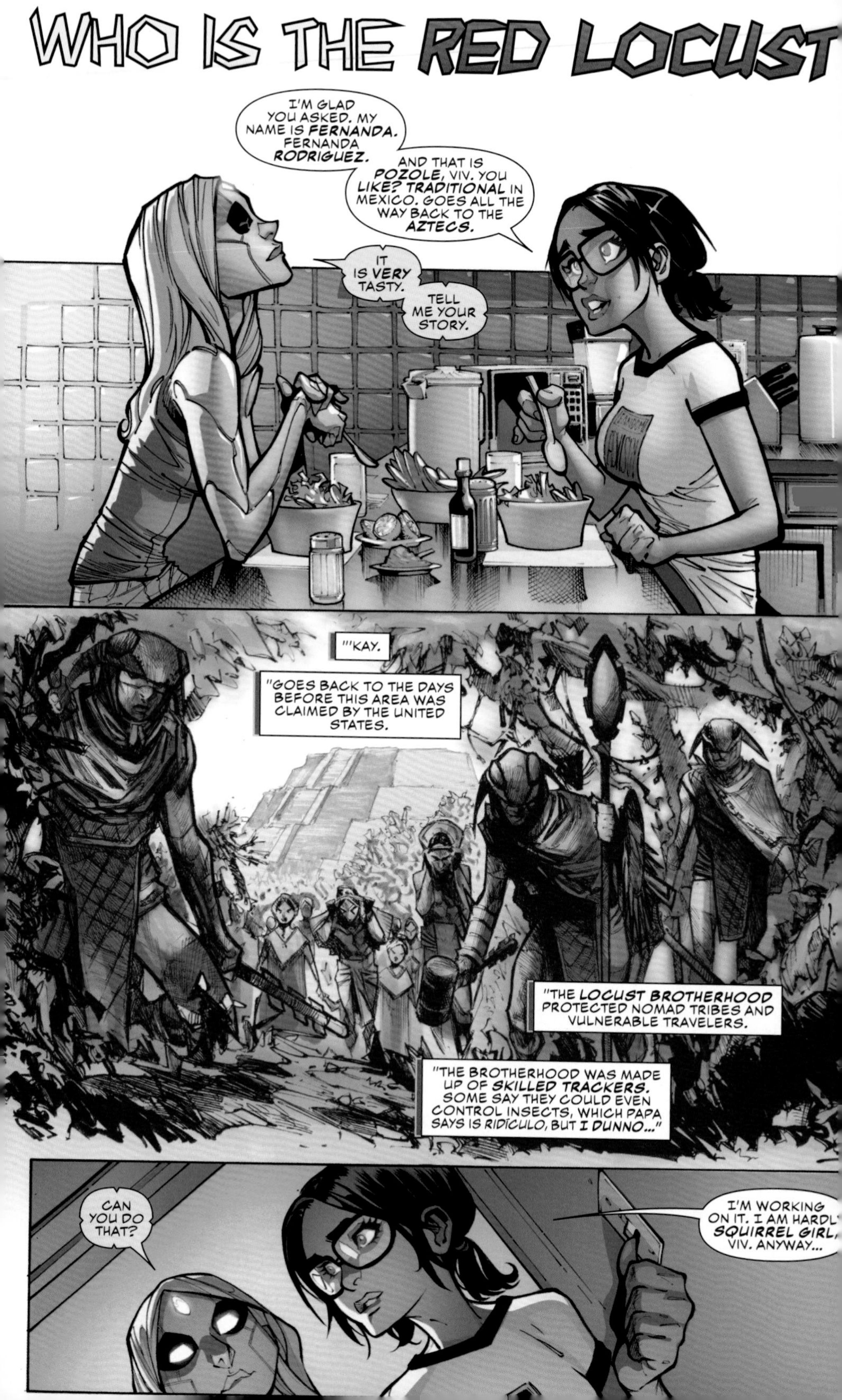
WHO IS THE RED LOCUST
I'M GLAD YOU ASKED. MY NAME IS FERNANDA. FERNANDA RODRIGUEZ.
AND THAT IS POZOLE, VIV. YOU LIKE? TRADITIONAL IN MEXICO. GOES ALL THE WAY BACK TO THE AZTECS.
IT IS VERY TASTY.
TELL ME YOUR STORY.
"'KAY.
"GOES BACK TO THE DAYS BEFORE THIS AREA WAS CLAIMED BY THE UNITED STATES.
"THE LOCUST BROTHERHOOD PROTECTED NOMAD TRIBES AND VULNERABLE TRAVELERS.
"THE BROTHERHOOD WAS MADE UP OF SKILLED TRACKERS. SOME SAY THEY COULD EVEN CONTROL INSECTS, WHICH PAPA SAYS IS RIDÍCULO, BUT I DUNNO..."
CAN YOU DO THAT?
I'M WORKING ON IT. I AM HARDL SQUIRREL GIRL, VIV. ANYWAY...

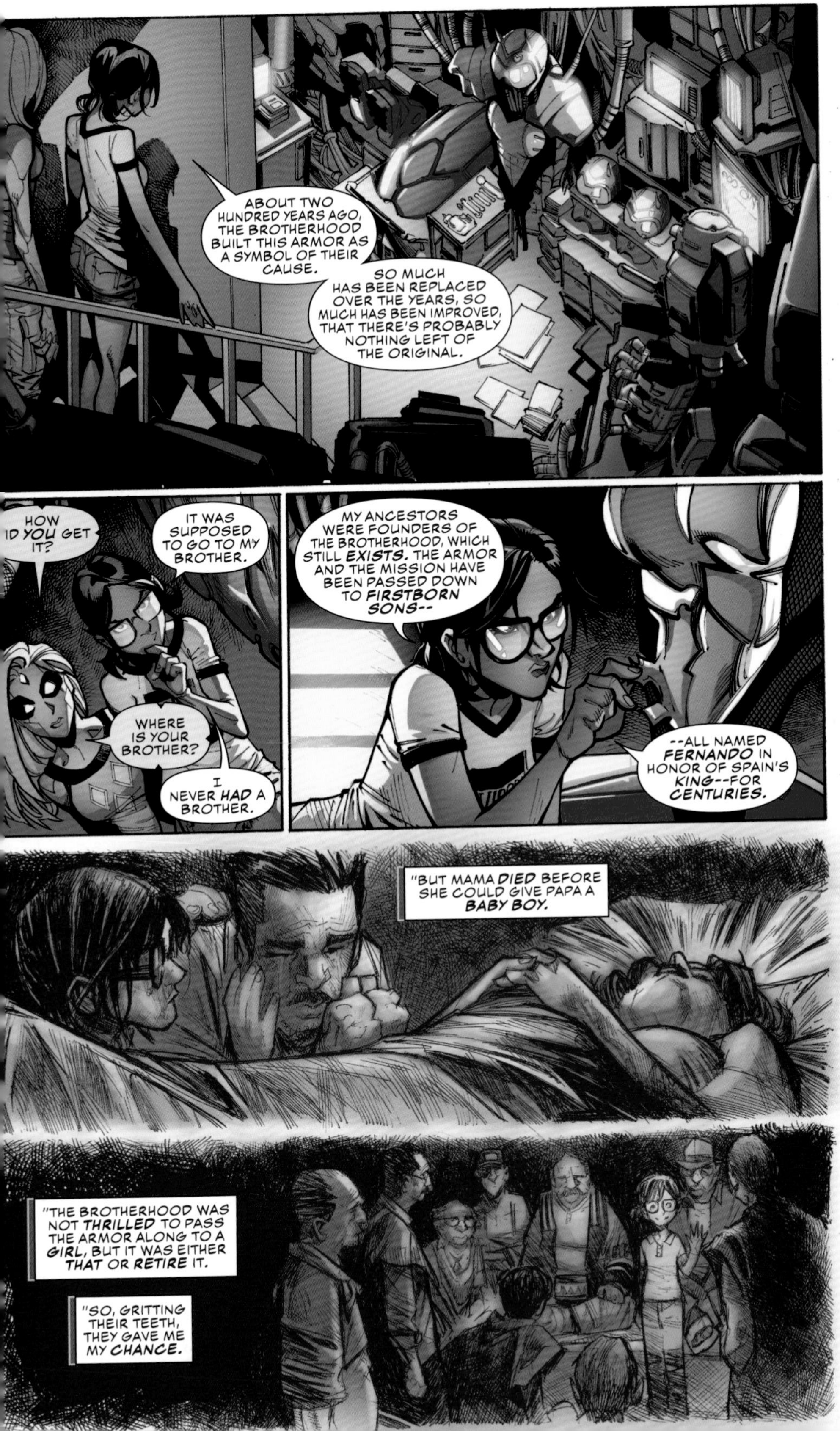

ABOUT TWO HUNDRED YEARS AGO, THE BROTHERHOOD BUILT THIS ARMOR AS A SYMBOL OF THEIR CAUSE.
SO MUCH HAS BEEN REPLACED OVER THE YEARS, SO MUCH HAS BEEN IMPROVED, THAT THERE'S PROBABLY NOTHING LEFT OF THE ORIGINAL.
HOW ID *YOU* GET IT?
IT WAS SUPPOSED TO GO TO MY BROTHER.
WHERE IS YOUR BROTHER?
I NEVER *HAD* A BROTHER.
MY ANCESTORS WERE FOUNDERS OF THE BROTHERHOOD, WHICH STILL *EXISTS.* THE ARMOR AND THE MISSION HAVE BEEN PASSED DOWN TO *FIRSTBORN SONS--*
--ALL NAMED *FERNANDO* IN HONOR OF SPAIN'S *KING*--FOR *CENTURIES.*
"BUT MAMA *DIED* BEFORE SHE COULD GIVE PAPA A *BABY BOY.*
"THE BROTHERHOOD WAS NOT *THRILLED* TO PASS THE ARMOR ALONG TO A *GIRL*, BUT IT WAS EITHER *THAT* OR *RETIRE* IT.
"SO, GRITTING THEIR TEETH, THEY GAVE ME MY *CHANCE.*

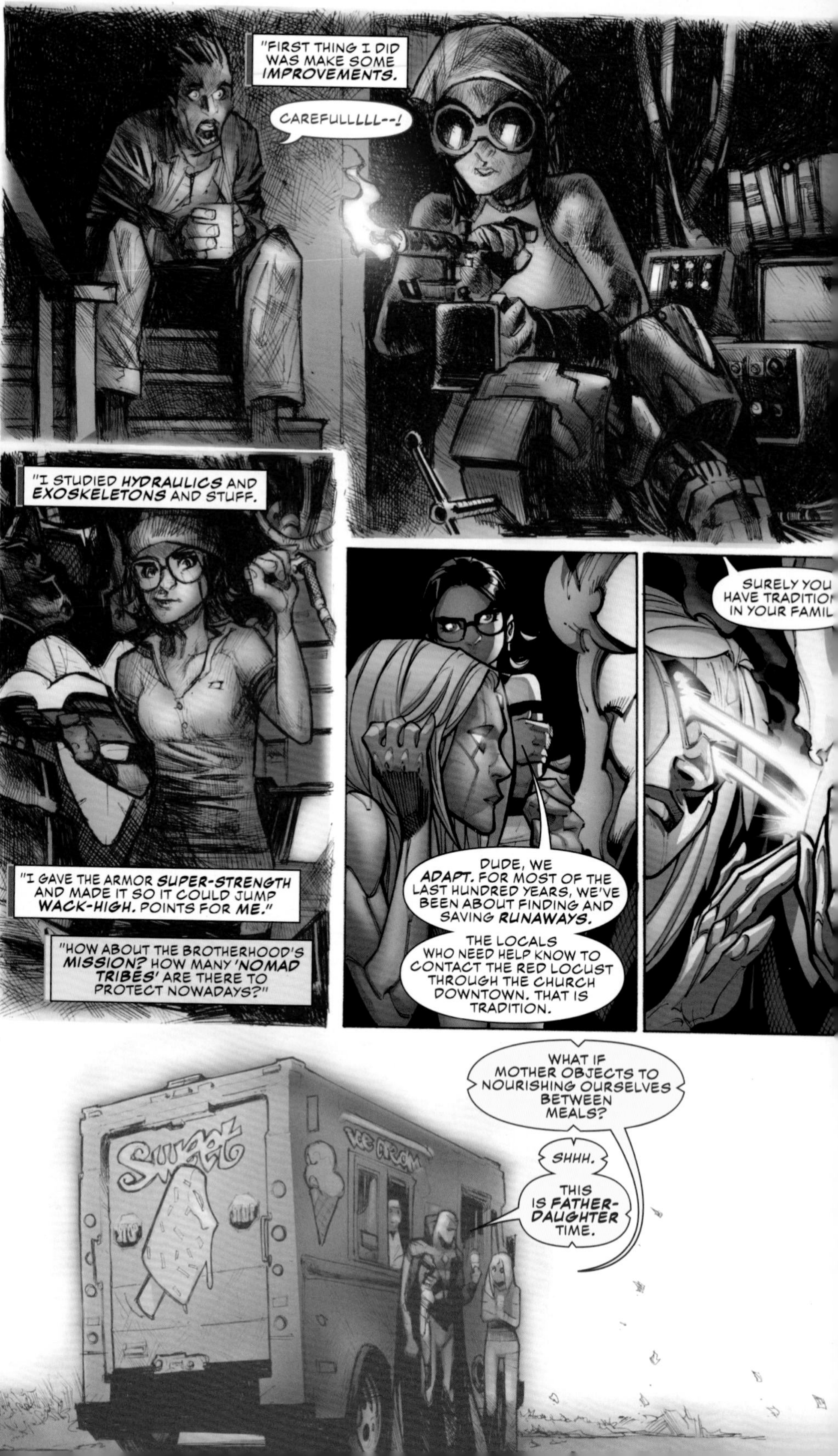
"FIRST THING I DID WAS MAKE SOME IMPROVEMENTS.
CAREFULLLLL--!
"I STUDIED HYDRAULICS AND EXOSKELETONS AND STUFF.
"I GAVE THE ARMOR SUPER-STRENGTH AND MADE IT SO IT COULD JUMP WACK-HIGH. POINTS FOR ME."
"HOW ABOUT THE BROTHERHOOD'S MISSION? HOW MANY 'NOMAD TRIBES' ARE THERE TO PROTECT NOWADAYS?"
DUDE, WE ADAPT. FOR MOST OF THE LAST HUNDRED YEARS, WE'VE BEEN ABOUT FINDING AND SAVING RUNAWAYS.
THE LOCALS WHO NEED HELP KNOW TO CONTACT THE RED LOCUST THROUGH THE CHURCH DOWNTOWN. THAT IS TRADITION.
SURELY YOU HAVE TRADITIO IN YOUR FAMIL
WHAT IF MOTHER OBJECTS TO NOURISHING OURSELVES BETWEEN MEALS?
SHHH.
THIS IS FATHER-DAUGHTER TIME.

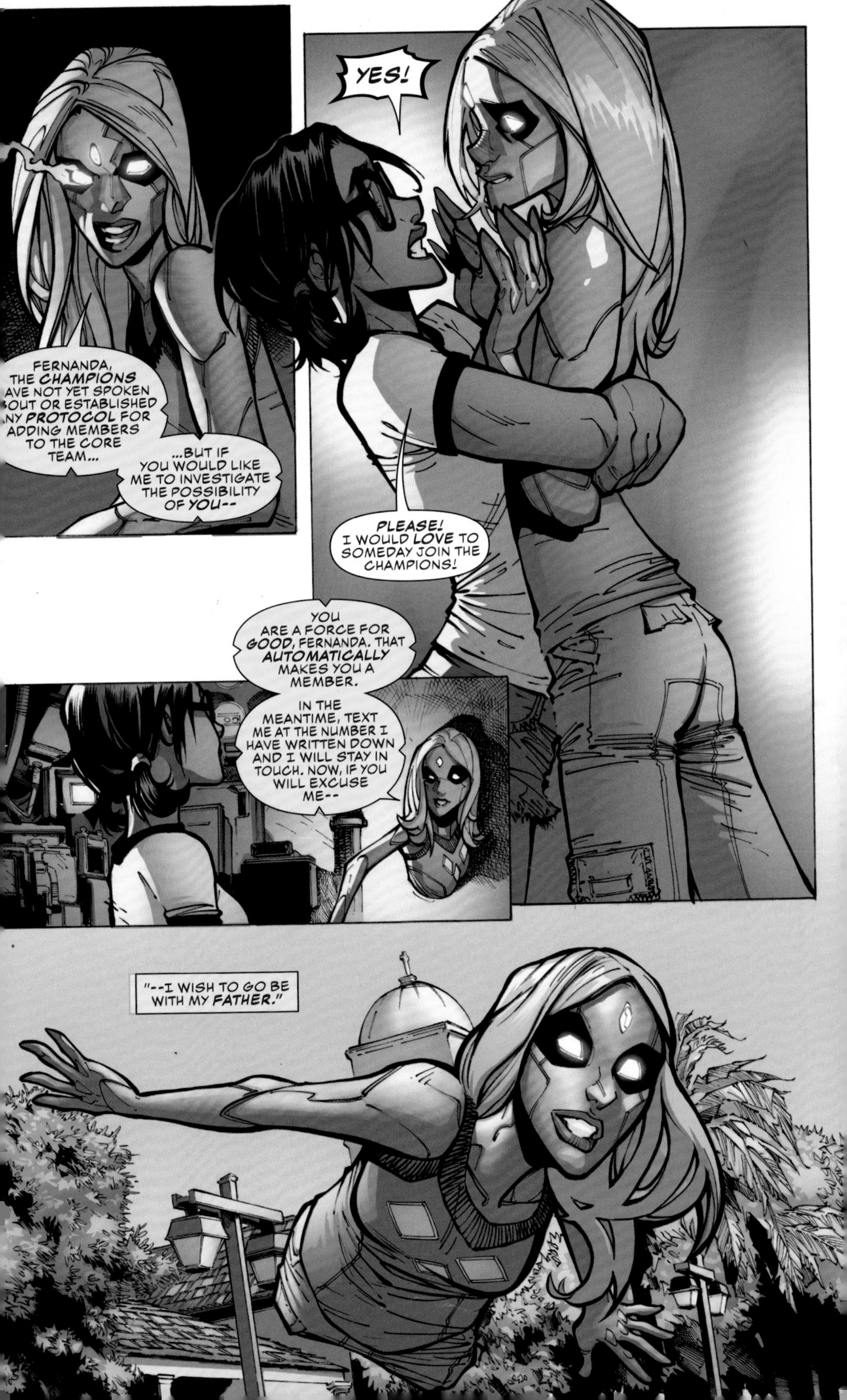

FERNANDA, THE CHAMPIONS AVE NOT YET SPOKEN BOUT OR ESTABLISHED NY PROTOCOL FOR ADDING MEMBERS TO THE CORE TEAM...
...BUT IF YOU WOULD LIKE ME TO INVESTIGATE THE POSSIBILITY OF YOU--
YES!
PLEASE! I WOULD LOVE TO SOMEDAY JOIN THE CHAMPIONS!
YOU ARE A FORCE FOR GOOD, FERNANDA. THAT AUTOMATICALLY MAKES YOU A MEMBER.
IN THE MEANTIME, TEXT ME AT THE NUMBER I HAVE WRITTEN DOWN AND I WILL STAY IN TOUCH. NOW, IF YOU WILL EXCUSE ME--
"--I WISH TO GO BE WITH MY FATHER."

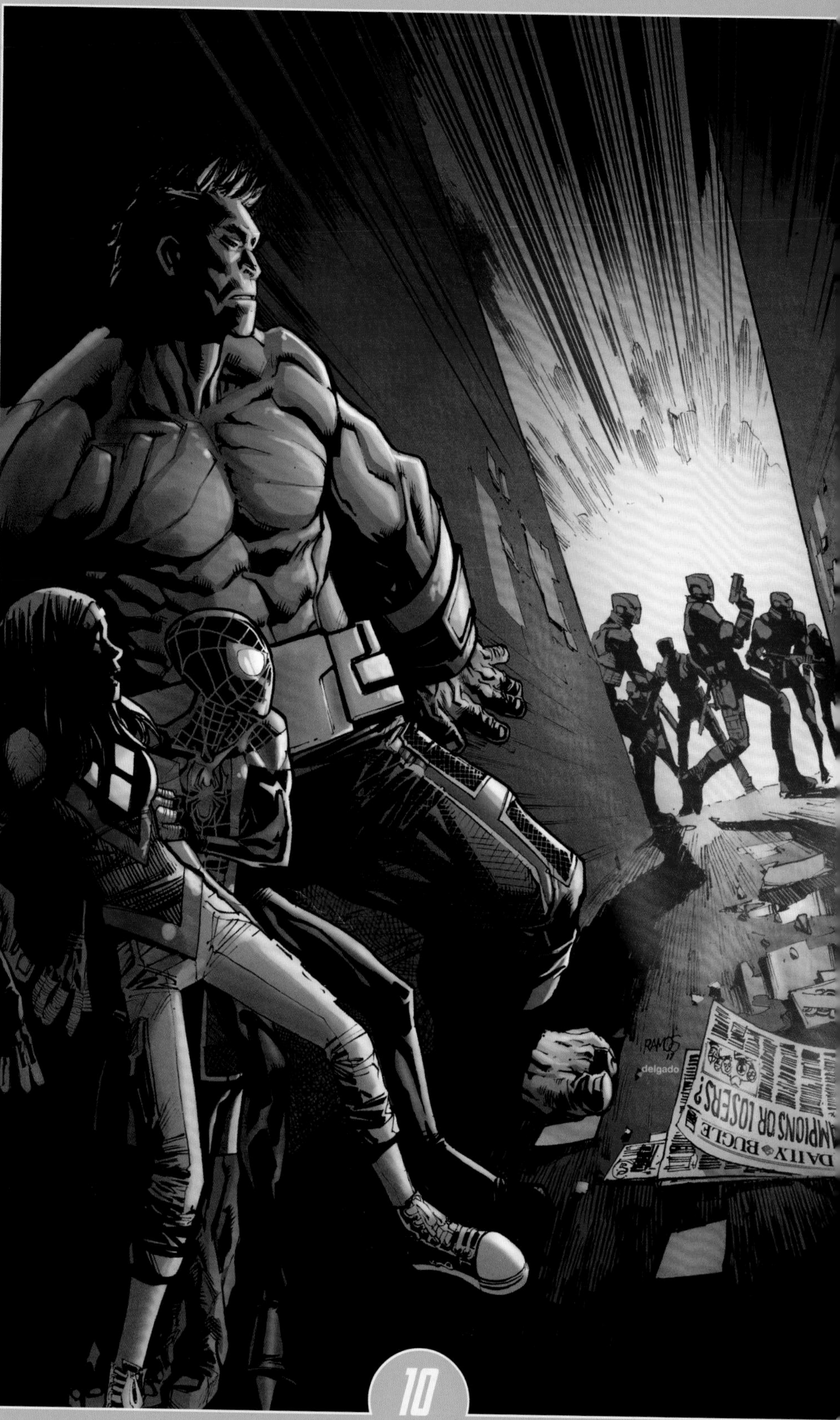
DAILY BUGLE
MPIONS OR LOSERS?
RAMOS 17
delgado

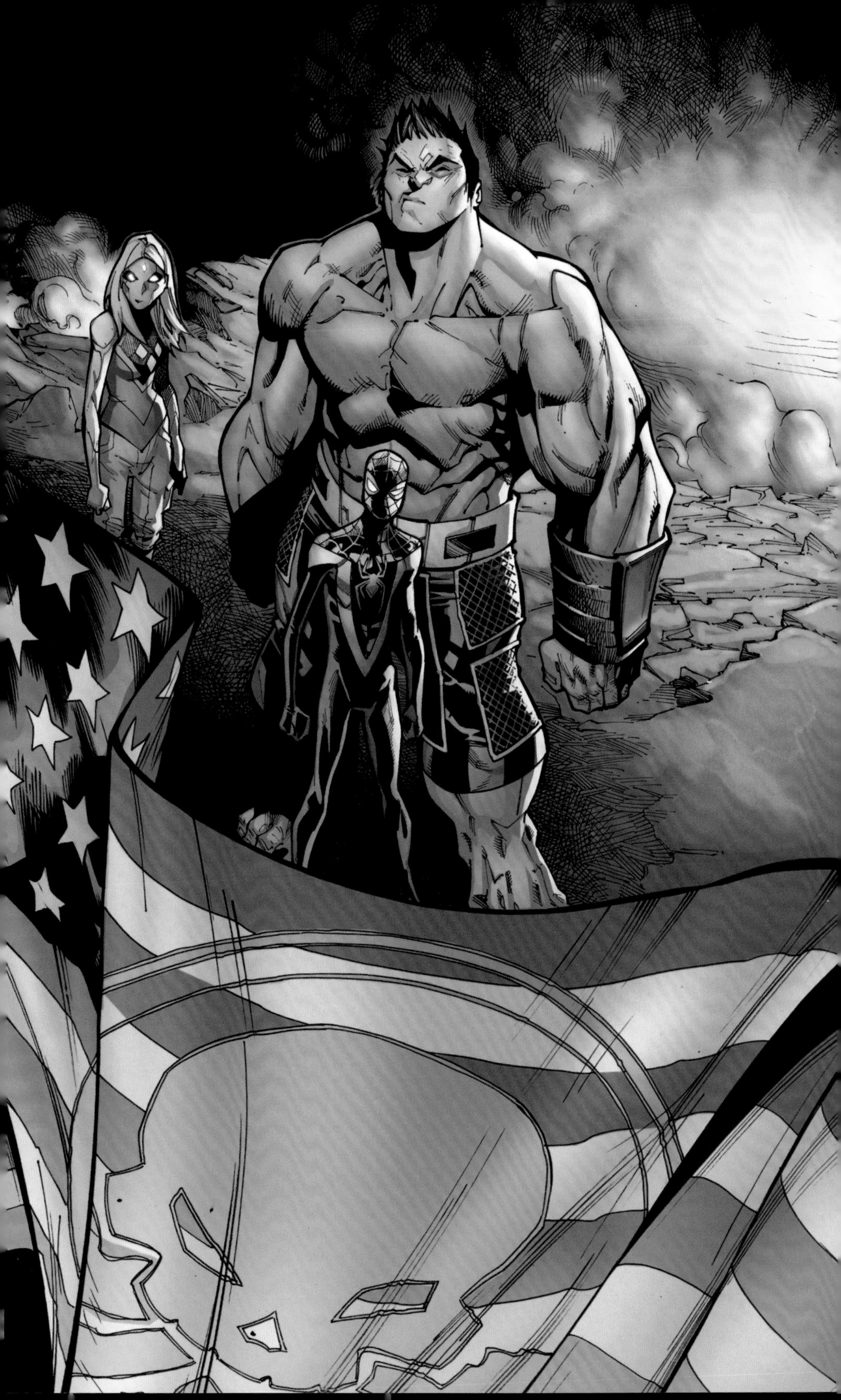

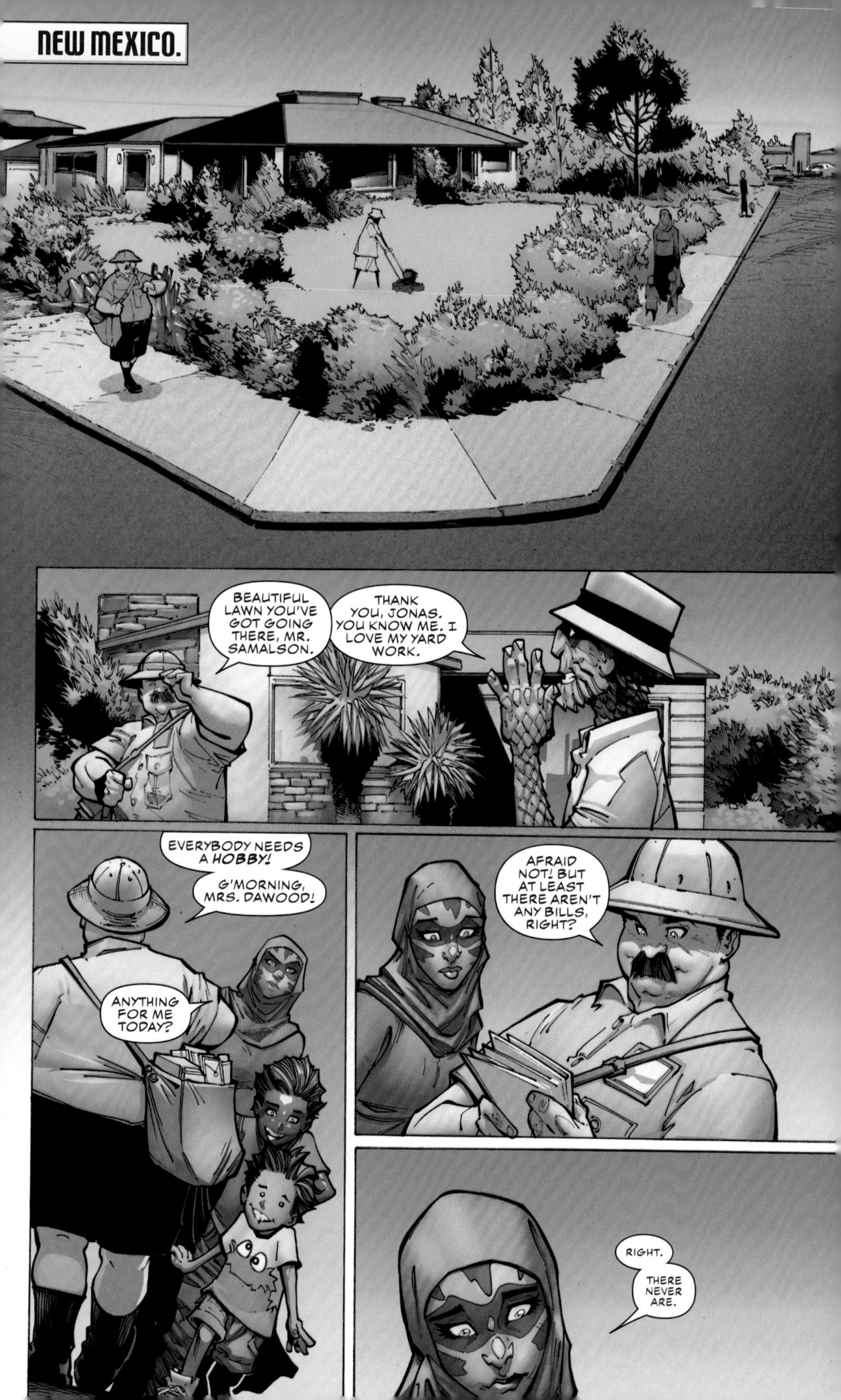
NEW MEXICO.
BEAUTIFUL LAWN YOU'VE GOT GOING THERE, MR. SAMALSON.
THANK YOU, JONAS. YOU KNOW ME. I LOVE MY YARD WORK.
EVERYBODY NEEDS A HOBBY!
G'MORNING, MRS. DAWOOD!
ANYTHING FOR ME TODAY?
AFRAID NOT! BUT AT LEAST THERE AREN'T ANY BILLS, RIGHT?
RIGHT.
THERE NEVER ARE.

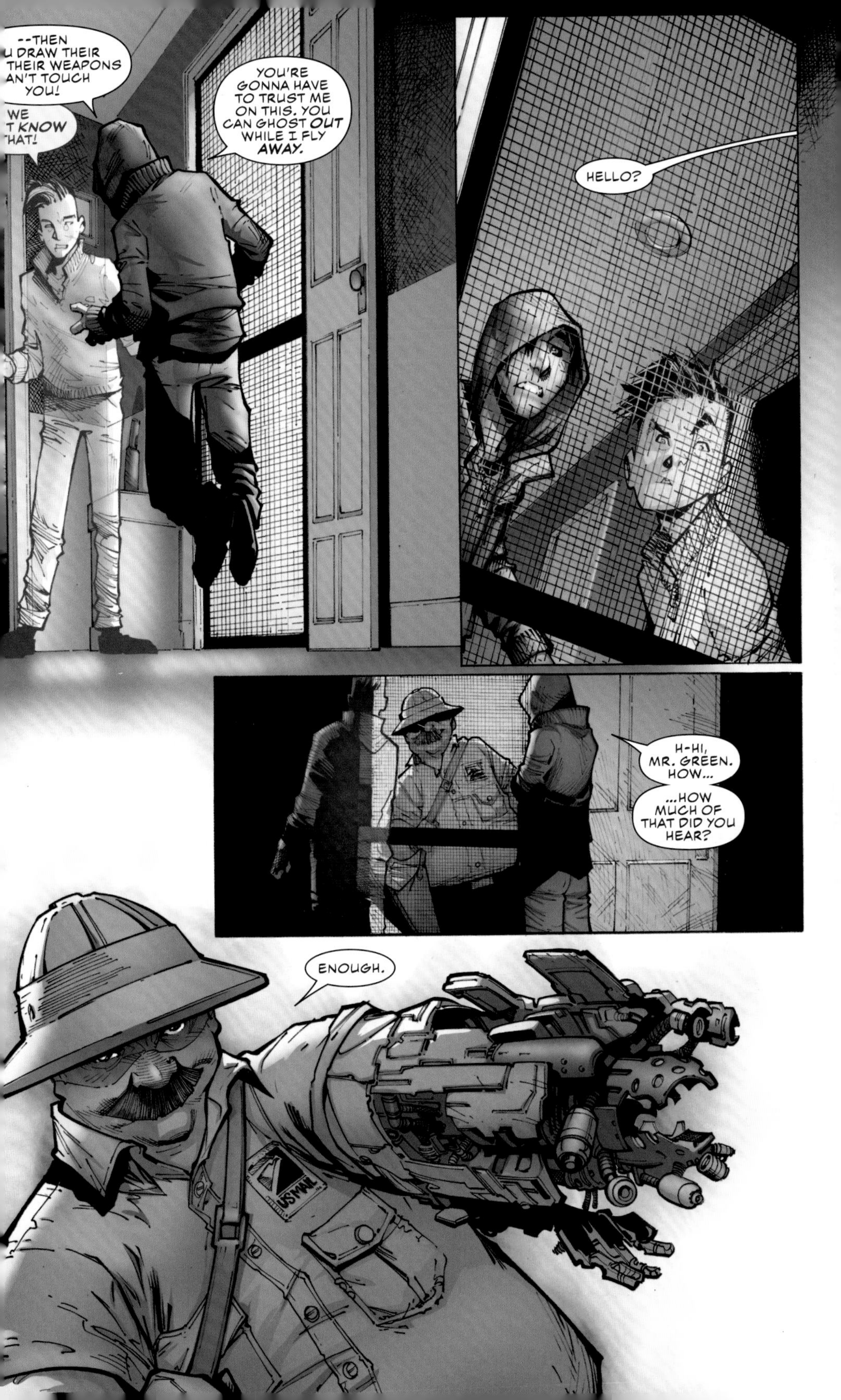
--THEN
U DRAW THEIR THEIR WEAPONS AN'T TOUCH YOU!
WE T KNOW THAT!
YOU'RE GONNA HAVE TO TRUST ME ON THIS. YOU CAN GHOST OUT WHILE I FLY AWAY.
HELLO?
H-HI, MR. GREEN. HOW...
...HOW MUCH OF THAT DID YOU HEAR?
ENOUGH.
US MAIL

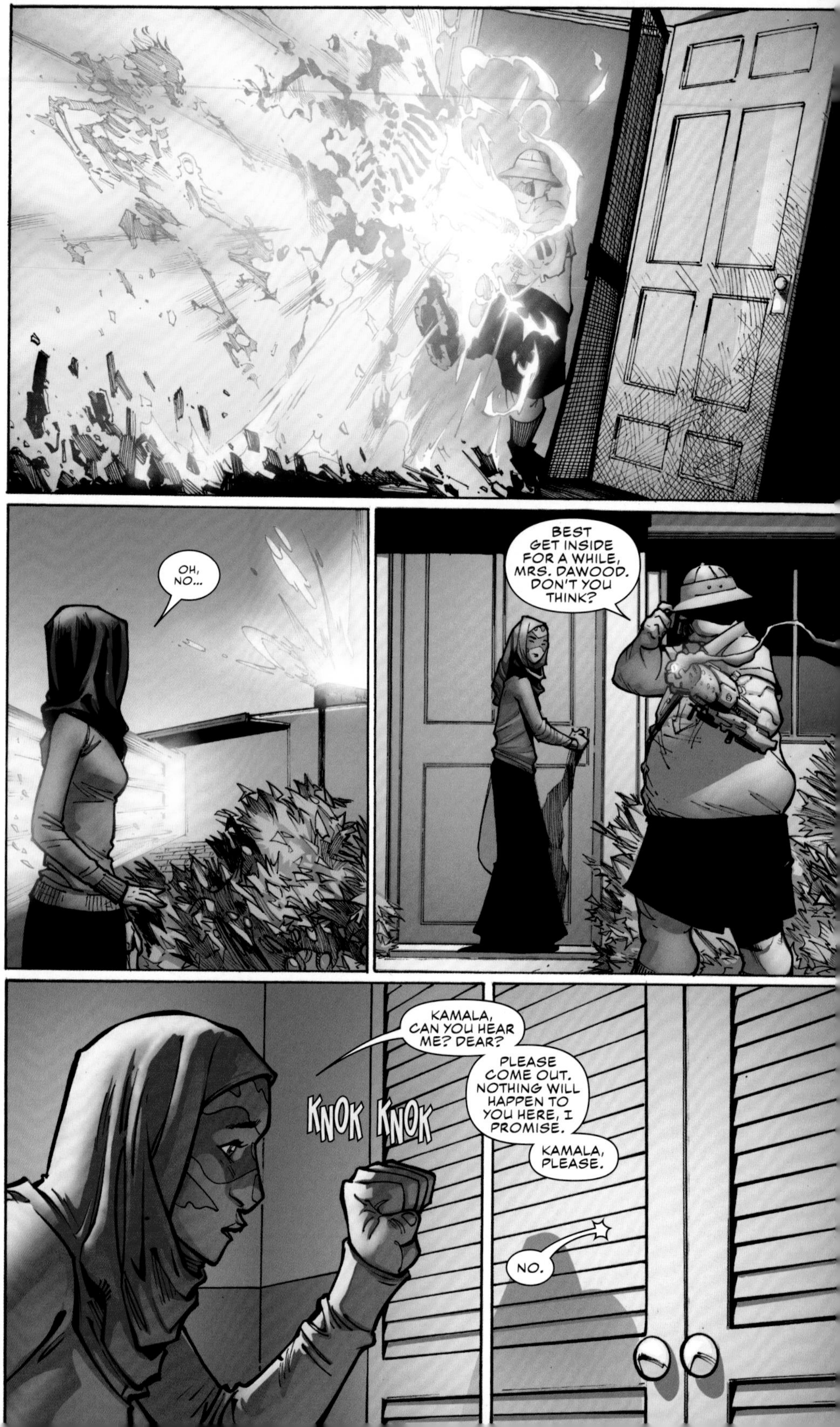
OH, NO...
BEST GET INSIDE FOR A WHILE, MRS. DAWOOD. DON'T YOU THINK?
KAMALA, CAN YOU HEAR ME? DEAR?
PLEASE COME OUT. NOTHING WILL HAPPEN TO YOU HERE, I PROMISE.
KAMALA, PLEASE.
KNOK KNOK
NO.

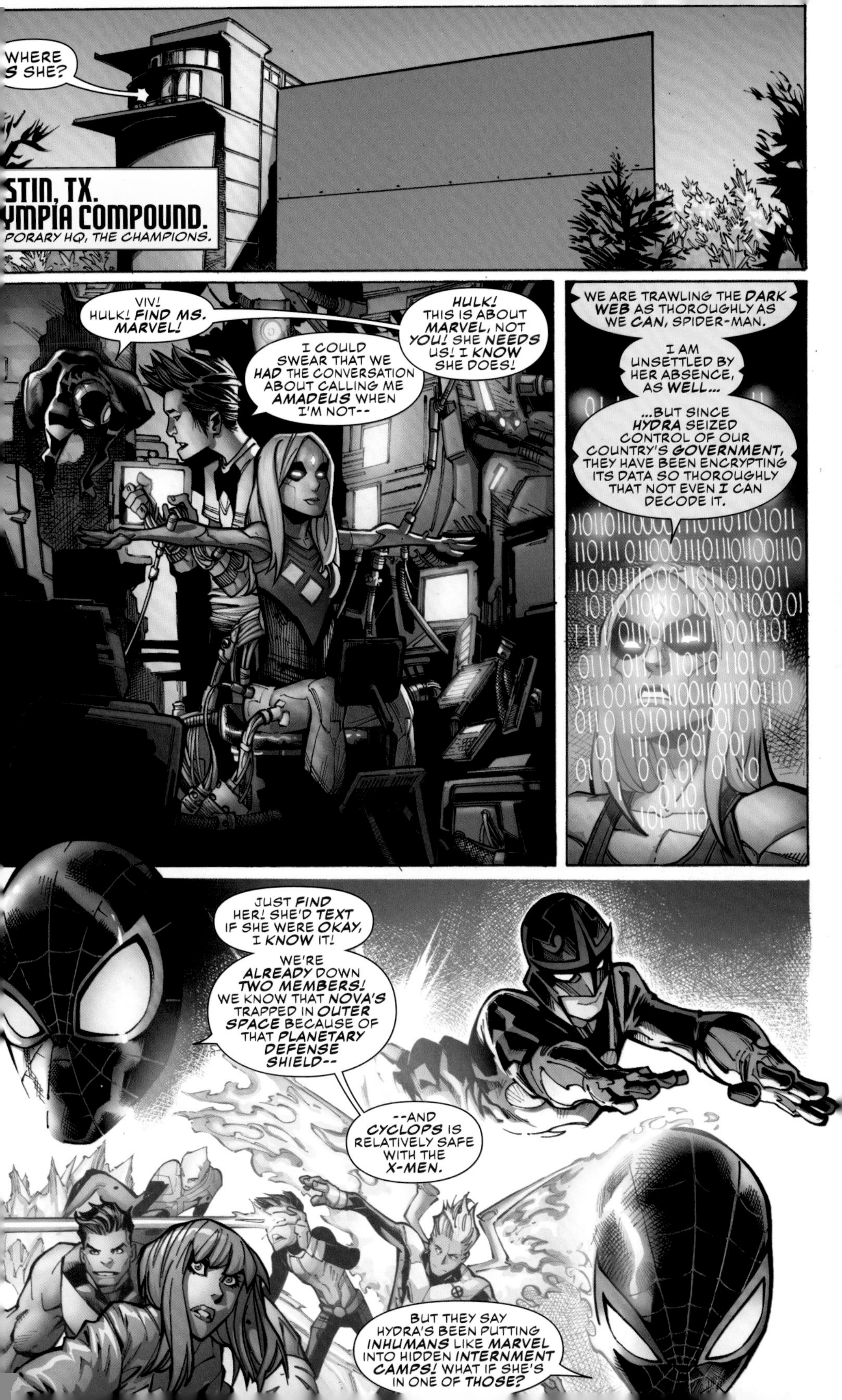
WHERE
S SHE?
STIN, TX.
YMPIA COMPOUND.
PORARY HQ, THE CHAMPIONS.
VIV! HULK! FIND MS. MARVEL!
I COULD SWEAR THAT WE HAD THE CONVERSATION ABOUT CALLING ME AMADEUS WHEN I'M NOT--
HULK! THIS IS ABOUT MARVEL, NOT YOU! SHE NEEDS US! I KNOW SHE DOES!
WE ARE TRAWLING THE DARK WEB AS THOROUGHLY AS WE CAN, SPIDER-MAN.
I AM UNSETTLED BY HER ABSENCE, AS WELL...
...BUT SINCE HYDRA SEIZED CONTROL OF OUR COUNTRY'S GOVERNMENT, THEY HAVE BEEN ENCRYPTING ITS DATA SO THOROUGHLY THAT NOT EVEN I CAN DECODE IT.
JUST FIND HER! SHE'D TEXT IF SHE WERE OKAY, I KNOW IT!
WE'RE ALREADY DOWN TWO MEMBERS! WE KNOW THAT NOVA'S TRAPPED IN OUTER SPACE BECAUSE OF THAT PLANETARY DEFENSE SHIELD--
--AND CYCLOPS IS RELATIVELY SAFE WITH THE X-MEN.
BUT THEY SAY HYDRA'S BEEN PUTTING INHUMANS LIKE MARVEL INTO HIDDEN INTERNMENT CAMPS! WHAT IF SHE'S IN ONE OF THOSE?

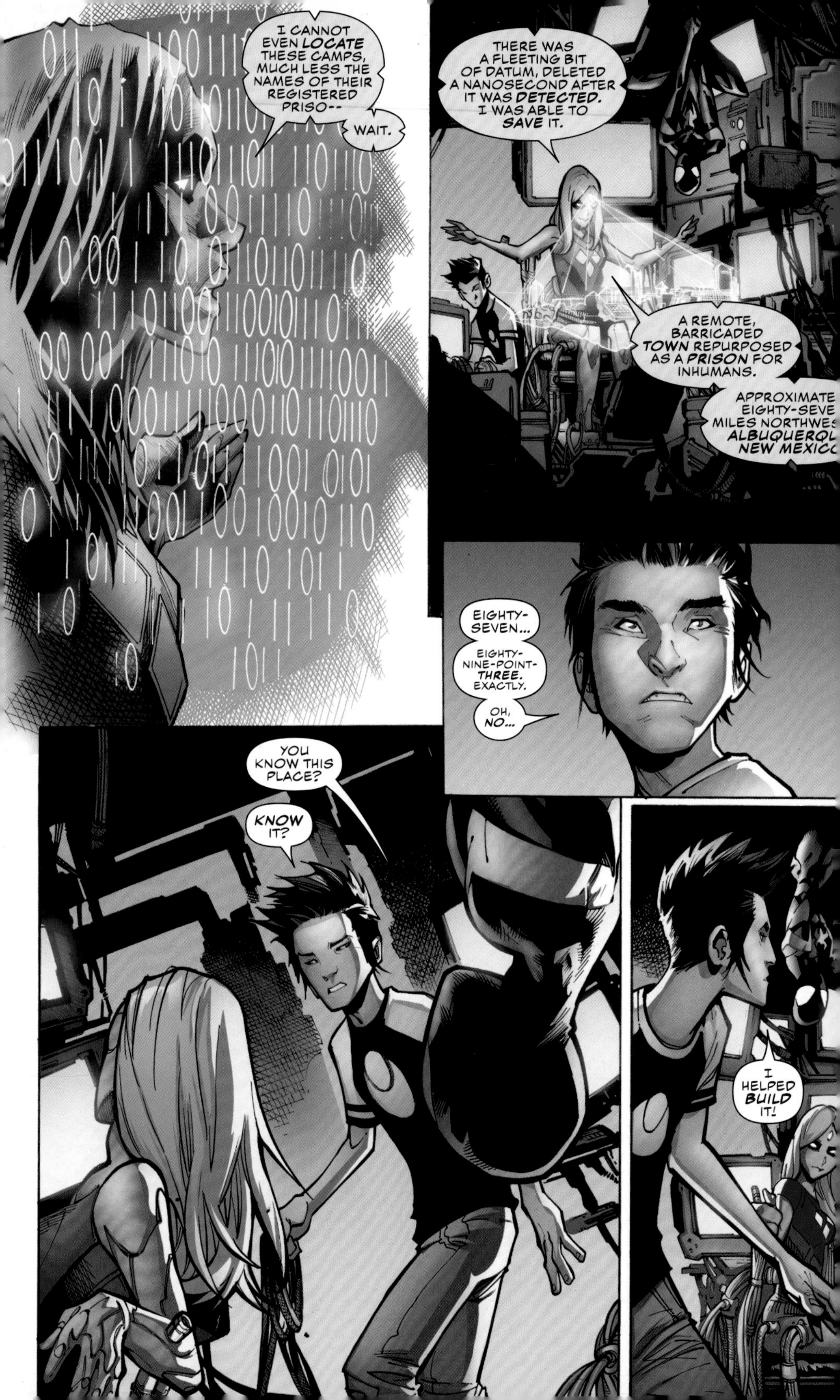
I CANNOT EVEN LOCATE THESE CAMPS, MUCH LESS THE NAMES OF THEIR REGISTERED PRISO--
WAIT.
THERE WAS A FLEETING BIT OF DATUM, DELETED A NANOSECOND AFTER IT WAS DETECTED. I WAS ABLE TO SAVE IT.
A REMOTE, BARRICADED TOWN REPURPOSED AS A PRISON FOR INHUMANS.
APPROXIMATE EIGHTY-SEVE MILES NORTHWES ALBUQUERQU NEW MEXICO
EIGHTY-SEVEN...
EIGHTY-NINE-POINT-THREE. EXACTLY.
OH, NO...
YOU KNOW THIS PLACE?
KNOW IT?
I HELPED BUILD IT!

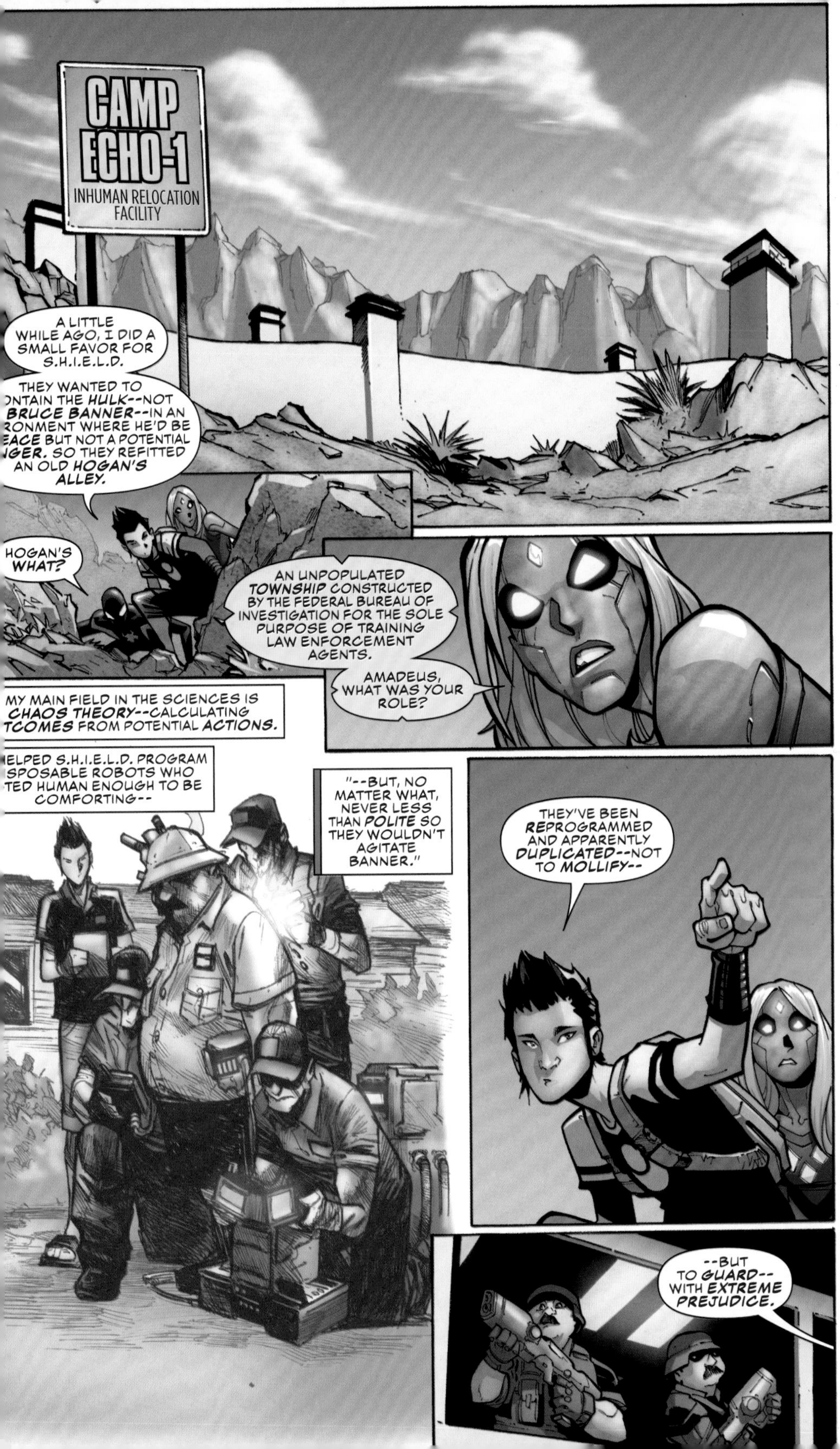
CAMP ECHO-1
INHUMAN RELOCATION FACILITY
A LITTLE WHILE AGO, I DID A SMALL FAVOR FOR S.H.I.E.L.D.
THEY WANTED TO ONTAIN THE HULK--NOT BRUCE BANNER--IN AN RONMENT WHERE HE'D BE EACE BUT NOT A POTENTIAL NGER. SO THEY REFITTED AN OLD HOGAN'S ALLEY.
HOGAN'S WHAT?
AN UNPOPULATED TOWNSHIP CONSTRUCTED BY THE FEDERAL BUREAU OF INVESTIGATION FOR THE SOLE PURPOSE OF TRAINING LAW ENFORCEMENT AGENTS.
AMADEUS, WHAT WAS YOUR ROLE?
MY MAIN FIELD IN THE SCIENCES IS CHAOS THEORY--CALCULATING TCOMES FROM POTENTIAL ACTIONS.
ELPED S.H.I.E.L.D. PROGRAM SPOSABLE ROBOTS WHO TED HUMAN ENOUGH TO BE COMFORTING--
"--BUT, NO MATTER WHAT, NEVER LESS THAN POLITE SO THEY WOULDN'T AGITATE BANNER."
THEY'VE BEEN REPROGRAMMED AND APPARENTLY DUPLICATED--NOT TO MOLLIFY--
--BUT TO GUARD--WITH EXTREME PREJUDICE.

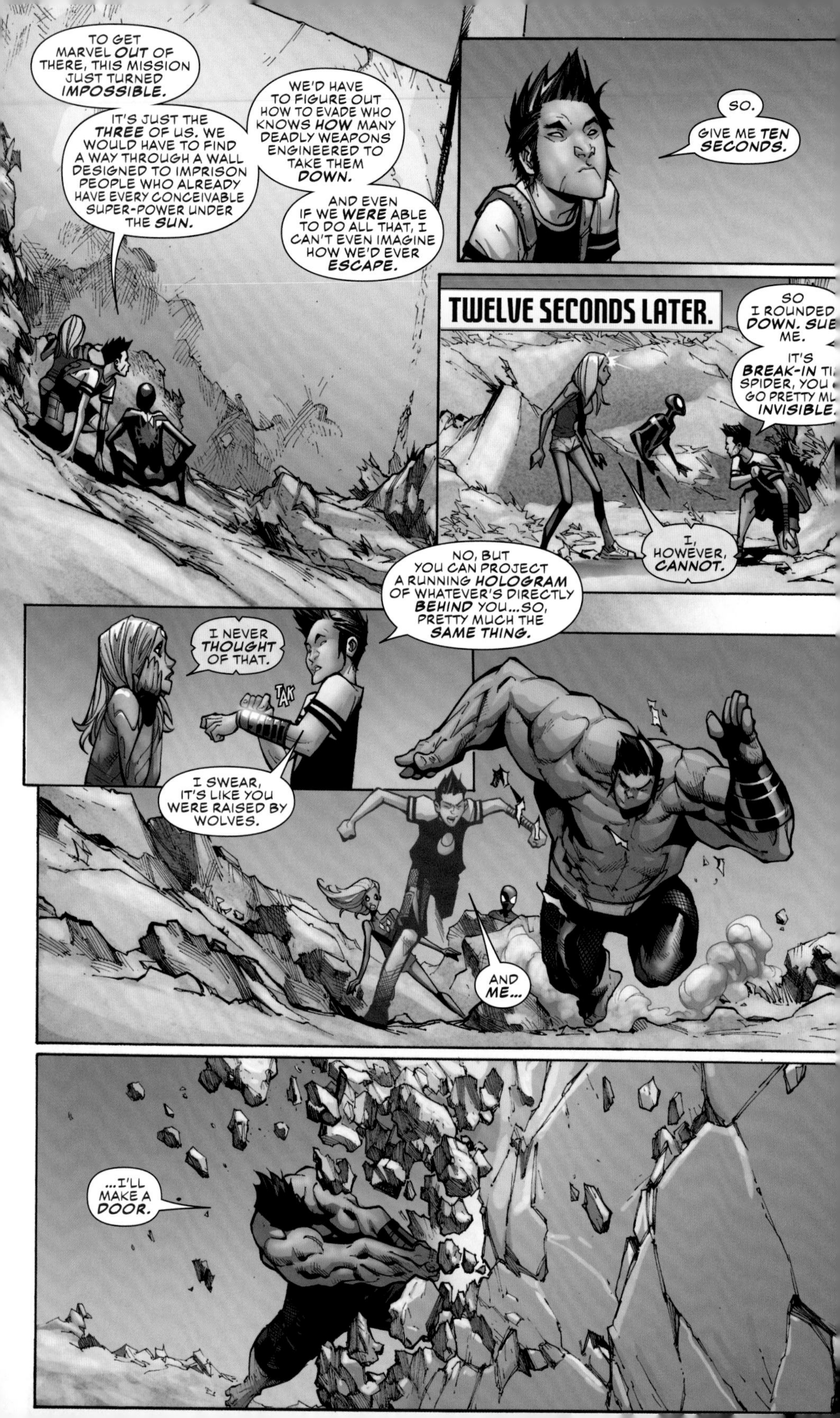
TO GET MARVEL OUT OF THERE, THIS MISSION JUST TURNED IMPOSSIBLE.
IT'S JUST THE THREE OF US. WE WOULD HAVE TO FIND A WAY THROUGH A WALL DESIGNED TO IMPRISON PEOPLE WHO ALREADY HAVE EVERY CONCEIVABLE SUPER-POWER UNDER THE SUN.
WE'D HAVE TO FIGURE OUT HOW TO EVADE WHO KNOWS HOW MANY DEADLY WEAPONS ENGINEERED TO TAKE THEM DOWN.
AND EVEN IF WE WERE ABLE TO DO ALL THAT, I CAN'T EVEN IMAGINE HOW WE'D EVER ESCAPE.
SO.
GIVE ME TEN SECONDS.
TWELVE SECONDS LATER.
SO I ROUNDED DOWN. SUE ME.
IT'S BREAK-IN TI
SPIDER, YOU
GO PRETTY MU
INVISIBLE.
I, HOWEVER, CANNOT.
NO, BUT YOU CAN PROJECT A RUNNING HOLOGRAM OF WHATEVER'S DIRECTLY BEHIND YOU...SO, PRETTY MUCH THE SAME THING.
I NEVER THOUGHT OF THAT.
TAK
I SWEAR, IT'S LIKE YOU WERE RAISED BY WOLVES.
AND ME...
...I'LL MAKE A DOOR.

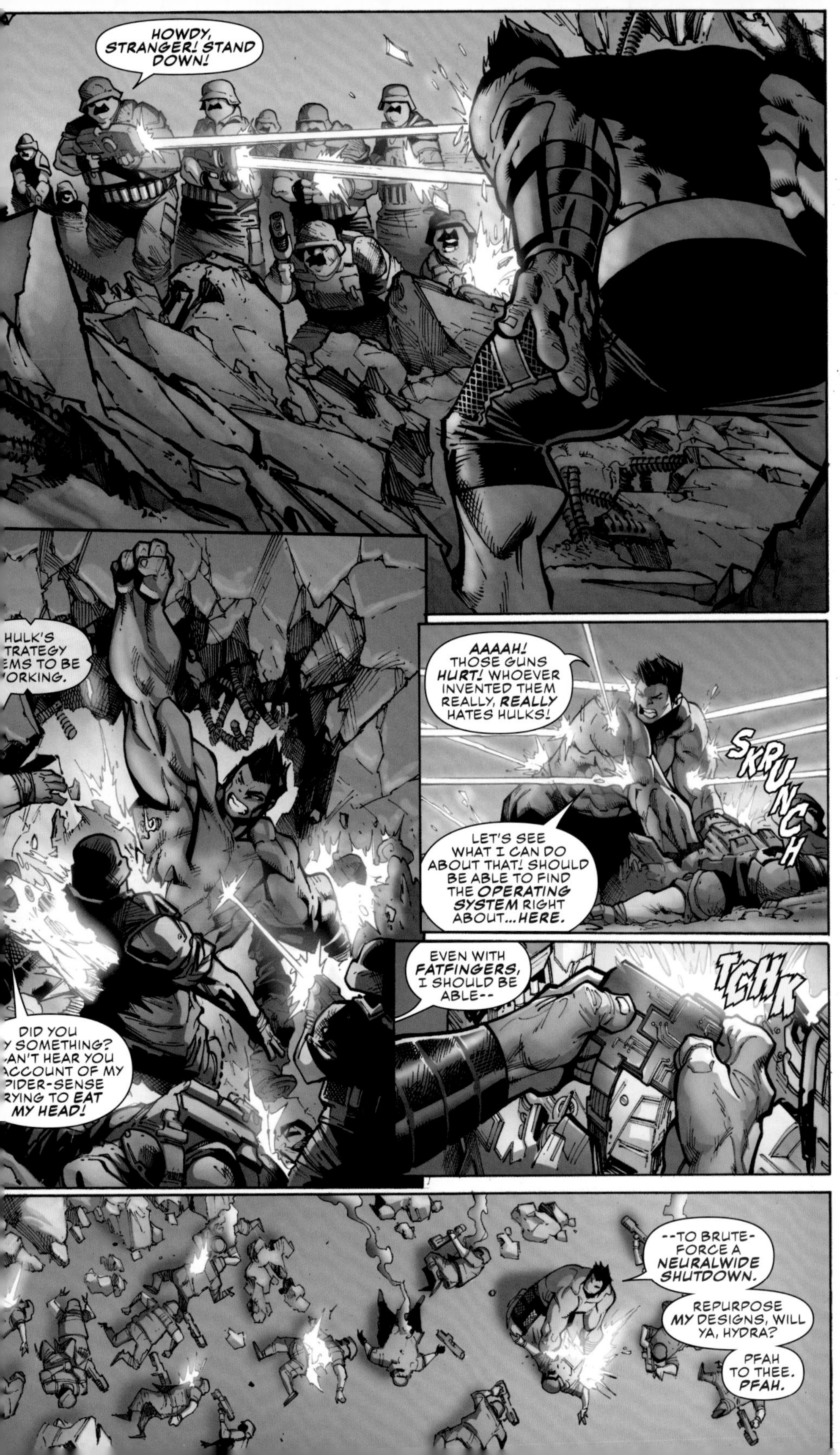
HOWDY, STRANGER! STAND DOWN!
HULK'S TRATEGY EMS TO BE WORKING.
DID YOU Y SOMETHING? AN'T HEAR YOU ACCOUNT OF MY PIDER-SENSE RYING TO EAT MY HEAD!
AAAAH! THOSE GUNS HURT! WHOEVER INVENTED THEM REALLY, REALLY HATES HULKS!
SKRUNCH
LET'S SEE WHAT I CAN DO ABOUT THAT! SHOULD BE ABLE TO FIND THE OPERATING SYSTEM RIGHT ABOUT...HERE.
EVEN WITH FATFINGERS, I SHOULD BE ABLE--
TCHK
--TO BRUTE-FORCE A NEURALWIDE SHUTDOWN.
REPURPOSE MY DESIGNS, WILL YA, HYDRA?
PFAH TO THEE. PFAH.

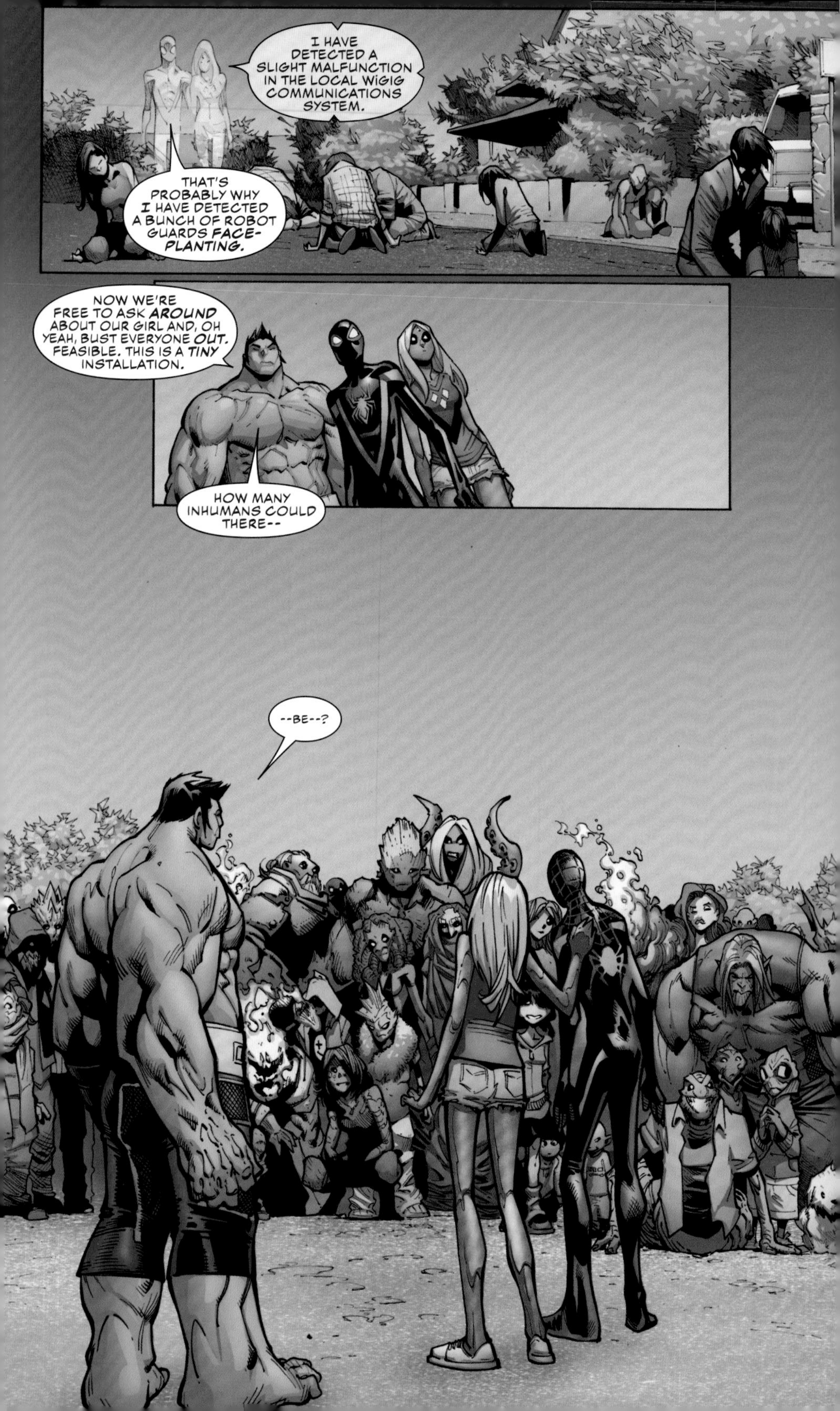
I HAVE DETECTED A SLIGHT MALFUNCTION IN THE LOCAL WiGIG COMMUNICATIONS SYSTEM.
THAT'S PROBABLY WHY I HAVE DETECTED A BUNCH OF ROBOT GUARDS FACE-PLANTING.
NOW WE'RE FREE TO ASK AROUND ABOUT OUR GIRL AND, OH YEAH, BUST EVERYONE OUT. FEASIBLE. THIS IS A TINY INSTALLATION.
HOW MANY INHUMANS COULD THERE--
--BE--?

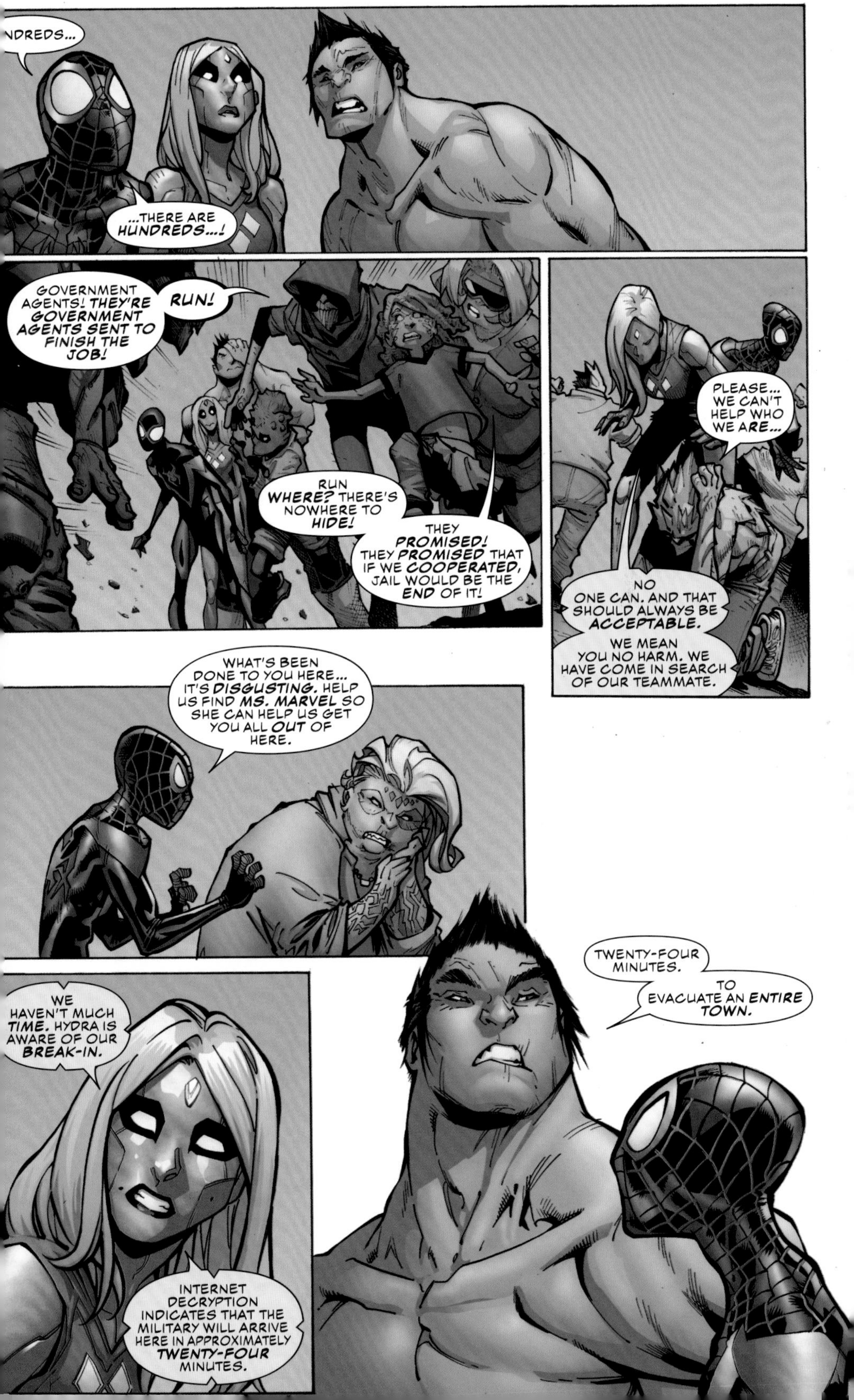

...NDREDS...
...THERE ARE HUNDREDS...!
GOVERNMENT AGENTS! THEY'RE GOVERNMENT AGENTS SENT TO FINISH THE JOB!
RUN!
RUN WHERE? THERE'S NOWHERE TO HIDE!
THEY PROMISED! THEY PROMISED THAT IF WE COOPERATED, JAIL WOULD BE THE END OF IT!
PLEASE... WE CAN'T HELP WHO WE ARE...
NO ONE CAN. AND THAT SHOULD ALWAYS BE ACCEPTABLE.
WE MEAN YOU NO HARM. WE HAVE COME IN SEARCH OF OUR TEAMMATE.
WHAT'S BEEN DONE TO YOU HERE... IT'S DISGUSTING. HELP US FIND MS. MARVEL SO SHE CAN HELP US GET YOU ALL OUT OF HERE.
WE HAVEN'T MUCH TIME. HYDRA IS AWARE OF OUR BREAK-IN.
INTERNET DECRYPTION INDICATES THAT THE MILITARY WILL ARRIVE HERE IN APPROXIMATELY TWENTY-FOUR MINUTES.
TWENTY-FOUR MINUTES.
TO EVACUATE AN ENTIRE TOWN.

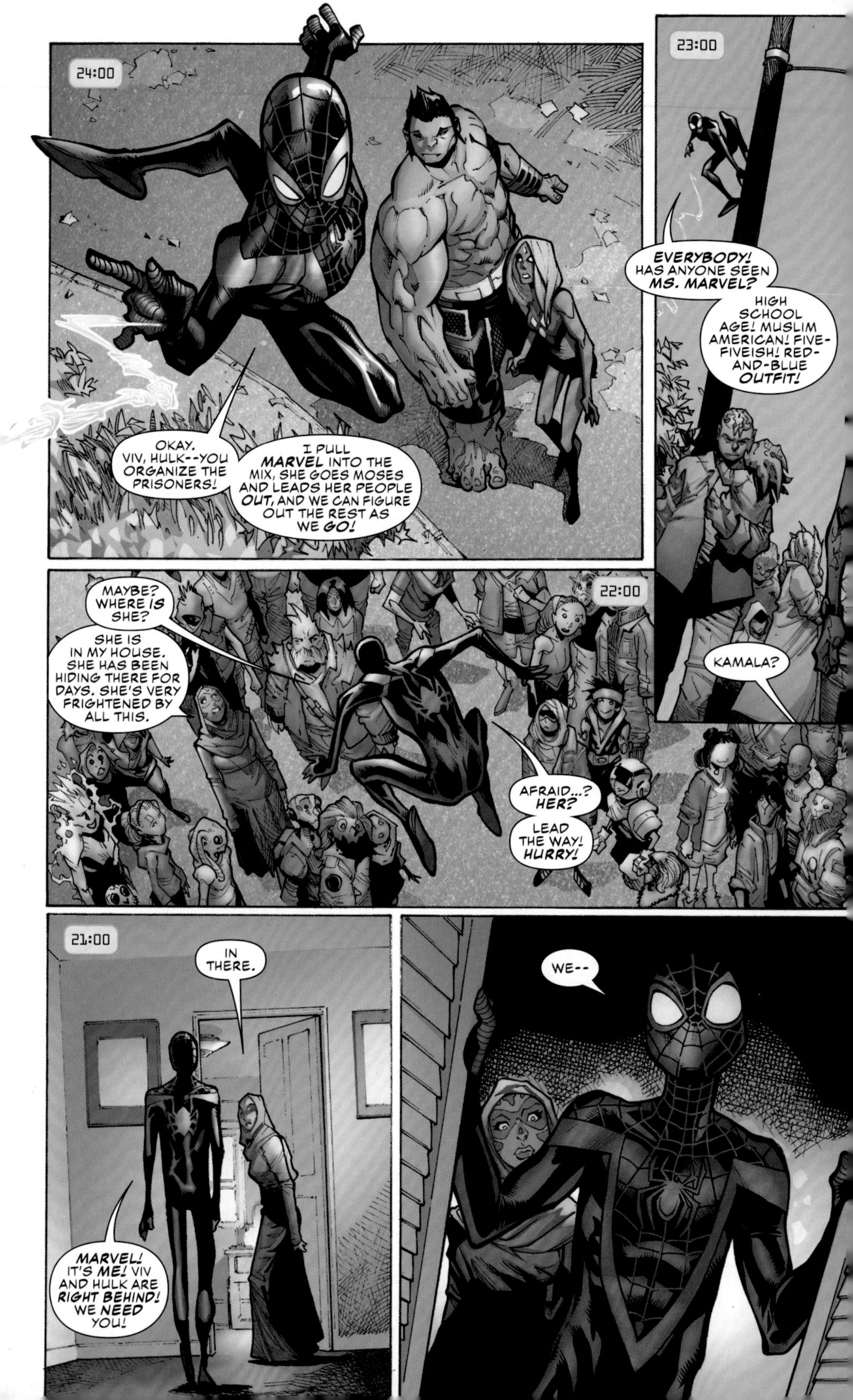
24:00
OKAY. VIV, HULK--YOU ORGANIZE THE PRISONERS!
I PULL MARVEL INTO THE MIX, SHE GOES MOSES AND LEADS HER PEOPLE OUT, AND WE CAN FIGURE OUT THE REST AS WE GO!
23:00
EVERYBODY! HAS ANYONE SEEN MS. MARVEL?
HIGH SCHOOL AGE! MUSLIM AMERICAN! FIVE-FIVEISH! RED-AND-BLUE OUTFIT!
KAMALA?
22:00
MAYBE? WHERE IS SHE?
SHE IS IN MY HOUSE. SHE HAS BEEN HIDING THERE FOR DAYS. SHE'S VERY FRIGHTENED BY ALL THIS.
AFRAID...? HER?
LEAD THE WAY! HURRY!
21:00
IN THERE.
MARVEL! IT'S ME! VIV AND HULK ARE RIGHT BEHIND! WE NEED YOU!
WE--

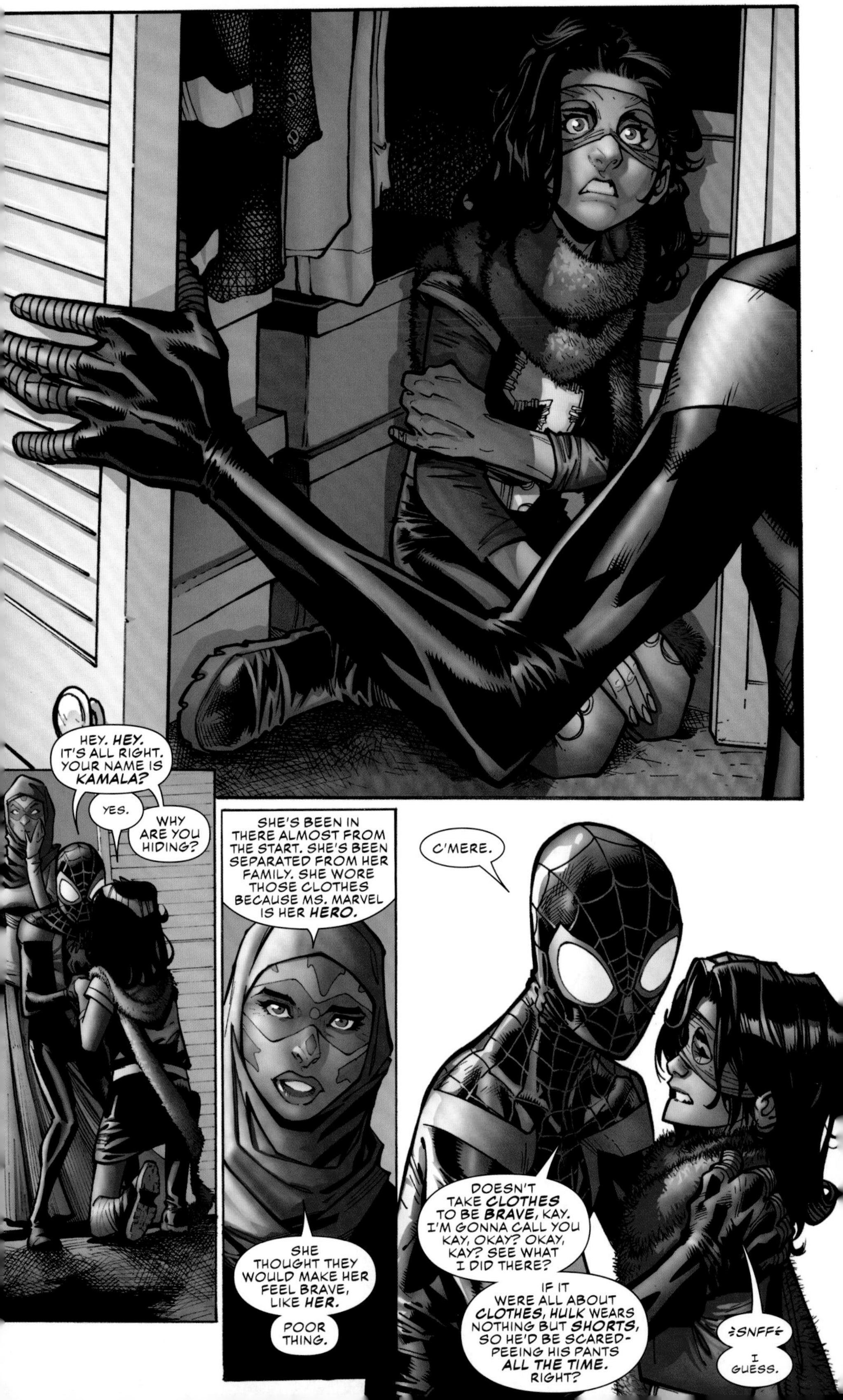

HEY. **HEY.** IT'S ALL RIGHT. YOUR NAME IS **KAMALA?**
YES.
WHY ARE YOU HIDING?
SHE'S BEEN IN THERE ALMOST FROM THE START. SHE'S BEEN SEPARATED FROM HER FAMILY. SHE WORE THOSE CLOTHES BECAUSE MS. MARVEL IS HER **HERO.**
SHE THOUGHT THEY WOULD MAKE HER FEEL BRAVE, LIKE **HER.**
POOR THING.
C'MERE.
DOESN'T TAKE **CLOTHES** TO BE **BRAVE**, KAY. I'M GONNA CALL YOU KAY, OKAY? OKAY, KAY? SEE WHAT I DID THERE?
IF IT WERE ALL ABOUT **CLOTHES, HULK** WEARS NOTHING BUT **SHORTS,** SO HE'D BE SCARED-PEEING HIS PANTS **ALL THE TIME.** RIGHT?
SNFF
I GUESS.

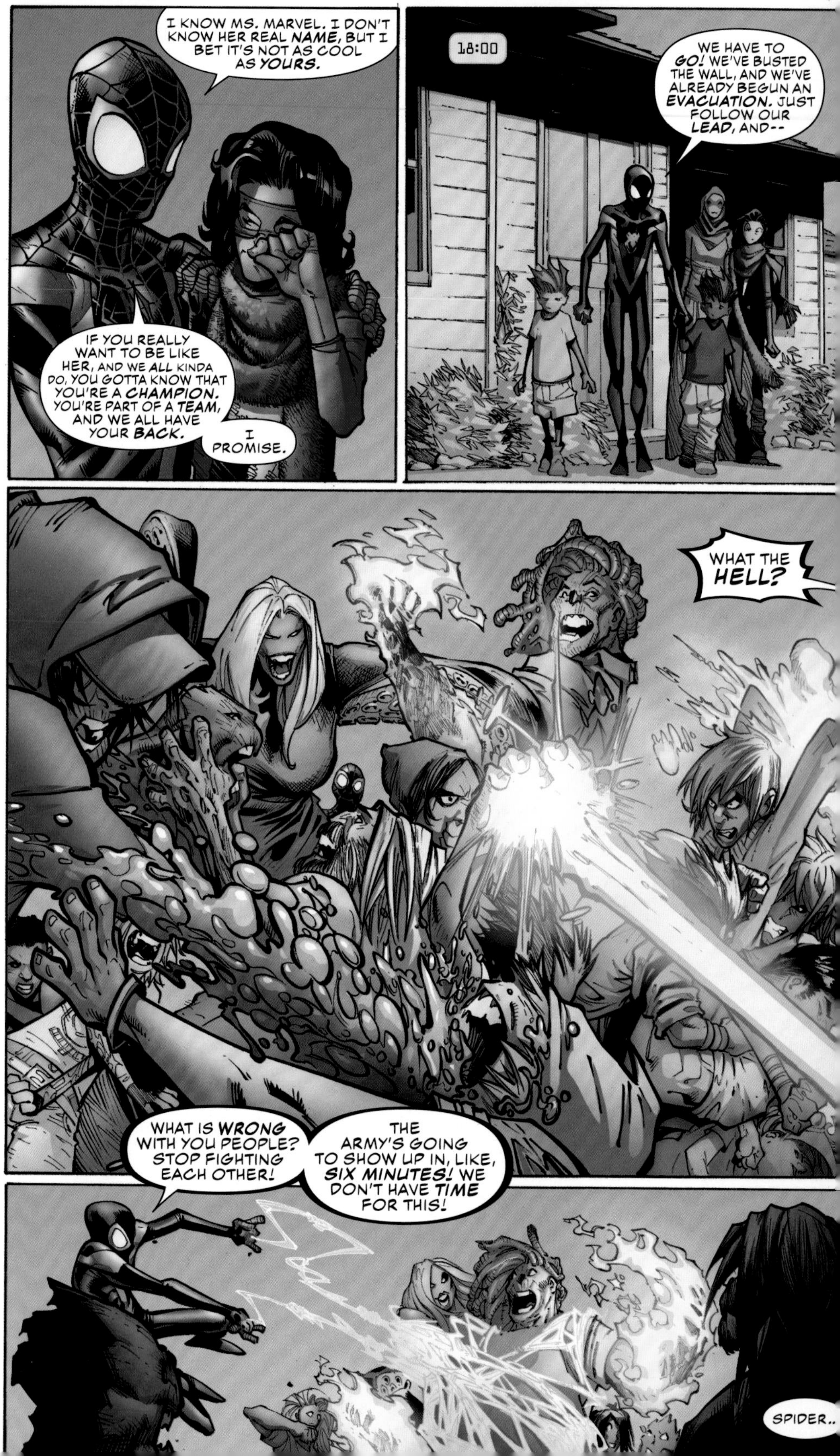
I KNOW MS. MARVEL. I DON'T KNOW HER REAL NAME, BUT I BET IT'S NOT AS COOL AS YOURS.
IF YOU REALLY WANT TO BE LIKE HER, AND WE ALL KINDA DO, YOU GOTTA KNOW THAT YOU'RE A CHAMPION. YOU'RE PART OF A TEAM, AND WE ALL HAVE YOUR BACK.
I PROMISE.
18:00
WE HAVE TO GO! WE'VE BUSTED THE WALL, AND WE'VE ALREADY BEGUN AN EVACUATION. JUST FOLLOW OUR LEAD, AND--
WHAT THE HELL?
WHAT IS WRONG WITH YOU PEOPLE? STOP FIGHTING EACH OTHER!
THE ARMY'S GOING TO SHOW UP IN, LIKE, SIX MINUTES! WE DON'T HAVE TIME FOR THIS!
SPIDER..

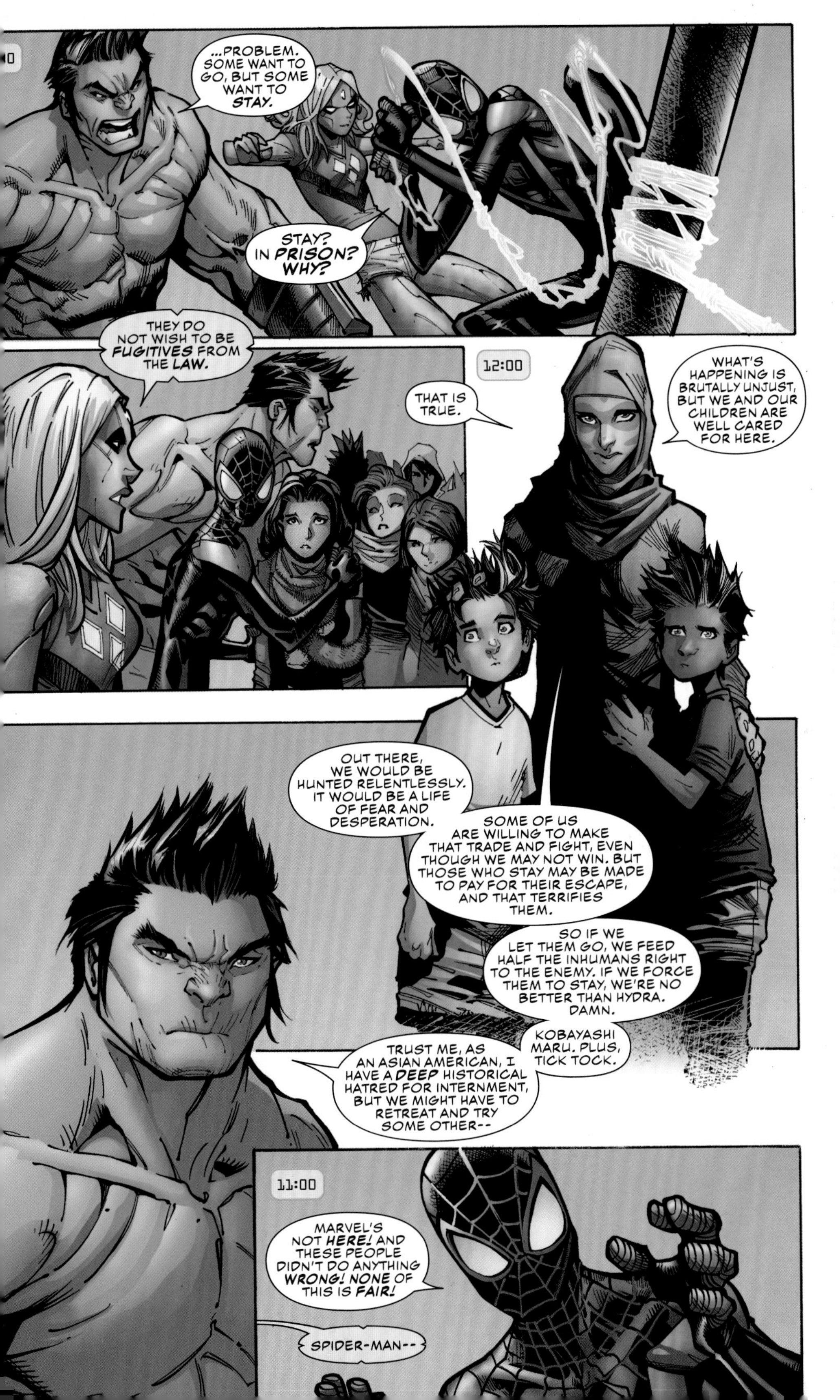
...PROBLEM. SOME WANT TO GO, BUT SOME WANT TO STAY.
STAY? IN PRISON? WHY?
THEY DO NOT WISH TO BE FUGITIVES FROM THE LAW.
12:00
THAT IS TRUE.
WHAT'S HAPPENING IS BRUTALLY UNJUST, BUT WE AND OUR CHILDREN ARE WELL CARED FOR HERE.
OUT THERE, WE WOULD BE HUNTED RELENTLESSLY. IT WOULD BE A LIFE OF FEAR AND DESPERATION.
SOME OF US ARE WILLING TO MAKE THAT TRADE AND FIGHT, EVEN THOUGH WE MAY NOT WIN. BUT THOSE WHO STAY MAY BE MADE TO PAY FOR THEIR ESCAPE, AND THAT TERRIFIES THEM.
SO IF WE LET THEM GO, WE FEED HALF THE INHUMANS RIGHT TO THE ENEMY. IF WE FORCE THEM TO STAY, WE'RE NO BETTER THAN HYDRA. DAMN.
KOBAYASHI MARU. PLUS, TICK TOCK.
TRUST ME, AS AN ASIAN AMERICAN, I HAVE A DEEP HISTORICAL HATRED FOR INTERNMENT, BUT WE MIGHT HAVE TO RETREAT AND TRY SOME OTHER--
11:00
MARVEL'S NOT HERE! AND THESE PEOPLE DIDN'T DO ANYTHING WRONG! NONE OF THIS IS FAIR!
SPIDER-MAN--

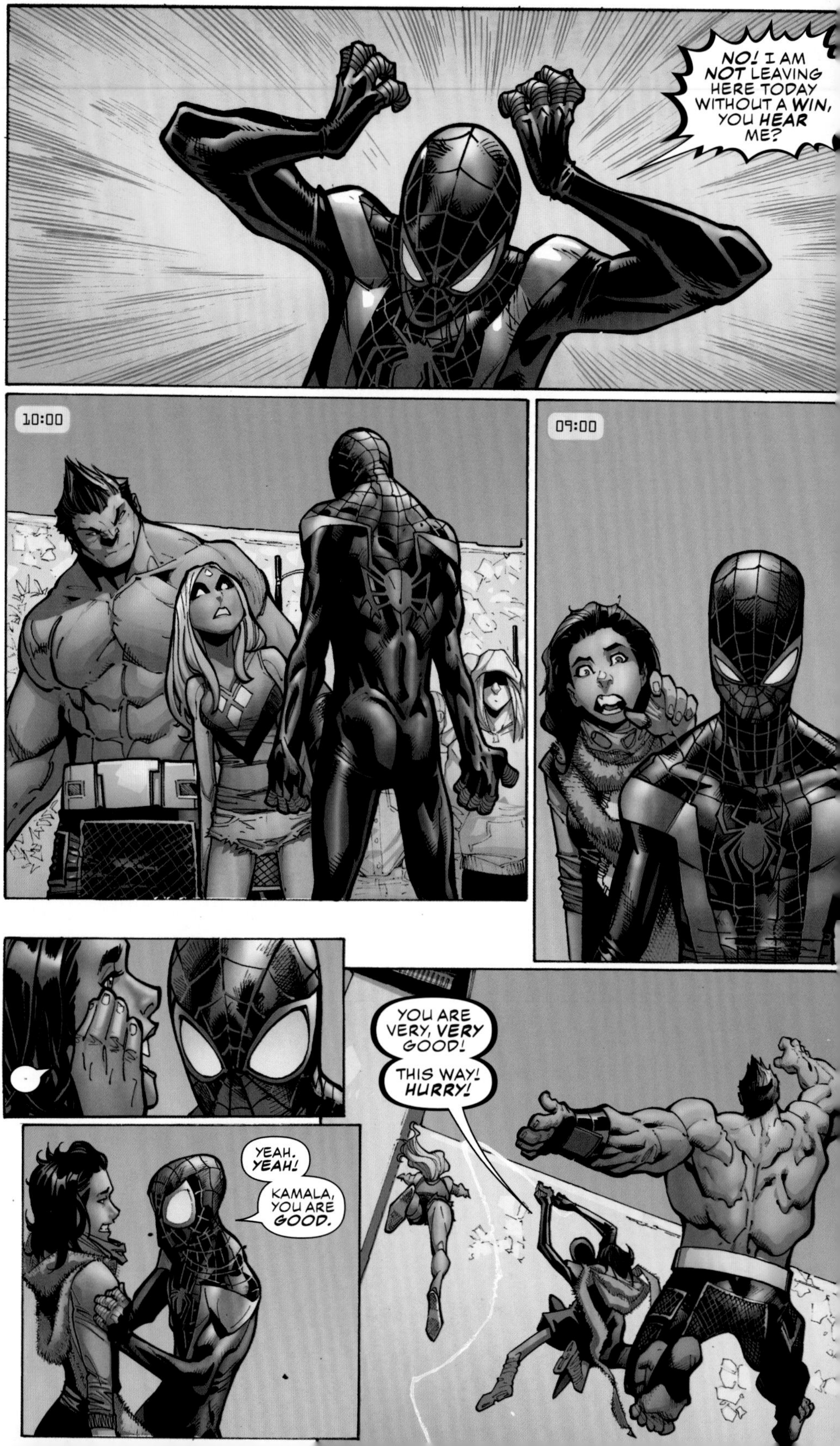
NO! I AM NOT LEAVING HERE TODAY WITHOUT A WIN, YOU HEAR ME?
10:00
09:00
YOU ARE VERY, VERY GOOD!
THIS WAY! HURRY!
YEAH. YEAH!
KAMALA, YOU ARE GOOD.

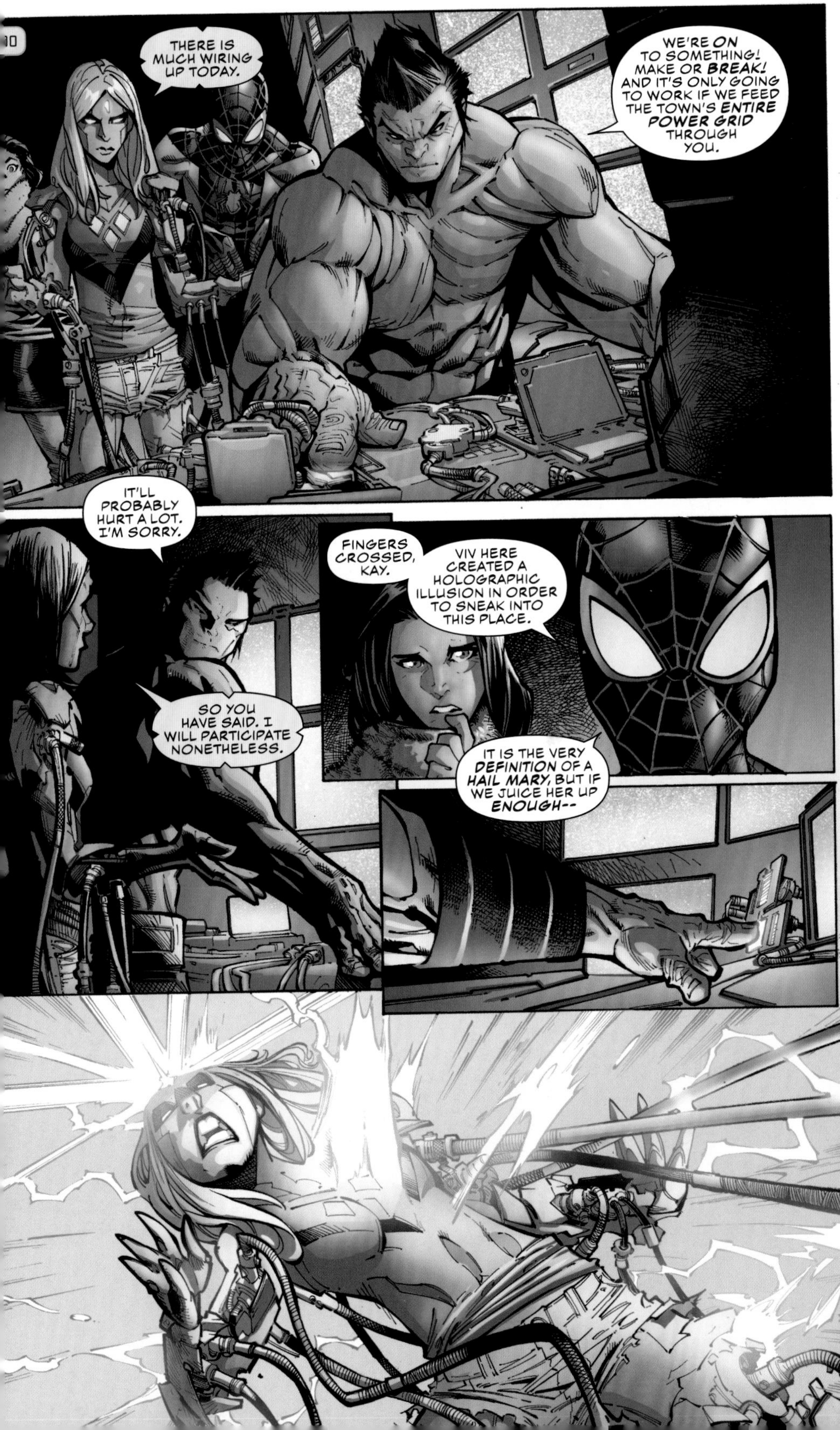
THERE IS MUCH WIRING UP TODAY.
WE'RE ON TO SOMETHING! MAKE OR BREAK! AND IT'S ONLY GOING TO WORK IF WE FEED THE TOWN'S ENTIRE POWER GRID THROUGH YOU.
IT'LL PROBABLY HURT A LOT. I'M SORRY.
SO YOU HAVE SAID. I WILL PARTICIPATE NONETHELESS.
FINGERS CROSSED, KAY.
VIV HERE CREATED A HOLOGRAPHIC ILLUSION IN ORDER TO SNEAK INTO THIS PLACE.
IT IS THE VERY DEFINITION OF A HAIL MARY, BUT IF WE JUICE HER UP ENOUGH--

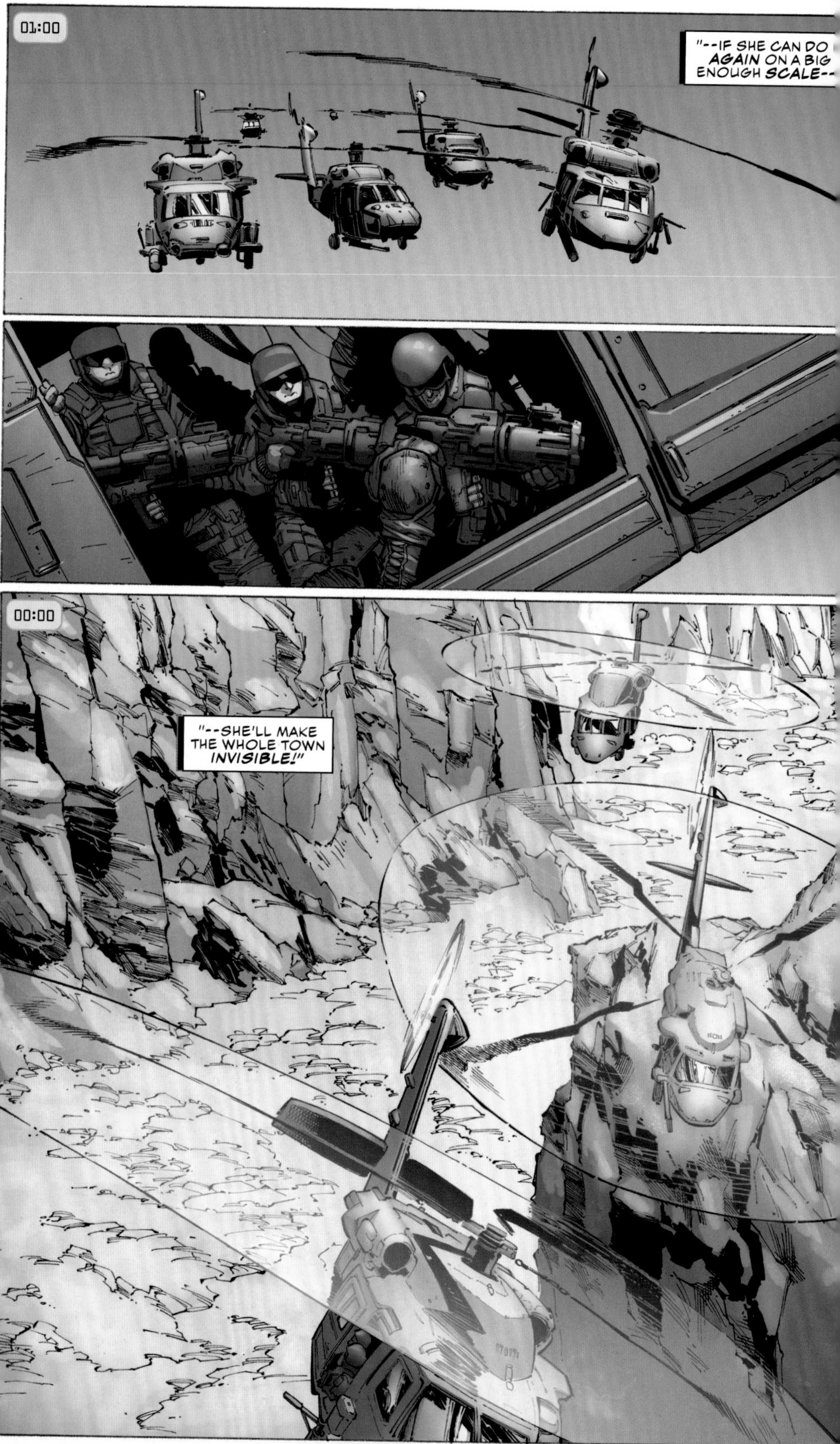
01:00
"--IF SHE CAN DO AGAIN ON A BIG ENOUGH SCALE--
00:00
"--SHE'LL MAKE THE WHOLE TOWN INVISIBLE!"

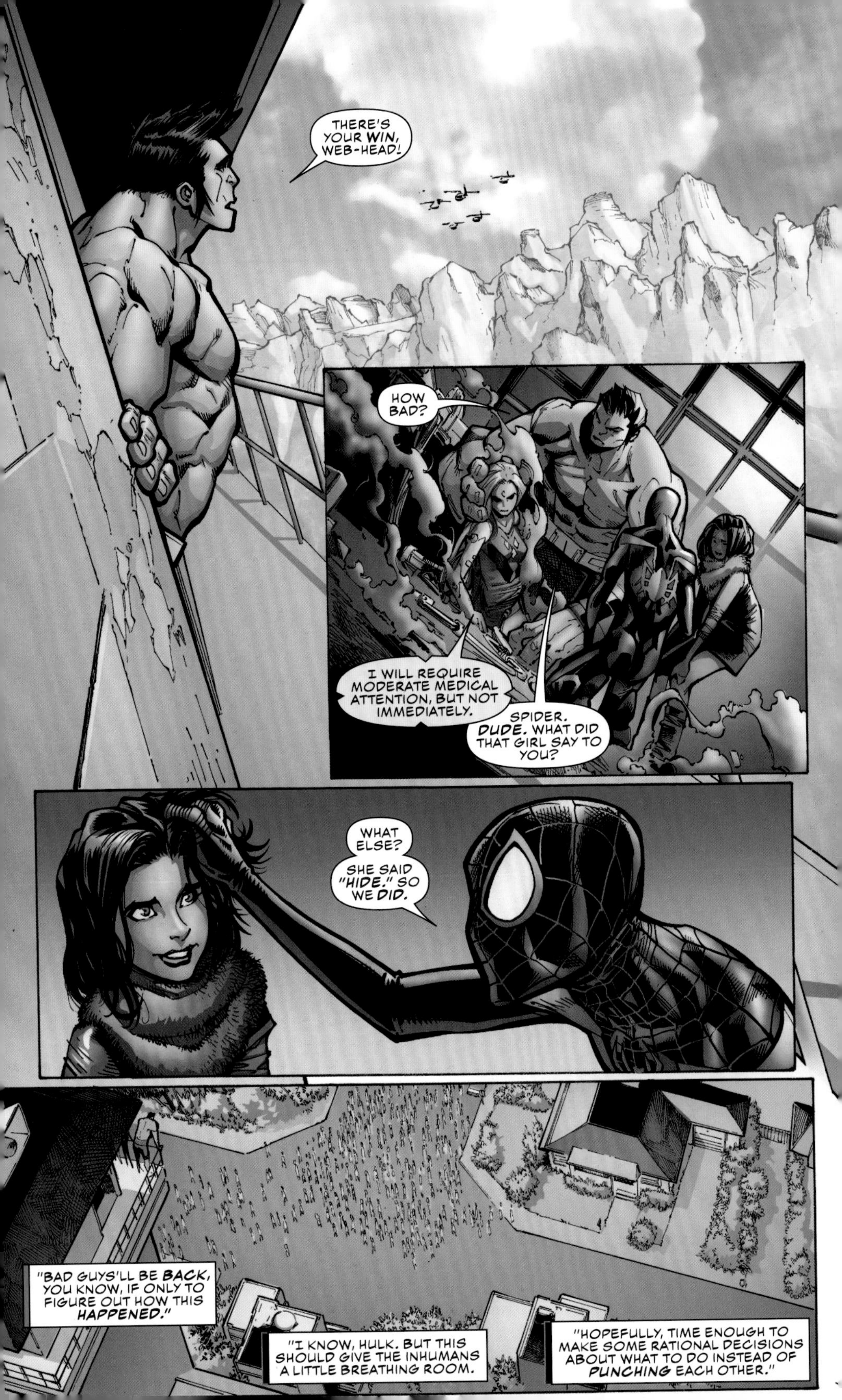
THERE'S YOUR WIN, WEB-HEAD!
HOW BAD?
I WILL REQUIRE MODERATE MEDICAL ATTENTION, BUT NOT IMMEDIATELY.
SPIDER. DUDE. WHAT DID THAT GIRL SAY TO YOU?
WHAT ELSE?
SHE SAID "HIDE." SO WE DID.
"BAD GUYS'LL BE BACK, YOU KNOW, IF ONLY TO FIGURE OUT HOW THIS HAPPENED."
"I KNOW, HULK. BUT THIS SHOULD GIVE THE INHUMANS A LITTLE BREATHING ROOM.
"HOPEFULLY, TIME ENOUGH TO MAKE SOME RATIONAL DECISIONS ABOUT WHAT TO DO INSTEAD OF PUNCHING EACH OTHER."

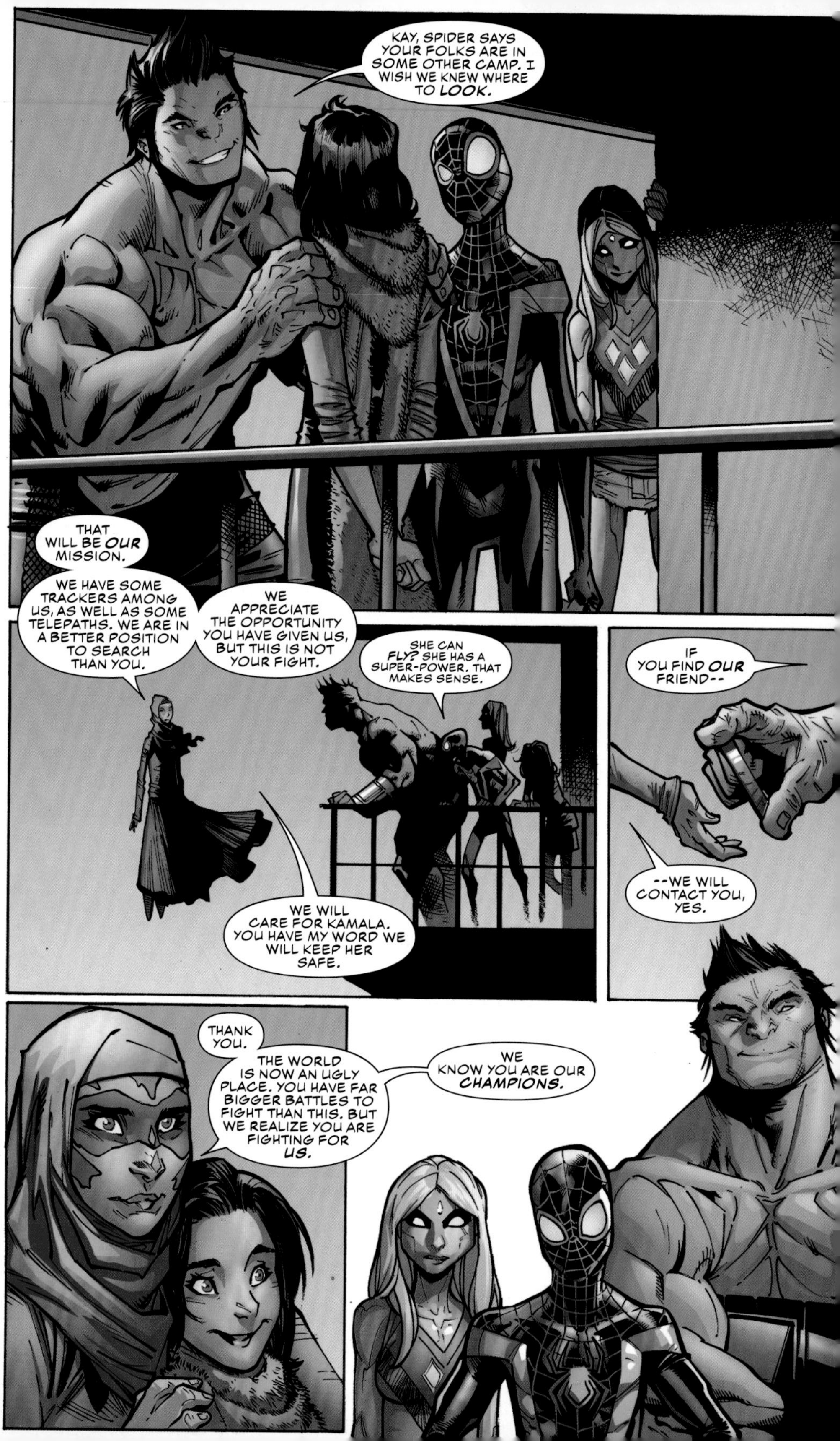
KAY, SPIDER SAYS YOUR FOLKS ARE IN SOME OTHER CAMP. I WISH WE KNEW WHERE TO LOOK.
THAT WILL BE OUR MISSION.
WE HAVE SOME TRACKERS AMONG US, AS WELL AS SOME TELEPATHS. WE ARE IN A BETTER POSITION TO SEARCH THAN YOU.
WE APPRECIATE THE OPPORTUNITY YOU HAVE GIVEN US, BUT THIS IS NOT YOUR FIGHT.
WE WILL CARE FOR KAMALA. YOU HAVE MY WORD WE WILL KEEP HER SAFE.
SHE CAN FLY? SHE HAS A SUPER-POWER. THAT MAKES SENSE.
IF YOU FIND OUR FRIEND--
--WE WILL CONTACT YOU, YES.
THANK YOU.
THE WORLD IS NOW AN UGLY PLACE. YOU HAVE FAR BIGGER BATTLES TO FIGHT THAN THIS. BUT WE REALIZE YOU ARE FIGHTING FOR US.
WE KNOW YOU ARE OUR CHAMPIONS.

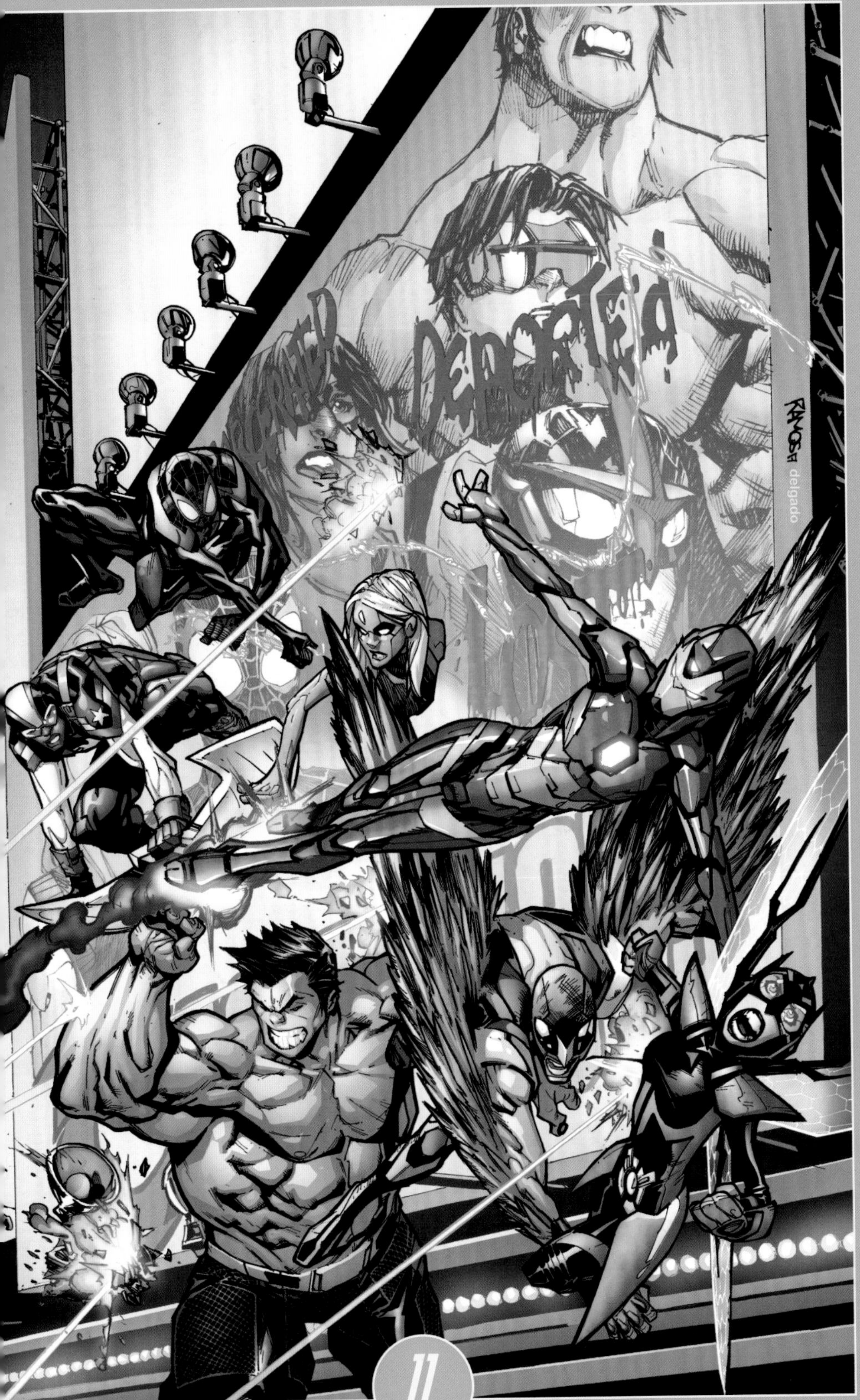
DEPORTED
RAMOS
delgado

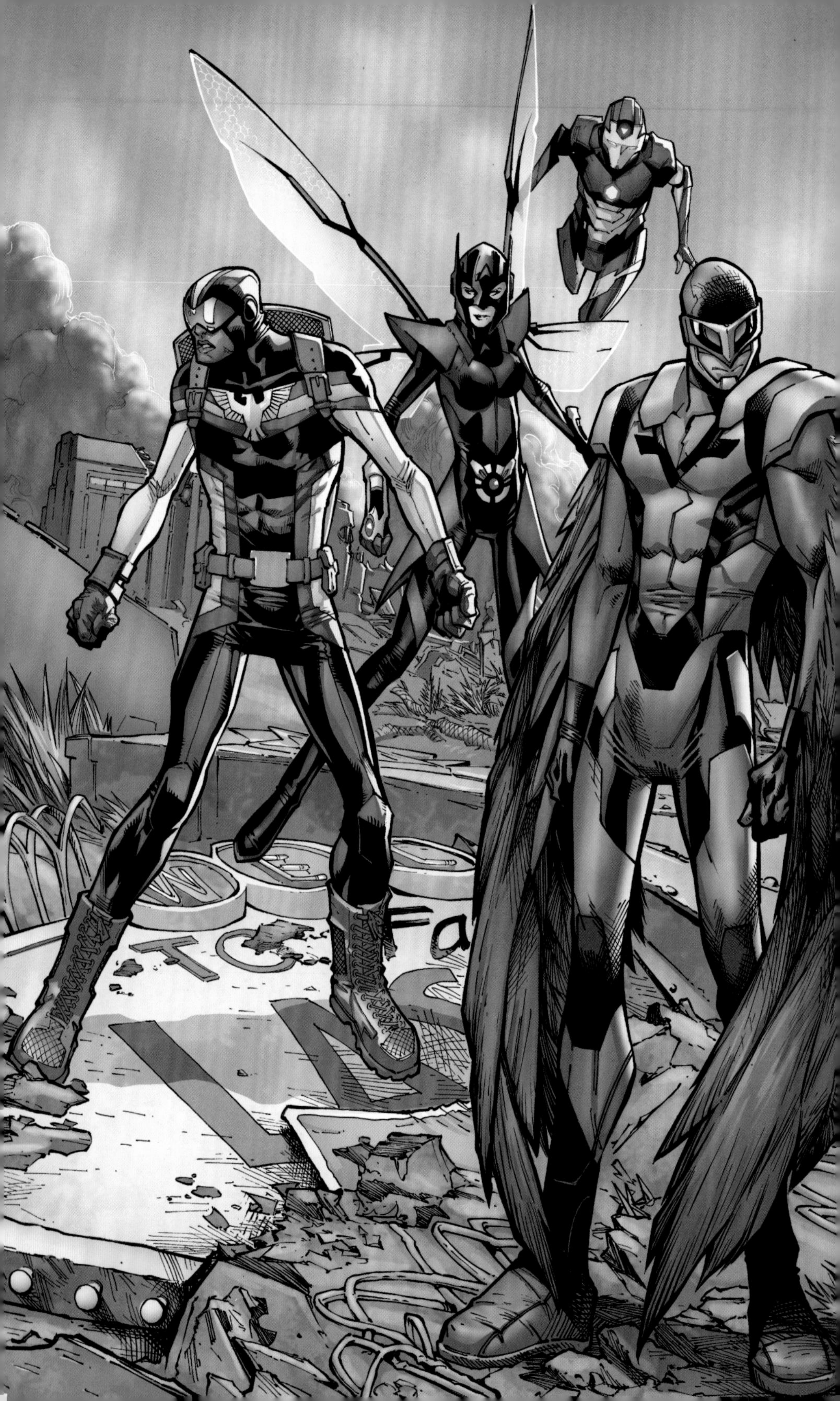

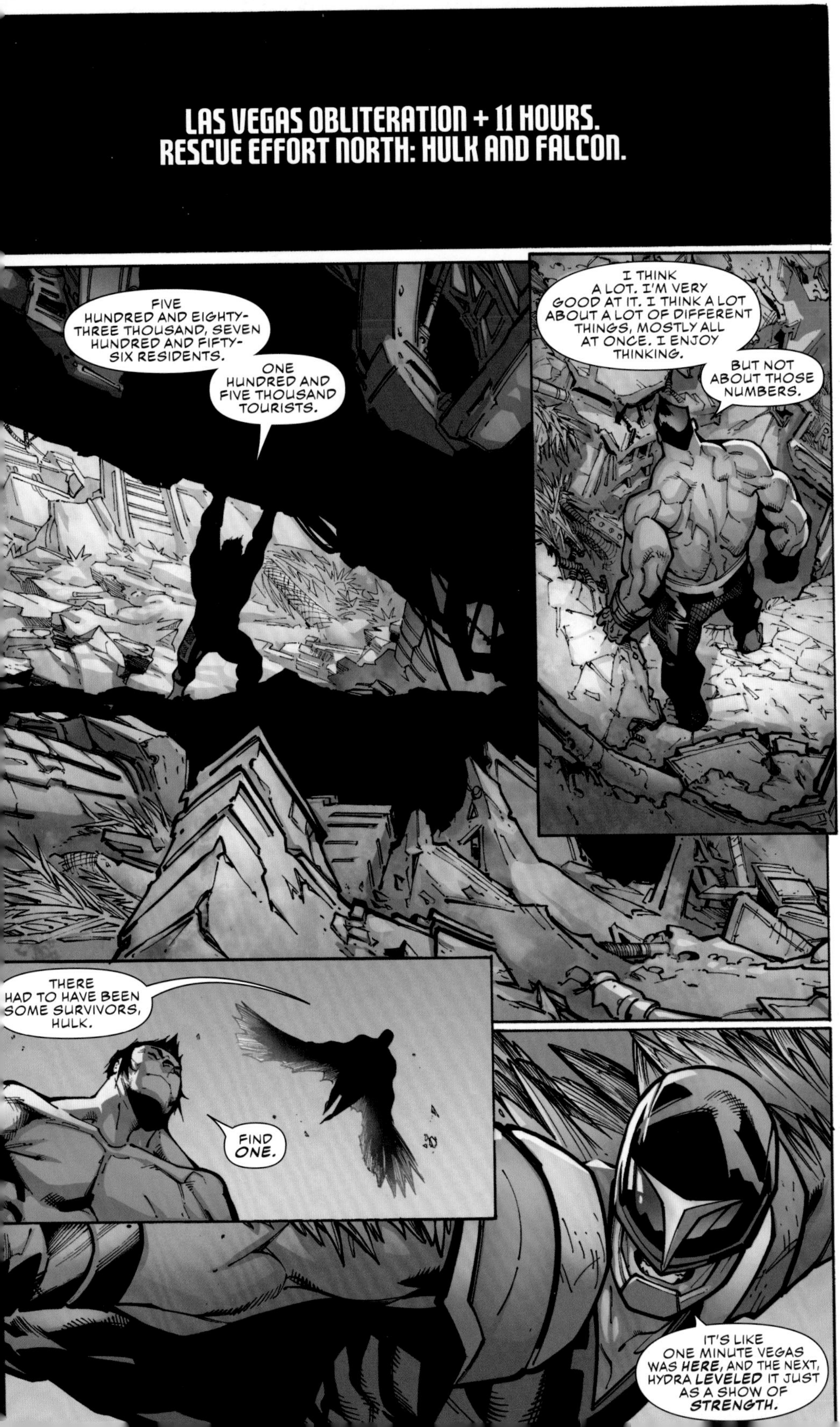
LAS VEGAS OBLITERATION + 11 HOURS.
RESCUE EFFORT NORTH: HULK AND FALCON.
FIVE HUNDRED AND EIGHTY-THREE THOUSAND, SEVEN HUNDRED AND FIFTY-SIX RESIDENTS.
ONE HUNDRED AND FIVE THOUSAND TOURISTS.
I THINK A LOT. I'M VERY GOOD AT IT. I THINK A LOT ABOUT A LOT OF DIFFERENT THINGS, MOSTLY ALL AT ONCE. I ENJOY THINKING.
BUT NOT ABOUT THOSE NUMBERS.
THERE HAD TO HAVE BEEN SOME SURVIVORS, HULK.
FIND *ONE.*
IT'S LIKE ONE MINUTE VEGAS WAS *HERE*, AND THE NEXT, HYDRA *LEVELED* IT JUST AS A SHOW OF *STRENGTH.*

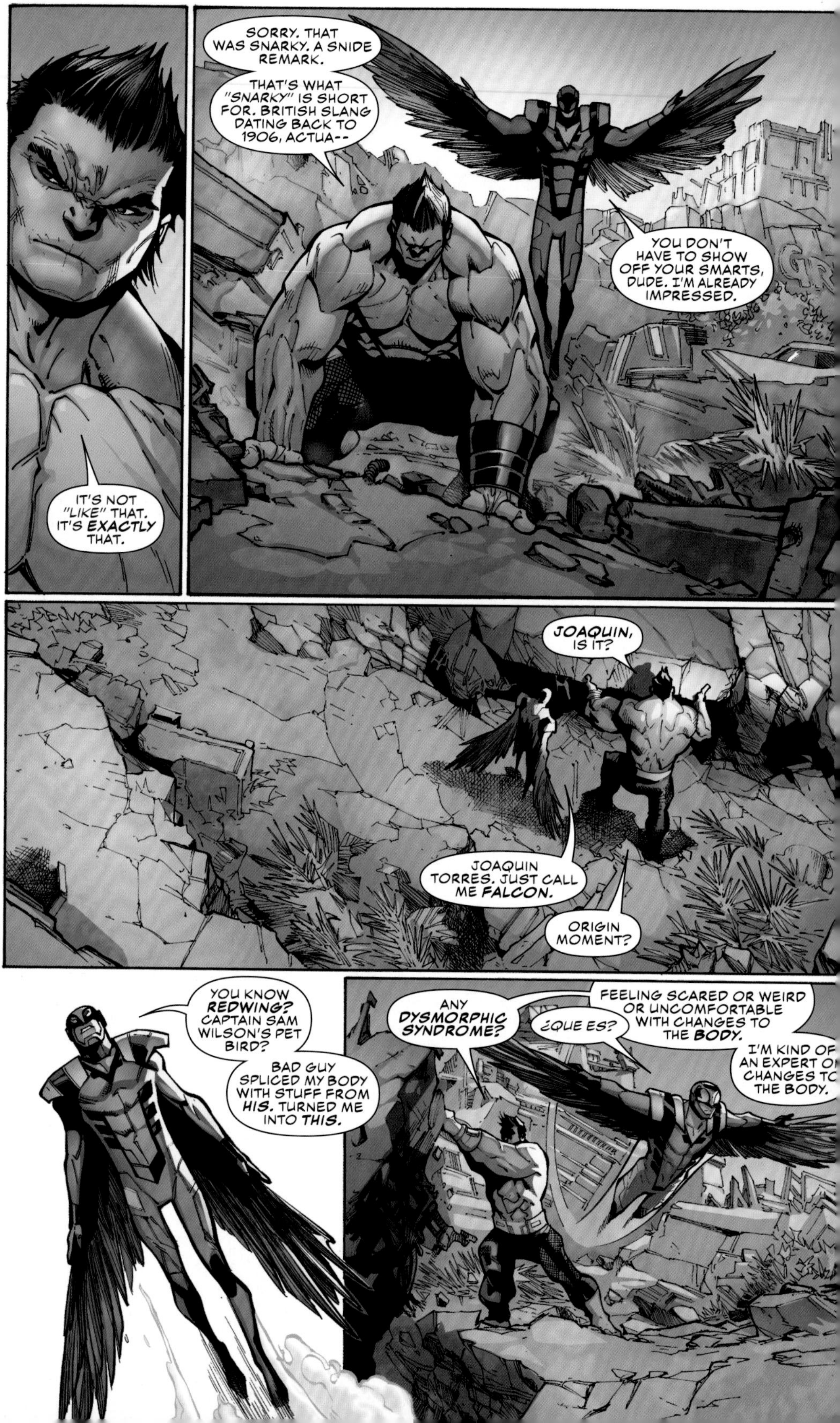
SORRY. THAT WAS SNARKY. A SNIDE REMARK.
THAT'S WHAT "SNARKY" IS SHORT FOR. BRITISH SLANG DATING BACK TO 1906, ACTUA--
IT'S NOT "LIKE" THAT. IT'S EXACTLY THAT.
YOU DON'T HAVE TO SHOW OFF YOUR SMARTS, DUDE. I'M ALREADY IMPRESSED.
JOAQUIN, IS IT?
JOAQUIN TORRES. JUST CALL ME FALCON.
ORIGIN MOMENT?
YOU KNOW REDWING? CAPTAIN SAM WILSON'S PET BIRD?
BAD GUY SPLICED MY BODY WITH STUFF FROM HIS. TURNED ME INTO THIS.
ANY DYSMORPHIC SYNDROME?
¿QUE ES?
FEELING SCARED OR WEIRD OR UNCOMFORTABLE WITH CHANGES TO THE BODY.
I'M KIND OF AN EXPERT ON CHANGES TO THE BODY.

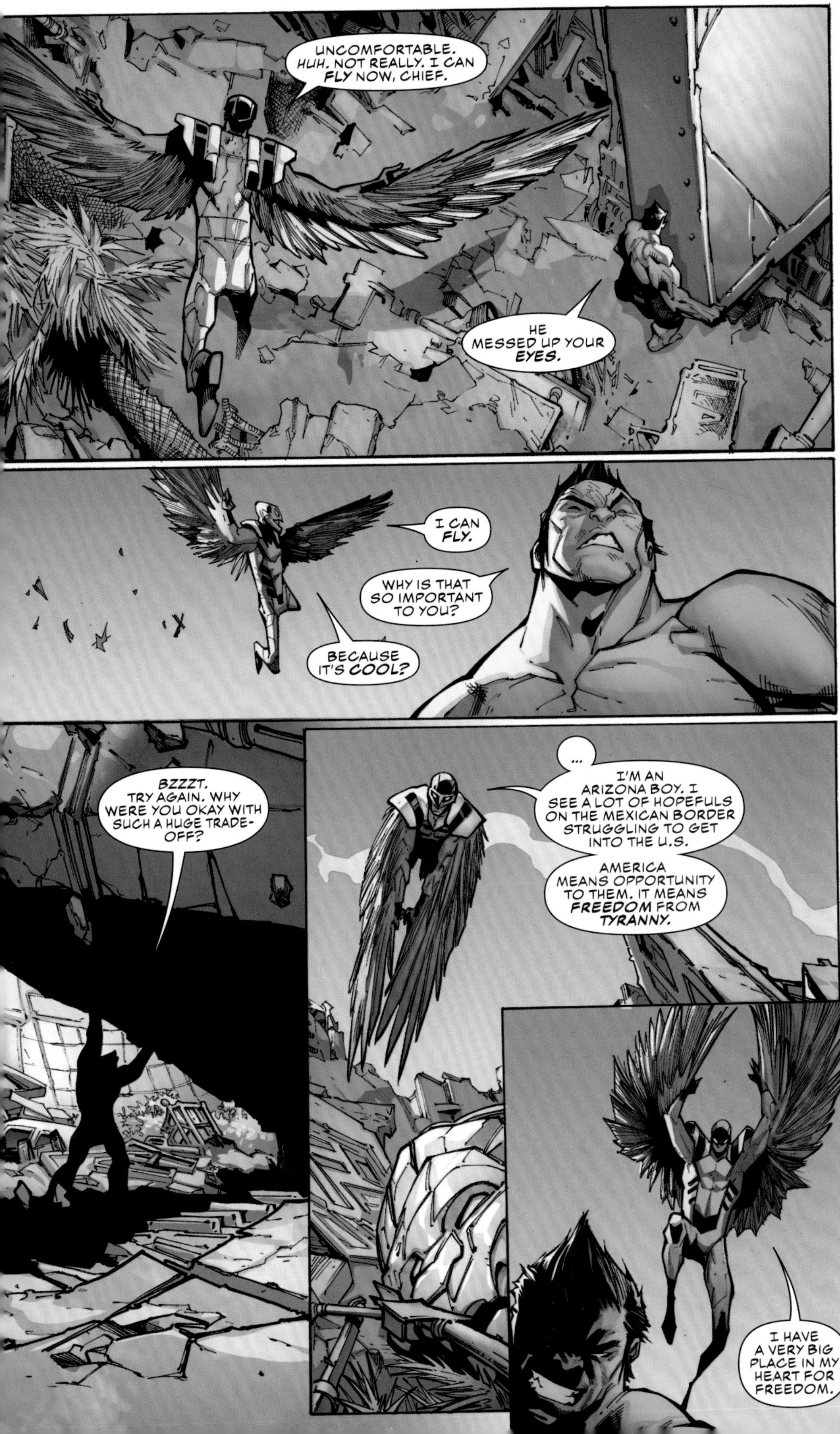
UNCOMFORTABLE. HUH. NOT REALLY. I CAN FLY NOW, CHIEF.
HE MESSED UP YOUR EYES.
I CAN FLY.
WHY IS THAT SO IMPORTANT TO YOU?
BECAUSE IT'S COOL?
BZZZT. TRY AGAIN. WHY WERE YOU OKAY WITH SUCH A HUGE TRADE-OFF?
...
I'M AN ARIZONA BOY. I SEE A LOT OF HOPEFULS ON THE MEXICAN BORDER STRUGGLING TO GET INTO THE U.S.
AMERICA MEANS OPPORTUNITY TO THEM. IT MEANS FREEDOM FROM TYRANNY.
I HAVE A VERY BIG PLACE IN MY HEART FOR FREEDOM.

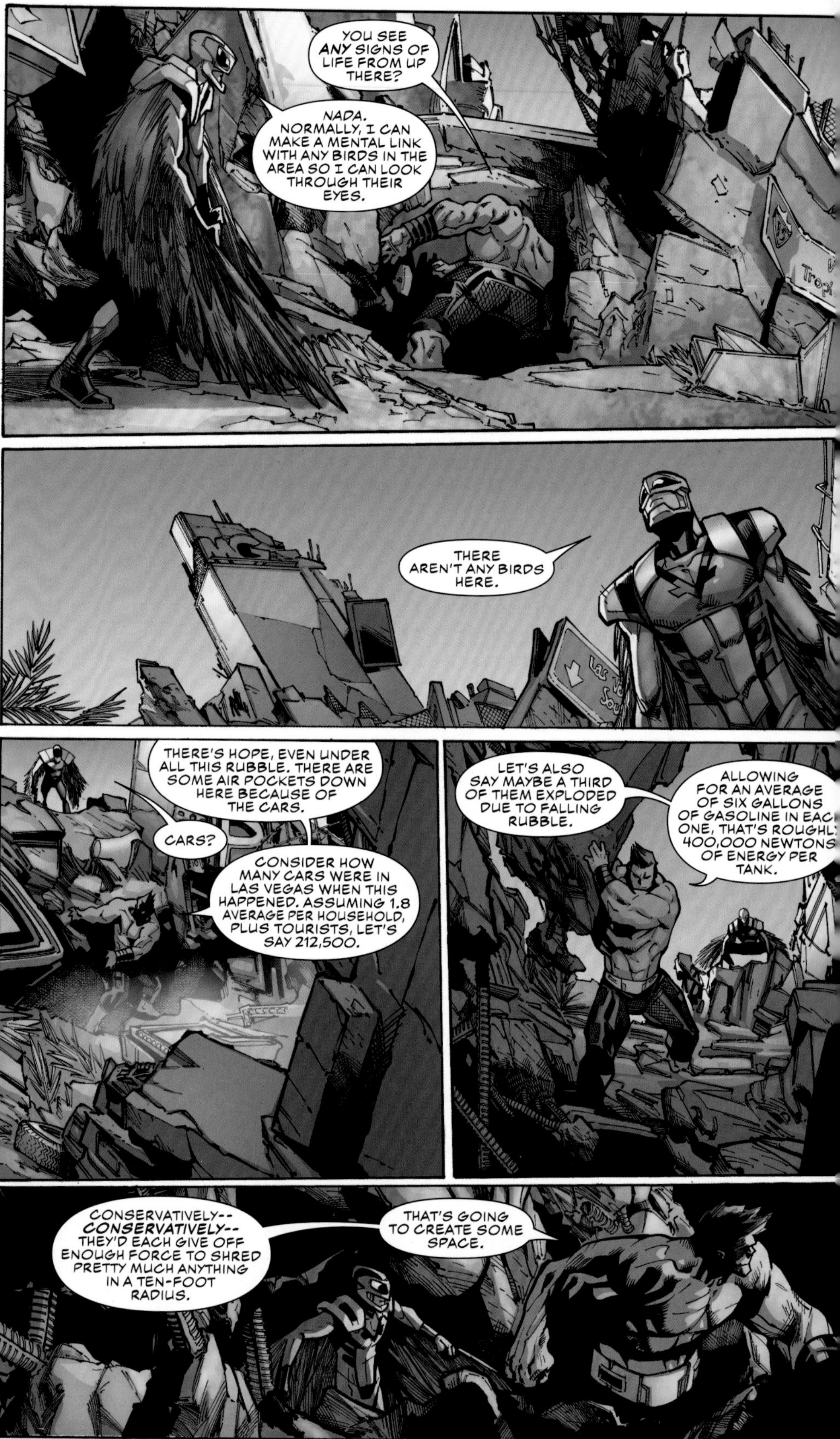
YOU SEE ANY SIGNS OF LIFE FROM UP THERE?
NADA. NORMALLY, I CAN MAKE A MENTAL LINK WITH ANY BIRDS IN THE AREA SO I CAN LOOK THROUGH THEIR EYES.
THERE AREN'T ANY BIRDS HERE.
THERE'S HOPE, EVEN UNDER ALL THIS RUBBLE. THERE ARE SOME AIR POCKETS DOWN HERE BECAUSE OF THE CARS.
CARS?
CONSIDER HOW MANY CARS WERE IN LAS VEGAS WHEN THIS HAPPENED. ASSUMING 1.8 AVERAGE PER HOUSEHOLD, PLUS TOURISTS, LET'S SAY 212,500.
LET'S ALSO SAY MAYBE A THIRD OF THEM EXPLODED DUE TO FALLING RUBBLE.
ALLOWING FOR AN AVERAGE OF SIX GALLONS OF GASOLINE IN EAC ONE, THAT'S ROUGHL 400,000 NEWTONS OF ENERGY PER TANK.
CONSERVATIVELY-- CONSERVATIVELY-- THEY'D EACH GIVE OFF ENOUGH FORCE TO SHRED PRETTY MUCH ANYTHING IN A TEN-FOOT RADIUS.
THAT'S GOING TO CREATE SOME SPACE.

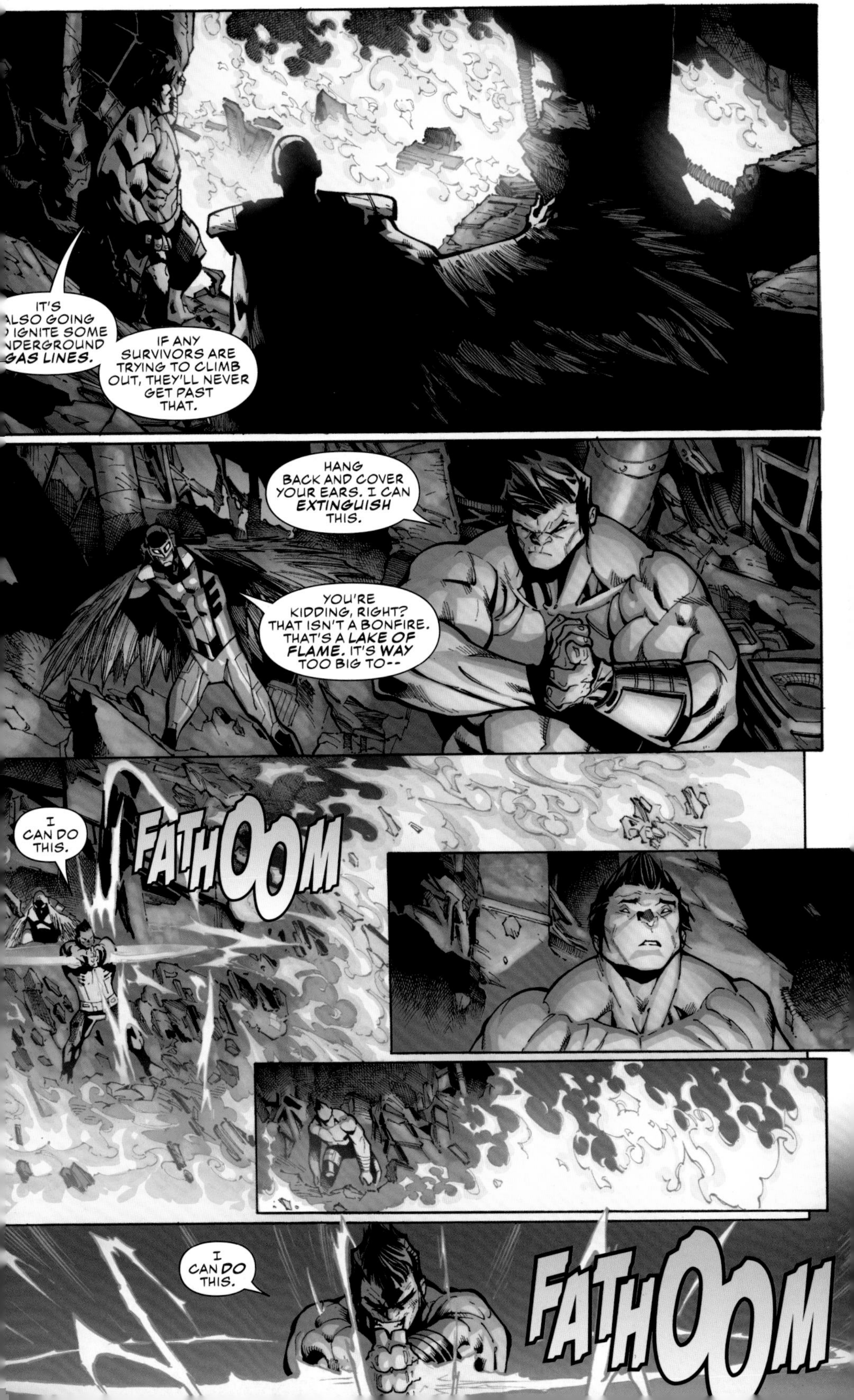
IT'S ALSO GOING TO IGNITE SOME UNDERGROUND GAS LINES.
IF ANY SURVIVORS ARE TRYING TO CLIMB OUT, THEY'LL NEVER GET PAST THAT.
HANG BACK AND COVER YOUR EARS. I CAN EXTINGUISH THIS.
YOU'RE KIDDING, RIGHT? THAT ISN'T A BONFIRE. THAT'S A LAKE OF FLAME. IT'S WAY TOO BIG TO--
I CAN DO THIS.
FATHOOM
I CAN DO THIS.
FATHOOM

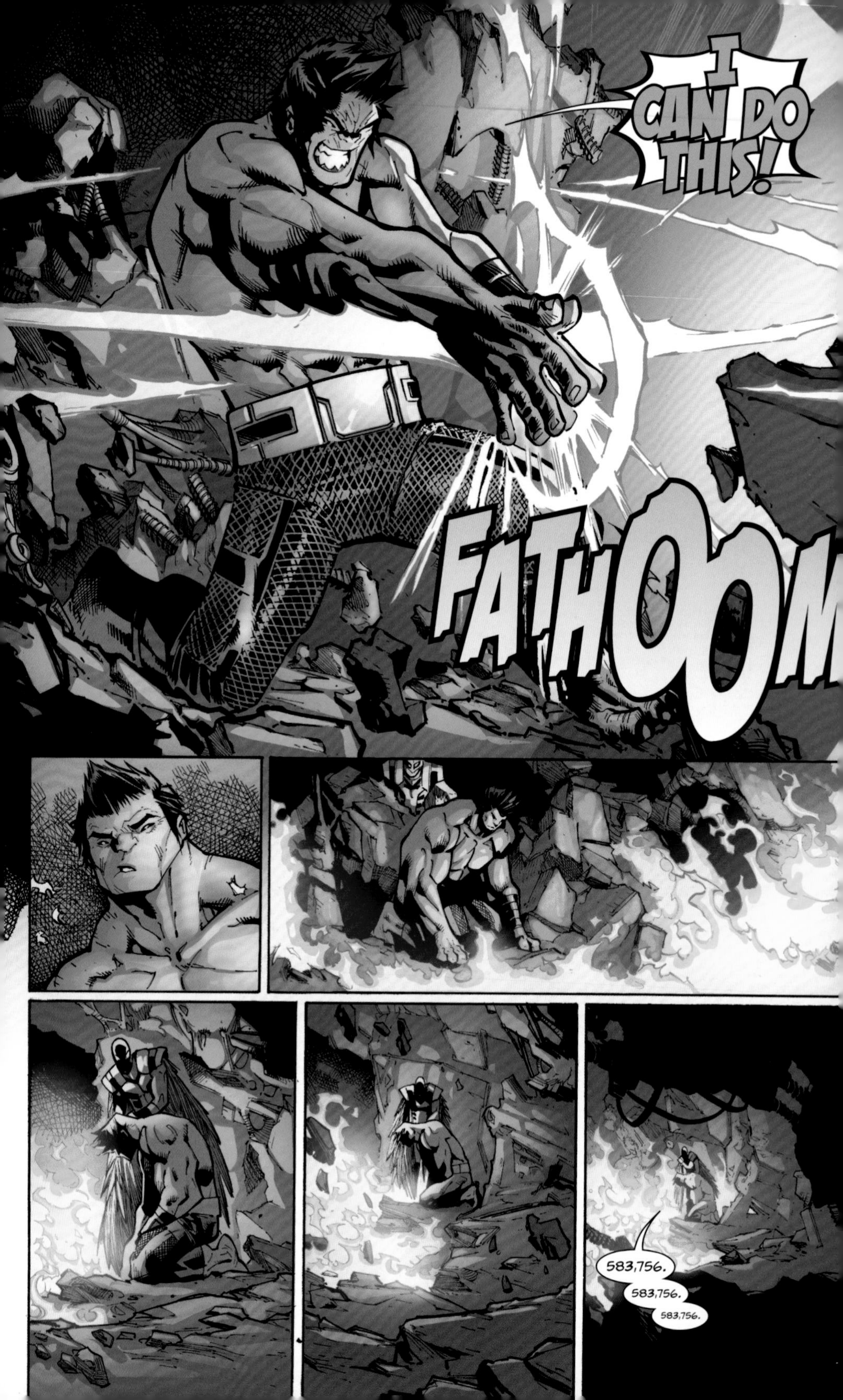
I CAN DO THIS!
FATHOOM
583,756.
583,756.
583,756.

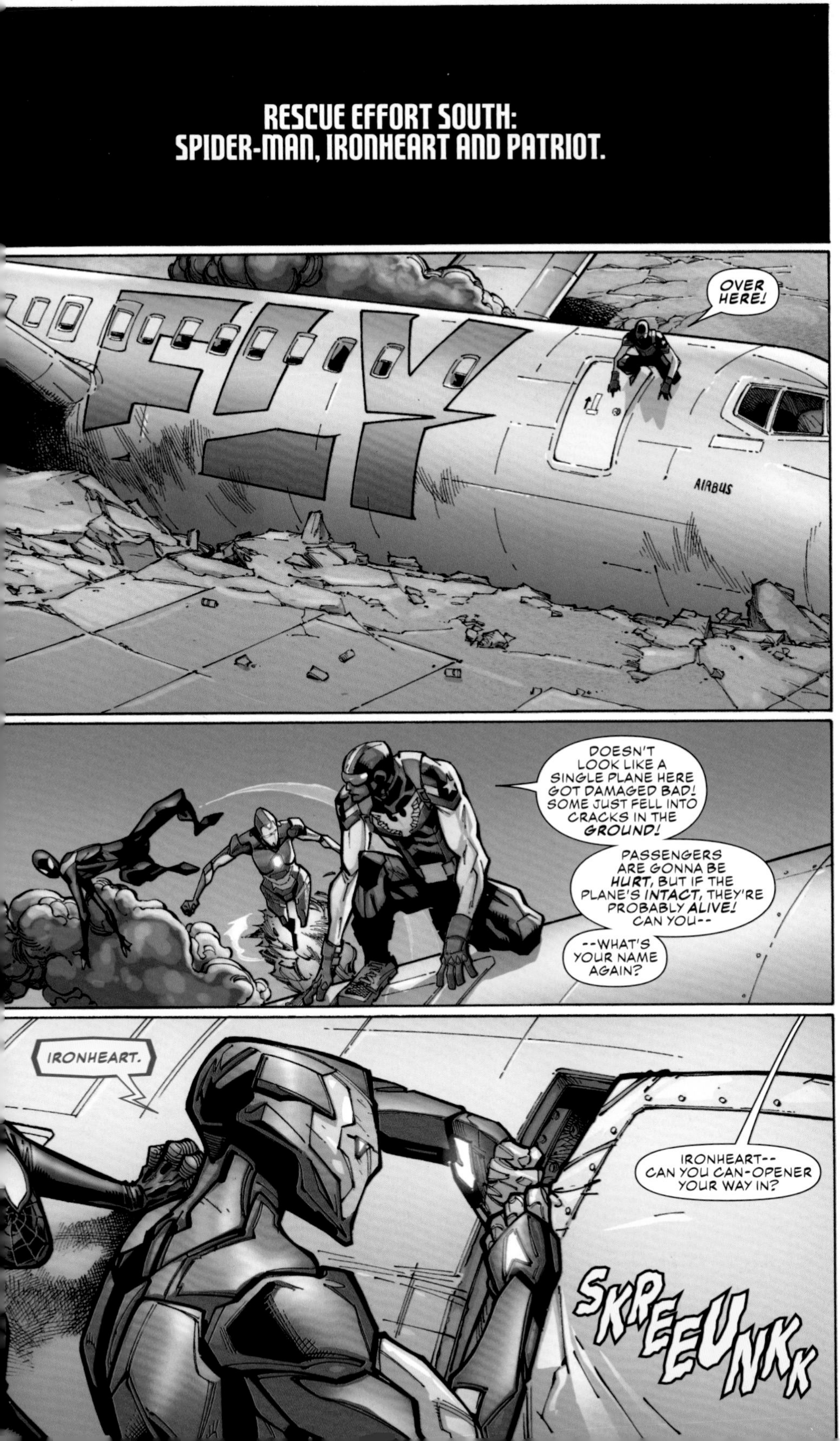
RESCUE EFFORT SOUTH: SPIDER-MAN, IRONHEART AND PATRIOT.
OVER HERE!
AIRBUS
DOESN'T LOOK LIKE A SINGLE PLANE HERE GOT DAMAGED BAD! SOME JUST FELL INTO CRACKS IN THE GROUND!
PASSENGERS ARE GONNA BE HURT, BUT IF THE PLANE'S INTACT, THEY'RE PROBABLY ALIVE! CAN YOU--
--WHAT'S YOUR NAME AGAIN?
IRONHEART.
IRONHEART-- CAN YOU CAN-OPENER YOUR WAY IN?
SKREEUNKK

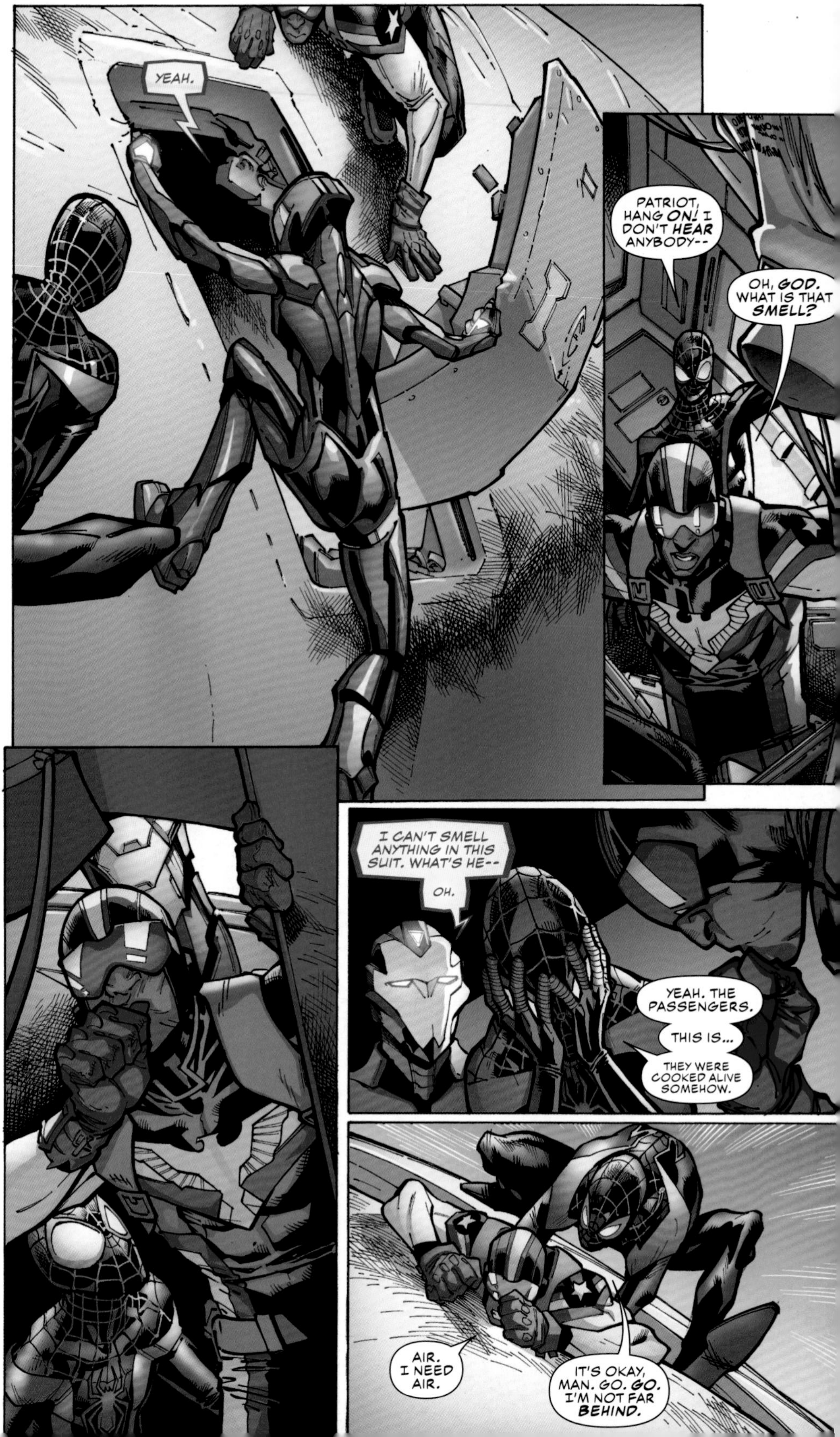
YEAH.
PATRIOT, HANG ON! I DON'T HEAR ANYBODY--
OH, GOD. WHAT IS THAT SMELL?
I CAN'T SMELL ANYTHING IN THIS SUIT. WHAT'S HE--
OH.
YEAH. THE PASSENGERS.
THIS IS...
THEY WERE COOKED ALIVE SOMEHOW.
AIR. I NEED AIR.
IT'S OKAY, MAN. GO. GO. I'M NOT FAR BEHIND.

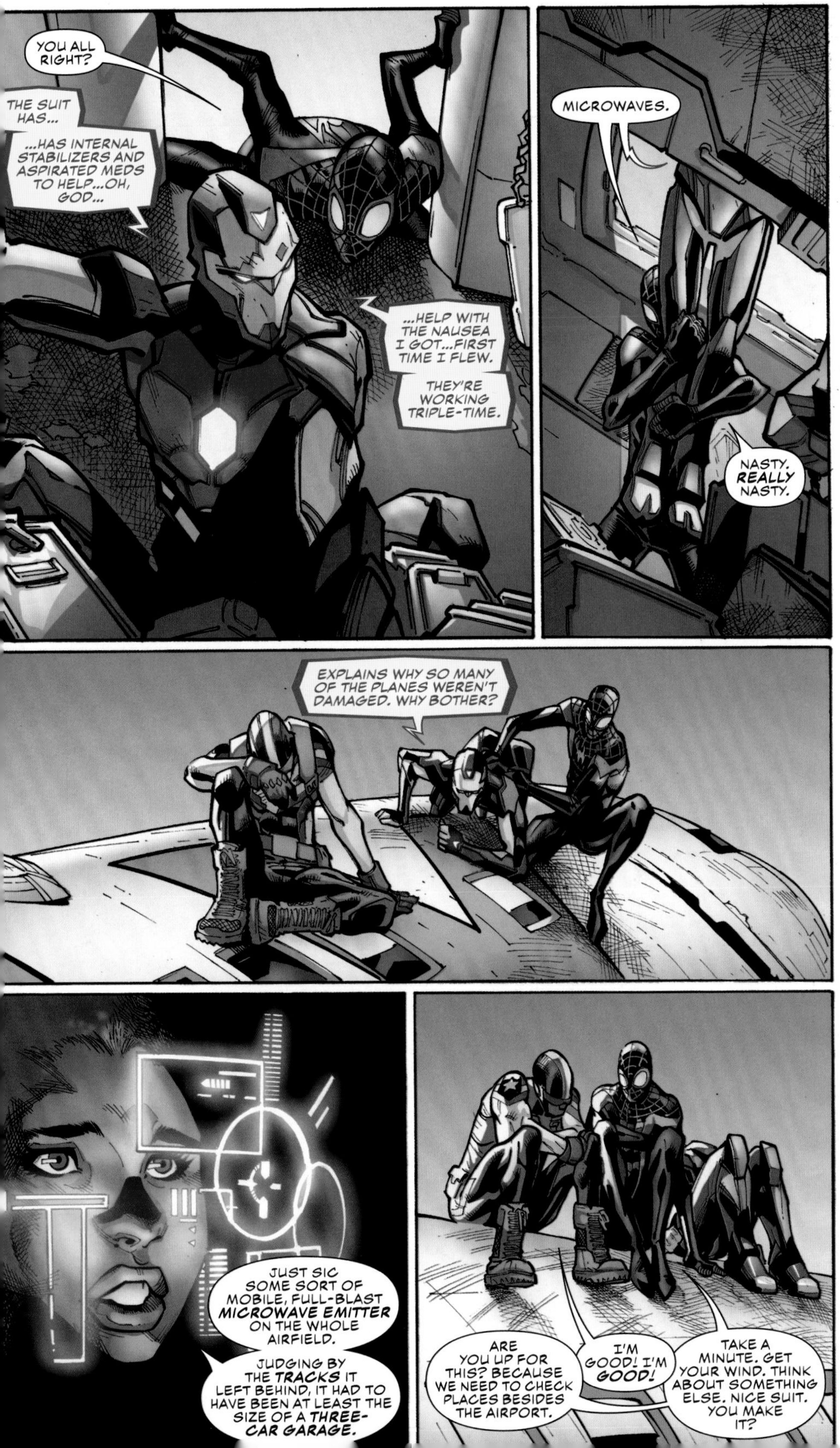

YOU ALL RIGHT?
THE SUIT HAS...
...HAS INTERNAL STABILIZERS AND ASPIRATED MEDS TO HELP...OH, GOD...
...HELP WITH THE NAUSEA I GOT...FIRST TIME I FLEW.
THEY'RE WORKING TRIPLE-TIME.
MICROWAVES.
NASTY. **REALLY** NASTY.
EXPLAINS WHY SO MANY OF THE PLANES WEREN'T DAMAGED. WHY BOTHER?
JUST SIC SOME SORT OF MOBILE, FULL-BLAST **MICROWAVE EMITTER** ON THE WHOLE AIRFIELD.
JUDGING BY THE **TRACKS** IT LEFT BEHIND, IT HAD TO HAVE BEEN AT LEAST THE SIZE OF A **THREE-CAR GARAGE.**
ARE YOU UP FOR THIS? BECAUSE WE NEED TO CHECK PLACES BESIDES THE AIRPORT.
I'M GOOD! I'M **GOOD!**
TAKE A MINUTE. GET YOUR WIND. THINK ABOUT SOMETHING ELSE. NICE SUIT. YOU MAKE IT?

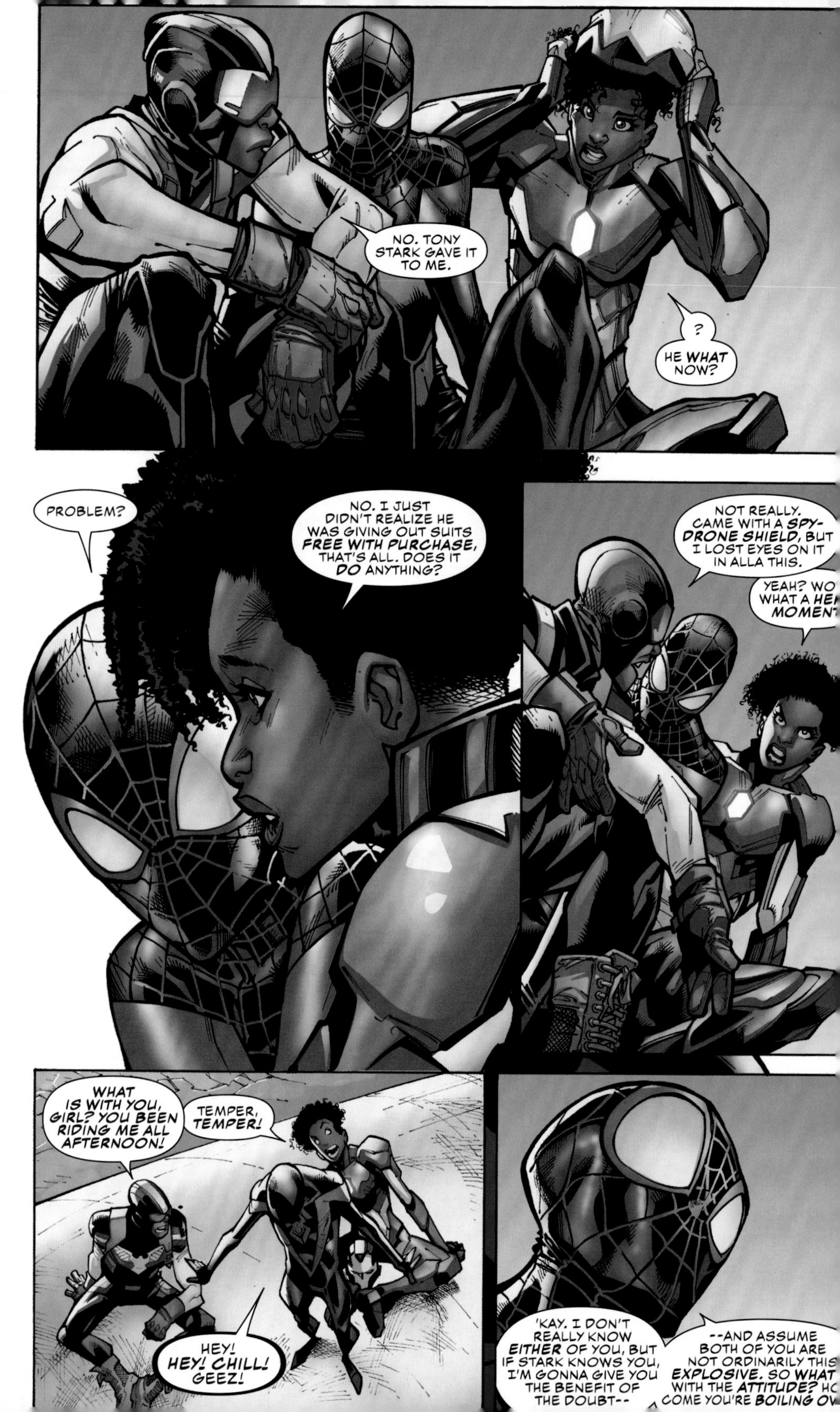
NO. TONY STARK GAVE IT TO ME.
?
HE WHAT NOW?
PROBLEM?
NO. I JUST DIDN'T REALIZE HE WAS GIVING OUT SUITS FREE WITH PURCHASE, THAT'S ALL. DOES IT DO ANYTHING?
NOT REALLY. CAME WITH A SPY-DRONE SHIELD, BUT I LOST EYES ON IT IN ALLA THIS.
WHAT IS WITH YOU, GIRL? YOU BEEN RIDING ME ALL AFTERNOON!
TEMPER, TEMPER!
HEY! HEY! CHILL! GEEZ!
'KAY. I DON'T REALLY KNOW EITHER OF YOU, BUT IF STARK KNOWS YOU, I'M GONNA GIVE YOU THE BENEFIT OF THE DOUBT--
--AND ASSUME BOTH OF YOU ARE NOT ORDINARILY THIS EXPLOSIVE. SO WHAT WITH THE ATTITUDE?

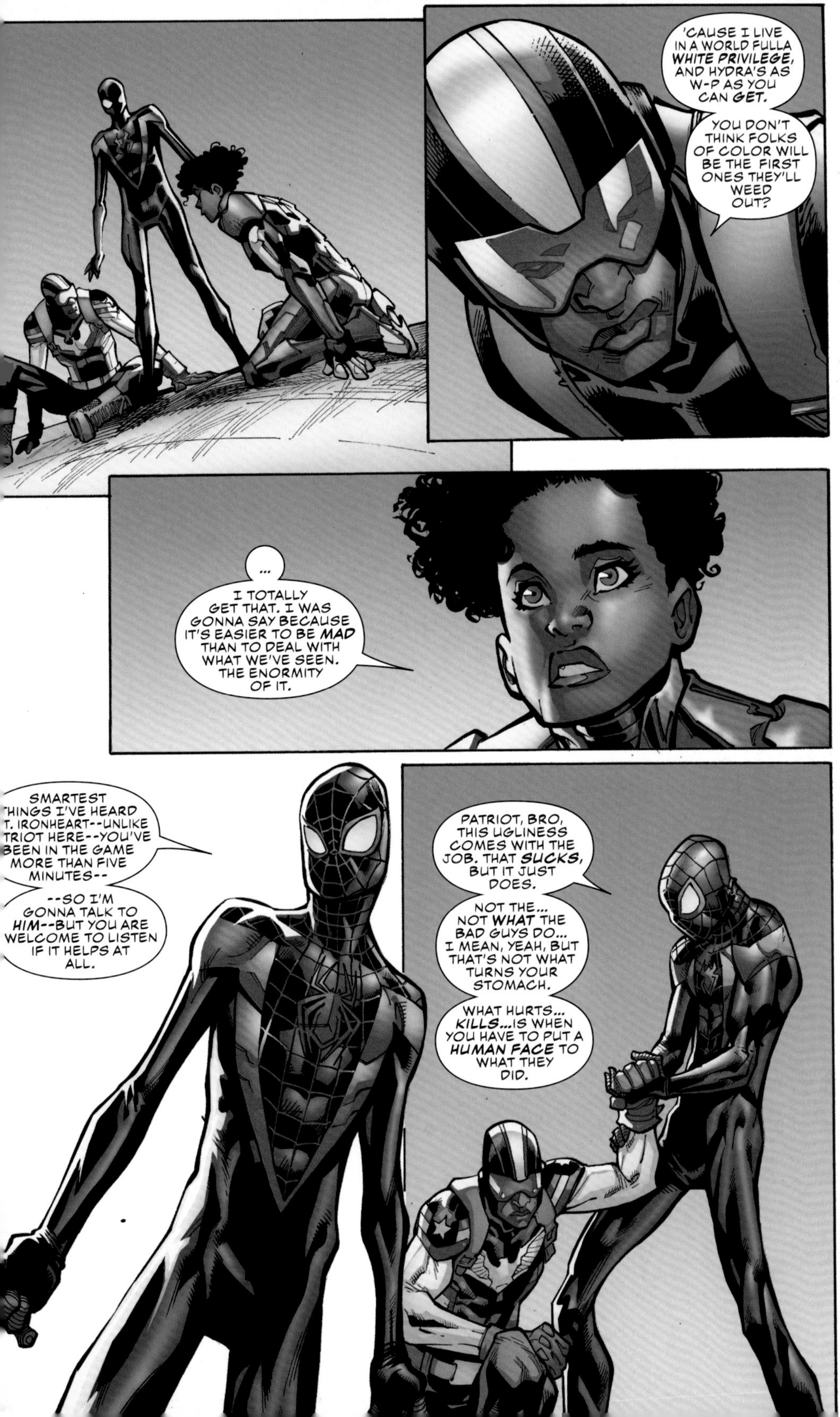
'CAUSE I LIVE IN A WORLD FULLA WHITE PRIVILEGE, AND HYDRA'S AS W-P AS YOU CAN GET.
YOU DON'T THINK FOLKS OF COLOR WILL BE THE FIRST ONES THEY'LL WEED OUT?
...
I TOTALLY GET THAT. I WAS GONNA SAY BECAUSE IT'S EASIER TO BE MAD THAN TO DEAL WITH WHAT WE'VE SEEN. THE ENORMITY OF IT.
SMARTEST THINGS I'VE HEARD T. IRONHEART--UNLIKE TRIOT HERE--YOU'VE BEEN IN THE GAME MORE THAN FIVE MINUTES--
--SO I'M GONNA TALK TO HIM--BUT YOU ARE WELCOME TO LISTEN IF IT HELPS AT ALL.
PATRIOT, BRO, THIS UGLINESS COMES WITH THE JOB. THAT SUCKS, BUT IT JUST DOES.
NOT THE... NOT WHAT THE BAD GUYS DO... I MEAN, YEAH, BUT THAT'S NOT WHAT TURNS YOUR STOMACH.
WHAT HURTS... KILLS...IS WHEN YOU HAVE TO PUT A HUMAN FACE TO WHAT THEY DID.

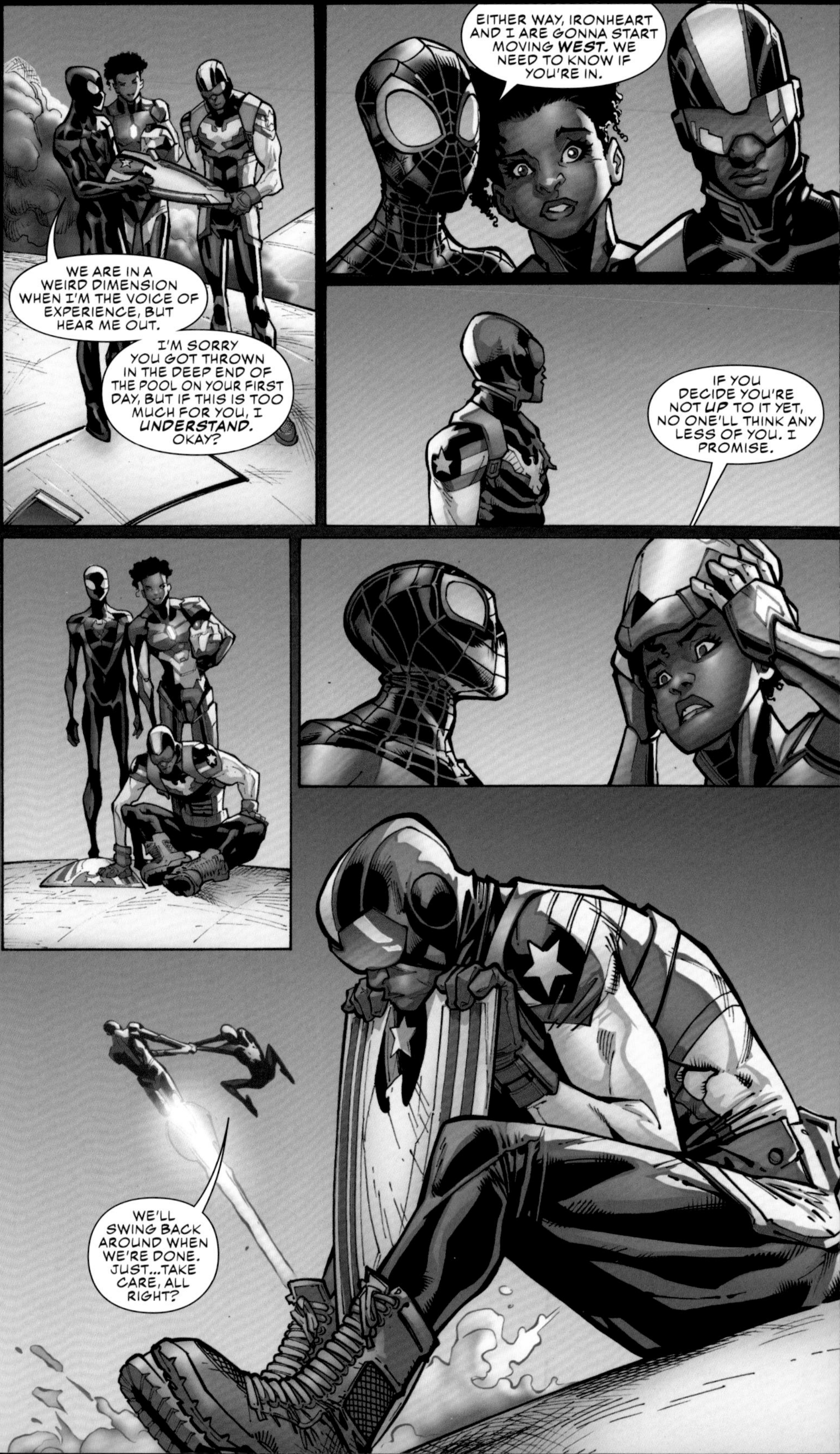
WE ARE IN A WEIRD DIMENSION WHEN I'M THE VOICE OF EXPERIENCE, BUT HEAR ME OUT.
I'M SORRY YOU GOT THROWN IN THE DEEP END OF THE POOL ON YOUR FIRST DAY, BUT IF THIS IS TOO MUCH FOR YOU, I UNDERSTAND. OKAY?
EITHER WAY, IRONHEART AND I ARE GONNA START MOVING WEST. WE NEED TO KNOW IF YOU'RE IN.
IF YOU DECIDE YOU'RE NOT UP TO IT YET, NO ONE'LL THINK ANY LESS OF YOU. I PROMISE.
WE'LL SWING BACK AROUND WHEN WE'RE DONE. JUST...TAKE CARE, ALL RIGHT?

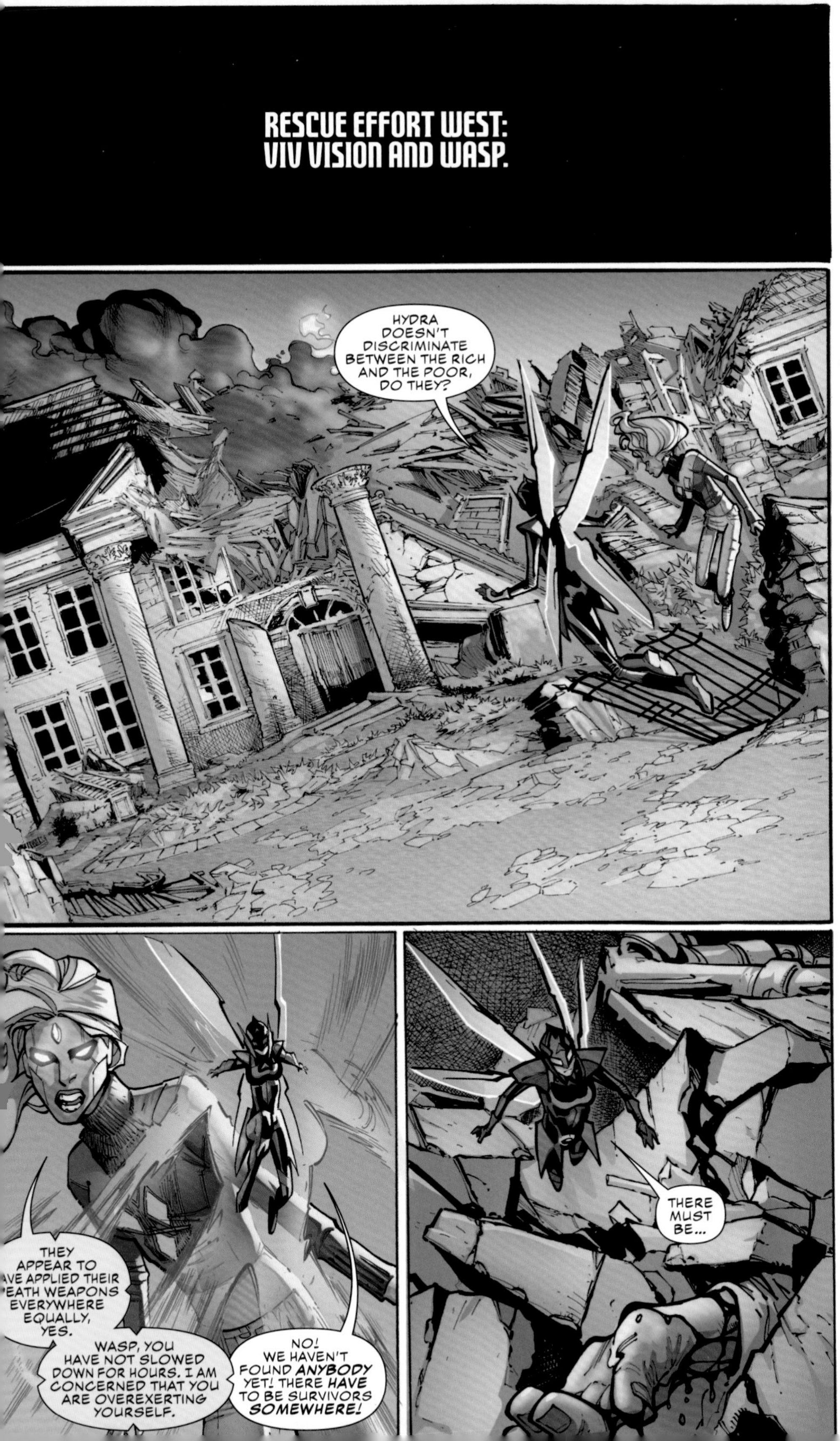
RESCUE EFFORT WEST:
VIV VISION AND WASP.
HYDRA DOESN'T DISCRIMINATE BETWEEN THE RICH AND THE POOR, DO THEY?
THEY APPEAR TO AVE APPLIED THEIR EATH WEAPONS EVERYWHERE EQUALLY, YES.
WASP, YOU HAVE NOT SLOWED DOWN FOR HOURS. I AM CONCERNED THAT YOU ARE OVEREXERTING YOURSELF.
NO! WE HAVEN'T FOUND ANYBODY YET! THERE HAVE TO BE SURVIVORS SOMEWHERE!
THERE MUST BE...

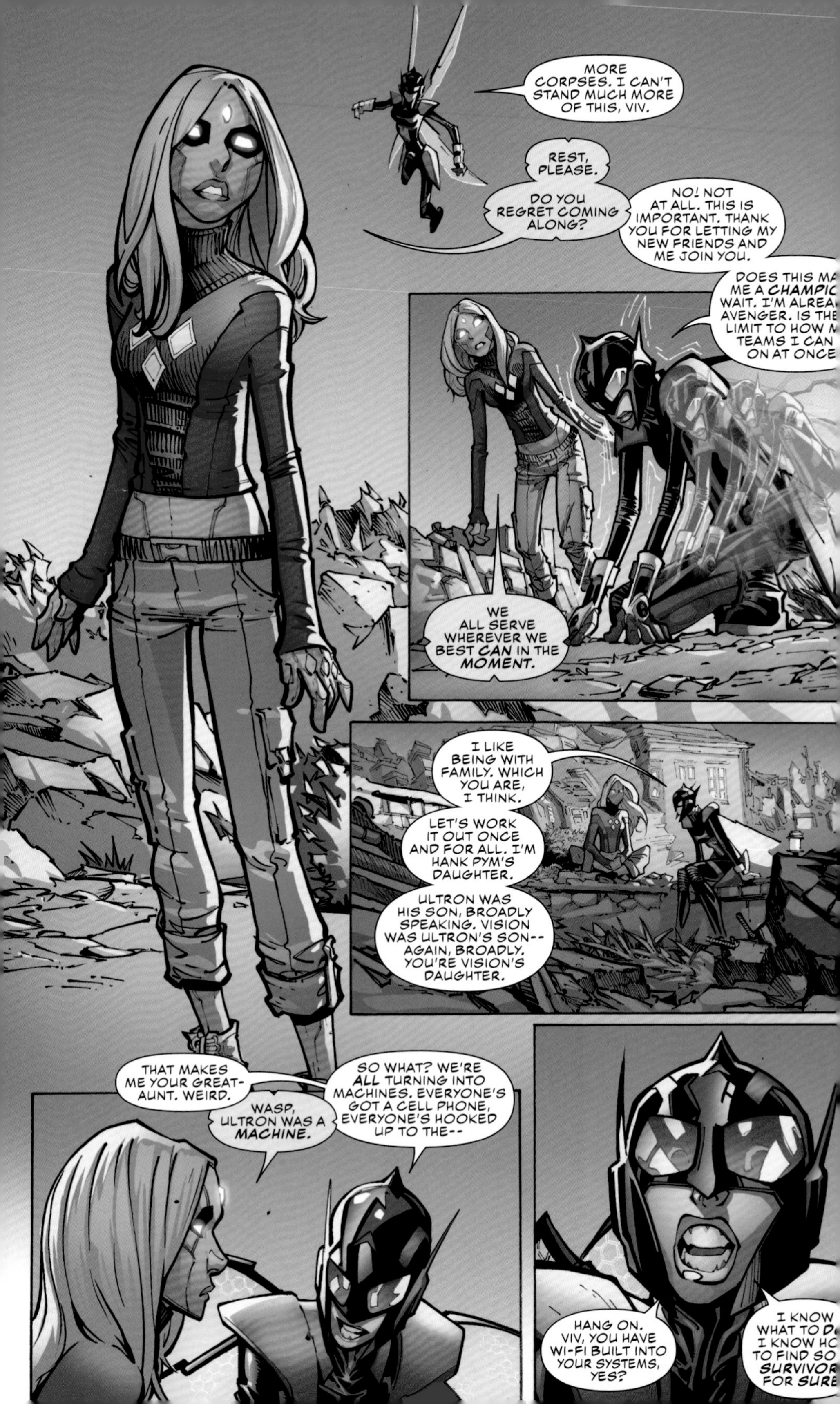
MORE CORPSES. I CAN'T STAND MUCH MORE OF THIS, VIV.
REST, PLEASE.
DO YOU REGRET COMING ALONG?
NO! NOT AT ALL. THIS IS IMPORTANT. THANK YOU FOR LETTING MY NEW FRIENDS AND ME JOIN YOU.
WE ALL SERVE WHEREVER WE BEST CAN IN THE MOMENT.
I LIKE BEING WITH FAMILY. WHICH YOU ARE, I THINK.
LET'S WORK IT OUT ONCE AND FOR ALL. I'M HANK PYM'S DAUGHTER.
ULTRON WAS HIS SON, BROADLY SPEAKING. VISION WAS ULTRON'S SON-- AGAIN, BROADLY. YOU'RE VISION'S DAUGHTER.
THAT MAKES ME YOUR GREAT-AUNT. WEIRD.
WASP, ULTRON WAS A MACHINE.
SO WHAT? WE'RE ALL TURNING INTO MACHINES. EVERYONE'S GOT A CELL PHONE, EVERYONE'S HOOKED UP TO THE--
HANG ON. VIV, YOU HAVE WI-FI BUILT INTO YOUR SYSTEMS, YES?

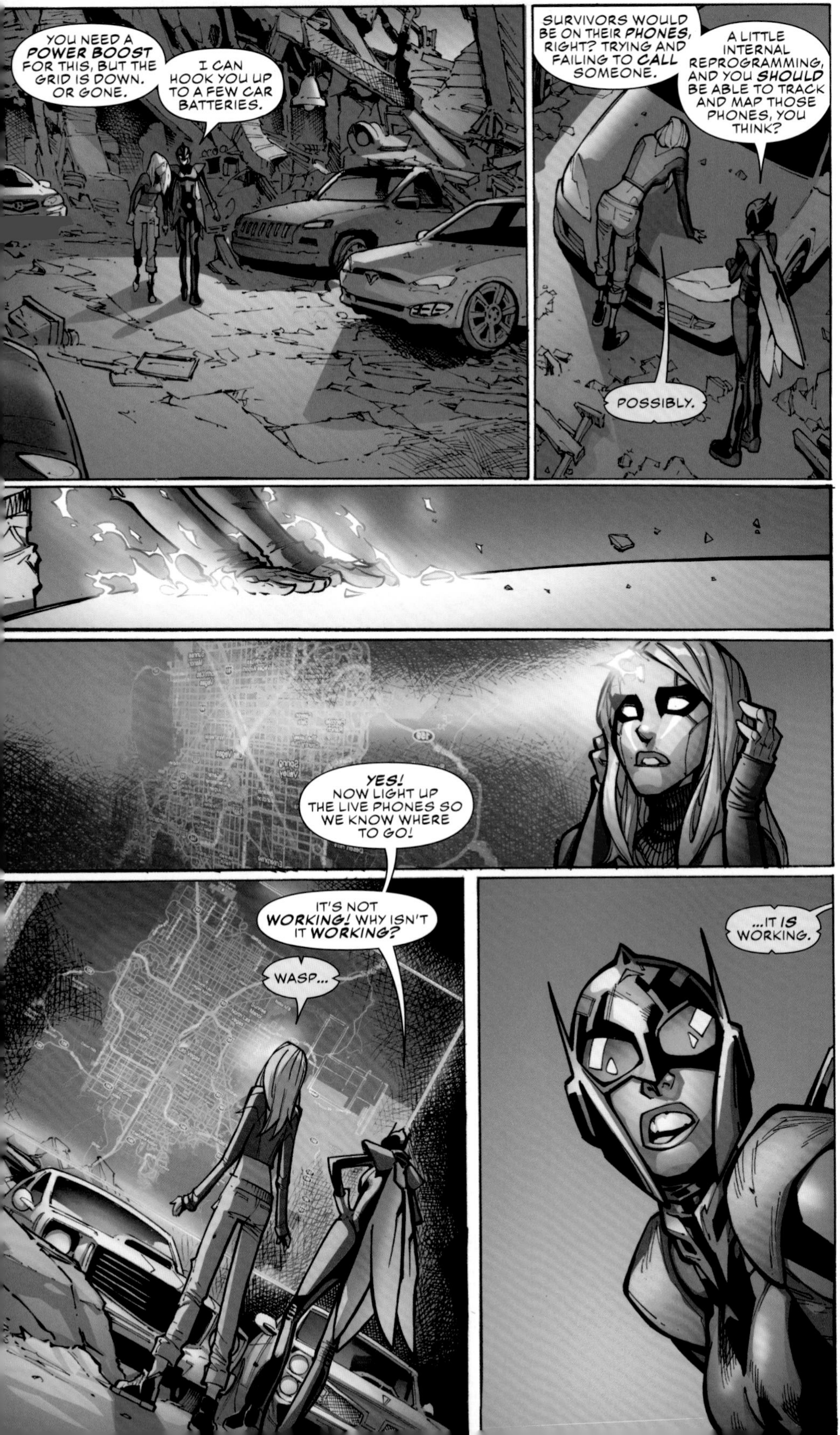
YOU NEED A POWER BOOST FOR THIS, BUT THE GRID IS DOWN. OR GONE.
I CAN HOOK YOU UP TO A FEW CAR BATTERIES.
SURVIVORS WOULD BE ON THEIR PHONES, RIGHT? TRYING AND FAILING TO CALL SOMEONE.
A LITTLE INTERNAL REPROGRAMMING, AND YOU SHOULD BE ABLE TO TRACK AND MAP THOSE PHONES, YOU THINK?
POSSIBLY.
YES! NOW LIGHT UP THE LIVE PHONES SO WE KNOW WHERE TO GO!
IT'S NOT WORKING! WHY ISN'T IT WORKING?
WASP...
...IT IS WORKING.

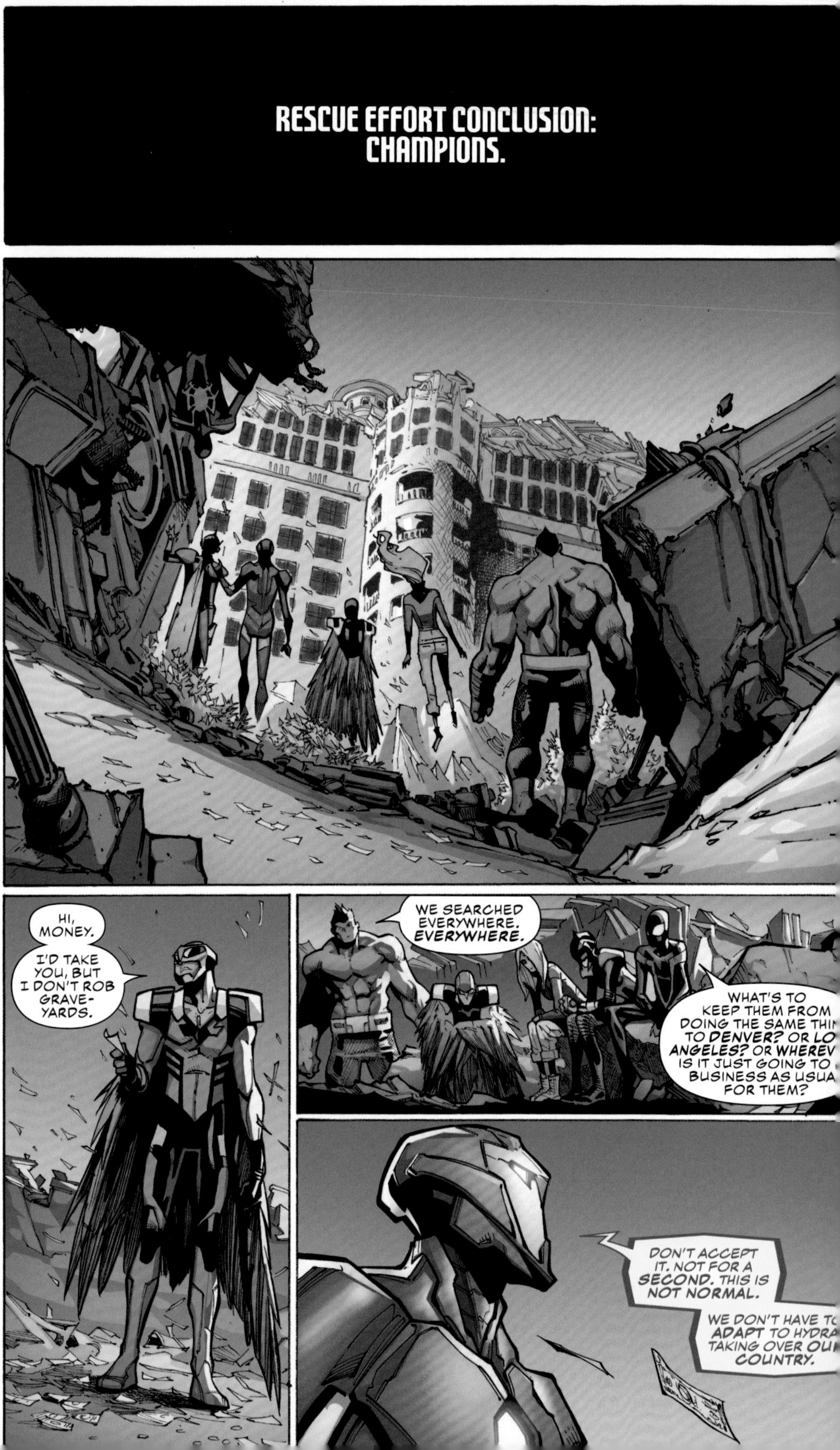
RESCUE EFFORT CONCLUSION: CHAMPIONS.
HI, MONEY.
I'D TAKE YOU, BUT I DON'T ROB GRAVE-YARDS.
WE SEARCHED EVERYWHERE. EVERYWHERE.
WHAT'S TO KEEP THEM FROM DOING THE SAME THI TO DENVER? OR LO ANGELES? OR WHEREV IS IT JUST GOING TO BUSINESS AS USUA FOR THEM?
DON'T ACCEPT IT. NOT FOR A SECOND. THIS IS NOT NORMAL.
WE DON'T HAVE TO ADAPT TO HYDRA TAKING OVER OU COUNTRY.

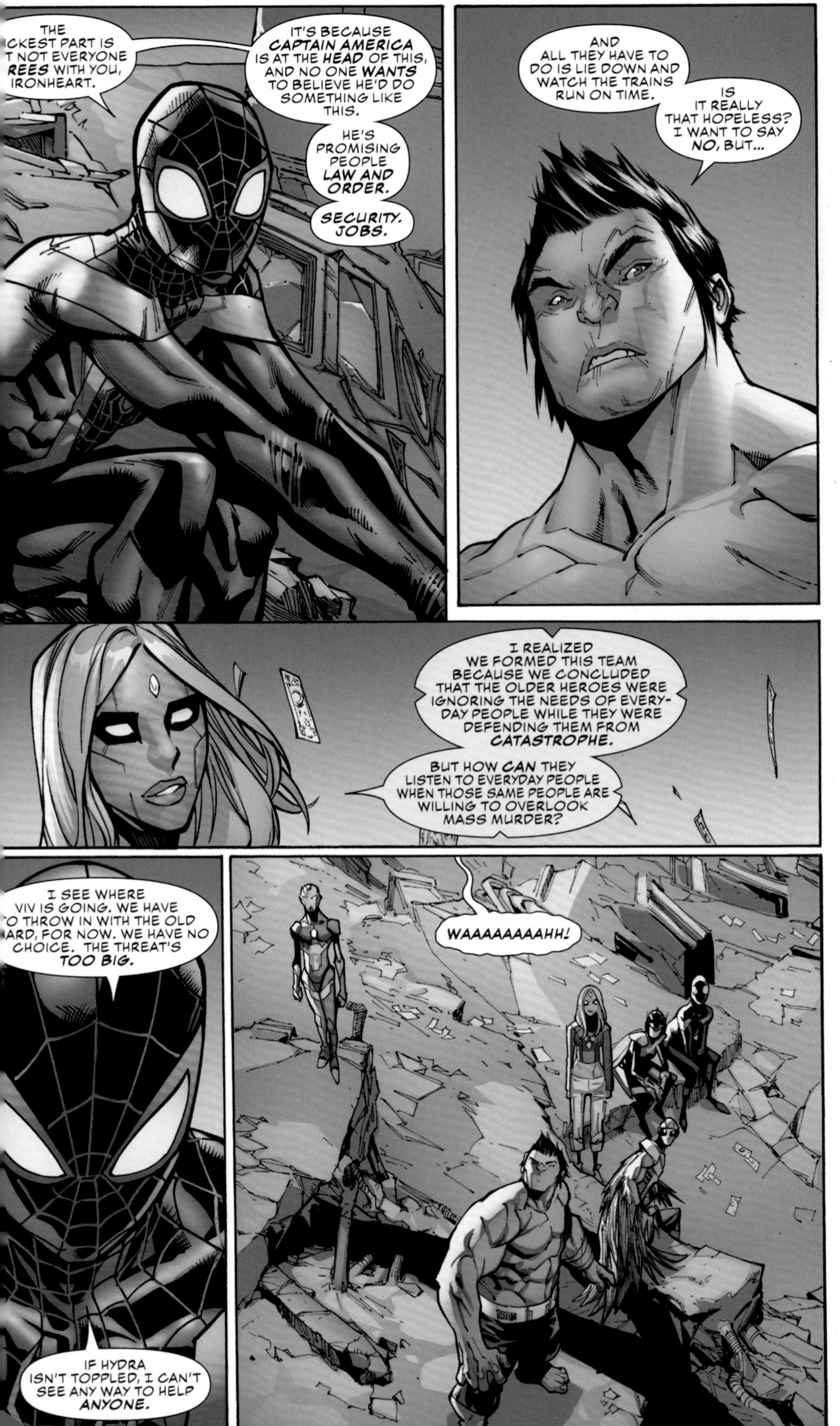
THE
CKEST PART IS
T NOT EVERYONE
REES WITH YOU,
IRONHEART.
IT'S BECAUSE CAPTAIN AMERICA IS AT THE HEAD OF THIS, AND NO ONE WANTS TO BELIEVE HE'D DO SOMETHING LIKE THIS.
HE'S PROMISING PEOPLE LAW AND ORDER.
SECURITY. JOBS.
AND ALL THEY HAVE TO DO IS LIE DOWN AND WATCH THE TRAINS RUN ON TIME.
IS IT REALLY THAT HOPELESS? I WANT TO SAY NO, BUT...
I REALIZED WE FORMED THIS TEAM BECAUSE WE CONCLUDED THAT THE OLDER HEROES WERE IGNORING THE NEEDS OF EVERY-DAY PEOPLE WHILE THEY WERE DEFENDING THEM FROM CATASTROPHE.
BUT HOW CAN THEY LISTEN TO EVERYDAY PEOPLE WHEN THOSE SAME PEOPLE ARE WILLING TO OVERLOOK MASS MURDER?
I SEE WHERE VIV IS GOING. WE HAVE
O THROW IN WITH THE OLD
ARD, FOR NOW. WE HAVE NO CHOICE. THE THREAT'S TOO BIG.
IF HYDRA ISN'T TOPPLED, I CAN'T SEE ANY WAY TO HELP ANYONE.
WAAAAAAAAHH!

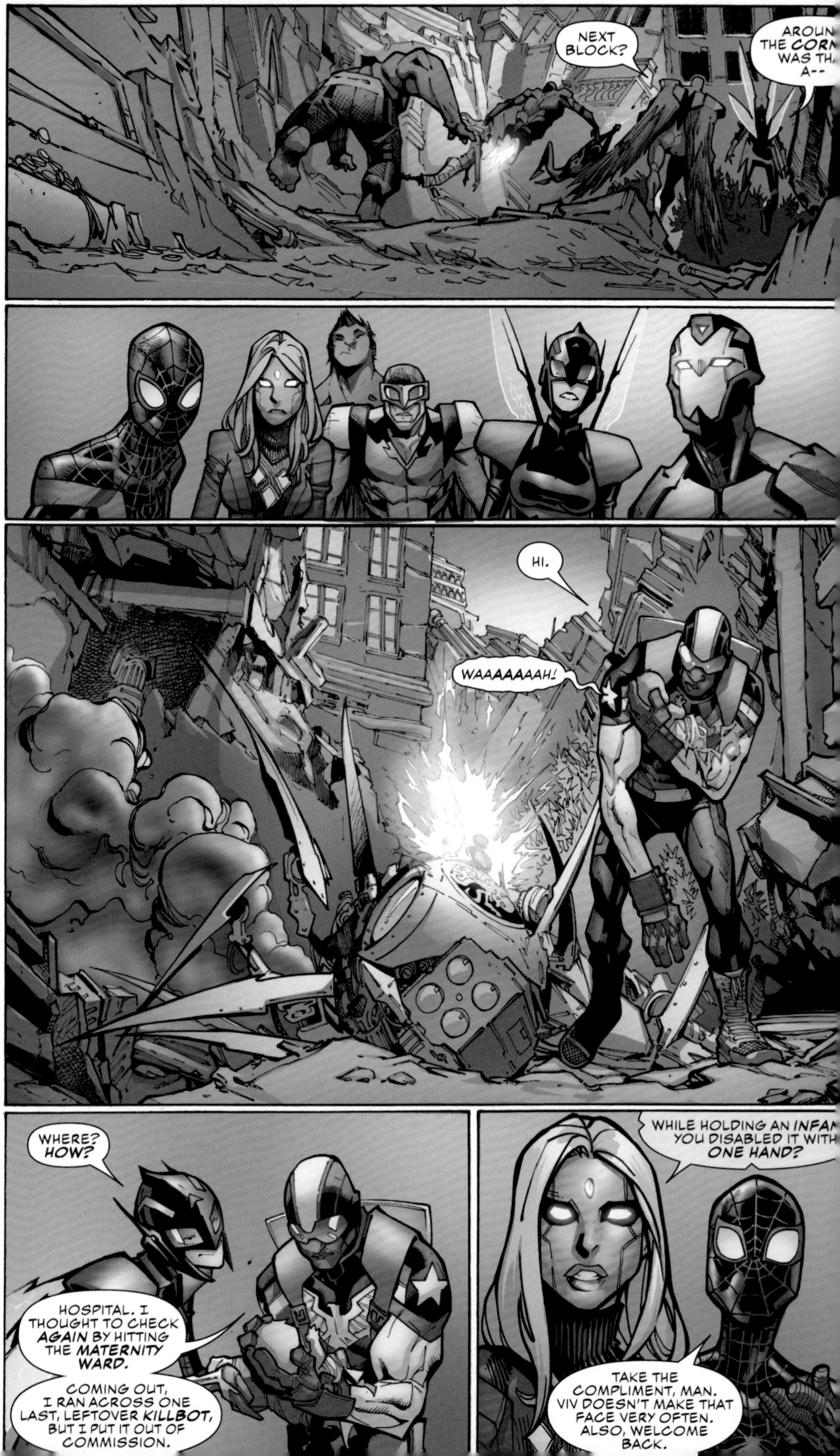

NEXT BLOCK?
AROUN THE CORN WAS TH A--
HI.
WAAAAAAAH!
WHERE? HOW?
HOSPITAL. I THOUGHT TO CHECK AGAIN BY HITTING THE MATERNITY WARD.
COMING OUT, I RAN ACROSS ONE LAST, LEFTOVER KILLBOT, BUT I PUT IT OUT OF COMMISSION.
WHILE HOLDING AN INFA YOU DISABLED IT WITH ONE HAND?
TAKE THE COMPLIMENT, MAN. VIV DOESN'T MAKE THAT FACE VERY OFTEN. ALSO, WELCOME BACK.

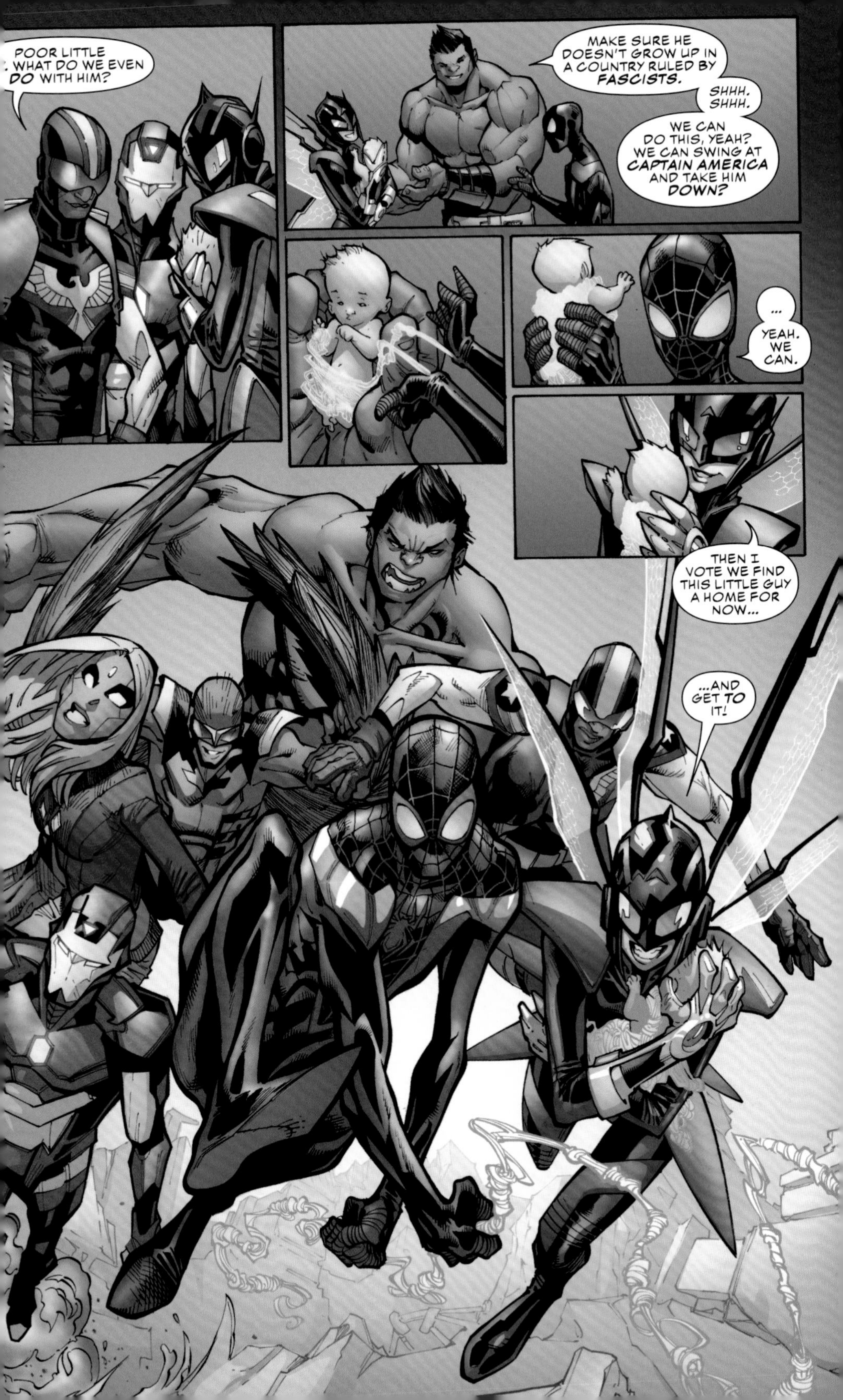

POOR LITTLE ... WHAT DO WE EVEN DO WITH HIM?
MAKE SURE HE DOESN'T GROW UP IN A COUNTRY RULED BY FASCISTS.
SHHH. SHHH.
WE CAN DO THIS, YEAH? WE CAN SWING AT CAPTAIN AMERICA AND TAKE HIM DOWN?
... YEAH. WE CAN.
THEN I VOTE WE FIND THIS LITTLE GUY A HOME FOR NOW...
...AND GET TO IT!

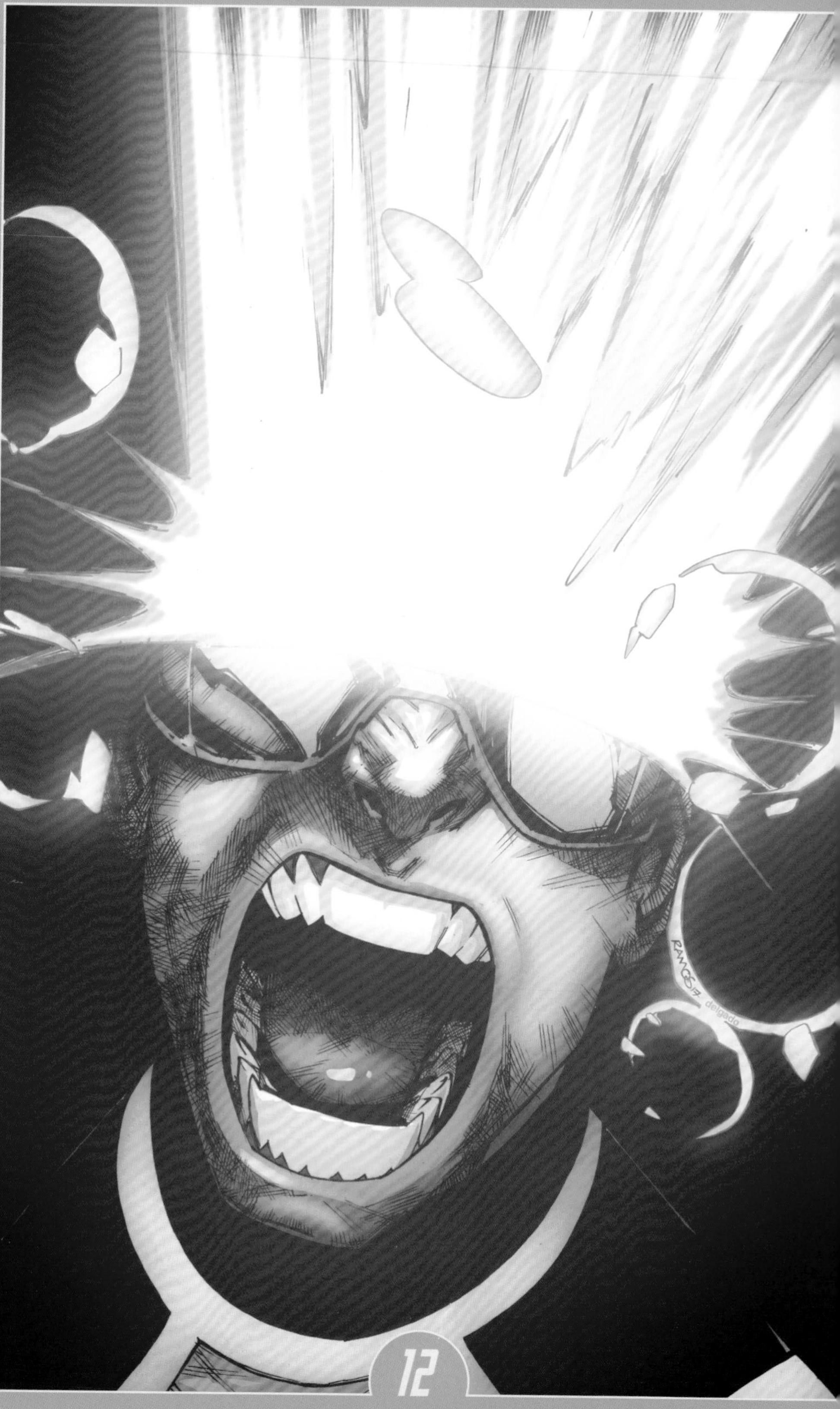

12

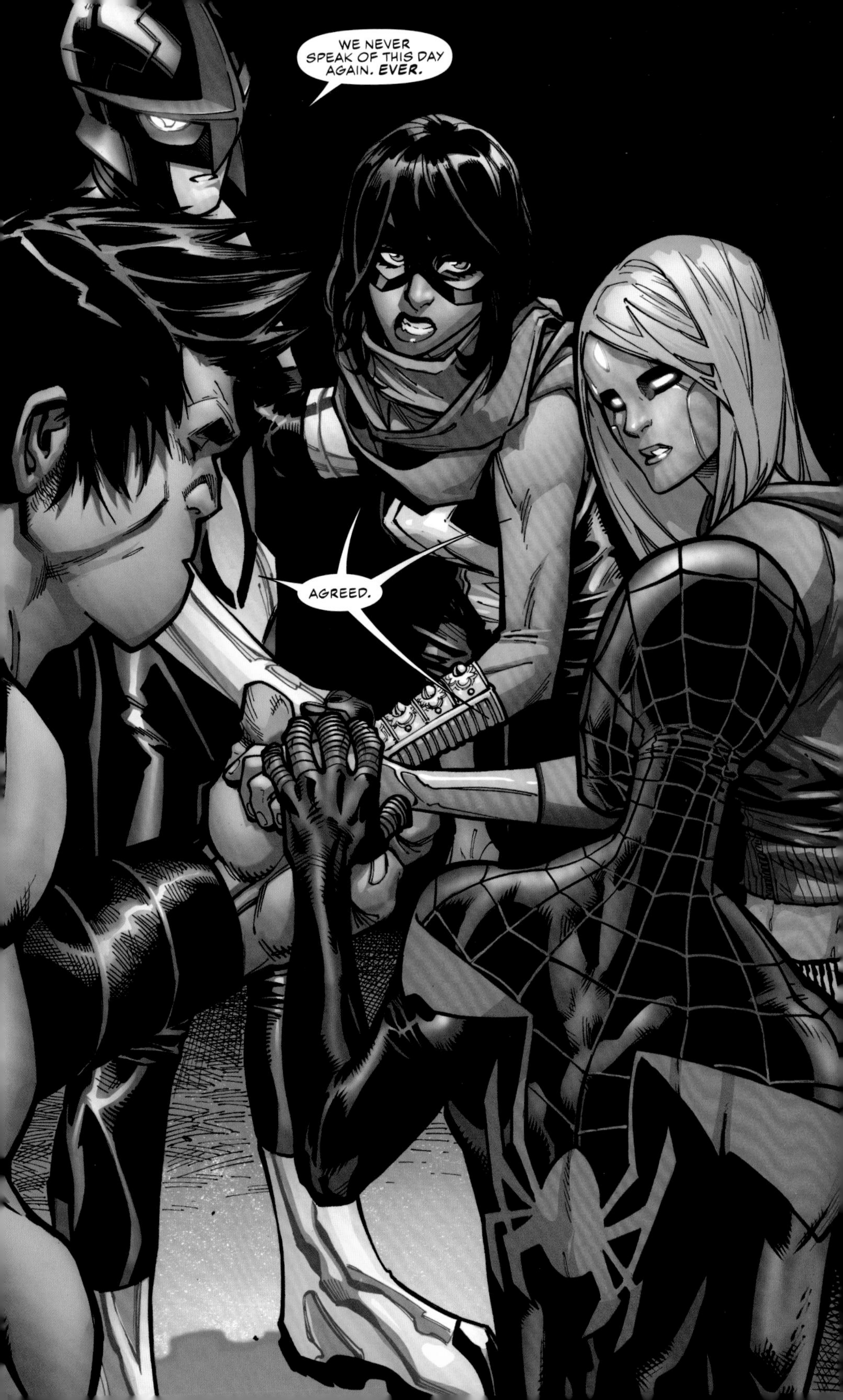
WE NEVER SPEAK OF THIS DAY AGAIN. EVER.
AGREED.

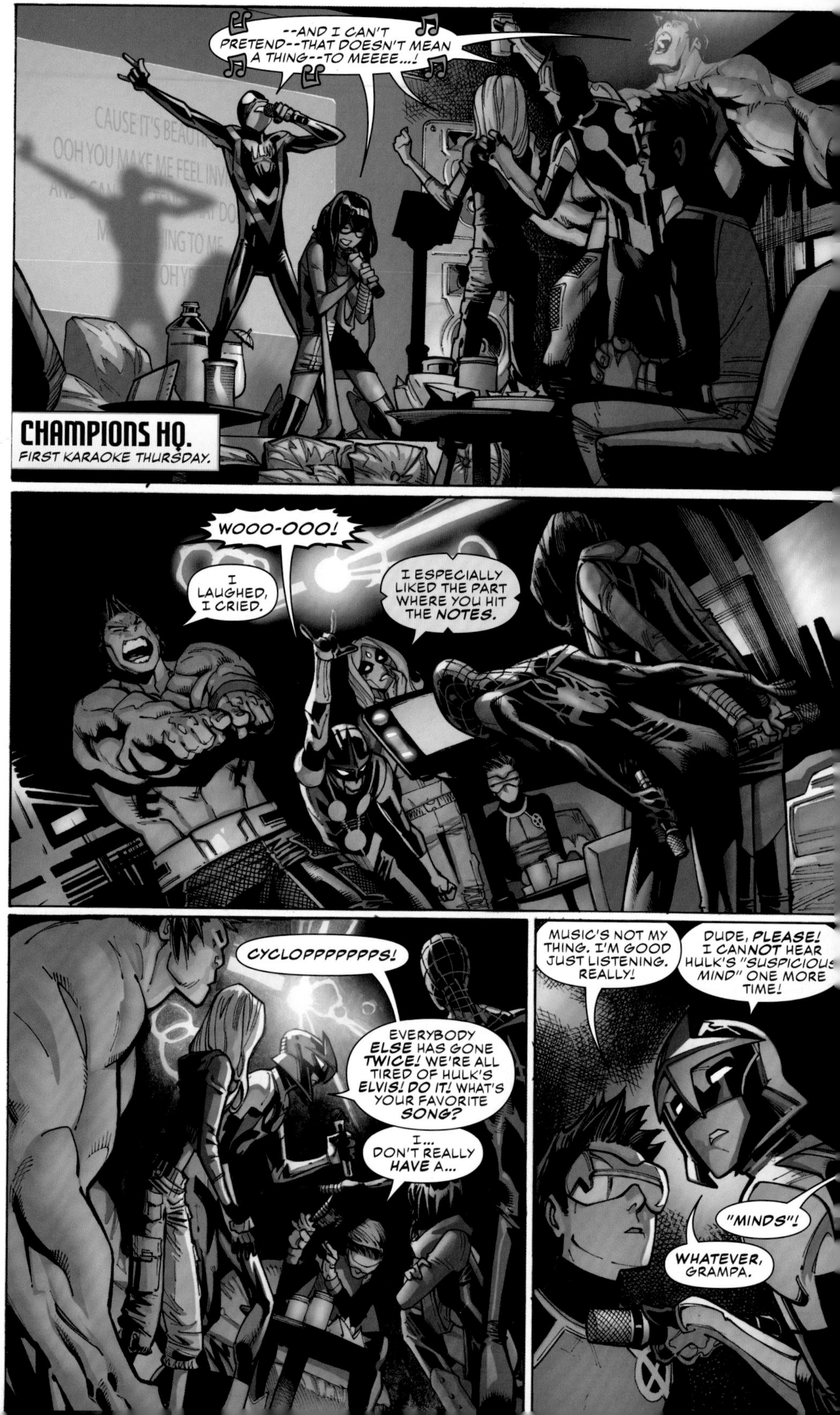
--AND I CAN'T PRETEND--THAT DOESN'T MEAN A THING--TO MEEEE...!
CAUSE IT'S BEAUTI
OOH YOU MAKE ME FEEL INV
ING TO ME
CHAMPIONS HQ.
FIRST KARAOKE THURSDAY.
WOOO-OOO!
I LAUGHED, I CRIED.
I ESPECIALLY LIKED THE PART WHERE YOU HIT THE NOTES.
CYCLOPPPPPPPS!
EVERYBODY ELSE HAS GONE TWICE! WE'RE ALL TIRED OF HULK'S ELVIS! DO IT! WHAT'S YOUR FAVORITE SONG?
I... DON'T REALLY HAVE A...
MUSIC'S NOT MY THING. I'M GOOD JUST LISTENING. REALLY!
DUDE, PLEASE! I CANNOT HEAR HULK'S "SUSPICIOUS MIND" ONE MORE TIME!
"MINDS"!
WHATEVER, GRAMPA.

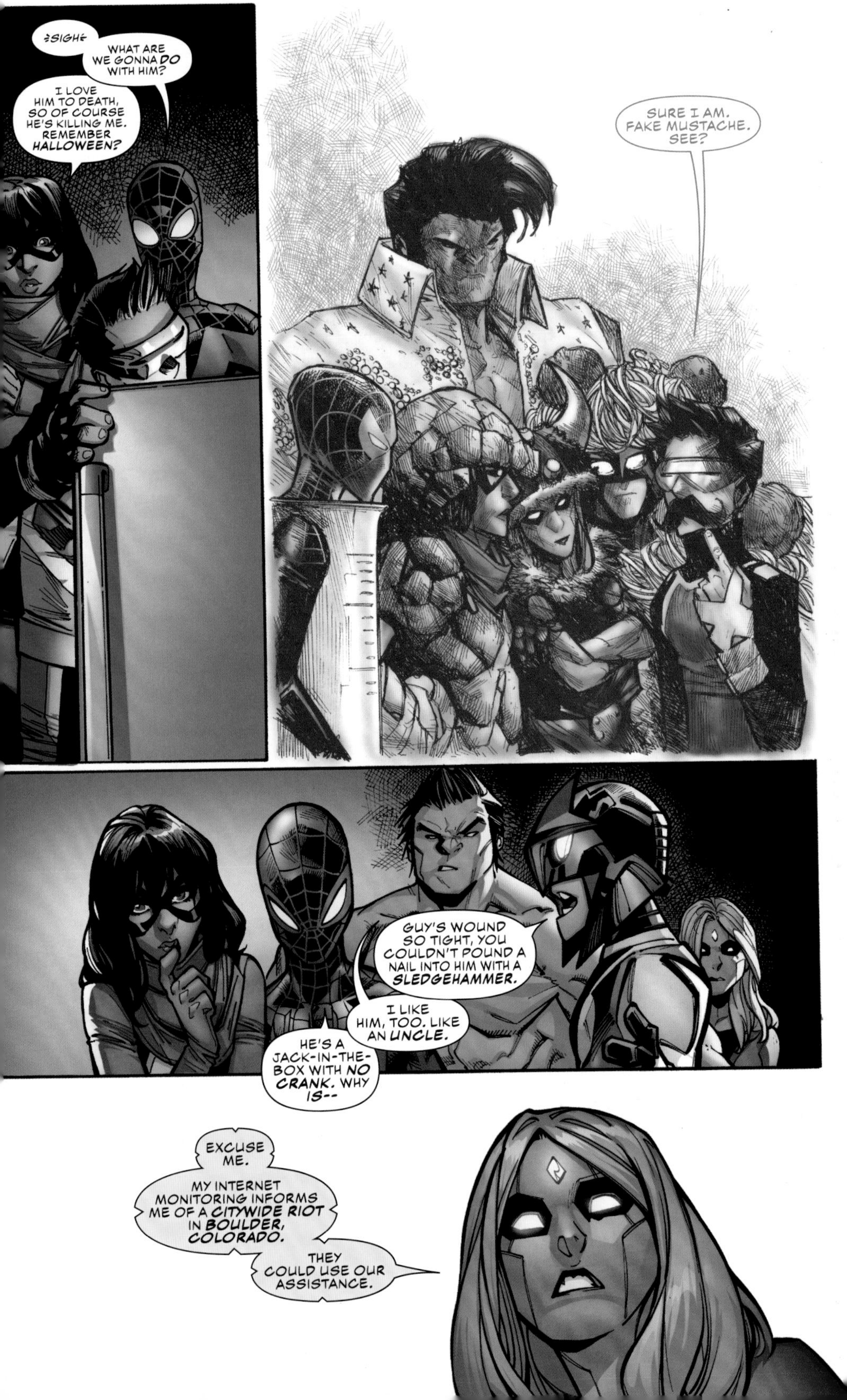

SIGH
WHAT ARE WE GONNA DO WITH HIM?
I LOVE HIM TO DEATH, SO OF COURSE HE'S KILLING ME. REMEMBER HALLOWEEN?
SURE I AM. FAKE MUSTACHE. SEE?
GUY'S WOUND SO TIGHT, YOU COULDN'T POUND A NAIL INTO HIM WITH A SLEDGEHAMMER.
I LIKE HIM, TOO. LIKE AN UNCLE.
HE'S A JACK-IN-THE-BOX WITH NO CRANK. WHY IS--
EXCUSE ME.
MY INTERNET MONITORING INFORMS ME OF A CITYWIDE RIOT IN BOULDER, COLORADO.
THEY COULD USE OUR ASSISTANCE.

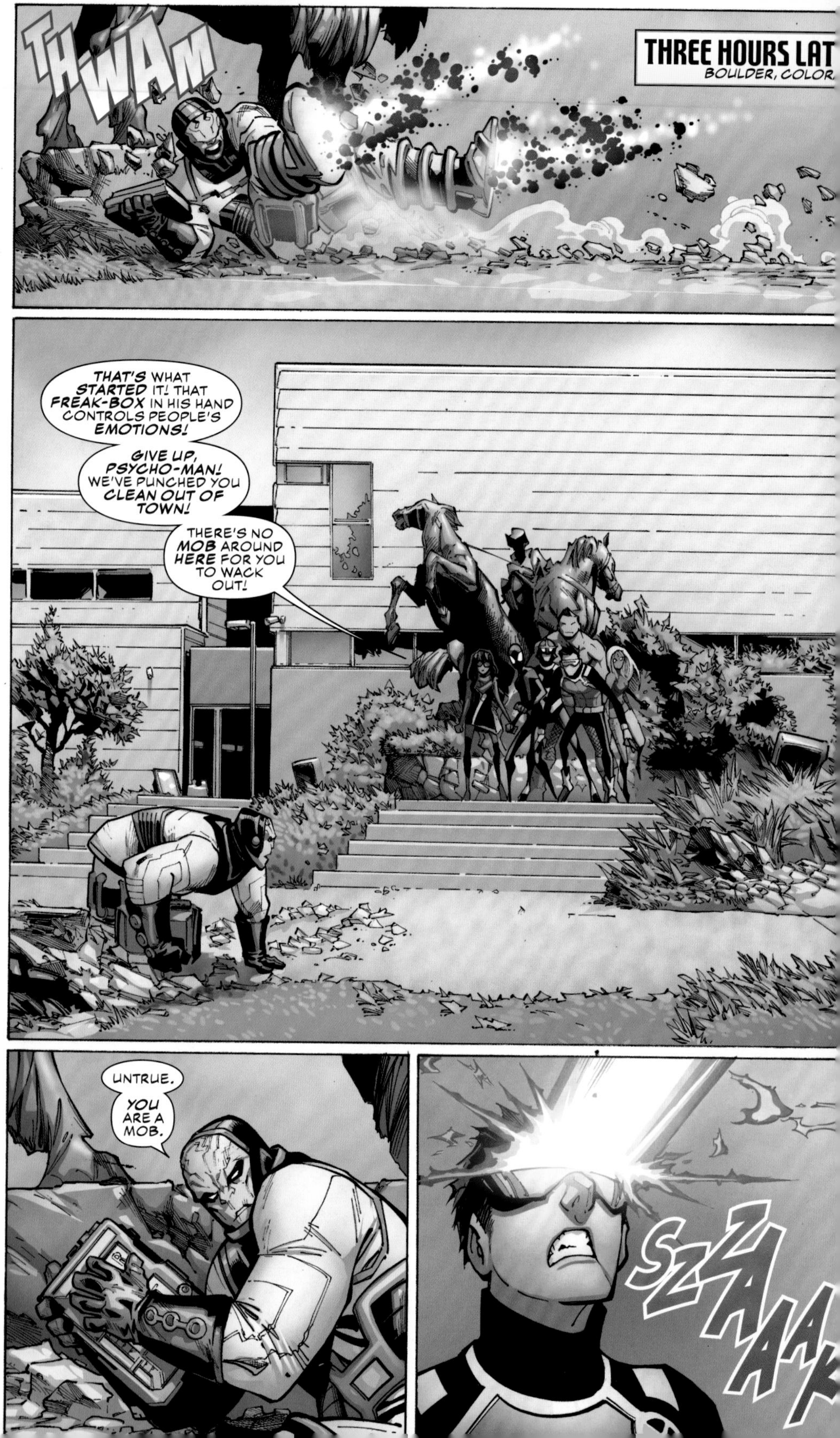
THWAM
THREE HOURS LAT
BOULDER, COLOR
THAT'S WHAT STARTED IT! THAT FREAK-BOX IN HIS HAND CONTROLS PEOPLE'S EMOTIONS!
GIVE UP, PSYCHO-MAN! WE'VE PUNCHED YOU CLEAN OUT OF TOWN!
THERE'S NO MOB AROUND HERE FOR YOU TO WACK OUT!
UNTRUE.
YOU ARE A MOB.
SZZAAK

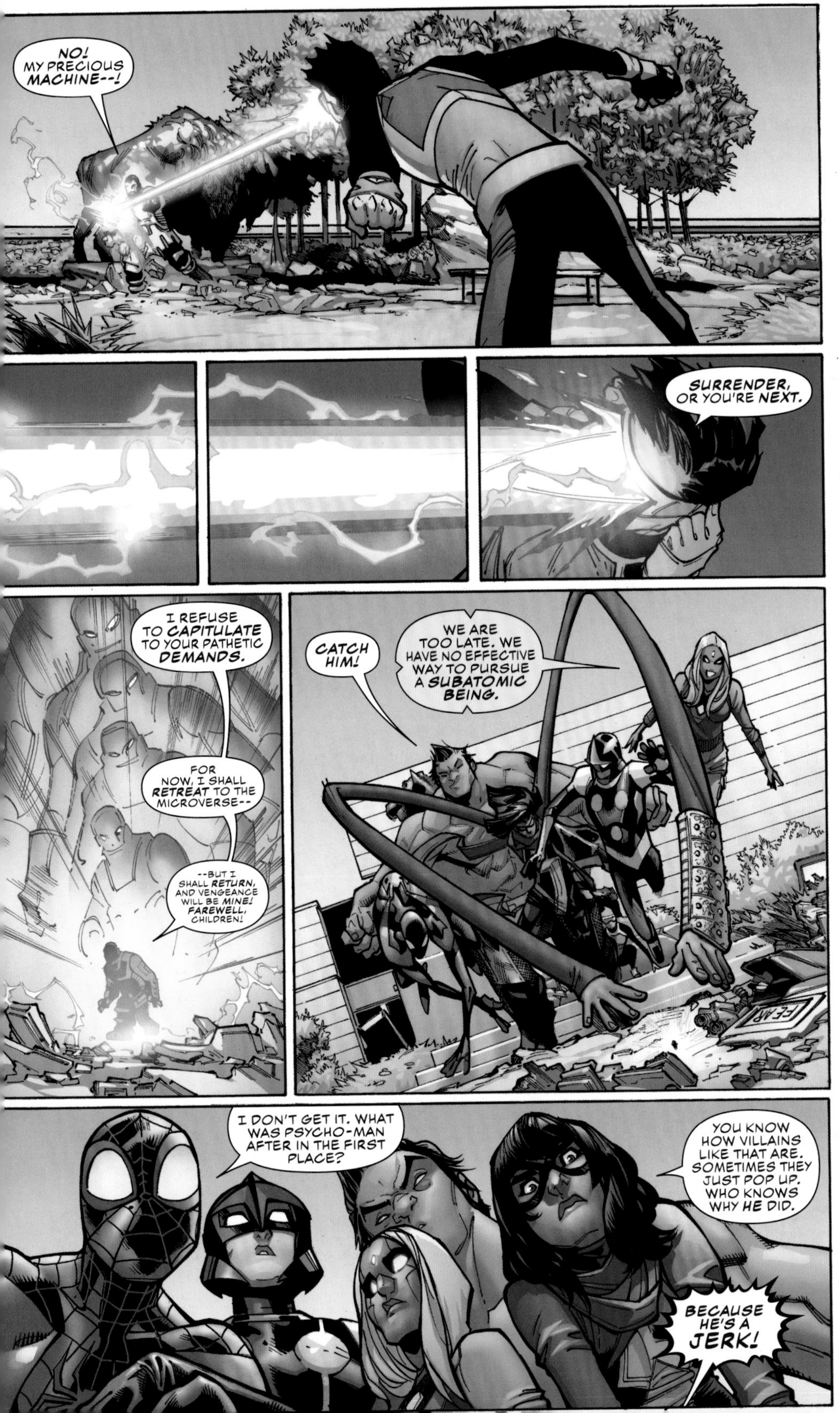
NO! MY PRECIOUS MACHINE--!
SURRENDER, OR YOU'RE NEXT.
I REFUSE TO CAPITULATE TO YOUR PATHETIC DEMANDS.
FOR NOW, I SHALL RETREAT TO THE MICROVERSE--
--BUT I SHALL RETURN, AND VENGEANCE WILL BE MINE! FAREWELL, CHILDREN!
CATCH HIM!
WE ARE TOO LATE. WE HAVE NO EFFECTIVE WAY TO PURSUE A SUBATOMIC BEING.
FEAR
I DON'T GET IT. WHAT WAS PSYCHO-MAN AFTER IN THE FIRST PLACE?
YOU KNOW HOW VILLAINS LIKE THAT ARE. SOMETIMES THEY JUST POP UP. WHO KNOWS WHY HE DID.
BECAUSE HE'S A JERK!

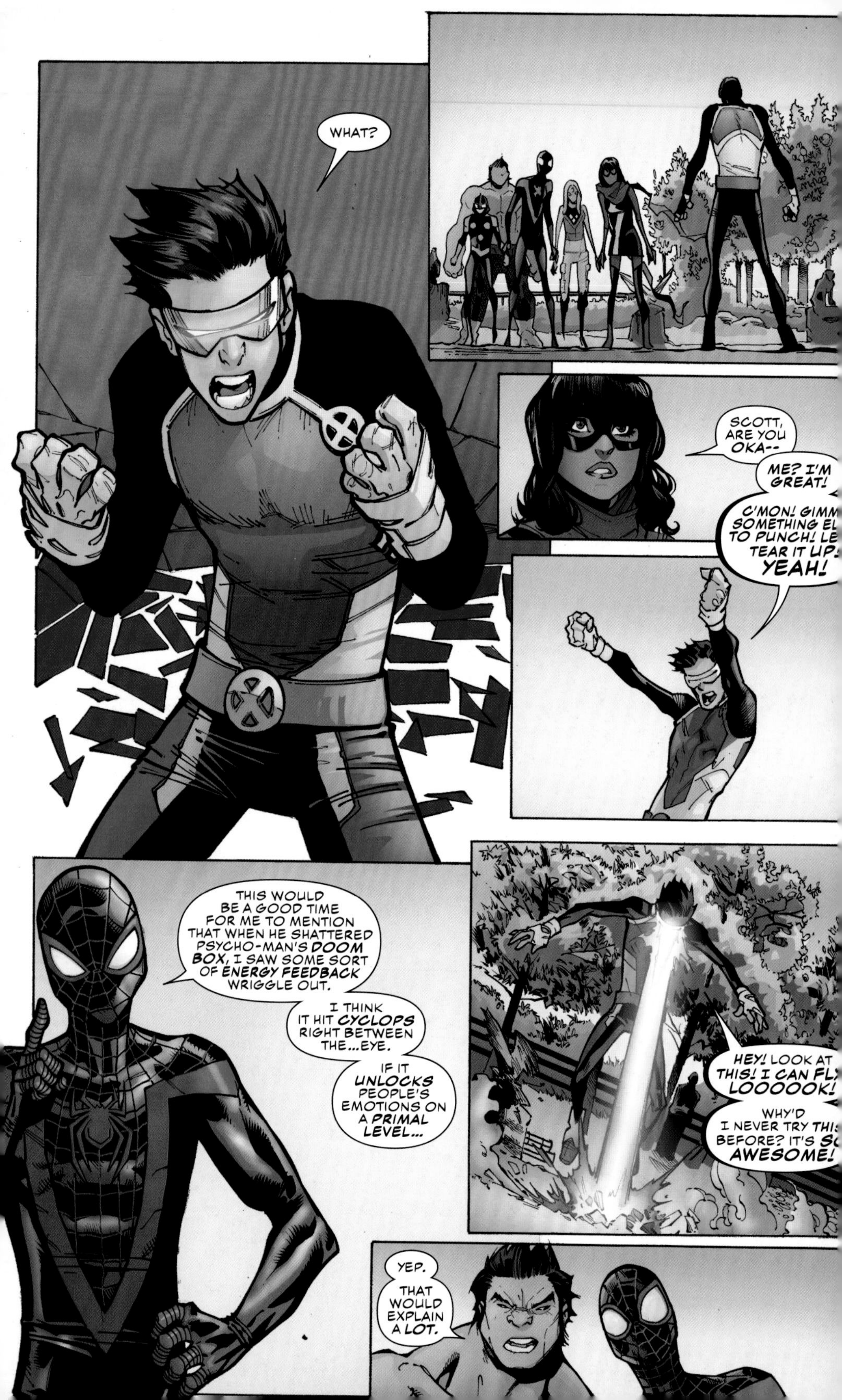
WHAT?
SCOTT, ARE YOU OKA--
ME? I'M GREAT!
C'MON! GIMM SOMETHING EL TO PUNCH! LE TEAR IT UP! YEAH!
THIS WOULD BE A GOOD TIME FOR ME TO MENTION THAT WHEN HE SHATTERED PSYCHO-MAN'S DOOM BOX, I SAW SOME SORT OF ENERGY FEEDBACK WRIGGLE OUT.
I THINK IT HIT CYCLOPS RIGHT BETWEEN THE...EYE.
IF IT UNLOCKS PEOPLE'S EMOTIONS ON A PRIMAL LEVEL...
HEY! LOOK AT THIS! I CAN FL LOOOOOK!
WHY'D I NEVER TRY THI BEFORE? IT'S S AWESOME!
YEP.
THAT WOULD EXPLAIN A LOT.

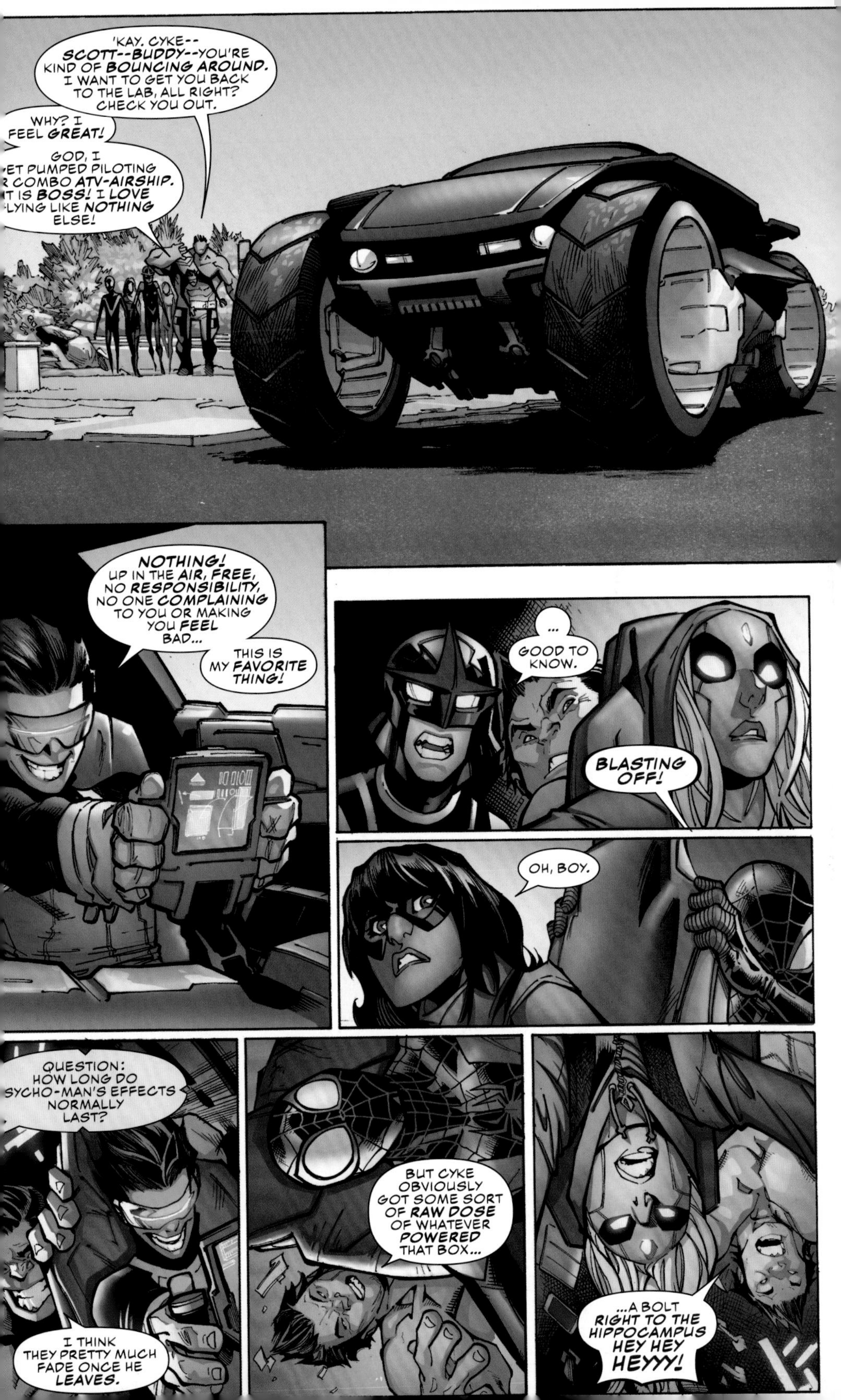

'KAY. CYKE-- SCOTT--BUDDY--YOU'RE KIND OF BOUNCING AROUND. I WANT TO GET YOU BACK TO THE LAB, ALL RIGHT? CHECK YOU OUT.
WHY? I FEEL GREAT!
GOD, I ET PUMPED PILOTING R COMBO ATV-AIRSHIP. T IS BOSS! I LOVE LYING LIKE NOTHING ELSE!
NOTHING! UP IN THE AIR, FREE, NO RESPONSIBILITY, NO ONE COMPLAINING TO YOU OR MAKING YOU FEEL BAD...
THIS IS MY FAVORITE THING!
... GOOD TO KNOW.
BLASTING OFF!
OH, BOY.
QUESTION: HOW LONG DO SYCHO-MAN'S EFFECTS NORMALLY LAST?
I THINK THEY PRETTY MUCH FADE ONCE HE LEAVES.
BUT CYKE OBVIOUSLY GOT SOME SORT OF RAW DOSE OF WHATEVER POWERED THAT BOX...
...A BOLT RIGHT TO THE HIPPOCAMPUS HEY HEY HEYYY!

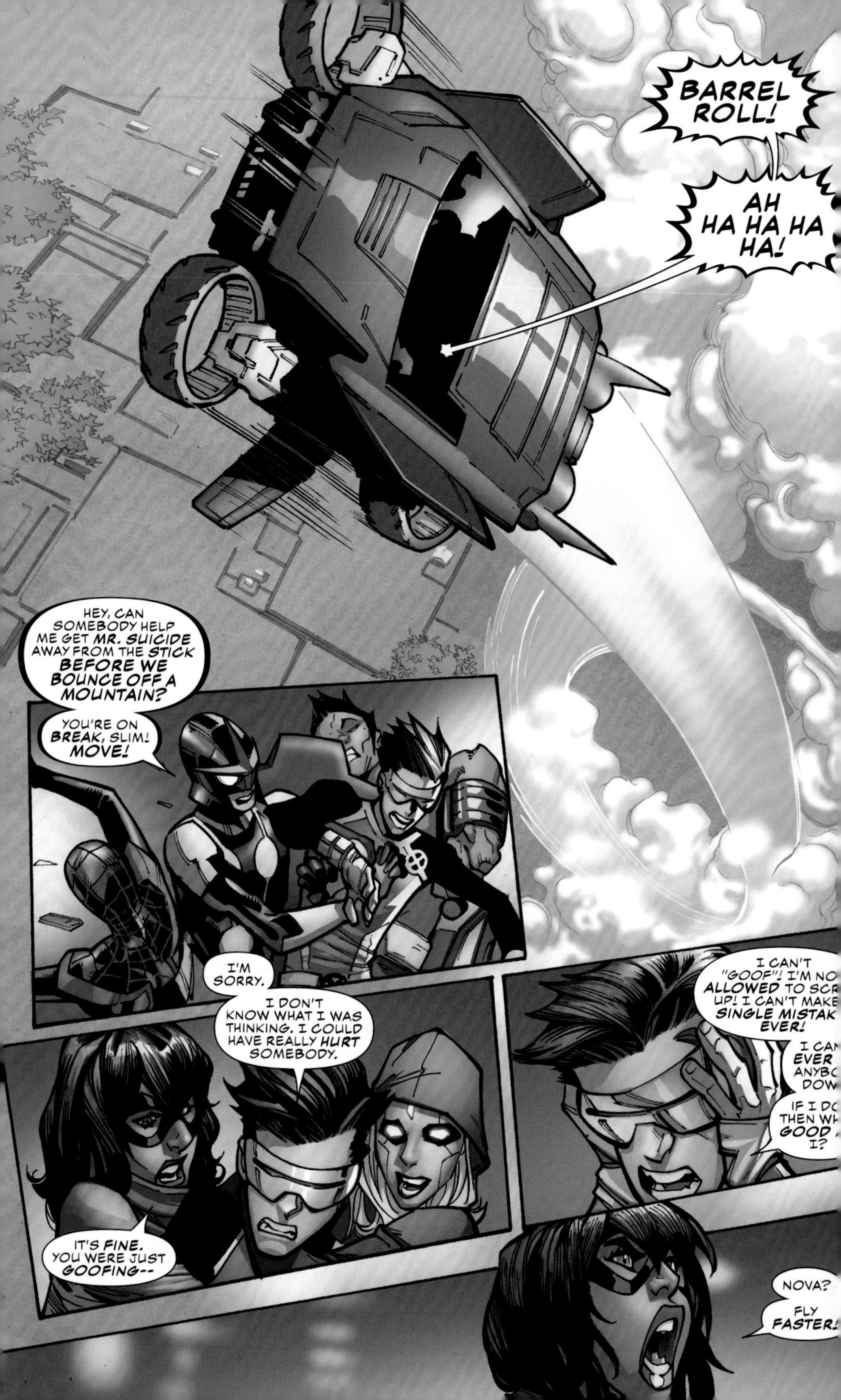

BARREL ROLL!
AH HA HA HA HA!
HEY, CAN SOMEBODY HELP ME GET MR. SUICIDE AWAY FROM THE STICK BEFORE WE BOUNCE OFF A MOUNTAIN?
YOU'RE ON BREAK, SLIM! MOVE!
I'M SORRY.
I DON'T KNOW WHAT I WAS THINKING. I COULD HAVE REALLY HURT SOMEBODY.
IT'S FINE. YOU WERE JUST GOOFING--
I CAN'T "GOOF"! I'M NO ALLOWED TO SCR UP! I CAN'T MAKE SINGLE MISTAK EVER!
I CA EVER ANYBO DOW
IF I DO THEN WH GOOD I?
NOVA?
FLY FASTER!

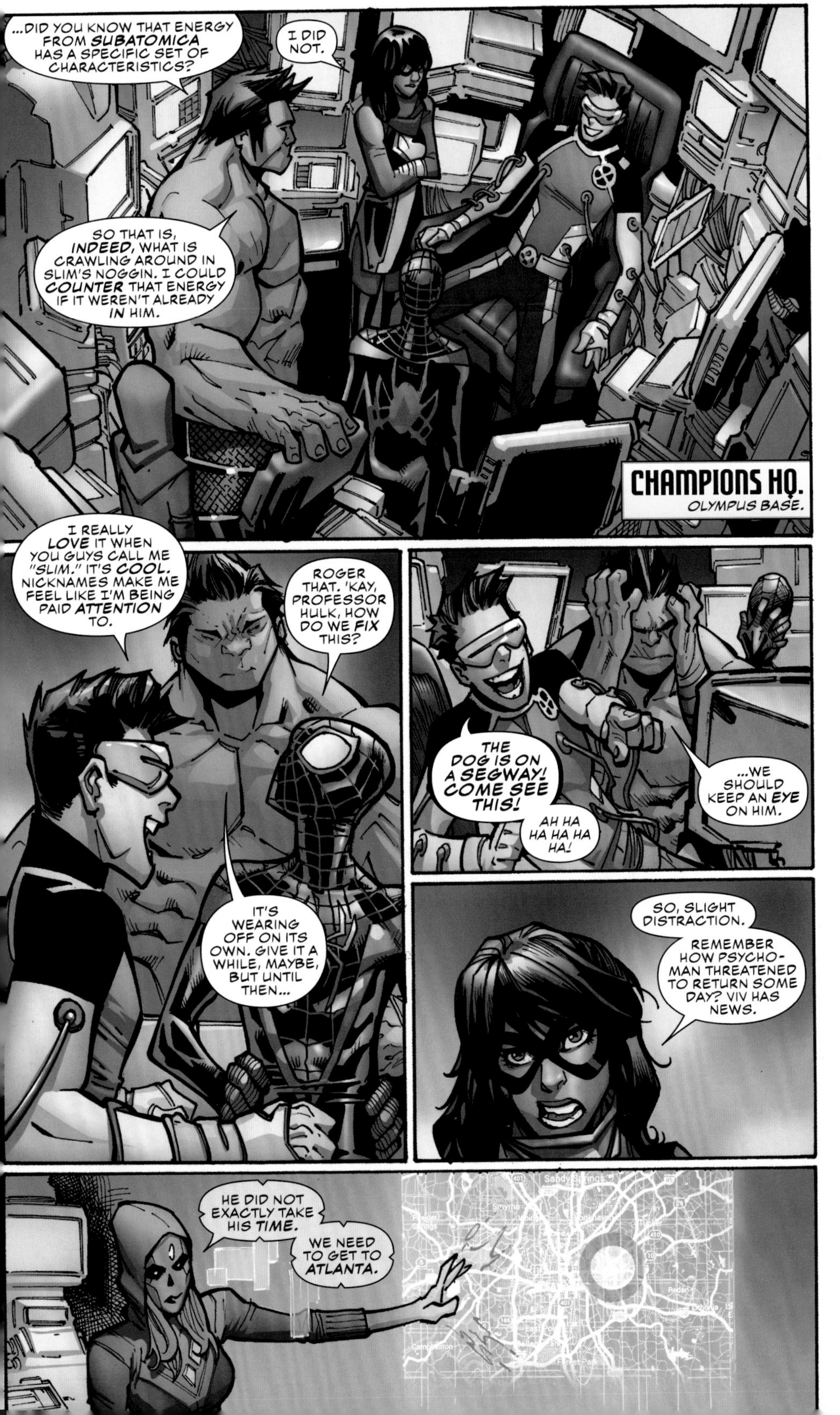
...DID YOU KNOW THAT ENERGY FROM SUBATOMICA HAS A SPECIFIC SET OF CHARACTERISTICS?
I DID NOT.
SO THAT IS, INDEED, WHAT IS CRAWLING AROUND IN SLIM'S NOGGIN. I COULD COUNTER THAT ENERGY IF IT WEREN'T ALREADY IN HIM.
CHAMPIONS HQ.
OLYMPUS BASE.
I REALLY LOVE IT WHEN YOU GUYS CALL ME "SLIM." IT'S COOL. NICKNAMES MAKE ME FEEL LIKE I'M BEING PAID ATTENTION TO.
ROGER THAT. 'KAY, PROFESSOR HULK, HOW DO WE FIX THIS?
IT'S WEARING OFF ON ITS OWN. GIVE IT A WHILE, MAYBE, BUT UNTIL THEN...
THE DOG IS ON A SEGWAY! COME SEE THIS!
AH HA HA HA HA HA!
...WE SHOULD KEEP AN EYE ON HIM.
SO, SLIGHT DISTRACTION.
REMEMBER HOW PSYCHO-MAN THREATENED TO RETURN SOME DAY? VIV HAS NEWS.
HE DID NOT EXACTLY TAKE HIS TIME.
WE NEED TO GET TO ATLANTA.

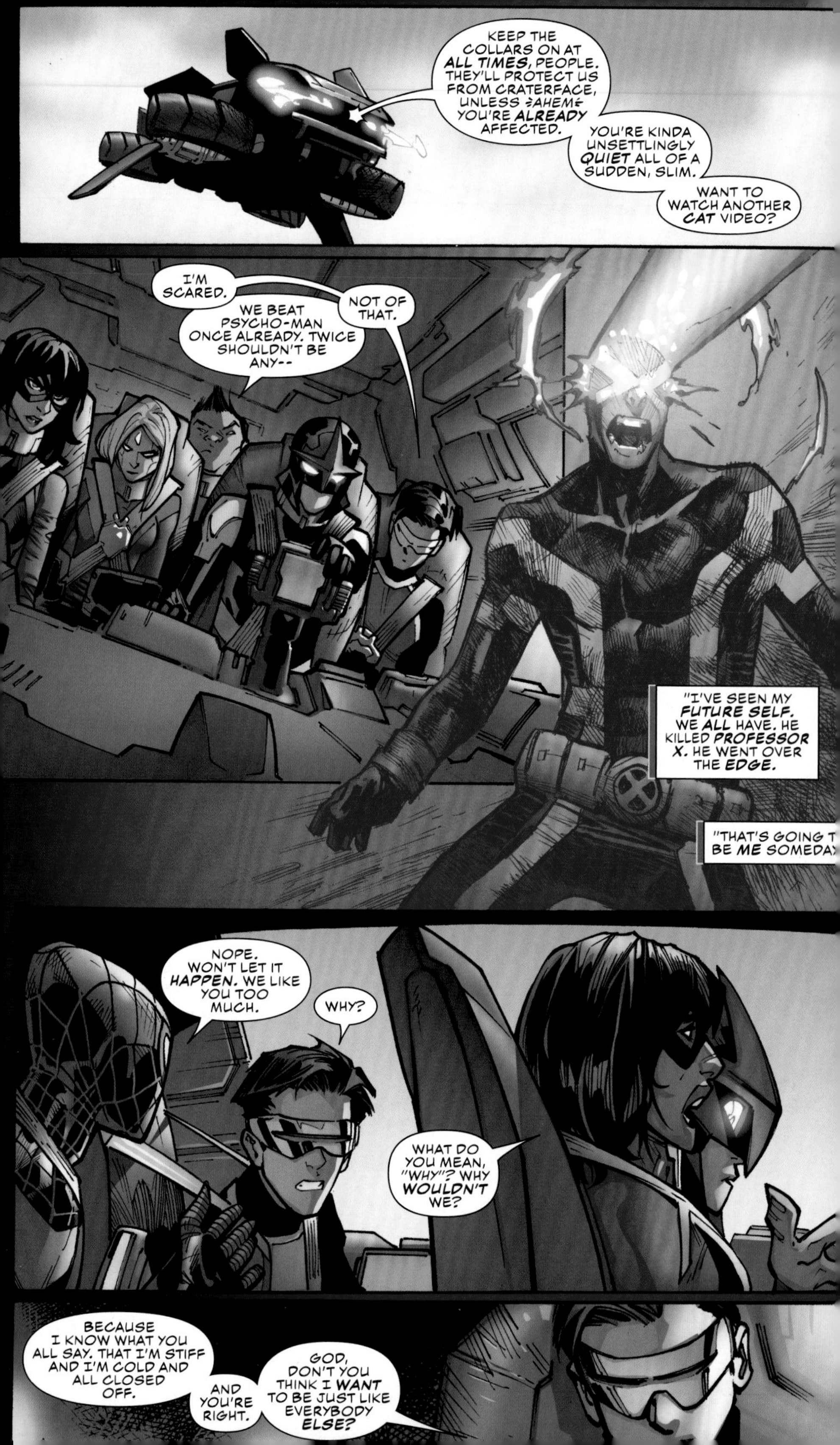
KEEP THE COLLARS ON AT ALL TIMES, PEOPLE. THEY'LL PROTECT US FROM CRATERFACE, UNLESS *AHEM* YOU'RE ALREADY AFFECTED.
YOU'RE KINDA UNSETTLINGLY QUIET ALL OF A SUDDEN, SLIM.
WANT TO WATCH ANOTHER CAT VIDEO?
I'M SCARED.
NOT OF THAT.
WE BEAT PSYCHO-MAN ONCE ALREADY. TWICE SHOULDN'T BE ANY--
"I'VE SEEN MY FUTURE SELF. WE ALL HAVE. HE KILLED PROFESSOR X. HE WENT OVER THE EDGE.
"THAT'S GOING T BE ME SOMEDAY
NOPE. WON'T LET IT HAPPEN. WE LIKE YOU TOO MUCH.
WHY?
WHAT DO YOU MEAN, "WHY"? WHY WOULDN'T WE?
BECAUSE I KNOW WHAT YOU ALL SAY. THAT I'M STIFF AND I'M COLD AND ALL CLOSED OFF.
AND YOU'RE RIGHT.
GOD, DON'T YOU THINK I WANT TO BE JUST LIKE EVERYBODY ELSE?

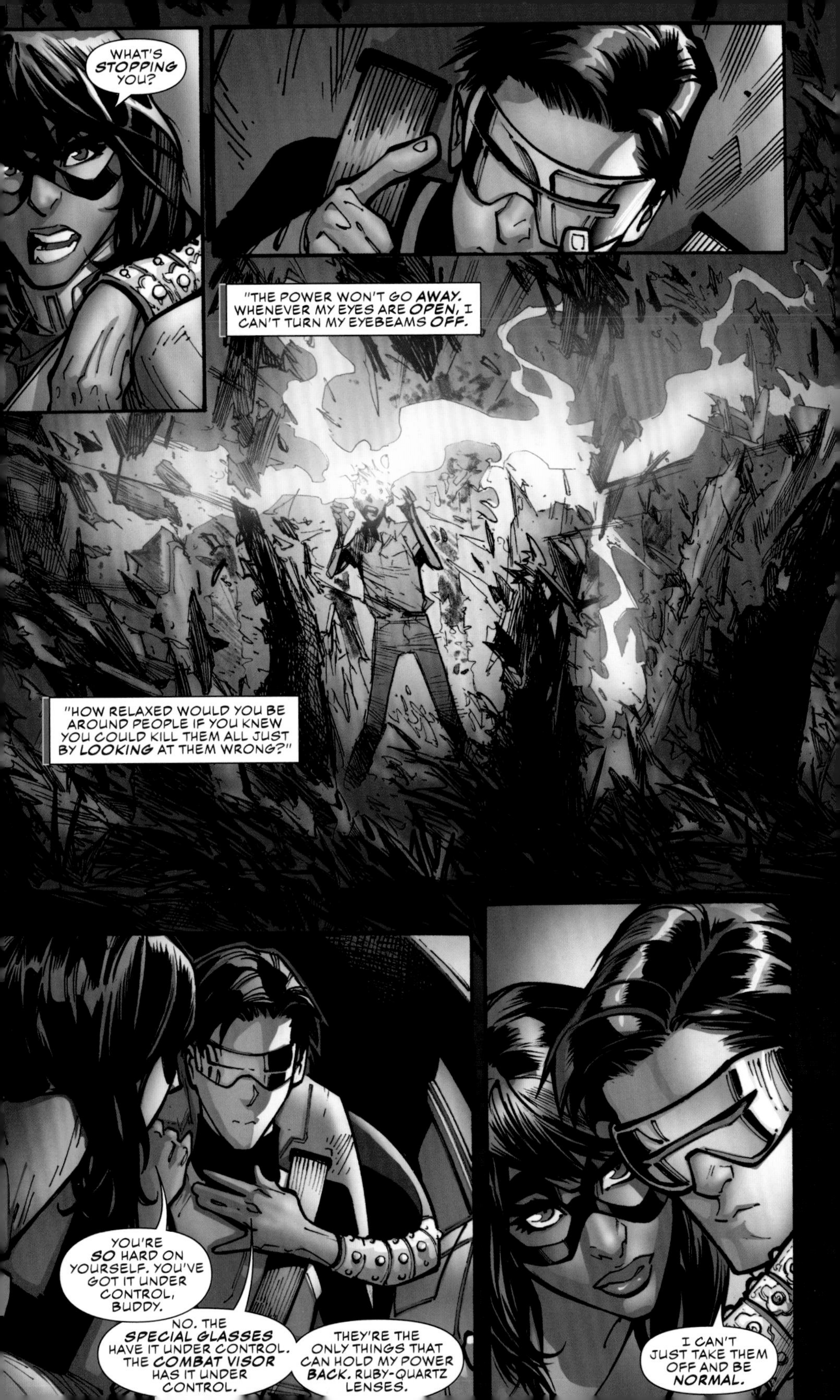
WHAT'S STOPPING YOU?
"THE POWER WON'T GO AWAY. WHENEVER MY EYES ARE OPEN, I CAN'T TURN MY EYEBEAMS OFF.
"HOW RELAXED WOULD YOU BE AROUND PEOPLE IF YOU KNEW YOU COULD KILL THEM ALL JUST BY LOOKING AT THEM WRONG?"
YOU'RE SO HARD ON YOURSELF. YOU'VE GOT IT UNDER CONTROL, BUDDY.
NO. THE SPECIAL GLASSES HAVE IT UNDER CONTROL. THE COMBAT VISOR HAS IT UNDER CONTROL.
THEY'RE THE ONLY THINGS THAT CAN HOLD MY POWER BACK. RUBY-QUARTZ LENSES.
I CAN'T JUST TAKE THEM OFF AND BE NORMAL.

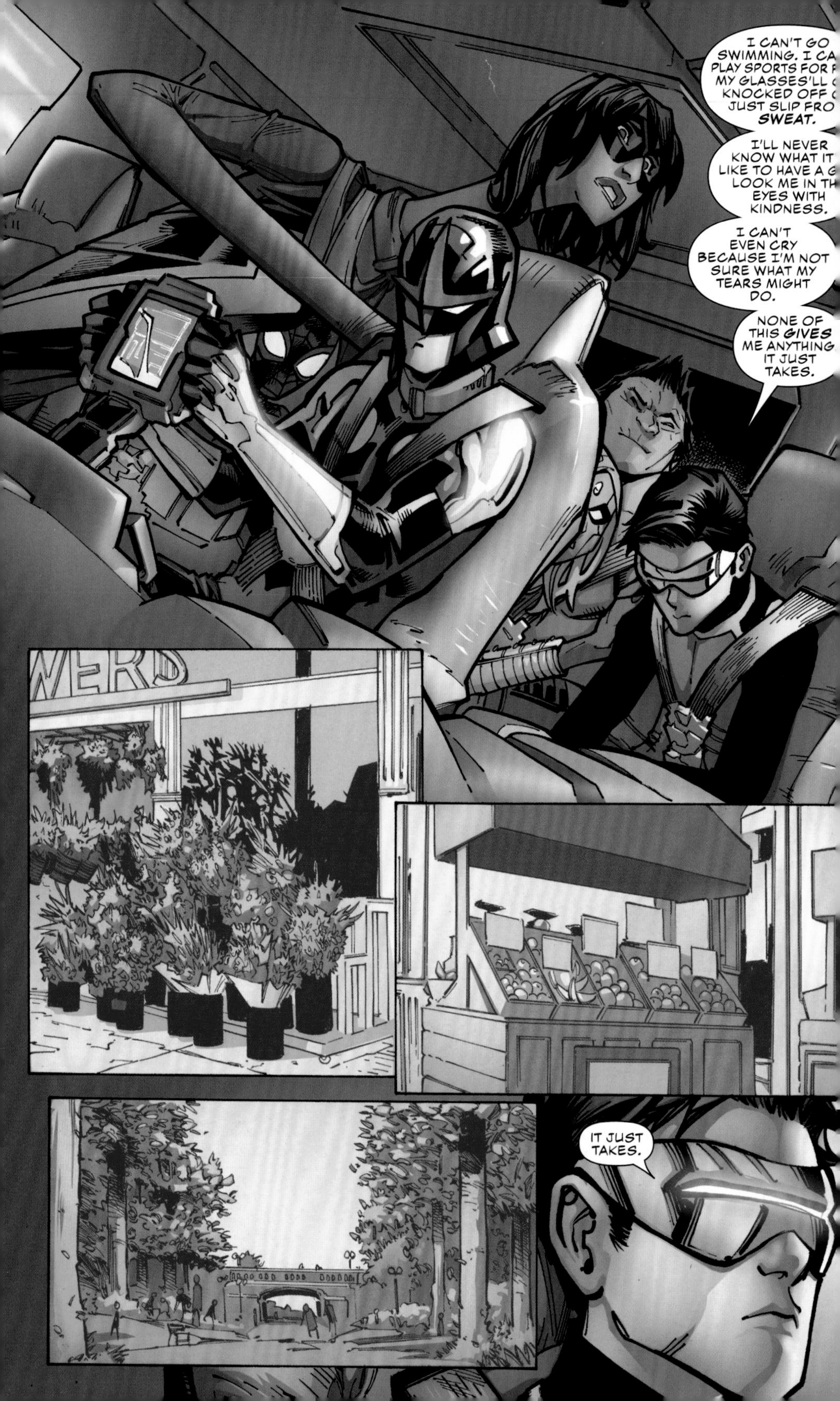

I CAN'T GO SWIMMING. I CA PLAY SPORTS FOR MY GLASSES'LL KNOCKED OFF JUST SLIP FRO **SWEAT.**
I'LL NEVER KNOW WHAT IT LIKE TO HAVE A G LOOK ME IN TH EYES WITH KINDNESS.
I CAN'T EVEN CRY BECAUSE I'M NOT SURE WHAT MY TEARS MIGHT DO.
NONE OF THIS **GIVES** ME ANYTHING IT JUST TAKES.
WERS
IT JUST TAKES.

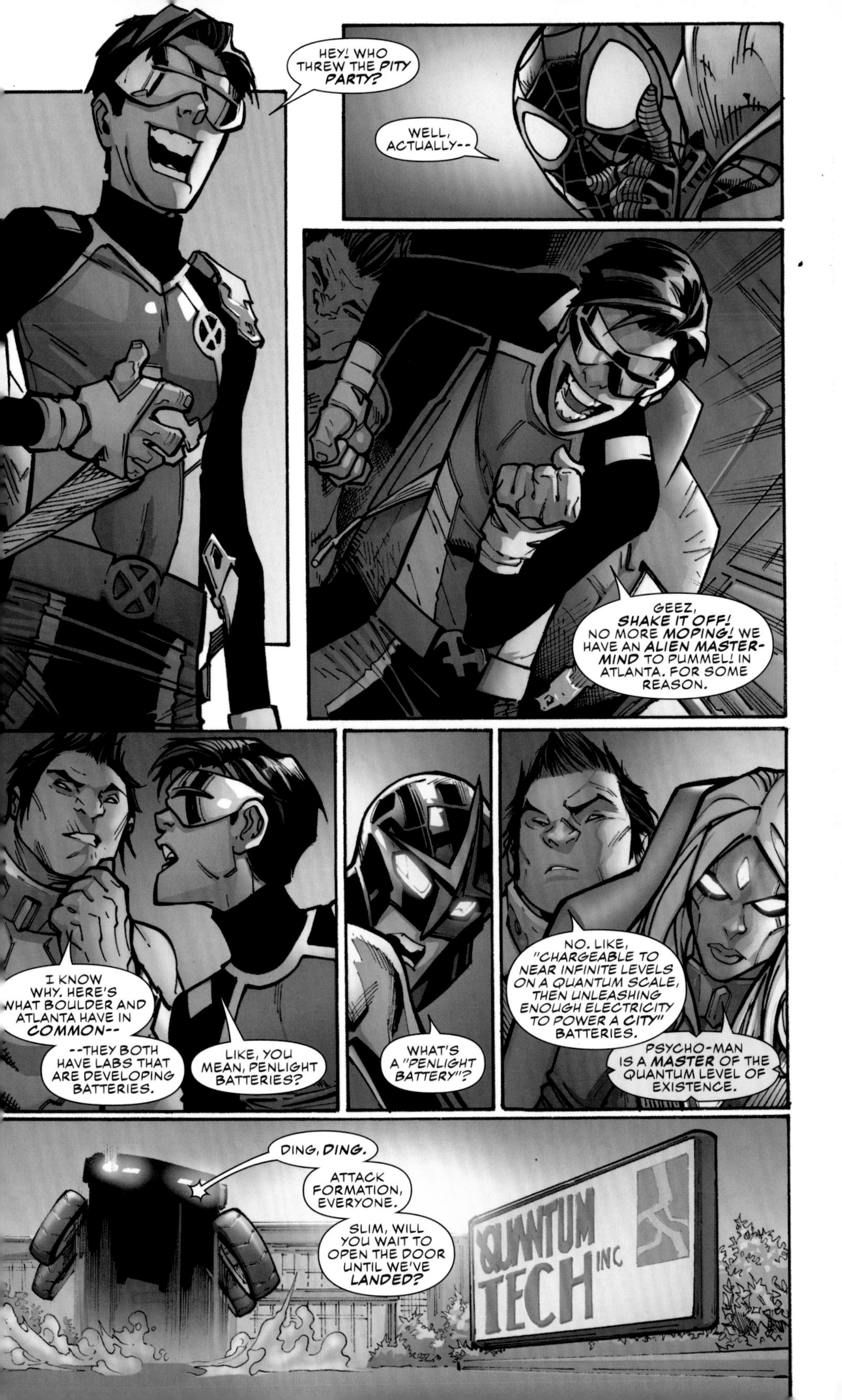
HEY! WHO THREW THE *PITY PARTY?*
WELL, ACTUALLY--
GEEZ, ***SHAKE IT OFF!*** NO MORE ***MOPING!*** WE HAVE AN ***ALIEN MASTER-MIND*** TO PUMMEL! IN ATLANTA. FOR SOME REASON.
I KNOW WHY. HERE'S WHAT BOULDER AND ATLANTA HAVE IN ***COMMON--***
--THEY BOTH HAVE LABS THAT ARE DEVELOPING BATTERIES.
LIKE, YOU MEAN, PENLIGHT BATTERIES?
WHAT'S A *"PENLIGHT BATTERY"?*
NO. LIKE, *"CHARGEABLE TO NEAR INFINITE LEVELS ON A QUANTUM SCALE, THEN UNLEASHING ENOUGH ELECTRICITY TO POWER A CITY"* BATTERIES.
PSYCHO-MAN IS A ***MASTER*** OF THE QUANTUM LEVEL OF EXISTENCE.
DING, ***DING.***
ATTACK FORMATION, EVERYONE.
SLIM, WILL YOU WAIT TO OPEN THE DOOR UNTIL WE'VE ***LANDED?***
QUANTUM TECH INC

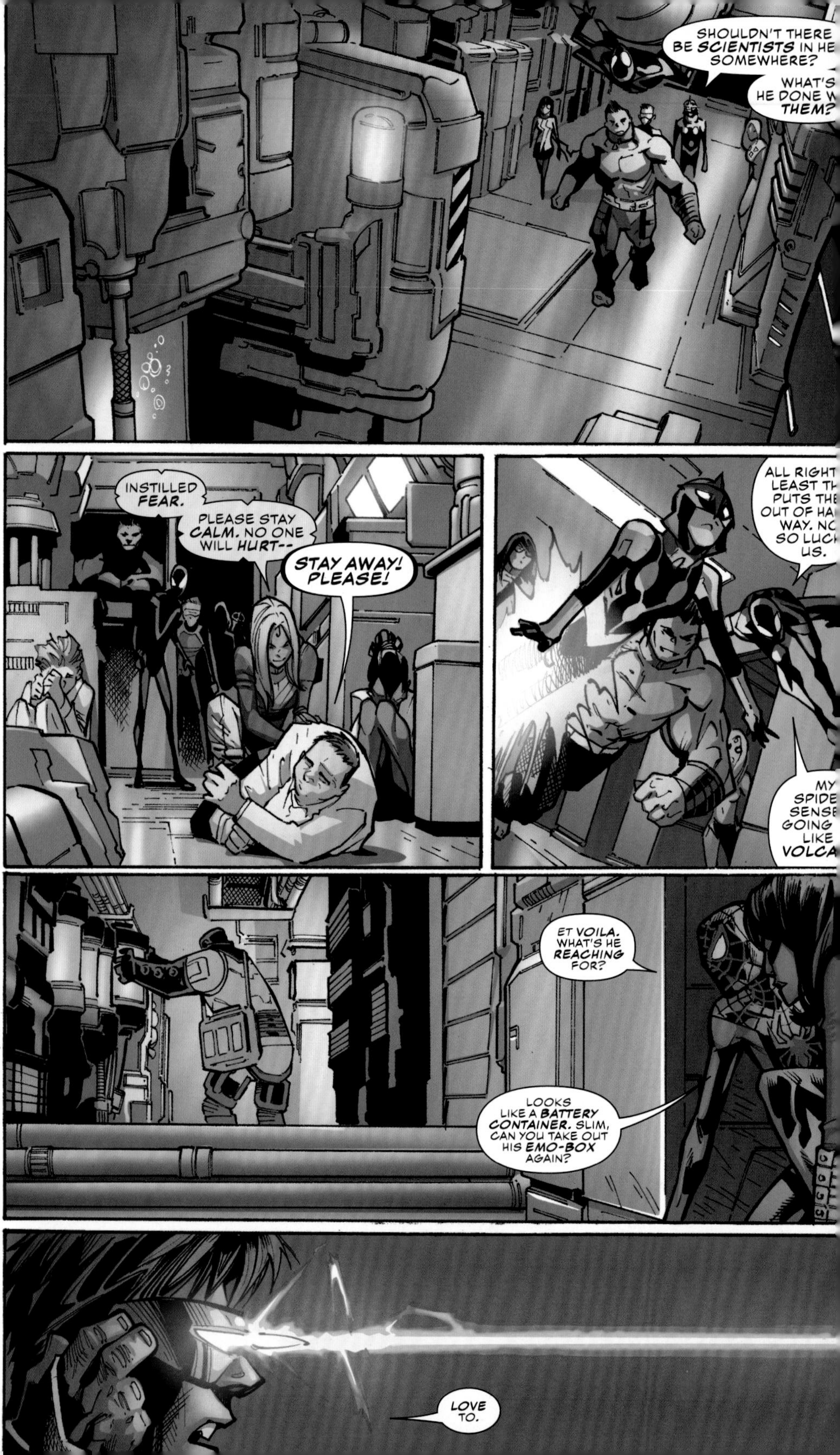
SHOULDN'T THERE BE SCIENTISTS IN HE SOMEWHERE?
WHAT'S HE DONE W THEM?
INSTILLED FEAR.
PLEASE STAY CALM. NO ONE WILL HURT--
STAY AWAY! PLEASE!
ALL RIGHT LEAST TH PUTS THE OUT OF HA WAY. NO SO LUCK US.
MY SPIDE SENSE GOING LIKE VOLCA
ET VOILA. WHAT'S HE REACHING FOR?
LOOKS LIKE A BATTERY CONTAINER. SLIM, CAN YOU TAKE OUT HIS EMO-BOX AGAIN?
LOVE TO.

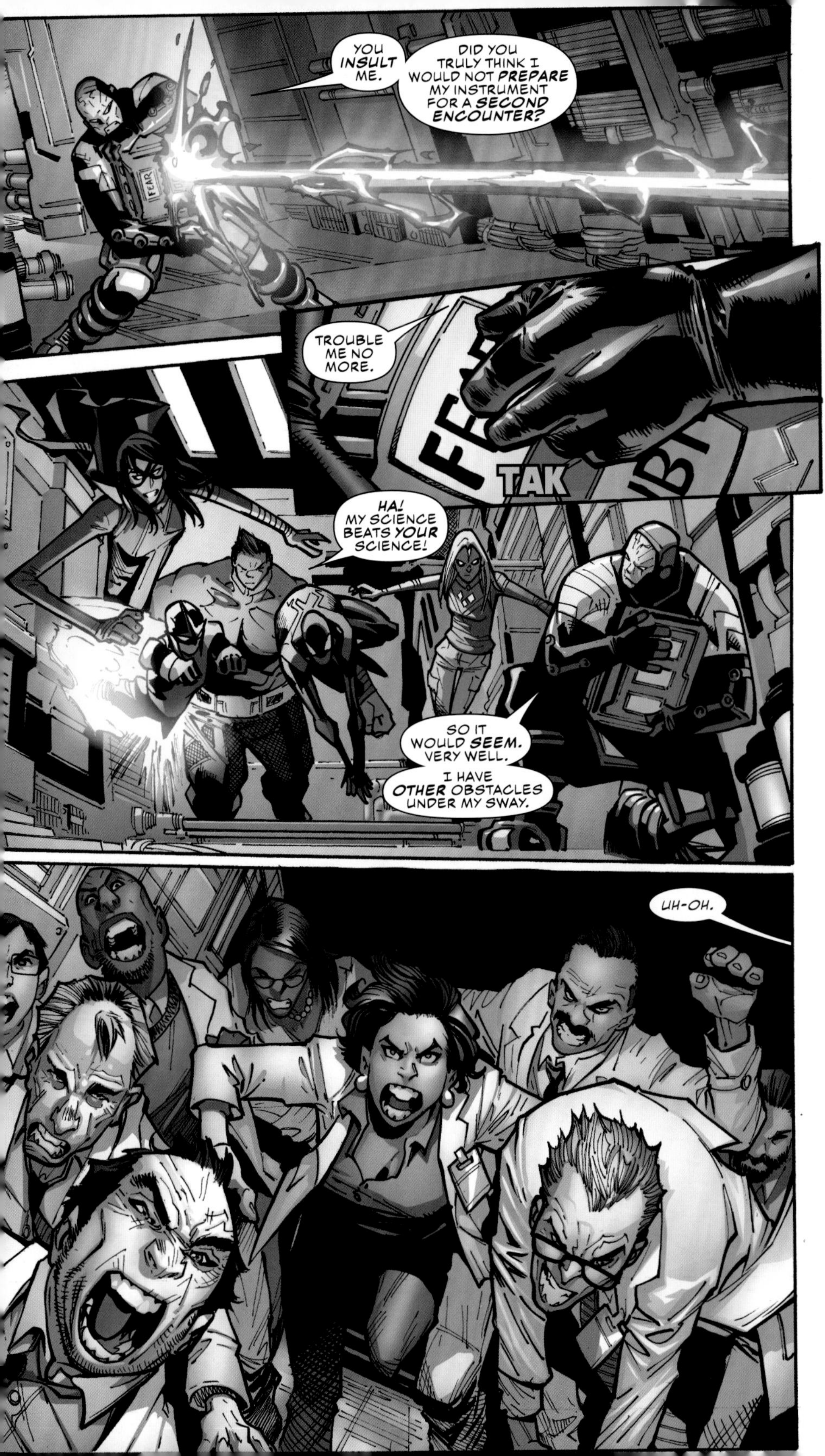

YOU INSULT ME.
DID YOU TRULY THINK I WOULD NOT PREPARE MY INSTRUMENT FOR A SECOND ENCOUNTER?
TROUBLE ME NO MORE.
FEAR
TAK
HA! MY SCIENCE BEATS YOUR SCIENCE!
SO IT WOULD SEEM. VERY WELL.
I HAVE OTHER OBSTACLES UNDER MY SWAY.
UH-OH.

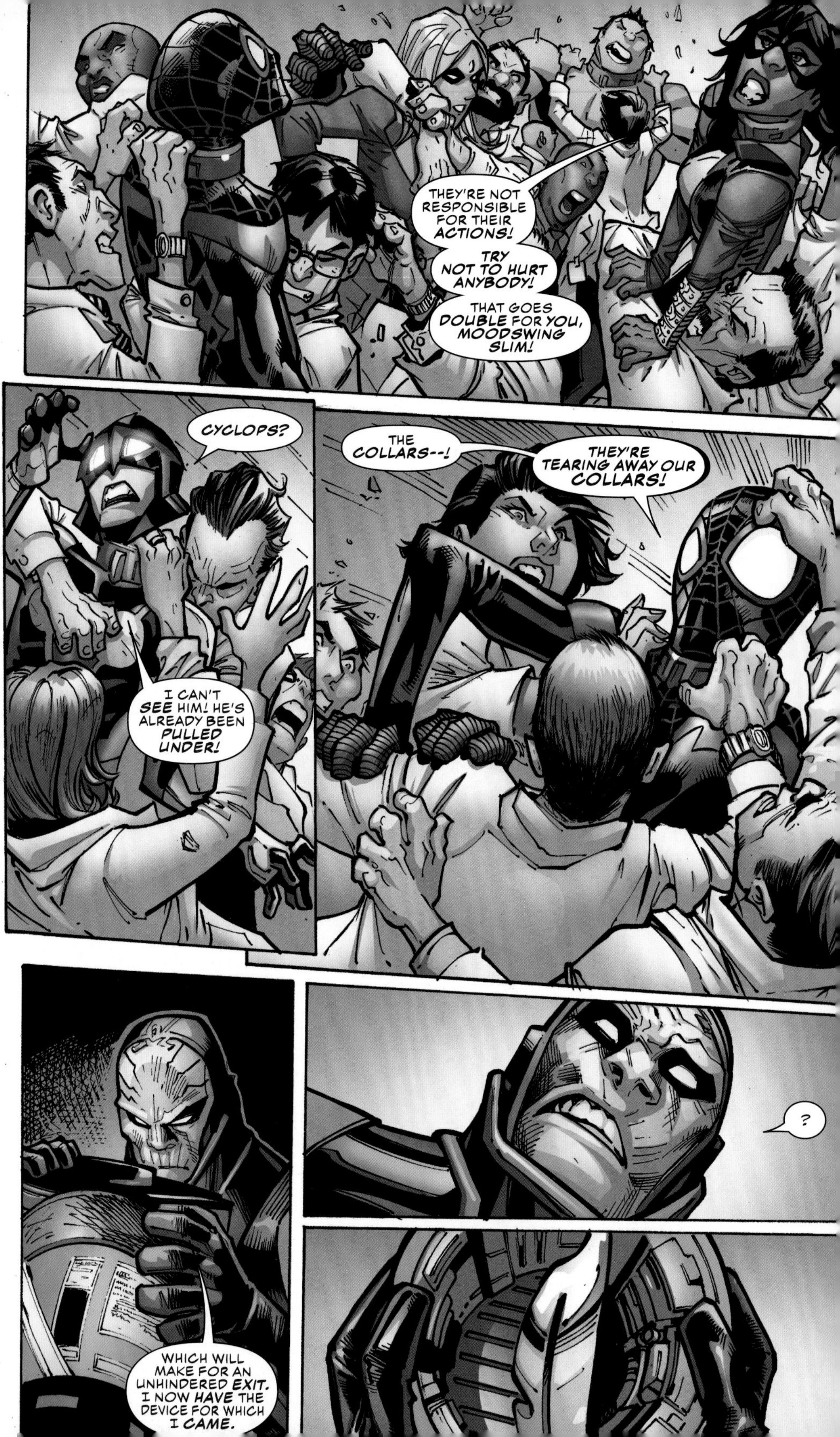
THEY'RE NOT RESPONSIBLE FOR THEIR ACTIONS!
TRY NOT TO HURT ANYBODY!
THAT GOES DOUBLE FOR YOU, MOODSWING SLIM!
CYCLOPS?
I CAN'T SEE HIM! HE'S ALREADY BEEN PULLED UNDER!
THE COLLARS--!
THEY'RE TEARING AWAY OUR COLLARS!
WHICH WILL MAKE FOR AN UNHINDERED EXIT. I NOW HAVE THE DEVICE FOR WHICH I CAME.
?

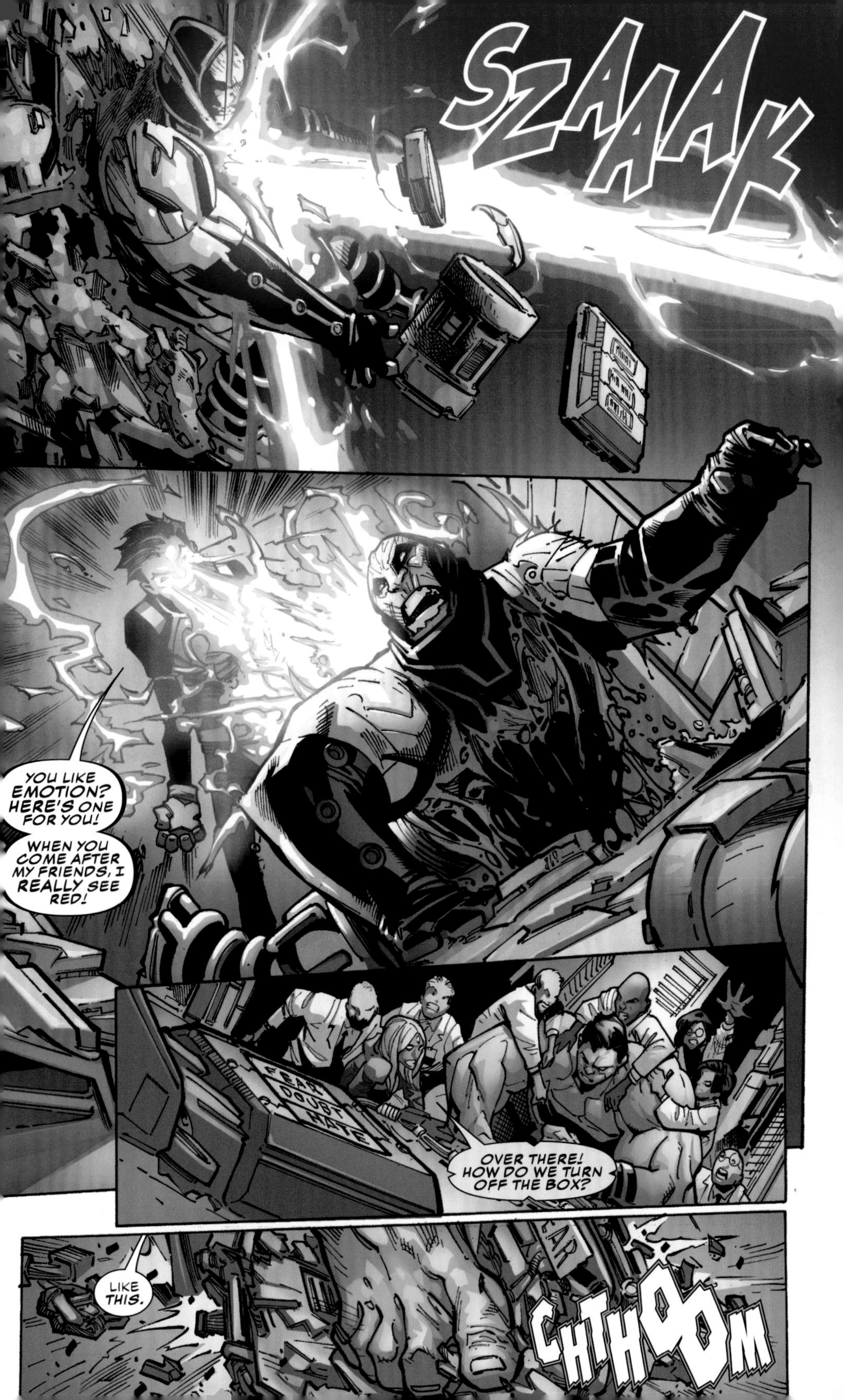
SZAAAK
YOU LIKE EMOTION? HERE'S ONE FOR YOU!
WHEN YOU COME AFTER MY FRIENDS, I REALLY SEE RED!
FEAR
DOUBT
HATE
OVER THERE! HOW DO WE TURN OFF THE BOX?
LIKE THIS.
CHTHOOM

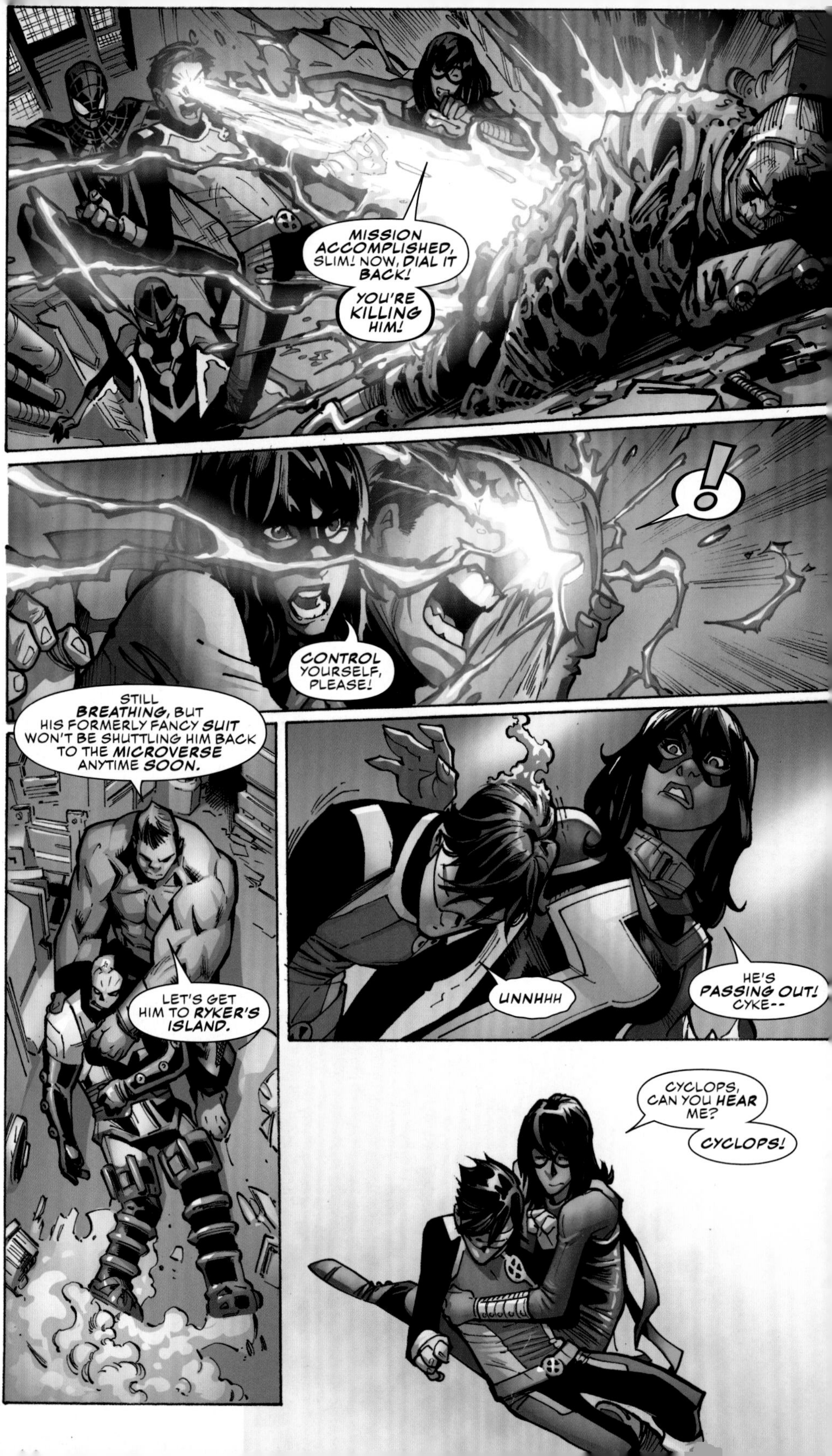
MISSION ACCOMPLISHED, SLIM! NOW, DIAL IT BACK!
YOU'RE KILLING HIM!
!
CONTROL YOURSELF, PLEASE!
STILL BREATHING, BUT HIS FORMERLY FANCY SUIT WON'T BE SHUTTLING HIM BACK TO THE MICROVERSE ANYTIME SOON.
LET'S GET HIM TO RYKER'S ISLAND.
UNNHHH
HE'S PASSING OUT! CYKE--
CYCLOPS, CAN YOU HEAR ME?
CYCLOPS!

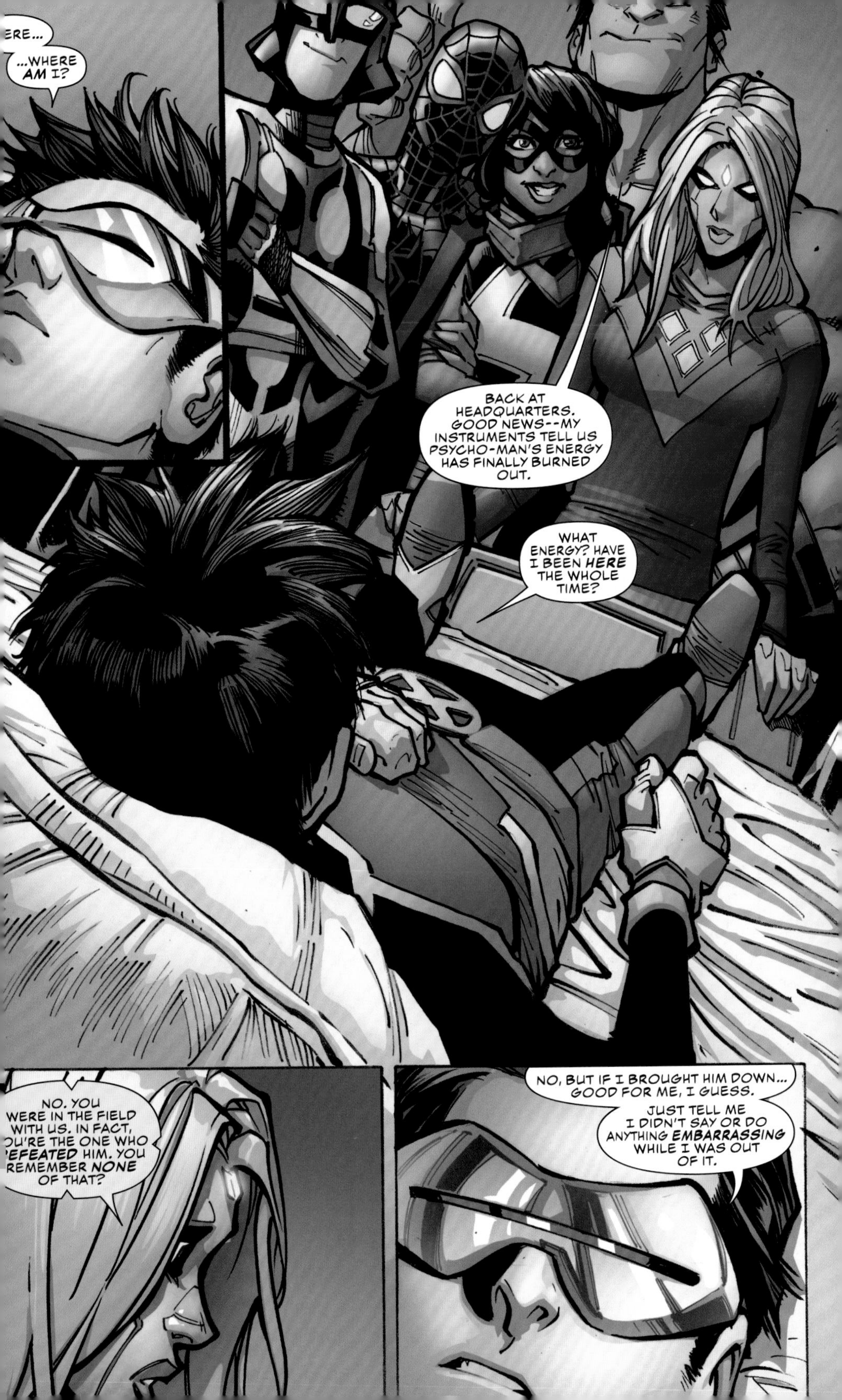

ERE...
...WHERE AM I?
BACK AT HEADQUARTERS. GOOD NEWS--MY INSTRUMENTS TELL US PSYCHO-MAN'S ENERGY HAS FINALLY BURNED OUT.
WHAT ENERGY? HAVE I BEEN HERE THE WHOLE TIME?
NO. YOU WERE IN THE FIELD WITH US. IN FACT, OU'RE THE ONE WHO EFEATED HIM. YOU REMEMBER NONE OF THAT?
NO, BUT IF I BROUGHT HIM DOWN... GOOD FOR ME, I GUESS.
JUST TELL ME I DIDN'T SAY OR DO ANYTHING EMBARRASSING WHILE I WAS OUT OF IT.

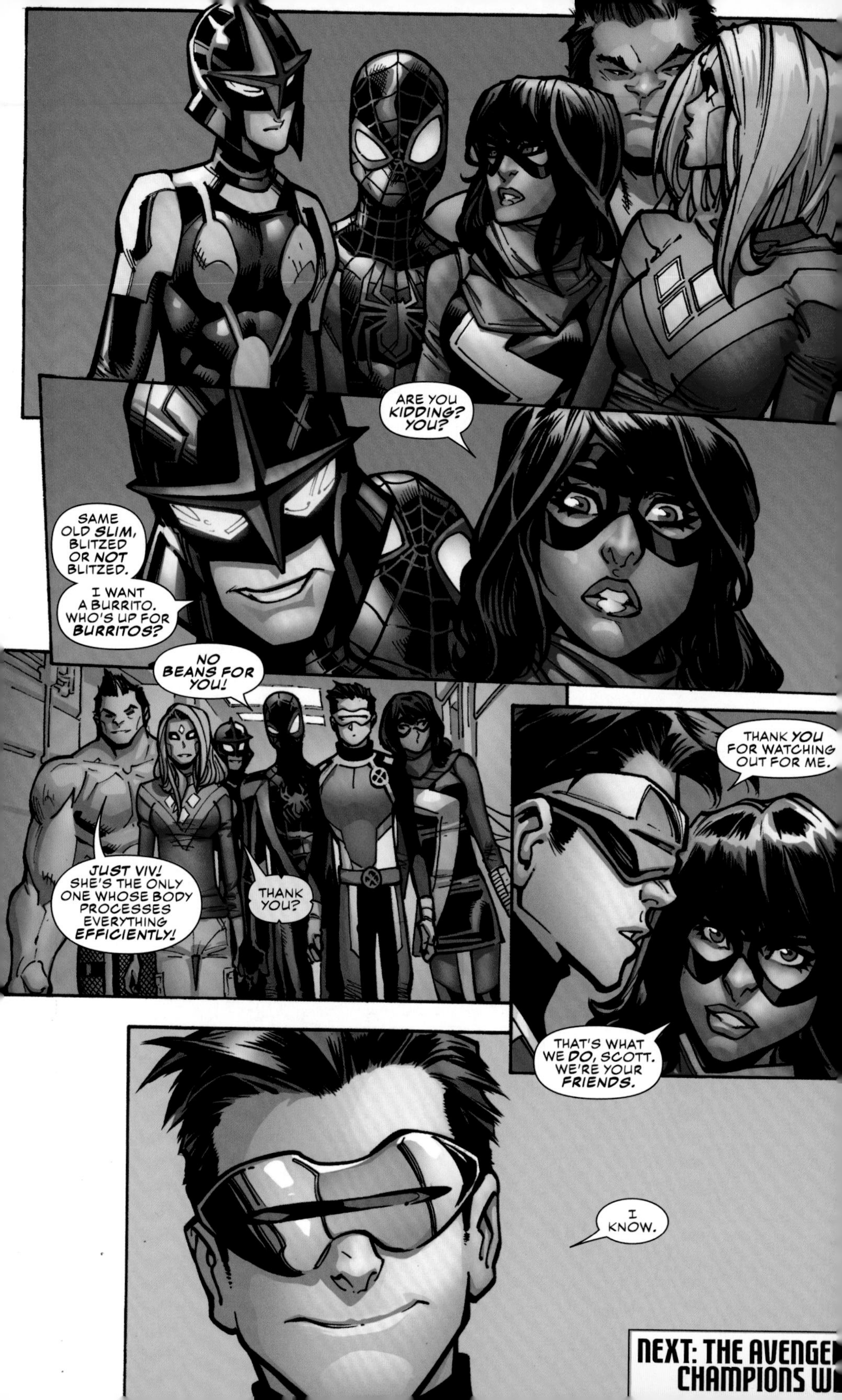

ARE YOU KIDDING? YOU?
SAME OLD SLIM, BLITZED OR NOT BLITZED.
I WANT A BURRITO. WHO'S UP FOR BURRITOS?
NO BEANS FOR YOU!
JUST VIV! SHE'S THE ONLY ONE WHOSE BODY PROCESSES EVERYTHING EFFICIENTLY!
THANK YOU?
THANK YOU FOR WATCHING OUT FOR ME.
THAT'S WHAT WE DO, SCOTT. WE'RE YOUR FRIENDS.
I KNOW.

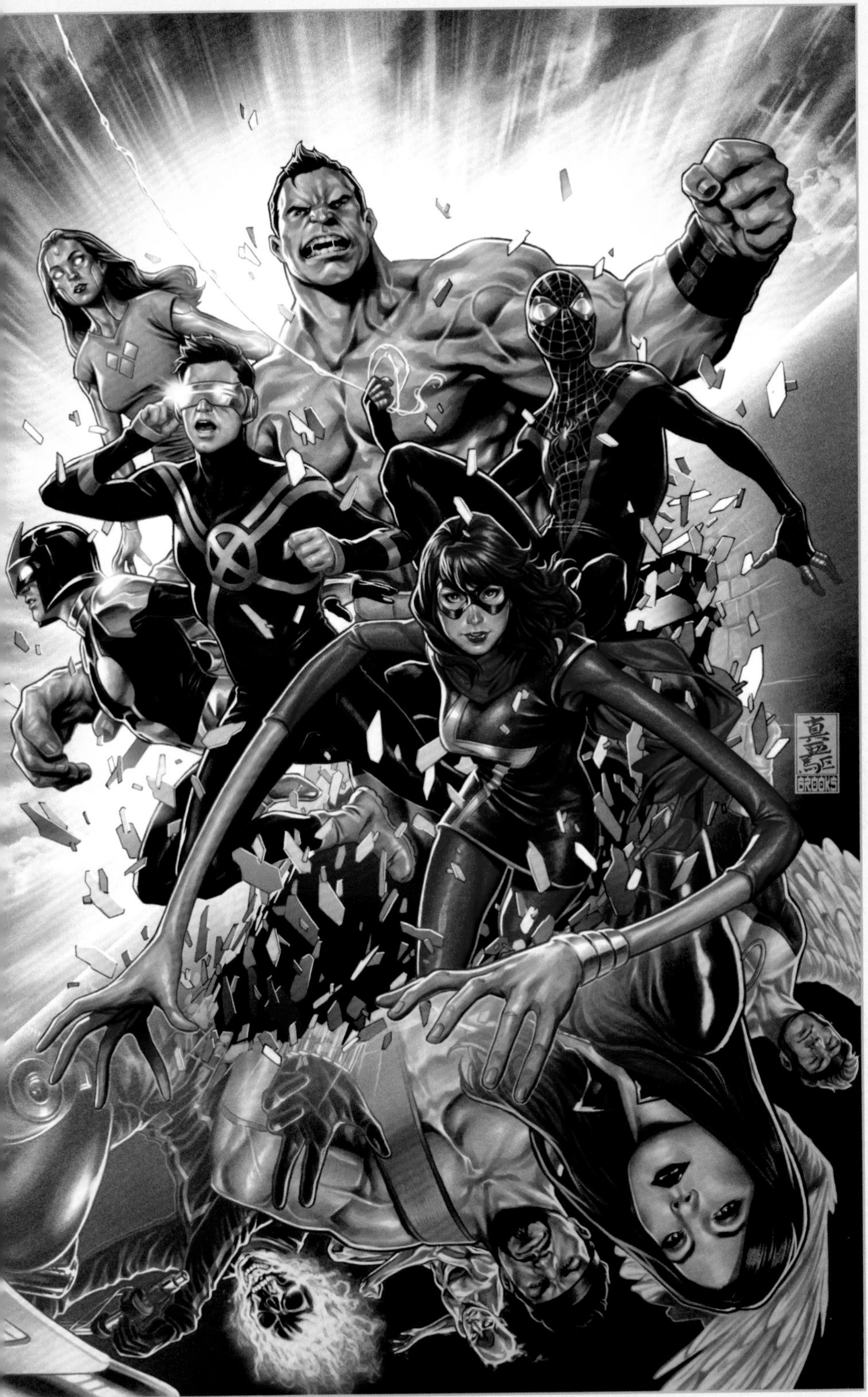
BROOKS

#1 VARIANT
BY MARK BROOKS

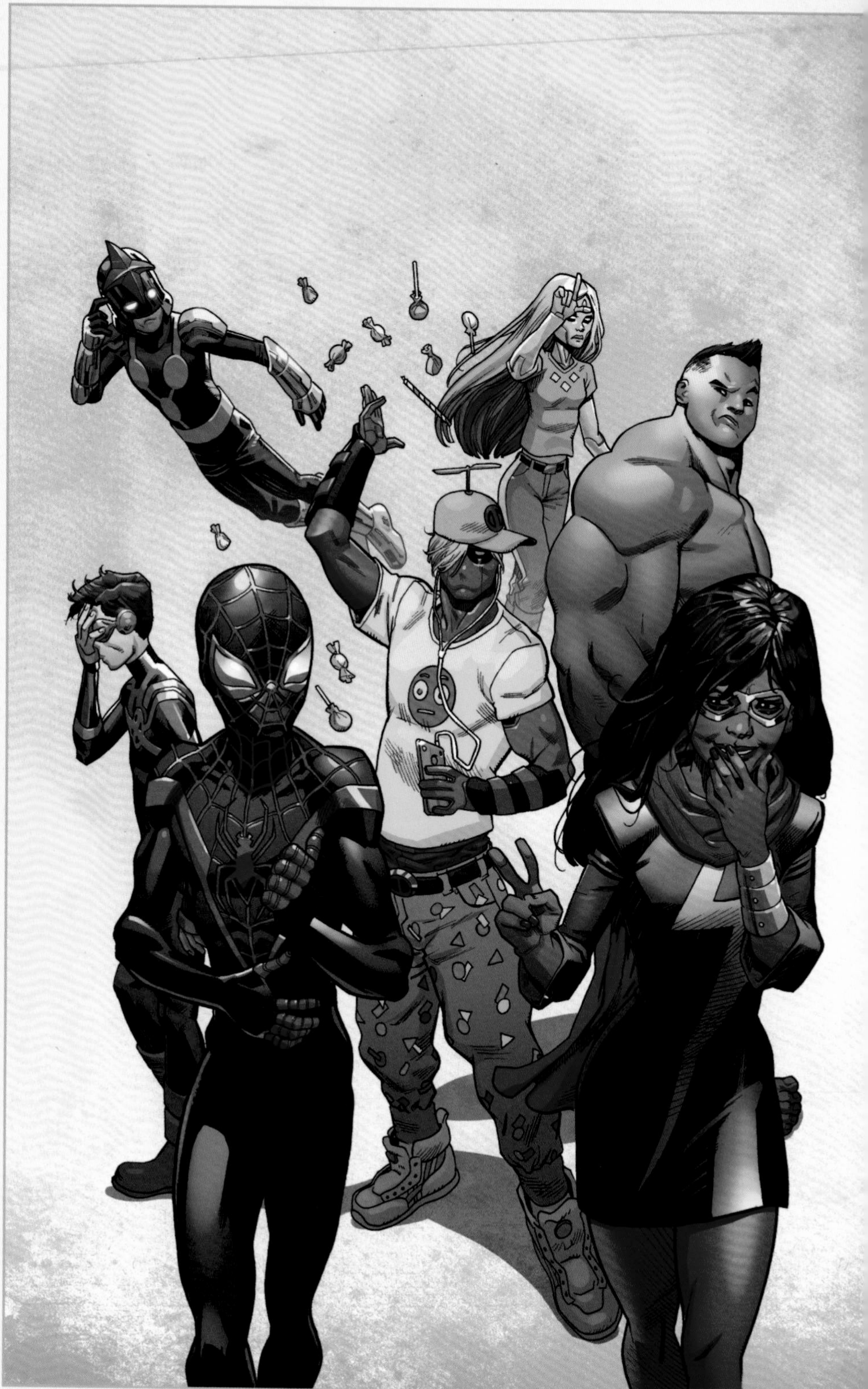

#1 VARIANT
BY MIKE HAWTHORNE & MATT MILLA

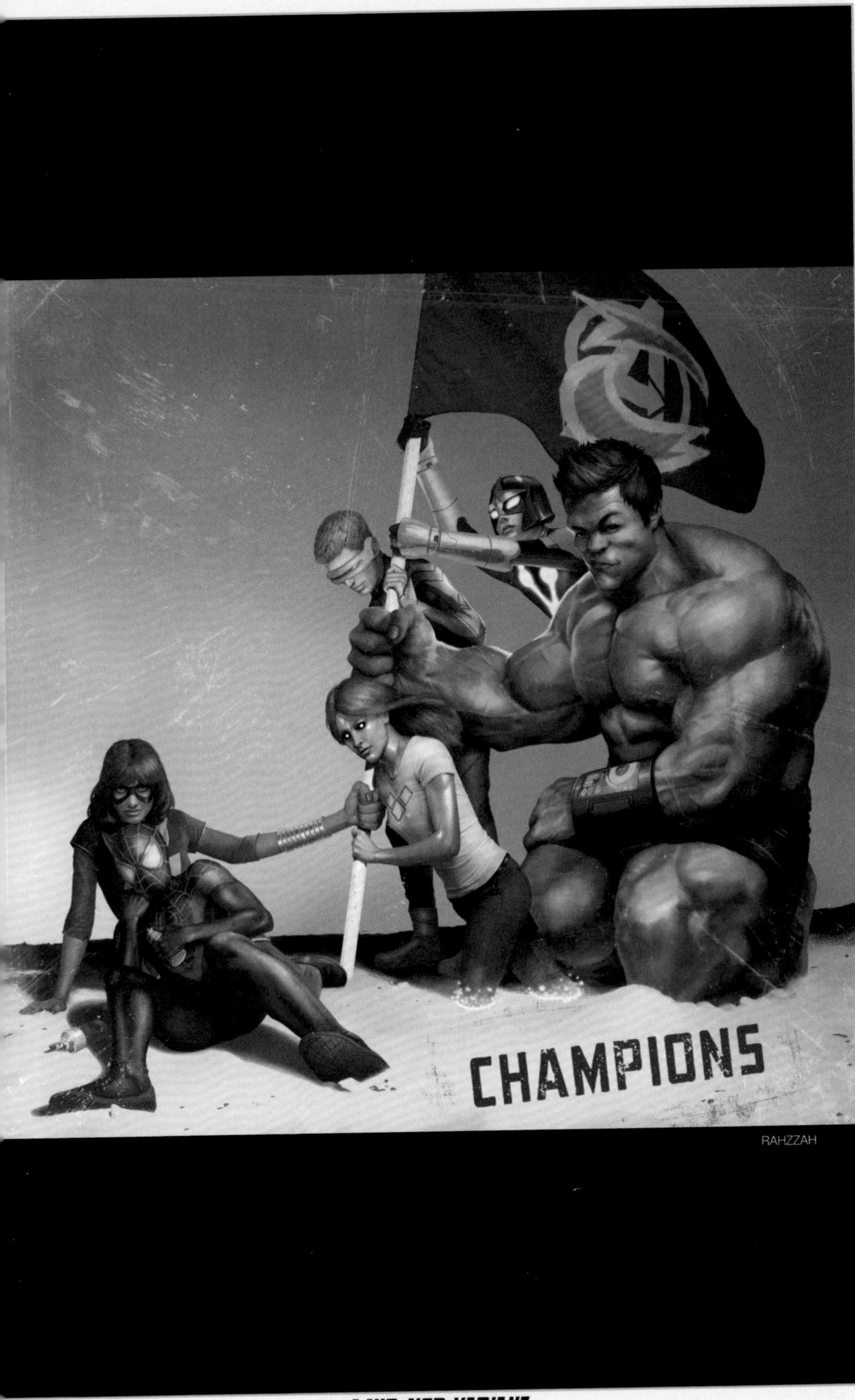
CHAMPIONS
RAHZZAH

#1 HIP-HOP VARIANT
BY RAHZZAH

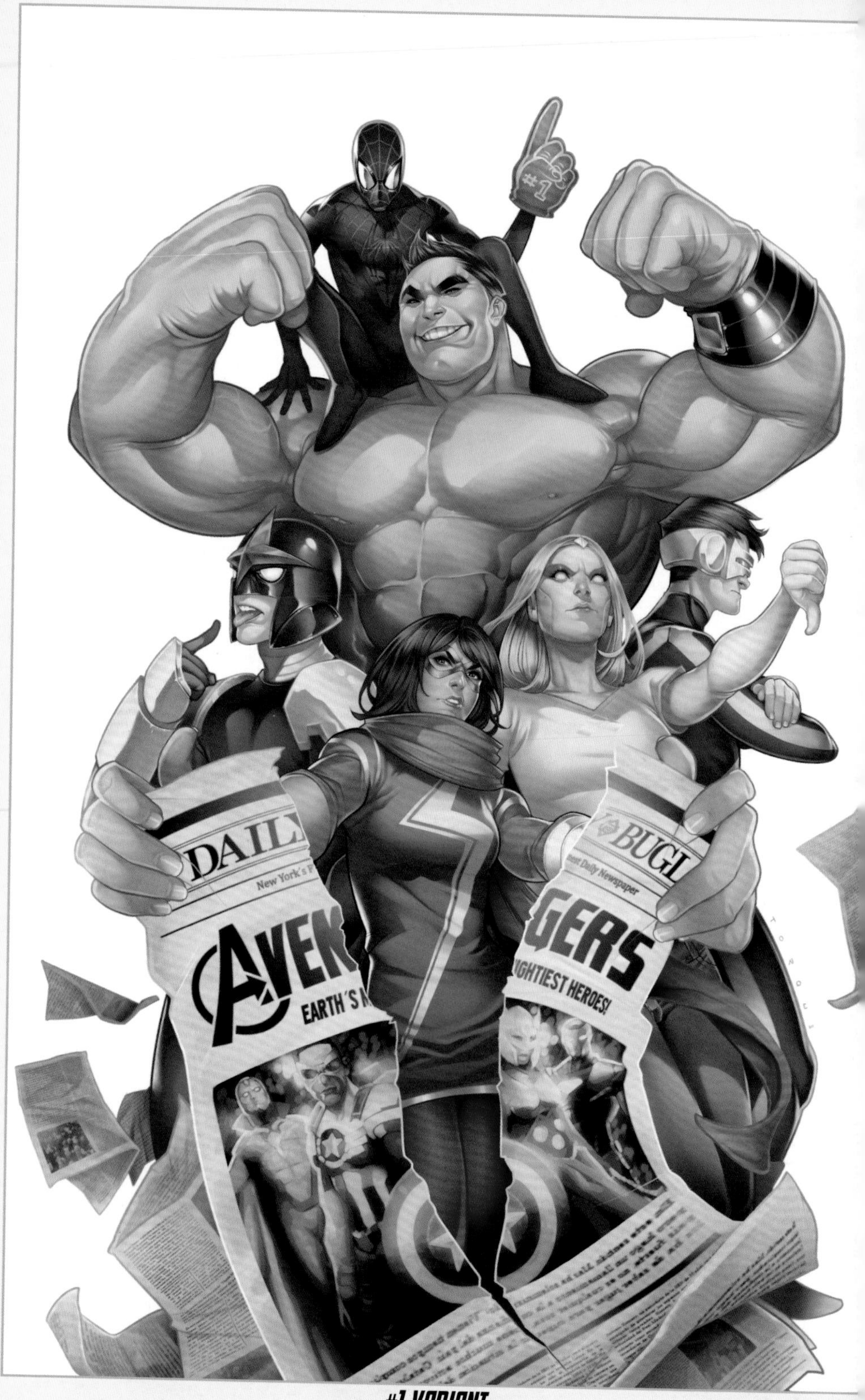
DAIL
New York's F
BUGL
Daily Newspaper
AVEN
GERS
EARTH'S M
IGHTIEST HEROES!
#1
TORQUE

#1 VARIANT
BY ELIZABETH TORQUE

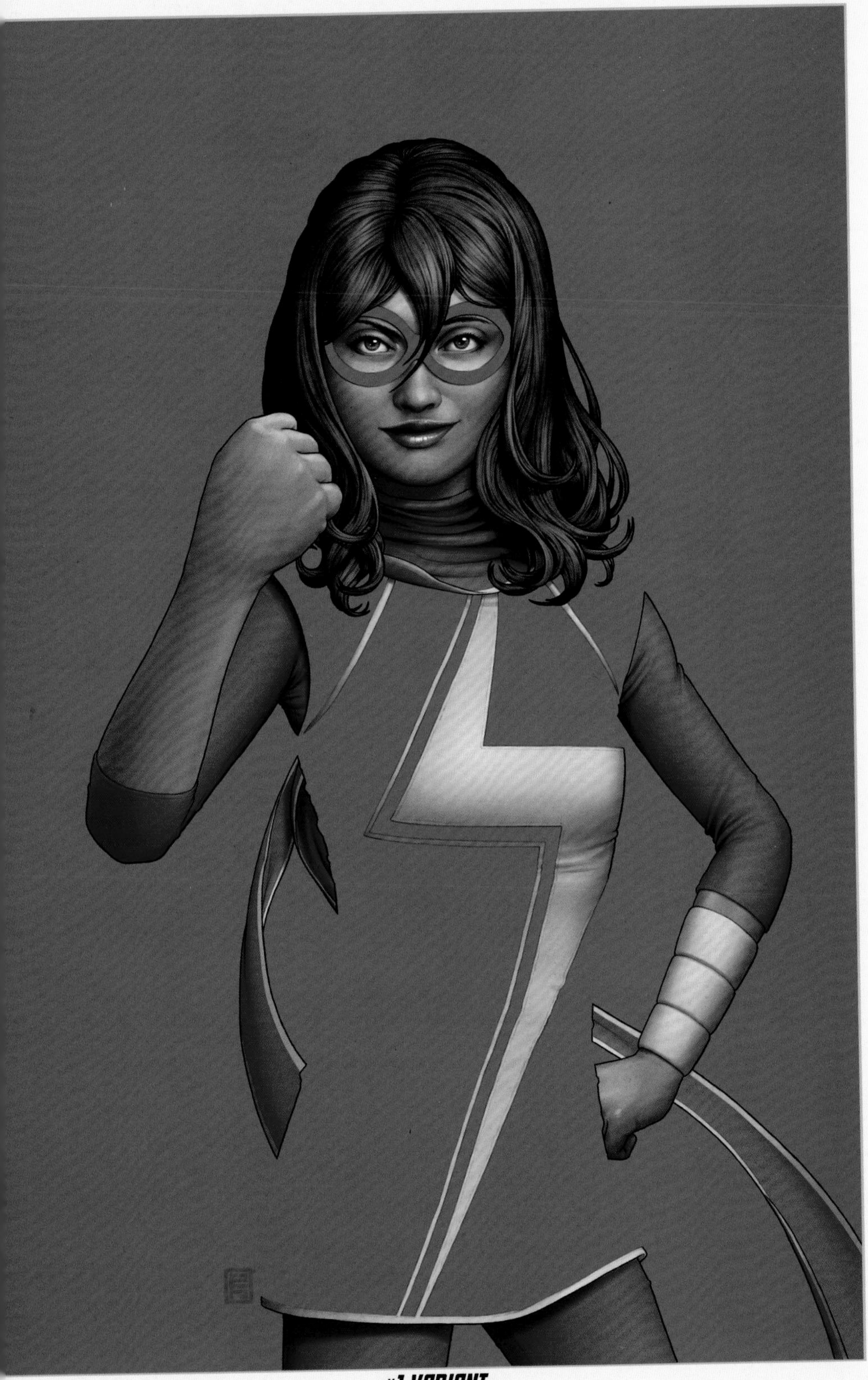

#1 VARIANT
BY JOHN TYLER CHRISTOPHER

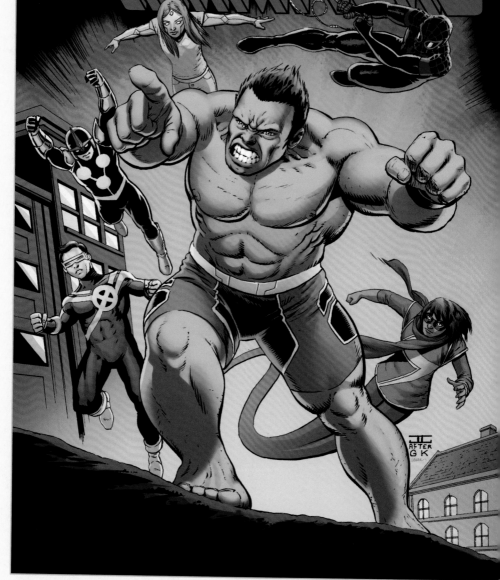

MARVEL COMICS GROUP

HULK! MS. MARVEL! NOVA! SPIDER-MAN! CYCLOPS! VIV VISION!

THE CHAMPIONS

#1 VARIANT
BY JOHN CASSADAY & LAURA MARTIN

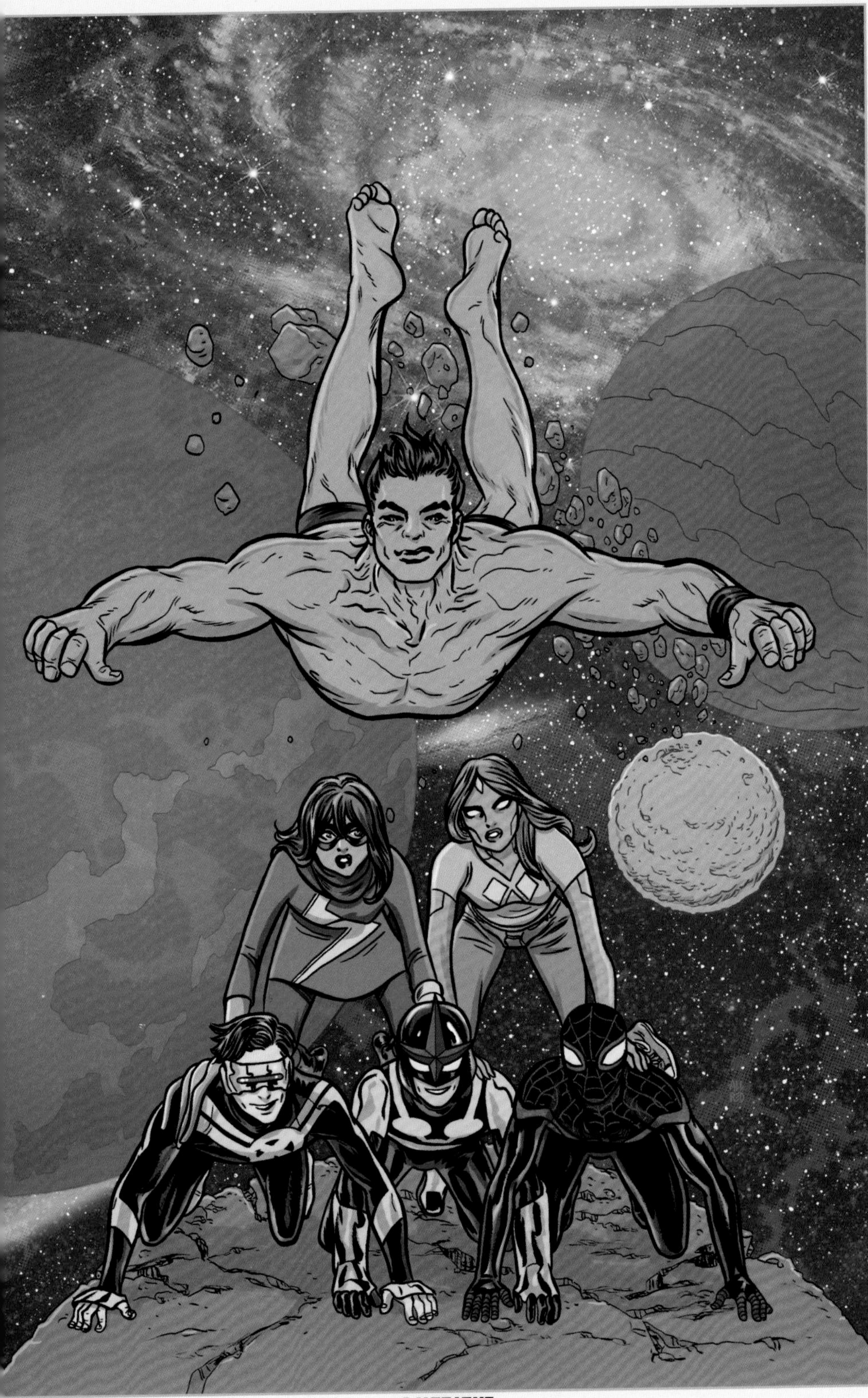

#1 VARIANT
BY MICHAEL ALLRED & LAURA MARTIN

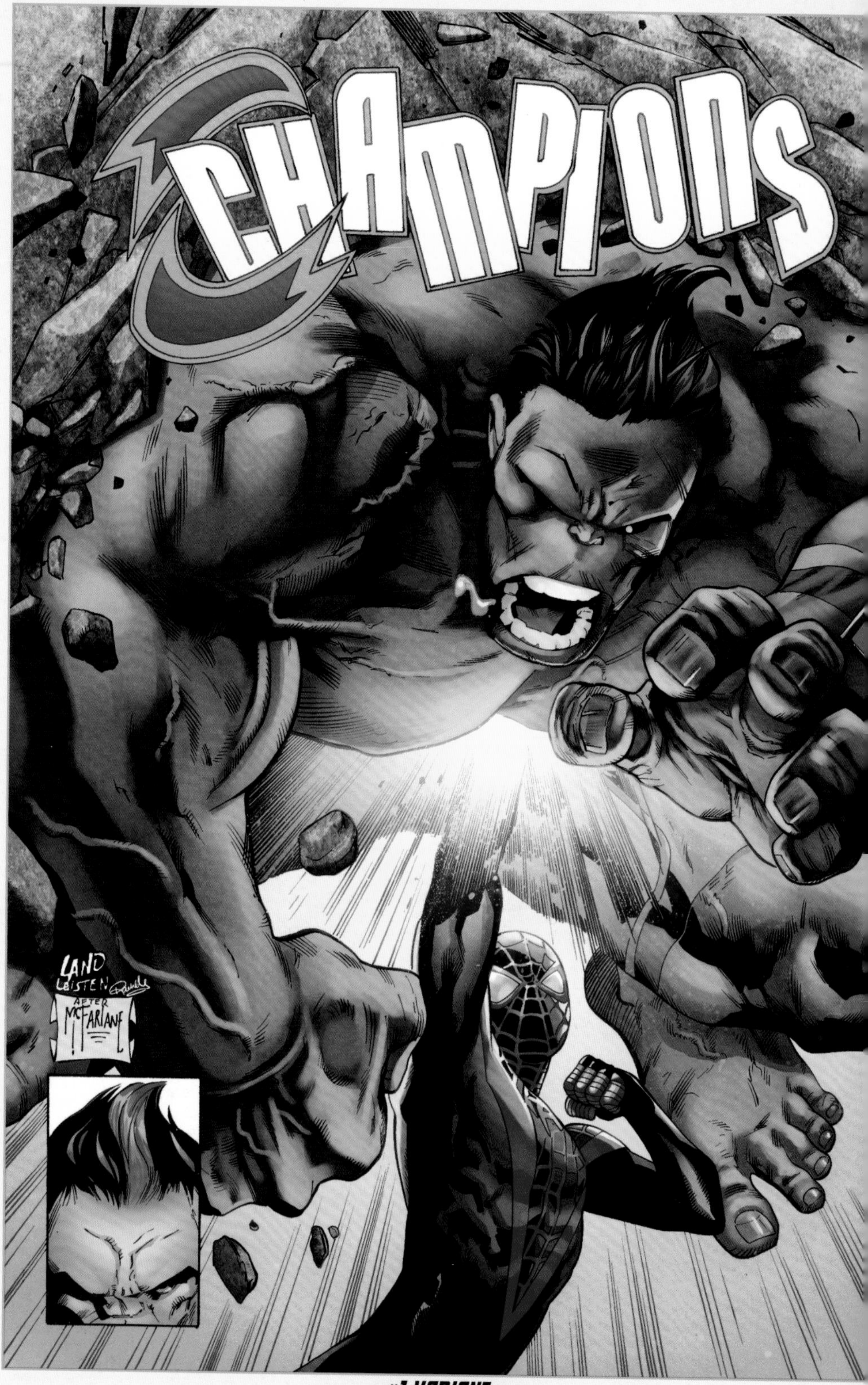
CHAMPIONS
LAND
LEISTEN
AFTER
McFARLANE

#1 VARIANT
BY GREG LAND, JAY LEISTEN & RACHELLE ROSENBERG

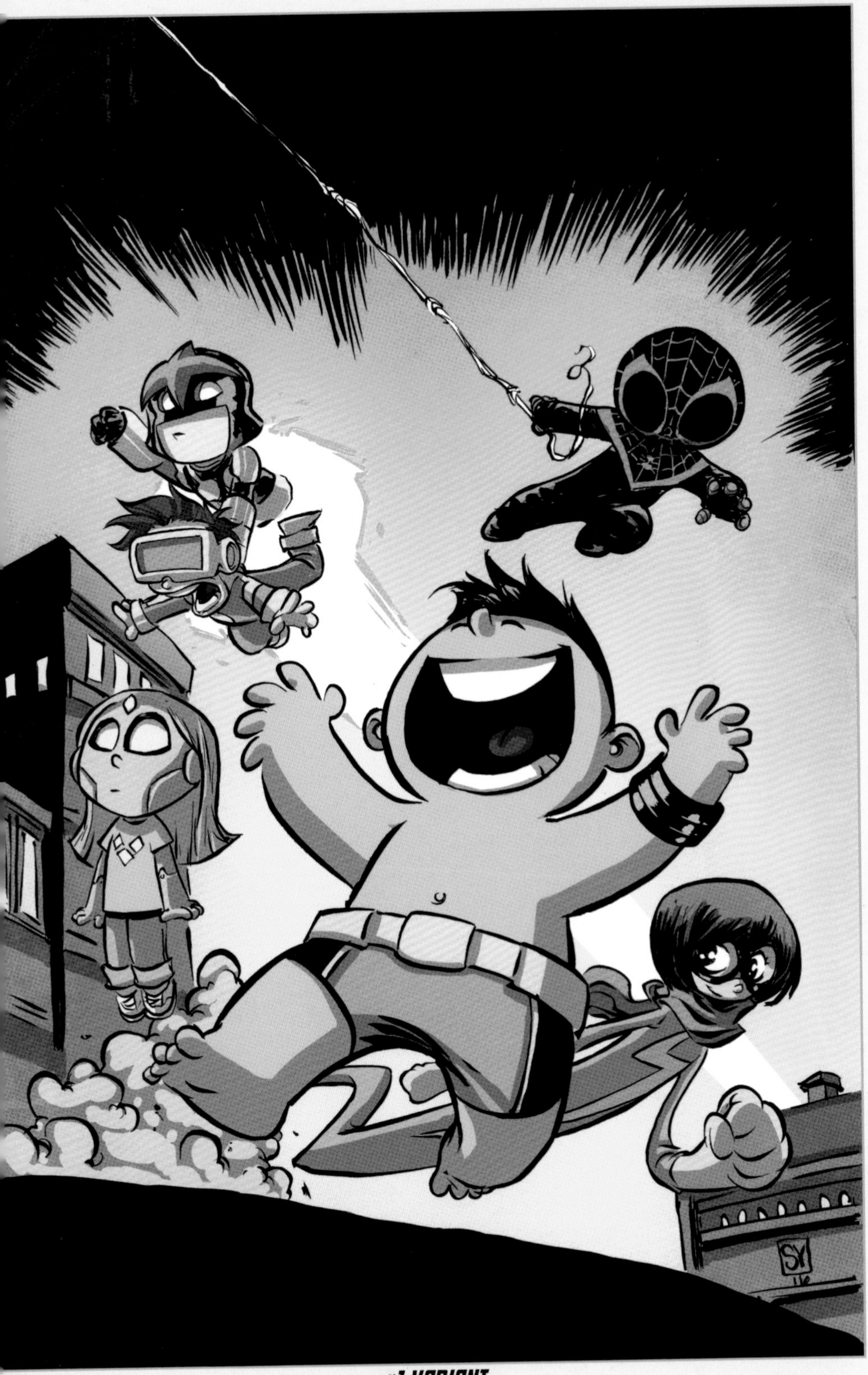

#1 VARIANT
BY SKOTTIE YOUNG

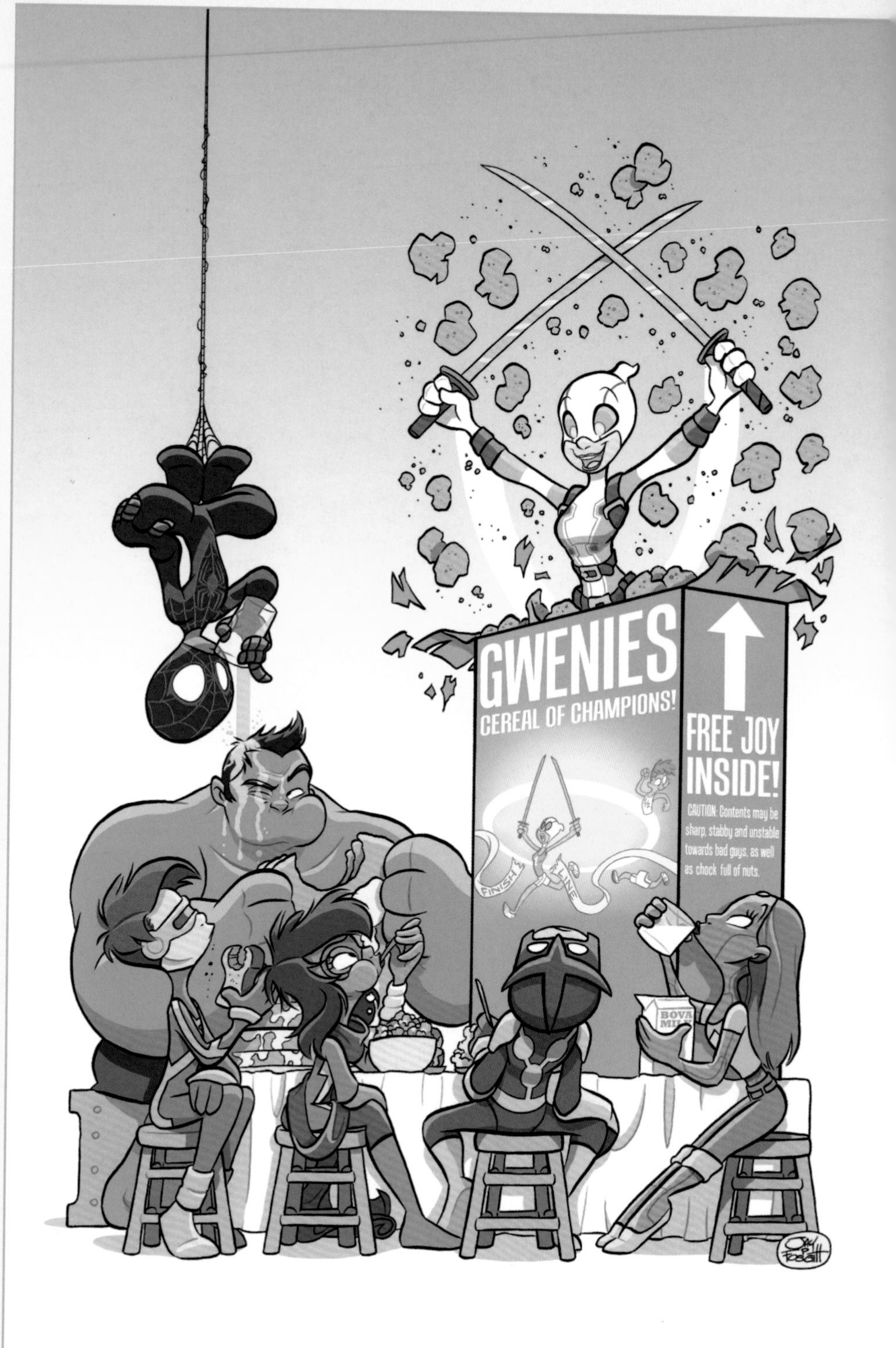
GWENIES
CEREAL OF CHAMPIONS!
FREE JOY INSIDE!
CAUTION: Contents may be sharp, stabby and unstable towards bad guys, as well as chock full of nuts.
FINISH LINE

#1 PARTY VARIANT
BY JAY FOSGITT

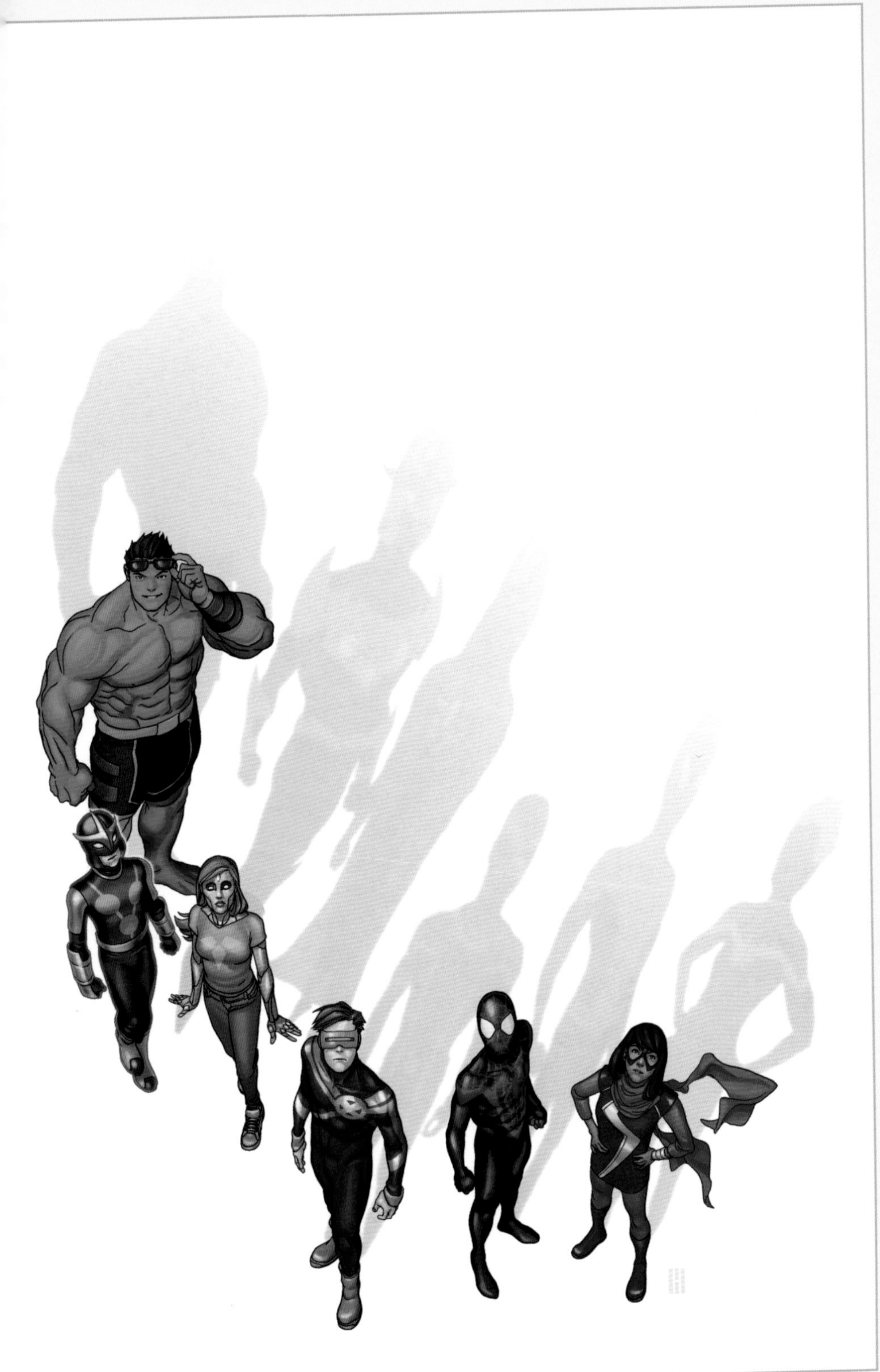

#2 VARIANT
BY MIKE CHOI

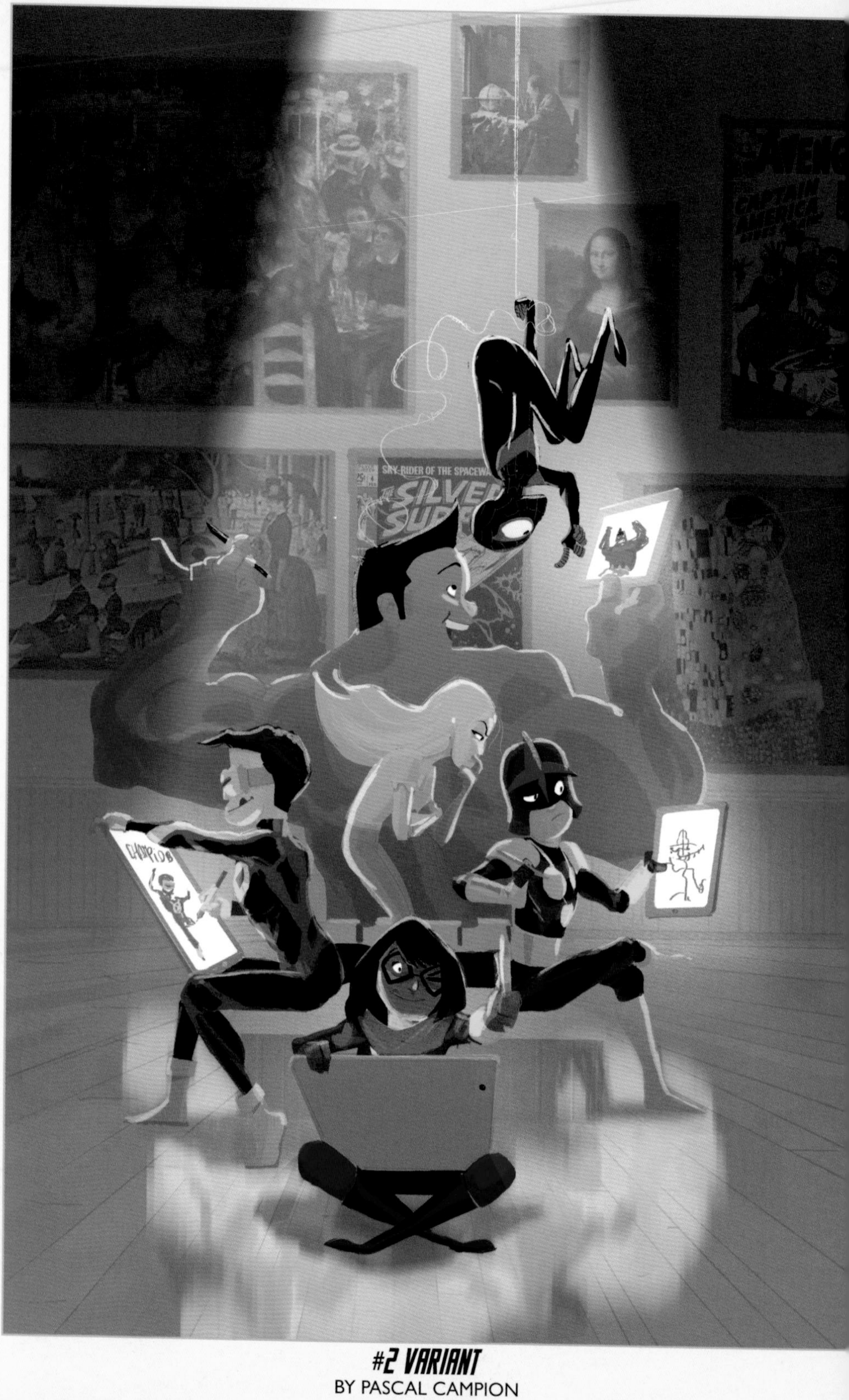
SKY-RIDER OF THE SPACEWA
SILVER
SURF
CAPTAIN AMERICA
CHAMPION

#2 VARIANT
BY PASCAL CAMPION

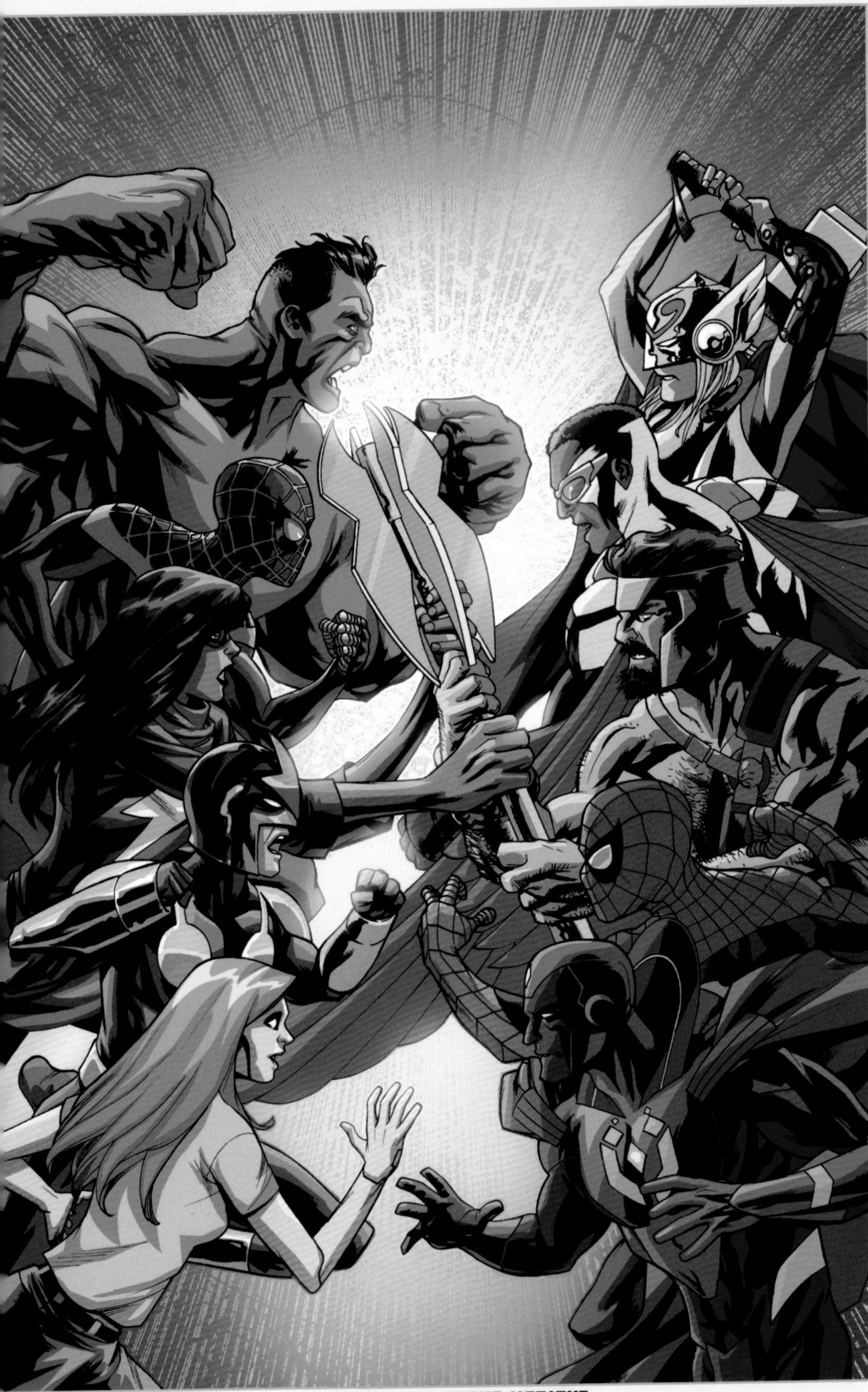

#2 DIVIDED WE STAND VARIANT
BY MIKE McKONE & ANDY TROY

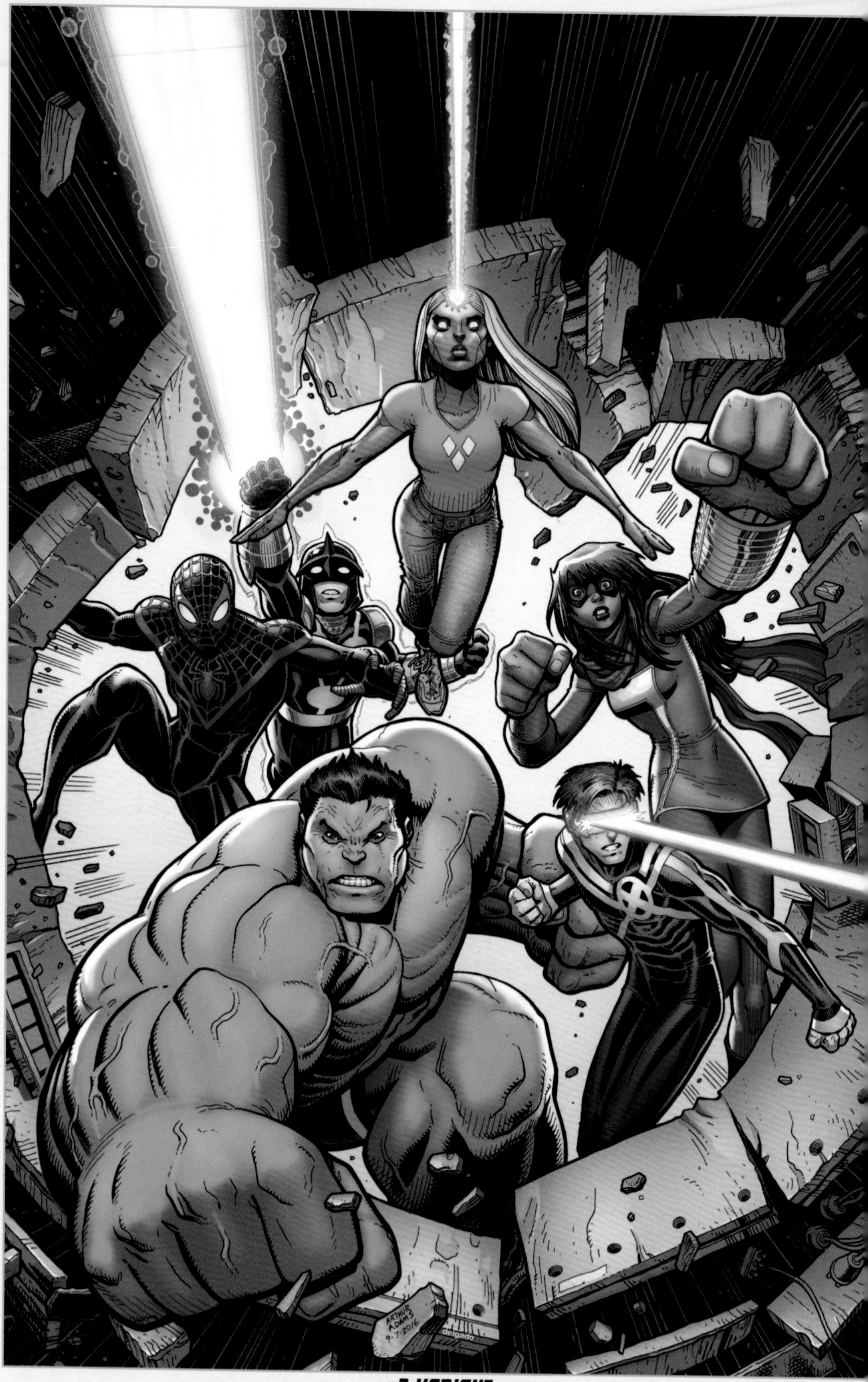
ARTHUR
ADAMS
9-7-2016
delgado

#3 VARIANT

BY ARTHUR ADAMS

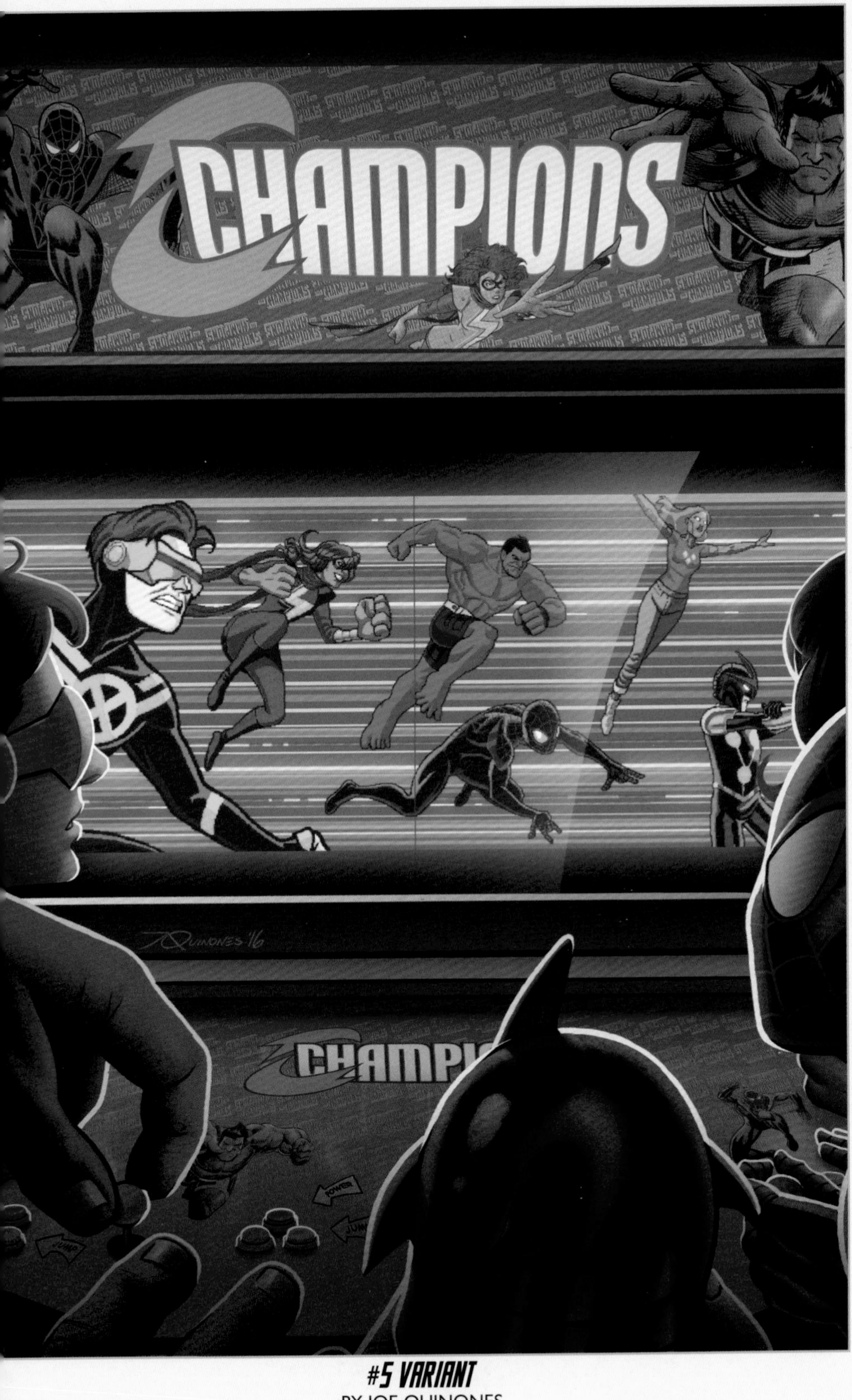
CHAMPIONS
JQUINONES '16
CHAMPIONS
POWER
JUMP
JUMP

#5 VARIANT
BY JOE QUINONES

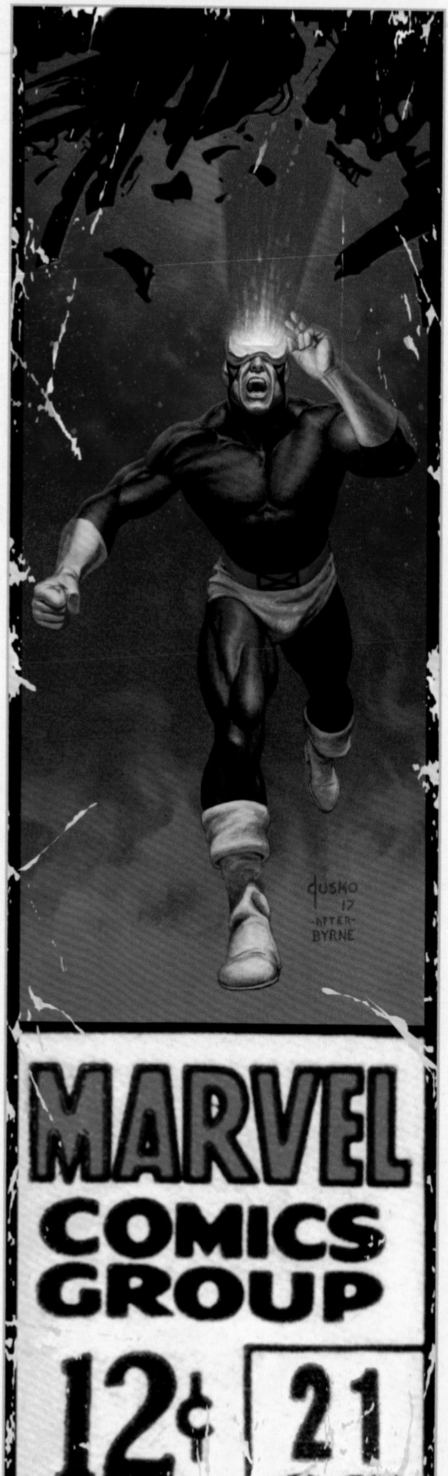
Jusko
17
-after-
Byrne
MARVEL
COMICS
GROUP
12¢
IND.
21
OCT

#5 CORNER BOX VARIANT
BY JOE JUSKO

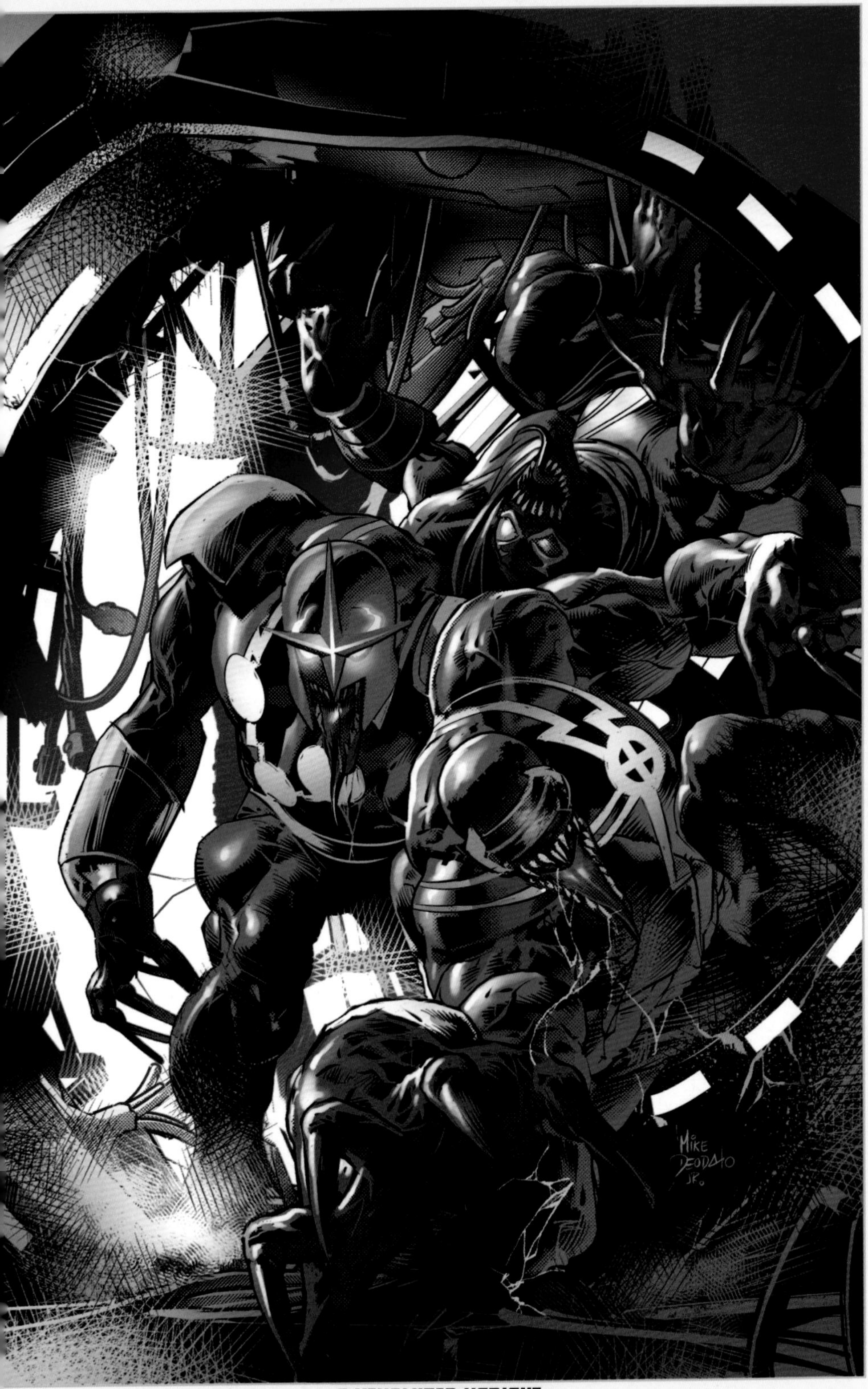
MIKE DEODATO JR.

#6 VENOMIZED VARIANT
BY MIKE DEODATO JR. & RAIN BEREDO

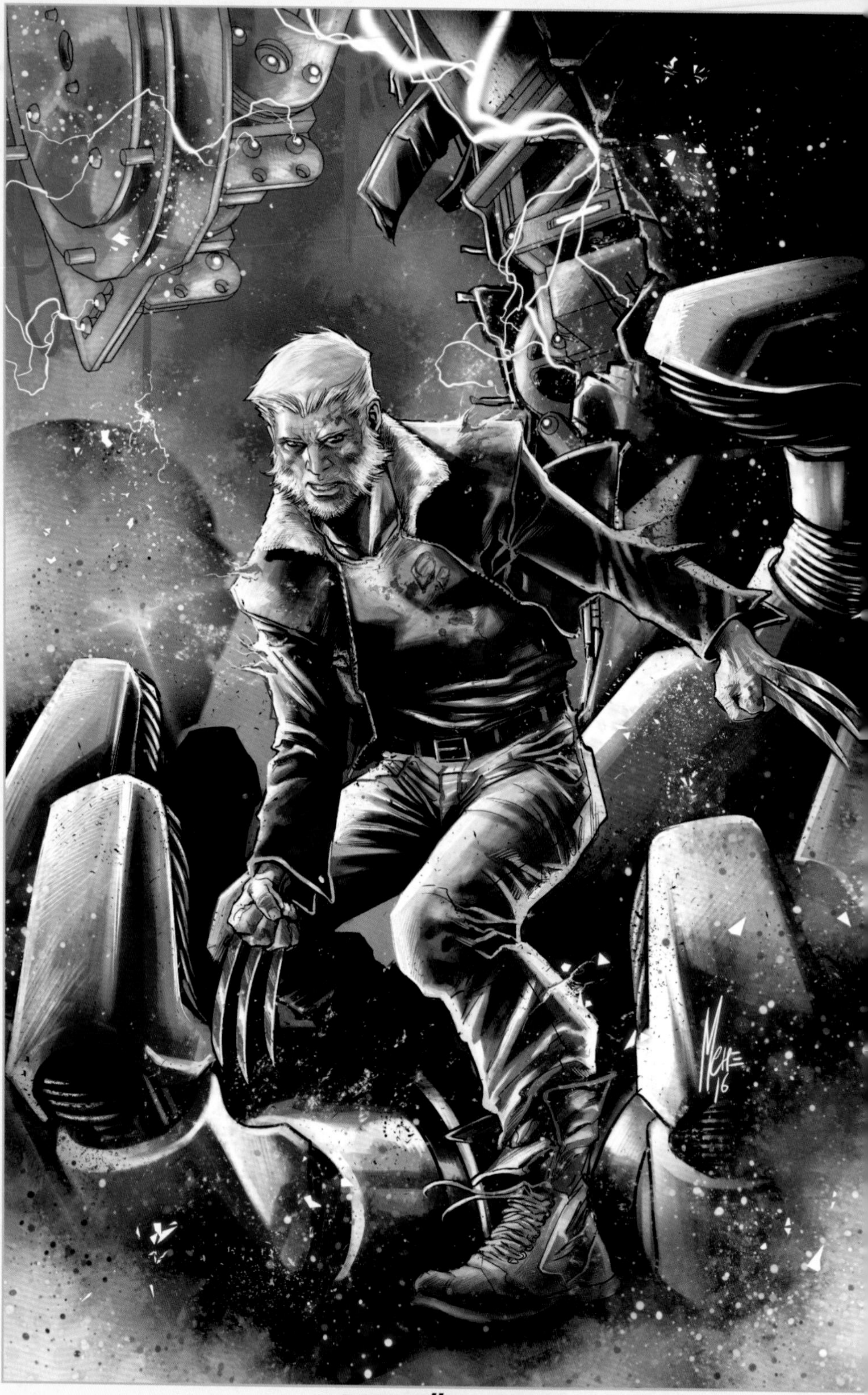

#7 RESURRXION VARIANT
BY MARCO CHECCHETTO

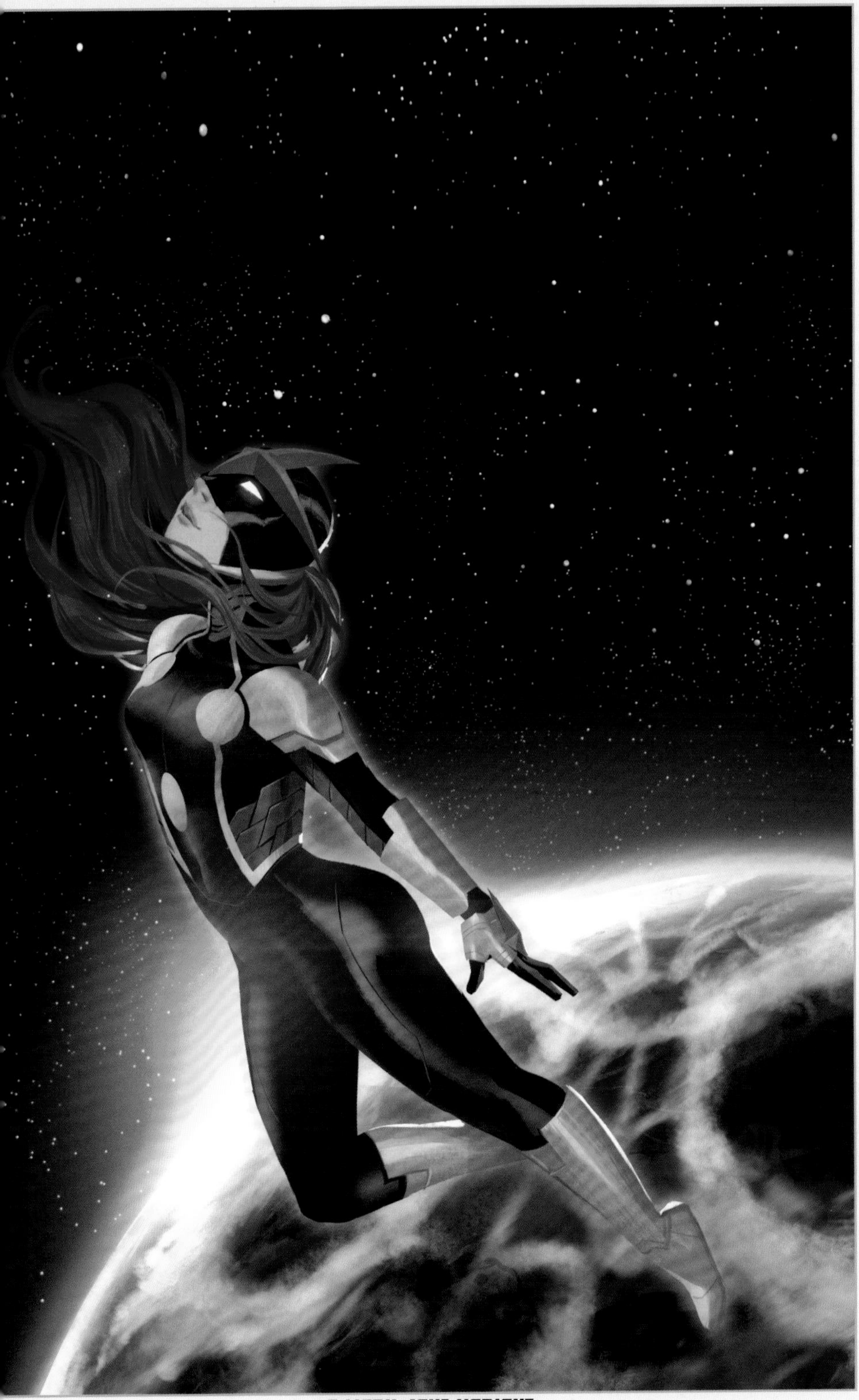

#9 MARY JANE VARIANT
BY HELEN CHEN

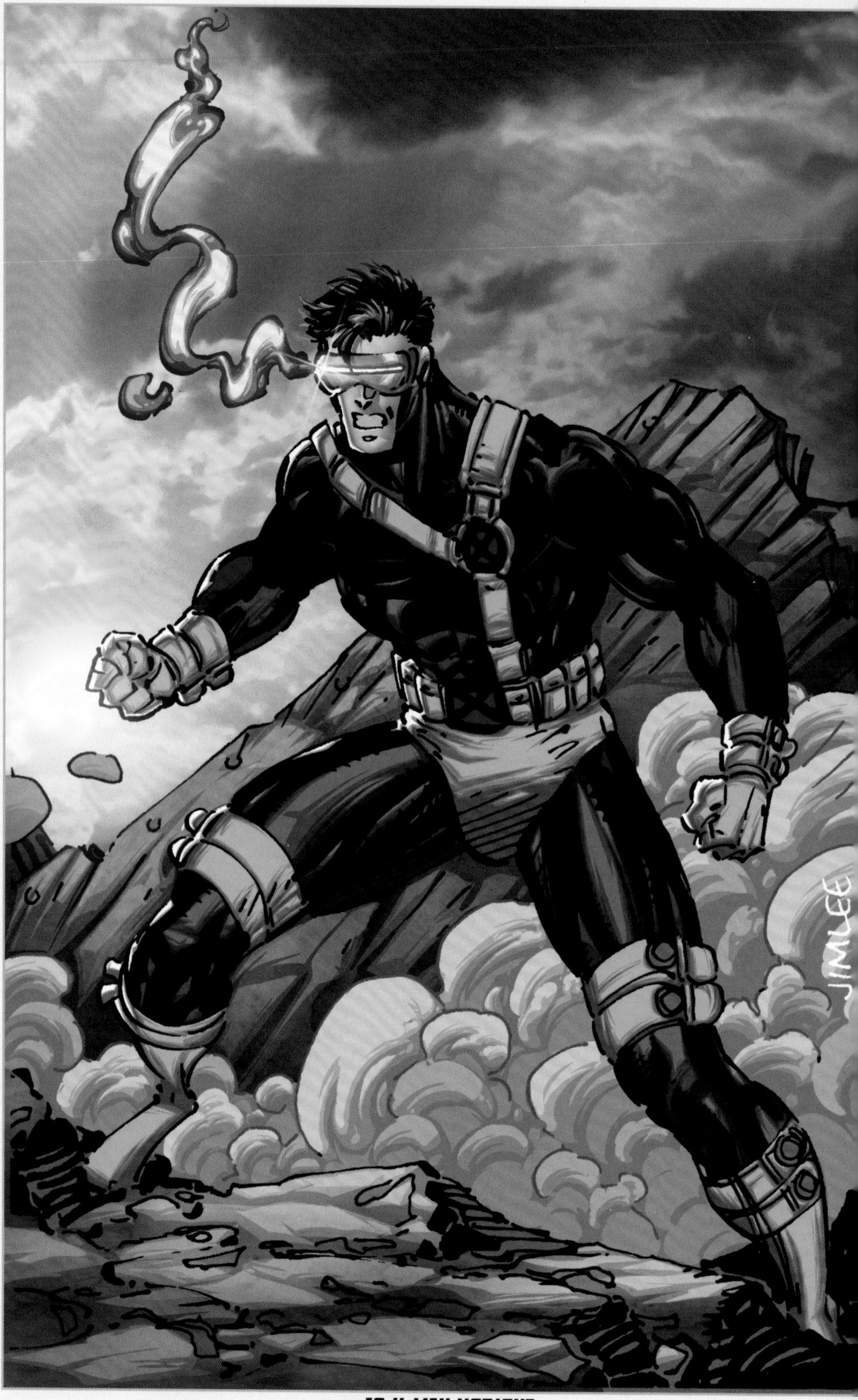
JIMLEE

#10 X-MEN VARIANT
BY JIM LEE & ISRAEL SILVA WITH MICHAEL KELLEHER

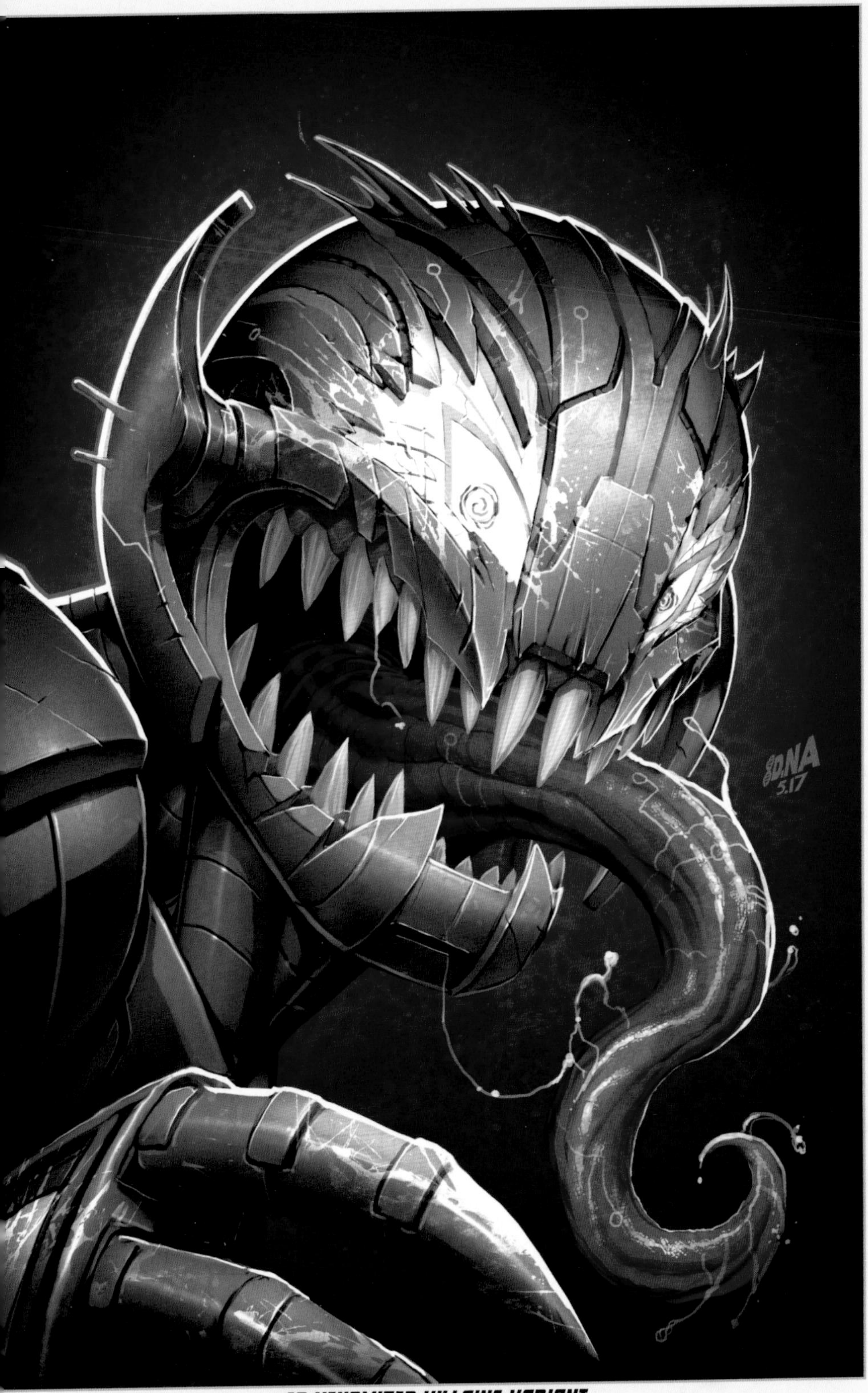
D.NA
5.17

#12 VENOMIZED VILLAINS VARIANT
BY DAVID NAKAYAMA

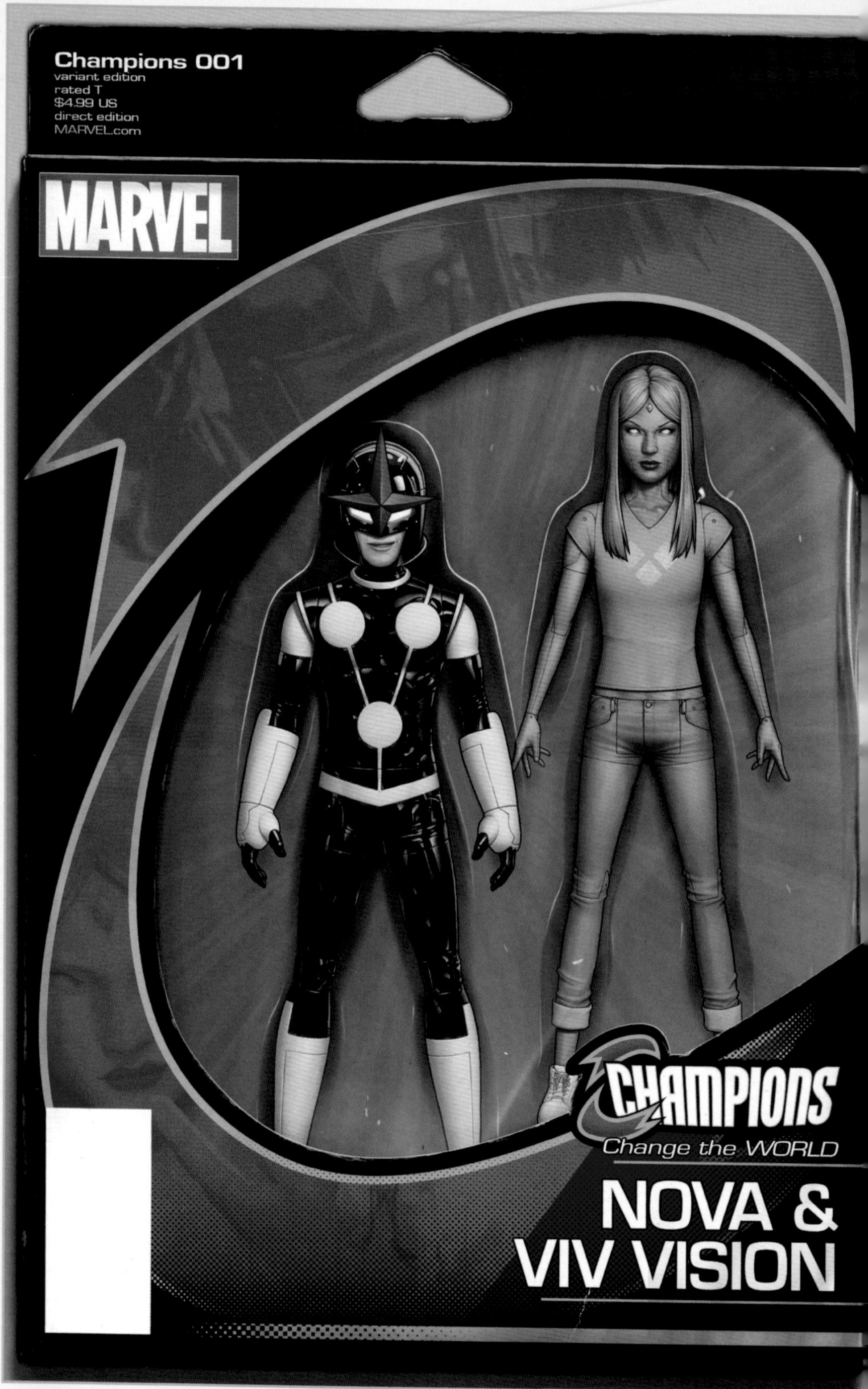
Champions 001
variant edition
rated T
$4.99 US
direct edition
MARVEL.com
MARVEL
CHAMPIONS
Change the WORLD
NOVA &
VIV VISION

#1 ACTION FIGURE VARIANT
BY JOHN TYLER CHRISTOPHER

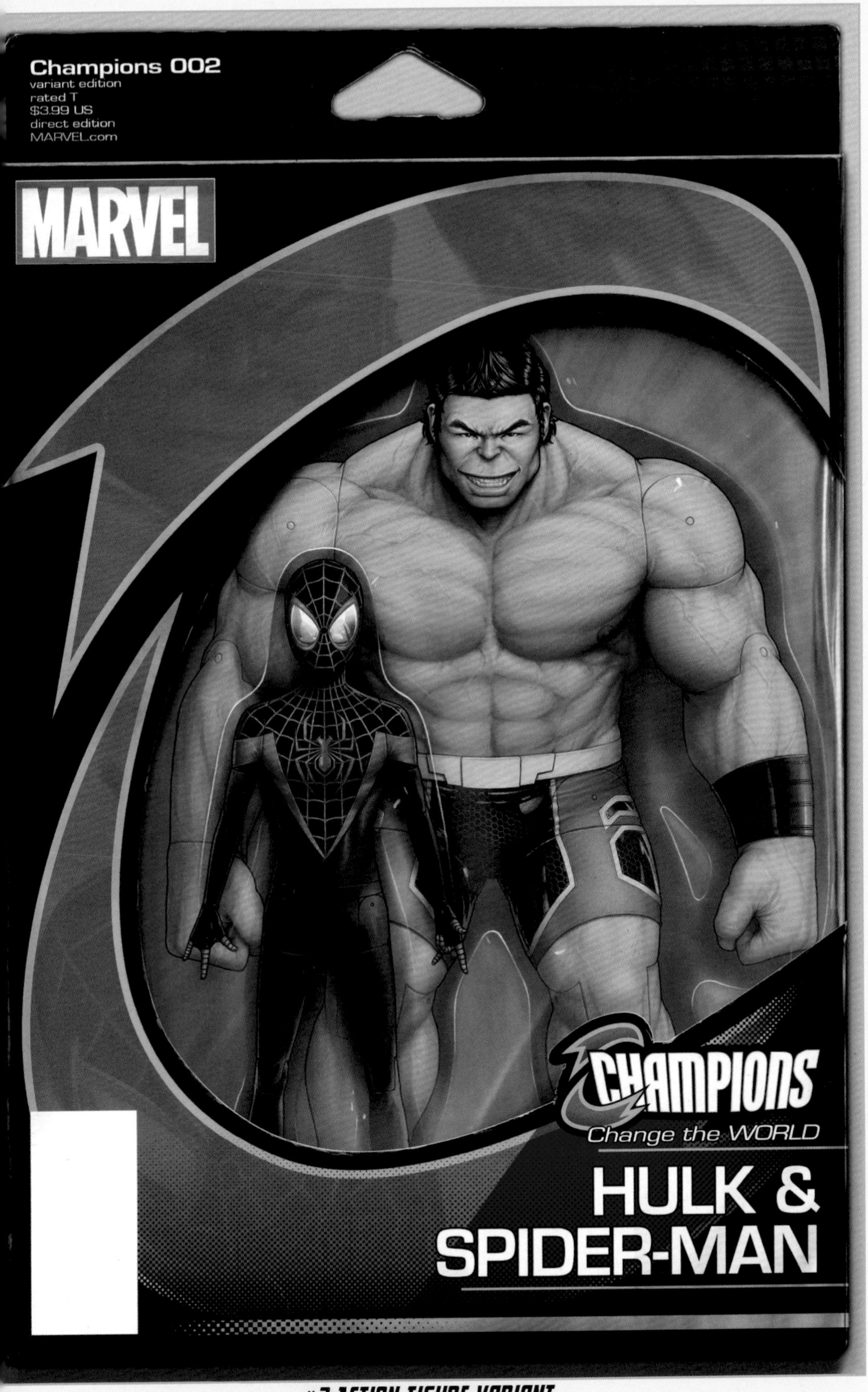
Champions 002
variant edition
rated T
$3.99 US
direct edition
MARVEL.com
MARVEL
CHAMPIONS
Change the WORLD
HULK &
SPIDER-MAN

#2 ACTION FIGURE VARIANT
BY JOHN TYLER CHRISTOPHER

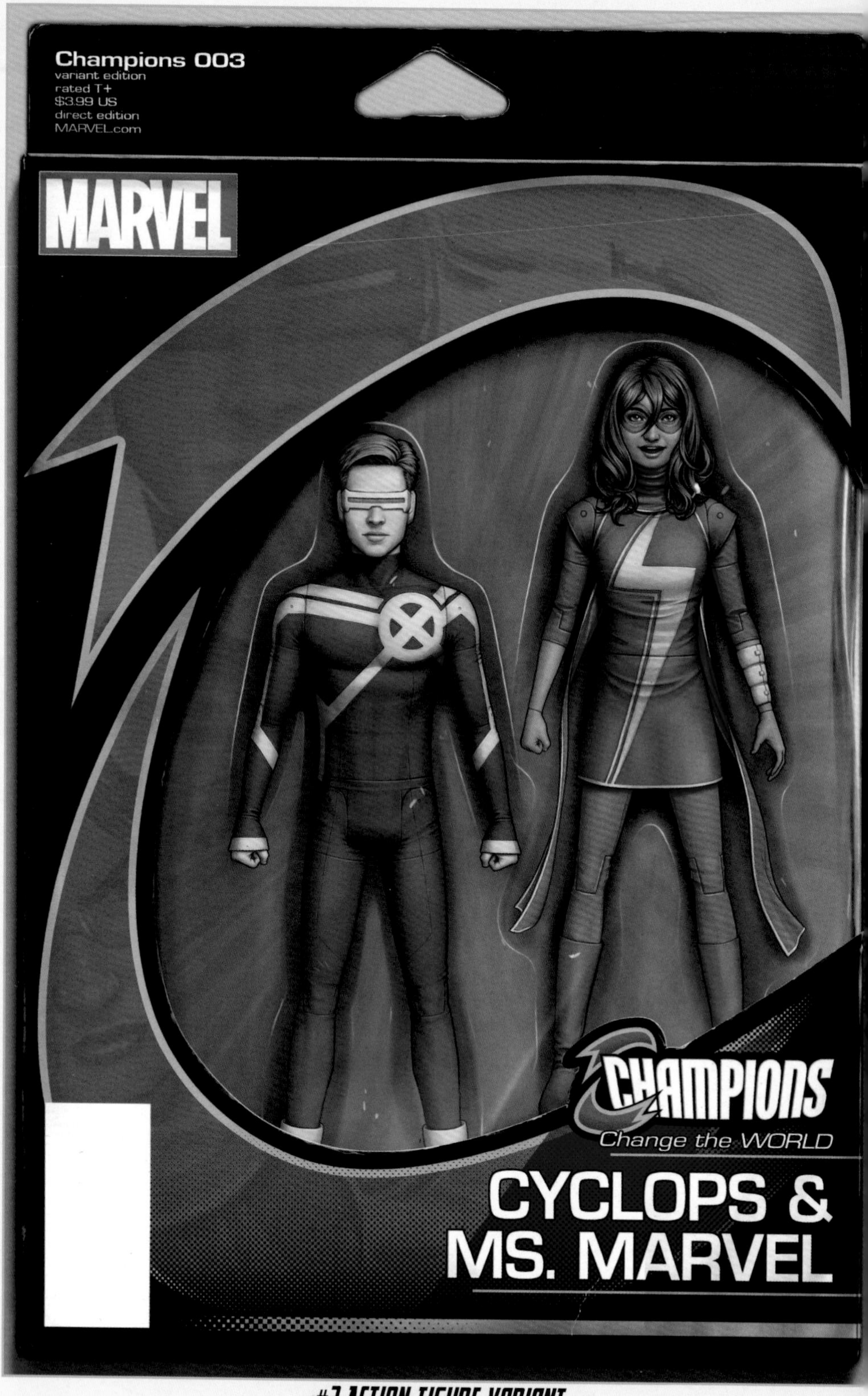
Champions 003
variant edition
rated T+
$3.99 US
direct edition
MARVEL.com
MARVEL
CHAMPIONS
Change the WORLD
CYCLOPS &
MS. MARVEL

#3 ACTION FIGURE VARIANT
BY JOHN TYLER CHRISTOPHER

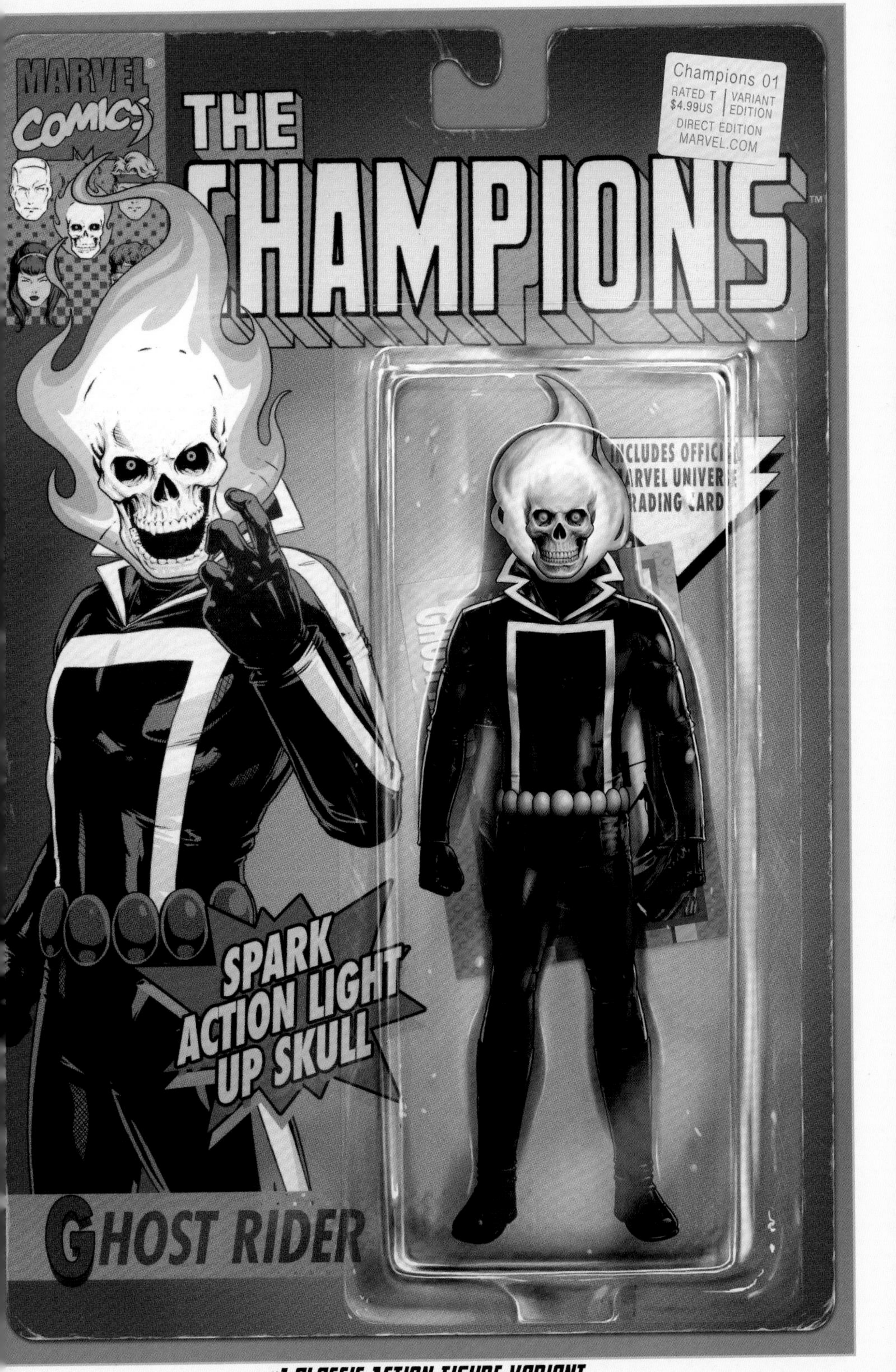
MARVEL COMICS
THE CHAMPIONS
Champions 01
RATED T
$4.99US
VARIANT EDITION
DIRECT EDITION
MARVEL.COM
INCLUDES OFFICIAL MARVEL UNIVERSE TRADING CARD
SPARK ACTION LIGHT UP SKULL
GHOST RIDER

#1 CLASSIC ACTION FIGURE VARIANT
BY JOHN TYLER CHRISTOPHER

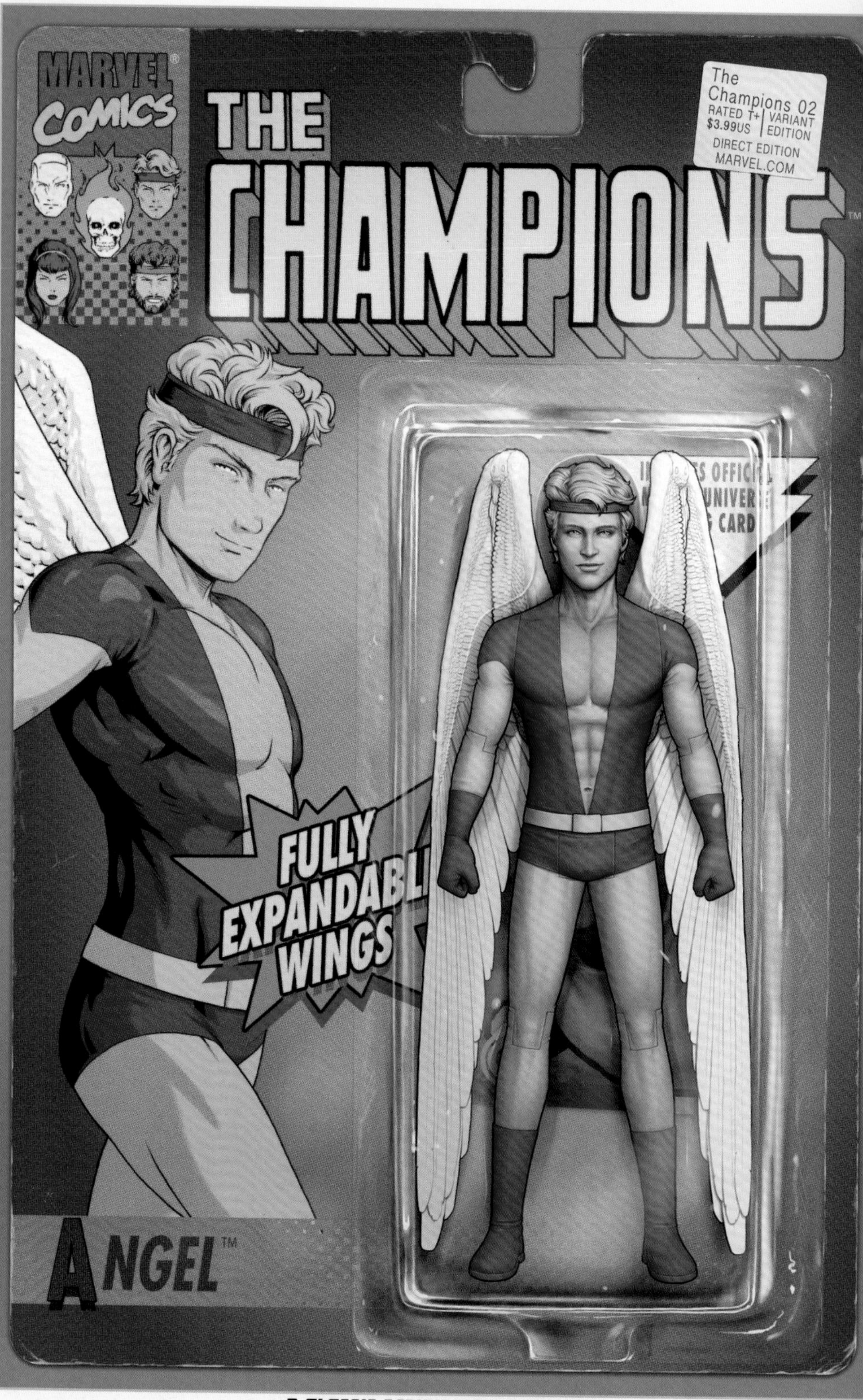

MARVEL
COMICS
THE
CHAMPIONS
The
Champions 02
RATED T+
$3.99US
VARIANT
EDITION
DIRECT EDITION
MARVEL.COM
FULLY
EXPANDABLE
WINGS
ANGEL

#2 CLASSIC ACTION FIGURE VARIANT
BY JOHN TYLER CHRISTOPHER

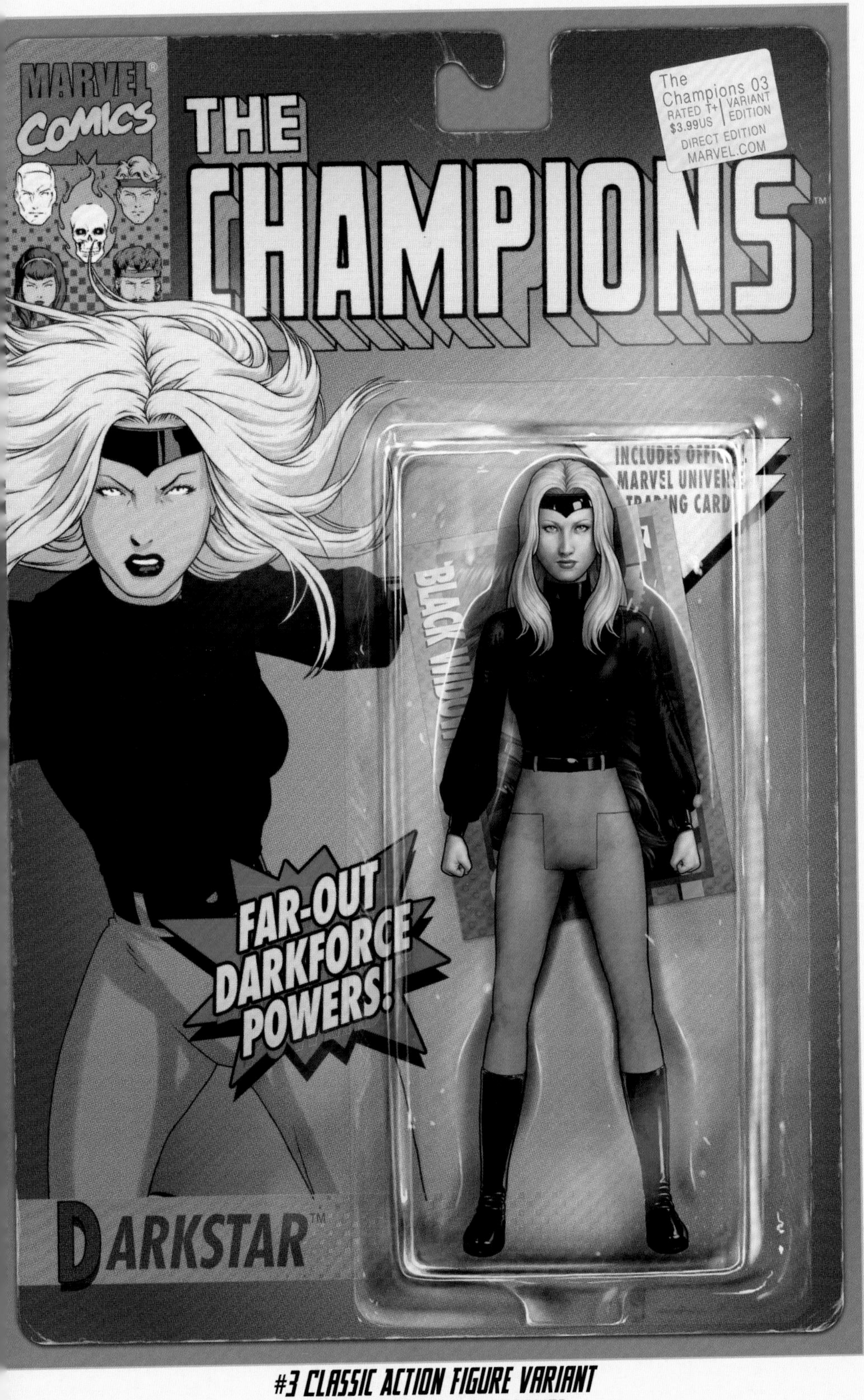
MARVEL COMICS
THE CHAMPIONS
The Champions 03
RATED T+
$3.99US
VARIANT EDITION
DIRECT EDITION
MARVEL.COM
FAR-OUT DARKFORCE POWERS!
DARKSTAR

#3 CLASSIC ACTION FIGURE VARIANT
BY JOHN TYLER CHRISTOPHER

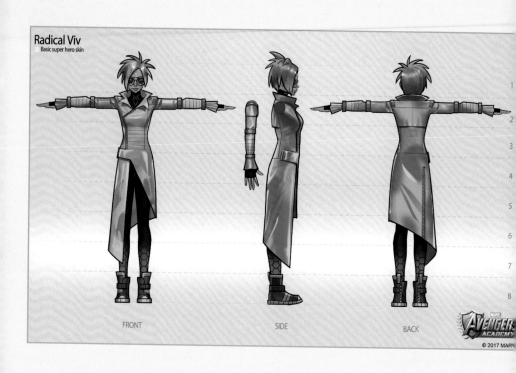

Radical Viv
Basic super hero skin

FRONT   SIDE   BACK

1
2
3
4
5
6
7
8

© 2017 MARV

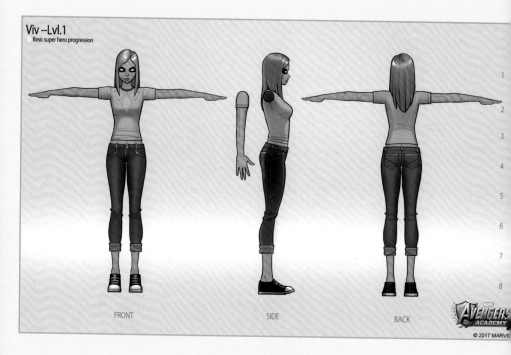

Viv --Lvl.1
Basic super hero progression

FRONT   SIDE   BACK

1
2
3
4
5
6
7
8

© 2017 MARVE

VIV VISION CHARACTER DESIGNS
FROM THE *AVENGERS ACADEMY* MOBILE GAME

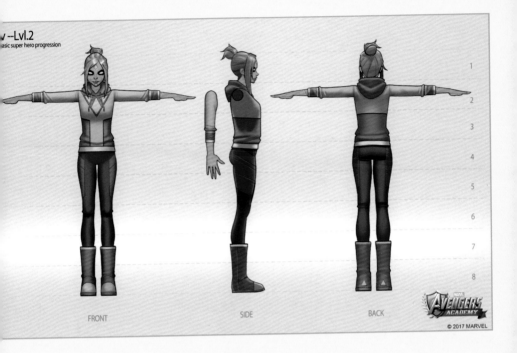

...v --Lvl.2
asic super hero progression

1
2
3
4
5
6
7
8

FRONT   SIDE   BACK

© 2017 MARVEL

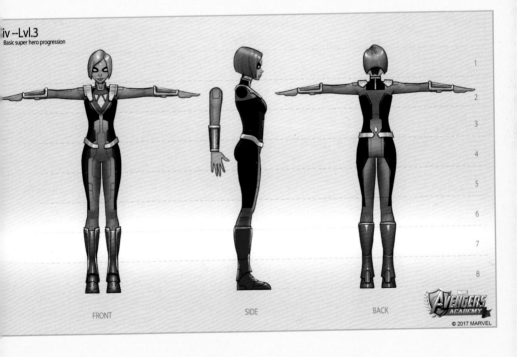

...iv --Lvl.3
Basic super hero progression

1
2
3
4
5
6
7
8

FRONT   SIDE   BACK

© 2017 MARVEL

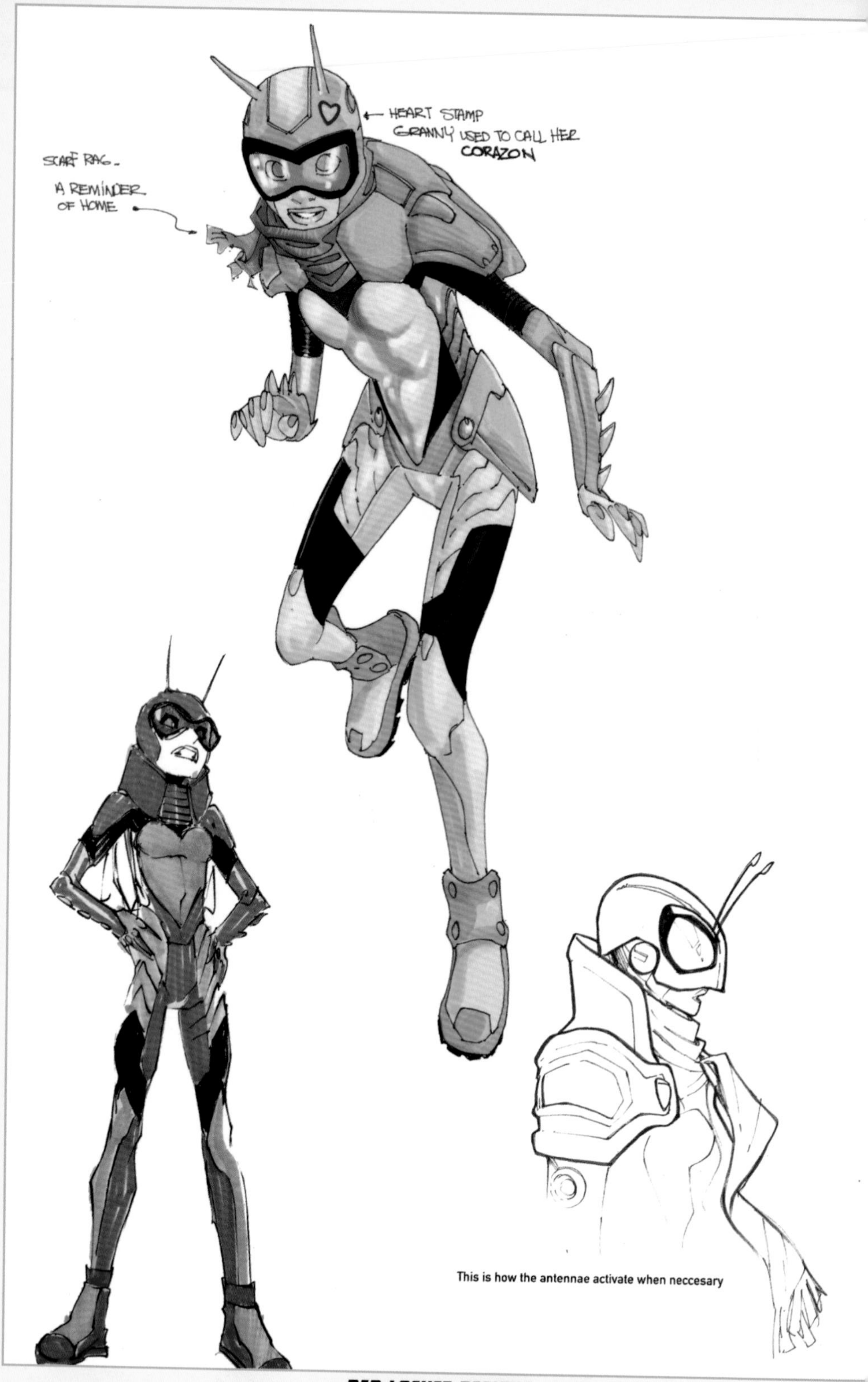
HEART STAMP
GRANNY USED TO CALL HER
CORAZON
SCARF RAG -
A REMINDER OF HOME
This is how the antennae activate when neccesary

RED LOCUST DESIGNS
BY HUMBERTO RAMOS

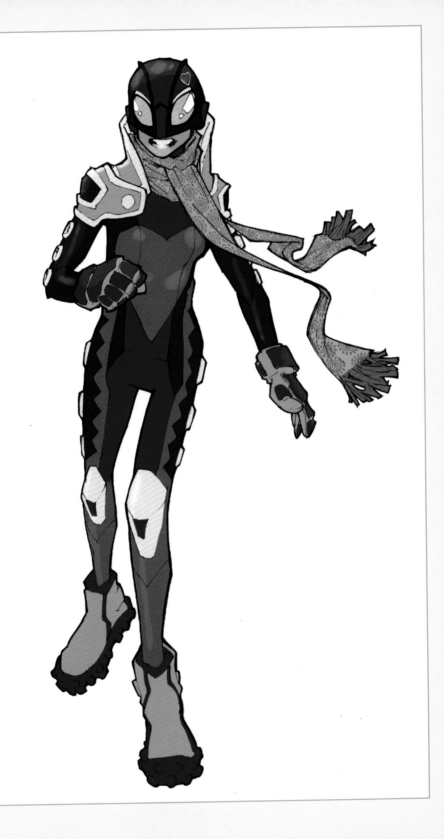

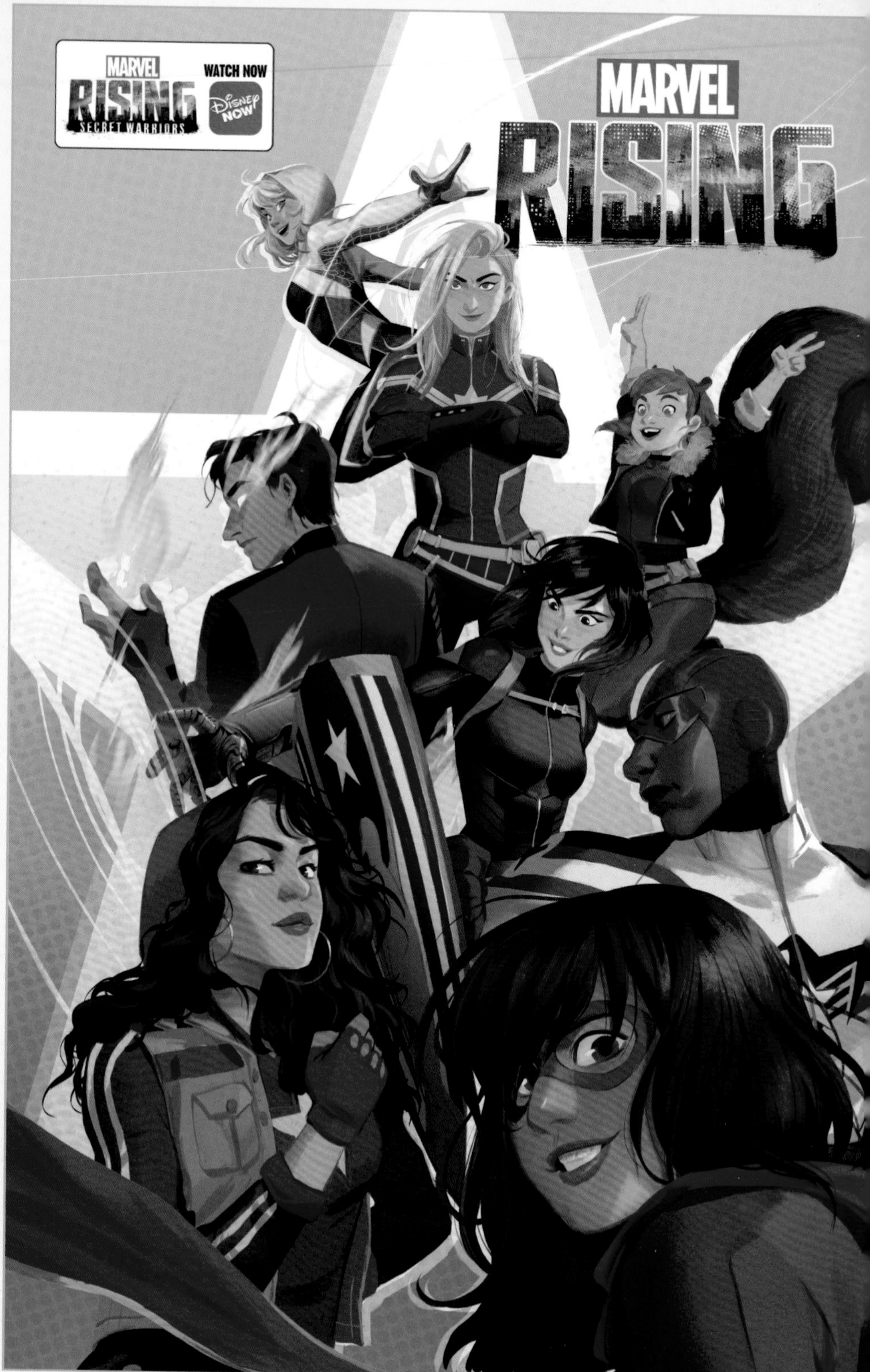
MARVEL
RISING
SECRET WARRIORS
WATCH NOW
DISNEY NOW
MARVEL
RISING

INTRODUCING MARVEL RISING!

MARVEL RISING

THE MARVEL UNIVERSE IS A RICH TREASURE CHEST OF CHARACTERS BORN ACROSS MARVEL'S INCREDIBLE 80-YEAR HISTORY. FROM CAPTAIN AMERICA TO CAPTAIN MARVEL, IRON MAN TO IRONHEART, THIS IS AN EVER-EXPANDING UNIVERSE FULL OF POWERFUL HEROES THAT ALSO REFLECTS THE WORLD WE LIVE IN.

YET DESPITE THAT EXPANSION, OUR STORIES REMAIN TIMELESS. THEY'VE BEEN SHARED ACROSS THE GLOBE AND ACROSS GENERATIONS, LINKING FANS WITH THE ENDURING IDEA THAT ORDINARY PEOPLE CAN DO EXTRAORDINARY THINGS. IT'S THAT SHARED EXPERIENCE OF THE MARVEL STORY THAT HAS ALLOWED US TO EXIST FOR THIS LONG. WHETHER YOUR FIRST MARVEL EXPERIENCE WAS THROUGH A COMIC BOOK, A BEDTIME STORY, A MOVIE OR A CARTOON, WE BELIEVE OUR STORIES STAY WITH AUDIENCES THROUGHOUT THEIR LIVES.

MARVEL RISING IS A CELEBRATION OF THIS TIMELESSNESS. AS OUR STORIES PASS FROM ONE GENERATION TO THE NEXT, SO DOES THE LOVE FOR OUR HEROES. FROM THE CLASSIC TO THE NEWLY IMAGINED, THE PASSION FOR ALL OF THEM IS THE SAME. IF YOU'VE BEEN READING COMICS OVER THE LAST FEW YEARS, YOU'LL KNOW CHARACTERS LIKE MS. MARVEL, SQUIRREL GIRL, AMERICA CHAVEZ, SPIDER-GWEN AND MORE HAVE ASSEMBLED A BEVY OF NEW FANS WHILE CAPTIVATING OUR PERENNIAL FANS. EACH OF THESE HEROES IS UNIQUE AND DISTINCT--JUST LIKE THE READERS THEY'VE BROUGHT IN--AND THEY REMIND US THAT NO MATTER WHAT YOU LOOK LIKE, YOU HAVE THE CAPABILITY TO BE POWERFUL, TOO. WE ARE TAKING THE HEROES FROM MARVEL RISING TO NEW HEIGHTS IN AN ANIMATED FEATURE LATER IN 2018, AS WELL AS A FULL PROGRAM OF CONTENT SWEEPING ACROSS THE COMPANY. BUT FIRST WE'RE GOING BACK TO OUR ROOTS AND TELLING A MARVEL RISING STORY IN COMICS: THE FIRST PLACE YOU MET THESE LOVABLE HEROES.

SO IN THE TRADITION OF EXPANDING THE MARVEL UNIVERSE, WE'RE EXCITED TO INTRODUCE MARVEL RISING--THE NEXT GENERATION OF MARVEL HEROES FOR THE NEXT GENERATION OF MARVEL FANS!

SANA AMANAT

VP, CONTENT & CHARACTER DEVELOPMENT

► **DOREEN GREEN** IS A SECOND-YEAR COMPUTER SCIENCE STUDENT — AND THE CRIMINAL-REDEEMING HERO THE UNBEATABLE SQUIRREL GIRL! THE NAME SAYS IT ALL: AN UNBEATABLE GIRL WITH THE POWERS OF AN UNBEATABLE SQUIRREL, TAIL INCLUDED. AND ON TOP OF HER STUDYING, NUT-EATING AND BUTT-KICKING ACTIVITIES, SHE'S JUST TAKEN ON THE JOB OF VOLUNTEER TEACHER FOR AN EXTRA-CURRICULAR HIGH-SCHOOL CODING CAMP! AND WHO SHOULD END UP IN HER CLASS BUT...

► **KAMALA KHAN**, A.K.A. JERSEY CITY HERO AND INHUMAN POLYMORPH MS. MARVEL! BUT BETWEEN SAVING THE WORLD WITH THE CHAMPIONS AND PROTECTING JERSEY CITY ON HER OWN, KAMALA'S GOT A LOT ON HER PLATE ALREADY. AND FIELD TRIP DAY MAY NOT BE THE BREAK SHE'S ANTICIPATING...

MARVEL RISING
PART 0

DEVIN GRAYSON
WRITER

MARCO FAILLA
ARTIST

RACHELLE ROSENBERG
COLOR ARTIST

VC's CLAYTON COWLES
LETTERER

HELEN CHEN
COVER

JAY BOWEN
DESIGN

HEATHER ANTOS AND **SARAH BRUNSTAD**
EDITORS

SANA AMANAT
CONSULTING EDITOR

C.B. CEBULSKI
EDITOR IN CHIEF

JOE QUESADA
CHIEF CREATIVE OFFICER

DAN BUCKLEY
PRESIDENT

ALAN FINE
EXECUTIVE PRODUCER

SPECIAL THANKS TO RYAN NORTH AND G. WILLOW WILSON

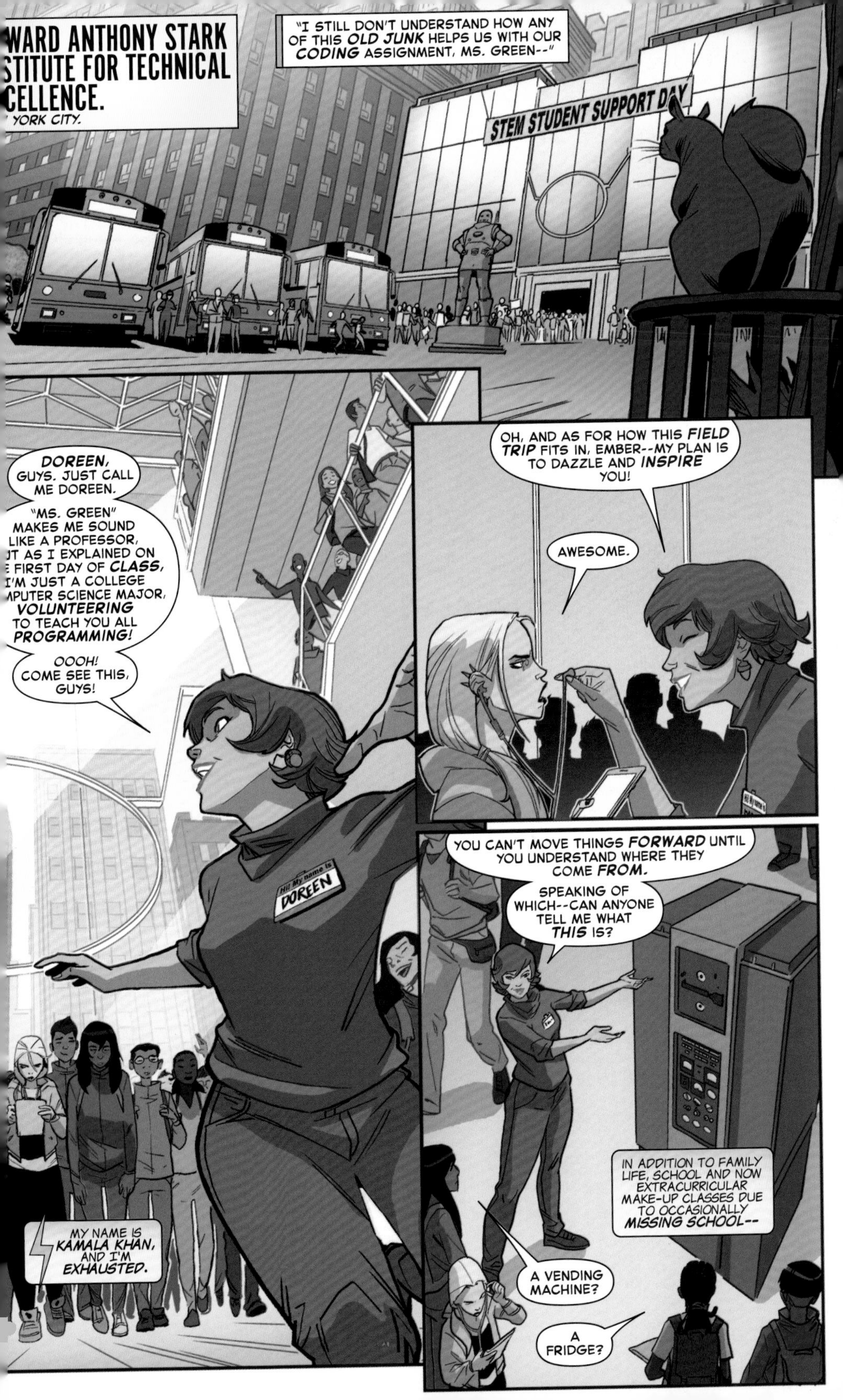
WARD ANTHONY STARK
STITUTE FOR TECHNICAL
CELLENCE.
YORK CITY.
"I STILL DON'T UNDERSTAND HOW ANY OF THIS OLD JUNK HELPS US WITH OUR CODING ASSIGNMENT, MS. GREEN--"
STEM STUDENT SUPPORT DAY
DOREEN, GUYS. JUST CALL ME DOREEN.
"MS. GREEN" MAKES ME SOUND LIKE A PROFESSOR, UT AS I EXPLAINED ON E FIRST DAY OF CLASS, I'M JUST A COLLEGE MPUTER SCIENCE MAJOR, VOLUNTEERING TO TEACH YOU ALL PROGRAMMING!
OOOH! COME SEE THIS, GUYS!
HI! My name is DOREEN
MY NAME IS KAMALA KHAN, AND I'M EXHAUSTED.
OH, AND AS FOR HOW THIS FIELD TRIP FITS IN, EMBER--MY PLAN IS TO DAZZLE AND INSPIRE YOU!
AWESOME.
YOU CAN'T MOVE THINGS FORWARD UNTIL YOU UNDERSTAND WHERE THEY COME FROM.
SPEAKING OF WHICH--CAN ANYONE TELL ME WHAT THIS IS?
IN ADDITION TO FAMILY LIFE, SCHOOL AND NOW EXTRACURRICULAR MAKE-UP CLASSES DUE TO OCCASIONALLY MISSING SCHOOL--
A VENDING MACHINE?
A FRIDGE?

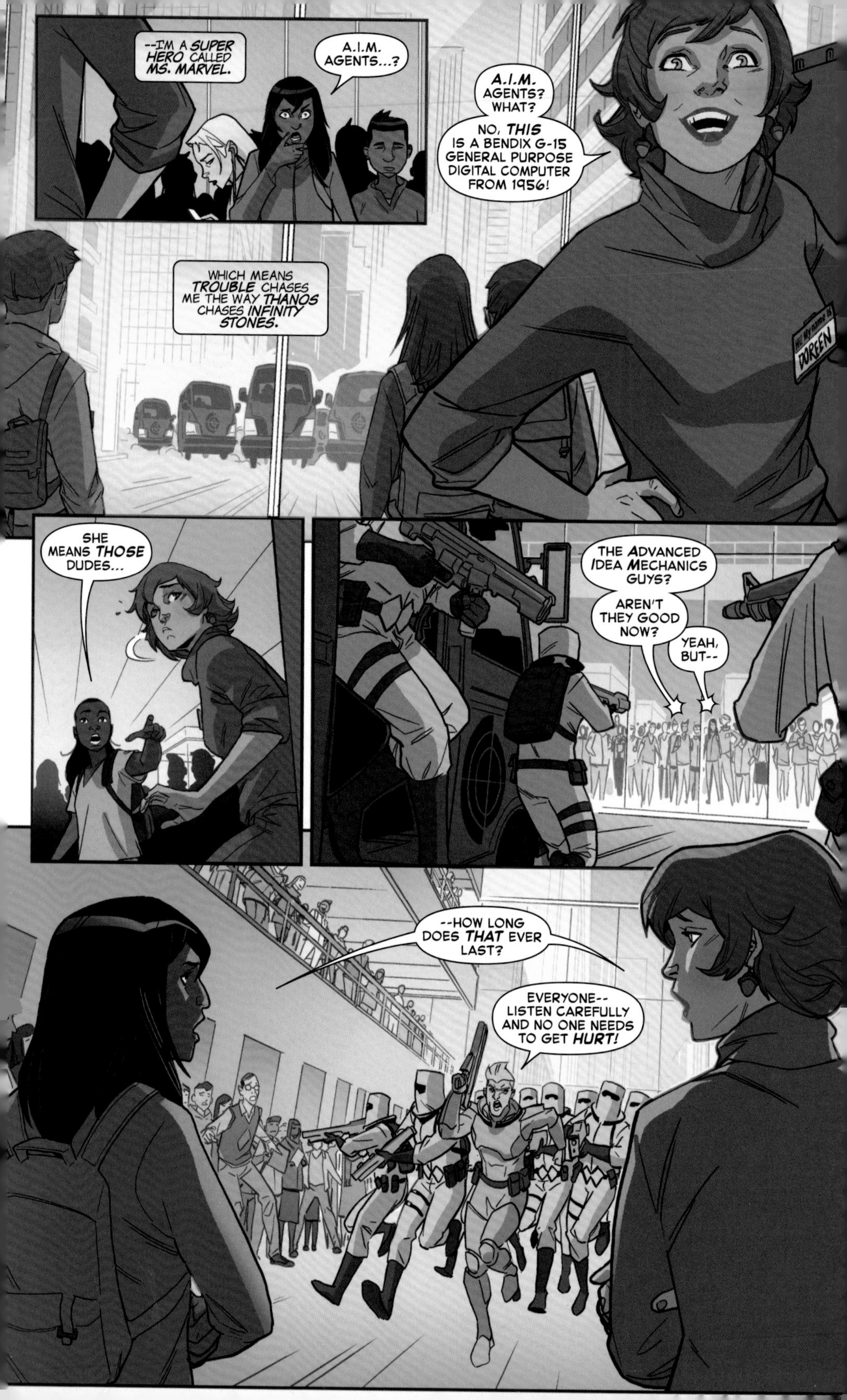
--I'M A SUPER HERO CALLED MS. MARVEL.
A.I.M. AGENTS...?
A.I.M. AGENTS? WHAT?
NO, THIS IS A BENDIX G-15 GENERAL PURPOSE DIGITAL COMPUTER FROM 1956!
Hi! My name is DOREEN
WHICH MEANS TROUBLE CHASES ME THE WAY THANOS CHASES INFINITY STONES.
SHE MEANS THOSE DUDES...
THE ADVANCED IDEA MECHANICS GUYS?
AREN'T THEY GOOD NOW?
YEAH, BUT--
--HOW LONG DOES THAT EVER LAST?
EVERYONE-- LISTEN CAREFULLY AND NO ONE NEEDS TO GET HURT!

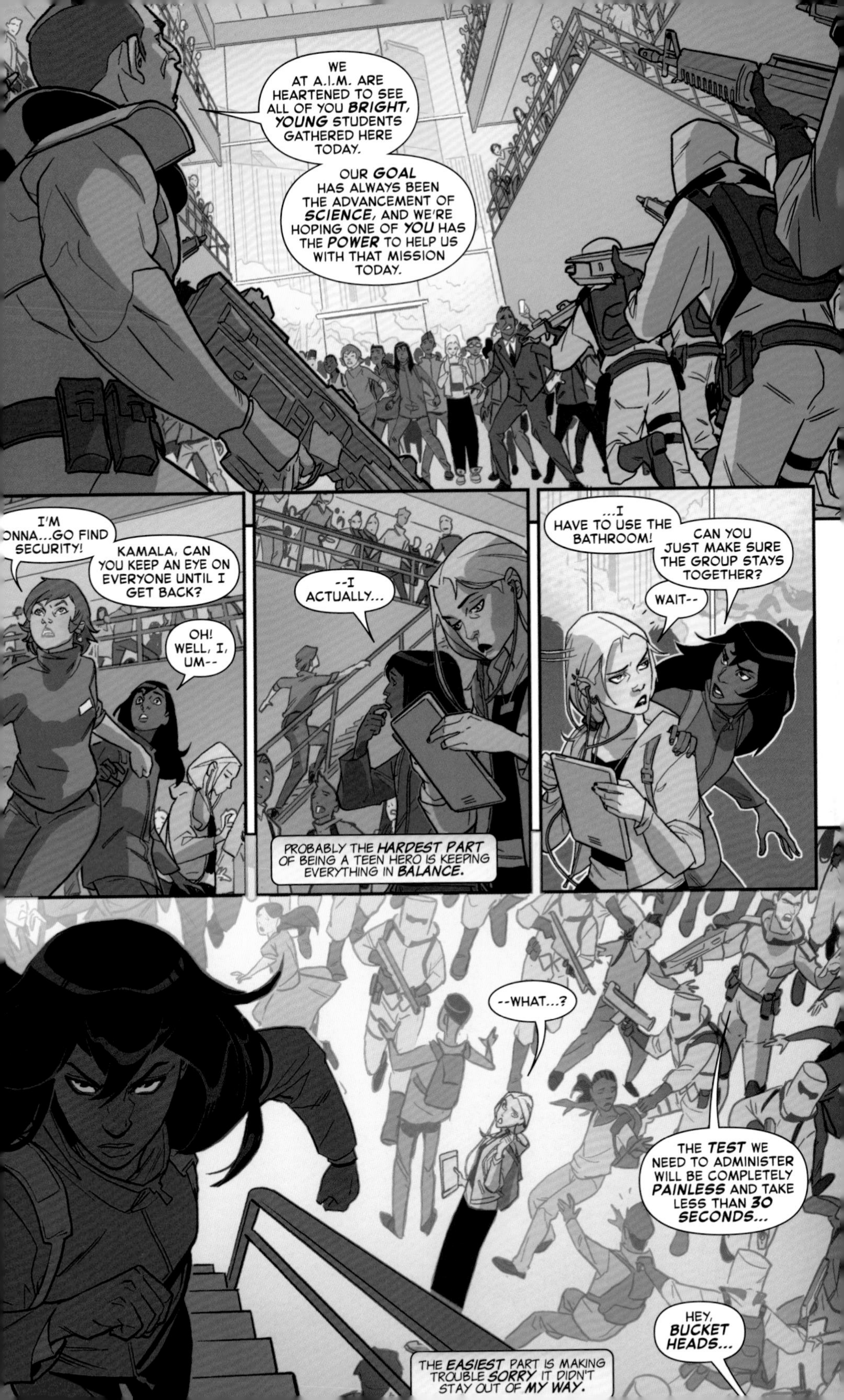
WE AT A.I.M. ARE HEARTENED TO SEE ALL OF YOU BRIGHT, YOUNG STUDENTS GATHERED HERE TODAY.
OUR GOAL HAS ALWAYS BEEN THE ADVANCEMENT OF SCIENCE, AND WE'RE HOPING ONE OF YOU HAS THE POWER TO HELP US WITH THAT MISSION TODAY.
I'M ONNA...GO FIND SECURITY!
KAMALA, CAN YOU KEEP AN EYE ON EVERYONE UNTIL I GET BACK?
OH! WELL, I, UM--
--I ACTUALLY...
PROBABLY THE HARDEST PART OF BEING A TEEN HERO IS KEEPING EVERYTHING IN BALANCE.
...I HAVE TO USE THE BATHROOM!
CAN YOU JUST MAKE SURE THE GROUP STAYS TOGETHER?
WAIT--
--WHAT...?
THE TEST WE NEED TO ADMINISTER WILL BE COMPLETELY PAINLESS AND TAKE LESS THAN 30 SECONDS...
HEY, BUCKET HEADS...
THE EASIEST PART IS MAKING TROUBLE SORRY IT DIDN'T STAY OUT OF MY WAY.

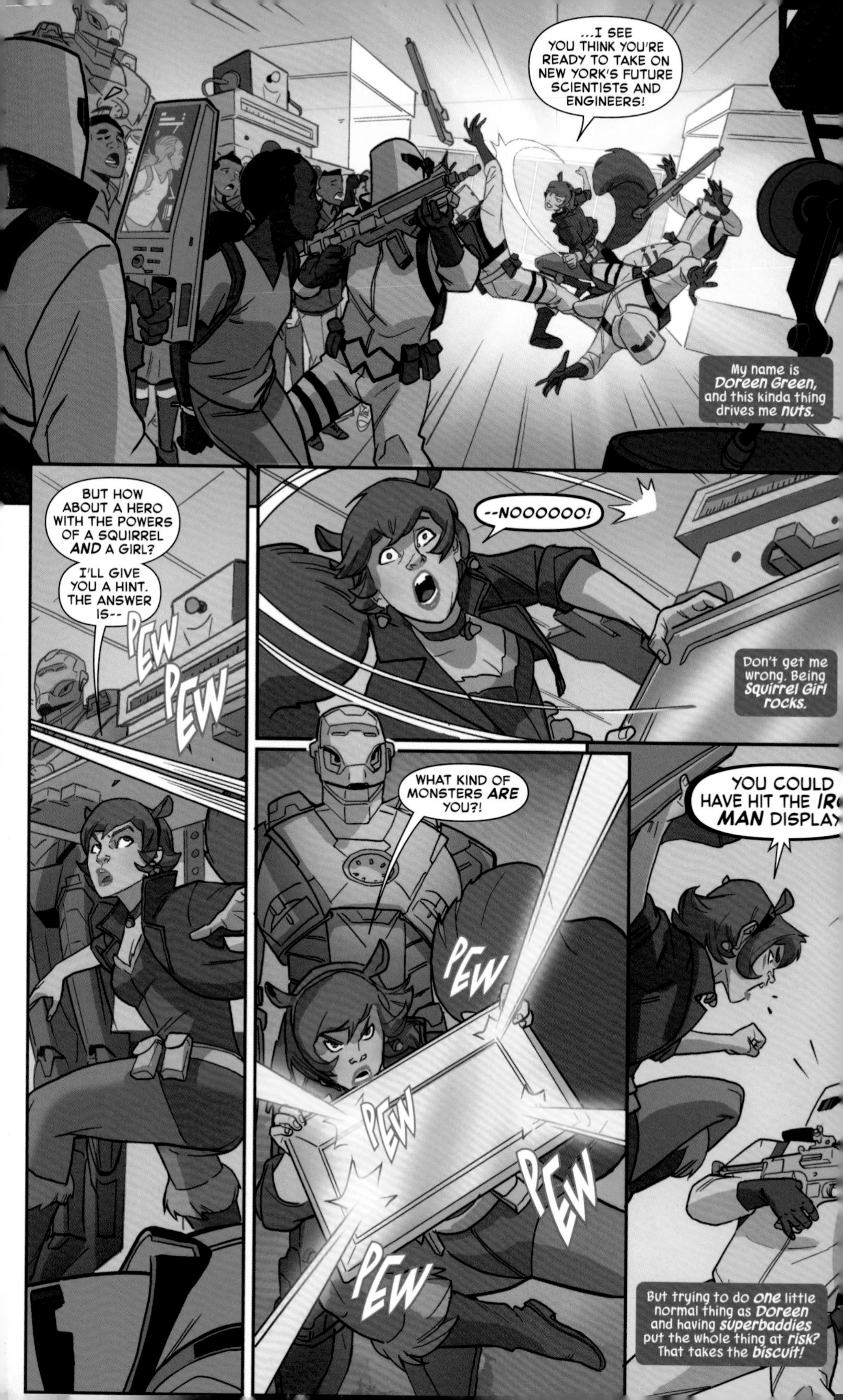
...I SEE YOU THINK YOU'RE READY TO TAKE ON NEW YORK'S FUTURE SCIENTISTS AND ENGINEERS!
My name is Doreen Green, and this kinda thing drives me nuts.
BUT HOW ABOUT A HERO WITH THE POWERS OF A SQUIRREL AND A GIRL?
I'LL GIVE YOU A HINT. THE ANSWER IS--
PEW
PEW
--NOOOOOO!
Don't get me wrong. Being Squirrel Girl rocks.
WHAT KIND OF MONSTERS ARE YOU?!
PEW
PEW
PEW
PEW
YOU COULD HAVE HIT THE IR MAN DISPLAY
But trying to do one little normal thing as Doreen and having superbaddies put the whole thing at risk? That takes the biscuit!

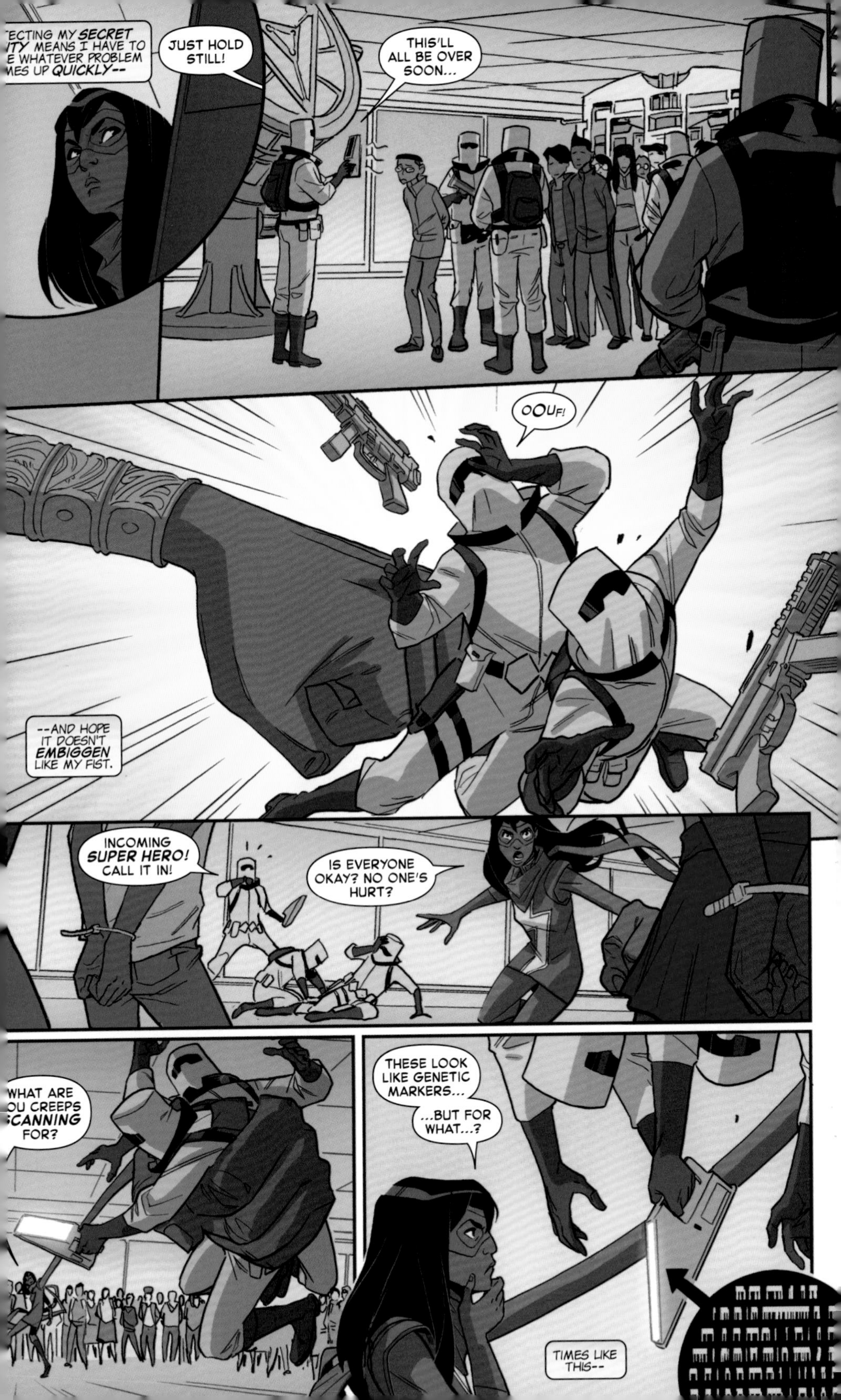

-TECTING MY SECRET -ITY MEANS I HAVE TO -E WHATEVER PROBLEM -MES UP QUICKLY--
JUST HOLD STILL!
THIS'LL ALL BE OVER SOON...
OOUF!
--AND HOPE IT DOESN'T EMBIGGEN LIKE MY FIST.
INCOMING SUPER HERO! CALL IT IN!
IS EVERYONE OKAY? NO ONE'S HURT?
WHAT ARE -OU CREEPS -CANNING FOR?
THESE LOOK LIKE GENETIC MARKERS...
...BUT FOR WHAT...?
TIMES LIKE THIS--

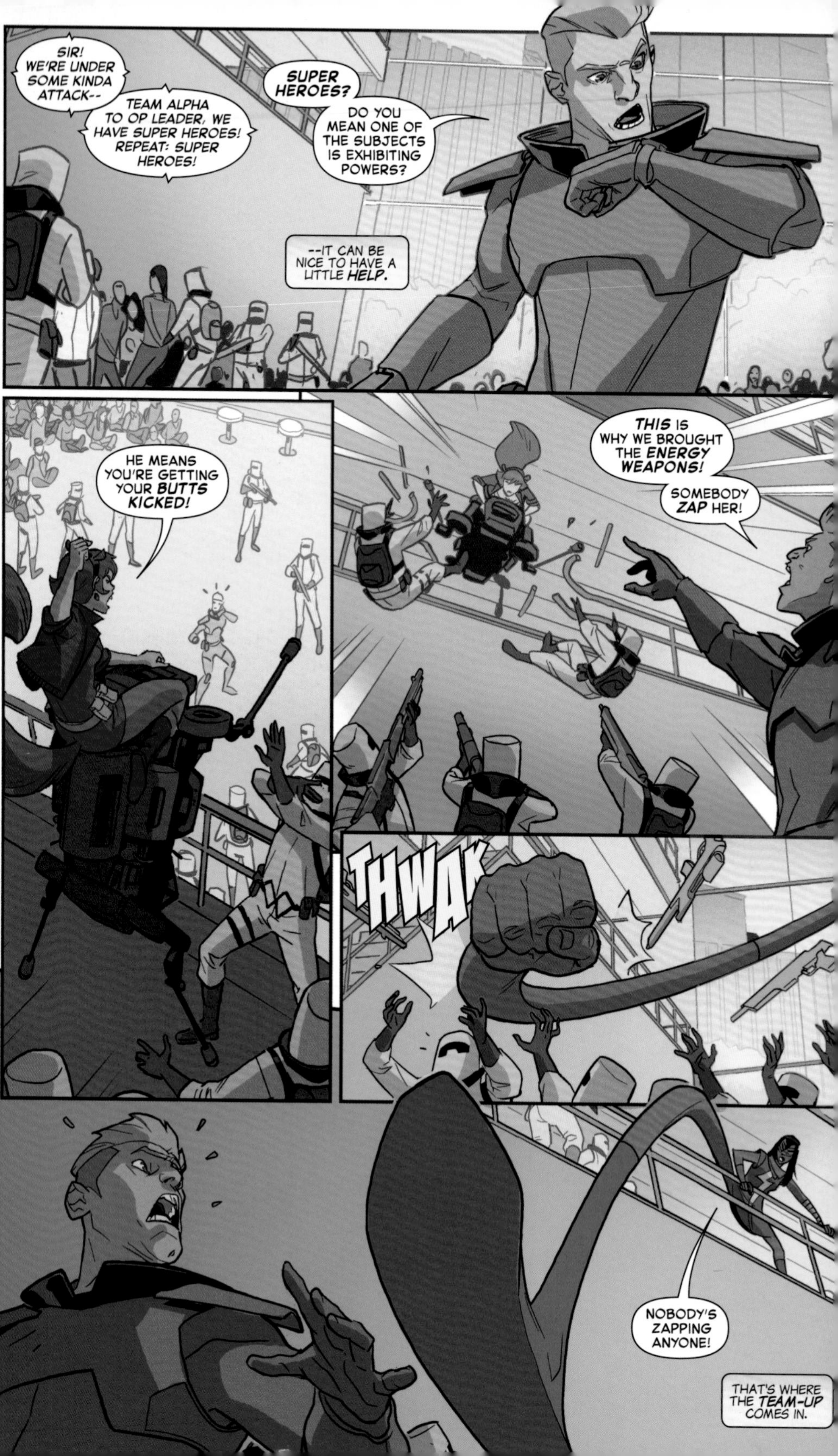
SIR! WE'RE UNDER SOME KINDA ATTACK--
TEAM ALPHA TO OP LEADER, WE HAVE SUPER HEROES! REPEAT: SUPER HEROES!
SUPER HEROES?
DO YOU MEAN ONE OF THE SUBJECTS IS EXHIBITING POWERS?
--IT CAN BE NICE TO HAVE A LITTLE HELP.
HE MEANS YOU'RE GETTING YOUR BUTTS KICKED!
THIS IS WHY WE BROUGHT THE ENERGY WEAPONS!
SOMEBODY ZAP HER!
THWAK
NOBODY'S ZAPPING ANYONE!
THAT'S WHERE THE TEAM-UP COMES IN.

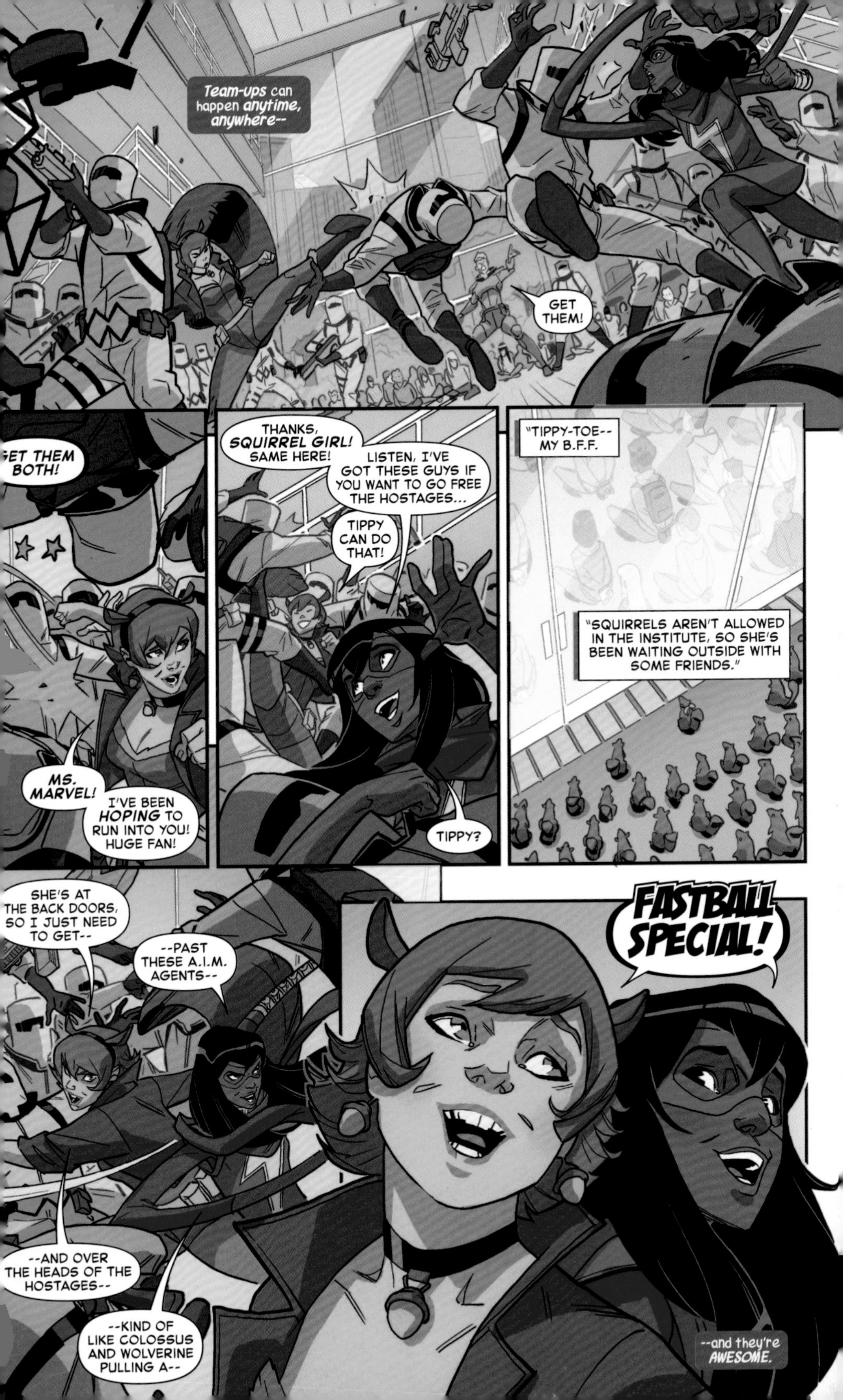
Team-ups can happen anytime, anywhere--
GET THEM!
GET THEM BOTH!
MS. MARVEL!
I'VE BEEN HOPING TO RUN INTO YOU! HUGE FAN!
THANKS, SQUIRREL GIRL! SAME HERE!
LISTEN, I'VE GOT THESE GUYS IF YOU WANT TO GO FREE THE HOSTAGES...
TIPPY CAN DO THAT!
TIPPY?
"TIPPY-TOE-- MY B.F.F.
"SQUIRRELS AREN'T ALLOWED IN THE INSTITUTE, SO SHE'S BEEN WAITING OUTSIDE WITH SOME FRIENDS."
SHE'S AT THE BACK DOORS, SO I JUST NEED TO GET--
--PAST THESE A.I.M. AGENTS--
--AND OVER THE HEADS OF THE HOSTAGES--
--KIND OF LIKE COLOSSUS AND WOLVERINE PULLING A--
FASTBALL SPECIAL!
--and they're AWESOME.

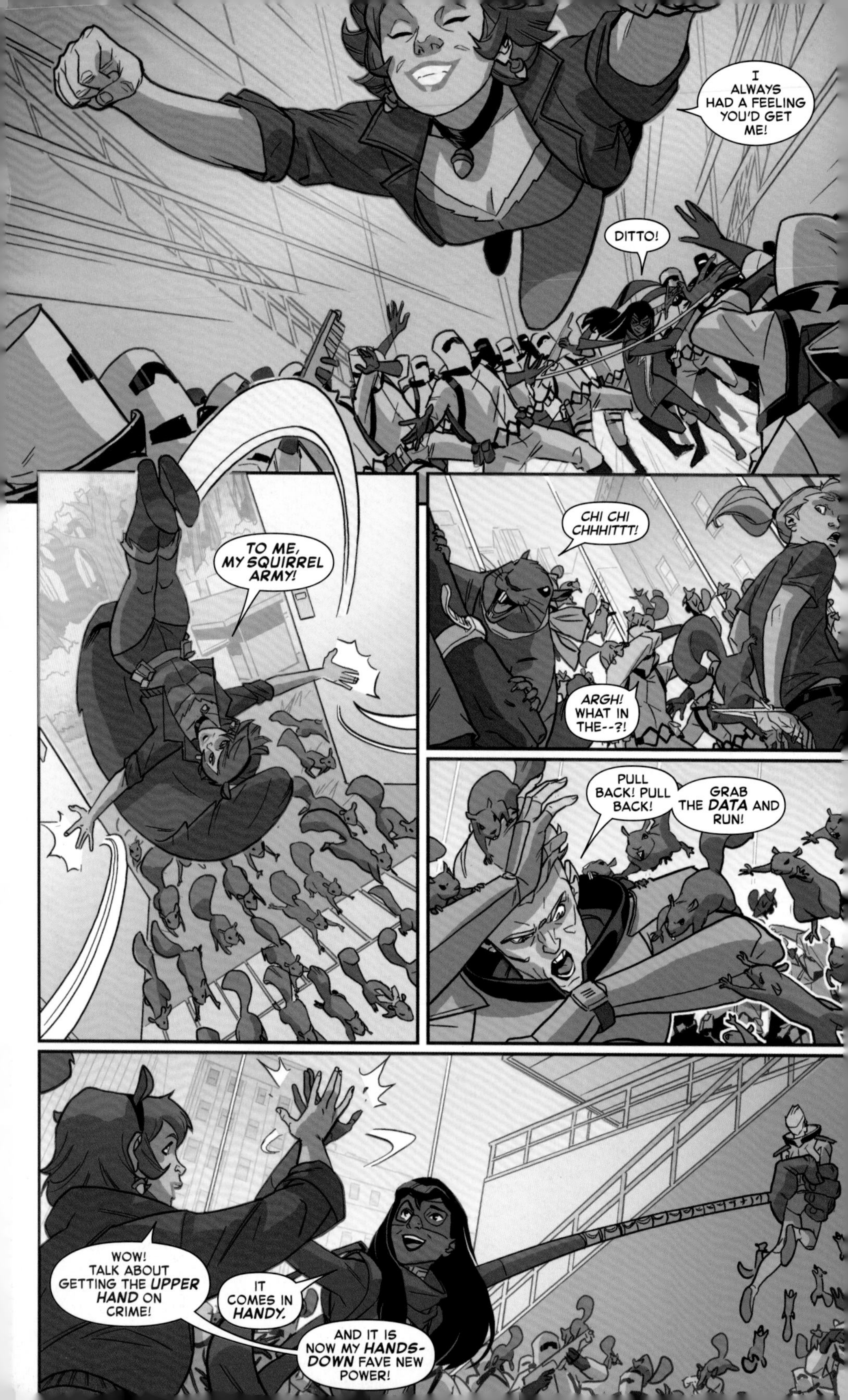
I ALWAYS HAD A FEELING YOU'D GET ME!
DITTO!
TO ME, MY SQUIRREL ARMY!
CHI CHI CHHHITTT!
ARGH! WHAT IN THE--?!
PULL BACK! PULL BACK!
GRAB THE DATA AND RUN!
WOW! TALK ABOUT GETTING THE UPPER HAND ON CRIME!
IT COMES IN HANDY.
AND IT IS NOW MY HANDS-DOWN FAVE NEW POWER!

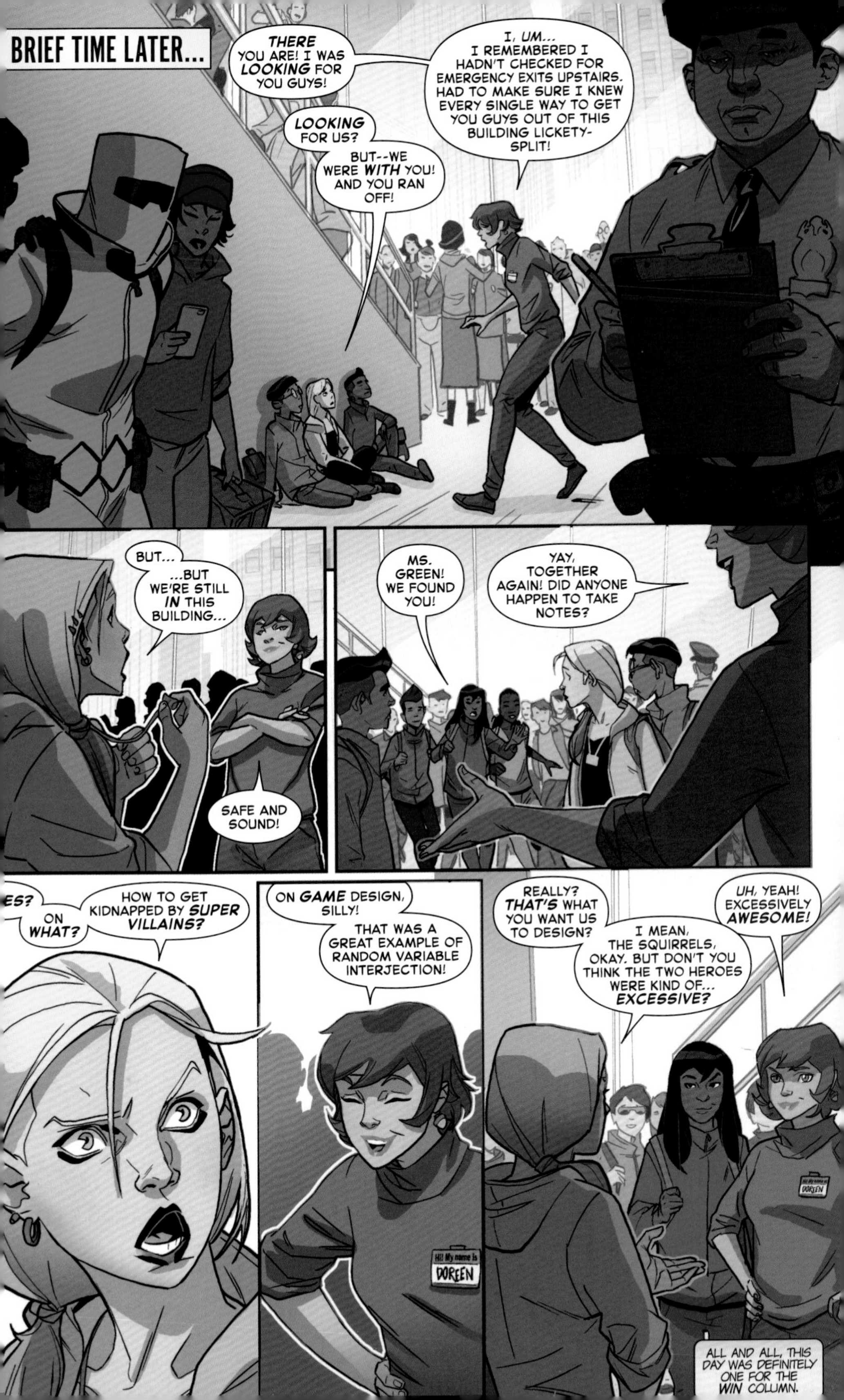
BRIEF TIME LATER...
THERE YOU ARE! I WAS LOOKING FOR YOU GUYS!
LOOKING FOR US?
BUT--WE WERE WITH YOU! AND YOU RAN OFF!
I, UM... I REMEMBERED I HADN'T CHECKED FOR EMERGENCY EXITS UPSTAIRS. HAD TO MAKE SURE I KNEW EVERY SINGLE WAY TO GET YOU GUYS OUT OF THIS BUILDING LICKETY-SPLIT!
BUT...
...BUT WE'RE STILL IN THIS BUILDING...
SAFE AND SOUND!
MS. GREEN! WE FOUND YOU!
YAY, TOGETHER AGAIN! DID ANYONE HAPPEN TO TAKE NOTES?
ON WHAT?
HOW TO GET KIDNAPPED BY SUPER VILLAINS?
ON GAME DESIGN, SILLY!
THAT WAS A GREAT EXAMPLE OF RANDOM VARIABLE INTERJECTION!
HI! My name is DOREEN
REALLY? THAT'S WHAT YOU WANT US TO DESIGN?
I MEAN, THE SQUIRRELS, OKAY. BUT DON'T YOU THINK THE TWO HEROES WERE KIND OF... EXCESSIVE?
UH, YEAH! EXCESSIVELY AWESOME!
ALL AND ALL, THIS DAY WAS DEFINITELY ONE FOR THE WIN COLUMN.

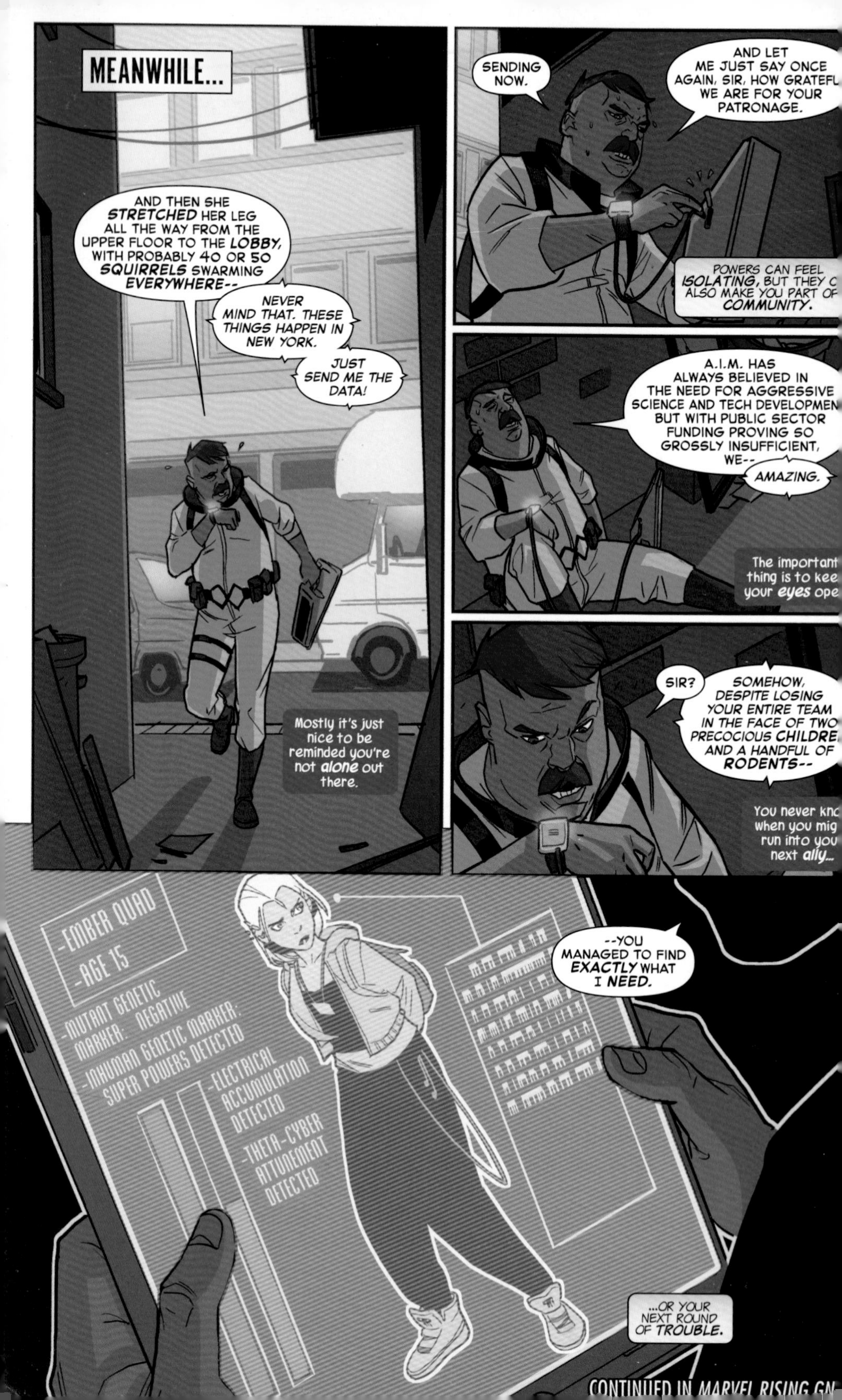
MEANWHILE...
AND THEN SHE STRETCHED HER LEG ALL THE WAY FROM THE UPPER FLOOR TO THE LOBBY, WITH PROBABLY 40 OR 50 SQUIRRELS SWARMING EVERYWHERE--
NEVER MIND THAT. THESE THINGS HAPPEN IN NEW YORK.
JUST SEND ME THE DATA!
Mostly it's just nice to be reminded you're not alone out there.
SENDING NOW.
AND LET ME JUST SAY ONCE AGAIN, SIR, HOW GRATEFL WE ARE FOR YOUR PATRONAGE.
POWERS CAN FEEL ISOLATING, BUT THEY C ALSO MAKE YOU PART OF COMMUNITY.
A.I.M. HAS ALWAYS BELIEVED IN THE NEED FOR AGGRESSIVE SCIENCE AND TECH DEVELOPMEN BUT WITH PUBLIC SECTOR FUNDING PROVING SO GROSSLY INSUFFICIENT, WE--
AMAZING.
The important thing is to kee your eyes ope
SIR?
SOMEHOW, DESPITE LOSING YOUR ENTIRE TEAM IN THE FACE OF TWO PRECOCIOUS CHILDRE AND A HANDFUL OF RODENTS--
You never kno when you mig run into you next ally...
-EMBER QUAD
-AGE 15
-MUTANT GENETIC MARKER: NEGATIVE
-INHUMAN GENETIC MARKER: SUPER POWERS DETECTED
-ELECTRICAL ACCUMULATION DETECTED
-THETA-CYBER ATTUNEMENT DETECTED
--YOU MANAGED TO FIND EXACTLY WHAT I NEED.
...OR YOUR NEXT ROUND OF TROUBLE.
CONTINUED IN MARVEL RISING GN